"Our wrinkles are the map to places our dreams have taken us"

Stephen Haughan

PESHWARI NANS

BEYOND THE BUCKET LIST

BY
STEPHEN HAUGHAN

PESHWARI NANS

In their twilight years two eighty-something sisters, Esther and Minnie, are coaxed from their easy chairs and their comfort zone of carpet slippers, crochet hooks, jigsaws and jumble sales to fulfil the dying wish of a dear friend.

They go on to undertake a road trip of sorts in Esther's beloved classic Trafalgar-blue 1965 Morris Traveller car, affectionately known as 'Vivien'. The trip however is no minor errand to return late library books: theirs turns out to be an epic undertaking of some seven thousand miles, all the way from London's Whitechapel to Raipur, deep in the the heart of the Indian subcontinent, passing through no less than ten countries along the way, including Poland, Russia, China and Tibet.

Esther and Minnie's saga of course does not go without the occasional hitch, but the sisters' eternal love for one another and their quintessential innocence and innate kindness stand them in good stead when they are faced with seemingly insurmountable odds.

CHAPTER ONE

For more than half a century there had been a greengrocer's on the corner of Vallance road and Whitechapel road opposite the Royal London Hospital in the heart of London's East End. Bought for ten shillings and run by three successive generations of the Reynolds family it proudly served the local community with the freshest of seasonal fruits and vegetables, which were meticulously displayed according to variety, size and colour as though contesting for a coveted county fair accolade.

Jack Reynolds, the most recent proprietor, would rise every morning before first light and drive his beloved powder blue Bedford three-quarter-ton van to Spitalfields market where he would sup strong hot black tea with his fellow greengrocers and hand-pick the most crisp and plump of produce and return home for the day's trading.

Along with his wife Esther and their daughter Elizabeth, Jack occupied a modest first-floor flat above the family business with very little in the way of modern conveniences, a walnut gramophone and a second-hand temperamental cast-iron Aga being amongst their most cherished possessions. The arrival of the so-called supermarket and the influx of Bengali, Pakistani and Sikh cut-price corner stores lured his once loyal customers away with the promise of two-for-one offers and a 'pile it high sell it cheap' mentality. But there was food on the table, a shovel or two of coke for the fire and a roof above their heads, a luxury presumably taken for granted by the lords and ladies strolling beside the Serpentine in London's Hyde Park, which although barely a couple of miles from the Reynolds greengrocer's, at times seemed a world away.

Eventually with Elizabeth having graduated at university and flown the coop and he and Esther approaching retirement age, Jack was forced to sell the business to a local Hindi family with the proviso that he and Esther live out their days rent free in the flat. But barely six months into a life of jigsaws, jumble sales and jaundice and during a particularly harsh winter, Jack contracted pneumonia and was admitted to the Royal London Hospital. Elizabeth returned home and she and her mother took it in turn to sit at his bedside offering words of comfort and an assurance that he would be home in a matter of days and life would resume as normal.

Jack's respiratory infection however showed no signs of abating and in fact his condition soon rapidly deteriorated and his wife and daughter were advised by clinicians to prepare for the worst.

"How?" Esther said, turning to Elizabeth at her husband's bedside as he slept entwined in a yard or more of oxygen tubing. "How do we prepare to lose him, tell me Lizzy. How?"

"I don't know, Mother, really I don't," Elizabeth replied with an emptiness and an aching growing in the pit of her stomach. Her father had been there since her very first steps with a steady hand to support her, the same hand that had dried her tears after a spurned adolescent crush and gave her away to her eventual husband. The void left by such a passing would be unimaginable.

Jack Reynolds did pass away peacefully in his sleep just three-and-a-half weeks after being admitted to hospital. The curtains were pulled around his bed to allow his wife and daughter the privacy of a final farewell.

"Love you, Daddy," Elizabeth sobbed, kissing her father's forehead several times and drying her streaming nose.

"He loved you too," Esther said, rubbing her daughter's back. "With all his heart, you're his little girl, you always have been." Esther herself stooped to kiss her husband, brushing his thinning hair behind his right ear as he himself had done for as long as she could remember. "Goodbye my darling," she said softly. "Goodbye love."

Jack was laid to rest in the East London Cemetery, a short distance away from his mother and father. The service was short with a touching eulogy read by a tearful Elizabeth, but was attended by very few mourners.

Richard, Elizabeth's eighteen-year-old son, sat between his now estranged parents with his face buried in his hands, having idolized his grandfather and helped out in his shop tirelessly during his formative years.

Esther's sister Minnie, aged eighty-four and two years her junior, arrived moments before the service ended, looking flushed and breathless. "Essy dear I'm so sorry," she said, removing her gloves and taking her sister's hand. "The perishing taxi got a flat and I had to wait an eternity for a bus, please forgive me."

"That's quite all right, my dear," Esther said, hugging her sister, who had travelled from her home in Hackney. "I think we're going to the grave in a moment. You missed Lizzy's speech. She did her father proud she did, and the poem was simply beautiful."

"Oh damn," Minnie cursed. "I'm so very sorry," she then said, stopping Elizabeth as she filed from the chapel. "I tried my upmost to be here, I really did."

"That's okay Aunt Minnie," Elizabeth replied with a peck to Minnie's cheek. "It's lovely to see you. Are you okay?"

"Yes, yes, I'm fine," Minnie said, taking a seat momentarily. "Just a little shortness of breath that's all, pay no attention dear."

"Nonsense, Auntie," Elizabeth insisted, thrusting her car keys into her son's hand. "Richard be a dear and fetch some water from the car for Minnie, there's a bottle on the back seat."

Peshwari Nans

"Is everything all right?" the vicar then asked, peering over Elizabeth's shoulder as Minnie clutched her chest. "Is there anything I can do?"

"I'm fine," Minnie assured him, smiling and patting her sister's knee. "Please don't fuss, really I'll be all right."

Richard returned with a bottle of spring water but Minnie was already back on her feet, arm in arm with her sister, "Thank you Richard, dear," she said, stroking the young man's shoulder. "But I couldn't possibly drink from a plastic container, no, no I'll be fine we'll have a nice cup of tea back at Essy's won't we dear?"

Esther led her unsteady sibling outside and followed the funeral cortège at a sedate pace some fifty metres or more to Jack's final resting place.

"Oooh look!" She gestured to an adjacent flower bed which had been recently hoed and edged. "Aren't those crocuses gorgeous, Minnie? And the daffodils. Beautiful, just beautiful." She then called to a cemetery gardener who was three flower-beds away: "I say, young man, you're doing a wonderful job, just wonderful!"

The understudy smiled and bowed his head respectfully without uttering a word and following strict cemetery protocol.

"Jack loved his daffodils," Esther remarked, crossing the narrow grass border to the graveside.

"Careful, Mother," Elizabeth said, taking her mother's arm. "Richard? Help your Aunt Minnie."

Richard took Minnie's hand and ushered her forward.

First looking to the heavens and then down at his Bible, the vicar began his solemn service of interment whilst Esther mopped her eyes with her handkerchief, comforted by her only child. Jack was lowered slowly into the ground and Esther stooped to scoop a quantity of earth from the graveside pile and scatter it down onto his polished coffin lid. She then felt a hand on her elbow and turned to see the young gardener holding a handful of pristine daffodils. "I'm sorry, but I heard you say he loved his daffodils," he said softly. It seemed even the strictest of protocols could be bent on occasions.

"Oh good heavens, thank you dear," Esther said, taking the blooms. "That's awfully kind of you."

"Thank you," Elizabeth also told him as he backed away respectfully and returned to his spade.

Kissing the flowers and bidding her love goodbye, Esther flung them down into the grave, where they lay splayed across the brass plaque.

"I'm sorry for your loss," the vicar said, approaching Elizabeth and her sobbing mother, as one-by-one the gathering dispersed. "If there is anything we can do for you please feel free to ask."

"Thank you," Esther said, blowing her nose, "Thank you, Vicar for a beautiful service."

Minnie took her sister's hand and peered down into the grave. "Bye, Jack," she said, almost buckling at the knee.

"I've got you Aunt Min," Richard said with an arm around her waist. "We don't want you going in after him, do we?"

Esther broke down in the rear of the car as it swept out through the cemetery gates. "Oh, Mother," Elizabeth said, cradling her in her arms. "It's alright, it's alright."

Stepping from the car outside what was now Aayushmaan's chemist shop, Esther and the others greeted by the young shopkeepers, who were husband and wife Ravi and Jasvinder. They were standing with their hands clasped and their heads bowed. "We are so sorry Mrs Reynolds," Jasvinder said, shaking her head.

"Thank you, Jazzy love," Esther replied in passing. "Thank you, Ravi."

Esther and Minnie sat side by side in the living room while several close family friends stood chatting in hushed circles. "Mother, I've been thinking," Elizabeth said, offering them tea. "Why don't you come and stay with me? There's no reason for you to be here on your own now is there? And after all it's not like we don't have the room."

"Or you could come stay with me, dear," Minnie added. "I've been on my own for so long now I could use the company."

Esther looked around her meagre flat with its peeling paper and tattered shade and shook her head. "No, no I couldn't possibly move," she told them. "Jack and I have so many happy memories of this place."

"But, Mother," Elizabeth said, kneeling before her. "We'd love to have you, wouldn't we Richard?"

"Yes Nan, come and live with us," her son reiterated. "We can keep an eye on you then."

"Whatever do you mean, keep an eye on me?" Esther said, a little perturbed at her grandson's remark. "May I remind you I'm quite capable of looking after myself! Now please don't fuss."

"Sorry, Gran I—I didn't mean..." Richard stammered.

"I know exactly what you meant," Esther intervened. "Sorry Richard dear, I know you mean well, but honestly I'll be fine."

"Well if you won't move, Essy dear," Minnie said, taking a rich tea biscuit from the table, "then I'll come stay with you."

"Don't be daft, Minnie dear," Esther insisted. "You have your house in Hackney. There's no reason for you to leave."

"Yes, I have the house," Minnie agreed. "But that's all I have. I've been on my own now for twenty years or more and to be honest with you it's getting a bit too much for me, all those rooms to dust, and for what? Nobody ever uses them, the only company I have for much of the time is a spider that sits on the soap dish occasionally while I soak my dentures. Oh and the Romanian fellow that lives beneath me who puts out my recyclables every Thursday, charming fellow, but that's just about it. I've been thinking about selling up for some time but you know what it's like. One week runs into the next and so on."

"Minnie dear," Esther exclaimed. "Why on earth would you want to come and live with me? We haven't shared a room in over sixty years, and from what I remember we were at each other's throats half the time, what with you wearing my nylons and me scratching your seventy-eights!"

"Well, Essy dear," Minnie replied, smiling, "I have my own nylons now and I took my seventy-eights to the church bazaar many years ago. Think about it Essy. It would be company for the both of us and we would want for nothing. I have a bit put by and what with the sale of the house we'd be able to spruce this place up and live quite comfortably."

"I'm sorry I can't think about that right now," Esther said, hanging her head. "Not now."

"Okay, Mother," Elizabeth said, backing away. "But I think it's a wonderful idea."

Esther was eventually left, albeit reluctantly, by her daughter and sister to her thoughts. She was sitting in her late husband's chair with his framed picture gripped in her arthritic fingers. That evening she boiled a saucepan of water and instinctively washed enough new potatoes for two and opened a tin of corned beef and garden peas, dining at the table by the window opposite an empty chair.

"Oh Jack," she said, her fork trembling in her hand. She forced down three potatoes and several peas before pushing her plate away and tugging the curtain aside, watching the steady flow of traffic as the signals turned from red to green over and over again.

Jasvinder and Ravi shut up the shop below her at 8 p.m. and were heard ascending the stairs to the attic room above

Peshwari Nans

Esther's home. Jasvinder's Uncle Dayanidhi, which in Hindu means 'kind person' did not live up to his name. In his case nothing could be further from the truth, for he was a strict taskmaster who insisted that the shop had to be open all year round from seven in the morning until eight at night without fail, and he would pay the young couple a pittance, stating that 'a roof over their heads was not a gift—it must be earned and paid for.' The pair were forever in his debt, having borrowed from him to travel to the UK with the promise of one day owning their own business to fund the family's rice farm back home. But Dayanidhi simply wanted cheap subservient labour for his own business and had no intention of ever letting them leave. Their single attic room contained a small electric fire, a kitchen sink perched on a broken base and a mattress on the floor without a single window. They would cook simple foods on a spirit burner which filled the room with acrid fumes and tainted their meal. But at least they were together, having only been married a matter of months.

Unbeknown to them, their Uncle Ravi had been working at night at a Brick Lane clothing factory, maintaining the machinery and baling the material scraps. He would leave the flat at around nine and return at six-thirty with just thirty pounds in cash to show for his efforts.

Jasvinder and Ravi saved every penny they earned apart from what they spent on a few essentials, in an old red Lipton's tea tin, circa 1920s, produced by the famous Lipton's tea merchants. It could be found in the corner of the attic, and was about four inches square and double that in height and it was in near perfect condition with its brightly coloured picture panels depicting happy plantation workers and the company's proud crest surrounded with gold bordering. It was a little tarnished maybe, but nevertheless provided a perfect savings depository.

Peshwari Nans

The husband and wife had managed to put by in excess of nine hundred pounds through sheer hard work at the cost of a good many nights' sleep. With the money they hoped one day to be able to return to their native Raipur in India and pay off the family farm's debts to the government and free them once and for all from their crippling interest rates and exorbitant taxes. Jasvinder herself sat up until the early hours beneath the bare forty-watt bulb that hung from the roof rafters, inserting advertising brochures into envelopes for a mailing company, earning on average fifty pence per hour. But each hour was fifty pence closer to their goal and that was all that mattered.

Over the days and weeks that followed, Esther busied herself as best she could, but during the nights she sat by the window facing that empty chair and watching those monotonous traffic signals changing, marking the passing of time. The situation soon began to eat away at her until one morning she rose half an hour earlier than usual and picked up the telephone. "Hello, hello is that you Minnie dear?" she asked when she got through. "Minnie, it's me, Essy."

"Ohhhh Essy dear, I'm sorry I didn't hear the phone," her sister replied in a flap. "I was just making a pot of tea, how lovely to hear from you. How are you, dear? How are you coping?"

"Well, well, that's why I'm calling you," Esther confessed. "It's been a little more difficult than I thought, in fact it's been damn near impossible at times."

"Oh dear, dear Essy," Minnie said, setting her teapot down and taking a seat. "Now I have all the time in the world, dear, so tell me what it is that's bothering you and we'll see what we can do to make things right."

"Oh thank you, Minnie." Esther sighed, lowering herself into Jack's chair. "I really don't know where to start. I mean I thought I'd be fine on my own but the truth of the matter is I'm not, I'm not fine, Minnie, I'm going to pieces and I don't know what to do. Lizzy's been in from time to time but I don't like to bother her."

"I know exactly what you mean, Essy dear," Minnie agreed, pouring her chamomile tea and rattling a silver spoon in her cup. "But you really don't have to be on your own you know, I told you that. I have a neighbour who's been wanting to buy my place for ages and, like I said, the company would be good for both of us."

"Would you really come and live here, Minnie dear?" Esther asked, looking about her flat. "I mean it's hardly what you're used to, is it?"

"It's fine, really," Minnie told her sister. "At my time of life I don't want a great deal and I doubt if you do either. I have a bit of money so we can splash out on the odd luxury I'm sure, maybe one of those flat screen televisions I've heard so much about and maybe a modern radiogram."

Esther heaved a sigh of relief. "Whatever you say, Minnie dear," she replied. "But to be honest I'd give it all for a cup of tea and a good old natter."

"Right so it's settled then," Minnie said abruptly. "I'll sort things out this end and in the meantime feel free to call at any time, day or night, do you hear?"

"Yes, Minnie dear." Esther smiled. "And thank you, thank you ever so much."

"Don't mention it at all," Minnie said, brimming with enthusiasm. "Now I'll get myself dressed and go and see my neighbour, I'll speak to you soon Essy, take care!"

Esther made herself a pot of tea, chamomile just like her sister's brew, one of few similarities between them, what with Minnie being more like their father: brash and irresponsible, and Esther taking after their mother, who had been a music hall singer with the voice of an angel and a glittering career spanning thirty years and who had travelled several continents singing alongside some of the legendary greats of her generation.

After a speedy sale—avoiding the costly estate agency fees—Minnie's property was sold and a date for the move arranged. Esther flitted around her flat early that morning in a heady daze, overjoyed at her sister's impending arrival. "Morning Jazzy dear," she said, opening her door as Jasvinder descended the stairs to open the shop. "Lovely day."

"Yes, yes it is Mrs Reynolds," Jasvinder replied, smiling. "Very lovely indeed."

Esther took the girl's hand. "Please dear, call me Esther," she said. "Christ, girl, your hands are freezing!" she then remarked, rubbing Jasvinder's hand in hers. "Is your heating on the blink or something?"

"No, no, it's perfectly fine," Jasvinder replied, not wanting to make a fuss. But the truth of the matter was that their aging electric fire had finally broken down, so the couple had resorted to going to bed fully clothed.

"If you'll excuse me, Mrs Reynolds," she added, sidestepping her neighbour. "I must open the shop, I cannot be late."

"Okay love," Esther said, watching her leave and shaking her head.

Minnie and her removal van arrived at noon with far more of her worldly goods than she ever needed to bring.

"Heavens, Minnie dear," Esther exclaimed as a constant stream of possessions passed by. "Where on earth are we going to put all this?"

"It's just a few things, Essy dear." Minnie smiled, directing operations. "Over there, dear!" she told a young man who was carrying a standard lamp. "No not there, to the left, a little more, not that's too far, back a tad, there that's it."

Peshwari Nans

The lad raised his eyebrows and returned to the van for more of her belongings. When the van had left the two sisters standing in a tiny space in the middle of the floor surrounded by some fifty or so boxes, a three-piece suite and side tables, seven lamps, a grandfather clock and a whole host of 'smalls' as they were known in the furniture trade. "It'll be fine, Essy dear." Millie smiled. "Once we've rearranged a thing or two."

"A thing or two!" Esther said, hemmed in between two boxes. "Millie dear, I'd like a cup of tea but I can't find the kitchen door, for heaven's sake!"

Eventually some semblance of normality was achieved after much huffing, puffing and panting and numerous pots of tea, although Esther's flat now closely resembled a cluttered second-hand shop, complete with stuffed Macaw, various chiming clocks, alabaster wall plaques and more carnival glass clowns than Esther felt comfortable with.

"Minnie dear," she said, opening the last of the boxes. "Why on earth have you bought so much shrimp paste?"

"Oh you found it, Essy dear," Minnie said, delighted to say the least. "I was worried I'd left it behind, I live on the stuff you see, the doctor told me to eat plenty of shellfish and quite frankly I find crab a little overbearing."

"Yes, but…" Esther said, surveying the crammed box of some sixty or so jars. "There's enough here to last a lifetime, surely?"

"Good heavens no!" Minnie laughed. "A month or two at the most I'd say."

Suddenly there was a knock at the door "I'll get it," Esther said, closing the box. "Hello Jazzy dear, do come in," she said, greeting Jasvinder.

"Just for a moment, Mrs Reynolds," Jasvinder said, clutching a covered plate. "I have baked your sister some samosas to welcome her. I hope you do not mind."

Peshwari Nans

"Oh no, of course not, Jazzy love," Esther said, taking the plate. "That's awfully kind of you, thank you. Jazzy this is Minnie, Minnie this is Jasvinder. She and her husband live upstairs and work in our old shop—you know, the chemist shop downstairs."

"Ahh yes, pleased to meet you dear," Minnie said, offering her hand. "Samosas you say? Well I don't usually go in for rich foods but I'll give them a try nethertheless. Thank you dear, it's a pleasure to meet you."

Jasvinder clasped her hands together and bowed. "And you too," she said. "But if you will excuse me I must be returning to the shop. I hope you enjoy your stay here."

"Thank you, love," Minnie said, seeing her to the door. "I hope to see you around. Pop in for a cup of tea whenever you wish."

"She works too hard," Esther said after Minnie had closed the door. "And that husband of hers, I've heard him go out late at night and come home exhausted in the morning. You really must try one of Jazzy's samosas though, dear, they're simply divine."

"Yes, yes indeed," Minnie said a little hesitantly. "Maybe with a touch of shrimp paste."

Esther looked down her nose at her sister. "Now Minnie dear," she said disapprovingly. "Jazzy is a wonderful cook so give her the benefit of the doubt before you go spoiling it with your potted paste."

"You're right Essy, I'm sorry," Minnie said, removing the foil and taking a piping-hot samosa and first nibbling the tiniest of corners. "Mmmm delicious!" she said, having barely tasted the snack. "She is a terrific cook like you say."

The following morning Minnie rose first at daybreak and tapped on her sister's door "Essy dear I've made you some tea," she called out, waiting momentarily for a reply. "Essy dear?" she added, tapping a little harder. "I've made a pot of tea!"

16

Peshwari Nans

A shuffling could be heard on the other side of the door and soon Esther appeared, fastening her robe. "Heavens Minnie, what time is it?" she said, bleary eyed. Her hair was in loose curlers.

"Six-fifteen, dear," Minnie replied, turning the pot three times on the table. "I never lie in, dear, not at my age, and neither should you, Essy love, we're on borrowed time as it is. I mean look at your Jack..." She then changed her tone, seeing her sister's eyes wander to Jack's photograph. "Oh Essy I'm sorry. I didn't mean it like that."

"It's alright Minnie." Esther sighed. "I've just never been one for early mornings me, you should know that."

"Yes I remember, dear," Minnie reminisced. "I had my breakfast, and yours for that matter, before you were even out of bed. I suppose that's why I've always carried a few extra pounds."

"Yes, it serves you right." Esther smiled. "I can't remember how many times I went to school hungry because of you."

Minnie always did have the more bulkier frame of the two ladies.

Later the sisters donned their hats, scarfs and woollen gloves and left the flat, each dragging a tartan trolley behind them, and set off for the market, which was now a daily feature of Whitechapel life and in full swing on their arrival, offering everything from replica Persian rugs, mobile phone accessories, fresh fish and discounted garments of all description.

The majority of the market stallholders now were Orientals, Asians and Somalis but a few of the old-time traders still stubbornly clung to their pitches, each and every one of them remembering the Reynolds family with fondness and respect.

Peshwari Nans

"Mawnin, Esther love!" a fellow greengrocer said, handing her a bag of conference pears. "Sorry to hear about Jack, me and him go way back ya know."

"Thank you, Freddie dear," Esther replied, knowing full well that to offer Freddie payment for his produce would be a gross insult. "I don't believe you've met my sister Minnie, have you?"

Freddie removed his time-worn cloth cap and offered Minnie his hand, after wiping the soil from his King Edwards onto his apron. "Pleased to meetcha, Love," he said before popping several juicy plums into a brown paper bag and spinning it closed. "There ya go me darling, them's me bestest Victorias, you won't get no better, not on this market thas for sure, ain't that right, Esther love?"

"That's right, Freddie dear." Esther smiled, popping her pears into her trolley. Without parting with a single penny throughout the market Esther accumulated a pound-and-a-half of smoked mackerel, a box of broken biscuits, a kilo of shelled Brazil nuts and an assortment of dented tinned goods, whilst Minnie purchased one or two gaudy items from the kerbside boutiques. "You surely don't intend to wear that, do you Minnie dear?" Esther asked when her sister held a strapless zebra print evening dress to her bust and eyed a full-length mirror.

"I happen to think black-and-white suits me," Minnie said, checking the price tag.

"Minnie, dearest," Esther said, snatching the garment and replacing it on the rail. "You're a pensioner not a ruddy penguin! Now do come along!"

On their return the ladies first visited Jasvinder in the chemist.

"Afternoon, Jazzy dear," Esther said, approaching the counter and producing her repeat prescription for glucosamine supplements to ease the crippling symptoms of osteoarthritis. "How's that charming young husband of yours?"

"Good afternoon, Mrs Reynolds," Jasvinder replied, producing a white paper bag from beneath the counter. "Ravi is fine thank you, he has gone…"

"—Ah ah ah!" Esther said, stopping Jasvinder in mid-sentence "What have I told you Jazzy dear, it's Esther, we've known each other long enough now to dispense with the formalities don't you think? And after all, we are neighbours."

"Sorry, Mrs Esther." Jasvinder smiled.

"Just Esther, dear," Esther informed her. "Or Essy, I don't mind either way. And what do you mean he's gone? Gone where?"

"Back to Raipur," Jasvinder said, hanging her head. "His father has contracted yellow fever and cannot run the family business."

"Oh dear," Esther said, her brow furrowed. "Jazzy I'm terribly sorry to hear that."

Minnie then piped up behind her sister: "Excuse me, love, but how much are your bunion patches?" she asked, holding a box aloft. But at that moment two wiry Oriental youths dressed in identical black designer suits entered the shop, putting Jasvinder immediately on edge.

"You got it?" one of the newcomers asked.

"Excuse me, young man!" Minnie intervened, thrusting her bunion patches under his nose. "I believe I was next."

"What?" the six-foot-plus bespectacled lad snapped back, towering over her.

"Please!" Jasvinder told the men, "Come back later, we close at eight o'clock."

"Look I told you!" he barked in reply "I want—"

"—And I told you, young man," Minnie said, interrupting him a second time. "I want my patches so I'm afraid you'll just have to wait."

19

Peshwari Nans

The Beijing-born youth, incensed at her intervention, instinctively reached into his jacket pocket, but his friend, who was pacing around, seeing the overhead CCTV camera pointing in their direction, tugged at his arm. "Let's go!" he told him, pulling his cap down to conceal his face. "Come on, Sotto!"

"Eight o'clock!" the man called Sotto growled, pointing a rigid finger at Jasvinder. "Have it ready!"

Esther cowered at the counter beneath him whilst Minnie continued to wave her box of patches "Will you pipe down!" she told Sotto. "And wait your turn!"

Sotto's companion wrenched him towards the door while Sotto himself maintained eye contact with Jasvinder until the door closed against his face.

"Frightful fellow," Esther remarked, loosening the white-knuckle grip she had on her purse.

"I am very sorry, Mrs. Reynolds," Jasvinder said, doey eyed. "Are you alright?"

"Yes, yes of course," Esther said, checking the door. "What was it they wanted?"

"I don't know Mrs Reynolds," Jasvinder said, sparing her neighbour the truth. "I have never seen them before."

"Ahem!" Minnie said still clutching the box of patches,

"Oh sorry, Miss Minnie," Jasvinder said, taking them from her, relieved at the distraction. "Three pounds twenty-five if you please."

"Thank you, dearie," Minnie said, handing over a five-pound note while her sister mulled over the situation.

"Are you sure you're okay, Jazzy dear?" Esther asked, still trembling somewhat.

"Yes thank you, I'm fine," Jasvinder replied, handing Minnie a bag and her receipt. "Your change Miss Minnie!" she added when Minnie turned away.

"Oh, thank you dear." Minnie smiled. "I'm sorry. I'm a little absent minded at times, aren't I, Essy dear?"

Peshwari Nans

Esther said nothing as Jasvinder rounded the counter and held the door open for her neighbours "You have a lovely evening," she told them, forcing a smile.

In fact Jasvinder knew the two gentlemen only too well. They were part of a small-time criminal organization, one of many to plague the UK streets. Sotto and his cohorts' principle illegitimate activities included the selling of counterfeit DVDs, stolen automobiles and narcotics, and that's where the young shop assistant came in. With cocaine and heroin shipments being increasingly intercepted by ever vigilant authorities, prescription drugs were growing in popularity. Drugs such as diazepam, otherwise known as Valium and pentobarbitone to name but a few.

Jasvinder and her husband had been leaned on by the Oriental thugs and forced to steal regular amounts from their uncle's business firstly at knifepoint. However, Dayanidhi had been going through the accounts and was growing increasingly suspicious.

Esther closed her flat door behind her. "I didn't like the look of those two," she said, dropping her keys onto the sideboard.

"What, dear?" Minnie replied, unwinding the scarf and removing her hat.

"Those men, dear," Esther insisted. "I didn't care for the way they were with Jasvinder."

"Yes, rather unsavoury I thought," Minnie agreed, donning her glasses and scrutinizing the labelling on her bunion patches. "Ooh they're medicated, dear," she added, tapping at the box.

"What?" Esther asked, slipping her gabardine coat from her shoulders and paying very little attention.

"My patches, dear!" Minnie smiled. "Isn't that marvellous. Aloe vera and jojoba."

"Yes dear," Esther said half-heartedly. "Quite."

Peshwari Nans

That evening, after a light supper of mackerel and boiled potatoes, the sisters settled in front of the television with both windows wide open to rid the flat of the heady aroma of the aforementioned smoked fish that lingered long after it had been consumed. Esther sat engrossed in her favourite weekly detective drama, one of several to buck the trend and feature a female lead after the likes of Morse and Frost had dominated the genre for many years, with Agatha Christie's detective Miss Marple being a classic exception to the rule.

"She's early," Esther said after a lengthy period of silence.

"Who is, dear?" Minnie asked, sitting in her wing-backed chair and looking over her spectacles without dropping a stitch of her knitting.

"Jazzy," Esther informed her. "It's seven forty-five," she added, looking up at the clock on the mantlepiece. "She never shuts up shop before eight p.m., never."

Jasvinder's footsteps were then heard hurrying up the stairs outside and then the slam of her attic door slamming shut. "How odd," Esther remarked.

"Mmmm," Minnie said, a tad disinterested. "If you say so, dear."

Eventually settling down once more, Esther was immediately startled by the sound of a booming stereo from a car that was arriving outside. "What on earth?" she said, clawing at the arm of her two-seater floral sofa and peering down through the open sash window.

"Close the window, Essy dear!" Minnie moaned with a look of abject disdain on her face. "I can't hear myself think with that awful racket."

"Shhhh, dear!" Esther said, waving a hand behind her. "It's those horrid men that were here earlier."

"Those what, dear?" Minnie asked, cupping a hand to her ear. "I'm sorry? What?"

Peshwari Nans

"Those men from Jazzy's shop," Esther said over her shoulder in a hushed whisper. "Asians, I think they are."

"Oooh those despicable wretches," Minnie sneered. "Come away from the window, why don't you?"

"Shhh! Be quiet!" Esther told her sister as she cautiously peered down over the window ledge.

Sotto was shoving against the chemist shop's door whilst his associate cupped his hands to the glass and peered inside. "It's closed, Sotto," he said, checking his wristwatch. "You did say eight o'clock, didn't you?"

"You know I did!" Sotto snapped, pounding on the door. "And so did that bitch!"

The time was seven fifty-eight. Jasvinder sat in darkness in the corner of her attic room with her hands clasped in prayer. Ravi was half a world away and she had no telephone.

"Sotto, Sotto!" the henchman said, tugging at his boss's arm as he tried to force his way inside. "She lives up top."

Sotto looked up as Esther ducked back inside. "Oh dear!" she said, clutching her chest and visibly shaking.

"What is it, dear?" Minnie asked, lowering her knitting "What's wrong?"

"Oh dear, oh dear," Esther repeatedly said, pacing the room. Soon the footsteps of Sotto and his subordinate could be heard ascending the stairs.

"What is it, dear?" Minnie asked again.

"It's Jazzy, dear," Esther told her sister, whilst wringing her hands. "I think she's afraid of those fellows and may be in grave danger. I'm going to telephone the police."

"Are you sure, dear?" Minnie asked, setting down her needles, rising from her chair and stepping into her corduroy slippers. "Good heavens!" she gasped, then, tugging a lengthy needle from her wool, she made for the door.

Peshwari Nans

"Minnie, no!" Esther barked, making a grab for her sister. "Don't be ridiculous! They're brutes the two of them, no no! This is a matter for the police, now do come away!"

"But Essy, dear," Minnie objected with a steely determination.

"No buts, Minnie dear," Esther insisted. They both then froze as the footsteps stopped outside their door, then continued up towards the attic.

"Hurry then, Essy dear!" Minnie said, looking up to the ceiling, knowing that Jasvinder's room was just above theirs. "Call the police at once!"

"Well I was trying to," Esther said with a contemptuous look. "And they'd be on their way by now if you hadn't been so cavalier."

"Yes, yes, alright," Minnie admitted, maintaining a firm grip on her sizeable needle. "But if they come through that door I'll, I'll stick the pair of them I tell you!" She thrust the needle several times with pursed lips and narrowing eyes.

"Hello? Hello? Is that the police?" Esther asked with the earpiece of her bakelite telephone pressed to her ear. "Yes, yes, the police, dear, that's what I said," she added when the operator asked which service she required. "Please do hurry."

In the meantime Sotto was pounding on Jasvinder's door, directly above the sisters' heads.

"BITCH, OPEN THE DOOR!" he yelled.

Jasvinder backed ever further into the corner, praying to the Hindu god Vishnu for salvation. Sotto's friend took a menacing blade from his jacket pocket and began hacking at the door frame adjacent to the lock. "OPEN THIS DOOR BITCH!" Sotto raged, kicking out.

"Yes. Yes. Hello!" Esther said, near panic stricken because of the chaos escalating above her. "You must come right away!" she told the officer. "There are two men! You must hurry!"

Peshwari Nans

The officer at the other end of the line attempted to calm Esther and glean a little more information. "Two men you say?" he asked.

"Yes, yes! Bad men," Esther insisted. "Do hurry!"

"Yes madam, we'll send someone right away," the officer told her. "If you could just tell me where you are?"

Once armed with the relevant facts, the officer advised Esther to stay inside with her door firmly bolted and not to approach the individuals in question, and informed her that a car was on its way.

As Esther put down her telephone, Sotto shoulder-barged the splintered door open and entered the attic. "Get up bitch!" he told Jasvinder while his man fumbled for the light. "I SAID GET UP!"

Jasvinder crawled sheepishly from the corner and clambered to her feet with her head bowed.

"Where are my drugs?" Sotto growled. "Are you forgetting that we had an arrangement?"

"Please!" Jasvinder said, shaking her head. "I cannot get you this anymore. My uncle, he suspects."

"You listen to me, Bitch!" Sotto snapped, grabbing at Jasvinder's throat. "You will do as I say, do you hear me? I want those drugs and I want them now!"

"Please, I cannot," Jasvinder wailed, sobbing with his grip ever tightening. "Please! Please!"

"DO YOU HAVE MY DRUGS!" Sotto bellowed into Jasvinder's face.

"No!" Jasvinder gargled, having been hoisted up onto her toes.

"Then I will get them myself," the Asian insisted. "Give me the keys."

"No, no, I cannot, please let me go," Jasvinder begged. "Please! I beg of you!"

"Let me make myself clear," Sotto snarled, plunging a clenched fist into Jasvinder's slender midriff, and then doing it again, and again, causing her to cry out and convulse.

"Here Sotto!" his associate said, plucking Jasvinder's keys from the inverted tea crate that doubled as a table.

"Thank you," Sotto said, snatching the keys and jangling them in Jasvinder's face. "Do not make me come looking for you again," he warned her, striking her temple hard with the metal Disney key fob, once for every word he spoke until he drew blood. He then thrust the distressed Hindi girl against the wall and released her before turning to leave.

Although dazed and in some considerable pain, Jasvinder could not allow her uncle's shop to be ransacked, so she staggered, clutching her bloody forehead and snatching a vase from a shelf, raised it above her head and screamed, "NOOOOO!"

Sotto's henchman spun on his heels wide eyed and without a moment's hesitation, thrust his knife deep into Jasvinder's side. Sotto himself looked over his shoulder unfazed, his face showing not a shred of emotion. Jasvinder let out a pitiful cry, her eyes fixed on her attackers as her punctured right lung began to fill with blood. As the vase fell she managed with gritted teeth to steer it towards the thug's head, shattering it into several pieces but inflicting very little in the way of harm, causing him more embarrassment than pain.

"Sotto's right," he said, twisting his blade. "You are a bitch!" So saying, the barbarian removed the knife and rammed it home again and again until Jasvinder collapsed to the floor coughing blood and haemorrhaging internally.

"Come!" Sotto barked at his man, making for the stairs. "Leave her!"

Straightening his jacket, Jasvinder's assailant wiped the blood from his blade on her headscarf that hung on the door and followed his master to the stairs and down.

Peshwari Nans

"Where the devil are they?" Esther said, looking through the window for any sign of the police while Minnie cowered behind the door, having heard enough of the attack above her to know that these men were ruthless and indeed cold hearted.

Once outside, Sotto and his man unlocked the chemist's shop and entered, and, as Jasvinder had feared, began smashing at the locked medicine cabinets. But no sooner had they begun to make headway than the sound of approaching sirens startled them and they both fled through the rear fire door and made their escape.

Knowing now that help was on its way Esther unbolted her door. "Minnie dear, bring them up when they arrive," she said ushering her sister downstairs before starting for the attic. "Jazzy, Jazzy dear?" she called, pushing the damaged attic door open. "Oh good heavens!" she cried, seeing her young friend lying in a pool of blood with both hands pressed to her side. "Jazzy dear, whatever's happened?" she asked, lowering herself down onto her knees with the aid of the tea crate.

Jasvinder's eyes were rolling and her mouth spattered with vomited blood. "Mrs, Mrs Reynolds," she spluttered, tugging at Esther's cotton shawl.

"Shhh, shh, don't speak dear!" Esther told her, reaching for a tea cloth to stem the flow of blood from her wounds. "I'll get you an ambulance," she attempted to leave but Jasvinder refused to relinquish her grip on her shawl.

"No, no, please!" she croaked with a pitiful acceptance of her diminishing chances of survival. "Wait!" She reached out and dragged the red vintage Lipton's tea tin from beneath her duvet.

"What's that, dear?" Esther asked, dabbing at the open cuts with the now sodden cloth.

"Give this, give this to Ravi," Jasvinder insisted, arching her back in agonizing pain. "Pleas Mrs Reynolds!"

"Ravi?" Esther said, taking the tin. "But Ravi's not here."

"Give it to Ravi," Jasvinder said, reeling.

Minnie stood on the edge of the pavement in her flannelette nightgown and waved the police car down. "Hurry young man!" she said as the officer stepped out to meet her.

"What's the problem, madam?" he asked, straightening his utility belt,

"Upstairs! Hurry!" Minnie said, ushering him to the open street door.

Clutching Jasvinder's tea tin Esther looked over her shoulder. "Do hurry!" she called to the approaching officer.

"Give it to Ravi," Jasvinder said again in a state of near delirium.

"Yes dear," Esther agreed. "I'll see to it I promise, I'll give it to your uncle he'll know what to do, now don't speak."

"No, no!" Jasvinder said, wide eyed. "Not my uncle!" She knew full well that Ravi would never see a penny of their savings if her unscrupulous Uncle Dayanidhi were the go-between. "No Mrs Reynolds—Ravi!"

The officer then arrived "Christ!" he gasped at the bloody scene. "Two-four, two-four," he then barked into his radio. "Requesting an ambulance at this location, quick as you can please."

"Please help her," Esther said, distraught by now.

Minnie eventually made it to the attic landing and immediately clasped a hand to her mouth. "Oh good God, Esther!" she cried, steadying herself at the door while the young officer attempted to prevent further blood loss from the young victim. But their efforts proved futile.

"What's her name?" the officer asked.

"Jazzy," Esther said, in a daze herself. "Sorry. It's Jasvinder."

Peshwari Nans

"Jasvinder stay with me, love," the officer told the traumatized Hindi girl. "An ambulance is on its way. What happened?" he then asked the sisters.

"Two beastly men did this to her," Esther replied, rubbing Jasvinder's hand. "I think they were Japanese or Chinese."

"They came into the shop this afternoon," Minnie interjected.

"Which shop would that be, madam?" the officer asked over his shoulder.

"The chemist's below us," Esther informed him. "Jazzy here runs it for her uncle."

Hearing the ambulance approaching the police officer left the ladies. "Keep talking to her," he said in parting.

"Yes, yes, of course," Esther said, stroking Jasvinder's face. "It's alright dear, help is on its way". She did her level best to reassure her friend, who by now lay awash with blood. Slipping in and out of consciousness, Jasvinder tapped at the tin on Esther's lap. "Give it to Ravi," she said, choking and fighting for every breath.

"Yes of course dear, but how?" Esther asked. "Ravi's gone, hasn't he?"

With her response garbled and inaudible, Jasvinder reached into a cardboard box that doubled as her larder and grappled amongst the provisions for a bag of basmati rice, thrusting it into Esther's arthritic hands, nodding in doing so.

"What's this?" Esther asked, bemused. "Jazzy, what do you mean?"

At that moment the paramedics hurried inside and ushered her aside. "Thank you madam, we'll take it from here," one of them said, taking a large green pack from his back.

"Oh yes, of course dear," Esther replied, pulling herself up and joining her sister.

Peshwari Nans

"I think she's been stabbed," the police officer said from the doorway. "Ladies, is there somewhere we can talk?" he then asked the distraught sister's.

"Yes, yes, downstairs," Esther told him without taking her eyes from Jasvinder. "She will be alright won't she?" she asked the crouching paramedics. "She's such a sweet girl."

The two ambulance men looked at one another with a degree of concern. "We need to get her to a hospital right away," one of them said, sending for a stretcher. "Jazzy, can you hear me?" he then asked, shining a torch into Jasvinder's glazed eyes. "Squeeze my hand if you can hear me, love."

Jasvinder did not respond to repeated questioning.

"Oh dear, the poor girl," Esther said, coaxed away by the policeman.

"She will be alright, won't she, young man?" Minnie asked once they were inside their flat.

"She's in good hands," the officer replied, taking out his pocketbook. "Now ladies, before we begin, are you both alright?" he asked. "Were you hurt in any way?" He looked Esther's bloodied garments up and down. "I can ask the paramedics to take a look at you if you like."

"No, no!" Esther insisted. "Let them see to Jazzy, we're fine, aren't we dear?"

"Just a little shook up, that's all," Minnie said, taking her seat.

Jasvinder was stretchered by the open door to a waiting ambulance as forensics officers arrived to examine the scene.

"Can I help?" a WPC said, following them upstairs and popping her head into Esther's flat. "Oh good grief," she then said, seeing Esther's bloodied state. "Are you okay, my darling?"

Peshwari Nans

"They could really do with a cup of tea, Susan," the policeman said, intervening. "Would you mind?"

"No, no, not at all." Susan smiled, heading for the kitchen. "Through here, is it?"

"Yes, dearie." Minnie nodded. "We both take chamomile if you don't mind, and thank you, you're so kind."

"My pleasure," Susan said, disappearing.

The two shaken sisters gave as good a description of Jasvinder's attackers as they could. "The taller of the two had a mark on the left side of his face," Minnie explained. "A mole I think."

"No dear, I think it was one of those tattoo things," Esther said, recalling a tiny dragon below Sotto's left eye. "A tiger I think. No, no, wait it was a dragon. Yes I'm sorry, it was definitely a dragon no bigger than my thumbnail, blue I think, or was it green? I'm sorry officer, I'm not being of much help am I?"

"You're doing great, Mrs Reynolds," the bobby said, writing feverishly. "Now have either of you seen these two gentlemen around these parts before? I mean would you say they're locals?"

"Oh no, never," Esther replied adamantly. "I would have recognized them for sure. We have a lot of Orientals on the market these days, and jolly nice people they are too, always very polite and accommodating, I buy my tea from a charming Thai lady who has a stall outside the station on Wednesdays and Fridays."

"I see," the officer said, lost for a moment. "Thank you, Susan," he then said as the WPC handed each of the sisters a cup of calming chamomile tea.

"Thank you, dear" Esther said, her hands still trembling somewhat as she took the cup and saucer.

While Jasvinder's humble bedsit was swabbed for prints and photographed thoroughly the ambulance crew fought desperately to revive her en route to the hospital after the young shopkeeper went into cardiac arrest for the third time.

"Do you think you'll catch them?" Esther asked the officers as she set down her china cup.

"Well you've painted a pretty good picture of these guys," the young man said, pocketing his notebook. "So I'm confident we'll get a result on this one sooner or later."

"Sooner, I hope," Minnie said, sipping her tea. "Nobody's safe with animals like that roaming the streets."

"You're quite right, my love," the WPC agreed, patting Minnie's hand. "Just try not to worry yourselves. Every bobby on the beat will be on the lookout for these two and I wouldn't be surprised if your descriptions aren't splashed all over tomorrow's papers."

"Oh, jolly good," Esther said, forcing a smile. "That's very reassuring to know."

Minnie stopped the two police officers as they got up to leave. "But why would anybody want to hurt such a sweet young girl?" she asked.

"Well if I were to hazard a guess," the policeman said, donning his cap, "I'd say it was drug related, what with…" He paused. "Jasvinder was the name, wasn't it?" he asked.

"Yes dear, that's right," Esther replied, rising to see them out.

"What with Jasvinder working in a chemist's and all," the officer continued. "We've seen a huge rise in the number of offences committed relating to so called 'legal highs' and over-the-counter prescription drugs."

"My word," Minnie gasped, appalled at the depths to which some people would stoop. "Do you think there's any chance these fellows might come back?"

"I very much doubt it, my lovely," the charming WPC replied, checking the door's antiquated locking mechanism. "But for your own safety and peace of mind I'd suggest you upgrade your locks. I can send someone over to have a chat with you if you like."

"Okay dear, if you really think it's necessary," Esther said, examining the door for herself. "But we've never felt the need before now. I mean nothing like this has ever happened before, and my husband and I have lived here for many many years."

"Where is your husband now, Mrs Reynolds?" the policeman asked, hoping there was a man about the house no matter how old he might be.

"Jack passed away I'm afraid," Esther said with a heavy heart. "Only just recently actually."

"I'm sorry to hear that, madam," the officer replied, removing his cap once more.

"Yes, that goes for me too," the WPC added, rubbing Esther's shoulder and glancing across at her wedding photograph the hung above the fireplace. "If you don't mind me saying so, he looked a very dashing man. The two of you look as though you were made for each other, and that dress it's gorgeous."

"Yes, yes, it was," Esther agreed. "Jack and I were childhood sweethearts you know. I fell in love with him the moment I set eyes on him., he was playing marbles in the school playground and I just marched right up to him and told him in front of all his friends that one day we would be married. We were only six and seven at the time and everybody found it highly amusing but I knew, I knew there and then, that one day Jack would be mine."

Esther's tale of a bygone age touched the young WPC with thoughts of her late grandparents who met in a shelter during the Second World War and were married within a matter of weeks. "You take care, my love," she told Esther and then slipped a card into her hand. "If you need anything, and I mean *anything* you can reach me on that number. Goodbye Minnie, lovely to meet you."

"Goodbye, dear." Minnie smiled, joining them at the door,

"Oh, oh!" Esther then called after the officers. "When can we go and see her? Jazzy I mean?"

"I'd wait until morning if I were you, Esther love," the WPC replied with a hand on the stair rail. "I think you'll find she'll be in surgery for much of the night, judging by her injuries."

"Oh the poor thing," Esther said, taking a tissue from her bloodied sleeve. "I do hope she'll be alright, she has no family here as such, there is an uncle but they're not at all close by all accounts."

"Well, she has you." The WPC smiled. "Now you get yourself on in and make sure you bolt that door, won't you?"

"Yes, yes, goodbye," Esther said, waving.

"My God, Essy dear," Minnie said as her sister closed the door and slipped the top and bottom bolts. "You simply must change out of those clothes—look at the state of you!"

"Yes, yes, in a moment, dear," Esther replied, looking across the road at the hospital with an expression of utter despair. "Why? Why her?" she said to herself.

"Come on, dear," Minnie said, with a neatly folded nightie over one arm and a bottle of sweet sherry in her hand. "Let's get you sorted and the two of us can have a little something to 'steady our nerves' so to speak."

"Thank you, Min," Esther said, pulling down the heavily painted sash window. "But just the one mind, I want to be over to check on Jazzy first thing in the morning. I'll get her some flowers, and a box of chocolates perhaps."

"Good idea," Minnie agreed, setting two crystal glasses down on the table. "I have one or two paperbacks she might like to take a look at while she's convalescing."

Peshwari Nans

The following morning, true to her word, Esther was up at the crack of dawn waking her sister with a cup of tea and after a trip to the newsagents for boiled sweets Esther and her sister chose fresh tulips and chrysanthemums from a close friend of Jack's who ran a stall on the market. "No, no Ron I insist!" Esther snapped, thrusting a five-pound note into his hand. "I appreciate the gesture but you have a living to make, and we all know money doesn't grow on trees now, don't we?"

"Yes I know Esther love, but," Ron said, reluctant to accept payment, "Jack was always good to me. I mean how many times did he slip an extra cauli into me bag or a buncha bananas? Ar don't forget nuffing me, ar tell ya it proper broke me art when they told me e'd passed away."

"Thank you, Ron," Esther said with a tender touch. "I have my sister now so I'm not alone."

"We av met," Ron said, offering Minnie a hand in a fingerless glove. "At Jack's seventieth. You don't remember me, do ya?"

"I can't say that I do," Minnie confessed, peering over her spectacles. "That was an awful long time ago and my mind's not what it was."

"Ar got you up on the dance floor." The cockney market trader smiled, hoping to jog Minnie's memory. "You trod on me foot arf way fru the waltz an ar twisted me hip!"

"No, no, I still don't remember," Minnie said, shaking her head. "But by the sound of things we were no Fred and Ginger, were we?"

"Oh ar dunno!" Ron laughed, twirling in his market apron. "Ar've ad two new hips since then so if you ever fancy a two-step girl, ar'm ya man!"

"Thank you Ron, I'll bear that in mind," Minnie said, taking the wrapped blooms.

Peshwari Nans

Crossing the road Minnie tapped at her sister's arm with a glint in her eye. "Essy dear, I do believe Ron may have the hots for me, what do you think?" she asked.

"I wouldn't get too excited dear," Esther said, stopping abruptly when a speeding cycle courier jumped the red light and narrowly missed them. "Ron has the hots for just about anything in a skirt, he's always been the same."

Armed with their get-well gifts the sisters entered the historic Royal London Hospital, which was founded in 1740 and originally known as the London Infirmary. Among the tens of thousands that had been treated within its walls was Joseph Merrick, also known as 'The Elephant Man', whose skeleton is now mounted on display in the hospital's very own school of medicine, but which cannot be viewed to this day by the general public.

"Excuse me, dear?" Esther said, approaching the reception desk. "A friend of ours was admitted last night. Jasvinder."

"Is that the surname?" the abrupt receptionist replied, tapping at her computer keyboard.

"Oh no dear," Esther told her. "I'm afraid I don't know her surname, she's a neighbour you see, she was brought in between half-eight and nine I'd say, wouldn't you agree, Minnie dear?"

"I couldn't really say," Minnie confessed. "It was all so chaotic, you see."

"Okay. Jasvinder you say?" the receptionist asked.

"Yes," Esther agreed. "I call her Jazzy but I believe it is Jasvinder. She came in by ambulance."

"Aaaand what was she admitted for, do you know?" the receptionist asked, retrieving the night book.

"The poor dear had been stabbed," Esther informed her, trembling at the very thought. "It was awful. There was blood evewrywhere."

Peshwari Nans

"Yes, yes, I can imagine," the receptionist replied, paying very little attention. "You might like to try A and E or possibly the ICU, down the hall, take a left at the end then second on the right, okay?"

"Yes, thank you," Minnie said, tottering after her sister, who was already on her way.

"I say!" Esther called to a duty nurse. "I say, I'm looking for Jasvinder, I don't know her last name I'm afraid but she was brought in last night and we were told to try the A and E or the IC something or other."

"ICU," the nurse replied, checking the watch that hung from her breast pocket. "Right. Let me take a look for you. Jasvinder was it?"

"Yes, yes, dear," Esther said, following the nurse.

"Oh!" the nurse said, stopping abruptly at a white board with scribblings that only somebody within the medical profession could decipher. "Shall we take a seat?" she added, ushering the ladies to a row of chairs. "I er, I'm afraid Jasvinder passed away last night. I am sorry."

"I'm sorry, what?" Esther said, cocking an ear. "What did you say?"

"She passed away, my love," the nurse said sympathetically. "Was she a friend of yours?"

"Passed away? But…" Esther said, lowering the flowers. "B-but she…"

Minnie hung her head and set down her bags at her sister's side while the nurse gave them a moment to digest the tragic news before explaining: "I'm afraid Jasvinder suffered multiple stab wounds to her abdomen and lungs. We did all we could but by the time she arrived here she had already lost so much blood and was ever so weak."

"Oh no, no!" Esther said with a hand to her mouth. "No not Jazzy, not Jazzy!"

Minnie put an arm around her sister. "I'm sorry dear," she said softly.

Peshwari Nans

Esther put her head in her hands and quietly sobbed for the life of an innocent friend and neighbour snuffed out like a breath of wind to a candle. "Can I see her?" she then asked. "Please. I'd like to say goodbye if I may."

"I'll have to check for you, one moment," the nurse said, leaving the ladies.

"Oh Min," Esther said, leaning into her sister's shoulder,

"I know, dear." Minnie sighed, shaking her head. "I know."

The nurse returned a short while later and ushered the sisters to a side room at the end of the corridor, where Jasvinder's body lay covered up. "We did our best to clean her," the nurse told them, dragging back the white sheet to reveal the girl's face.

"Oh dear God!" Esther gasped rocking backwards.

"Are you alright?" the nurse asked with a steadying hand on her arm.

Minnie looked upon the deceased girl briefly before heading for the door. "I'm sorry I can't," she said on leaving and clutching a handkerchief to her mouth. "I just can't."

Esther took a moment to compose herself. "Can I have a moment alone with her?" she asked the duty nurse. "Do you mind?"

"No, not at all," she was told. "Take as long as you like."

"Thank you dearie," Esther said, watching her leave. Once alone Esther sat at Jasvinder's side. "Oh Jazzy darling," she said with a lump in her throat. "I'm so very sorry I couldn't do anything to help you, really I am."

Jasvinder lay as though asleep, with the faintest traces of blood visible in the creases of the corners of her mouth and in her jet-black shoulder-length hair. "I have your tin my darling," Esther continued. "I promise I'll do whatever I can to make sure that Ravi gets it. I have the rice too but for the life of me I just can't see the significance, I really can't."

Esther sat with the young Hindi girl, reluctant to leave her cold and alone until Minnie entered the room once again. "I'm sorry Essy dear, I should never have left you," she said with her head bowed. "Forgive me." She stood at the opposite side of the bed.

"Look at her," Esther told her sister. "She looks so beautiful, I keep expecting her to open her eyes."

"It really is such a shame," Minnie added, running her hand gently along the sheet. "A crying shame."

"I have to find her husband," Esther told her sister. "I made a promise to her, a promise I aim to keep if it's the last thing I do."

"That's very noble of you, Essy dear." Minnie smiled, unaware of Ravi's location and not wanting to press the point at that particular time. Instead she stood in quiet contemplation, almost ashamed at having lived for so long when Jasvinder had barely had a chance at life.

Eventually the sisters had to leave, saying their goodbyes, Esther leaning down to plant a tender kiss on Jasvinder's forehead. "Sleep tight my child," she whispered, dabbing her eyes with a tissue. "Sleep tight."

Leaving the hospital in sombre mood and crossing the Whitechapel Road, Esther and Minnie were met outside the chemist's shop by Jasvinder's uncle.

"The police came to see me," he told Esther, "asking all sorts of questions about my business. The shame of it."

"Your business!" Esther snapped. "Jasvinder is dead for heaven's sake and all you care about is your damn business!"

"The girl was a fool," Dayanidhi said, enraging Esther further. "I should never have hired her."

"She's your niece god damn it!" Esther stormed, baring her teeth. "Have you no decency, man?"

"Yes, yes I have," Dayanidhi said in his defence. "I will see to it that her body is flown back to Raipur."

"Well that's the least you can do," Minnie said, adding her own two pennyworth.

"She has a month's wages owing to her," Dayanidhi informed the sisters. "That will more than cover the fare."

"You mean to say," Esther said, positively seething, "that you won't even pay the blasted fare?"

"Times are hard," Dayanidhi said, holding up his hands. "And I have to pay for my shop to be repaired because of that girl."

"Why you!" Esther raged, lunging with a clenched fist, but was immediately restrained by Minnie.

"Don't dear, he's not worth it," her sister said, looking down her nose at the unfeeling shop owner.

"Watch your tongue, Mrs Reynolds," Dayanidhi warned. "If our agreement was not in writing I would see you out on the street."

This time it was Minnie who had to be restrained. "Why you horrid little man!" she snarled. "If I were a man I'd beat you black and blue I would."

Feeling a tad intimidated Dayanidhi beat a hasty retreat back into his shop and bolted the door.

"Hideous man," Esther said, opening the side door.

"Don't worry dear," Minnie said behind her. "He'll get his comeuppance one of these days—you mark my words."

"I sincerely hope so," Esther said, still raging inside. "If only Jack were here he'd have torn him off a strip, I've no doubt of that."

Even at the ripe old age of eighty-five Jack Reynolds was still a commanding figure in and around the neighbourhood, respected for his forthright manner and chivalrous attitude where women were concerned.

"There there, dear," Minnie said, handing her sister a cup of chamomile tea and sitting beside her. "So, Essy dear," she asked. "Where exactly is Jazzy's husband? Ravi isn't it?"

"Yes," Esther replied, blowing on her tea. "In Raipur, dear."

"Raipur!" Minnie exclaimed, aware of her limited geographical knowledge. "And where pray tell is that?"

"Why, India of course," Esther explained. "It's where Jazzy was born. Ravi was forced to return only just recently to help out on the family farm. He'll be devastated when he hears the news, they were so close. Jazzy said it broke his heart to have to leave her but it was only meant to be until his father recovered from his illness."

"Oh the poor dear," Minnie said, setting her teacup down and picking up the Lipton's tin. "And what on earth's this?" she asked.

"It's their life savings," Esther said, taking it from her and cradling it. "Jazzy practically begged me to get it to Ravi and to not under any circumstance give it to her uncle."

"Well you can see why," Minnie scoffed. "The man's a heartless... excuse my profanity dear, but the man's a bastard. An absolute bastard!"

"You're quite right," Esther agreed. "It's the only way to describe such a wretch."

"But, but how?" Minnie asked. "I mean how are we going to see that Ravi gets this money? He is in India after all."

"We'll take it to him," Esther blurted out without hesitation. "It's the only way."

"What?" Minnie gasped. "Take it to India!"

"Yes, why not?" Esther said abruptly. "Like I said, I made a promise and I intend to keep it."

"But Essy dear," Minnie said, struggling to get used to her sister's outlandish plan.

Peshwari Nans

"But nothing!" Esther snapped. "My mind's made up Min, so there's no use trying to talk me out of it."

"Yes I know, but," Minnie added, but then stopped, knowing full well that once her sister had set her heart on something nothing on God's green earth could stop her, like the time she decided to try her hand at snowboarding whilst holidaying in the Swiss Alps. Against all advice she took to the slopes and managed to stay upright for a full minute-and-a-half before colliding with a conifer and badly bruising her coccyx.

"But how will we find him?" Minnie asked, "and what's with the basmati rice?"

"We?" Esther asked in surprise.

"Of course!" Minnie said adamantly. "You don't think I'd let you go on your own do you? Good heavens no!"

Esther placed the bag of rice on her lap and sat tapping her finger on it. "The clever girl!" she then shrieked. "That's what she was trying to tell me, look!" The rice in question was produced on Ravi's family farm and had been brought to the UK as a fond reminder of home. "It has the address on it, dear!"

"So it does Essy, so it does." Minnie smiled, but then thought for a moment. "But, but, how will we get there, Essy dear? You can't fly, remember?"

Esther had been advised by her family practitioner to refrain from any form of air travel after a particularly troublesome case of deep vein thrombosis, contracted during her one and only foreign holiday with her late husband.

"Yes I must say I hadn't thought of that," Esther confessed. "I don't suppose there's a ferry."

"To India, dear?" Minnie laughed. "I very much doubt it. It's halfway around the world isn't it? I cruised the Med with a man friend of mine once but I think that's about as far as they go. I mean I could be wrong, dear, anyway we ran aground off the coast of Majorca and had to be towed in to port for repairs, cost us three days of our holiday although I wasn't complaining at the time. Cyril and I, that was his name, we met at a rotary club dinner and dance one Christmas eve, charming man, had the bluest eyes I'd ever seen and the most supple hips."

"Get to the point, dear!" Esther said, struggling to see a shred of relevance in her story.

"Oh yes, sorry dear." Minnie smiled, recalling her nautical affair with fondness. "Anyway, Cyril was married at the time to a horrid librarian by the name of Rita, who made the poor man's life a living hell, or so he said, but we had the most enchanting three days stranded in Palma Nova, and when I say that we barely left the hotel room I think you'll get the picture."

"Yes, yes, Minnie dearest!" Esther snapped. "But what the devil are you getting at?"

"Oh yes," Minnie said with the broadest of smiles on her face and the thought of Cyril's supple hips running through her mind. "Where was I? Oh yes, that's right, we found out later that the reason we ran aground was the fact that our captain was three sheets to the wind at the time, it seemed he abused his rum rations on a regular basis. Well that put me off sailing ever since."

"Riiiight," Esther said, weighing up their options, which were rapidly dwindling,

"We could always mail it to Ravi," Minnie suggested. "After all, we do have the full address."

"Yes, yes we do," Esther replied. "But somehow just popping the tin in the post with the very real chance of it going astray would not be fulfilling Jasvinder's dying wish, now would it?"

"It's getting late, dear," Minnie eventually said after the pair had sat in quiet contemplation for some time. "I think I'll turn in."

Peshwari Nans

"Me too, Min," Esther replied, taking the cups through to the kitchen and turning out the lights.

"Goodnight dear," Minnie said from her adjacent single bed. "Sleep well."

"You too, dear." Esther smiled, winding several rollers into her silver hair.

Esther lay awake for much of the night, oblivious to the sounds of the city outside. Her head was a jumble of thoughts, amongst them Jasvinder's dying plea, Ravi, Raipur and the bag of basmati rice. Sheer exhaustion finally got the better of her at around four a.m., and she drifted into a deep but discontented sleep.

Minnie rose around nine and busied herself with breakfast while her sister slept. Standing at the kitchen counter she watched a group of children playing ball against the rear garages. "That's it!" she shrieked, dropping her buttered toast. "That's it, that's it! Esther dear, come quick!"

Esther hadn't heard her sister's euphoria and lay motionless with her satin duvet pulled up around her ears.

"Essy, Essy dear!" Minnie said, bursting into the bedroom. "Essy, wake up! I have it!"

Minnie then began coughing and rocked back against the linen press, clutching her chest.

"Min," Esther said, rubbing her eyes. "Minnie is that you?"

Minnie's cough rattled from her lungs, causing her to bend double.

"Minnie dear!" Esther said, clambering out of bed and hurriedly donning her dressing gown. "Minnie are you alright?"

Minnie's face was crimson as she clawed at the knobs on the pine dresser. "Your tablets!" Esther cried, opening the drawer and removing Minnie's medicine box, made of Tupperware with tiny compartments, each containing two yellow pills to be taken daily. "I'll fetch you some water," she told her sister, placing the tablets into her hand. "Wait there."

Esther hurried through to the kitchen, giving the slice of toast on the floor a sideways glance in passing. "There you go, dear," she said, returning with a plastic beaker. "Slowly, slowly, dear," she added as her sister grappled with the cup. "I wish you wouldn't get so worked up," she then said, rubbing Minnie's back. "It's really not good for you. Anyway, what was all the fuss about? I hardly slept a wink last night and you come crashing in here like, like heaven knows what, and by the way do you know there's a slice of toast on the kitchen floor?"

Still catching her breath, Minnie took her sister's hand.

"What is it dear?" Esther asked whilst being dragged back to the kitchen. "Can't it wait?"

"No, no, it can't," Minnie said, wheezing. "I have it Essy, I have the answer."

"What answer? What are you talking about, dear?" Esther asked, still half asleep.

"How to get to Raipur, Essy," Minnie croaked, almost beside herself with excitement.

"How?" Esther asked, following her sister's gaze out of the window and still very much none the wiser.

"Vivien!" Minnie said proudly. "You do still have her, don't you?"

"Vivien?" Esther said, looking down at their corner garage with its peeling turtle-green hand-painted doors. "Er, er yes, b-but," she stammered. "Of course Minnie dear. But you aren't seriously suggesting that we drive to Raipur are you?"

"Yes, yes I am," Minnie replied, brimming with enthusiasm. "And why not Essy? Why not?"

"Why not?" Esther laughed. "I've never heard anything so preposterous in all my life."

Peshwari Nans

"Just think about it, Essy," Minnie said, forcing the point. "You don't fly and I don't sail, so apart from a couple of bow-legged donkeys that only leaves the road!"

"But Vivien!" Esther exclaimed. "She hasn't seen the light of day in well over a decade."

Vivien was Esther and Jack's one and only luxury in life, a 1965 Morris 1000 Traveller in Trafalgar blue, lovingly named after Vivien Leigh, the screen siren who starred opposite Clark Gable in the 1939 all-time classic movie *Gone with the Wind.*

The Morris Traveller with its distinctive ash wood framing to its side windows and rear doors was very much the roadster of its day, used by vacationing families the length and breadth of the country and Jack, Esther and baby Elizabeth were no different, although not taking as frequent holidays as many. Locked away during the winter months, Vivien was only brought out on Sundays and bank holidays when the weather permitted. Their destination of choice was predominantly the Essex coastal town of Leigh-on-Sea with its bustling cockle sheds, striped deckchairs and enough ice cream to cover a small child from head to toe (Elizabeth was covered like this time and time again). But with Elizabeth eventually reaching an age where the lure of destinations further afield divided the family somewhat, so the need for Vivien's services dwindled and she spent more and more time locked away.

"Well?" Minnie asked after Esther had stood speechless for a moment or two. "What do you think?"

"What do I think?" Esther said, still dumbfounded by her sister's seemingly ridiculous proposition. "What do I think? I think you must have fallen out of bed this morning and bumped your head, that's what I think."

"But Essy dear," Minnie replied, convinced of her plan's validity. "You always said that Vivien never once let you down. You said that, didn't you?"

Peshwari Nans

"Yes I did, Min love, but that was years ago," Esther told her.

Jack had bought Vivien for Esther on their silver wedding anniversary and wrapped her in the biggest brightest yellow bow he could find, such was his love for her.

"Besides," Esther went on. "How on earth would we get to India by road? I doubt that even crossed your mind did it?"

"Well no, actually it didn't," Minnie confessed. "But if there is a way then I believe we should at least consider it. Or have you forgotten the promise you made to Jasvinder already?"

"No of course I haven't!" Esther snapped. "How could you even think that I would? Jazzy meant the world to me, and you're right I did promise her so okay I will consider it, but I think you'll find that Vivien isn't the answer, there's a distinct possibility that she'll never run again."

"Well what about that grandson of yours?" Minnie asked, switching on the kettle and rinsing two china cups "Robert isn't it?"

"Richard," Esther said, reaching for the chamomile. "What of him?"

"Richard, that's it." Minnie smiled. "He's always tinkering with that sporty little car of his, isn't he? Maybe he could take a look at her for us."

Richard was indeed one of life's tinkerers, with a natural penchant for all things mechanical, having helped service his grandfather's delivery van as a child.

"Well, yes he is," Esther admitted. "But—"

"—Right that's settled then," Minnie said, cutting her sister short. "You're to telephone him today and arrange a viewing, and tell him to bring his tinkering tools. Somehow I think he's going to need them."

"Okay," Esther said, warming to the idea. "I will."

47

Peshwari Nans

The two ladies sat side by side on the sofa sipping their tea. "Oh wait!" Minnie suddenly said, rising and disappearing into the bedroom where she tore at the packing tape on the last of her removal boxes. "Got it!" she smiled, retrieving a tattered and dog-eared world atlas. "Remember this, Essy dear?" she said, rejoining her sister and wiping the dust from the faded cover. "As children we used to sit and plan our grand adventures to far off continents, jungles and Arabian deserts, didn't we?"

"You still have it," Esther said, taking the much-loved reminder of their innocent youth.

"Yes of course," Minnie replied, nestling into her sister's shoulder as she carefully turned the fragile pages where there was a spattering of crudely drawn crayon stick figures, depicting the sister's epic circumnavigation of the globe, and all done from the safety and comfort of the box room they shared.

"Oh look, dear!" Esther laughed at their transformation of the Isle of Wight to a cannibal-infested treasure island complete with volcano, snake pit and the all-important 'X to mark the spot'. "I remember that as though it were yesterday, dear," she added. "We were boiling alive in the cannibals' pot when a bouncy baboon named Bobo rescued us. My, what imaginations we had in those days."

"Yes I remember that." Minnie chuckled. "And the treasure chest was filled with liquorice and gum drops."

"Riiight now let me see," Esther said, looking at the globe as a whole. "Well *if*, and this is a huge *if*, we are able to revive Vivien and set off by road to Raipur then it's obvious we'd first have to leave this island of ours and cross the channel to the Continent."

"Well that's easy, dear," Minnie said confidently. "Before our ill-fated Mediterranean cruise Cyril and I crossed over the pond to Calais for a spot of Parisian passion."

Peshwari Nans

Esther turned to her sister. "Oh Minnie you didn't!" She smirked.

"More than once, dear." Her sister laughed. "Well I did say he had supple hips didn't I?"

"Yes you did indeed," Esther said, tugging her spectacle case from between the sofa cushions. "Okay so Calais it is then."

Esther traced several lines with her finger while being watched intently by her sister. "This could work I suppose," she said, tapping the page. "If we pass through Germany and into Prague."

"Oooh Prague!" Minnie interjected. "I've always wanted to visit Prague. I hear it's wonderful in the summer."

"Do pay attention, dear," Esther said, glaring over her spectacles.

"Oh sorry, dear," Minnie replied, nestling closer. "Do carry on, this is exciting."

"Right. From Prague we can cut through Poland to enter Ukraine and then on to Russia."

"Russia!" Minnie gasped. "My word Essy, wouldn't that really be something?"

"Yes dear!" Esther said, angered at the constant interruption. "A miracle if Vivien gets us that far."

"But if she does," Minnie said, fidgeting. "If she does, what next?"

"Well," Esther said, turning the page, "we would have to reach China of course, but to do so we would need to pass through..." she held the atlas a little closer to focus, "Uzbekistan I think it is."

"Uzbeki what, dear?" Minnie asked. "I never knew there was such a place."

"Neither did I, dear," Esther confessed.

"Oooh you simply must remind me to dig out my polaroid, dear," Minnie told her sister. "We really should document our journey."

Peshwari Nans

"Yes, quite," Esther said, still not one hundred per cent confident. "Okay so let's just say that by some divine miracle we do reach the Chinese border." She continued tracing a possible route.

Of the two sisters Esther was the one who had gleaned a little geographical knowledge from her early years at the Central Foundation School for Girls, which was established in London in 1726 in Spital Square, adjacent to her husband's beloved Spitalfields Market. "It would be on through Kathmandu to Nepal," she told her sister.

"Oooh Nepal, where the Dalai Lama lives!" Minnie squealed.

"Yes dear." Esther laughed. "Where the Dalai Lama lives, then from Nepal it's a simple border crossing into India. But what am I saying?" she then asked herself. "We're two octogenarians driving a fifty-year-old car. Nothing could be less simple."

"What have we got to lose?" Minnie asked. "And you never know Minnie dearest, we might even find that chest of gumdrops after all."

The two of them sat as they had done as children, planning another epic adventure, only this time they would be throwing caution well and truly to the wind and leaving all their home comforts behind them.

The following day Esther telephoned her grandson Richard with Minnie squirming at her side. "I'm doing it, dear!" she said, fending her sister off. "I said I'd call him and I am. Oh hello Richard dear, it's me, Granny."

"Oh, hi Gran," Richard replied, setting down his game controller. "What's up? Are you okay?"

"Yes, yes, I'm fine, dear." Esther smiled. "How are you?"

"Ask him dear, ask him!" Minnie said, tugging at her sister's cardigan sleeve.

"Alright!" Esther snapped.

"I'm good, thanks Gran," Richard told her. "I've been meaning to pop over and see you. I took some flowers to granddad's grave a few days ago and sat with him for a while."

"Oh that's very kind of you, dear," Esther said, evading Minnie's prodding finger. "Listen Richard. I was wondering if I might ask a small favour. Well actually it might be a huge favour but I'll let you be the judge of that. It's Vivien. Would you be kind enough to take a look at her for me?"

"Vivien?" Richard said bemused, not having seen the car since he was a child. "Who's Vivien?"

"My car, dear," Esther informed him. "In the garage, you remember. Your grandfather sat you behind the wheel while he changed her oil."

"Your car!" Richard recollected. "You still have it?"

"Yes, dear," Esther replied. "I could never part with her and I know you're good with that sort of thing. I was hoping to take her for a little jaunt sometime." Esther failed to disclose the magnitude of 'the jaunt' as she called it.

"Yeah, sure Gran," Richard agreed. "I'll pick up my things and pop over this afternoon."

"Only if it's no trouble, dear," Esther told him. "I don't want to put you out."

"Don't be daft, Gran." Richard laughed. "Like I said, I've been meaning to pop over anyway."

"Oh you are a good boy," Esther said, giving her anxious sister the thumbs-up.

"Yes!" Minnie shrieked playfully, shaking her sister.

"Will you let go!" Esther snapped. "No not you Richard dear," she then told her confused grandson. "It's your Aunt Minnie. You know how she is."

"Oh okay Gran I'll see you around three," Richard said. "Seeya."

"Lovely to speak to you, dear," Esther replied. "Bye bye, bye bye."

Peshwari Nans

Minnie was at sixes and sevens all of a sudden. "I should start packing!" she cried, gathering several of her belongings, including a stained-glass table lamp.

"Will you stop, dear!" Esther said, snatching it from her "We don't even know if Vivien can be resurrected at all, so I wouldn't get my hopes up if I were you."

"Oh she'll run," Minnie said, tucking one or two hardback books under her arm. "Now where did I put my travel trousers? The elasticated waist is an absolute godsend on long journeys."

"Minnie stop, will you?" Esther barked. "We can't just up and leave straightaway with a blasted lamp and a few books! We need to plan for the journey ahead, familiarize ourselves with local customs and such."

"Yes I know that, dear," Minnie said, lying through her teeth. "But I'll still need my travel trousers."

Richard arrived at three o'clock sharp sounding his car's horn outside the rear garages. "He's here, dear," Esther told her sister, who hadn't sat still for the entire day.

"Do you have the keys, dear?" Minnie asked, taking her coat from the door.

Esther merely jangled Vivien's keys under her sister's nose and opened the door.

"Hi Gran, hi Aunt Min," Richard said, greeting them both with a kiss. "You alright?"

"Yes dear, all the better for seeing you." Esther smiled.

Richard's friend then stepped from his hatchback, an acne-smothered seventeen-year-old 'goth' with upwards of a dozen piercings about his face including nose and lip rings, forehead studs and a pair of ear-stretching hoops you could poke a finger through.

"Oh good heavens!" Minnie shrieked, turning and meeting him face to face.

Peshwari Nans

"Gran, Aunt Min, this is Slider," Richard said, introducing the lad. "He's a very good friend of mine and a much better mechanic than I'll ever be."

"Ladies," Slider said, offering his hand courteously, something which took the sisters completely by surprise because of his outward appearance.

"Oh hello," Esther said, eyeing his tattooed knuckles before taking his hand. "Pleased to meet you. Slider did you say?"

"Yeah that's right," Slider replied. "I went down the Becton Ski slope on my backside when I was thirteen and the name's stayed with me ever since. My real name's Billy but somehow I prefer Slider."

"Well I think it's charming, dear," Esther said for want of a better reply. "So you're a whizz with automobiles so Richard tells me?"

"Yeah I'm a proper petrolhead, me." Slider smiled.

"A what, dear?" Minnie asked, transfixed by the lad's metalware.

"Petrolhead, Aunt Min," Richard explained, giving his friend a playful hug. "This boy could strip a Ferrari to its nuts and bolts and put it back together with his eyes closed."

"Well I don't have a Ferrari, dear," Esther informed him. "But I think you may have met you match with Vivien."

"No problem," Slider said confidently. "Richy told me what you got: Morris Thousand Traveller, water cooled four cylinder, eight valves giving you 49 brake horse power at 5100 rpm, four speed manual box, rear-wheel drive, torsion bar suspension on the front and leaf springs at the back with rack and pinion steering."

"Impressive, dearie," Minnie said, her head now spinning with Vivien's technical specifications "You seem to be just the fellow we're looking for."

Peshwari Nans

"Told ya," Richard said, ruffling Slider's hair. "Between the two of us we should be able to get your old car running in no time, Gran."

"Vivien," Esther said proudly. "Her name is Vivien and she's not just any old car she's a member of the family."

"Yeah, sorry Gran," Richard said, rubbing his grandmother's shoulder and remembering his place. "I know Granddad got her for you."

"Don't worry." Slider smiled. "I'll treat her like she was my own."

Minnie eyed Slider's gothic band tee shirt, featuring a newborn baby on a crucifix, but because of his supposed mechanical prowess decided not to voice her objections.

"Shall we take a look at her then?" Richard asked, heading for the family garage.

"Yes, yes, of course," Esther said, hurrying behind him. "Help me with this, will you?" she then said, struggling with the lock. "It appears to be rusted solid, dear."

"Hang on," Slider said, retrieving a tin of lubricant from his toolbag. "This'll sort it."

Sure enough, after a few squirts and a wiggle of the key, the lock sprang open.

"Wonderful, dear," Esther said, patting his back. "Perhaps you could use that on my back? I creak like a barn door first thing in the morning."

Minnie helped to pull open the aged double doors, and for the first time in many many years the sunlight illuminated Vivien's front bumper and then her bonnet. Esther immediately clasped her hand to her mouth, unable to stem the flow of tears.

"Ohhh Gran," Richard said, wrapping his arms around her. "It's alright, it's alright."

"There, there, Essy dear," Minnie said, knowing only too well that the last time her sister set eyes on Vivien she and Jack were heading to the coast for a blissful day by the sea.

"May I?" Slider said, asking her permission to enter.

Esther nodded, mopping her eyes.

"She's a beauty!" Slider said, running his hand across the bonnet and tracing a line in the accumulated dust.

"Yes," Esther agreed, pulling herself together. "Yes she is."

Slider took the keys from Esther's trembling hand and gingerly opened the driver's door. "Oh wow!" he said as a whiff of nostalgia washed over him.

"Start her up! Start her up!" Minnie cried, clinging to her sister.

"No way!" Slider said, popping the bonnet open. "That's the worst thing you can do to a car that's been left standing as long as Vivien here has. The oil would have completely drained to the sump you see, so the pistons will be bone dry. If we turn her over now we could do all sorts of damage. I'll have to crank the engine over manually to make sure she's not seized."

"What's he talking about?" Esther asked her grandson.

"Never mind, Gran." Richard smiled. "Believe me, he knows what he's doing. I tell you what, why don't you and Aunt Min go and put your feet up for an hour or so and leave us to it? I'll call you when she's done."

"Okay dear," Esther said, arching her back. "I do have trouble standing for any length of time these days. Thank you dear, and thank you too, Slider."

"No worries, Mrs Reynolds," Slider said, removing several ratchets and spanners from his bag. "I promise I'll be real gentle with her."

"What a charming young man," Minnie commented as the two made their way back to the flat. "I'll admit I didn't care for him at all when I first saw him, but I suppose you can never judge a book by its cover do you agree Essy dear? Do you?"

"Absolutely not, dear," Esther agreed. "It takes all sorts, after all."

Richard and his best friend checked Vivien over meticulously, cleaning her spark plugs with emery cloth, overhauling her distributor and wire brushing the corrosion from her battery terminals. And while Slider got down to the technical side of things, Richard brushed away the dust, polished her chrome accessories and buffed her Trafalgar blue paintwork to a gleaming shine. Slider then drained the ancient petrol from Vivien's tank and poured in a gallon of new fuel from his can.

"Nearly there," he said, checking that there was sufficient power in the battery to turn over the engine. "We're gonna have to jump her" her told Richard. "Give us a hand, will you?" Releasing the handbrake the two of them rocked Vivien back and forth to release the rusting brake shoes from the drums, before rolling her out onto the forecourt.

The varnish on Vivien's woodwork had tarnished somewhat but apart from that she looked magnificent, resplendent in fact, with the sun glinting from her Morris emblem on the bonnet. Richard connected one end of his positive and negative jump leads to his own battery and the other to Vivien's and left his car idling for several minutes to transfer some charge.

"Ready?" Slider asked leaning into Vivien's driver's door with one foot on the accelerator,

"Yeah, go for it," Richard replied, stepping back.

Vivien's engine turned over countless times as Slider pumped the accelerator pedal. "Come on, come on," Richard said, biting at his thumbnail, but Vivien flatly refused to start. "Try it again!" he then said when Slider emerged, shaking his head. "Please, Slider!"

Peshwari Nans

Slider held the starter for a longer period of time but again Vivien was reluctant to stir from her lengthy slumber.

Esther watched from her kitchen window, rocking back and forth as the boys toiled over her beloved car. "Come on darling," she mouthed, willing Vivien to wake up. "There's a good girl."

"I'm gonna check the fuel line," Slider said, grabbing a screwdriver and leaning into the engine bay. "There's nothing getting through," he soon added. "Richy? Pump the pedal, mate!"

Richard did so while his friend stripped pieces from the carburettor "That's it keep the ignition on!" Slider yelled.

Minnie took a chocolate biscuit from the barrel and stood nibbling at her sister's side "What's happening dear?" she asked, depositing crumbs at her feet.

"They've been at it for ages God bless them," Esther told her sister, looking disapprovingly at the kitchen floor. "Do watch what you're doing, Minnie dear," she told her, fetching a dustpan and broom. "We'll be running alive with rodents at this rate."

"Never mind that, dear," Minnie said, craning her neck to see the boys. "What about Vivien? Any luck?"

"I'm afraid not by the looks of things," Esther replied, kneeling at her sister's feet. Binning the crumbs she joined the vigil at the window. "It's hopeless, dear," she added. "I'm afraid we're scuppered."

Even with the carburettor overhauled, spark plugs cleaned, distributor dismantled and points cleaned and gap checked, the air filter grime brushed away and the battery fully charged, Vivien remained in an auto comatose state.

"Give it another go," Richard said, checking his watch with the light fading.

"We've checked everything," Slider told him after repeatedly tuning the key. "I don't know why she won't start."

57

"A little love," Richard suddenly said. "Granddad always said every car needs a little love and she'll never let you down, just like his Essy he used to say."

"Well what do you expect me to do then?" Slider laughed. "Get on my hands and knees and kiss her back doors?"

"No, you idiot!" Richard chuckled, fetching a tin of polish and a cloth from the garage. "Just keep turning that key."

Richard sat in the passenger seat beside his friend and sprayed the pine scented polish onto Vivien's dashboard. "Come on, baby," he said affectionately, cleaning her central clock face. "Come on my beauty!"

With Esther and Minnie watching in abject anticipation from the window and Slider pumping the pedal, Vivien suddenly gave a splutter.

"That's it, girl!" Richard smiled, buffing her rear-view mirror. "You can do it!"

Slider then tried his hand at coaxing Vivien to life "Come on, gorgeous!" he yelled, buffing her door with his sleeve. "Come on, you hot smokin' mumma!"

Vivien coughed and spluttered again with the two jubilant boys bobbing in their seats.

"COME ON YOU BEAUTY!" Richard shrieked.

It seemed that a little love could indeed work miracles as Vivien's aging engine suddenly caught and whirred into life. "YES! YES! WE DID IT!" he laughed, punching the air.

"YEEEEEEEHAAA!" Slider yelled, high-fiving his friend and revving Vivien's accelerator, sending a plume of smoke from the dust-filled exhaust pipe.

"Look dear, look!" Minnie shrieked after her sister had turned away. "She's back! Vivien's back!"

"What?" Esther said, dashing to the window. "My God, so she is!"

Peshwari Nans

Richard waved frantically from the passenger window, overjoyed at their meteoric accomplishment. "COME ON GRAN, COME SEE!" he yelled beckoning to the sisters.

"Oh my dearest Vivien," Esther said, hugging her sister. "We'll have a sherry or two tonight, dear, that's for sure."

"Ohh yes, dear," Minnie replied. "And I'll open a packet of ginger snaps."

Shuffling across the car park, Esther embraced her grandson as he got out to greet her. "Oh my dear boy," she said, welling up in tears again. "I can't begin to thank you enough, I never thought I'd hear that sweet sound again, how on earth did you do it?"

"With a little love, Gran," Richard replied, shaking the tin of polish. "Isn't that what Granddad used to say?"

"Yes, yes, it is, my love," Esther said with a tear tracing a line down her wrinkled cheek. "You remembered."

Slider then emerged from the car, beaming.

"And you, young man," Esther added, taking her purse from her coat pocket, "you must tell me how much I owe you."

"Not a bean, Mrs Reynolds," Slider said with an arm around his friend. "Not a bean. Getting her going was reward enough for me."

"Thanks, Slider," Richard said, squeezing him tight. "Thanks mate."

"Yes, thank you indeed," Esther said, drying her eyes while Minnie stood in awe of their handiwork. "She looks amazing." She could see her reflection in the chrome bumper. "You really have done a remarkable job, truly remarkable."

"Haven't they just?" Esther agreed, lowering herself into the driver's seat. "Hello Vivien," she said softly. "It's so good to see you again."

"Come on Aunt Min," Richard said, holding open the passenger door. "In you get."

Peshwari Nans

"Why thank you, young man." Minnie smiled, hitching up her skirt. "Oh my!" she then gasped. "Look at her, Essy dear, she's shining like a new pin!"

Esther said nothing, with her hands inches from the wheel. "Go on, dear," Minnie urged. "She is yours after all."

Tentatively wrapping her fingers around Vivien's fifty-year-old steering wheel, Esther instantly felt a connection like a surge of electricity coursing through her veins. "Vivien," she whispered.

Richard and Slider meanwhile posed for photographs using their mobile phones, posting the pictures to their social media pages. The cherry on the cake came when Esther gave a playful honk of Vivien's horn, bringing a ripple of laughter from everyone and startling a nearby slumbering rooftop tabby cat. "Yes!" Esther said, shaking her sister's knee.

"So, Gran," Richard said at the window. "I suppose you and Aunt Min'll be off to Leigh-on-Sea now you've got Vivien back."

"No dear," Esther said, straight faced. "We're off to India."

Richard's jaw dropped momentarily. "What?" he said assuming his elderly grandmother was joking. "Don't be silly Gran. Seriously, where are you going?"

"I told you, dear," Esther reiterated. "Minnie and I are off to India. Raipur to be exact."

"India!" Richard exclaimed. "What, India as in, 'India that's halfway around the world' India?"

"Yes dear, that India," Esther replied.

"Cool." Slider smiled as he stood at Richard's side. "That's one hell of a road trip. Respect, ladies."

"Thank you, Slider," Esther replied. "And it's all thanks to you two wonderful boys."

Peshwari Nans

"But Gran," Richard said with a hand to his head. "You can't. I mean it's thousands of miles away. If you don't mind me saying, you're both in your eighties, and as for Vivien, well…"

"She'll be fine, dear," Esther said, cutting him short. "She's awake now so if anyone can get us there Vivien can."

"But Gran, she's an antique!" Richard said, doing his level best to dissuade her.

"So am I dear," Esther informed him. "But that's not going to stop me."

"India," Richard said again. "Gran, why?"

"To keep a promise, dear," his grandmother told him. "Don't worry, Minnie and I will be just fine. Right now I need you to reverse Vivien back into the garage for me Richard, there's a good boy. I always was much better at going forwards than backwards."

"And you want to drive to India, Gran?" Richard said, helping her from the car.

"Yes dear." She smiled. "Forwards all the way I hope."

Richard raised his eyebrows as Minnie clambered from the car. "Well at least let me and Slider work on her some more at the weekend," he said as he backed Vivien into the garage.

"Yes of course, dear," Esther said, closing the doors. "If you feel it necessary."

"Yeah Mrs R," Slider said excitedly. "I'll sort you out some bangin' mods for the old girl."

"Banging mods?" Esther exclaimed. "Dear boy, Vivien is a lady I'll have you know, not some cheap hussy!"

"Don't worry," Slider said confidently. "I'm just gonna upgrade the cams, retune the carb and renew the transmission, oil changes for the engine and the differential, oh and overhaul the brakes and fit her with a new set of boots."

61

Peshwari Nans

"Boots?" Minnie asked. "Whatever do you mean?"

"Tyres." Slider laughed. "She'll run like a dream and twice as fast, nought to sixty in twenty seconds I reckon."

"Is that miles per hour?" Esther asked.

"Yes, Gran," Richard told her "Slider's Corsa does it in eight-and-a-half flat, but he does have nitrous injectors and a V8 under the hood."

"Richard, dearest," his grandmother said. "I haven't the foggiest idea what you are talking about but I'll tell you this. Vivien and I won't be going nowhere near as fast as sixty miles per hour that's for sure, after all we're not trying to break the land-speed record, dear boy."

Richard and Slider laughed. "Gran at that rate it'll take you forever to get there."

"Yes but we'll arrive alive, dear," Esther informed him. "Not in a pine box."

"Oh I don't know, Essy dear," Minnie said, siding with the boys. "Cyril had a Harley Davidson which did a whopping seventy-five miles per hour and I once rode pillion and almost peed myself with excitement."

"Way to go Aunt Min!" Richard said, holding his hand up for a high five but got nothing in return. "Don't worry Gran," he said, slowly lowering his hand. "We'll look after her. I tell you what, I'll fit you a satnav so you won't get lost."

"A what, dear?" Esther asked.

"A satnav," Slider interjected. "It uses satellites orbiting in space to pinpoint your global position."

"Statellites!" Minnie gasped. "Did you hear that, Essy dear? We're going to get a statellite, from space! How exciting. Richard what exactly is a statellite, dear boy?"

"*Satellite*, Aunt Min." Richard laughed. "Well it's a…" He thought for a moment how best to describe the billion-dollar piece of aeronautical hardware to two elderly ladies.

Peshwari Nans

"It's like a, like a sort of spaceship I suppose, sending signals down to us."

"Oh, I don't know about that, Richard dear," Esther said, fearing Vivien would be corrupted by modern technology and lose her olde-worlde charm.

"It's just an accessory, Gran," her grandson told her with an arm around her shoulders. "It'll be there in case of emergencies. You can switch it off and on whenever you want."

"Well in that case," Esther said, kissing Richard's cheek, "we'll take your statellite thingy but pass on the nitrous injectors."

Richard and his friend left the sisters at the foot of their stairs and headed back to their car, eager to scour the Internet for accessories and modifications suitable for a car of Vivien's social standing. "Oh Gran!" Richard called back. "Have you told Mum?"

"No, dear!" Esther confessed. "I was rather hoping you would break the news for me, you know what a worrywart she can be."

"Me!" Richard exclaimed. "Why me? She's gonna go ballistic, you know that don't you?"

"Well I'll just have to deal with that when the time comes, won't I?" Esther told him. "After all, she's my daughter, not my mother."

Elizabeth had always been overprotective of her parents and, as Esther thought, overbearing at times, but all in the name of love as she so often explained.

"Er, okay!" Richard said, dreading the impending conversation with his mother. "Seeya Saturday!"

"Bye dear!" Esther called back. "Bye Slider!"

"Yes byyyyyye!" Minnie said, waving over her sister's shoulder.

That evening at the dinner table Richard sat quietly toying with his spaghetti "Are you okay darling?" his mother asked, pouring herself a glass of wine. "You don't seem yourself tonight. Is something wrong?"

"No, nothing Mum I'm fine," Richard replied, wondering how best to broach the subject. "I er, I went to see Gran today."

"Why? What's wrong? Is she okay?" Elizabeth asked, setting down the wine bottle with a thud. "Tell me Richard, what's happened?"

"Nothing's happened," Richard said, having anticipated her reaction.

"Is it Aunt Min then?" Elizabeth said, tensing somewhat. "Has she been taking her tablets?"

"Yes, Mum," Richard said abruptly. "Aunt Min's fine, and so is Gran. Slider and I just went to get Vivien started, that's all."

"Vivien?" Elizabeth gasped. "What on earth does your gran want with Vivien for God's sake?"

Richard put his head down and tucked into his bolognese, red faced.

"Richard!" his mother snapped. "Tell me! What does my mother want with Vivien? She hasn't driven in years."

"Well," Richard said hesitantly.

"Well, what?" Elizabeth said, pressing the point. "There's something you're not telling me. Now what is it? Come on, out with it!"

"Okay!" Richard said, slamming down his knife and fork and buckling under her interrogation. "If you must know, Gran and Aunt Min are going on a road trip."

"A trip!" Elizabeth said, glass in hand. "A trip where for heaven's sake, Richard? What do you mean 'They're going on a trip'?" She was exasperated at this point. "Where to?"

Richard took a deep breath and a mouth full of orange squash.

"India," he said as his mother raised her glass to her lips.

Peshwari Nans

Immediately her eyes dilated and she spat the Merlot across the table, coating Richard in the process.

"INDIA!" she cried, pushing her chair back and springing from the table. "What do you mean, India?"

"They're going to India, Mum," Richard said, mopping his face with his napkin and pushing his spattered plate away. "Gran knew you'd react like this."

"*React like this!*" Elizabeth said, pacing the room. "There is no way my mother is driving to India, especially not in Vivien, the car's a blasted relic!"

"She's adamant, Mum," Richard explained. "She made a promise to a friend of hers and you know how stubborn she can be."

"Yes I do," Elizabeth agreed. "But this time she's gone too far. India! I've never heard something so ridiculous. I'll go straight round there in the morning and put a stop to this, you see if I don't."

With that, she poured herself a brimming glass of wine and drained it almost to the bottom.

"She's your mum, Mum," Richard said in an attempt to calm the situation. "She's old enough to do what she wants. Slider and I are gonna make sure Vivien's safe and roadworthy so you'll have nothing to worry about there."

"Richard!" his mother snapped. "It's not going to happen, I'm telling you! I'll put a stop to it tomorrow and that'll be the end of it!"

This was truly going to be an epic battle of wills and one that Richard would not want to witness. Although he and his mother were close, when push came to shove his allegiances lay firmly in the opposite camp.

CHAPTER TWO

Elizabeth arrived at her mother's flat the following morning, intent on putting a stop to her madness, but after letting herself in she found that nobody was at home.

"Mother!" she called, tapping on the bathroom door. "Mother? Are you in there?" She anxiously paced the flat for a full fifteen minutes until she heard her mother's voice on the stairs outside.

"Mother!" she said, opening the door and peering down. "Where have you been? I've been here for ages."

"Hello, Lizzy dear," her mother said in reply. "How lovely to see you. Minnie and I have been to the library, take these, will you dear?" She handed her daughter a 'bag for life' containing some six or seven reference books on the subject of world travel, survival skills, and 'an idiot's guide to motor repairs' amongst others.

"And these, dear," Minnie added, handing over her own bulging bag. "The young man at the library was extremely helpful, apparently he's just returned from a kibbutz in Tanzania, I didn't like to ask what a kibbutz is because he was being so charming."

Kibbutz is a Hebrew word meaning 'communal settlement' and has been adopted by aid organizations the world over to improve the lives and living standards of the impoverished and the needy.

"Mother, listen, I need a word!" Elizabeth said, following the sisters inside. "Mother!"

Esther knew exactly why her daughter had decided to visit but skirted around the subject. "Would you like some tea, Lizzy dear?" she asked, disappearing into the kitchen. "Minnie and I are having a cup."

"Mother, I've spoken to Richard," Elizabeth said, pressing the point.

Peshwari Nans

Minnie slipped out of her coat and offered Elizabeth the biscuit barrel. "Garibaldi, dear?" she asked, taking one for herself and standing between Elizabeth and her mother.

"No, Minnie, I haven't come for tea, or biscuits for that matter!" Elizabeth said, losing her cool whilst Esther busied herself filling the kettle. "You know why I'm here, Mother!" she called over Minnie's shoulder. "India, Mother! Really!"

Minnie replaced the lid on the biscuit barrel. "It's not as bad as you think, Lizzy dear," she said, attempting to soften the blow.

"Not as bad, Min?" Elizabeth exclaimed. "Not as bad! My son informs me that you two intend to drive Vivien, *Vivien* of all things, to India, not Leigh-on-Sea or even Yarmouth! India! Have you both completely lost your minds?"

Esther emerged from the kitchen and slipped a cup into her daughter's hand. "Have some tea, Lizzy dear," she told her before slipping away.

"Mother!" Elizabeth snapped. "Will you please stop what you're doing and listen! I don't know what on earth's got into you both but whatever it is you can just forget all about it. You're not going and that's that! I simply forbid it."

"What?" Esther said, turning to confront her daughter. "What do you mean, you forbid it? This is your mother you're talking to, not some dizzy child."

"Well you're behaving like one!" Elizabeth replied. "Both of you. Thinking you can just up sticks and set off around the world at the drop of a hat, at your age, Mother, *at your age*, and don't even get me started on Vivien, yes we had some wonderful years with her but she's past it now."

"Like me!" Esther snapped back. "Am I past it too, eh?"

"What I meant, Mother, was..." Elizabeth said, backtracking.

Peshwari Nans

"I know full well what you meant, Lizzy dear," Esther said with her blood beginning to boil. "You think we're too old, too worn out and senile."

"No, no, of course not," Elizabeth said, reaching for her mother's arm.

"Let me finish!" Esther said, pulling away. "Minnie and I may have the combined age of one hundred-and-seventy-one, but we're not quite ready for the old folks' home yet! I can still do *The Times* crossword, solve the countdown conundrum and fasten my own shoelaces."

"Quite right, dear," Minnie agreed. "And we don't dribble our soup or soil our petticoats either."

Elizabeth raised her hands. "All I'm saying…" she said, backing away from the fuming pensioners.

"I know what you were saying, Lizzy," her mother interjected again. "But you can save your breath. We've made up our minds and that's that."

"But why, Mother?" Elizabeth pleaded. "Why India of all places? I mean is it *even possible* for Christ's sake?"

"Yes of course it's possible, Lizzy dearest," Minnie informed her, tapping the atlas. "We've chartered our course, so to speak."

"Elizabeth!" Esther said with a determined glare. "We are going."

Elizabeth threw her hands up in the air. "Just tell me why? Mother, please!" she asked. "Why now? And why on earth India?"

"Because I made a promise!" Esther stormed, lowering herself onto the sofa. "To Jasvinder, that's why!"

Since she was aware of Jasvinder's death, Elizabeth sat beside her mother, changing her tone somewhat. "I er, I heard about Jazzy, Mum. And I know how fond of her you were."

"Yes. Yes I was," Esther said, screwing her handkerchief in her hands.

Peshwari Nans

"Your mother has an obligation," Minnie, sitting down opposite them, told Elizabeth. "It was Jasvinder's wish that she deliver a package to her husband personally, and as Ravi is currently back home in Raipur then that is where she must go. With me at her side, obviously."

"But…" Elizabeth said, with the grounds for her argument dissipating, "it must be thousands upon thousands of miles away."

"Approximately seven-and-a-half thousand," Minnie informed her. "Give or take a few miles."

"Seven-and-a-half thousand!" Elizabeth gasped. "My God!"

"We'll be fine dear," Esther said reassuringly. "Young Richard and his friend are giving Vivien the once over and the two of us are doing our homework." She gestured to the stack of library books on the coffee table.

"Yes," Minnie said, taking one from the top. "I even have an Uzbeki phrase book—the young man at the library said it had never been out on loan before."

"I'm not surprised." Elizabeth smiled, her temper subsiding. "I doubt there's much call for it in the East End of London."

"Oh I think it's a fascinating language, Lizzy," Minnie told her. "I managed to pick up one or two phrases on the bus home." She then attempted to string together a jumble of Uzbek words from memory, but only succeeded in telling Elizabeth that 'her mother's camel rides a blue bicycle'.

"What does it mean?" Elizabeth asked, impressed to say the least.

"It means 'I am feeling unwell and am in need of a doctor'," Minnie said proudly. "It really is quite simple when you get your head around it."

Peshwari Nans

"Well done you," Elizabeth said, feeling a little more at ease. "Well at least you won't have any trouble communicating, will you?"

"Absolutely not, dear." Minnie smiled, puffing out her chest. "I'm going to try my hand at Chinese next."

Elizabeth took her mother's hand. "Well I'd still rather you didn't go, Mother," she said giving her a gentle squeeze. "Since Daddy died you're all I have left."

"Exactly, dear," her mother told her. "Your father has gone and I don't just want to sit around and wait my turn."

"Please don't say that," Elizabeth said with one hand on her heart. "I don't know what I'd do."

"Lizzy, dearest," Esther said, looking her daughter in the eye, "you have to let me do this. Please darling, I can't stress enough how important to me this is."

Elizabeth looked to the ceiling for a moment and then back at her mother. "But it's so dangerous, Mother," she said, finding it hard to imagine how two eighty-somethings could possibly undertake such an arduous journey. "I mean, what do you want me to say, eh?"

"I want you to say good luck and God speed," her mother replied adamantly.

Elizabeth now knew that there was absolutely no way she was ever going to get them to reconsider. "You will look after her, Minnie, won't you?" she said, maintaining the grip on her mother's hand. "At all times."

"Of course, my dear." Minnie smiled, looking up from her Uzbek phrase book. "Or as the Uzbeks say…" She then proceeded to announce in their native tongue that 'she is serviced by her three husbands regularly'.

"I'm sorry, what?" Elizabeth asked.

"Yes, I'll look after her," Minnie said, setting the phrase book down. "After all, she's all I have too, you know."

Peshwari Nans

"Well I've voiced my objections," Elizabeth told the two sisters. "I can see it's of no use, so I suppose I had better lend a hand."

"Lend a hand?" Minnie asked.

"Yes," Elizabeth replied, taking another book from the pile. "A venture of this magnitude will need meticulous planning and that's one thing I'm particularly good at."

"You always were, dear," her mother said affectionately. "If I found one of your lists about the house I must've found a hundred."

"That's right," Elizabeth said proudly. "So fetch me a pen and some paper and let's get started, shall we?"

Esther smiled as she headed for her writing desk.

"Okay," Elizabeth said with her pen poised above the paper. "Day one."

With the atlas and reference books strewn across the coffee table, Elizabeth and the sisters formulated a detailed schedule of events, day-by-day and country-by-country, listing the various visas, currencies and provisions required and deducing that if unhindered the journey should be completed in around two-and-a-half months, allowing of course for Vivien's sedate speed.

"You say Richard's fixing her up for you?" Elizabeth asked. "Vivien?"

"Yes, dear." Minnie nodded. "With the help of his friend Smiler"

"Slider, dear," Esther said, correcting her sister. "His name is Slider."

"Oh Slider." Elizabeth sighed, relieved that Vivien was in capable hands. "He's very good and one of Richard's oldest friends."

"Yes, such a charming young man," her mother added. "Despite the…" She gestured to her face.

"Piercings?" Elizabeth said, reading her thoughts. "Yes, but each to his own, eh Mother?"

Peshwari Nans

"Indeed, dear," Esther replied, mulling over her daughter's numerous notes. "What's an iPad, dear?" she asked, checking the extensive kit list.

"It's a tablet, Mother," her daughter replied, noting the various time zones and expected weather conditions throughout the journey. "I'll lend you mine, that way we can skype or face time to keep in touch."

"Skype!" Esther said confused by her daughter's terminology. "Face time? What on earth?"

"Don't worry, Mother." Elizabeth smiled, knowing her mother was one of life's true technophobes. "I'll give you a masterclass before you set off."

"But, I still have my old reliable," her mother said, delving into her handbag for the mobile phone her daughter had given her some years earlier.

"That old thing," Elizabeth scoffed. "You really should have let me upgrade that a long time ago."

"It suits me just fine, dear," Esther said, wiping the screen.

"Yes, Mother, when you bother to switch it on," Elizabeth said, taking the brick-sized phone from her. "And when did you last charge the darn thing?"

"Charge it, dear?" Esther said, snatching it back and popping it into her bag. "Oh I don't know, maybe a month or so ago. I don't want to overfill it you see."

"Over*charge*, Mother!" Elizabeth laughed. "And you can't so don't fret about it. Promise me you'll charge it before you go and I'll buy you a travel plug so you can keep it topped up along the way. Mother, this is important. You don't want to be stranded in Timbuktu or God knows where."

"Kathmandu," Minnie piped up.

"Wherever," Elizabeth said, adopting a more authoritative tone.

Peshwari Nans

"Now if you two foolish ladies are going through with this ridiculous venture then I'm afraid I'm going to have to lay down a few ground rules, and these are non-negotiable. Do I make myself clear?"

Esther was about to object when her daughter cut her off. "I mean it, Mother! Firstly, as I say you are to keep your mobile phones and the tablet fully charged at all times. Now I have seen a solar charger online for when, God forbid, you are miles from civilization. So there should be absolutely no excuses, okay?"

"Yes, dear," Esther and Minnie said simultaneously.

"Secondly," Elizabeth continued laying down the law, "you are to keep your windows and doors locked at all times and never, I repeat never, speak to strangers."

"Lizzy dear," Minnie said, raising a hand. "We're going abroad, darling. Everybody will be a stranger, won't they?"

"Yes, but…" Elizabeth replied, stumped for a moment. "You know what I mean. Odd types and such."

"Make a note of that, dear," Esther joked with her sister. "Avoid all odd types."

"Mother!" Elizabeth frowned. "You really must take this seriously. There could be murderers and highwaymen out there, you just don't know do you? Right. Next, if either of you are feeling unwell and wish to abandon this… this—"

"—Trip of a lifetime, dear?" Minnie said over the top of a reference book.

"Well I wouldn't put it quite like that," Elizabeth continued. "What I'm trying to say is—"

"—Turning back just isn't an option, Lizzy dear," her mother intervened. "A promise is a promise after all. But should anything untoward occur then we will deal with it accordingly. Now will there be anything else? Minnie and I would like a cup of tea, wouldn't we dear?"

"Oooh yes, I'm positively parched, dear." Minnie smiled.

"Tea, Mother?" Elizabeth said, eager to dictate proceedings.

"Yes dear, haven't you heard?" Esther said, rising from the sofa and straightening her back. "Everything stops for tea."

"And biscuits," Minnie added, reaching for the barrel. "Garibaldi, dear?"

"No, Aunt Min," Elizabeth said, compiling a detailed kit list. "I do not want a Garibaldi, now we'll have to get the pair of you seen by your GP."

"But Lizzy, I've had my winter flu jab," Minnie replied, depositing yet more crumbs on the carpet. "But maybe he could take a look at my haemorrhoids, dear, you see I can't sit for too long without them creating merry hell if you know what I mean. Maybe he has some cream or a whoopee cushion perhaps."

"Aunt Min!" Elizabeth frowned. "I was thinking more along the lines of a rabies inoculation, tetanus and TB, heaven only knows what the two of you could pick up along the way."

"Ooh I wouldn't worry too much, dear," Minnie said with a blasé air. "An apple a day should suffice."

"Aunt Min, this is serious," Elizabeth reminded her, getting a little hot under the collar at this point. "You must adhere to my strict instructions if you are to have my blessing, is that clear?"

Minnie wasn't listening, she was busy rummaging around in the biscuit barrel amongst the Hobnobs and Bourbons. "Esther dear!" she called out. "Have we any more Garibaldis?"

"Aunt Min!" Elizabeth snapped, tapping her pen on the edge of the notepad. "Shall we continue?"

"Esther dear!" Minnie called a little louder. "The Garibaldis!"

Peshwari Nans

"Pardon dear," Esther said, popping her head around the kitchen door.

"Mother!" Elizabeth said, holding her pad aloft. "We really must…"

"Have we any more Garibaldis?" Minnie asked, cutting Elizabeth short. "You know I can't have my tea without a Garibaldi."

"I'll take a look, dear." Esther smiled.

"Will you two forget about the damn biscuits!" Elizabeth raged.

Both sisters stopped and stared at her. "Forget the biscuits, dear?" Minnie said, aghast. "Oh good God, no!"

"Now you listen here, Little Miss Bossy Trousers," Esther added, wagging a motherly finger. "There are some things in life that simply can't be forgotten, and a cup of tea and a biscuit is one of them, so while you're making your confounded list I suggest you add a packet of Garibaldis or two, or you may have a riot on your hands."

"Oooh yes," Minnie agreed. "And don't forget the boiled sweets, to prevent my ears from popping."

"What?" Elizabeth said, having completely lost track. "You're driving, Aunt Min, not flying. I thought the pair of you had done your homework," she scoffed.

"I have, dear," Minnie said, producing a folded piece of paper from her pinnie pocket. "'The province of Kathmandu'," she read, "'Sits at approximately four-and-a-half thousand feet above sea level, high enough for the air pressure to cause mild discomfort'." She neatly folded the paper and pocketed it once again.

"You were saying, dear?" Esther asked her daughter with a wry smile.

Elizabeth begrudgingly added biscuits and boiled sweets to the manifest.

Esther returned with a tray of tea. "There dear," she said, handing her sister a packet of Garibaldi biscuits. "I always keep a spare in the bread-bin in case of emergencies."

"Wonderful, dear." Minnie smiled.

"So, Mother, why did you buy the Bourbons?" Elizabeth asked, finding herself sucked into the whole biscuit debate.

"Oh they were for Jazzy, dear," Esther said, setting the tray down. "She often popped in for a chat, God rest her soul, and the Hobnobs are for Dr Kumali. He calls once a month to take a look at my feet. I do suffer terribly with them, you see."

"Mother!" Elizabeth exclaimed yet again. "How on earth are you two going to make it halfway around the world what with Minnie's piles and you and your blasted feet!"

"Medication, dear," her mother replied simply. "I spoke with Dr Kumali only this morning and ordered several months' supply in advance."

"And a nip of sherry works wonders too, my dear," Minnie added. "I spoke to the nice man at the Coop and he's agreed to put a case aside for us."

Elizabeth sat speechless once again while the sisters sipped tea and nibbled biscuits.

"Okay," Elizabeth later said, having filled three pages with notes. "Next we need to shop. I'll be round at eight-thirty sharp in the morning, so I expect the pair of you washed, dressed and ready."

Minnie leaned across to her sister. "Has she always been like this?" she asked, kicking the crumbs from her feet.

"Absolutely," Esther replied. "At four years of age she ruled her fellow pre-school pupils with a rod of iron, insisting on politeness and punctuality at all times."

"You must have order, Mother," Elizabeth said in her own defence. "Without it there is chaos and chaos, as we know, leads to anarchy, and that will not be tolerated."

Peshwari Nans

Elizabeth left her mother and Minnie that evening with a to-do list as long as their arms and promised to return the very next morning for stage two of their preparations.

"Sherry, dear?" Minnie asked her sister, who sat there attempting to absorb her daughter's strict instructions.

"Most definitely, dear," she replied, lowering her spectacles so that they hung from the string around her neck. "I'll give her that she's thorough," she added, waving the notes. "Apparently we need ant, wasp, wolf and even bear repellent aboard, and not to mention distress flares, pepper spray, a mosquito net and a hunting knife."

"A hunting knife?" Minnie gasped, handing her sister a glass of sweet sherry. "I can assure you I won't be hunting anything for our table, dear, I've a good supply of potted shrimp paste to see me through so I'll be just fine."

Elizabeth was surprised the following morning when she arrived to find the sisters up, washed, dressed and sitting in their overcoats. "You did say eight-thirty sharp, didn't you dear?" Esther asked, looking at the clock on the mantlepiece, which read eight thirty-five.

"Oh," Elizabeth said at first. "You're serious about this then?" She had hoped a good night's sleep may have had them seeing sense or at least a glimmer of doubt as to the trip's feasibility.

"Of course," Esther said abruptly. "Now, shall we go?" She and Minnie marched past Elizabeth, shopping bags at the ready. "Well, come along, dear." Esther beckoned to her lacklustre daughter from the door. "Time is of the essence."

While the three ladies boarded the Tube train to Stratford's Westfield Shopping Centre, Sotto and five of his Oriental associates sat languishing in police custody thanks to the detailed description Esther had supplied. Sotto himself had refused to answer the charges put before him, however his minions had each folded under intense interrogation, selling one another out, including their lord and master. But without a confession from the gangland boss, the police were floundering for a conviction.

"Look, Sotto!" the breathless Detective Inspector barked, having questioned the Chinese mobster for some five hours. "We've got you bang to rights this time, your boys have all pointed the finger your way and taken the deal, so you may as well roll over and save us all a lot of time and money."

"No ... comment," Sotto said, leaning across the table with a defiant glare and his hands tightly cuffed.

"You're only making more difficult for yourself," the DI threatened. "We've got enough on you as it is, but if you sign and sweeten the deal maybe the judge will take your cooperation into consideration."

Sotto's lawyer, a fellow Oriental, whispered into his ear, advising his client to sign and plead for leniency.

"NO!" Sotto yelled, shoving the man with his cuffed fists. "What am I paying you for, eh?"

His lawyer bowed his head and scrutinized the written accusations. "My client denies all charges against him," he told the attending officers.

Arriving at Stratford, Elizabeth and the sisters alighted and walked the short distance to the shopping centre. "Oh Essy, look!" Minnie said, in awe of the glitzy mall with its polished marble floors, perpetually moving escalators and designer stores. "It's like a magical wonderland!"

Esther looked around open-mouthed, craning her neck at the vaulted atrium overhead.

"This way!" Elizabeth said, ushering the gawping sisters along. "In here" she added, herding them into a popular outdoor activities' retailer.

"Can I help you, madam?" the burly sales assistant asked, looking every inch the mountaineering type, with his athletic physique and tough-looking outdoor attire.

Peshwari Nans

"Yes, yes, you can," Elizabeth said, smiling. "We're looking for protective clothing for extreme conditions, you know? Boots, hats, gloves, quilted overcoats, etcetera."

Meanwhile, out of Elizabeth's sight, the sisters toyed with a rack of ice axes, snow goggles and crampons.

"Well you came to the right place," the assistant said, taking a tape from around his neck and approaching Elizabeth. "We custom fit all of our clothing here, so if I might just take a few measurements—"

"—Oh no!" Elizabeth said, backing away. "No, no, it's not for me, it's for my mother and her sister." She looked around the aisle to see Esther and Minnie, each with a tangled climbing harness over their head.

"I beg your pardon?" the assistant said, bemused.

"Mother!" Elizabeth snapped, freeing the sisters from the harnesses. "Do behave please! Sorry, yes," she told the young man. "They do feel the cold at their age."

"Er yes, b-but..." the assistant stammered, "madam I think M&S or possibly Dorothy Perkins would be a more appropriate place for such clothing, don't you think? No offence, but we cater for the more adventurous types."

"Young man, we *are* adventurous types!" Minnie insisted. "My sister Essy and I aim to drive seven thousand miles across the globe unaided, so I'd say we more than qualify. What do you think?"

"You're doing what?" the gobsmacked assistant asked.

"I'm afraid it's true," Elizabeth said, rolling her eyes. "I know how this may seem, but believe me you won't find a more determined pair."

"I say!" Minnie asked, taking a shine to an axe with a gleaming blade. "How much is this please, young man?"

"Minnie? Put that down!" Elizabeth barked, attempting to disarm her. "You don't need that."

"Let me be the judge of that, Lizzy dear," a defiant Minnie said, slipping it into her basket along with two sets of crampons in case the two of them encountered ice and snow. She also took down a coil of climbing rope. "Be prepared, dear," she told her sister, handing her a similar axe.

In a state of disbelief, the sales assistant measured the sisters for arctic clothing and robust footwear as they filled their baskets with various survival aids, outdoor catering equipment and the various insect repellents from Elizabeth's lengthy lists.

During the spree the sisters behaved like two childish schoolgirls, giggling and trying on all manner of outlandish headgear designed for climbers and white-water rafters alike. "Will you two stop!" Elizabeth laughed, taking a divers harpoon from Minnie and a menacing looking crossbow from her mother. "And what on earth are you doing with this?" she asked, removing a twenty-two calibre pistol from Minnie's basket. "I'm sorry, I really can't allow this, you'll kill somebody for heaven's sake, or one another for that matter."

"But, Lizzy dear!" Minnie protested.

"No, Min, I won't hear of it!" Elizabeth said, handing the weapon over to the assistant. "You can see what I'm up against can't you?" she told him.

Walking around the bustling mall with armfuls of bulging bags, the ladies feasted on doughnuts, hot dogs and pick-and-mix sweets from bags. Elizabeth soon found herself lagging behind, fatigued, while the sisters revelled in their very first mall experience.

"Come down, Minnie!" Elizabeth called, coaxing Minnie from yet another pointless escalator ride. "No, no, no, no!" she then said, dragging the hysterical ladies from the window of the Victoria's Secret store, with its revealing lacy lingerie on display for all to see, and guided them towards a shop that was more fitting for their declining years. "You'll be needing thermals where you're going, Mother," she said sternly. "Not thongs!"

Soon Esther and Minnie were both kitted out with knee-length woollen undergarments, cotton vests and winceyette blouses to fend off the merest drop in temperature.

"I don't know about you, Minnie dear, but I'm famished," Esther said, pausing outside a popular pizzeria. "Shall we?" She and her sister ducked inside, leaving Elizabeth dumfounded.

"Where the hell are they putting it?" she asked herself.

Meanwhile back at Bow Road Police Station the DI was becoming more and more exasperated with the ever more belligerent Sotto, who taunted him at every opportunity. But as he was about to launch into another fuming tirade there was a knock at the door.

"WHAT?" the DI yelled, incensed at the interruption.

"Might I have a word?" his direct superior said, popping his head into the interview room. "*Now*, Detective Inspector."

The DI was then informed that Sotto was to be transferred to Paddington Green Police Station to answer more serious allegations in connection with his intercontinental narcotics and prostitution dealings.

"You've got to be kidding me!" the frustrated DI stormed, kicking out at an empty chair. "He's mine, Guv! I'll get him to talk—you wait and see. Five more minutes sir, give me five more minutes."

The DI was then reminded in no uncertain terms of his rank and relative position to the other man, and begrudgingly relented. "Get him out of here!" he told his fellow detectives.

Sotto smiled as he was frogmarched from the interview room and out to a waiting van.

Facing a possible fifteen years in prison if convicted, the career criminal sat, staring into the eyes of the officer opposite him, unnerving him somewhat as the van made its way through the rush-hour traffic.

"What are you grinning at?" the officer asked. "They'll soon wipe that smug smile off your face where you're going, you mark my words." But no sooner had the words left his mouth than the van slowed yet again. There was an almighty bang and the police vehicle was thrown onto its side, tossing its occupants around like peas in a can. Sotto was thrown across and on top of the startled officer, because his younger and even more unhinged brother, Lee, had stolen a concrete lorry at gunpoint from a nearby construction site, and driven it, complete with its spinning load, directly into the side of the police van.

Lee leapt from his crumpled cab, brandishing a semi-automatic weapon in broad daylight without a care, spraying bullets at the underside of the toppled van, sending the emerging driver diving back inside for cover.

"SOTTO!" he yelled as pedestrians and fellow road users fled the chaotic scene. "SOTTO!"

Sotto grappled with the escorting officer with his cuffed hands around his throat, eventually butting him on the bridge of the nose,

"SOTTO GET BACK!" his brother screamed, firing a volley of shots into the van's fortified rear door.

Onlookers in nearby offices and restaurants were stunned by the audacious attempt, many capturing the unfolding drama on their smartphones.

Lee tugged at the buckled doors after pouring some twenty or so bullets into the lock mechanism.

With his guard now incapacitated, Sotto began kicking out from the inside until the doors finally gave way.

"SOTTO, QUICK!" Lee barked, dragging his bruised brother clear and thrusting a loaded pistol into his cuffed hands.

Peshwari Nans

"Wait!" Sotto yelled as his brother turned to flee. Sotto leapt back inside the stricken van, tugging at the keys fastened to the groaning officer's belt, then struck him about the head with the butt of the pistol when he reached out to restrain him.

"SOTTO! HURRY!" Lee yelled, leaning inside whilst keeping any have-a-go heroes at bay with his smoking gun. "SOTTO!"

Wrenching the keys free Sotto scrambled clear once again and fled with his brother into a side street, barging passers-by out of the way, screaming obscenities in their native tongue. Unable to backtrack to his own vehicle, Lee was forced to step into the road and flag down an approaching delivery van and force its petrified driver out and to lie face-down on the ground.

The brothers made good their escape with the sound of police sirens in the background, mounting the curb occasionally to skirt the lumbering traffic. Sotto freed himself from the handcuffs and tossed them from the window before ruffling his brother's hair "Excellent Lee, excellent!" he said, checking his blooded forehead in the visor mirror.

All 'shopped out' at Westfield, Elizabeth and the sisters left the awe-inspiring mall and returned to the Tube station, adequately equipped for extremes of temperature at either end of the scale and for life on the open road.

"I quite fancied the harpoon, Essy dear," Minnie moaned as they boarded the train. "If we were to run into ferocious bears or wolverines I could've let the blighters have it in the backside and sent them packing."

Elizabeth shook her head. "I'd rather you just locked your doors and sounded your horn," she said, opting for the non-violent and far safer approach. "Better still, stay at home."

Peshwari Nans

"Now now, dear we've been through all this," her mother reminded her. "We are going, in fact we're setting off on Sunday at noon."

"Sunday!" Elizabeth gasped, startling her fellow passengers. "This Sunday? But Mother, you're not ready. It's Friday for heaven's sake and there's still so much to do!"

"Noon on Sunday it is, dear," Esther said defiantly. "Ready or not."

"Mother, you really are incorrigible!" Elizabeth said, turning away.

The sisters tinkered with their purchases during their journey home, trying to fathom the direction of true north with their compass, while they were several metres below street level. "The darn thing's defective," Minnie said, watching the constantly spinning pointer. "At this rate we'll be going round in circles."

Esther then dropped a stack of aluminium cooking pots onto the train floor, startling each and every person in the carriage with the resounding clang.

"Will you two behave!" Elizabeth said, scolding the pensioners as though they were children. "This is the last time I'm taking you anywhere, I swear it."

The two sisters looked at one another and burst out laughing at the sheer absurdity of the situation, as did several adjacent passengers. "Don't mind her," Esther explained. "She's just tossing her teddy out of the pram!" The hysteria increased, leaving Elizabeth red-faced and humiliated.

Dragging her heels behind the giggling grannies Elizabeth mumbled under her breath, "Never, never again."

"Put the kettle on, dear," Esther told her sister once they were home and she was flinging her bags onto the sofa. "I'm positively pooped."

Peshwari Nans

"It's Sunday, Mother," Elizabeth said, joining them. "Really!"

"Oh do be quiet, Lizzy dear," her mother replied, tired of her daughter's constant objections. "If you haven't anything constructive to say then I suggest you say nothing at all."

Elizabeth set the remainder of the shopping bags down with a thud. "Right, I'll be off then," she said abruptly, expecting an immediate apology, which of course wasn't forthcoming. "I said I'll be off!" she added, with her hand on the door handle,

"Goodbye dear," Esther said without turning her head.

"Look, Mother," Elizabeth then said in a last ditch attempt to dissuade them from going. "Would it help if I begged you to reconsider? It's such a long way and the two of you aren't in the best of health, are you?"

Esther merely gave her daughter the look she had given her as a child whenever she'd overstepped the mark.

Elizabeth marched from the flat while Minnie made tea. "She should've had more children," Esther said, busying herself with unpacking.

"I beg your pardon, dear?" Minnie replied, leaning into the room from the kitchen.

"Elizabeth," Esther explained. "She should have had more children, then she'd never have had time to get so het up about things, and she has too much coffee and red meat. I keep telling her it's no good."

"Yes, quite," Minnie said, disappearing back into the kitchen as the kettle's whistle sounded.

Moments later there was a resounding thud on the door. "I told you, Lizzy dear," Esther said, hanging up her coat and opening the door. "We're going and that's—"

She gasped on seeing that it wasn't her tempestuous daughter after all. It was Sotto, leaning against the door frame.

"Good evening," he said, grinning as her pushed past Esther, knocking her aside.

"What? What are you doing here?" Esther remarked with her hand against her pounding chest. "Get out! Get out I say!"

"No I'm afraid I can't do that," Sotto said, shoving the door closed and dragging Esther toward the sofa and tossing her down amongst the plastic bags. "Are you alone?" he asked, dabbing at his weeping head wound with his woollen sleeve and looking around the flat. "I said *are you alone?*" he barked, brandishing a knife.

Minnie glanced over her shoulder and immediately froze upon seeing Sotto and the blade. Then, while his back was momentarily turned, she ducked behind the kitchen door with her hand over her mouth.

"Yes, yes, of course I am," Esther said defiantly, enraged to suddenly be face to face with one of Jasvinder's assailants. "I'm here on my own. Now what do you want? Is it money?" she asked, popping her handbag onto her knee.

Sotto sat down opposite her. "Money is good," he snarled, "but revenge is sweeter."

"Revenge!" Esther snapped. "What about young Jazzy? You, you *murderer!*"

"You're quite right," Sotto said, rocking back in his seat. "I am a murderer, many times over, so if I were you I would hold my tongue. You see I know you spoke to the police and gave them my description—a foolish act on your behalf, a very foolish act indeed—you have hurt my organization, so I am here to repay the favour, an eye for an eye so to speak. But on this occasion I think we'll begin with a finger." Sotto leaned across the coffee table and grabbed at Esther's right hand, holding the knife to her skin.

Peshwari Nans

Minnie peered cautiously around the door and, seeing her sister in imminent danger, she pursed her lips and clenched a fist. But what could she do against a crazed psychopath who was about to slowly dismember her sibling?

Sotto looked deep into Esther's eyes and it unnerved him somewhat that he saw no fear, just the merest wince when he pressed the blade a little harder above her knuckle. "You surprise me, old woman," he told her. "Many would be begging for their life right now."

"I wouldn't give a worm like you the satisfaction," Esther replied, catching sight of her sister and covertly shaking her head, silently insisting she stay put.

Minnie looked around the kitchen for a weapon, but all the carving knives were stashed away in the cutlery drawer and would undoubtedly alert Sotto if retrieved.

Sotto's brother sat outside reclining in his car seat, knowing his kin would not want to rush his premeditated slaying.

"Beg!" Sotto grimaced, pressing the blade ever harder onto Esther's index finger. "Beg for your life, old woman!"

"I hope you rot in hell," was Esther's response through gritted teeth as the pain increased tenfold.

Panic-stricken, Minnie grabbed a heavy iron frying pan, which hung beside the cooker, and held it to her chest, with her heart now racing and her hands trembling uncontrollably. Taking a deep breath she slowly rounded the door in full view of her sister, who again shook her head while Sotto delighted at the sight of broken skin and the first glimpse of Esther's blood. "I can't hear you," he said, craving her pleas for mercy.

Minnie shuffled in her silent slippers across the shag pile carpet, gripping the frying pan's handle with whitened knuckles until she was close enough to smell his expensive cologne.

Peshwari Nans

Sotto removed the glinting blade from Esther's nearly severed finger. "Perhaps I will take that eye after all," he said, smiling. "I promise that you will beg for what's left of your pathetic life."

With no time to lose, and summoning what little courage she possessed, Minnie raised the frying pan above her head and took a step towards the wing back chair. But in doing so she kicked over the biscuit barrel she had left beside it, spilling her beloved Garibaldis across the floor.

"What?" Sotto snapped, spinning the blade in his hand. "Bitch!" he cried, seeing Minnie brandishing the frying pan and prepared to slay the pair of them.

With the roles now reversed and her sister in danger, Esther quickly reached into her handbag for her trusty aerosol.

"HEY YOU!" she yelled, attracting Sotto's attention before unloading half the can into his face.

"ARRRRRRGGH! BIIITCH!" the crime boss screamed, his retinas burning and his vision instantly impaired. "BITCH, BITCH, BIIITCH!" he roared, clawing at his streaming eyes.

"NOW MINNIE, NOW!" Esther yelled, nodding to her quivering sister. "NOW FOR PETE'S SAKE!"

"Oh!" Minnie said, coming to. "Oh yes!"

With all the strength she could muster, she swung the cumbersome pan up high and brought it down onto the side of the reeling gangster's head.

"Arrrrrrggh! Fuuuuck!" Sotto again screamed, lashing out blindly with his blade. "You're dead old woman! DEAD!"

"Hit him again, dear!" Esther insisted, backing away from the flaying knife. "*Hit him again!*"

Minnie grunted as she swung the frying pan again at the knifeman's head, and then did it a third time, until the screaming Sotto collapsed from the chair onto the floor at Esther's feet.

"My God, Essy dear!" Minnie said, unable to hold the heavy pan a moment longer. "Are you alright?"

"I, I, don't know," Esther replied in a state of shock, with her hand running with blood. "What were you thinking of?" she then snapped at her sister. "You could've got yourself killed!"

"I, I, I, I, I," Minnie stammered, visibly shaking. "I'm sorry I just couldn't, I couldn't, stand by and let him hurt you, Essy dear."

Esther stepped across the unconscious Sotto and embraced her weeping sister. "It's all right, Minnie dear," she said with a comforting squeeze. "Thank you, dear," she added, planting a kiss on her cheek.

The pair stood for a moment, peering over the back of the sofa at Sotto's lifeless body.

"Is he dead?" Minnie eventually asked. "Have I, have I killed him, Essy?"

"I don't think so, dear," Esther replied, although Sotto's battered head was awash with blood, and his rapidly swelling chest was heaving.

"What was that anyway, dear?" Minnie asked, looking down at the can in Esther's hand. "Mace?"

"No, dear," Esther replied, managing a half smile under the harrowing circumstances and showing her weapon of choice. "It was lily of the valley."

"An excellent choice, dear," Minnie agreed.

"Ditto, dear," Esther replied, looking across at the blood-spattered pan.

"What do we do now?" Minnie asked, hearing the faintest of groans from the battered Oriental. "Shall I hit him again, dear?"

"No dear," her sister told her. "We're not like him. Quickly now dear, go and fetch the rope."

Peshwari Nans

Emptying the rest of the shopping bags, Minnie proceeded to uncoil the fifty or so metres of brightly coloured climbing rope.

"Help me get him up, Min," Esther said, tugging at Sotto's arm. The two pensioners puffed and panted as they heaved the battered Chinaman from the floor and back into the wing-back chair. "That's it, dear," Esther added when her sister began winding the rope around and around him, over and over, using the entire length until he was securely bound.

The sisters dropped, breathless, onto the sofa, clutching one another tightly. "The card, dear," Esther eventually said, looking over her shoulder. "In the bureau."

Minnie retrieved the contact details the WPC had given them. "Here we are, dear," she said, collecting the telephone too.

"Thank you dear," Esther said, still shaking as she dialled the number. "Hello? Hello?" she said as it was answered. "Hello dear, it's Mrs Reynolds, yes that's right dear, you were here for Jazzy. Well actually no we're not alright," she said when asked. "That awful man I told you about, well he came back. Yes dear, he's here."

"He's there!" the WPC said, clicking her fingers to alert her superiors. "Are you okay? Has he hurt you?"

"As well as can be expected, dear," Esther replied. "Just a minor flesh wound, that's all."

"Flesh wound!" the WPC gasped. "We're on our way, stay calm. Where is he now?"

"He's here, dear," Esther said, looking across at the trussed fugitive with her sister standing over him, frying pan in hand. "But don't worry. He's quite incapacitated."

The WPC and several fellow officers, including the Detective Inspector who'd interviewed Sotto earlier that day, raced to the scene, running red lights with piercing sirens and blue lights flashing.

Peshwari Nans

"Esther! Minnie!" the woman officer called, vaulting the stairs three at a time, and bursting through the door brandishing her night stick. "Thank God!" she sighed, seeing them alive but shaken. "How on earth?" she then asked, checking Sotto's vital signs. "Did you do this?"

"Of course we did, dear," Esther said, clutching a handkerchief to her blooded hand. "With Minnie's frying pan."

"And Essy's lily of the valley spray," her sister added as the DI entered the room.

"What the blazes?" he asked, also looking about the place for Sotto's assailant. "Who did this?"

"They did, sir," the WPC said, tongue-in-cheek. "Proper have-a-go heroines, wouldn't you say?"

"You?" the DI said in disbelief. "You mean to tell me that you beat and subdued this man?"

"It's less than he deserves," Esther said defiantly. "I'd have strung the blighter up by the neck if I'd had my way."

Sotto began moaning and wriggling in his restraints.

"Well, well, well." The DI smiled, gesturing to his men to cuff the mobster and unravel the numerous coils that bound him. "It seems you'll be signing that confession after all, eh Sotto? Unless that is you want me to put the word about that you were overpowered and restrained by the bingo mafia here—no offence ladies," he added, bowing ever so slightly.

"None taken, Officer," Esther replied, retrieving the villain's blade from the floor, and for a brief instance contemplated doing the shell-shocked Sotto further harm.

"I'll take that please, Esther love," the WPC said, well aware of her possible intentions. "He'll get exactly what's coming to him now, don't you worry."

Sotto was frogmarched out of the flat by armed officers while the DI expressed his sincere gratitude.

Peshwari Nans

"Ladies, can I just say that what you did was nothing short of heroic," he told them. "We would usually advise people against facing up to dangerous criminals and taking the law into their own hands, but as we were foolish enough to let him escape in the first place you have my wholehearted thanks and admiration. I'll see to it personally that you two are put forward for one of our outstanding citizen awards. You showed true grit in the face of adversity." The DI left the ladies but insisted that the WPC should remain there to help steady their nerves.

"Esther? Minnie? How about a nice cup of chamomile tea?" she asked. "I just can't get enough of it since I saw you last, and I don't suppose you have any more of those delicious Garibaldis, do you?"

"It just so happens we do, my dear." Minnie smiled, retrieving the barrel and feeling more at ease with the officer's presence.

The WPC dressed Esther's hand over tea. Fortunately it was indeed only a flesh wound, despite the blood making it look more serious. The officer couldn't help but ask: "So what did you mean when you said you attacked him with lily of the valley?"

The three of them roared with laughter when Esther described how she'd immobilized her aggressor with a tin of vintage perfume.

"What's with all the books?" the WPC also asked. "You're doing what?" She then gasped when informed of their impending road trip. "That's incredible. And all for Jasvinder! Wow, you two really are an inspiration do you know that? An inspiration to women of all ages."

"Thank you, dear," Esther said, her own nerves having steadied somewhat. "To tell you the truth after recent events Minnie and I will be glad to get away."

"Yes, yes, I'm so sorry you had to endure that," the WPC replied. "It's our fault. We had him in custody and we made a right pig's ear of it. He's a very dangerous man by all accounts—the two of you are lucky to be alive."

"Oh he's the lucky one, dear," Minnie said, producing her newly acquired ice axe. "Lucky it was only the frying pan I clobbered him with!"

The WPC left the sisters later that evening, vowing to return to see them off on their trip.

Dressing for bed, Esther embraced her sister. "Thank you, Minnie dearest," she said, giving her a peck on the cheek. "That was immensely brave of you. Stupid, but immensely brave."

"You're welcome, Essy." Minnie smiled, kicking off her slippers and slipping into bed with her Uzbeki phrase book. "I'm sure you'd have done the same if the tables were turned."

"Oh without hesitation, dear," Esther replied, reaching for her dog-eared Mills and Boon book. "Without hesitation."

At around 7 a.m. the following morning the slumbering sisters were woken by the doorbell being repeatedly rung from the street below. "Minnie dear, did you forget to pay the window cleaner?" Esther asked, donning her spectacles and dressing gown.

"No dear," Minnie said in broken Uzbek, having sat up half the night. "I mean no dear, he called round on Thursday while you were at the chiropodist."

Sliding the sash widow above her head Esther leaned out to see a bank of reporters and associated cameramen eager for the scoop, having been tipped off by their paid police contacts.

"MRS REYNOLDS!" one of them called up. "I'm Peter Schofield from the *Mirror*. Mrs Reynolds, we were hoping you'd agree to an interview!"

Peshwari Nans

"Good heavens!" Esther gasped, clasping her robe around her neck. "An interview? The *Mirror*? What on earth for?"

The fact that she and her sister had beaten and bound an escaped Category-A prisoner had temporarily slipped her mind.

"Sotto, Mrs Reynolds!" another jostling reporter called out, urging his cameraman to get a shot of her.

"Will you stop that please?" Esther snapped, tugging at her curlers. "I haven't done my hair, and as for an interview I'm afraid you'll just have to wait. Minnie and I haven't had our crumpets." With that she slammed the window down, leaving the reporters bemused and frustrated.

"Who was it, dear?" Minnie asked, buttoning up her cable-knit cardigan.

"Reporters, dear," Esther told her, heading for the kitchen.

"But we haven't had our crumpets yet, Essy dear," Minnie said, glancing out of the window towards the flashing cameras.

"I know dear, set the table," Esther said, popping four crumpets into the toaster and retrieving their home-made marmalade from the cupboard. "They'll just have to wait."

The sisters sat at the table enjoying a pot of tea and nibbling their crumpets for a good twenty minutes before clearing the dishes away.

"Okay, let them in, dear," Esther said, ducking into the bedroom to dress. "They're obviously not going to leave otherwise."

Esther and her sister gave a full and frank account of their ordeal, and posed for accompanying photographs, brandishing the rope and the can of perfume. The story was then rushed to Fleet Street in time to make the late editions, but the sisters had chosen to omit giving them the greater scoop, having tucked the reference books out of sight. The reporters would have loved to report the fact that two eighty-plus sisters were about to undertake a journey of epic proportion, never before attempted by someone of their advancing years. It would have been a true story of heroism in the face of adversity.

Richard and Slider arrived at around eleven in their performance cars, accompanied by a group of like-minded friends who had replied to their rallying call on social media, agreeing to assist in prepping Vivien for the gruelling seven-and-a-half-thousand-mile trip and, God willing, the return journey.

"Hey Gran!" Richard said, giving Essie a hug. "Everyone's buzzing about your road trip you know. I've set up a Facebook page for you, and you've already got over five hundred-and-forty 'likes'."

"A what book page, dear?" Esther asked, cupping a hand to her ear.

"Likes?" Minnie asked. "Like what?"

"*Likes* Mrs Minnie." Slider laughed. "Friends."

"It's just Minnie, dear, not Mrs," Minnie reminded him. "And I only have three friends at the bridge club."

"Not any more, Aunt Min." Richard smiled. "Check it out!"

He showed the sisters the page he had created on his smartphone. "You're getting messages from all over the country. Look, there's a lady from Ayrshire sending you love and best wishes, the Tunbridge Zumba foursome have made a banner for you, a bedsheet reading 'Go Ess and Minnie we're behind you all the way!'"

Richard's posting had indeed caused the slightest of ripples in the infinitely expanding social media pool. Some ripples ebb away and disperse, but others rise to become an all-engulfing feverish Tsunami, trending the world over, but on this occasion only time would tell.

Peshwari Nans

The truth was that the news was out there in cyberspace and the fledgling story had struck a faint chord with the general public, amid a bleak journalistic backwash of wars, austerity and the all-consuming general election news.

"And the Longfield lawn bowls team," Richard continued, "have mowed your names into their green and even sent a proposal of marriage from the vice-captain. I tell you Gran, it won't be long before we see the two of you in the daily papers."

"Maybe sooner than you think, dear," Esther said, choosing to keep her grandson in the dark for the time being.

"Do what, Gran?" he asked.

"Oh, nothing dear," Esther said, diverting his attention. "So I know young Slider, but I can't say I've met the other chaps."

"Oh, sorry Gran." Richard smiled. "This here's Smudger, that's Rabbit, Ketchup, Grover, the littlun's Tinkerbelle and the greaseball in the Nova is Two Beers."

"Two Beers?" Minnie said, eyeing the blushing lad. "Dare I ask why he's called that?"

"Coz that's all it takes!" all of his friends said in unison.

"Naaaah, that's where you're wrong!" the youth said, springing from his hatchback to his defence, having been constantly ribbed for his lack of stamina. "Me and Ketchup done a bottle of vodka between us at Rabbit's party, didn't we, Ketchup mate?"

"Er, no I don't think so," Ketchup replied, denying all knowledge of it. "You had your usual coupla tinnies and passed out on the patio. I know because I painted your toenails and fake tanned ya face!"

"SO IT WAS YOU!" Two Beers (AKA Pete) stormed, chasing his friend around his car with a healthy Mediterranean glow to one side of his face.

Peshwari Nans

"Okay you guys!" Richard said, opening the garage. "Let me introduce you to Vivien, the feistiest thing on four wheels."

The lads gathered round, clambering over Vivien like a pack of safari-park baboons.

"Right, Tinkerbelle!" Richard said, orchestrating proceedings. "You sort the electrics, Ketchup you fit the boots, Rabbit, get to work on the carb, Smudger you know what you're doing with the sounds, yeah?"

"Yes, mate," Smudger said confidently. "Digital Kenwood with two twenty-five watt Sonys and a ten-inch sub woofer in the back, got it."

"Nice one," Richard agreed. "Two Beers, you polish the rims and sort the rust out on the wheel arches," he told his semi-tanned friend. "Slider? You can give me a hand with the brakes. Okay guys, let's do this!"

Vivien was wheeled from the garage and set upon by the enthusiastic mechanics.

"My word!" Esther exclaimed, seeing much of Vivien's panelling stripped before her eyes.

The boys barked instructions constantly back and forth amongst themselves, working in complete harmony with one another while the sisters popped to the corner newsagent for refreshments.

In a space of time that a formula-one pit crew would be proud of, Vivien was transformed from a tired vintage classic into a pumped-up pulsating powerhouse of a car beneath her ever-chic exterior.

"She's not a lady any more, Gran," Richard said, running a cloth over one of Vivien's headlights.

"She's not?" Esther replied, disappointed to say the least.

"No, Gran," Richard added. "She's a Duchess."

"A Duchess!" Esther smiled. "Did you hear that Minnie dear? Our Vivien's a Duchess. How wonderful!"

Peshwari Nans

"Remarkable," Minnie said, peering into the engine compartment, where brightly coloured accessories had been fitted. "Quite remarkable."

Esther handed out bottles of cold beer to the diligent crew, leaving Two Beers until last. "And this is for you dear," she said, offering him a panda pop instead. "I don't think you're quite cut out for the hard stuff, do you?" She smirked, eyeing his two-tone complexion. "But thank you kindly for you help nethertheless. I'm eternally grateful, really I am."

Two Beer's friends found this hysterical but hugged their comrade all the same.

"You off tomorrow then, Gran?" Richard asked.

"Yes dear, at noon," Esther informed him.

Richard updated the 'London to Raipur' Facebook page, detailing the course of events.

"Me and the guys'll come and see you off, if that's okay," he told her as he climbed into his sporty roadster.

"Yes, yes, of course, do," Esther replied, while Minnie personally thanked each of his friends.

"Ketchup? What an interesting name," Minnie said, shaking hands with the last of the lads.

"You don't wanna know!" Slider, Smudger and Rabbit said simultaneously, sparing Minnie the sordid details of the boys carnal condiment cravings.

With Vivien now as ready as she'd ever be and safely tucked away for the penultimate evening, the sisters retired to the comfort of their living room. "Did you leave a note for the milkman, dear?" Minnie asked, individually wrapping the bone-china tea set in newspaper, in readiness for their journey.

"Yes, dear," Esther replied, packing an ample supply of wool and needles to occupy them in their down time.

"And cancel the *Mail on Sunday*?" Minnie added.

Peshwari Nans

"Yes, dear," Esther again replied, looking over her spectacles.

"And throw away the cottage cheese from the refrigerator, would you, Essy dear?" Minnie was constantly fussing.

"Yes, dear!" her sister snapped. "And I've frozen the leftover lasagne, left enough treats with the neighbours for the stray cats and packed the portable commode!"

"Wonderful, dear," Minnie said, breathing a sigh of relief. "And I trust you packed the quilted tissue, dear? You know how the value tissue chaffs my haemorrhoids something awful."

"Yes, dear!" Esther said, a little exasperated. "Three ply, just like you asked for."

"Marvellous, dear." Minnie smiled, wrapping the crystal cruet set.

The ladies sat up in bed that evening unable to sleep. Esther was working on her cryptic crossword and Minnie was eating her tea and biscuits, and of course depositing crumbs all over her eiderdown. Apprehension was not the reason for their temporary insomnia. It was excitement, a tingling sensation which ran from their heads to their arthritic toes, the kind intrepid explorers must experience when stepping bravely into the unknown.

The alarm clock rattled across the bedside table between them just two-and-a-half hours after the pair had finally drifted off to sleep.

"Heavens, no it can't be," Esther said, reaching out blindly. "Where is the darn thing?" The clock had tumbled into her knitting basket and lay rattling, nestled amongst the Lavender Aran wool.

"Switch the darn thing off will you, Essy dear?" Minnie said, stirring. "Essy!"

"I'm trying to, dear!" her bleary-eyed sister snapped over her shoulder.

Peshwari Nans

"Thank you, dear," Minnie eventually said when Esther silenced and replaced the tacky floral timepiece.

"Today's the day then, dear," Minnie said, rising and massaging the base of her aching spine.

"Indeed it is, dear," Esther replied, taking her teeth from a Tupperware tumbler. "Now are you absolutely positive you want to come along, Minnie darling? You know I wouldn't think any the worse of you if you were to have second thoughts."

"Just you try and stop me," Minnie said, tugging on her surgical supports. "I've been waiting for a chance like this my whole life. It's just sad that it takes a tragedy to kick-start an adventure."

"You're quite right, dear," her sister agreed, folding back her bed sheets and tucking them neatly beneath the mattress in readiness for their return.

After having a reviving cup of tea and the last of their crumpets, the sisters perused their kit list.

"Woollies? Yes. Underwear? Yes. Torch? Yes," Esther reeled off. "Passports? Yes. Monies? Yes. Visas? Yes. Potted shrimp paste—"

"—Two dozen jars?" Minnie piped up. "You know I can't go a day without it."

"Yes, dear," Esther said, rolling her eyes, having endured the fishy odour ever since her sister had come to stay. "Don't I know it."

There was then the distinctive three knocks on the door and the jangle of keys that could only be Elizabeth, but arriving at a much earlier hour than usual.

"Mother!" she barked, storming in, brandishing a copy of the morning paper. "What on earth's going on?"

Esther and Minnie's faces were splashed across the front page, accompanied by the obligatory cheesy headline.

Peshwari Nans

"Morning, Lizzy dear," Esther replied, clearing the breakfast things into the kitchen while Minnie kept her head down.

"Mother!" Elizabeth said, following her. "Listen to this: 'Capturing escaped gangsters'! Mother, really!"

"Would you like some tea dear?" Esther enquired, adding, "I'm making a fresh pot. You'll have to make do with a mug though, my darling, because Minnie has packed the Royal Albert."

"Christ, Mother, what were you thinking?" Elizabeth asked, taking the tea caddy from her mother and slamming it down on the counter. "You could have been killed, damn it! First your ridiculous road trip, or attempted suicide as I call it, and now this. I just don't know what's got into you lately, Mother, I really don't. And what's happened to your hand, Mother? Let me take a look."

"Chamomile or lemon-and-ginger, dear?" her mother asked, unfazed.

"Grrrrrrrr you are impossible Mother, do you know that?" Elizabeth stormed, screwing up the newspaper and marching from the kitchen. "And no, Minnie!" she barked at her aunt. "I do *not* want a blasted Garibaldi before you ask. You two really have gone too far this time."

"I'm afraid I've packed the Garibaldis, dear," Minnie informed her. "But there may be one or two custard creams in the bottom of the barrel if you're peckish."

"What?" Elizabeth said, seething.

"Custard creams, dear," Minnie reiterated, offering the biscuit barrel as an olive branch. "They're out of date and a little soft, but tasty nethertheless."

"You two!" Elizabeth raged. "You're as bad as one another, I swear it." She dropped into the wing-back chair and sat strumming her fingers. "Do you know, I'm actually glad you're going away."

"No you're not, dear," her mother said, returning with more tea. "I can always tell when you're lying, your nose twitches and you can't look me in the eye."

"I am!" Elizabeth insisted, lying of course. "You're killing me, Mother, my blood pressure's through the roof, I haven't slept a wink in days, my nerves are shot to pieces and I've completely lost my appetite."

"My dear girl!" Esther said, somewhat concerned. "You're not taking drugs by any chance, are you?"

"No, Mother of course I'm not taking drugs!" Elizabeth said, with her heart rate rising.

"Well you have all the symptoms, dear," Esther exclaimed, returning to the kitchen. "I'll fix you a sandwich."

"Mother it's not drugs that are responsible, for heaven's sake!" Elizabeth called after her. "It's you and Aunt Min! You're driving me insane!"

"Perhaps a sherry might help, dear?" Minnie suggested.

"Do you know what?" Elizabeth said, springing from her seat and reaching for the bottle. "Perhaps it will."

So saying, she poured a large measure into a long-stemmed glass and sank it in one. "Oh good God!" she cringed, screwing up her face. "That's disgusting!"

"I'm not surprised, dear." Minnie smirked. "That's my twelve-year-old malt, the sherry's in the decanter."

Elizabeth examined the label before hastily replacing the bottle. "I'll have that tea after all, Mother!" she called out, feeling a tad queasy.

"There, dear," Esther said shortly afterwards. "Will you please calm down? Minnie and I are fine. Now drink your tea and be a dear and help us pack, will you?"

"Give me your hand, Mother!" Elizabeth said, reaching out.

"I'm fiiiine." Her mother smiled. "Now where did I put that list of yours?"

Peshwari Nans

The soothing chamomile worked its herbal magic and within minutes Elizabeth's frustrations had subsided somewhat. "Okay, give it here, Mother," she said, taking charge as she so often did as she pulled the list from her mother's hand. "Right, passports," she said, reeling off the inventory. "Aunt Min—how much potted shrimp paste are you taking?"

"Enough, dear," Minnie replied, taping up a box.

Elizabeth noticed a carton marked 'china'. "This isn't on my list," she remarked. "Is it going into storage?"

"No, dear," Esther informed her. "That's the Royal Albert and it's coming with us, and before you say a word let me tell you there is absolutely no comparison to a cup of tea in a china cup. It's sophistication personified, my dear."

"As is the three-ply quilted," Minnie added, packing a dozen rolls of deluxe toilet tissue.

"Quite right, dear," her sister agreed.

Elizabeth and the sisters diligently packed the essentials and necessities for the road ahead and ferried them to the garage, where they were loaded under Elizabeth's strict instructions. "No, no, Mother!" she said, removing the first-aid kit. "This rides up front with you, in case of immediate emergencies."

Esther took down the family's pre-war tent from the garage shelf and proceeded to load it into the car.

"Mother, what on earth do you want with that old thing?" her daughter asked, not having seen it since she was eleven during their trip to the Cotswolds. "I really must insist that you and Aunt Min find a hotel at every opportunity."

"And if the opportunity doesn't arise?" her mother replied, stowing it securely. "What then?"

"But surely you aren't considering…" Elizabeth began.

"We are considering every eventuality, my dear," Esther told her. "It's better to have than have not, wouldn't you agree?"

"Yes, b-but..." her daughter stammered. "I definitely won't be able to sleep knowing that you may be roughing it beside a dirt road in some hellish backwater."

"Oh we won't be roughing it, dear," Minnie said, handing her a pair of hot-water bottles and a neatly rolled eiderdown quilt. "We'll be as snug as two bugs in a rug, won't we, Essy dear?"

"Undoubtedly, dear," Esther agreed. "Now I believe that's everything," she added, donning her driving gloves and buttoning her powder-blue knee-length overcoat, her flowing floral skirt hanging to her ankles beneath it. "You will remember to lock up, won't you dear?" she said, eager to be off.

"Yes, yes, of course, Mother," Elizabeth fussed. "Okay, now let me just double-check a few things," she insisted. "You both have your passports, mobile phones, chargers, etcetera?"

"Yes, dear," the sisters replied together.

"You have the tablet I gave you?" Elizabeth rambled on. "And you remember how to skype me?"

"Yes, dear," Minnie replied, rolling her eyes. "I turn on the app thingy and wait for it to load."

"That's right, Aunt Min," Elizabeth said, adjusting both their woollen hats. "And the two of you, don't forget your medications. I've left a note to remind you in the glove compartment."

"Of course you have, dear." Esther smiled, checking her Tiffany time piece. "Will that be all, only it's approaching noon and we have a ferry to catch."

Handing her sister Jasvinder's Lipton's tea tin, Esther climbed behind the wheel.

Peshwari Nans

"Mother, promise me you'll be careful," Elizabeth said, leaning in to kiss her mother's cheek. "You too, Aunt Min."

"I'm sorry dear, what?" Esther said, turning the key to produce a resounding roar from the engine, and closing the door. "Right!" she then said, fastening her seat belt. "Ready Min?"

"Absolutely, dear," Minnie replied, gripping the tin that was on her lap.

"Mother, Mother!" Elizabeth yelled, tapping on the window.

"What is it, dear?" Esther said, winding it down, frustrated at the apparent delay.

"I, I, just wanted to tell you that I love you," Elizabeth said with her heart in her mouth as she clung on to the door. "And I know I haven't told you this, but I'm immensely proud of you, both of you in fact. But that won't stop me worrying about you, mind."

"I'm sure it won't, Lizzy dear." Esther smiled. "And I love you too. Please do close the garage door behind you, there's a good girl." With this, she gripped the gear stick. "Now if I remember rightly," she said, much to her daughter's dismay, "first gear is this way." With a crunch of gears, she eased Vivien out of the garage for the start of their gargantuan quest. "Oh my word!" she suddenly said, turning right and seeing the road ahead packed with well-wishers.

"Heavens above!" Minnie gasped as well.

Richard and all of his friends had turned out to see them off, as had the charming WPC, Dr Kumali (who had advised them not to travel), twenty or so market traders who had also got wind of their plans, and upwards of a hundred social media followers, many of them wielding home-made banners emblazoned with good-luck messages such as 'Go go Ladies' and 'Do it for the Nans', their cameras flashing furiously to document the momentous occasion with selfies galore.

"You're off then, Gran?" Richard said, leaning on Vivien's door. "I just wanna say you're amazing, and you too Minnie."

"Thank you, dear," Minnie said, waving graciously to the crowd.

"And thank you for Vivien, dear," Esther added, patting the boy's hand. "She's purring like a kitten."

"Take it easy though, Gran," Richard warned her. "Because there's a tiger under the bonnet."

The crowd parted to an echoing cheer and the sisters proceeded along the road, with Vivien polished and glinting to a showroom finish.

"Good byyyyyyye!" the sisters called out. "Bye byyyyyye!"

With the lights in their favour they turned onto the Whitechapel Road and they were off.

"Parma Violet, dear?" Minnie asked, offering her sister an open packet of sweets.

CHAPTER THREE

Behind the wheel of her beloved Vivien, the memories came flooding back to Esther. Although she realised that her driving left a little to be desired, especially as Britain's roads now resembled more of a battlefield, with ten times the amount of vehicles jostling and vying for position.

"Good Lord!" she shrieked when an articulated lorry cut across her path without indication or warning. "I beg your pardon!" she then called out to an irate London cabbie who was frustrated at her sedate speed.

"Careful, careful dear!" Minnie gasped, edging across her seat and indicating that her sister was far too close to adjacent vehicles.

"It's alright, Minnie dear." Esther smiled. "Vivien and I are just getting reacquainted, that's all."

"Well please be quick about it dearest, won't you?" Minnie replied, wincing at the sight of the double-decker bus towering over them.

The road layout, signals and street signs had also changed considerably over the years, giving Esther greater cause for concern. "No, no, no, this isn't right," she said, turning into a cul-de-sac and having to make a juddering three-point turn to rejoin the dual carriageway. Her haphazard attempt at exiting the huge roundabout beneath the Bow flyover was just as daunting, with the tiny Morris going around and around for a nail-biting seven times.

"I think it was that one, dearest," Minnie said, looking over her shoulder.

"I'll get it next time around, dear," Esther said, waving courteously to the bemused onlookers. "Oh damn it!" she consequently cried when failing to choose the correct lane to exit. "Next time it is, dear!"

Peshwari Nans

"Please do make it next time, Essy darling," Minnie insisted. "I'm beginning to feel a tad queasy."

"There!" Esther eventually smiled when they were free of the roundabout's hypnotic grip. "That wasn't so bad after all." Minnie gave her a sideways glance and popped another sweet into her mouth.

"Ahhhh, some things never change," Esther remarked on entering the Blackwall Tunnel, which meandered beneath the River Thames. "Jack and I took Lizzy to Broadstairs for the Dickens Festival in the summer of eighty-five, what a scorcher that was. Jack fell asleep on the beach and burnt his knees, the fool."

Cruising at forty miles per hour on the M2 motorway, Esther had the broadest smile on her face. "I should never have given up driving," she said, relishing every moment.

Minnie reached behind her and rummaged for her packed lunch, unfolding the neat foil parcels on her lap.

"Surely you're not hungry already, dear?" Esther asked, the pair having eaten a hearty meal of corned beef and boiled potatoes before setting off.

"It settles my nerves, dear," Minnie said, tucking into a shrimp-paste sandwich. "I never was the best of passengers."

"What?" Esther said, dumbfounded. "Well why didn't you say so, dear? After all, we are driving to India, remember."

"Oh that's quite alright," Minnie said reassuringly. "I have plenty of potted shrimp, don't worry." After three rounds of rye bread and shrimp paste and a sip of elderflower cordial, Minnie breathed a sigh of relief.

"Minnie dear, I must ask," Esther said, increasing her speed to forty-eight miles per hour. "What are you doing with all those confounded jars?"

Peshwari Nans

Minnie had amassed a collection of some seventy-two glass shrimp-paste jars which she kept in an old suitcase beneath her bed.

"I just can't bring myself to throw them out, dear," she replied, replacing the remainder of her lunch. "I thought we could keep buttons and pins in them and maybe scented candles. I brought one or two along in case of emergencies."

"Splendid idea, Min," Esther agreed, a huge advocate of the recycling movement herself, having grown parsley and thyme in baked-bean tins on her kitchen window sill, made a patchwork blanket and matching cushions from thrift store remnants, and hand-crafted money and memento boxes from milk cartons.

"There dear, Dover! Look!" Minnie cried, herding her sister into the correct lane for the ferry terminal. "Fifteen miles! I'm so excited I could pee!"

Esther looked across at her squirming sister. "Minnie dearest, you did go before we left, didn't you?" she asked, fearing for Vivien's upholstery.

"Oh yes, dear." Minnie smiled. "I even had a movement, dear."

"I don't wish to know that, thank you," Esther said, screwing up her face. "A simple yes or no would suffice."

"Yes, dear," Minnie replied. "Ooooh look, look Essy!" she eventually shrieked, catching her first glimpse of the English Channel and the world-renowned white chalk cliffs of Dover. "It gives me goose pimples every time I see the sea, I don't know why."

Their hulking passenger ferry sat gently swaying in her berth. "Thank you, young man," Esther said at the terminus, having queued for a full fifteen minutes behind fellow passengers and a convoy of freight trucks. "Yes, yes, dear I'm coming!" she said when beckoned by a frustrated crew member. The ever cautious Esther proceeded steadily

109

up the boarding ramp at a walking pace to the sound of honking horns behind her, a sound that had dogged her from the onset.

"Patience is a virtue!" she called out of the window.

"ANY TIME YA LIKE LOVE!" a disgruntled trucker yelled, stomping on his brakes yet again.

Once safely and securely stowed, Vivien was left on the lower deck and the ladies ventured topside. "Well this is it, dear," Esther told her sister, with the brisk sea breeze in her face. "No turning back now."

"As if we would, dear," Minnie said, gripping the rail and dodging a swooping gull.

The mooring lines were eventually slipped and the ferry inched away from the dockside, using her powerful starboard thrusters to churn up the emerald swell. Esther took Minnie's hand and gently squeezed. "Thank you, dear," she said with true fondness. "Thank you for being here I mean."

With the ferry out into open water and her turbines turning at full speed, Esther and Minnie retired to the lounge. "Can I get you ladies anything?" a stewardess asked, approaching their table. "Coffee? Or tea?"

"Oooh yes, may I have a cream tea, dear?" Minnie replied, fidgeting with anticipation. "And a slice of your lemon drizzle cake. I must say it looks absolutely delicious."

"It is." The stewardess smiled. "Take it from me."

"Where do you put it, Minnie darling?" Esther asked, shaking her head. "Just a tea for me, dear," she added.

"Certainly," the stewardess said, wiping their table and rearranging the nautical coasters.

Esther suddenly sat bolt upright, the colour draining from her face "My dear, the tin!" she said, rising to her feet.

"I have it, dear!" Minnie told her, opening her bag. "It's quite alright."

Peshwari Nans

"Oh thank heavens." Esther sighed, lowering herself back into her tub chair. "Thank you Minnie darling, I swore I'd never let it out of my sight, after all Ravi and his family are counting on us."

The Channel crossing passed without incident and the sisters delighted in seeing the French coast looming ahead of them.

"Bonjour, bonjour!" Minnie called to the predominantly British crew as they drove from the ferry. "Au revoir!"

Sailing swiftly through passport control, the ladies drove off with Minnie barking directions with a lap full of maps. "Left, dear, left!"

"I'm sure we've been this way before, Minnie dear," Esther said, driving around the Calais backstreets. "Turn on the statelite thingy, will you?"

"What, and get zapped by a laser beam from space?" Minnie replied hesitantly. "Not blooming likely!"

"Oh don't be so daft." Esther laughed, reaching for the satnav, but she, too, suddenly had reservations looking up into the clear blue sky above them. "Okay, okay, but turn the map up the right way, will you, dear?" she said, erring on the side of caution.

"Bonjour!" Minnie called to a gendarme who was resting on his bicycle.

"That'll do, dear," Esther said, chastising her sister. "We don't want to appear too familiar. Being merely courteous will suffice."

"Very well, dear," Minnie replied, waving regally instead. They then began a lengthy conversation on Anglo-French relations, covering the recent port blockades by striking dockyard workers, their churning appetite for amphibious limbs and the historical naval battle led by Admiral Horatio Nelson in which the powerful French fleet were defeated in the legendary battle of the Nile off the Egyptian coast in 1798.

111

Peshwari Nans

"They're rather an odd bunch, the French," Minnie mused. "On one hand pig-headed and arrogant, and on the other, charming and romantic with a language that weakens the knees. Cyril and I would quite often make love to his Charles Aznavour 78s, now I tell you, that man's voice could melt butter, Essy dear."

"No, no, no, dear," Esther argued. "The Italians for me have the monopoly on aural arousal. By that I mean singing, dear, you do know that, don't you? Anyway Jack and I always wanted to visit Rome, Sicily and Venice but the closest we ever got was a cornetto and a punt at Henley-on-Thames."

While navigating the ring road surrounding the city of Lille, the sisters could barely make out the spire at the top of the Eiffel Tower in the far distance.

"Look, dear!" Minnie shrieked. "Look! Oh can we please stop for a photograph? Pleeeeease Essy?"

"Oh must you, Minnie dear?" Esther moaned, eager to put as many miles as she could between them and the coast on day one.

"Oh please Essy, it's for my scrapbook," Minnie explained. "I've had it a year and I've only got an X-ray of my gallbladder and a set of commemorative stamps depicting the birth of Will and Kate's baby boy, young Prince George."

"What on earth for?" Esther asked, aghast.

"Well, why not?" Minnie replied nonchalantly. "He's a charming little chap and the spitting image of his mother, wouldn't you say?"

"No, dear!" Esther exclaimed. "The X-ray. Why?"

"Oh that, well," Minnie explained, "I had a stone which funnily enough bore an uncanny resemblance to his Royal Highness the Duke of Edinburgh, and of course I knew nobody at the women's institute would ever believe me, so

Peshwari Nans

I asked the rather ravishing young surgeon for a copy and he happily obliged."

"The Duke of Edinburgh?" Esther scoffed.

"Yes. I swear it's quite remarkable," Minnie replied proudly. "I wanted to keep the stone and have it mounted on a pendant but it was far too large to pass whole so they pulverized it with a laser beam."

"Best thing for him, dear." Esther smirked, directing her quip at the troublesome Duke.

"Who, dear?" Minnie asked, losing track completely.

"Never mind, dear," her sister replied.

Within twenty miles of the Belgian border Minnie tapped her sister's arm. "Ahem Essy dearest, I'm in need of the bathroom," she said, clenching her knees together.

"Are you sure, dear?" Esther said, counting down the miles to country number three. "Can't it wait?"

"Sorry, dear," Minnie said, writhing in her seat. "It's the elderflower cordial you see, it plays havoc with my pipes."

Esther accelerated to forty-nine in an attempt to make the border but Minnie's constant groaning forced her to pull in at a rest stop.

"Please be quick, Minnie dear," she told her sister, who wrenched her seat belt free and flung open the door. "I'm not stopping again until we're deep into Belgian territory," Esther called after her. "So please make sure it's a lot more than two squirts and a drip, do you hear me?"

"Oh it'll be more than that, I assure you!" Minnie yelled over her shoulder, shuffling inside. "Oh good grief!" she immediately said on seeing the ladies toilet out of order. "Damn you!" she added, cursing the entire population.

With the coast clear and apparently deserted, Minnie pushed open the door to the gents toilet.

"Bonjouuuuuur!" she called softly. "Hello? Bonjouuuuur?"

113

Peshwari Nans

Since there was no answer she bravely ventured inside and was instantly struck by the acrid stench of stale pee. "Filthy beasts," she said with a hand to her mouth.

Firstly eyeing the urinal trough and contemplating hoisting a leg up, she eventually opted for a cubicle, choosing the one with the least right-wing graffiti and caked-on faeces.

"Desperate times," she told herself, grabbing fistfuls of her flowing dress up to her hips. The pan rim was spattered with dried-on pee and the occasional spring-like pubic hair, things which turned Minnie's stomach, so she decided, as most do, to 'hover', wriggling out of her M&S bloomers. "Oooh, ahh, oh ahh," she said, her back creaking as she bent her knees ever so slightly, with one hand barely touching the grime-encrusted wall.

Thirty or so seconds of sustained flow later, Minnie was startled by the sound of chanting voices apparently heading her way. "What on earth?" she asked, wrenching on her bloomers. The chanting grew louder, and before Minnie could flee, the door outside was barged open by upwards of twenty Paris Saint-Germain soccer fans, who were en route to the Cup Final against their bitter rivals, Marseille.

The supporters' coach had stopped to relieve the inebriated and boisterous fans and was parked alongside Vivien. Jostling for urinal space, the jeering lads crammed into the two adjacent cubicles. Several of them had severely bloated bladders, and were urinating on the floor.

"Oh dear, oh dear, dear, dear," Minnie said as the puddle seeped under her door. The chanting of "Allez Paris Saint Germain! Allez Paris Saint Germain!" (Go Paris Saint Germain) reached fever pitch, as did their abhorrent behaviour. Toilet rolls were flung around the lavatory and a playful fight ensued, with the culprits bouncing off the cubicle doors, sending Minnie cringing into the corner, wedged between the cistern and the wall, fearing for her life.

One or two of the louts then turned their attentions to Minnie's bolted door, wanting to antagonize the user within.

"HEY! HEY!" they yelled, pounding on the fragile surround and tossing wads of paper over the top along with crumpled cans, spattering her with remnants of beer and cider.

"Stop! Please stop!" she cried, unheard above the rousing soccer anthem. Their pounding grew more aggressive as did their intentions towards the cubicle occupant, many of them spoiling for a fight "Essyyyyyy! Esyyyyyy!" Minnie cried, close to tears.

With his fellow compatriots thumping at the door with boots and fists, one young lad—eager to impress—climbed onto the adjacent lavatory cistern and peered over the top, bottle in hand but immediately staggered back, planting a foot squarely into the stinking pan beneath him.

"ARRETEZ, ARRETEZ!" he yelled, urging his fellow supporters to stop at once "NON, NON, ARRETEZ, GRAND-MERE, GRAND-MERE, ARRETEZ!" he yelled, wrenching his baying friends from the door. The young lad stood guarding the cubicle. "Grand-mere!" he said, shoving several of them back.

"Grand-mere?" a few of his friends said as the singing subsided.

"Oui, oui," the lad said, turning and tapping softly on the door. "Grand-mere?" he called to Minnie. "Pardon, pardon." (meaning 'I'm sorry.') The lavatory duly fell silent and moments later Minnie crept cautiously from the corner from whence she was crammed and gingerly slid the bolt aside.

"Grand-mere!" many of the fans gasped, tugging their red, white and blue hats from their heads. "Pardon, grand-mere, pardon grand-mere," echoed around the lavatory as the supporters each respectfully bowed their heads, sobering rapidly.

"Well!" Minnie snapped, quietly seething but still visibly shaken from her ordeal. She removed her own woollen hat, which dripped with their discarded alcohol. "You should all be ashamed of yourselves, wholeheartedly ashamed! Do you hear me?"

Many of the belittled supporters understood nothing of what she had said but the manner and tone of her scolding had their tails tucked firmly between their legs. "Look at you, you drunken louts!" Minnie continued, with her assailants well and truly on the back foot. "You're a disgrace, a disgrace I say, and look at this place!" She wrenched a mop from the cleaner's bucket and thrust it into one heavily tattooed hoodlum's hand. "Clean it up at once!" she barked.

With his own beloved grandmother in mind, the man did exactly as he was told, mopping the torrent of pee from the floor. "Well don't just stand there!" Minnie gestured to his friends. "Chop chop!"

The army of subservient fans set to work with lavatory brushes and fistfuls of paper towel, scrubbing with vigour under Minnie's authoritative eye.

Meanwhile, Esther sat strumming her fingers on Vivien's wheel, smiling courteously at the coach driver beside her. "Where on earth is she, Vivien?" she asked.

Before long the gents lavatory was beginning to show some semblance of normality and hygiene. The tiled walls were scrubbed and buffed as was the porcelain ware. "Splendid!" Minnie said, overseeing operations. "Splendid!"

The lad that had discovered her offered Minnie his own woollen bobble hat in his team's colours.

"Oh, thank you," Minnie said, accepting the olive branch so to speak, and dropping hers into the waste bin.

Peshwari Nans

"Well gentleman I'll bid you all good day," she told them, turning for the door, which several of the chaps fought over to open for her.

Pulling on the Paris Saint-Germain hat, Minnie left the toilets surrounded by the French fans, each of them attempting to sing the British National Anthem to appease her. "No, no, no!" Minnie called out over them. "It's seeeeend herrrrr viiiictooooorious, haaaaapy aaaand gloooorious!"

Esther looked across the car park and did an immediate double take, seeing her sister amid the soccer thugs, belting out 'Rule Britannia' at the top of her voice.

"Excellent, excellent!" Minnie told the cheering supporters on reaching the car, where Vivien's door was held open for her. "Now," she said, addressing her new-found friends. "I'll expect each and every one of you to conduct yourselves with a little more decorum in future, do I make myself clear?"

The lads chanted in reply: "GRAND-MERE, GRAND-MERE, GRAND-MERE!"

"What the devil happened?" Esther asked when her sister sat beside her. "Minnie dear, what on earth have you been doing? And what have you got on your head, for Pete's sake?"

"Oh it's a gift from the boys," Minnie replied, waving goodbye to the football supporters as they boarded their coach, many of them retrieving their discarded cans while doing so.

"Have you been drinking, dear?" Esther then asked, getting a distinct whiff of ale.

"Of course not, dear!" Minnie insisted, still waving to the departing fans. "You know I never touch a drop before seven-fifteen. Shall we go?"

Esther drove from the car park, glancing quizzically at her sister, who sat humming the Parisian soccer team's anthemic chant and smiling to herself at having taught their fans an all-important lesson in respect and humility.

"Minnie, dear," Esther said, winding down her window as they rejoined the motorway. "You smell like a bar tender's apron my dear, here." She handed her sister her ever-present lily-of-the-valley perfume. "Use it sparingly, darling," she told her. "It's all I have until we return home."

"Sandwich, dear?" Minnie asked as they were crossing into Belgium.

"Do you know I think I will, dear," Esther replied, her stomach rumbling. "Anything but shrimp paste, please."

"Right you are, dear," Minnie said, reaching for their provisions. "Oh hell!" she then cursed, hunting for a plate. "Did you pack the Denby, dearest?" she asked, concerned for her classic kitchenware.

"Of course, dear, I wrapped it in my woollens this morning," Esther informed her sister. "But it's towards the rear, you'll just have to make do without it for now."

Minnie was all fingers and thumbs with the bread, butter knife and preserves on her lap. "Ahaaa," she suddenly said with a flash of inspiration, buttering Esther's slice on the rear of Elizabeth's tablet computer.

"How resourceful, dear." Esther smiled, pinching a slice of red Leicester. "It's like a futuristic cheeseboard."

Minnie handed her sister her sandwich triangle then scooped a dollop of piccalilli from the tablet's camera lens. "Whoops," she said, licking her finger.

The night was drawing in and fatigue was beginning to get the better of the two travellers, their joints stiffening. "Look out for a motel please, Minnie dear, would you?" Esther asked, putting a hand to her open mouth. "I'm positively pooped and I have a feeling Vivien could do with a rest too."

Peshwari Nans

Vivien's temperature gauge had been straying from the normal position towards the hot zone, despite her recent overhaul.

Entering the picturesque town of Namur, where the two mighty Sambre and Meuse Rivers collide, Minnie directed her sister to a truck stop that was complete with a restaurant and motel. "Ten euros per couple," Minnie exclaimed. "My, that's excellent value, what do you think, dear?"

"Yes, well done, dear." Esther smiled, approving of her sister's find and parking in full view of the reception.

"Ooooh, ahhh, ahhh, ouch," the pair groaned as they climbed from the car and straightened their backs.

Esther massaged her rear, unaccustomed as she was to Vivien's sagging upholstery. "I don't know about you," she puffed, "but I feel as though I've been kicked by a prize heifer. I shall definitely need a soak in a hot tub to ease the pain, dear."

"Me too, dear," Minnie agreed, aware of a temporary stoop to her spine. "I took the liberty of purchasing some soothing salts from the Chinese herbalist before we left, Essy, so I'll happily share them with you."

"Oh you are a dear," Esther said, collecting her case from Vivien's rear and locking all of her doors.

"I say, helloooooo?" Minnie called as she stood in front of the empty desk. "Hello? Cooeeeee? I sayyyyy!"

The door behind them opened and a middle-aged pot-bellied trucker entered, escorting a noticeably younger brunette in glitzy heels and wearing a short skirt that barely covered her bottom.

It so happened that the truck stop was a notorious hotspot for prostitutes and lecherous lorry drivers alike, many of the shameless girls bedding up to a dozen in a single day in the aptly named 'service station'. By day they would flit from cab to cab plying their trade, but by night they would avail themselves of the motel's basic amenities, grabbing the chance to rid themselves of the stench of diesel and hydraulic fluid.

"Excuse me," Esther said, raising a finger. "Could you please tell us how we acquire a room for the night?"

The lusty trucker barely acknowledged the sisters, instead whispering his depraved wishes into the girl's ear and mauling her pert buttocks.

"I say, young lady," Esther insisted. "Would you be so kind as to—"

The heavily made-up girl popped the gum in her mouth and simply pointed to the bell on the wall at the end of the counter before entering a code into a keypad and disappearing through to the motel corridor.

"Oh I see, thank you!" Esther called after her. "The bell dear, ring the bell," she told her sister, who by now was flagging somewhat.

Setting down the Lipton's tin, Minnie went over and prodded the button three times. "Try it again, dear," Esther said, checking the open door behind the counter.

Minnie did so over and over again. "What are we going to do, dear?" she asked.

"Leave it to me, dear," her sister said, taking the phone from her pocket and dialling the number on the reception wall. The payphone on the counter top soon began ringing continuously until a bleary eyed youth emerged from the back room, his eyes glued to his hand-held games console.

"Ahhh, hello," Esther said, raising a hand, but the lad, with his head down and thrash metal playing in his headphones, ignored her, answering the telephone instead.

"Bonjour?" he said, turning down the volume on his MP3 player.

"Hello," Esther said into her phone, whilst waving in his direction. "We'd like a room please."

"A room?" the lad said, whilst completing his current level of death droids game and showing very little professional courtesy.

"Yes. A room," Esther reiterated. "It's *me*, on the phone, over here!"

The lad put a finger up to silence Esther while he dealt with his telephone enquiry.

"Well I never," Esther exclaimed, taking from a pocket the panic alarm her daughter had given her to fend off undesirables. She pressed it to the mouthpiece. "Cover your ears Minnie dear," she told her sister, before giving a deafening blast, which had her own ears ringing.

The inept receptionist immediately dropped his games console and wrenched the phone from his ear, wincing before slamming the receiver down, assuming he had been the unwitting victim of a prank call. "Arsehole!" he cursed, fumbling at his feet for his console.

"I say?" Esther said, her finger poised on the button "Now about that room."

"You want a room?" the lad said, coming to.

"No," Minnie replied sarcastically. "We'd like haddock and chips twice and two pickled eggs! Of course we want a room, you foolish boy!"

"Sign please," the lad said, offering the register—still apparently very much deaf in his right ear.

Esther paid and was given a four-digit code for the door.

"Twenty-one," the receptionist added, handing Minnie a swipe card.

"Thank you," Minnie said, collecting the Lipton's tea tin. "What time is breakfast?"

The lad merely pointed to a sparsely filled vending machine in the corner of reception. "Twenty-four hour," he informed them, slamming the register closed.

"Oh," Minnie scoffed, unimpressed to say the least. "Well perhaps a pot of tea, say at around seven-thirty? And if you do happen to have chamomile that would be delightful."

The young man gave no response, merely donning his headphones and shuffling out of sight.

"It's hardly the Marriot, dear, is it?" Minnie said as Esther entered the code and proceeded through to the corridor.

"Twenty-one, twenty-one," Esther mouthed, having to press the time sensitive light switch repeatedly. "Ahh here we are, dear, now one assumes you slide the card through here." She tried the swipe card several times but to no avail. "Oh for heaven's sake!" she cursed, in no mood for further delays. "And they call this progress! What's wrong with a good old fashioned key?"

"Try the lucky rub, dear," Minnie insisted.

"The lucky *what*, dear?" Esther asked, never having been privy to such wizardry.

"The lucky rub," Minnie said, taking the card and rubbing it vigorously on the sleeve of her overcoat. "It works wonders with my bingo membership. I'm afraid everything's either swiped or pin-and-chipped these days."

"Do you expect me to believe that just by—" Esther was about to question her sister's magical prowess when Minnie ran the card through the slot once more and opened the door. "Oh," she said abruptly. "The lucky rub, you say?"

"Yes, dear." Minnie smiled, picking up her case and proceeding inside. The two sisters then stood in the doorway, letting their cases slip from their tired fingers in abject horror when they saw the rooms archaic condition. The curtains either side of the window were mismatched, the window itself had a piece of cardboard taped over a gaping hole, the remnants of its fractured state still visible on the threadbare carpet. The catalogue of horrors only increased when they noticed the three-legged bed supported on one corner by a pile of telephone directories and covered in a pale green polyester bedspread, complete with questionable staining.

"You were right, dear," Esther agreed. "It is hardly the Marriot."

"Shall I ask the young man to move us?" Minnie said, turning for the door,

"I wouldn't bother, dear," her sister said, having been through hell and high water already with the incompetent boy. "You'd have more luck resurrecting the dead."

The plug from the kettle had been stolen, along with the complimentary tea, coffee and creamers.

"I think I'll turn in, dear," Minnie said, dragging the bedspread and sheet from the bed by her thumb and forefinger and tossing it aside with a look of disgust, while Esther removed the pillowcases. "Would you turn out the light, Essy dear?" Minnie asked, stretching out on the bare mattress fully clothed.

Esther tugged at the cord beside the door, but the powerful one-hundred-watt light bulb remained illuminated. "Blast!" she said, grimacing.

"What's the matter, dear?" Minnie asked, shielding her eyes. "Switch it off, will you?"

"I'm trying to, dear," Esther said, tugging a little harder. "I don't want to break the damn thing."

But as she said it, the entire ceiling rose and a huge section of plaster came away, showering her with debris. "Oh. Oh, oh Minnie!" she cried, ducking and shaking the flaking paint from her hair.

"You were saying, dear?" Minnie said, turning away from the light.

Peshwari Nans

"Good grief, this place is a death-trap," Esther said, surveying the damage—it had clearly occurred as a result of a former botched repair.

Unable to reach the light bulb to remove it, the sisters lay on the bare sunken mattress with their eyes clenched tightly shut.

"It's no use, dear," Esther said after a short while. "I can't sleep like this."

"Shall I throw a shoe at it, dear?" Minnie asked, fumbling on the floor beside the bed but picking up a discarded condom instead.

"What on earth?" she said, struggling to focus beneath the glare. "Good God, how revolting!" she cried out, horrified at her find and flinging it across the room. "I can't stay here, Essy," she moaned. "I'll catch the bubonic plague or something a whole lot worse, I'm sure of it. And as for that perishing light!"

"Calm down dear," Esther said, taking control of the dreadful situation. "I have an idea."

She slipped from the bed and opened her suitcase. "Here you are, dear," she said, offering Minnie a pair of her reinforced knickers.

"Essy dear, what's this?" Minnie began, but then seeing her sister slip them over her head as a makeshift blindfold, she soon cottoned on. "Very good, dear," she said, following suit.

The two ladies looked totally ridiculous lying side by side on the mattress in their overcoats with spotted undergarments covering their faces.

"Splendid, dear," Minnie said in a muffled tone through the cotton gusset. But just when the dozing ladies thought their motel experience couldn't possibly deteriorate any further, the trucker and his paid bed mate began their carnal acrobatics in the bed directly behind theirs.

Peshwari Nans

"YES, YES, YES!" the girl screamed in a bid to convince the wheezing lothario of her apparent enjoyment.

"Who am I? Tell me! Tell me!" he yelled with their headboard pounding the wafer-thin dividing wall. "WHO AM I?"

"POOH BEAR, BABE!" the girl replied, raising her eyebrows while he groaned from behind her.

"Oh yes, that's right!" he panted. "And you've been a baaaaad piglet, haven't you? Haven't you?"

The call girl agreed, concentrating solely on the handsome bonus she had bartered for to indulge his farcical fantasy.

Esther and Minnie's own bed juddered in time with his rhythmic thrusting, driving Esther to distraction. "Oh really, this is impossible!" she barked, raising her knickers above one eye, squinting in doing so.

"Reminds me of my Cyril." Minnie smiled, listening intently. "You've got to admire the fellow, haven't you?" she told her fuming sister. "He has the stamina of an ox."

"Admire him?" Esther moaned. "I'd like to give him a piece of my mind and wash his filthy mouth out with carbolic soap! Why does he have to be an English lorry driver? If he was French, at least I wouldn't know what he was saying!"

After her speech, Esther pushed the ends of her handkerchief into each ear, left Minnie, and settled in the one and only armchair, pulling her temporary blackout down firmly over her face. "Revolting man," she mumbled.

Esther spent the next two hours twisting and turning, accompanied by the bumping and grinding noises of epic proportions from the adjacent motel room.

The young prostitute concluded that the only logical explanation for his near God-like sexual performance was the empty packaging from his 'blue rampant rhino' pills, that were strewn around the room. At one point she halted proceedings to renegotiate an extended verbal contract.

The following morning Minnie collected several packets of cheese biscuits from the vending machine and returned to the room, smiling knowingly at the depraved trucker as she passed him by.

"Essy, Essy dear," she said, gently nudging her sister, who was sitting upright in the chair, mouth wide open with her knickers askew. "Essy dearest, it's nine thirty-five, we wanted to be away at eight."

"What? What?" Esther said, stirring and removing her mask. "Oh hell!" she immediately cried at the blinding light.

"Nibbles, dear?" Minnie said, offering a packet.

"Heavens no," Esther sneered while her sister tucked in, swatting the crumbs from her cardigan. "I need a cup of tea, a hot bath and a nit comb. This place is alive with the damn things, I'm sure of it."

Little did they know that the motel had been forced to close on three separate occasions by health officials, and each time had been thoroughly fumigated throughout to combat the ever-increasing cockroach, lice and bedbug infestations.

"A bath, you say?" Minnie replied, having surveyed the washroom facilities. "I'm afraid you'll have to make do with a cat's lick, dear, there are no towels or hot water and there's a ring around the tub you could write your name in."

"WHAT?" Esther raged, climbing from her chair and scratching at her neck. "This, this, *fleapit* should be razed to the ground I tell you, razed to the ground!" Hastily gathering her things, Esther noticed the iPad on the bed was illuminated. "Is that thing okay?" she asked, betraying her total lack of technical knowhow.

"Oh yes, dear," Minnie said excitedly. "Young Richard telephoned this morning. I told him you were asleep and

126

filled him in on our progress. Apparently Elizabeth is furious that you haven't been in touch."

"Of course she is." Esther sighed.

"Anyway," Minnie continued, retrieving the tablet. "While we were chatting, Richard talked me through this skype thingy. Essy dear, you know it's quite remarkable. I could actually see him as clear as day while we spoke. Don't ask me how—I suppose it's another of those statelites, but it's incredible nethertheless."

"Really," Esther replied, decidedly unimpressed, having been eaten alive for half the night.

Minnie followed her sister around the room, eager to share her new-found wisdom. "He also explained the Book face to me."

"Isn't it Facebook, dear?" Esther said, hunting for her right shoe.

"That's the one." Minnie smiled. "Anyway, I now know how to post, poke, nudge, wink, share and update, oh and apparently if we want more likes we should post and update regularly."

"I don't want a damn *like!*" Esther snapped, slamming her case closed. "I want a hot bath!"

"Yes dear, but," Minnie said, oblivious to her sister's apparent distress. "Do you know our page now has over a thousand likes?"

"Minnie, dearest!" Esther stormed, in no mood for a social network masterclass. "You can go poke your likes."

"Oh no, dear," Minnie said confidently. "You can't poke a like."

Minnie had omitted to tell her sister that while she slept she had taken several photographs of her wearing her knickers on her head and her mouth wide open and posted them to their Facebook page for all to see. This single posting alone was to quadruple their popularity within the hour, with 'shares' reverberating as far afield as Tokyo, Japan.

"You should try it, dear," Minnie said, clutching the tablet to her chest, completely hooked and eager to learn everything that cyber networking had to offer.

Their hellish night at the near derelict motel had been fully documented in the minutest detail, with Minnie eventually mastering the virtual keyboard after a jittery start. Included in her account were details of the sinful activities of their neighbours.

Facebook friends around the world soon found themselves distracted from their everyday lives, glued to their devices, eagerly awaiting another posting. Minnie obliged them by snapping several of their accommodation's more memorable features, such as the condoms, the cardboard window, the lavatory seat minus one half, and the gaping hole in the ceiling where the light switch once hung. "He's going to teach me how to tweet this afternoon," Minnie said enthusiastically.

"Tweet?" Esther said, raising the hem of her dress to claw at her ankles. "Listen, Minnie dear," she added angrily. "If I'd wanted a blasted budgerigar I'd have bought one."

Minnie tried to explain. "No, no, dear it's—"

"—It's ridiculous that's what it is," Esther sneered. "A grown woman tweeting. Whatever next?"

"Blogging apparently, dear," Minnie informed her. "Then there's tagging, hash tagging, newsfeed and hootsuite, oh and I need to find out what a flash mob is."

"Marvellous, dear," Esther said, flinging open the door, keen to distance herself from the mangy motel, the owner of which was now seated at the front desk.

"Mesdames," he said, smiling, having deduced their nationality by Minnie's constant attempts to educate her sister. "I trust you enjoyed your stay with us. Perhaps if it is not too much trouble, you would like to leave a comment in our visitors' book?"

"A comment?" Esther snapped, snatching the pen from his hand. "Yes I'll leave you a blasted comment alright!" Whilst scratching at her neck she scrawled a scathing condemnatory passage in block capitals, pressing so firmly she pierced the paper several times "There!" she said, slamming the pen down when she was finished.

Minnie used the iPad to snap the stunned face of the hotelier. "Oh and, er," she added, pointing to the empty vending machine, "I wouldn't hold my breath on that Michelin star if I were you either."

The ladies left and loaded their things back into Vivien. "Wait, dear, wait!" Minnie said, backing across the car park to include her sister, Vivien and the motel in the picture "Now give us a smile!"

"You have got to be kidding," Esther said, barely managing a frown.

"That'll do," Minnie said, posting the picture to their page like a pro. "Now according to google, dear," she said as they were about to set off.

"Who?" Esther asked, using an entire packet of wet wipes in an attempt to rid herself of the room's distinctive odour,

"Google, dear," Minnie explained. "He's this fellow on the world wide net, and a very clever one at that."

"Get to the point, Minnie," Esther said, starting Vivien first pulling out the 'choke' button. "You're beginning to bother me as much as these damn lice! God, I need a bath."

"Well that's what I'm trying to tell you, dear," Minnie said, looking extremely pleased with herself. "According to Mr Google, there's a municipal baths around six or so miles from here. We have to pass it en route."

Peshwari Nans

"Really?" Esther said, changing her tone drastically. "Well what are we waiting for? Oh and be sure to thank Mr Google wholeheartedly on my behalf, won't you, dear?"

"Will do, dear." Minnie smiled with the Lipton's tin of cash tucked firmly between her legs.

Esther, her skin now crawling, applied a little more pressure to Vivien's accelerator pedal, taking her to a jaw-dropping fifty-two miles per hour.

"Steady, dear," Minnie said as they cornered at apparent speed. "Arrive alive, remember?"

"I won't if these blighters have their way," Esther moaned, scratching feverishly at her neck once again and pulling into the car park of the local municipal baths on the outskirts of the city of Liège. "Thank heavens," she sighed, wrenching her seat belt free.

"Oooh, hang on dear, we have a call," Minnie said, opening 'Skype' on their tablet. "It's Elizabeth."

"Mother, Mother!" Elizabeth said, clearly irate and now visible on the tablet's screen to the sisters.

"Not now, dear," Esther said, switching the tablet and her daughter off in mid flow.

Back in England, Elizabeth fumed: "Mother, switch your damn phone on, will you!" Then her screen went blank. "Mother!" she cursed to herself. "Oh this really is too much!"

"Quickly, dear," Esther then said, half a continent away from her daughter, and unaware of her feelings. She shuffled to the entrance steps with a change of clothes and her costume tucked under her arm. "Two please, yes with towels," she told the attendant with a growing sense of urgency. "Hurry Minnie dear," she called behind her, slipping through the turnstiles and into the changing rooms.

After showering and disinfecting their feet the sisters stepped gingerly into the shallow end of the Olympic sized pool, and waded until they were waist deep. "Hopefully the chlorine will kill whatever's eating me," Esther said, ducking beneath the water several times to exterminate the last of her unwanted guests.

"Better, dear?" Minnie asked, attempting an awkward breaststroke.

"Much better, thank you." Her sister smiled, wiping the water from her face.

Suddenly, while the ladies were happily wallowing, there was a huge splash beside them as three German youths leapt in, buttocks first, engulfing the startled sisters in a drenching wave. "Excuse me!" Esther spluttered, drying her eyes.

"Yes, yes, watch what you're doing please!" Minnie added, having been swept aside.

"Ahhhh, English," one of the Berlin-born lads said, looking down his nose at the bathing ladies. "What right have you got to tell us what to do, eh? If you don't like it get out and go back home."

"Leave it, Mikel," one of his friends said with a greater degree of courtesy. "Sorry ladies."

"Sorry!" Mikel snapped. "Why do we have to be sorry? These English with their strawberries and cream, Wimbledon and Ascot. Pompous and meddlesome that's what they are, always sticking your nose in where it is not wanted."

"How rude!" Esther said, whilst at the same time a tad intimidated.

"Now you listen here!" Minnie snapped, his attitude getting her back up somewhat. "We didn't come here to be insulted by the likes of you, so I'll thank you to keep a civil tongue in your head, young man!"

"Mikel, come," the lad's other friend said, tugging at his arm. "Come. Let's dive."

Peshwari Nans

Eager to save face, Mikel thrust a handful of water into Minnie's face and swam away with his friends towards the deep end and the towering three-stage diving boards, the highest of which was a staggering ten metres, or some thirty-three feet above the water.

"Are you alright, dear?" Esther asked, sweeping the hair from Minnie's face.

"I think I swallowed some—" Minnie coughed. "—Some water." Spluttering, she struggled to catch her breath. "Those brutes! I'll, I'll…"

"Leave it, dear," Esther urged. "It's not worth it. Besides, what can we possibly do?"

Minnie, enraged, hardly took her eyes off Mikel as he and his friends climbed the concrete steps towards the top board. At the second level he paused. "This is high enough don't you think?" he told the other two in their own language. They were just ahead of him.

"No, no, no." His friends laughed. "We must dive from the top. What's the matter? You're not chicken, are you?"

"No, no, of course not," Mikel replied, although he seemed extremely hesitant. "I have dived from there many times."

This was, of course, a blatant lie. His fear of heights had been kept from all but his immediate family.

"Come, come," they said, racing upwards with Mikel following at a lesser pace.

"Let's all go together?" one lad suggested, brimming with confidence.

"No, no, no, you two go," Mikel replied, clinging to the rail. "I'll—er—I'll be right behind you, I promise."

Minnie observed this discussion, guessing what was going on even though she couldn't understand German, while her sister bobbed on her back.

Mikel's two friends stood side by side, smiling at one another before leaping into the air in tandem, shrieking loudly as they turned three consecutive summersaults and a twist, entering the water below with the minimum of disturbance. "COME MIKEL!" one of them yelled once he had surfaced. "LET US SEE YOU DIVE!"

"Okay, yes, one moment!" Mikel barked back. "I'm just, I'm just, preparing myself."

He began to tremble as he looked down at his friends, who seemed like tiny sprats in an ocean below him.

"MIKEL!" they both called, beckoning to him.

"He can't do it," Minnie then said to herself with a wry smile.

"Do what, dear?" Esther asked, treading water as best she could.

"Nothing, dear," Minnie replied. "I'll be back in a moment."

"Where are you going, Minnie dearest?" Esther asked, standing up and drying her face once more. "Minnie? What on earth are you doing?"

"Just a little payback, dear," Minnie said, clambering from the pool.

"What? What? Minnie, come back!" Esther said, unaware of her sister's intentions.

"It's alright dear," Minnie called back. "Just wait right there, I won't be a moment."

While Mikel's friends were goading him, Minnie began to climb the diving board steps, much to their astonishment and obviously to the amazement of her sister.

"What the devil?" Esther said, bemused. "Minnie? Minnie? Get back here at once!" She gestured.

But Minnie had only one thing on her mind: sweet revenge, and although she was frail and breathing, she made her way slowly up to the top board.

"What, what are you doing here?" Mikel asked her.

"Diving, dear." Minnie smiled. "Aren't you?"

Peshwari Nans

"Yes, yes, but," Mikel stammered "Y-You cannot do it. Look at you? You are too old."

In her gaudy one-piece bathing suite Minnie hardly resembled an Olympic athlete, she looked more like a wrinkled turtle, but she did possess the one thing that Mikel sadly lacked: gumption, and she had it in spades. "Well," she said nodding in the pool's direction. "What are you waiting for?"

"I—I can't. Not with you here," Mikel said, looking down once again, his head spinning and his stomach churning.

"Well I'm not going anywhere, dear," Minnie insisted. "Apart from off the end of this thing."

"YOU?" Mikel gasped. "You are really going to dive off here!"

"This is a diving board, is it not?" Minnie said, edging towards him.

"GET BACK!" Mikel cried, fearing for his life. "Get back, please!"

"Jump," Minnie said, steely eyed.

"What?" Mikel replied with his heart beating fast and his back to the water.

"You heard me," Minnie said, grimacing. "I said jump!"

She had her man cornered and relished every second.

"MIKEL COME ON! DIVE WILL YOU?" his friends yelled, piling on the pressure.

"You heard them," Minnie added. "Go on, get on with it, I haven't got all day."

Mikel's bottom lip began to quiver as his fear got the better of him.

"Dive, you pathetic wretch!" Minnie insisted.

"No, no, please I'm sorry," Mikel began to weep, clasping his hands together.

Peshwari Nans

His friends watched in horror as Mikel begged for forgiveness from the old woman he had mocked. "Mikel, what are you doing?" one of them asked.

"Minnie, get down from there at once!" Esther called, but Minnie was savouring the moment.

"Pleeeeeeease!" Mikel said with genuine tears of remorse.

Minnie eventually stepped aside, unable to stomach his grovelling a moment longer. "Get out of my sight," she said, watching him scurry by and down the stairs, crying like a scolded child.

"What?" his friends cried out as Mikel raced to the changing rooms, his reputation and manhood in tatters.

Minnie herself attempted to leave but then the chanting began: "ENGLISH! ENGLISH" ENGLISH!" the German youths called up, egging her on.

"Me?" Minnie said, looking down.

The lads both nodded and continued to coax her: "ENGLISH! ENGLISH!"

"Oh hell," Minnie said, turning back to the edge.

"What are you doing, Minnie dear?" Esther called, waving frantically. "Get down!"

The chanting grew louder, drowning out Minnie's frantic sister, and everybody within the pool and poolside stopped and stared.

"Don't you dare!" Esther said under her breath, watching intently. "Minnie *please don't!*"

Minnie hadn't dived from a board since the summer of seventy-three at the now derelict Poplar Baths when, once before, she had been goaded into doing it, that time by her own friends. But that board had been half the height of this one, and she had been considerably more supple.

Inching forward until her toes gripped the edge, Minnie went over her supposed performance in her head. Should she tuck, roll or flop? And with or without the customary half pike seen in so many professional routines?

"Minnie, no!" Esther pleaded. "Don't be ridiculous!"

"ENGLISH! ENGLISH! ENGLISH!" echoed around the pool, with many foreign nationals contributing.

With a huge gulp of air, Minnie stretched out her arms beside her. "My God, she's going to do it," Esther said to herself, with a hand to her heart. "Heavens Minnie, no, dear!"

In that one moment with the crowd willing her, Minnie felt a conflicting mixture of emotions: true elation, the kind an Olympian feels when they have the audience with them, combined with a rush of pure adrenalin, like a suicidal bridge jumper must experience moments from certain death.

The crowd then suddenly fell eerily silent as Minnie clasped her hands tightly together and bent her knees in readiness. "God no!" Esther gasped.

All eyes were now on the courageous pensioner in her one-piece, high above the pool.

"Oh well," she said to herself, trembling somewhat. "Here goes."

And then, as if in slow motion, Minnie leaned forward until gravity took control and pulled her from the board.

"OH, OH AHH, OHH ARRRRRRGHH!" she cried, tumbling with her legs splayed like an acrobatic starfish, and all thoughts of a refined and honed routine were well and truly out the window.

The entire gathering gasped as she fell with all the grace of a gangly goose, and looking as though she would break every bone on impact with the water. Esther looked away, tensing her body, but somehow Minnie miraculously straightened her aging frame moments before she hit, and entered the water with a resounding splash, but she remained intact nethertheless.

Peshwari Nans

A rapturous cheer rang out around the pool as everybody surged towards the deep end.

"MINNIE!" Esther cried, turning back to find her sister out of sight. "MINNIE!"

Minnie broke the surface to a heroine's welcome, letting out the deep breath she had been holding. "Minnie, oh thank God!" Esther shrieked.

Mikel's friends swam to her and helped her to the side.

"Crazy English!" One of them said, laughing and patting her back. She was then hoisted from the water by her now adoring fans, each jostling to shake her hand and be part of the awe-inspiring spectacle.

"Minnie, dear!" Esther called, leaving the water and nudging her way to her sister. "Minnie, you fool!" she said, hugging her dripping sibling. "What in God's name were you thinking?"

"I, I, don't know," Minnie said, shivering. "But I tell you what Essy, d-d-dear, I'd d-d-do it again."

The crowd went wild, applauding her tenacity and zest for life. "Ohhh no," Esther said, tugging her sister towards the shallow end. "I couldn't go through that again, you fool, you could've got yourself killed."

"Excuse me, ladies," a Dutch spectator said. "Are you by any chance driving to India? I noticed your car outside."

"Yes, yes, we are," Esther replied. "But how do you know who we are?"

"Oh I am a huge fan of yours." The gentleman smiled and was joined by his wife and three children. "This is my wife Sara and these are our children: Fleur, Lucas and Noah. We have followed your progress on the Internet and think you are both amazing, truly amazing. I can't believe you are here with us now."

"Well it's jolly nice to meet you," Esther said, shaking each of their hands, as did Minnie.

"You dived from there?" young Lucas said, wide-eyed, pointing way up to the top board.

"Yes I did, young man," Minnie replied, crouching at his side.

"Were you scared?" the boy asked.

"Petrified, my dear." Minnie laughed. "But that's the best part by far—overcoming the fear and taking that 'leap of faith' so to speak."

"Look," the boys' father said, producing his smartphone. "I have it all here."

He replayed the whole remarkable event, which included the terrified Mikel's departure. "Do you mind if I upload it?" he asked.

"If you *what,* dear?" Esther asked unsure of his terminology.

"Upload to the Internet," he explained. "To your Facebook page, and of course to my YouTube account."

"I don't see why not," Minnie replied, noticing more and more cameras pointed her way, and receiving just as much adulation as a supreme athlete winning a gold medal for their country.

"Will you please excuse us?" Esther eventually said, ushering her sister towards the changing rooms. "We must be on our way."

A roar of applause echoed around the cavernous pool house, coaxing a parting wave from Minnie.

"What's got into you, Minnie dear?" Esther asked, whilst towelling herself dry.

"Life, dear," Minnie simply said, smiling. "Or what's left of it. I tell you at times like this I think about my own mortality and say to hell with it, what's the worst that can happen?"

"Well it was damn foolish if you ask me," her level-headed sister said, flinging her lice-infested clothes into the bin. Minnie followed suit, and the pair left feeling altogether cleansed and respectable.

"Oh my!" Esther gasped on seeing as many as fifty of their supporters surrounding their car, eager for a parting autograph. "Oh er, okay," she said, unaccustomed to such adoration. "Thank you, thank you so much," she told her well-wishers while being dragged from pillar to post by enthusiastic 'selfie' aficionados. "I'm sorry but we really must be going," she eventually told them all, as they loaded their bags into Vivien. "Goodbye, goodbye!"

"Bye bye," Minnie said, shaking several hands. "It was lovely to have met you all, thank you. And you, dear."

Waving as they departed, Minnie held the tablet out of the car's window and snapped the jubilant gathering. "What a jolly nice bunch," she said, posting the picture online with increased dexterity. "It's quite easy when you get the hang of it." She smiled at her achievement.

"Well there's absolutely no way you'd ever get me up on that diving board, that's for sure," Esther said, as they joined the busy dual carriageway.

"No, no, not doing the dive, dear," Minnie said, scrolling through their social network site. "I mean this Facebook thing, oh look, dear! Albert from Bridlington has carved our faces into his prize marrow. How clever. Mind you, mine's not a bad likeness but I'm afraid yours leaves a little to be desired."

"Where? Show me!" Esther barked, glancing over.

The pair burst out laughing at Esther's ludicrous likeness. "I look like the Wicked Witch of the West, dear," Esther chuckled. "Surely my nose isn't that big, is it?"

"Well," Minnie said, comparing the two. "At least he captured your double chin, dear."

"Oooh, the cheeky beggar!" Esther frowned.

The ladies navigated the busy Belgian back roads and bypasses and finally made it to the German border at around 3 p.m. that afternoon, with Minnie snapping just about every road sign and marker along the way, both of them blissfully unaware of their growing popularity at home and abroad: such was the immense power of the Internet.

Soon marriage proposals would come trickling in from aging suitors from the most unlikely places, such as Christmas Creek, Western Australia, Nome in Alaska and Hokkaido in Northern Japan. But this was merely the tip of an ever-expanding iceberg, for as Minnie's heroic high dive entered the cyber domain the clip instantly went viral worldwide, breaking all previous records for views and downloads in a single day.

Marketing executives were feverishly constructing ad campaigns around them for items such as age-defying creams, lotions and potions, hoping for the sisters' endorsement, with potential profits anticipated from customers in the senior community to run into the tens of millions of pounds.

"Sandwich, dear?" Minnie asked, turning the iPad over to butter her bread.

Soon Vivien was cruising the German autobahns at a leisurely forty-nine miles per hour with just about every other road user overtaking at more than double their speed.

"Good heavens!" Esther gasped, winding down her window and barking at the passers-by, many of them appearing as a blur. "SLOW DOWN YOU MANIACS!" The sound of honking horns unnerved her somewhat. "This is preposterous, Minnie dear," she told her sister. "Shall we stop for tea and let them all pass?"

"Splendid idea, dear." Minnie smiled, having prepared several rounds of shrimp paste and cottage cheese sandwiches, but instead of waiting for the next service area some seven kilometres ahead, Esther immediately pulled across the inside lane and stopped on the hard shoulder beside an adjacent field, as hundreds upon hundreds of motorists thundered by at breakneck speed.

"Did you pack the blanket, dear?" Esther asked, applying the handbrake and stepping out as a convoy of articulated lorries rumbled by, the slipstream they'd created almost sweeping her from her feet. "Oh my word!" she gasped, with her back pressed firmly against Vivien. "What ghastly things."

Minnie opened Vivien's rear doors and removed their picnic basket, several pieces of their Royal Albert chinaware from its protective newspaper wrapping, and her cellophane-covered sandwiches.

Clambering awkwardly over the three-bar fence to access the field, Esther took the basket from her sister. "Isn't this simply enchanting, dear?" she said, finding herself in a wild flower-filled meadow, their trip exquisitely coinciding with the spectacular blooming of poppies, plantains and purple loosestrife, to name but a few of the flowers.

"Crikey, yes!" Minnie agreed, flicking the tartan blanket out in front of her and laying it down. While Esther pumped their primus stove, Minnie heaped three tablespoons of chamomile tea into their china pot and filled the aluminium kettle with bottled water. "Scotch egg, dear?" she then said, opening a Tupperware box in their breathtaking surroundings, even though their rural bliss was punctuated by the constant drone of the autobahn behind them.

"Remember Camber Sands, Essy dear?" Minnie asked, harking back to their childhood and another budget family holiday in a tired and windswept chalet, when two shillings each had to last them the entire week. "Remember these?" she added, plucking daisies to form a chain.

Peshwari Nans

"Like it was yesterday, dear," Minnie said, following suit until the two sisters were exchanging garlands and bracelets, just like they had done so many years previously.

The whistling kettle sent a nearby nesting skylark fleeing from the tall grass as Esther filled their gold-rimmed floral teapot and stirred it three times. "Almost ready, dear," she said, extinguishing the stove. The two of them then kicked off their shoes and stretched out on the blanket, staring up into the pale blue sky whilst surrounded by sweet-scented blooms, with the occasional buzzing bumblebee plundering their rich pollen.

Esther pointed up to the wisps of cloud floating serenely by on the breeze. "Churchill," she said, gesturing to a particular plump formation of clouds. "Look Minnie dear! It looks just like Winston Churchill!"

"My word, so it does," Minnie agreed, removing the blade of grass from her mouth. "And look over there, dear, it's Andy Pandy," she said, reminding her sister of one of their TV favourites from the black-and-white era.

"Aaandy Pandy," Esther sighed. "God I haven't heard that name in, well, I don't know, it must be over fifty years or more."

While the pair lay reminiscing, CCTV cameras mounted on the autobahn's overhead gantries had picked up their vehicle's apparently 'stranded' position, and the police had been alerted.

"Another sandwich, dear?" Minnie asked, having devoured hers and the remainder of the scotch eggs.

"No thank you, dear," Esther said, running her hand lazily through the swaying meadow grass.

Soon a marked four-by-four police vehicle pulled up behind Vivien and two officers got out in readiness to assist with the breakdown.

Peshwari Nans

"GUTEN TAG!" one of them called out, having located the ladies and asked if they were okay. "ALLES IN ORDNUNG?"

"What the devil?" Esther said, sitting up. "Oh, oh hello!" she called back. "Minnie dear, I think it's the police. GOOD AFTERNOON OFFICERS!"

"Ahhh, English!" the second officer said from across the fence. "Are you alright?"

"Yes, yes fine thank you, dear!" Esther replied, the two of them now resembling festival-going hippy chicks with their floral accessories. "Just enjoying a spot of tea!"

"Well what is wrong?" the first officer asked, trying to ascertain the reason for their illegal 'pit stop'.

"What's wrong?" Minnie replied. "Well I have a fly in my chamomile, shrimp paste on my cardigan and my ankles have swollen, but apart from that everything's tickety boo, thank you."

"No, with your vehicle!" the officer said in a more direct tone, gesturing to Vivien with her rear doors wide open.

"Nothing's wrong, dear!" Esther called back. "She has a full bill of health. I tell you what, though, while you're here officer, if you wouldn't mind flagging down a few of those reckless fools behind you and reprimanding them I'd be more than grateful. There really is no need for all this speed."

"Quite right, dear," Minnie agreed, fishing the drowning bug from her tea.

"But you cannot stop here!" the officer replied, as he and his colleague mounted the fence and began clearing their belongings away. "This is not a service area, it is too dangerous to stop, come you must go!"

"Oh, but I haven't finished my tea," Minnie moaned. "I say, would you gentlemen care for a cup? I could make a fresh pot if you like. Essy dear, light the primus."

"Splendid idea," Esther agreed. "Oh and do help yourselves to the Garibaldis."

"No, no, you must come," the officers insisted, packing the basket hastily. "It is not safe."

"Safe, dear?" Esther asked, looking around for a stray bull or a harvesting tractor perhaps. "What could be safer than this, young man? Would you like a daisy chain?"

"Come, come, quick!" the officer barked, swatting the flowers from her hand. "*Please* you must go!"

"Oh very well, dear." Minnie smiled. "If you're sure you can't stop for tea. It is jolly good, you know."

The sisters were helped back over the fence and respectfully reprimanded, the officers deciding not to press charges. However they didn't see the funny side either.

"Oh, don't look so miserable the two of you," Minnie said while loading up their things. "Here, help yourselves to a scone, no, no, no I insist!" The officers reluctantly obliged and stood nibbling Minnie's home-made treats.

"Bye bye, bye bye!" the sisters said, climbing aboard their car. "Oh and I wouldn't hang around here if I were you," Esther told them from the window. "It really isn't safe, my dears!"

The stunned motorway cops cringed as Vivien backfired and rejoined the rapidly moving flow of traffic.

"I don't know about you, dear," Minnie told her sister on the road to Frankfurt, "but I think all this fresh air has done me the world of good." She toyed with her floral bracelet as the tablet at her feet vibrated. "Oh it's Elizabeth again, dear," she told Esther, opening the Skype app. "Hello, Lizzy dear," she said, holding her face far too close to the camera to produce a decent image. "How are things back in Blighty?"

"Never mind Blighty!" Elizabeth snapped. "Where are you? And how is my mother?"

"I'm fine, dear!" Esther called at the wheel. "Bobbing along quite nicely thank you!"

"Aunt Min," Elizabeth said, back in England, leaning back from her own PC with Minnie's face taking up the entire screen. "Would you kindly hold the tablet a little further away? I can see every whisker on your chin and you're frightening the cat!"

"Oh I am sorry dear, how's that?" Minnie replied, setting the tablet on the dashboard. "How are you anyway, Lizzy?"

"Fine!" Elizabeth said, in no mood for pleasantries. "Will you please tell me what on earth's going on? I knew I should never have let you two go on this ridiculous trip of yours. High diving Minnie? Really! The damn video's everywhere for Pete's sake. I'm just glad my mother wasn't up there with you that's all."

The video clip, which had gone viral, had been shown online alongside British Olympian Tom Daley's flawless feats, with countless viewers voting in favour of the pensioner for sheer guts and gumption. Minnie had even had a mention in the House of Commons, when the Conservative leader compared her to a former Prime Minister—the late Baroness Thatcher, such was her growing popularity. "I mean, whatever next?" Elizabeth asked.

"Who knows, dear?" Esther said, leaning over to see her daughter momentarily. "I thought I might try my hand at white water rafting, I hear it's rather exhilarating."

"Don't you dare, Mother!" Elizabeth stormed.

Richard then peered over his mother's shoulder. "Hi Gran, hi Aunt Min!" he said, waving. "Aunt Min, oh my God, your dive was absolutely awesome, everybody's talking about it, me and my friends are so going on a road trip next year."

"Oh no you're not," Elizabeth said, ever the worrier. "I don't think my nerves could stand it, be a dear and fetch my neurofen will you? Now Mother, Aunt Min," she said turning back to the sisters on the screen. "I really must insist that you refrain from any form of exertion. Please remember your age."

"How can we forget it, dear!" Esther replied, with one eye on the road. "It's hanging over us like the executioner's damn blade."

"Oh please, don't say it like that, Mother," Elizabeth said, clutching her chest. "What I meant was—"

"—I know what you meant, dear, and it's duly noted," Esther said, putting her daughter's mind at rest momentarily. "But if Minnie and I feel the urge to strip to our stockinged feet and skip through the streets of Berlin, Beijing or even Bangalore for that matter, then so be it."

Esther had once again grown tired of her daughter's constant dictatorial stance, and had decided enough was enough. "And I'm sorry to say, Lizzy dear, but there isn't a damn thing you can do about it."

Elizabeth flopped back into her chair as Richard handed her two tablets and a glass of water, something he had grown accustomed to doing ever since his grandmother and her sister had left for Raipur.

"How's Vivien running, Gran?" he asked while his mother hyperventilated.

"Wonderful, dear!" Esther smiled, caressing the wheel. "We're twenty kilometres outside of Frankfurt at present, and making excellent time."

"Richard, dear," Minnie said, puffing out her chest. "I've got to grips with the Facebook thingy and the other whatsit."

"Twitter." Richard smiled. "Yeah I've noticed. I've been following you, well done. Did you see that the Beckhams have tweeted you a good-luck message from LA, and even

Sir Cliff Richard at Wimbledon has done so too, it's nuts Aunt Min, it really is!"

"Anything from Paul O'Grady, dear?" Minnie asked, hoping that the housewives' favourite may have expressed an interest. "Essy and I never miss his show."

"Errrr, nothing as yet, Aunt Min," Richard replied, checking their Twitter feed. "But you now have more followers than Andy Murray, McBusted and Michael Schumacher, so you must be doing something right."

"Thank you, dear," Minnie replied, taking the tablet from the dashboard. "We'll speak again soon, dear, bye bye for now."

"No wait, mother!" Elizabeth yelled, but Minnie had already signed off.

"Don't worry, Mum, they're doing great," Richard said reassuringly.

"Worry!" Elizabeth said, reaching for another tablet. "I'm beyond worry, Richard." She then tossed the tablet across the room. "I really must phone Dr Meadows. These darn things aren't working."

Soon the thunderous roar of a high powered motorcycle could be heard approaching the sisters from behind, and then another, and another until one by one, well over a hundred-and-fifty machines overtook them, many with pillion passengers, some carrying brightly coloured teddy bears strapped to their backs.

"Oooh, how lovely!" Minnie remarked, waving to one or two of them.

The riders were on their annual pilgrimage, nicknamed 'The bear on a bike' rally to the mecca to just about anyone with a lust for speed, be it on two or four wheels. This was the Nürburgring, Germany's thirteen-mile twisting slice of asphalt heaven.

Peshwari Nans

Home to the country's Formula One Grand Prix, the track is also open to the public for the sum of twenty-seven euros per lap.

Aptly christened *The Green Hell* by racing legend Jackie Stewart, the track carves its way through lush forest, with nail-biting hairpin bends that over the years have claimed so many vehicles, and on many occasions people's lives.

"Look, dear, they're camping!" Minnie added excitedly. "Oh Essy, can we camp too? Pleeeease? I haven't camped in years, well decades actually. Oh please, Essy darling?"

Minnie's persistent grovelling eventually paid off.

"Oh alright Min, for heaven's sake!" her sister snapped at last, unable to concentrate. "But you must help me erect the tent, do you hear? I can't do it all by myself."

"Yes, yes, of course." Minnie smiled, but Esther knew only too well from past experience that her sister would willingly begin a task with the best of intentions, but very soon would allow herself to become distracted and leave her with the lion's share of the work.

"Follow them dear, follow them!" Minnie gestured, eyeing the stragglers bringing up the rear,

"Yes, yes, alright, dear," Esther said, accelerating to a further two miles per hour. "I'm going at breakneck speed as it is."

"Oh she's got plenty more in her yet, dear," Minnie said with every faith in the work done by Richard and his team of friends.

"She may well have plenty in her, Minnie dear," Esther said, straight lipped. "But I do not."

The riders whooped and punched the air in jubilation, arriving at their destination with Vivien following a short distance behind. "We'd like to camp for the night, my dear," Esther told the gate attendant, who looked Vivien up and down. "If we may?" she added.

Peshwari Nans

"How many laps?" the attendant asked, with pitch perfect pronunciation.

"Oh you speak English?" Esther remarked.

"Of course," the attendant replied, checking the growing queue behind them. "How many laps, please?"

"Laps? What do you mean, laps?" Esther asked, bemused.

"Laps of the track," the attendant replied, handing them a flyer in English that detailed the Nürburgring's amenities. "One or two laps?"

"Oh good heavens, no," Esther said, shaking her head.

However, Minnie had other ideas. "Two please!" she said, leaning across her sister and thrusting several notes into his hand.

"Minnie!" Esther snapped, glaring at her sister. "What on earth are you doing?"

"Follow the yellow signs please," the attendant said, raising the barrier and waving them on.

"Yes but I…" Esther said open mouthed, with two tickets in her hand.

"Oh don't be such a stick-in-the-mud, dear," her sister said as they proceeded. "After all we don't have to use them."

"No you're right!" Esther said defiantly, tossing the tickets over her shoulder. "We don't!"

While the motorcyclists erected their tents in high spirits Esther and Minnie reversed alongside them in a picturesque wooded glade. "Oh how beautiful, dear," Minnie said, straightening her back once again and wandering off amongst the towering pines.

"Minnie, dear!" Esther called after her. "The tent!"

"Oh yes, yes, of course," Minnie replied. "One moment, dear!"

As usual, Esther was left to unpack while Minnie delighted in all of the flora and fauna the place had to offer, coaxing a red squirrel down from a Larch tree with a parma violet. "There you are my little darling," she said, watching the inquisitive creature cupping the scented sweet in both paws, pricking up its ears at the strange but somehow appealing taste.

"Minnie, dear!" Esther repeatedly called into the wood with a jumble of poles, pegs and canvas at her feet. She then almost jumped out of her skin when two shaven-headed Hell's Angels appeared at her side, each sporting chest-length beards.

"D'you need some help with that?" one of them asked with a smile.

"Oh good grief, you gave me such a start!" Esther said, clutching her chest. "But yes, yes please. My sister is around somewhere but she's absolutely hopeless at this kind of thing."

"No problem," the other biker said, stooping to gather several poles. "Blimey!" He smirked. "Does Captain Mainwearing know you nicked his tent?" He and his friend roared with laughter, attracting yet more bikers, each of them referring to the long running classic BBC television comedy *Dad's Army* featuring a World War Two regiment of the Home Guard, a bunch of bickering senior citizens under the command of the ever bolshie Captain Mainwearing (pronounced 'Mannering'), played by the late family favourite actor Arthur Lowe.

Before long the chuckling bikers had erected the dated and threadbare tent and cleared the surrounding area of rocks and fallen branches.

"Thank you," Esther said. "Thank you all, that's extremely kind of you."

"You're welcome, love," one or two of them replied.

"Excuse me," the spouse of one of the bikers said. She was clad from head to toe in leather "We're having a bit of a get-together later tonight. You're more than welcome to join us if you like, oh and can I just say I absolutely *love love love* your car. She's beautiful!"

"Thank you, my dear." Esther smiled. "But my sister and I will be turning in shortly after supper. It's very kind of you to ask us though."

"Ahhhh, okay," the girl replied. "Well you know where we are if you change your mind."

Minnie returned moments later with a sprig of oak leaves in her hair and a contented smile on her face. "Oh, I'd have helped with that, Essy dear," she said, surveying the taught and sturdy tent.

"Yes, dear," Esther said, raising her eyebrows. "Of course you would. Now come along and help me with the stove."

Bikers and motoring enthusiasts alike pitched their tents in nearby clearings, each of them polishing and tweaking their beloved machines in readiness for the following days' exhilarating experience.

Firstly making a pot of herbal tea, the sisters then prepared their supper of pasta spirals with a carbonara sauce. "Here, dear," Minnie said, fetching her sister a folding chair from the back of Vivien and another for herself, while their meal gently simmered in the aluminium pan.

"It smells delicious, dear," Esther said, ladling a serving onto Minnie's china plate and sitting beside her between Vivien's open rear doors and the tent. "Crikey, this takes me back," she then remarked, handing her sister the salt and pepper pots, Royal Albert, of course.

The sisters sat eating in the dappled shade as the sun dipped slowly behind the dense forest to their right. "Fetch a lamp would you, dear?" Esther asked as the light faded fast. "I've dropped my spoon and I'll be damned if I can find it."

Peshwari Nans

Minnie was busy tossing the remains of her pasta to an inquisitive jackdaw and hadn't heard her sister.

"Minnie, dear!" Esther insisted. "The lamp!"

"Oh, oh yes, of course, sorry dear," Minnie said, rising and startling the feeding bird, sending it fleeing to its roost high above them. Minnie retrieved their brass paraffin lamp and used a wooden taper to light the fragile mantle.

"That's better, thank you," Esther said with their campsite now illuminated. "Oh and there's my spoon."

Later that evening, with the china and silverware washed, dried and safely stowed, the sisters prepared their bedding and locked Vivien up for the night. "Shall we retire, dear?" Esther asked.

"Well," Minnie replied, enjoying her surroundings. "I'm not in the least bit tired but I suppose we should."

Extinguishing the lamp, the ladies stooped, their backs creaking as they crawled on their hands and knees inside their tent. "Ooooh ow, ow!" Esther moaned as she lay beside her sister. "Minnie dear, will you please take your elbow out of my ear?" she added, attempting to undress.

"I'm trying to, dear," Minnie moaned, with her face pressed to the canvas and her hip close to dislocation.

Anybody passing could have quite easily mistaken their contorted groaning for the orgasmic ecstasy of a newlywed couple. "Will you please sit still, dear!" Esther snapped, having been swiped more than once by her sister's outstretched hand.

"Sorry, but I have a twist in my nightie, Essy dear," Minnie cursed, tugging at her hem.

Eventually the two donned their hairnets and wriggled beneath their duvet. "Oh hell!" Esther almost immediately said, sitting upright. "I haven't taken my tablets. Have we any water, Minnie dear?"

"Water dear? Yes dear," Minnie said, switching on her tiny flashlight. "I'll fetch it for you."

"Oh you are a dear," Esther replied, rummaging for her medication. "Oh and you might like to fetch the cotton balls too, Minnie darling, that lot over there are making the most dreadful racket. However is one expected to sleep under such conditions?"

"Whatever you say, dear" Minnie said, raising the zip and crawling back outside. "Damn it!" she then cursed, stumbling on a tent rope, the flashlight flickering occasionally.

"What are you doing, dear?" Esther asked when the tent was wrenched to one side. "Please be careful!"

Minnie opened Vivien's rear doors and shone her torch inside. "I have it, dear!" she called, tugging the plastic container from a storage box.

"Please be sure to lock Vivien, dear!" Esther reminded her sister. "And bid her good night!"

"Of course, dear!" Minnie said, doing as she was told. "Oh now come on you confounded thing," she then cursed when her torch batteries finally gave up the ghost. With the water tucked under her arm she beat the torch on the palm of her hand in the relative blackness of their woodland site.

"Minnie, what on earth are you doing?" Esther asked, growing ever more impatient. "Please come back inside at once."

"Yes I'm trying to, dear," Minnie said, feeling her way "OH, OH NO!" she suddenly cried, her foot becoming entwined around a tent rope. "ESSYYYYYYY!" Minnie stumbled forward with her arms outstretched, dropping her torch and the water container.

"Minnie, Minnie dear!" Esther called from inside. "Minnie, are you alright? What happened?"

Minnie fell to her hands and knees with a jolt that reverberated through her tired bones. "Oooooooh blast!" she cried.

Peshwari Nans

"Minnie!" Esther again called, crawling from beneath her blanket. "Talk to me Minnie, are you alright?"

"Yes, yes, I think so, dear," Minnie said in some degree of pain. "I came a cropper on one of these blasted ropes, it's my own fault. I suppose I should have lit the lamp."

Esther emerged from the tent and, fumbling around, helped her sister to her feet. "Now are you sure you're alright, dear?" she asked, stroking her sister's brittle frame. "You really should be more careful in future."

"Damn it, the water!" Minnie suddenly said, looking down around her feet. "Ahh, here it is," she added, stooping with the aid of her sister. "Oh no, dear," she cursed on finding it empty minus the lid. "I had it, dear, I had it I swear! Oh bother, I'm such a clumsy oaf at times."

"No you're not, Minnie," Esther told her. "Now stop all that nonsense. It was an accident, plain and simple."

"But your medication, Essy," Minnie reminded her. "You must take it. Dr Kumali gave strict instructions, remember he was most insistent."

"Yes I remember, but if we have no water," Esther replied, still clutching her tablets, "It'll just have to wait until morning. Now come on inside will you?"

Minnie looked over her shoulder at the bikers' glowing campfire. "Wait. I'm sure those chaps will have some water to spare, dear," she said, tugging at Esther's nightie. "Let's go and ask shall we"

"No dear we don't want to bother them," Esther said, heading for the tent opening. "Now do come inside, dear, God only knows what creatures could be roaming these parts in the dead of night."

"No, dear," Minnie said defiantly. "They did say to join them if we wished so I doubt they'd mind, and you really do need your medication. So we're going and that's that."

"Yes, but…" Esther said.

"Ah, ah ahhhh," Minnie replied, opening Vivien's rear doors once again. "We'll take the lamp with us so that nothing untoward will happen, oh and as for the creatures, dear, I doubt they'd come within a mile of this place—not with all those beefy biker types around anyway."

"Minnie, dear, I really don't mind waiting," Esther protested, while her sister lit the lamp.

"Come, dear," Minnie said, taking her sister's hand and having none of her nonsense. "Watch your step now, follow me and stay close."

The majority of the Nürburgring's visitors were still awake and sat around their respective campfires.

"Cooooeeee!" Minnie called out, making her way toward the closest of the fires with the lamp in her hand outstretched. "I say, helloooooo!"

The revellers had their CD player thumping and were enjoying a cold beer after a long hot day on the road. "Coooooooeeeee!" Minnie called again, breaking cover. "I sayyyy!"

"Oh hello, ladies," a biker chick said, rising to greet them. "Please do come and join us."

"Oh no, dear," Minnie replied, gesturing to the empty container in her hand. "We were just wondering if you good people could spare a little water."

"Water!" The girl laughed. "I think we can do better than that my lovely. Baz, Geoff, shift over will ya? Let the ladies sit down."

"Oh no, dear that really isn't necessary," Esther told her, not wanting to cause a disturbance.

"Don't be daft." The girl smiled. "We've got a ton of beer and hot dogs and jackets on the go, now come on sit yourselves down."

The bikers made room for the sisters and refused to take no for an answer. "There ya go," a denim clad chap said, thrusting an open beer bottle into each of their hands.

"Oh no, it's quite alright we don't…" Minnie said, shaking her head.

"Yes ya do," the biker insisted. "Now what do ya want in ya dog? Red, brown or mustard?"

"Dog?" Minnie asked.

"Hot dog." The biker laughed. "What's it gonna be?"

"Oh a little mustard please," Minnie said, not wanting to offend their hosts. "And my sister here is rather partial to ketchup, aren't you, dear?"

"Oh no thank you, I'm quite alright," Esther said, eyeing the girl's many tattoos.

"Ketchup it is then," the chap said, scooping a frankfurter from the pan of boiling water on the fire.

Extinguishing the lamp, each of the sisters sat amongst the rowdy bikers with a hot dog in one hand and a bottle of beer in the other, not knowing quite what to do or say for that matter.

"My, these really are delicious," Esther eventually said, nibbling tentatively at one end of her bun whilst Minnie devoured half of hers in two bites, licking the English mustard from her top lip in the process.

"Indeed, dear, indeed they are," she said, sniffing at the beer before braving a sip. "Oooh," she said, letting out the tiniest of burps. "I can't say I've ever had one of these but it's not half bad."

Esther looked at her sister disapprovingly and jabbed at her with her elbow, but Minnie pushed her sister's bottle to her lips. "Take your tablets, dear, go on," she urged her, watching intently while Esther did so before screwing up her face.

"Oh that's ghastly!" Minnie said, but then seeing the smiles drop from the many faces around her she obligingly took another sip. "But um," she added, "let's not be too hasty eh? In for a penny as they say."

Peshwari Nans

Esther and Minnie were given a further two hot dogs each by the bikers and another bottle of beer once the first was drained, under their watchful eyes.

"So where you off to, ladies?" a smiling Hell's Angel asked, clinking his bottle with theirs. "Well you didn't come here to ride the ring, did ya?"

"Raipur," Esther replied, belching into her hand. "Pardon me!"

"It's in India," Minnie informed the bemused bikers. "Where the basmati rice comes from, apparently."

"Oh my God!" one of the gang gasped. "It's them!"

"Aye?" his friend asked. "What d'ya mean?"

"Them!" the biker exclaimed, pointing at the sisters, wide eyed. "Them! The Peshwari Nans!"

"The what?" Esther asked, unaware of their pseudonym.

The newspapers back home had got wind of their story, owing to its ever-increasing Internet presence, and in true Fleet Street fashion had appointed them with the hilarious handle of the 'Peshwari Nans'.

All heads turned in their direction as a murmuring of "Peshwari Nans!" echoed around the fire.

"You!" the girl beside them gasped. "You're the Peshwari Nans! Oh my God, I've been following you two! Ted, Ted get a picture, quick!" She put an arm around Minnie's shoulder while her husband captured the moment.

"Wait!" another biker called, rising to his feet holding out his cellphone. "Which one of you is Minnie?"

Minnie cautiously raised her hand. "Me," she said softly.

"Oh your dive, man!" The biker smiled, tapping his phone's screen. "I must've watched it more than a dozen times I tell ya, you're a legend I swear." Many of his friends surged forward to clink bottles with the bewildered sisters, showering them with snacks of all description.

Peshwari Nans

Minnie turned to Esther and couldn't help but laugh. "The Peshwari Nans, Essy dear," she said, clinking her sister's bottle respectfully. "I rather like it, don't you?"

"Yes, dear," Esther replied proudly. "Yes. I rather think I do."

Welcomed deeper into the bosom of the group, Esther and Minnie found themselves bombarded with questions.

"Excuse me," another biker said, phone in hand. "Could you both say hello to my son, Daniel? He's seven-and-a-half, the children at his school have been painting pictures of you and your car, and of course Minnie's dive. He's a massive fan of yours."

"Of course, dear," Minnie said, taking the mobile. "Hello, hello my dear?" she said, cupping her hand to the screen. "I hear you've been painting pictures of us. It's Minnie, dear, yes the mad diving lady." Minnie then had to hold the phone a short distance away from her ear while young Daniel howled with excitement. "Would you like to say hello to my sister Essy?" she asked the hysterical boy. "She'll tell you all about Vivien, our super car."

Esther indulged the besotted boy, promising to post a photograph of his father with their Morris Traveller, thereby making him the envy of all of his peers, and his teachers for that matter.

Engrossed in conversation around the smouldering campfire, Esther and Minnie hardly noticed the time, or more importantly the amount of alcohol they were each consuming, their inhibitions dwindling with every bottle passed their way.

"I don't mind if I do, dear," Esther giggled, accepting another beer. "It's really rather nice when you get used to it." The pair bobbed and swayed on their log seat to each of the rock anthems being played.

"Oooh! Ooh! Turn it up a little please!" Minnie asked, swinging her shoulders back and forth. "This is one of my favourites." She began to warble, occasionally sipping from her bottle. "Oh yes, it was the summer of sixty niiiine, me and some fellows from schooooool, we had a band and we tried ever so haaaard!"

The bikers found her perfectly punctuated rendition of the phenomenally successful Bryan Adams hit hilarious.

"But when I look back then," she continued, "the summer seemed to last forever, foreeeeeeveeeeeeer!"

Soon the entire fireside ensemble joined her, ecstatic at discovering the much loved and respected Peshwari Nans in their midst, also those from neighbouring camps joined the raucous singalong, their voices echoing throughout the German forest.

A team of Austrian riders approached the sisters with their helmets in their hands and introduced themselves: "Hello we are from Salzburg," their team captain said. "We would consider it a great honour if you would sign our helmets please."

Minnie and Esther obliged in permanent ink, Minnie still singing to herself. "Those were the best days of my liiiiiiife!".

One by one the weary motor racing enthusiasts departed to their tents, bidding the ladies goodnight, in doing so leaving them and a handful of stragglers to finish the last of the beer.

"Light bulbs!" Minnie called after them.

"No, no, Minnie dear," Esther stammered. "I think the expression is *weights, lightweights.*"

"Are you sure, dear?" Minnie asked, unconvinced and steadying herself on the log.

"Positive, dear," Esther said confidently.

"Would you like me to see you back to your tent, ladies?" Sheila, their new friend, asked, yawning. "It's three in the morning and we're meant to be riding at nine."

"No, no, dear we'll be fine," Esther told her, sharing the last bottle with her sister. "You get yourself off to bed, go on now, off you go."

"Okay, if you're sure you'll be alright," Sheila said, mildly concerned. "I can stay if you like."

"Sheila, dear," Esther said abruptly. "The last thing that we need is a chaperone, we are more than capable of looking after ourselves, aren't we, Minnie dear?"

"More than capable, Essy dear." Minnie smiled. "But if you do have any more of this delicious beer we'd be eternally grateful, wouldn't we dear?"

"Eternally," Esther added.

"Sorry Minnie love, that's the last of it I'm afraid," Shelia said, observing the numerous empties at their feet. "Look are you sure you'll be alright?"

"Absolutely dear, now off you go," Esther insisted. "Night night!" she handed the near empty bottle to her pie-eyed sister.

"Yes, nighty night!" Minnie said, struggling to focus. "Don't let the bogbugs bite!"

"Bedbugs, dear," Esther reminded her.

"That's what I said, dear," Minnie replied, draining the bottle and discarding it with the others.

"No dear, you said bogbugs," Esther said insistently.

"I did not!" Minnie snapped. "Did I, Sheila dear?"

"I'm not getting involved, good night ladies," Sheila said, backing away. "See you in the morning. Oh what am I saying? It is the morning! Well good night anyway, it was lovely meeting you."

"I didn't say bogbugs, did I?" Minnie asked her sister.

"Yes dear, yes you did." Esther laughed. "What is a bogbug anyway?"

The two intoxicated sisters roared with laughter, rocking back and forth on the log. "I don't know!" Minnie howled. "But I wouldn't want to be bitten by one, that's for sure!"

160

Peshwari Nans

Hells angels and hardened drinkers alike had long since waned and retired for the night, but the unlikely party animals soldiered on, Esther finding a half bottle of Jameson's behind their log.

"After you, dear," she said, removing the cap and offering it to her sister.

"Why thank you, my dear," Minnie slurred, cringing after the initial sip. "Not bad," she soon added after three more. She wiped her mouth and returned the bottle.

"Well a wee tot before bed never hurt anybody," Esther said, swigging the spirit as though it were cordial. She then waved the bottle in the air. "Don't let the bogbugs bite'cha bottom." She chuckled. "DON'T LET THE BOGBUGS BITE'CHA BOTTOM!"

Woodland creatures and campers alike stirred as the ladies grew increasingly raucous. "*I got my first real six string!*" they sang arm in arm "*I bought it at the five and dime, I played it until my fingers bled, that was the summer of sixty niiiine!*"

"GO TO SLEEP!" a voice called out from a distant tent.

Esther and Minnie shuffled from their log and hoisted themselves to their feet, Minnie tossing the empty Jameson's bottle into the glowing embers of the fire. "The lamp, dear" Esther said, steadying her sister. "Fetch the lamp."

"I'm on it like a scotch bonnet, dear," Minnie replied, stooping for the handle. "I'M ON IT EVERYONE!" she then yelled, brandishing the lamp. "ON IT LIKE A SCOTCH BONNET!"

With the lamp swaying in her hand Minnie clung to her sister as they made their way back precariously through the trees. "What was that?" Esther said, stopping dead in her tracks.

"What was what, dear?" Minnie asked, listing to one side.

Peshwari Nans

"That!" Esther reiterated as an owl ruffled its feathers above them.

"I haven't the foggiest, dear," Minnie confessed. "Perhaps it's one of those bogbugs?"

"Oooh, perishing things." Esther cringed with one hand on her bottom. "Come, dear, let's not wait around to be bitten by the blighters."

The lady of the lamp and her sister stumbled through the pine, larch and oaks, colliding with the occasional trunk and at one point passing within a hair's breadth of their tent but pressing on with a blind determination. "Somebody's moved it, dear," Minnie said minutes later.

"The devils!" Esther cursed.

From above the sister's lamp must have resembled a meandering firefly, turning this way and that in the dead of night to the sound of breaking twigs beneath their carpet slippers and the occasional Bryan Adams lyric. "We should have left a trail of biscuits, dear," Minnie said, tugging her sister's arm. "Just like Hansel and Gretel."

"You mean we could have," Esther said, glaring at her sister in the lamplight, "if you hadn't eaten all the Garibaldis. Now where is that blasted tent?"

They edged deeper and deeper into the surrounding forest, the dense canopy above shielding any moonlight that may have assisted in their search.

"Let's turn back, dear," Minnie moaned, looking over her shoulder into the blackened abyss.

"Turn back,? Turn back where, dear?" Esther asked, staggering into a leafy thicket. "Oh, oh help me, Minnie!" she cried, becoming entangled in the rambling undergrowth. "Minnie dear!"

"Oh Essy dear, I've got you, I've got you!" Minnie said, but found she was only making matters worse. Soon the two of them were thrashing helplessly in the thorny shrubbery which tore at their flimsy winceyette nighties.

Peshwari Nans

"HEEEEEEELP, HEEEEELP!" Minnie cried, dragging a foot free and in doing so dropping the storm lantern, shattering the wafer-thin mantle and extinguishing their one and only source of light.

"Oh Minnie, you fool!" Esther yelled, dragging her sister clear of their leafy snare. "Now look what you've gone and done!"

The pair stood rooted to the spot in near complete darkness, swaying ever so slightly and clenching one another's hand as tightly as they could. "Oh Essy, what are we to do?" Minnie asked, catching her breath, her hair an unruly mess.

"We're going to press on, that's what we're going to do," Esther said with a belly full of alcoholic courage. "I have a feeling we're close."

In fact nothing could be further from the truth, for the sisters, hardly dressed for night manoeuvres, were a yard short of a mile from Vivien and the relative comfort of their tent.

"Right you are, dear." Minnie smiled, trusting in her elder sibling. "Best foot forward as they say!"

Esther and Minnie continued to beat a path in the wrong direction, having consumed more alcohol in one night than in the previous three years combined. "Ahhh this looks familiar, dear," Minnie said, stroking one of a thousand near identical trees. "You were right, we are close, thank heavens."

Up ahead the crescent moon illuminated a clearing. "At last!" Esther said, breaking through the lower woodland limbs. "Oh!" she then added, finding herself at the side of the tarmac roadway known in motoring circles as the Nürburgring.

"I knew you'd get us back dear," Minnie said, brushing a branch out of her way to join her sister. "Oh!" she too said, equally disappointed. "Essy, where are we?"

"God only knows," Esther replied with her hand to her forehead, looking left and then right along the deserted track. "I know this road leads back to camp," she said, scratching at her scalp and in doing so plucking out several twigs. "And my gut feeling says we go left."

"No, no, dear it's right!" Minnie insisted. "Trust me, dear I orienteered with the guides in Penrith in my teens remember, so if either of us has a penchant for directions I think it's me."

"Are you sure, dear?" Esther asked, looking left, her feet now throbbing. "I just have this distinct feeling that's all."

"Well we can't risk our lives on a feeling, now can we?" Minnie said with her hands on her hips. "Trust me, Essy love, that's the north star over yonder so we need to proceed due east which is this way, to the right." She started off along the track, keeping tabs on what she presumed was the north star or Polaris, but was in fact the international space station circling the earth, and therefore constantly on the move.

"I hope for your sake you are right, Minnie," Esther said, reluctantly starting after her.

"My dear, I'd put my pension on it," Minnie replied, brimming with misplaced confidence. "Every penny of it."

Had Minnie placed such a wager she would have undoubtedly have lost every penny. To their left, as Esther had guessed, a hundred or so metres around the very first bend, was the starting line of the race, manned by track officials twenty-four-seven. To their right on the other hand, lay thirteen miles of twisting desolate tarmac flanked by the very same woodland that had ensnared them in the first place.

Soon the sisters' breathless stagger was reduced to an agonizing shuffle. "Never mind your pension," Esther wheezed, walking several paces behind her sister. "I wouldn't put a brass farthing on you and your pathetic north star. Where is the darn thing anyway?"

Minnie looked up, but of course the space station had long since passed over and wouldn't be visible again for at least another hour or so.

"That's it, I can't go on," Esther said, rubbing her aching knees. "Minnie, please stop will you?"

It was now four-thirty in the morning and all around them was stillness. "Oh do come along Essy, my love," Minnie moaned. "I swear it's just around the next corner."

"You promise?" Esther replied, now at her wits' end.

"Absolutely, dear," Minnie said, digging deep and forging on. "Ah," she then said, peering around the bend. "Maybe I was a little hasty."

"Hasty!" Esther stormed, joining her a moment or two later. "I told you to go left Minnie! But oh no, ohhhh no, you were an orienteer remember? Navigating by the blasted north star! Well the truth of the matter is you haven't the foggiest idea what you are doing, have you? And we, my dear, are lost, plain and simple!"

"How preposterous!" Minnie laughed. "Of course we're not lost, my dear." Minnie scanned the skies but the blanket of cloud obscured any trace of a celestial body. "Anyway," she added, turning her attentions back to the road ahead. "It's a circular track, Essy, so how can we possibly be lost?"

"Yes, I know that!" Esther exclaimed, exasperated to say the least. "But it's as plain as the nose on your idiotic face that we are walking in the wrong direction and have been for the last half hour! Oh why did I ever listen to you in the first place? We should turn back at once."

"Please Essy, bear with me," Minnie begged, looking ahead towards the next of a series of punishing bends. "I'm never wrong about these things, trust me, you'll be tucked up in our tent in no time."

Peshwari Nans

Looking behind over her shoulder, Esther was in far too much pain to argue any further. "Oh very well Min, but you'd better be right!" she snapped "Or the pair of us will perish out here, for sure."

"Here, take my arm, dear," Minnie said, supporting her sister as they made their way wearily around the Nürburgring. "There look!" Minnie then suddenly said, seeing the outline of a man-made structure ahead. "What did I say, dear? I told you I'm never wrong about these things."

"Thank heavens," Esther said, tiring considerably.

"Ah," Minnie added on closer inspection. What she had presumed was their sanctuary was in fact an observation shelter at the track's halfway point, used by camera crews and track maintenance operatives, open to the elements on three sides with a shingle roof and a hard wooden bench, and offering nothing in the way of creature comforts. The two bedraggled ladies stood staring forlornly at their find, which was barely a bus stop.

"Trust me, you said," Esther growled. "I'm never wrong about these things, you said."

"Well," Minnie said, offering no retort. "Perhaps it's around the next bend instead."

"No, Minnie," Esther said defiantly. "My feet, my knees and my back are all killing me. Let's just sit for a moment, catch our breath and rest our bones, then I'll decide if we press on or turn back, alright?"

"Very well, dear," Minnie agreed, her own muscles and joints screaming for her to stop. "Just for a moment then."

"Ahhhhhh," Esther sighed, lowering her bottom onto the pine bench and resting her back against the wall. "I ache in places I never thought possible," she confessed.

"Oooooh me too, dear," Minnie said, massaging her thighs and flexing her ankles. "I'm sorry, dear," she added, still feeling the effects of the Jameson's. "This is all my fault. If I'd listened to you we probably wouldn't be in this pickle right now. I'm such a fool at times." She shuffled alongside her sister, nestling in close.

"Yes, yes, you are," Esther agreed angrily, but glad of her sister's presence all the same. "I'm the fool, Min," she then confessed. "I should have thought things through properly."

Their desperate situation soon had a sobering effect on the elderly women. "I mean what was I thinking," Esther went on. "Look at us, we're hardly cut out for a trip like this, are we? We could be seriously injured or far worse for that matter. No Min, it's me who should apologize to you for even believing it was possible."

"Esther!" Minnie barked, looking her sister in the eye, using her full name as a way of signifying her sincerity. "You may be my elder sister but I'm going to say this all the same. You're not to talk like that ever again, do you hear me? I simply won't have it! We're here because we chose to be and for no other reason. Now come what may we will succeed, even if there are a few hiccups along the way."

"You call this a hiccup?" Esther interjected.

"Yes, dear, that's all it is," Minnie replied in a forthright tone. "A hiccup. We're alive, we have shelter and more importantly we have each other." Minnie's rallying speech melted her sister's apprehensive heart.

"Yes, but," she said, clutching Minnie's hand.

"Ah, Ah," Minnie snapped. "That's enough dear."

"Very well, dear," Esther agreed, shuffling closer.

Minnie soon began humming contentedly to herself. "I got my first real six string…" she began to sing.

"Min!" Esther said, stopping her sister short. "That's quite enough of that, thank you."

Exhausted and mildly intoxicated Esther and Minnie's eyes soon grew heavy and, with their heads resting on one another, they soon drifted into the deepest of sleeps, with

Peshwari Nans

their legs outstretched, revealing the holes worn in their carpet slippers.

CHAPTER FOUR

Esther and Minnie sat motionless in the shelter for a full four hours, snoring loudly as they often did after a nip or two of sweet sherry. They didn't know that the track had in fact recently opened and the first wave of exhilarated riders and drivers were making their way around at full throttle and with their 'pedals to the metal' as it were.

"What? What?" Esther slurred as a powerful red Ducati motorcycle thundered by with its rider's head down, leaning into the bend. "Good God!" she shrieked, the sound of the engine pulsating in her fragile head.

"Turn it off, Essy!" Minnie said without opening her eyes, assuming her sister had the television set turned up too loud and they were safe in their one-bedroom flat. Even the numbness in her backside hadn't brought her to her senses.

Three yellow Porsches then came into sight, each jostling for the inside line, one of the drivers having a momentary lapse of concentration as he caught a glimpse of the sisters sitting in their night attire.

"Ohhhh, my head!" Minnie moaned. "My head, Essy, it's pounding."

Esther sat nursing her own horrendous hangover, wincing at the bright morning sunlight and the steady flow of Nürburgring fanatics. "Ooh, ow, ow, ow!" she squealed, clambering to her feet and rocking back against the shelter's wall, having long since forgotten the harrowing effects alcoholic overindulgence can have on a person. "Minnie dear, where on earth are we?" she asked, feeling disorientated.

"Whitechapel, dear," Minnie replied stretching out on the bench. "What is that dreadful noise?"

Peshwari Nans

"Get up, Minnie you fool!" Esther barked, even the sound of her own voice causing her extreme pain.

"Have you made the tea, dear?" Minnie asked, pushing herself into the upright position, faltering as she did so. "Oh!" she then said, opening one eye. The enormity of their situation flooded back to her.

"Oh indeed!" Esther said, angrily. "If I remember rightly, the root cause of our present predicament lies in your incompetent sense of direction. Because of you I've hiked miles through treacherous woodland inhabited by heaven only knows what, my nightclothes are in shreds and so is my lower back for that matter, and oh God my feet, my poor aching feet, I don't know whether I have bunions, blisters or boils for Pete's sake. MINNIE!" she snapped, noticing her sister's eyes begin to droop. "Are you listening to me?"

"Mmmm what? Oh yes," Minnie said croakily. "Of course, you have a blister on your bunion."

"Get up!" Esther said, prodding her sister back to life. "We can't stay here. This racket is driving me insane."

Minnie was helped to her feet, where she staggered, unsteady and woozy. "Everything's spinning, Essy," she whined, clinging pathetically to her sister's arm. "Make it stop, please make it stop!"

"For God's sake pull yourself together!" Esther said, weighing up their limited options. "We must get back to our tent, somehow."

The two dishevelled sisters stood beside the track, huddled and clinging to one another as a steady stream of racing enthusiasts rocketed by, a plethora of performance machines tuned to perfection for that one moment of motoring madness, a chance to live the dream from the driving seat and not the armchair.

One by one the riders and drivers snatched their necks to the right to gawp at the extraordinary spectacle of a pair of pensioners in tattered floral nightwear with their hair resembling ravens' nests. Minnie held out a thumb in the hope that a Good Samaritan might stop and offer them a ride, but the motor cars and bikes were exiting the nearby bend at such a rate that any form of braking would be deemed suicidal.

"It's no use, dear," Esther said despairingly. "We'll just have to retrace our steps."

"What?" Minnie gasped, recollecting their hellish journey of some four-and-a-half miles over the roughest of terrain. "Surely you can't be serious, Essy dear?"

"I'm afraid we have no choice, dear," Esther replied, trudging along the grass verge, her sodden slippers barely clinging to her feet.

Rounding the first bend the sisters were confronted by a procession of up to sixty motorcycles, the majority of them Harley Davidsons, some of them ridden by Sheila, her husband and many of their friends.

"What the?" Sheila gasped, immediately spitting a fly from her open mouth. "ESTHER!" she yelled, waving and almost coming a cropper and causing a dozen or so of her Hell's Angel 'chapter' to swerve erratically. "OH MY GOD!"

"Oh look Essy, it's Sheila, from the campfire!" Minnie exclaimed as the bikes roared by, unable to stop for fear of the carnage it would undoubtedly cause.

"Ohhhh no," Esther sighed, watching them disappear out of sight. "Shanks's pony it is then," she added, referring to the long walk ahead of them.

But Sheila wasn't about to leave the ladies high and dry, radioing to her husband on their helmet two-ways, she convinced him to accelerate for another thirteen-mile lap of the Nürburgring to rescue the dishevelled damsels in distress.

Peshwari Nans

Risking life, limb and certain death at speeds in excess of one hundred miles per hour, Sheila and her spouse put their throbbing machines through their paces, navigating the chicanes, hairpin bends and blind brows with pinpoint accuracy.

Next around the bend ahead of Minnie and Esther was a vintage VW split-screen camper van, driven by a pot-smoking surfer and his friends. "WOAAAAAW DUUUDE!" he cried, passing the sisters and checking them in his rear-view mirror. "Girl, did you see that?"

"See what, babe?" a starry eyed hippy chick replied, leaning from the back and snatching the joint from his lips, having been making out with her boyfriend the whole way round the track.

"The old lady chicks, man!" the young surfer exclaimed. "One of them looked like my grandmother, I swear it."

"You gotta lay off this shit, man," the girl told him, taking a long drag herself. Her near-naked lover then reached out and dragged her back to their bunk to continue the high-speed canoodling.

The sisters cringed at the close proximity of many of the racers, who strayed towards the grass verge, wrestling to maintain control of their vehicles. "It's really rather exciting, isn't it dear?" Minnie said with one foot on the tarmac, watching as a group of Ferrari fanatics raced by.

"Come away, dear!" Esther said, dragging her carefree sister clear just as a low profile Pirelli tyre clipped the verge in passing, showering the two of them in mud, grass and gravel.

"Oh, oh, OW!" they each squealed, cowering with their heads in their hands.

Suddenly, when all seemed just too much to bear, a familiar voice called out: "ESTHERRRRRR! MINNIIIIIIE!"

Peshwari Nans

Wiping the mud from their faces as best they could, the ladies looked up to see Sheila and her husband slowing on the approach.

"Oh thank heavens," Esther said with tears in her eyes. "Sheila my darling, please help us!"

Pulling onto the verge and removing their helmets, the husband and wife, both members of the Crawley chapter of the Hell's Angels from rural Sussex, dismounted. "Ladies, what on earth are you doing out here?" Sheila asked, wrapping a comforting arm around the tearful Esther. "My God, look at you! What happened?"

"We got lost," Minnie confessed, clinging helplessly to Sheila's husband, elated to see them.

"Lost!" Sheila exclaimed. "Your tent was, like, a few metres from our fire. How did it happen?"

Esther glared at her sister. "Christopher perishing Columbus here, that's how!" she said, seething.

Sheila removed her studded biker jacket, as did her husband, wrapping them around the ladies' shoulders. "Put these on," she told them, still very much aghast at finding them in such a pickle. "Come on, let's get you back, hop on."

"On there?" Esther said, looking the Harley low rider motorbikes up and down.

"Yes you'll be fine." Sheila smiled. "Look, if we don't get you two out of here you'll either die of exposure in those nighties or get yourself killed by one of these idiots." She gestured to a pair of rally cars, whose wheels were completely clear of the tarmac as they vaulted the brow of a hill.

"Oooh I'd love to," Minnie said, clambering fearlessly onto her husband's bike and gripping the handlebars.

"No, on the back, my love." He laughed, helping her to the heavily padded pillion seat before swinging his leg back over to mount the bike. "Hold on tight, you hear me?"

Peshwari Nans

"Yes dear, holding on tight," Minnie replied, gripping the belt loops of his leather trousers.

"Come on, Esther love." Sheila beckoned. "Let's get you back and cleaned up eh? It really isn't safe out here."

Esther had never been a huge motorcycle fan since she had been locked inside her father's motorbike side car, and subsequently had to be cut free by the fire brigade. "Are you sure, dear?" she asked apprehensively.

"Essy," Minnie said, dehydrated and near hypothermic. "Will you please just get on the motorcycle and stop being such an old woman about it!"

"Minnie dear, I am an old woman!" Esther said angrily. "An old woman who should have been tucked up beneath her duvet the whole night, instead of chasing a wandering star halfway to Timbuktu!"

"Esther!" Minnie insisted, "I'm going to say this for your own good: just shut the hell up and get on the damn bike!"

Esther was momentarily taken aback by her sister's wrathful outburst, albeit out of character.

"Well if I must," she said, hitching up her begrimed nightie, stepping onto one of the chromium foot rests and clambering on behind Sheila.

"Okay?" Sheila asked, selecting first gear.

"Hardly, dear," was Esther's grimaced reply as they set off.

Rounding a series of gut-wrenching bends, the sisters clung to their riders with fingers and thighs at a dramatically reduced pace from their previous lap.

"Does this thing go any faster, dear?" Minnie asked, tapping at the biker's shoulder.

"Will you please slow down!" was Esther's muffled cry as Sheila leaned a few degrees to the left.

Again startled motorists looked on open mouthed in passing.

174

Peshwari Nans

"Morning!" Minnie called out, waving to a rallying Subaru driver and his perplexed passenger. "Lovely day!"

Esther clenched her eyes tightly shut and buried her head into Sheila's back while Minnie relished every moment and, dared for a few seconds to release her grip and hold her arms outstretched with the wind rushing through her silvery hair. The pair of them were sporting their heavy biker jackets that were emblazoned with the 'Angel's Forever' motto.

"Oh thank heavens," Esther eventually said on completing two thirds of the Nürburgring and seeing their encampment ahead.

"YEEEEEHAAAAA!" Minnie squealed, punching the air triumphantly. "I say, can we go around again?"

"I can't get off," Esther moaned, having stiffened somewhat in the saddle.

"Here, let me help you," Sheila said, putting her head beneath Esther's arm and hoisting her clear. "Are you alright?" she asked, noticing the pensioner unsteady on her feet.

"I am now, my dear." Esther smiled, a little woozy to say the least.

Minnie was prised from her seat, having contemplated a solo lap on the biker's beloved Harley. "I say, where would one purchase such a machine?" she asked, green with envy, the lure of leather and chrome proving to be a powerful aphrodisiac.

"Come on," Sheila laughed. "Let's get you two cleaned up and respectable, you must be half starved as well."

"Famished actually," Esther agreed. "I could eat a dozen crumpets and half as many rounds of buttered toast."

"Oooh I could eat..." Minnie said excitedly, having reluctantly dismounted.

"Don't tell me," Esther said, still vexed with her sibling. "Shrimp paste?"

"Well," Minnie replied, her mouth watering, "I was going to say an entire Battenberg and a packet of Garibaldis, but now that you mention it, a half dozen shrimp-paste triangles would go down a treat right now."

Sheila and her husband turned up their noses at the culinary thought as they led the ladies back to their tent.

"Morning Vivien," Esther said, tapping the car's headlight. "I trust you slept a little better than Minnie and I did."

"Vivien?" Sheila said, taking her jacket from Esther's shoulders. "Why Vivien?"

"Because when I first saw her, my dear," Esther explained, looking upon her car lovingly, "I thought she was the most beautiful thing I'd ever seen, just like Vivien Leigh."

"*Gone with the Wind!*" Sheila exclaimed. "God I love that film."

Her husband rolled his eyes, having endured the epic love story (that had a running time just short of four hours) as many times as he cared to remember.

"We both do, don't we babe?" Sheila added.

Her husband turned and left without saying a word.

"He does love it," Sheila whispered with a smile.

Gathering fresh clothing and towels the sisters were directed to the complex's shower block and of course the cafeteria, from which they emerged a full two-and-a-half hours later, having eaten a hearty meal-and-a-half, and cleansed themselves of all woodland detritus.

"At this rate," Esther said, binning her ragged nightie, "soon we won't have a stitch to wear."

Their wardrobe had indeed depleted considerably and the sisters were still in the fledgling stages of their trip.

"That's okay, dear," Minnie said confidently. "There has to be a thrift shop en route."

Peshwari Nans

Characteristically, thrift shops were a bit of a hobby for the sisters, Esther and Minnie having three of them within a short walk of their Whitechapel home. On a Tuesday afternoon, after the pair had collected their weekly pension allowance, they would visit them all in sequence. Firstly Cancer Research, then the Heart Foundation and finally the British Red Cross. Here they would rummage through the racks of donated knitwear and cast-offs, delighting in the various collectables on offer, from tea cosys to teaspoons to novelty egg timers, of which Esther was particularly fond, her own private collection swelling to a jaw-dropping two hundred-and-twelve.

"I do hope so, dear." Esther sighed while her sister snapped pictures of the surroundings with their tablet.

"I say, Sheila darling," Minnie asked when they were back at camp. "Would you mind?"

"No, not at all," Sheila replied, gathering her fellow Angels for a group photograph. Several more were then taken with the sisters astride various chopper bikes with an array of headgear, some sporting ram's horns and even antlers.

"Thank you, my dear," Esther told Sheila. "For coming so valiantly to our rescue, and for being so charming. We can never repay you for what you have done."

"Ahhhhh, you're welcome Esther, it's been an absolute pleasure," Sheila replied, kissing Esther's cheek. "And you, Minnie darling," she added. "You crack me up you do, my lovely."

With the help of their new friends, Vivien was packed with their camping equipment, which on that occasion had barely been used. She was then topped up with oil and water and her windshield 'debugged'.

"Are you taking her round?" Sheila asked.

"Round?" Esther asked. "Round where?"

Sheila gestured to the track.

Peshwari Nans

"Oh good heavens no!" Esther laughed. "No, no, no that's quite out of the question, she's a thoroughbred my dear, not a gelding."

"Oh Essy dear, why not?" Minnie pleaded. "We're here, Vivien's here, it would be a crime not to do it, in my opinion."

"My dear." Esther smirked. "If you remember rightly, it was your opinion that almost got us killed!"

"Oh you must take her round," Sheila said, adding weight to Minnie's argument. "You can take it as slowly as you like, go on, we'll join you."

Many of her fellow bikers voiced their opinions too until Esther was forced to concede.

"Ohhh very well," she said, climbing behind the wheel. "But I assure you we won't be taking the chequered flag or breaking any records."

With the Crawley chapter of the Hells Angels riding alongside like a flock of migrating geese, providing safe passage for the sisters in their vintage automobile, the procession made its way sedately around the Formula One track at quite possibly the slowest time ever recorded, frustrating the sixty or so riders and drivers behind them, who dared not pass the Angels.

Hogging the centre of the road and avoiding the obvious racing line, Esther refused to accelerate or mount the steep chicanes, which had earned the track its notorious reputation as a 'widowmaker'. Minnie sat beside her, snapping away blissfully, uploading each and every image to their social network forums and pages, food for their rapidly increasing army of fans who were hungry for news of their progress.

Back in England, Elizabeth's house had been besieged with reporters from three European countries, falling over themselves for her 'take' on her mother's decision to undertake such an arduous trip, and offering monies in exchange for any inside information, or, as hacks put it, 'dirty laundry', of which of course there was none.

Richard himself had taken to sneaking in via the rear entrance over the neighbour's fence in order to avoid the constant probing. "Can you believe that lot, Mum?" he said, peering around the front-room curtains.

"Yes, yes, I can," his mother replied with her arms folded. "This is your Gran and your Aunt Min we're talking about, remember."

"Oh my God, what now?" Richard laughed, checking their online pages. "Are those, are those *Hell's Angels* Gran's with?"

"WHAT?" Elizabeth stormed, craning her neck to see. "What on earth are they doing with that bunch of cut-throats?"

Predictably, Elizabeth had jumped to all the wrong conclusions with regard to the Angels' behaviour, as so many had done before her, failing to heed another of their mottos which read: *"Always remembered for the wrong we do, but forgotten for the right".*

"Being escorted by the looks of things," Richard informed her. "How cool is that? And at the Nürburgring of all places."

"God, I need a Scotch," Elizabeth said, heading for the cabinet, drinking whisky being a luxury that had become more of a habit of late.

"Isn't it a little early, Mother?" Richard asked, concerned at his mother's alcohol consumption.

"Richard, darling," she replied, spinning the bottle's cap open. "My mother, aged eighty-seven, is openly associating with the Hell's Angels for God's sake! How on earth can it be too damned early?"

Arriving at the finish line flanked by their leather-clad outriders to tumultuous applause from visitors and track officials alike, the sisters eventually bade a fond farewell to

179

Peshwari Nans

Sheila and the gang and left the Nürburgring with mixed emotions. On one hand they had shared a campfire with some of the most respectful individuals they had ever encountered, and with whom they had promised to remain friends, and on the other hand the Nürburgring had almost claimed another two lives—even though these casualties would have been on foot rather than in or on a vehicle.

Determined to make Prague before nightfall, Esther pressed on, despite her obvious fatigue. "Here, dear," Minnie said, offering her another glass of elderflower cordial and a spam-and-piccalilli sandwich.

"Thank you, dear." Esther smiled, the effects of their colossal alcohol consumption still very much evident.

The border crossing into the Czech Republic was relatively insignificant, but a blessing nethertheless. "My dear," Minnie said, taking her credit card from her purse. "I think we've earned the very best the fair city of Prague has to offer, what do you say?"

"Well let's not be too hasty, Minnie dear," Esther replied—she was a tad more frugal than her sister. "I'm all for comfort as you know but only if it's at a price that suits the pocket."

Esther was right to err on the side of caution because the very best accommodation the city of Prague had to offer was the five-star Alchymist Grand and came at a hefty price. The sixteenth-century Baroque-style hotel and spa sat just a few steps from Prague castle, with its rooms heavily influenced by the castle's palatial style. Its rates at times were in excess of three hundred euros per person per night.

"I tell you what," Esther suggested. "Why don't you ask that nice Mr Google of yours? Perhaps he may have visited the city himself and could recommend somewhere? You never know, dear."

"Well, I could ask," Minnie replied, tapping the most polite of requests into the tablet.

"Oh how wonderful!" she said seconds later, when an extensive list of the city's tourist accommodation appeared before her. "How does he do it?"

"He's obviously at a loose end, dear," Esther said, hinting that 'Mr Google', as she called the all-powerful search engine, was some sweet fellow swinging his legs in an empty office somewhere with nothing better to do than answer to their every whim and fancy. "But we don't want to bother the poor chap too much, do we Minnie dear?" she added, concerned he may find them somewhat tiresome at times.

"Oh he's alright." Minnie smiled. "Google. Do you think that's Scandinavian dear?" she asked.

"I haven't the foggiest," Minnie replied, entering the name of the city. "It could be Chinese for all we know."

Scrolling through the dozen or so online pages, Minnie suddenly piped up: "Oooh dear I have it!" she squealed. "At a mere snip look, The Albatross. Isn't it just charming? And on the river, dear."

The Hotel Albatross was a floating hotel moored on the Vltava river on the edge of the picturesque old town of Prague, within walking distance of the old town square, Wenceslas square, and the municipal hall. The striking red-and-white vessel with over eighty rooms/cabins was a popular destination for tourists unable to afford a more opulent stopover, but still boasted four stars and offered superb views across the river.

"He's even given us directions, dear," Minnie said, tapping a polite 'thank you' into Mr Google's search box. "I wonder what he looks like?" she pondered.

"Who, dear?" Esther asked, stopping at a red traffic signal.

"Mr Google," Minnie replied dreamily. "I'd imagine he has a touch of Sean Connery about him, perhaps with neatly trimmed greying facial hair."

Peshwari Nans

Likening 'Mr Google' to the actor who first played the fictitious British secret agent with a license to kill, made Minnie momentarily weak at the knees. "Or maybe Kenny Rogers," she went on. "Oh I loved him with Dolly Parton." She then began to sing, which made her sister cringe: "Islands in the streaaaam, that is what we are, sail away with me…"

"Yes, alright dear," Esther said, proceeding at the lights' green phase. "That's quite enough of that."

Minnie rotated the tablet in her hands to get her bearings. "Take a left here, dear," she said, steering her sister towards the river. "Right then another left."

"Well I never!" Esther said, impressed to say the least when arriving at the quayside as directed. "Who needs a statelite when you have Mr Google, eh Minnie dear?"

"Quite right, dear," Minnie agreed. "Thank you," she said into the screen before closing it down and marvelling at the glamorous vessel beside them.

"Oh my!" Esther gasped, stepping from Vivien, in awe at her surroundings. "Minnie dear, we've really come up trumps this time, haven't we?"

"Welcome Madames," the smartly dressed doorman said at the foot of the gangway whilst eyeing Vivien over their shoulders. "Such a beautiful car." He smiled.

"Isn't she just?" Esther replied, handing him her bag. "Now I trust you have adequate dining facilities and hot and cold running water?" The memory of her recent motel nightmare was still fresh in her mind.

"But of course, Madam," the doorman replied, taking Minnie's belongings too. "Please follow me."

A little unsteady on their feet on the shifting gangway, the sisters clung to the rail. "Not so fast, young man!" Esther called after their escort. "I have arthritis and Minnie here has fallen arches, don't you dear?"

Peshwari Nans

"Yes, it was those perishing roller skates of ours, dear," Minnie said, reminding her sister of the skates they shared as children. "Damn near crippled me they did."

"Well Father did make them from trolley wheels and biscuit tins, dear," Esther informed her. "What did you expect? After all he was hopeless at DIY. Remember the clothes horse he made for Mother from garden canes and raffia? The darn thing collapsed under the weight of her wet whalebone bodice and skewered the cat!"

"Ahhh, Mr Jinx." Minnie sighed, recalling their beloved family pet found impaled on the crudely assembled clothes horse.

"My apologies," the doorman said, pausing on deck. "Please mind your step."

The interior foyer with its fine wood panelling and highly polished brassware made the ship look every bit the regal steamer that she was.

"We'd like a twin please, my dear," Esther told the girl at the counter.

"Yes, the best you have," Minnie piped up. "It's okay, dear," she reassured her sister. "It's well within budget, in fact we can afford to push the boat out. Oh I say, push the boat out? How apt."

The sisters were shown to an aft room, indeed one of the finest that the Albatross had to offer, with crisp white towels lovingly crafted into swans, two on either bed. "Oh this is just wonderful," Minnie said, handing the bellboy a two euro tip, which he duly pocketed with a disgruntled sneer.

"Indeed," Esther replied, heading for the lavish bathroom to fill the tub with hot lathered water. "Do you mind if I bathe first, Minnie darling?" she called through.

"That's okay, dear!" Minnie called after her. "You go right ahead, and leave the water in will you!"

Peshwari Nans

Minnie and her sister habitually shared their bathwater back home, just as they had done in their childhood tin tub beside a roaring open fire, only these days they used a soft sea sponge and a loofa, as opposed to the hard wooden floor brush their mother Iris would scrub them with, leaving their skin red and raised for some time afterwards.

Minnie opened her case on the bed of her choosing, the one closest to the window, taking out a lilac twinset and setting it out in readiness. She then opened the window and looked across the river at the city of Prague, in awe of its architectural heritage and grandeur.

Esther emerged almost an hour later, wrapped in towels and dabbing at her dripping hair. "Crikey, Minnie dear, I feel like a new woman," she told her sister, who was busy replying to a series of tweets from several media moguls, requesting an audience at the earliest opportunity.

"Persistent blighters these lot," she said, barely acknowledging her sister. "No matter how many times I tell them we are not interested they just won't take no for an answer."

"Just ignore them, dear," Esther said, selecting her own outfit for their evening meal. "They'll forget all about us in due course, you wait and see."

But Esther had grossly underestimated the media furore that surrounded them, and the inevitable knock-on effect. For instance more and more families were opting out of the mundane packaged beach holidays, and taking to the road instead, spurred on by the sisters' success. What's more, countless infant girls were being given the names Esther and Minnie, just as the norm had been of late to give baby boys names once popular in bygone times, such as Frank, Walter and Jack, to name but a few.

"You're quite right, dear," Minnie agreed, heading for the bathroom. "Essy, dear!" she called back. "You drained the water!"

Peshwari Nans

"Oh Minnie dear, I am sorry," Esther replied, looking out at the beautiful Vltava river and the characteristic red-tiled roofs of the city. "But I think we can allow ourselves this one eccentricity."

When they were dressed, the sisters gathered their handbags and of course the Lipton's tin, and left their room, making their way along the narrow corridors to the Albatross restaurant.

"Good evening," Esther said, tapping a young waitress on the shoulder. "Table for two please."

"Certainly, Madam." The girl smiled, tucking two menus under her arm. "Where would you like to sit? By the window perhaps? There is going to be a beautiful sunset tonight."

"That would be wonderful, my dear, thank you," Esther replied with Minnie in tow.

Seating the sisters, the waitress offered them the wine list. "Something to drink for you?" she asked.

"Oh good God, no!" Esther sneered, recalling their fireside binge. "Not for me. Do you have any Camp coffee by any chance?"

"We have Columbian," the girl replied, unfamiliar with Esther's bottled request.

"Hmmmm." Esther thought for a moment. "Perhaps then I'll just have a pot of tea if it's all the same, my dear."

"Certainly, Madam." The girl smiled politely. "And for you, Madam?" she asked Minnie, who sat perusing the list.

"I'll have a sweet sherry, my dear," she insisted.

"Of course," the waitress said, leaving the ladies to ponder over the menu.

"I can't see any faggots on here, dear," Minnie said, looking over the top of her spectacles. "Did you find the pease pudding?"

"No, dear," Esther said disapprovingly. "No I did not." She put her hand in the air. "I say!" she called to the waitress, who hurried across with their drinks. "Do you have any steak and kidney pudding, my dear? A Fray Bentos perhaps?" She was referring to her beloved tinned classic, of which her larder was never without at least three at any given time.

"Bentos?" the girl said quizzically. "I'm afraid we do not have this bentos. We have goulash, schnitzel, fried cheese, dumplings and…"

"Fried cheese!" Minnie said, interrupting her and turning up her nose at the Czech delicacy. "Don't you have any corned beef and cabbage? We like corned beef and cabbage, don't we, Essy dear?"

"Yes, yes, we do, dear," Esther reiterated.

"I am afraid I do not know this," the girl said, scrutinizing her own menu. "Perhaps some soup?"

"Oh yes, soup." Minnie smiled. "I'll have mulligatawny my dear, with a nob of buttered bread please, and I know Essy will have the same won't you dear? We usually share a dented tin you see."

"We have sauerkraut," the waitress said, eager to please. "But not this mully, mullyga—"

"—Mulligatawny, dear," Minnie said, sipping at her sherry. "We get three for two at Betterbuys, don't we dear?"

"Quite right, dear," Esther said, stirring her tea. "Four if the tins are damaged."

Esther soon relented. "Okay, we'll have the sauer whatsit, but do make sure it's piping hot mind, nothing worse than tepid soup."

"No dear, nothing worse," Minnie agreed.

On the food's arrival the sisters sniffed cautiously at their continental soup, Minnie taking the first tentative sip. "Not bad," she told her sister, who looked on for the verdict. "Just like leek and potato."

Peshwari Nans

Having sampled a taste of Czech cuisine the sisters dared to order the fried gruyere cheese, goulash and potato pancakes. "I say," Minnie said, offering the girl the electronic tablet and posing with her sherry glass. "Would you take a photograph please?" she asked.

"Of course, madam," the waitress agreed, stepping back.

"Excuse me, ladies," a woman with an American accent suddenly intervened, having left her table. "My husband Larry and I were just having a disagreement over there," she told the startled sisters. "I said you were," she continued, "and that meat-head said you were not."

"I'm sorry, were not what?" Esther asked, lowering her teacup.

"The Peshwari Nans!" the woman said, a little exasperated. "You are, aren't you? You gotta be! I mean I should know—me and the girls at the bowls club talk about you two all the time."

"You do?" Esther said, bemused. "I mean yes, yes we are but—"

"—SEE LARRY YA MORON!" the broad Brooklyn-born housewife yelled across the restaurant. "I TOLD YA, I TOLD YA IT WAS THEM DIDN'T I!"

Her husband sat with his head bowed as his wife caused heads to turn and raised eyebrows throughout the restaurant.

"Oh you're having a picture, great," the woman then said, rounding the table and crouching between the sisters. "LARRY? GET OVER HERE!" she called to her red-faced husband. "COME ON YA KNUCKLEHEAD WE'RE TAKING A GOD DAMN PICTURE HERE, WILL YOU GET OFF YOUR FAT ASS AND GET ON OVER HERE!"

Larry slithered from his table, well aware of the unwanted attention. "Hi, please to meetcha," he said, shaking the ladies' hands politely. "I must apologize for my wife, she's a little neurotic."

"I am not neurotic!" his wife barked, pulling him to her side and straightening his tie. "Okay now shut up and smile," she told him. "Can you take one with mine?" she asked the waitress, thrusting her camera into her hand. "My friends at the club will simply die when they see me with these folks." She then clicked her fingers above her head. "HEY EVERYBODY!" she yelled, getting everyone's attention.

"No, no, please don't," Esther said, just wanting to have a quiet evening with her sister. But the American lady had other ideas.

"HEY Y'ALL!" she again yelled. "LOOKY HERE, IT'S THE PESHWAAAAARI NAAAAANS!"

Within seconds the majority of the restaurant's diners had surrounded the sisters' table.

"Oh really!" Esther said, burying her head in her napkin whilst Minnie relished the limelight, signing her own napkin for one frantic fan.

"Yes of course, dear," Minnie told another admirer, sitting her bouncing baby on her knee and smiling sweetly for her camera.

"They're friends of mine!" the pushy American boasted to everyone. "This is Esther, and that there's Minnie."

"Actually, I'm Minnie," Minnie informed her, causing her mild embarrassment. "But you are right, we are friends, all of us, isn't that right everyone?"

Her humble gesture brought a cheer from their followers who, once satisfied, returned to their tables, texting and mailing their loved ones to tell of the highlight of their vacation.

"Listen sweeties," the American said as she was being torn away by her husband, "if you're ever stateside look me up, ya hear? I'll take you to the club, then maybe lunch at Bloomingdales!"

"Leave them be, honey!" her husband said, standing up to her for once in his miserable life. "My apologies once again, ladies, enjoy the rest of your evening!"

"Oh that's quite alright, dear!" Minnie smiled, catching the waitress's eye to order another sherry. "And could we please have the cheeseboard too, my dear?" she asked, having polished off the soup, the main course and one-and–a-half baked apples for dessert. "My sister and I are quite partial to a slice or two of Port Salut if you have it."

The pasteurized cow's milk cheese from the Loire Valley was indeed a favourite of the sisters, mainly consumed by them around Christmas time, or sometimes on birthdays. The rest of the time the more mundane cheese triangles were usually the order of the day, especially when Mr Nazir at the minimart had a glut of them, and offered a two-for-one promotion.

"Yes we have Port Salut, madam," the waitress replied. "And perhaps you would like to try some of our traditional Abertam farmhouse cheese? Made from the first sheep's milk."

The sisters looked at one another and then at the waitress, saying simultaneously: "I don't think so, dear."

"We'll stick to the Port Salut if you don't mind," Esther told her. "And a wedge of Wensleydale if it's not too much trouble."

"But you really should try our—" the waitress said before Minnie interrupted her.

"—That'll be all, dear," she said, turning away.

The sisters later returned to their cabin, having had their fill and grown tired of the video cameras pointed in their direction, capturing their every move. "I now know how Sinatra and Munroe must've felt," Esther said, closing the door behind her and dropping onto the end of her bed to

189

release her patent shoe buckles. "It's like being a damn fish in a bowl."

"Oh I don't know, dear." Minnie smiled, flopping back on her bed with her arms outstretched. "I rather enjoy it, sometimes it makes me feel like the Duchess of Windsor."

Minnie had long since been a fan of Wallis Simpson, the American socialite born in Pennsylvania in 1896, who found eternal fame when she fell in love with, and consequently had a relationship with, the then king of England, Edward VIII, who paid a hefty price for her hand by sensationally abdicating his throne to marry her, earning her the title of 'Duchess', which she kept until her death in the Bois De Boulogne, Paris, France in 1986.

"That harlot!" Esther sneered, having been a staunch objector to the whole affair. "Edward was a damn fool to fall for that woman, what he ever saw in her heaven only knows."

"Essy dear, they were in love." Minnie smiled dreamily. "I think it was tremendously romantic."

"You would, dear," Esther scoffed, removing her pearls.

"Wow Essy, come and look!" Minnie later said at the window, the cool evening breeze ruffling her nightie. "Isn't it just beautiful?" she marvelled at the illuminated spectacle of Prague castle reflected majestically in the Vltava river.

"Hmmm," Esther replied over her shoulder. "Not a patch on the Houses of Parliament, dear."

Minnie waved at a passing boat that was crammed with late-night revellers.

"Come away, dear," Esther said, ducking behind the curtains. "You look as though you're touting for business for Pete's sake!"

One of the drunken passengers joked with his friends before turning round and dropping his trousers to shake his lily-white bottom in Minnie's direction.

Peshwari Nans

"Well I never!" Minnie said, aghast. "Well two can play at that game, young man!"

"What are you doing?" Esther yelled as her sister tugged at her nightdress. "Oh no you don't, get away from there, get away this instant!" She wrestled Minnie to her bed and quickly drew the curtains after catching a fleeting glimpse of the mooning drunk. "Filthy beast!" she cursed. "What's got into you, Minnie?" she asked. "It's the sherry isn't it? I knew it! You're to lay off it from now on, do you hear me? Minnie? Minnie?"

But her sister had passed out instantaneously on top of her bed sheets. "Ohhhh, damn and blast!" Esther fumed, slipping into her own bed and turning out the light.

The following morning, after both of the sisters had enjoyed a restful night's sleep, albeit that it was punctuated by Minnie's occasional snoring, the sisters rose, washed and popped along to the restaurant for breakfast.

"I say, do you have kippers, my dear?" Esther asked the waiter.

"I'm sorry," he replied blankly. "Kippers?"

"Yes, you know," Esther said, tray in hand. "Kippers—smoked mackerel."

"Ahhhh, fish." The waiter smiled. "Yes we have this."

"Splendid!" Esther smiled too. "I'll take a pair with a lightly boiled egg please."

"Yes, I'll have the same please," Minnie informed him. "And two rounds of buttered toast. Do you have Hovis, dear?"

"Of course they don't, dear," Esther scoffed. "You're not at home now you know."

"Hovis? Hovis?" the waiter said, producing an array of oddly shaped breads.

"No, no, dear," Minnie said disapprovingly. "It's a square loaf, medium sliced, just right for my Marmite."

"Oh you and your Marmite!" Esther said, turning up her nose at the mention of the savoury topping. "How could you?"

"Okay," Minnie told the waiter, whilst ignoring her sister's protestations. "I'll make do with a slice of the pumpernickel, but do be a dear and shake off the seeds, I have a mild allergy you see."

"Please take a seat," the waiter replied, placing two teas on their trays. "I will bring your food."

"Oh that's awfully kind of you, thank you," Minnie said, plucking a handful of sweeteners from a bowl. "I'd like my kippers well done if I may, young man," she added, departing for their window table.

"Yes, yes, no problem," the waiter replied, turning for the kitchen.

"Charming man," Minnie commented. "What are you doing, dear?" she then asked her sister, who donned a pair of dark glasses,

"I'm incognito, dear," Esther replied furtively. "In case those ghastly Americans put in an appearance."

"Oh I thought she was rather sweet, dear," Minnie said, a little more tolerant than her elder sister. "And the husband reminded me of a young Richard Attenborough—rather dashing I thought."

Several minutes later the waiter reappeared, carrying two shining platters.

"Ahhhh thank you, dear," Esther said, sitting upright, but her expression of delight suddenly turned to one of dismay when he set down a meal of boiled sturgeon and deep fried eggs before them. "What in God's name is that?" she asked, looking down her nose and raising her dark glasses.

"Kipper?" the waiter said, with absolutely no knowledge of the age-old British favourite.

Peshwari Nans

"Don't be ridiculous!" Esther sneered. "Kippers are brown, flat and full of bones. This on the other hand—" She prodded the gelatinous grey cubes swimming in brine with her fork "—Is not. No no no, take it away at once!" she insisted. "I'll just have the cornflakes instead, thank you."

Minnie plucked the toast from her plate before also pushing it away. "I know you mean well, dear," she told the confused waiter, "but a kipper is a kipper and there are absolutely no substitutes. Now do be a dear and fetch us some more tea, will you?"

The waiter left looking quizzically at his sturgeon. "Kipper?" he said under his breath.

Somewhat fortified after breakfast, the sisters decided to spend the rest of the morning seeing the sights of the city, firstly crossing the world renowned Charles Bridge, constructed of Bohemian sandstone in 1357 and completed in 1402. The statue-lined crossing had featured in blockbusting movies such as *Casino Royale*, *Les Misérables* and *Amadeus*.

"Excuse me, would you mind?" Minnie asked a Japanese visitor, offering him the tablet and backing her sister to the side with the castle as a majestic backdrop to the picture. "Thank you, dear," she said, checking the picture. "Excellent. Do enjoy your stay, won't you?" The tourist and his wife bowed politely and shuffled away, taking his own memorable snaps.

"Now, Minnie dear," Esther told her sister, "I know you'd love to see the sights as I would, but we do need to purchase some more clothes, after all we've already thrown away half of our wardrobe."

"New clothes?" Minnie asked expectantly.

"Don't be ridiculous, dear," Esther said, pinching the pennies in her pocket. "No, no, I'm sure Prague has its fair share of thrift shops, and I do know how you love a bargain, dear."

Minnie did but she hung her head all the same, not having purchased anything new to wear in quite some time.

"Oh don't look like that, dear," Esther warned her. "Remember that hooded duffle coat I bought you, that was an absolute steal at two pounds twenty-five?"

"But Essy, dear," Minnie protested. "It had three buttons missing and a hole in the hood."

"Yes and I sewed the hood if you remember rightly!" Esther snapped at her ungrateful sibling. "And I stitched on new buttons."

"Yes, odd buttons at that," Minnie reminded her. "I looked like a damn rag doll."

"Ooooh you can be so finicky and fastidious at times Minnie, do you know that?" Esther said, pursing her lips. "I was down to my last three pounds and it was the dead of winter if you recall."

"Oh er yes, sorry Essy," Minnie said, changing her tone. "I didn't mean it like that, I know you only had my best interests at heart. Come on, let's track down those thrift shops shall we? You never know, I may even find another silver spoon for my collection."

Crossing the road, Minnie observed a beautiful horse and carriage heading in their direction. "Essy dear, can we?" she asked, bobbing up and down on the spot. "Please!"

"Absolutely not, dear!" Esther replied sternly. "Those majestic creatures are exploited by those ruthless brutes, made to work all hours of the day until they're too weak to stand."

Esther objected adamantly to the use of any animal for monetary gain, and she was right to, for the vast majority of all carriage horses used in countless major cities around the world led a pitiful existence, worked for upwards of twenty hours a day, whipped and beaten and very often housed in derelict buildings instead of the lush pasture they deserved. Animal rights organizations such as PETA (People for the Ethical Treatment of Animals) continue to lobby heads of state in order to see a worldwide ban on horse-drawn street carriages introduced, backed by many stars of screen and stage.

"If I had my way I'd round up all those gorgeous animals and set them free to roam and live out their lives with dignity," Esther went on. After her rant she stepped down from the kerb and in doing so planted her right foot squarely in a freshly deposited pile of horse manure. "Ooooh! Damn those wretched creatures!" she cried.

"Oh I say!" Minnie laughed, capturing the moment with her tablet for the amusement of their army of followers. "That's quite unfortunate, dear."

"Don't you dare," Esther said as Minnie posted the pic online.

"Too late." Minnie smiled mischievously. She then examined the deposit. "Perhaps we could take some home for the roses, dear? What do you think? It is a beauty after all."

"Perhaps you could be quiet!" Esther barked, hoisting her foot clear and clinging to her sister whilst teetering awkwardly.

"Here, dear," Minnie said, reaching into her oversized handbag. "I have a pair of flats you can wear."

"Thank you," Esther said, still seething as she kicked off her brogues and deposited them in a nearby litter bin, slipping on Minnie's emergency flatties. She would lose very little sleep over the discarded shoes, having only paid a pound for them in the Cancer Research charity shop in Bethnal Green.

"Looks like we'll be needing to find a thrift shop sooner than we thought, dear," Minnie said as the horse and carriage trundled by.

Peshwari Nans

"I SAY STOP THAT, DO YOU HEAR?" Esther yelled at the driver for his overzealous use of the whip. The Albanian driver turned and muttered several obscenities under his breath in her direction.

"I'd like to take that whip to him," she added, wishing for an end to the barbaric practice.

Minnie held up her hand and hailed one of Prague's many trams.

"Wenceslas Square, please," Esther said, dropping several coins into the driver's tray. "I've heard so much about it, Minnie dear," she told her sister. "It'd be a crime not to visit while we're here."

"Lead on then, dear," Minnie said, following her sister to the rear of the tram humming *'Good king Wenceslas'*.

The sisters sat and marvelled at all that the beautiful city of Prague had to offer them, and after alighting and two-and-a-half hours of rigorous sightseeing, the pair turned their attentions to the backstreets and the many thrift shops that had their eyes lighting up with anticipation.

"This one!" Minnie squealed.

"No, no, this one!" Esther insisted. "Look they have hundreds of hardbacks and a jigsaw of Prague castle!"

"A jigsaw you say?" Minnie said, pushing past her sister and entering the cluttered premises. "My word!" she gasped at the virtual Aladdin's cave of pre-owned paraphernalia. Esther and Minnie were in their element, rolling up their sleeves to rummage like true champions, donning their spectacles to scrutinize every china cup and teaspoon for hallmarks and imperfections, filling an ample box for the price of a packet of tea.

Then it was the turn of the clothes rails to undergo a thorough thumbing. They chuckled as they tried on traditional Czech garments, snapping one another in gaily coloured robes and bonnets and, again, posting them online, showing off their tat and trinkets, something which caused a ripple of hilarity throughout the world wide web.

This was a ripple that would extend to Wilmington Ohio in the good old U S of A, where a young games designer by the name of Karl Bodine lived in the basement of his great aunt's house. His eureka moment came when the sisters popped up on his newsfeed, knee-deep in knitwear, novels and pointless novelties. Karl immediately leapt from his bunk, flinging his half-eaten pizza across the room and setting to work, feverishly converting his fledgling idea into Internet code.

Weighed down with pre-worn woollens and associated junk, Esther and Minnie returned to the Albatross, taking up four seats on the tram. "All in all a very productive day, dear," Minnie said later, loading their wares into Vivien and proceeding back on board the boat.

"We'll be checking out in an hour, young man," Esther told the desk clerk. "And I must say it's been a very pleasant experience indeed. I'll be penning a glowing review of your floating hotel at the earliest opportunity."

"Thank you, madam," the clerk said, smiling politely. "It has been a pleasure having you and may I wish you the best of luck on your journey ahead, you are very brave."

"Oh," Esther said, still unconvinced of their popularity. "You know too, do you?"

"Of course!" the clerk said, turning his computer screen towards them to reveal the sisters and Vivien as his screen saver. "Everybody knows."

Making the most of the Albatross's facilities, Esther and Minnie bathed once more and filled their bellies with tea and toast, having decided to drive through the night onwards towards Poland, their fifth country including their own. "Ready, dear?" Esther said as she sat behind the wheel.

"You bet." Minnie smiled, handing her sister the last of their Parma violets.

Making their way through Chlumec nad Cidlinou and on towards Náchod the sisters settled down to life on the road once more, playing I spy and spot the yellow car to relieve the boredom. Esther made yet another fuel stop in the dead of night at a deserted service station on the outskirts of Jaroměř, and being deserted they were forced to pay at the pump.

"Damn!" Minnie groaned, peering through the station window at the tasty snacks within. "I rather fancied a Walnut Whip." She'd noticed the Czech equivalent of the English confectionery chocolatey favourite.

"Oh yes!" Esther said, joining her sister, their noses pressed to the glass. "And there's a packet of jelly babies."

Minnie began banging on the door with the palm of her hand. "Helloooo!" she called. "Anybody there?" such was her craving for the sweets. "Helloooooo!"

"To hell with it, dear," Esther said tearing her sister away. "If I remember rightly there's half a packet of liquorice allsorts left in the picnic basket."

"Well why didn't you say so, dear?" Minnie said, hurrying to Vivien to retrieve the said sweets.

Pressing on across into Dolina, a few miles the other side of the Polish border, the sisters shared the last of the liquorice and also some of the elderflower cordial. "How far to Krakow, dear?" Esther asked, having planned much of their route in advance.

"Now let me see," Minnie said, retrieving the tablet from beneath her seat. "I'll ask our friend Mr Google, that is of course if he's up and about at this ungodly hour."

"Oh don't wake him on my behalf, dear," Esther said, concerned that they had already been a burden on their fictitious cyber friend.

Peshwari Nans

"It's quite alright, dear." Minnie smiled. "He must be an insomniac. Look he says it's eighty kilometres from our present position, oh and look, he's even drawn us a map."

"Oh, how marvellous!" Esther exclaimed. "We really should send him a little thank you, what do you think? Maybe some cufflinks, or a tie perhaps? Jack always loved a new tie."

"Splendid idea," Minnie agreed.

Some four-and-a-half thousand miles away in Wilmington, Karl Bodine had drawn up the preliminary synopsis for his computer game: it was a spin on the hugely popular but grotesquely violent *Grand Theft Auto*, a game where players get to act out their sometimes sadistic fantasies by carjacking innocent drivers, running riot in a virtual city landscape and murdering or maiming random members of the public, all in the name of entertainment.

The gaming industry was one of the most lucrative of enterprises, with net profits running into the tens of billions, but as Karl had deduced, they had so far overlooked an un-tapped market: the elderly, many of them becoming more and more computer literate, as Minnie was, with more time on their hands and, more importantly, more disposable income than the average jobless teen. They often had a retirement fund perhaps, a nest egg like a rich seam of gold waiting to be mined, and Karl Bodine of Wilmington, Ohio was about to go prospecting.

Unlike the original eighteen-certificate game, Karl's would feature a pool of sweet old ladies that the player could choose from in a range of appropriate attire: woollens and gabardine in pastel shades. Next, like many driving games on the market, the players would have a choice of vintage automobiles, from Austins to Ford Zephyrs or even a Morris Traveller, just like Vivien. The aim of the game was simple: to visit as many thrift shops as

199

possible and amass the largest collection of second-hand clothes, knick-knacks and general 'tat' to win.

His very own Grand Theft Auto rip-off would be entitled Gran *Thrift* Auto with the very first edition available as a completely free download—while it might seem foolhardy business sense, the idea was that once hooked, the player would pay handsomely for his extension packs and future editions, of which there would be many. With the senior citizens of the world already getting to grips with such classics as *Candy Crush* and *Angry Birds*, *Gran Thrift Auto* was set to take the geriatric gaming industry by storm and to make Karl a very wealthy young man in the process.

Dawn was fast approaching as the sisters in their Morris Traveller meandered from village to village, town to town, towards Krakow, a name synonymous with Jews the world over.

Nestling on the river Vistula it's known to be one of the oldest cities in the country of Poland, and one with the most turbulent of pasts.

After the German invasion during World War Two, almost all the Jews were rounded up and forced into confinement inside a walled zone, later known as the infamous 'Krakow ghettos'. From there tens of thousands were transported to Hitler's concentration camps, such as Auschwitz or Bergen Belsen, to await their fate in horrendous conditions. Those that were not gassed, shot or mutilated, perished from disease and malnutrition, leaving but a few to be liberated by the allies in 1945.

"Oh I am sorry, dear," Minnie said, opening her eyes and stretching, having dozed off. "How long have I been asleep?"

"That's quite alright, dear," Esther said, patting her sister's knee. "Just an hour or so."

"An hour!" Minnie exclaimed. "Oh Essy, you should've woken me, darling, you shouldn't have driven through the night alone."

"It's alright." Esther laughed. "Really, dear I don't mind. Anyway it's only another fifteen kilometres to Krakow now, we can stop for breakfast and freshen up there."

"Wonderful idea," Minnie said, rubbing her tired eyes. "I could just eat a full English."

"Well dear, you may have to settle for a full Polish," Esther informed her.

"Oh yes, of course." Minnie smiled. "How silly of me." She wound down her window to keep from drifting back to sleep. "Krakow," she then said, turning to her sister. "Wasn't your Jack there for a spell during the war?"

"Yes, yes, he was," Esther replied, remembering in vivid detail the conversations she had with her husband on his return. Jack had become separated from his regiment during fierce fighting in Germany. Shell-shocked and half starved, he had hidden out in an abandoned barge for ten days, surviving on rainwater and grain scraps before being picked up by an American unit en route to Poland.

Cut off and unable to return Jack to his regiment, the marines fed and watered him and took him along with them, their arrival coinciding with the long overdue liberation of the Auschwitz Birkenau concentration and extermination camp in Oswiecim, where the Soviet Union were the first to enter after the notorious SS had fled. The horrific scene that greeted them would haunt every man for the remainder of their days. Over one million human beings had perished in the camp during its relatively brief spell in operation.

Survivors clung to the barbed wire fences just as the rags clung to their skeletal bodies. Jack wept uncontrollably as he carried the weak emaciated inmates to the waiting trucks

201

and helped to bury those that the SS hadn't had time to cremate.

The most harrowing of all for him was seeing the bodies of a young brother and sister found huddled together in the snow, the siblings being no older than seven and eight and barely weighing anything at all. Dressed only in what could be described as a striped nightshirt, they were frozen solid together. Jack scooped them up into his arms and held them close for a moment, looking skyward for the answer to the question on everybody's lips: why? Jack looked deep into their matching hazel eyes, eyes that would be forever etched into his mind.

"Can I help you?" a Soviet officer had asked him, offering a hand.

"No, no, I've got this," Jack replied, seeing to their burial personally. The children's thin shirts, grossly inadequate for the weather conditions, had thawed somewhat from the warmth of his beating chest.

Known only as a series of numbers at the time the siblings, whose names were in fact Jacob and Anna, had witnessed their father gunned down in the Krakow ghetto for objecting to their removal. They had also seen their grandparents dragged from their bed and shipped to Bergen Belsen in northern Germany, and their mother taken to the gas chamber just days before their liberation. Jacob and Anna sadly and ironically perished just hours before the Soviets arrived. This was indeed genocide on a galactic scale and a testament to man's inhumanity to man.

One of the most influential of all Jewish victims was a young innocent fifteen-year-old girl by the name of Anne Frank who, until her capture, had hidden out in a room concealed behind a bookcase in her father's former workplace. During that time Anne kept a detailed journal or diary which was preserved by a friend and handed to her only surviving family member, Otto Frank, after her death.

Peshwari Nans

It was published under the title *The Diary of a Young Girl* in 1947.

The Frank sisters Anne and Margot remained together throughout their hellish incarceration and died just days apart, probably from typhus which at the time was at epidemic levels. The girls were buried in a mass grave with thousands of their fellow inmates, but through Anne's diaries their legacy will live on forever.

Many who witnessed the horrors during the liberation never spoke of them again but Jack confided in his love, and through their intimate counselling he found a degree of inner peace. But he never ever forgot Jacob and Anna, lighting two candles, year-in year-out on the anniversary of their burial, the look in their frozen eyes as vivid on the day he himself died as it was back then in 1945.

"If you don't mind, Minnie dear," Esther said solemnly, "I'd like to see it for myself—the camp, I mean."

"Yes, yes, of course," Minnie said, hearing the distinct break in her sister's voice. "Here, dear," she said, offering her handkerchief. "We'll do whatever you want, Essy, you know that."

"Thank you, Min." Esther smiled, squeezing her sister's hand. "Thank you."

With the help of the tablet, Minnie located Oṣwiecim and directed her sister accordingly towards the former SS camp, the pair filled with trepidation as to what they might find.

Within a few kilometres of Auschwitz, Esther pulled over at a roadside cafeteria. "Oh no dear, let's press on," Minnie said, tired but understanding of her sister's need to visit the site.

"Nonsense, dear," Esther insisted. "You need a coffee and so do I for that matter."

Availing themselves of the washroom facilities, the sisters freshened their faces but applied very little in the way of make-up. Their onward journey to the camp would demand more in the way of respect, as such luxuries were expressly denied to the female population.

"Two coffees please, young lady," Esther told the waitress. "Black and strong, with half a sugar in each. What would you like to eat, Minnie dear?"

"Well you know me, Essy dear." Minnie smiled, eyeing the gut-busting daily special. "I'll have the terminator please, my dear," she said, requesting the aptly named 'calorific colossus'. "With an extra sausage and fried bread if you don't mind."

Esther smiled at her sister's fortitude. "Just a cheese sandwich for me, dear," she told the girl, handing back her menu.

"You go to Auschwitz?" the waitress asked, returning with the coffee and looking out of the window along the road.

"Yes my dear, we are," Esther replied, a little uneasy at appearing to be just another tourist come to gawp at the macabre place. "It's a personal visit," she hurriedly added.

"Ahhh, I see," the girl said, forcing a smile. "My grandmother was there."

"Oh darling, I'm so sorry," Esther said, presuming she had too perished along with so many others.

"No, no, she survived," the waitress informed the sisters. "She told us of the day when the German soldiers came for her and her brother Frederick, who was crippled with lupus."

Esther and Minnie listened intently as the raven haired waitress opened her heart to them, fulfilling her grandmother's wishes to pass on what had occurred, so that lessons could be learned and the dead not be forgotten.

"Is your grandmother still with us?" Minnie asked.

"No, no, she died just three weeks ago," the girl replied, toying with her grandmother's ring that hung on a chain around her neck. "I was with her and closed her eyes. It was sad but also a beautiful moment."

"Ahhh, you must have been close to her," Esther said, taking the girl's hand. "And Frederick? Is he..." She stopped talking, not daring to ask.

"No, Frederick was put on another train," the waitress said, clearly upset at this point. "We do not know what happened to him."

"Oh my dear, I am sorry," Minnie said, clutching her heart, the thought of a brother and sister separated in such a way almost too much for her. But Frederick's condition had sealed his fate, for those with any form of disability or disfigurement were deemed worthless and subhuman to the so-called 'master race' and were exterminated, sometimes within hours of their arrival at the concentration camps.

"I am sorry, I will fetch you food," the waitress said, noticing her boss glaring at her from the counter.

"That's quite alright, dear," Esther told her. "Take your time."

Esther ate half of her sandwich, then sat and watched as Minnie dissected, dismantled and devoured her brimming plateful with all the precision and dexterity of an open-heart surgeon, an awe-inspiring spectacle for her sister and for those on the adjacent tables, for that matter.

"More coffee?" the waitress later asked, filling their cups. "I am sorry," she then said. "I did not mean to speak of these things."

"Nonsense, my dear." Esther smiled. "It's wonderful to hear that you and your grandmother were so close. I have a grandson—Richard—and we get along just fine."

"Yes, we were very close," the young waitress said, eyeing Minnie as she mopped up the remains of her breakfast with her fried bread. "She was like you," she told her with a smile.

Peshwari Nans

"A good looking woman then," Minnie said, licking her fingers clean.

"No, no, not at all," the waitress said, unaware of any offence she may have caused. "I mean her appetite was like yours. You know I once saw her eat an entire babka cake to herself." The sweet yeast 'babka cake', sometimes drizzled with milk chocolate and a favourite at Christmas and Easter, would usually feed a family of four, with a slice or two left over for supper.

"Oooh, what's a babka cake?" Minnie asked, having already consumed double her recommended calorie intake in a single sitting.

"This," the waitress said, pointing to half a babka cake that was beneath the counter.

"Mmmm, can we have two slices to go, please Adriana?" Minnie said, having noted the girl's identification badge. "I tell you what, make it three," she added. "God only knows when we'll stop to eat again, and I—er—I don't suppose you have any Garibaldis, dear, do you?"

"I'm sorry, what is this?" Adriana asked, surveying her own menu. "It is a drink, yes?"

"No, no, dear," Esther explained. "It's a biscuit, about so big." She held out her hands, palms held apart. "With raisins in the middle."

"Raisins!" Minnie exclaimed. "I could have sworn they were prunes, dear."

"Don't be ridiculous, dear." Esther laughed. "Why on earth would they be prunes?"

"Well, Essy dear," Minnie said calmly, "they've always had a laxative effect on me. I remember I was stuck in the loo at Saint Pancras for over an hour after nibbling a packet on the seven-fifteen."

"No, no, dear, you're mistaken," Esther informed her. "They're definitely raisins."

"Are you positive, dear?" Minnie asked, unconvinced.

Peshwari Nans

Adriana left the sisters embroiled in a heated discussion as to the contents of the much-loved family favourite.

"Well why do you eat them then, dear?" Esther asked, getting nowhere with her obstinate sister.

"For my bloating, dear," Minnie said, confiding in her sibling. "Dr Kumali specifically told me to eat a portion of prunes at least three times a week."

"But they aren't prunes, dear!" Esther said, exasperated to say the least.

"Are you sure, dear?" Minnie asked yet again after a moment or two of contemplation.

"Will you please stop saying that! Of course I'm sure!" Esther stormed. "I can categorically say that Garibaldi biscuits do not, and never have, contained prunes in any way shape or form! Now let that be the end of it, please."

Minnie sat, slowly stirring her coffee whilst gazing out of the window. "Well," she said, plucking up the courage to approach her agitated sister. "Which biscuits do contain prunes?"

"Oh for heaven's sake!" Esther said, throwing her hands in the air.

"Okay, okay, I'm sorry!" Minnie said, attempting to calm her sister, who was beginning to cause several heads in the café to turn in their direction.

Leaving Adriana a generous tip and bidding her farewell, the sisters climbed into Vivien and left the waitress waving from the window. "Charming girl," Minnie said, waving back as they pulled away.

"Wasn't she just?" Esther agreed.

Despite her promise to Jasvinder, which was never far from her mind, Esther allowed herself this emotional detour of seeing the site of the concentration camp, since they were so close and most probably would never come here again. "I think she'd understand, dear, don't you think?" she asked her sister.

"Who, dear?" Minnie asked, getting to grips with a particularly sticky toffee wrapper.

"Jazzy of course," Esther said, following the signs to Oswiecim.

"Oh undoubtedly, dear," Minnie replied, unable to shake the wrapper from her thumb. "Besides, it's just a day. We'll make it up in no time."

"Yes, yes, you're right," Esther said, now convinced of her excursion's validity.

Thousands upon thousands of visitors regularly flocked to the cluster of camps, some of which were now in ruins. In 1979 the place was named as a UNESCO world heritage site, so that it could be preserved as a memorial, a constant reminder of the atrocities that occurred within. The trip these tourists made in modern air conditioned coaches and high speed locomotives was a far cry from the plight of the Jews, Roma and Soviet prisoners-of-war, who had been crammed into filthy goods wagons or *Guterwagon*. And unlike modern-day visitors the vast majority did not have the luxury of a return journey.

"Are you alright, dear?" Minnie asked when they were within a few kilometres of the camp, noting the needle on Vivien's speedometer creeping from forty-five to below thirty miles per hour.

"Sorry?" Esther said, snapping out of her daze.

"Are you alright, dear?" Minnie again asked with a hand on her sister's arm. "You were grinding your teeth, dear."

The tales that Jack had told her of his time in the region weighed heavily on Esther's mind. "Was I, dear?" she asked. "Sorry I was…" She paused.

"I know, dear," Minnie said with a loving squeeze. "I know."

Following closely behind a snaking line of tour buses, Vivien was eventually hemmed in between them as more and more arrived. Esther and Minnie sat craning their necks to catch a fleeting glimpse of the infamous death camp entrance, with its rusting steel transportation train tracks disappearing inside.

"My God!" Minnie said under her breath as they inched ever closer at a snail's pace. Minnie's reference to the almighty was an echo of a million or so past prayers uttered on that very site that sadly went unanswered.

Once parked, the sisters tagged on the end of a party of Koreans, who followed the Italians, who in turn followed the Danes, each and every soul stunned into a solemn silence that gripped them by the throat the moment they alighted and followed in the footsteps of those who had been condemned, half a century ago.

Doctors, lawyers and entire families spanning several generations looked upon those gates as they did that day, with its wrought-iron insignia above spelling out the words: *ARBIET MACHT FREI* which when translated read *WORK WILL SET YOU FREE*. Constructed by those detainees with a metalworking background in 1940, the sign was merely a ruse to instil a false sense of hope into all those who passed beneath it.

Esther took two white roses that she had purchased from a roadside seller and, pausing, stooped to place them beside a memorial stone. One was for Jacob and the other for his sister Anna. She stood and clenched her own sister's hand ever so tightly.

"Lovely, dear," Minnie said, welling up with tears herself. "Jack would be so proud of you."

Esther and Minnie were not regular church attendees but muttered a line or two of the Lord's Prayer under their breaths all the same, their feet rooted to the spot as though in concrete, as if to walk away would be disrespectful to the siblings' memory. And as there was no official headstone to make their eternal resting place, this memorial would have to suffice. The thought of those two children perishing

209

together in the snow was enough to wrench at the heart of any parent.

"Min," Esther eventually said softly, "you never speak of Sophia, do you?"

"I can't, dear," Minnie said, already shedding a tear for the Jewish children. "Not now." She looked round to see that they were now alone. "Essy, we should go, dear," she added, a timely distraction from a particularly thorny subject.

Unlike Elizabeth, Esther's daughter who had grown and gifted her mother with a grandchild, Sophia was Minnie's only child, fathered by a man she met and fell in love with at the age of seventeen. Sophia had contracted meningitis one week before her fifth birthday, which in many cases during that era and even sometimes today, was misdiagnosed as flu. The medication prescribed of course had no effect, and within a week her beloved child slipped into a coma and died. After that Minnie's world understandably fell apart, as the relationship with her then fiancé crumbled under the weight of such grief. For a mother to look upon the face of her lifeless child was beyond consolation and was a horror spared to that of Jacob and Anna.

Minnie undoubtedly hit the rails and the bottle at the age of twenty-two, partying hard with the wrong crowd, dabbling with the drug of choice at that time, marijuana and eventually getting arrested for affray at Trafalgar Square. The magistrate spared her a custodial sentence when her court-appointed solicitor informed him of Minnie's extremely difficult circumstances. Bound over to keep the peace she vowed never to bring another child into her world and that vow had stood firm. A string of short-term relationships followed, keeping her suicidal tendencies at bay until she eventually taught herself to suppress all thoughts of Sophia, burying them deep inside.

Peshwari Nans

Esther scurried after her sister, calling, "Minnie dear! I'm sorry. But it really doesn't do to bottle thing up, believe me I know."

"Essy!" Minnie snapped. "Please!"

"Alright, dear," Esther replied as they were about to enter the second gate, which was wrapped in twisted barbed wire. "Good grief!" she then added as the sheer scale of the camp hit home. "Jack was right."

Choosing not to follow the multilingual tour guides, Esther instead looked down at the dirt floor, imagining where her husband may have walked.

Peering through an open door with their hearts in their mouths, the sisters were first greeted by the eerie sight of a huge pile of spectacles.

"My word!" Minnie gasped, daring not to enter. But Esther was there to see it all and it was just as Jack had described, minus the dead and emaciated survivors.

Next were the shoes, thousands of them in all shapes and sizes. "God, no!" Minnie cried, clutching her handkerchief to her mouth to stifle her screams upon seeing a child's leather sandal, probably belonging to a four or five-year-old, the same age as her Sophia.

"I've got to get out," Minnie cried, "I've got to get out, Essy!" She was flying into a panic. "Essy, Essy I've got to!"

"It's alright, dear," her sister told her, giving her a comforting cuddle. "It's alright. You go and wait outside, I won't be long, I promise."

"I'm sorry," Minnie said, hurrying to the door. "I'm so sorry, Essy."

Esther, equally shocked, proceeded, passing a group of weeping nuns who had their hands clasped in prayer.

Minnie sat on a hard stone slab outside, struggling to catch her breath.

"Excuse me," a voice said beside her. "Would you like some tea?"

"Sorry, what?" Minnie said, mopping her eyes. "Oh you're English."

"Yes," the middle-aged gent in a tweed jacket replied. "And I presume you are too."

"Yes, of course," Minnie said, pocketing her sodden handkerchief.

"I er, I saw you were upset," he told her, sitting alongside Minnie. "And I just thought you could do with some tea." He produced a thermos flask from his attaché case. "I know I need one."

"Yes, thank you, that's awfully kind of you," Minnie said, mustering a smile. "I saw the shoes and I just went to pieces."

"Me too," the man replied, filling two plastic cups with tea. "I thought I'd be okay but how wrong I was. Sorry, I'm David by the way, David Jenkins." He offered his hand. "I have a group of sixth formers here from Newcastle-under-Lyme."

"Oh you're a teacher?" Minnie deduced. "I see. The name's Minnie, or Min for short. I'm here with my sister Essy, Esther. Her husband was here during the liberation."

"Really?" David exclaimed. "How fascinating. I mean I know it must have been deeply distressing at the time." He then thought for a moment, wondering how best to broach the subject. "Listen, er, do you think he might be able to speak to my students? It would help enormously with their coursework."

"I'm afraid Jack recently passed away," Minnie informed him. "That's why Essy's here, you see."

"Oh, please excuse me," David said, red faced. "I am so very sorry, do forgive me."

"That's quite alright, dear," Minnie said, sipping her tea and recovering somewhat. "So am I right in thinking you're a history teacher?" she said, grateful for the distraction.

Peshwari Nans

"Yes that's right," David said topping up her cup. "Thirty-two years next month, and I absolutely love it."

"You're a lucky man to have such a vocation," Minnie told him. "I for one could never quite get to grips with history as a child. Too many damn dates to remember you see."

"I know exactly what you mean." David smiled, tucking his shoulder-length mousey hair behind his ears.

"What a godforsaken place this is," Minnie said, looking around the stark yard at the crumbling red-brick buildings.

"Yes," David said solemnly. "This is my fourth time here and it doesn't get any easier I tell you."

"Crikey!" Minnie gasped. "Once is more than enough for me, I assure you."

Minnie and David sat on the makeshift bench in the open air whilst Esther and David's students explored the horrors within.

"Excuse me," Esther said, brushing past the shell-shocked six formers to visit the crematorium, where several of the ovens remained intact. It's difficult to say how many bodies were cremated at the height of the camp's evil, reduced to dust and discarded without a shred of dignity, but the numbers were inconceivable nethertheless.

Esther stood staring, as did the students who followed behind. "That's where they burned 'em," one girl said, notebook in hand. Esther wanted so much to correct her terminology, but somehow the words failed her.

Unbeknown to her, Jack had stood on that very spot, gripped in the moment as she, only the scene confronting him was vastly more grotesque. For instance there was the ash-littered wooden floor, complete with camp staff footprints, many of them detainees themselves, forced to cremate their countrymen at the empty promise of freedom. But they too would most likely visit that place themselves, stripped naked on a rusty trolley, just like the countless numbers of people that they had themselves dispatched.

Jack had stood dry-mouthed, just as his spouse now did. The ovens which worked around the clock were still warm to his touch, as were the bricks of that bakehouse, which would take several days to finally cool. The deathly silence that Esther witnessed was a far cry from the crematorium's heyday, when the clatter of the trolley procession forced many workers within to stuff their ears with wax, as if the insanity of their forced occupation wasn't enough to drive them insane.

While Esther shuffled pensively around the former SS camp her path criss-crossed with Jack's, all those years ago, sending an occasional shiver the length of her spine, but giving her a strange sense of closeness, just knowing that he'd been there.

On the opposite side of the globe however, the young games designer, Karl Bodine, eagerly watched the counter in the corner of his computer screen totting up the number of downloads of his brainchild *Gran Thrift Auto*. Like the continuous ticking of his Red Hot Chili Peppers wall clock the numbers slowly increased, as gamers from around the world sampled his free offering. Soon though the counter was notching up an incredible six hundred downloads per minute as Karl worked on the second edition, appropriately priced of course.

The Internet and gaming forums buzzed with news of the game's release and schoolchildren and the elderly alike clambered to add it to their devices. Its addictive formula of innocent retail addiction made it an instant hit. It was fresh, innovative and requiring absolutely no age restrictions, further increasing its market appeal. Word spread like a raging bush fire, causing several Internet servers to crash. Heads of vast gaming companies barracked their minions for not spotting this albeit obvious market trend. Karl himself, a self-confessed techno junkie and loner, instantly found himself the centre of attention, with his high school cheerleader, who rapidly ditched her macho soccer 'beef cake' boyfriends to date him. It seemed that the holy grail of gaming had been found, a cash cow that would lead a thunderous stampede the world over.

Meanwhile back at Auschwitz Birkenau, unlike many of its less sensitive visitors, Minnie for once refrained from documenting her experience with photographs. The powerful images and the thoughts conjured would prove enough and live on with the sisters as clear as any celluloid picture.

"All right, dear?," Minnie asked as her sister emerged, pale and shaken to the core.

"No," Esther replied, finding it hard to speak at first. "No. Actually I'm not."

"You must be Esther," David said, offering his hand and getting up to offer her his seat. "Please, have some tea. It helps, believe me."

"He's right, dear," Minnie agreed. "It's steadied my nerves a treat."

David drained his cup and refilled it, handing it to Esther. "It's still hot," he told her.

"Thank you," she said, wrapping her hands around it and cupping it to her lips. "That's very kind of you."

"David's a teacher," Minnie informed her sister. "From Newcastle."

"Under Lyme," David said, correcting her. "Pleased to meet you. Minnie here tells me your husband was at this place during the liberation. That's quite remarkable. Oh and she also informed me that he recently passed away. I'm so very sorry."

"Thank you, dear," Esther replied, lowering her teacup. "A teacher you say?" she added. "Well I fear we all have much to learn from this place, wouldn't you say?"

"Yes indeed," David agreed.

The three of them sat side by side in quiet contemplation until it was time to leave. In passing, Minnie clasped the barbed wire fence, looking out across the camp's exterior as those before her had done and imagining the trembling hands that had also gripped that very wire, some clenching so tight it would draw blood, enraged as they were at their forced separation from their loved ones.

"Come, Minnie," Esther said, taking her sister's hand. "I've seen enough."

"Goodbye ladies," David said, herding his students onto their coach, one or two of them playing the very game inspired by Esther and Minnie's quest "It was a pleasure meeting you."

"You too, my dear," Minnie replied. "And thank you so much for the tea, it was an absolute godsend."

"Yes, yes, it was," Esther agreed. "Thank you, David."

As the coach left the sisters were standing beside Vivien. David could be seen surrounded by several excited students waving their devices and pointing to the sisters. "What?" David gasped, looking over his shoulder as they disappeared out of sight. "You mean to tell me that was the Peshwari Nans!"

Minnie studied the map while Esther drove them from the harrowing site and back towards the motorway. "We could overnight in Krakow dear," she said, counting the kilometres.

"I'd rather not if it's all the same to you," Esther said, having had her fill of holocaust reminders for one day. "Find us somewhere remote, will you Minnie dearest?"

"As you wish, dear," Minnie agreed, plotting a course that would avoid Krakow by twenty or so miles. "Leave it to me."

Minnie consulted with her Mr Google, requesting a calm and tranquil setting to spend the night. "I have it, dear!" she soon said, after trawling several web pages. "The village of Mielec."

"I've never heard of it," Esther said, looking across at the tablet momentarily. "Why there?"

"Well," Minnie explained, "they have a retreat that looks absolutely idyllic, with a spa, a solarium and a masseur. Now I don't know about you, dear, but I could kill for a back rub."

"Ooooh yes, dear," Esther said, cherishing the thought. "What a simply splendid idea. How far?"

"Ninety kilometres, dear," Minnie replied, checking the stats. "And only half a day's drive from from the Ukraine border. It's perfect, don't you think?"

"Absolutely, dear." Esther smiled, relishing the prospect of a back massage in surroundings that didn't evoke the kind of nightmares that Auschwitz did.

CHAPTER FIVE

Having exhausted the last of their toffees, parma violets and elderflower cordial, the sisters trundled into the city of Mielec a little stiff and saddle-sore, having endured the Polish back roads that were littered with potholes, debris and belligerent dairy cows, many refusing point blank to stand aside, even when Esther leaned on Vivien's horn. "Stubborn beasts!" she occasionally cursed, looking them in the eye with her window wound firmly up.

Arriving at Tajny Ogrod, which when translated loosely means 'the secret garden', a palatial chateau set on the outskirts of town, Esther pulled in from the adjacent lane towards the three-storey house that dated back to the eighteenth century. Cosmetically dilapidated but structurally sound, having been overlooked during the German occupation, the house merely appeared tired.

Vivien's whitewall tyres crunched the sweeping gravel drive, which was overrun in places with nettles and bramble.

"Is this it?" Esther asked disapprovingly, on seeing the peeling willow-green paintwork, the shabby shutters and the precarious guttering.

"Yes, dear," Minnie said, tucking the tablet and Lipton's tea tin into her bag. "Looks can be deceiving, isn't that what they say, dear?"

"Hmmm, I do hope you're right, dear," Esther said, parking beneath a weeping birch tree.

While Esther and Minnie gathered their bags from Vivien's rear, the chateau's heavy mahogany doors opened and a rotund red-faced woman appeared, drying her hands on her lace-edged pinnie. "Dzien dobry, Witam, witam!" she called, which translates to: "Good morning, welcome, welcome." With her arms outstretched, she headed their way, elated to see potential guests, having struggled to fill a room in previous months. "Czesc, Jak sie masz?" she went on (meaning: "Hi, how are you?")

"I'm sorry but we don't speak the language I'm afraid," Esther said, locking Vivien. "We'd like a room if that's possible, my dear."

"Ahhh yes, of course," the woman replied displaying a basic grasp of the English language. "You want a room, yes?"

"Yes that's right, dear," Minnie replied. "Mr Google sent us."

"Mr?" their host replied, bemused.

"Yes, you know," Minnie explained. "Charming man, looks a little like Sean Connery, very helpful. Perhaps he's stayed here himself at some point?"

"I do not know this, Sean Canary," the chateau owner said, picking up their bags. "Please, come, this way, this way."

The sisters gasped on entering the chateau, which in comparison with the exterior was immaculately well kept, the brassware polished to a dazzling shine, the rugs beaten free of dust twice daily, and the antique furniture showing very little sign of wear and tear.

"Wow!" Esther said, taken aback. "Well I must say I wasn't expecting this, that's for sure."

"You like?" the wheezing woman asked, mopping her brow with a flour-covered hand. "Sorry," she told them. "I was baking when you arrive."

"Yes, we like it very much." Minnie smiled. "And whatever it is you're baking smells delicious."

"Monique," the woman said, wiping her hand once again and offering it. "I am Monique, welcome, welcome to Sekrenty Ogrod, sorry I mean welcome to Secret Garden chateau."

"Secret Garden?" Esther smiled. "Sounds heavenly. I'm Esther and this is my sister Minnie."

"Pleased to meet you, Monique," Minnie said, shaking her hand, then wiping the flour onto her own thigh. "I love this place, it's simply adorable."

"Thank you," Monique said, brushing the perspiration from her top lip. "It has been in my family for many years."

"Well, we'd like a room please," Esther asked. "A twin if you have it."

"Of course, of course, come!" Monique said, starting up the stairs, her huge bottom swaying from side to side, bringing a smile to the sisters' faces. "Come, come!" she insisted.

The sisters looked at one another as they followed behind, checking the faded family portraits as they ascended.

"I give you best room," Monique told them proudly as they set down their cases and opened the double doors to the master bedroom.

"Oh my!" Minnie said, peering inside at the towering four-poster bed complete with twin burr walnut dressing tables and an enamel chamber pot.

"It's, it's wonderful!" Esther said, venturing inside.

"Just what the doctor ordered." Minnie smiled.

"Indeed it is, dear," her sister agreed, prodding the mattress. "Indeed it is."

"Thirty euro per night," Monique informed them. "This is okay, yes?"

"Sixty euros is more than reasonable, dear." Minnie smiled. "Don't you think, Essy?"

"No, no, for two!" Monique added. "This is for two!"

"Are you sure, dear?" Esther asked, looking at their lavish surroundings.

"Yes, yes, this is good," Monique replied, throwing back the heavy drapes and beating one corner of the jammed sash window with her fist to free it and let in the cooling breeze and thus airing the room, which hadn't been occupied in quite some time, although it appeared to have been kept spotlessly clean in readiness.

Minnie ventured to the window. "Oh Essy, look!" she said, gazing down on a neatly laid out kitchen garden with formal beds of leeks, spinach, potatoes and sprouts amongst many other vegetables. Climbing beans were supported with a network of interlaced canes and plump ripe strawberries hung from just about every conceivable recycled container, from a coal scuttle to a pair of old wellington boots. "Isn't it marvellous?"

"Yes, dear," Esther agreed. "Monique, do you do all this yourself?"

"Yes, now I do," Monique replied, looking over their shoulder. "It was my father's love but he cannot do this no more."

"Oh I see," Minnie said, craning her neck to see beyond a row of flowering lilacs that were some twenty or so feet tall, at the rear of the vegetable garden. "And what's beyond there?" she asked.

Monique smiled knowingly. "The Secret Garden of course, or as we say 'Sekrenty Ogrod'," she said, turning for the door. "I will serve dinner at six, I hope you like chanterelle."

"Chanterelle?" Minnie said quizzically.

"Wild mushroom, dear," her sister enlightened her.

"Oh, yes, thank you, Monique dear!" Minnie called after their host. "That would be wonderful, thank you."

Esther and her sister sat resting in the window seat "Sekrenty Ogrod" Minnie said, looking towards the lilacs.

"Hmmm," Esther pondered.

Monique left the sisters to take in the grandeur and opulence of their surroundings.

Peshwari Nans

"Well we've really come up trumps this time, dear, haven't we?" Minnie said, unpacking her case on the bed and setting out her evening wear. "Shall we visit the spa, dear?" she asked, taking out their towels. "I could do with a steam and that back rub."

"Absolutely," Esther said, joining her and hanging the majority of her clothes in the adjacent closet.

Donning their dressing gowns, Esther and Minnie left the room to avail themselves of the amenities advertised: the steam room, plunge pool, gymnasium and of course the fully qualified masseur. "Coooeeeeee!" Minnie said as they descended the stairs. "Oooh oooooh!"

Suddenly Monique's father, Ludwik, appeared at the foot of the stairs. He was frail and bent over, leaning heavily on his briar cane, his thinning grey hair lathered to his freckled head with lashings of Brylcreem. Ludwik's eyes immediately lit up when he saw two females in housecoats heading in his direction.

"Oh hello," Esther said when she was on the bottom step. "We were looking for the steam room."

The bent-backed gent dressed in a neatly pressed linen suit and highly polished shoes, attempted to straighten his body and puff out his pigeon chest. With the appearance of somebody decidedly older than the sisters, Ludwik was in fact a good ten years their junior. A fall whilst tying his grape vine in the garden had left him severely debilitated, and the extended spell of inactivity that followed had aged him considerably. Until that fateful day Ludwik had worked tirelessly in his beloved garden, a self-enforced distraction since the death of his wife in the late eighties. He cupped a hand to his ear and said nothing in reply to Esther's question.

"The steam room, dear!" Minnie interjected. "And the pool. Which way?"

"Father!" Monique then called, emerging from the kitchen. "Father, come." she took him by the arm. "My apologies," she told the sisters, smiling politely.

"Oh that's quite alright, dear," Esther replied, stepping down. "We were looking for the steam room and the pool."

"Yes, yes," Monique replied, pointing along the hall while escorting her father back to his seat in the drawing room.

"Oh thank you," Esther said, uneasy as she noticed the man's lecherous leering look as he glanced over his shoulder.

"Father, come!" Monique barked, tearing him away.

"This way, dear," Minnie said, with her towel tucked tightly beneath her arm. "Last one in's a rotten egg!"

She turned the key and pushed open the door at the end of the panelled hall. "Oh," she then said, popping her head around the door jamb.

"What is it, dear?" Esther asked, pushing past her. "What the...?" she gasped on discovering a large open room with a vaulted ceiling and very little in the way of therapeutic facilities, apart from an enamel hot tub in the window bay, something vaguely resembling a wrought-iron hospital bed, two rusting thirty-five-kilo dumb-bells and a cast-iron log burner in the corner.

"Where's the pool?" Minnie asked.

"I think this is it," Esther sneered, running her hand along the hot-tub rim.

"Oh, right," Minnie replied, decidedly disappointed. "Are you sure, dear?"

Esther opened another door, only to find several buckets and a mop and broom. "Quite sure, dear," she added, looking dishevelled and deflated.

"Oh well," Minnie said, ever the optimist. "We're here now, dear, so we may as well make the most of it. Which end would you like?" she asked, popping the plug in the bottom of the tub and turning on the taps. "At least the water's piping hot," she remarked, slipping out of her dressing gown. "And more than big enough for the both of us, come on it'll be just like old times, won't it?"

Minnie and Esther hadn't bathed together since they'd shared a tin tub in front of a roaring open coal fire in 1935. Minnie sniffed at a bottle of rose-scented bubble bath before pouring a large quantity in as the tub filled. She was about to step in completely naked when out of the corner of her eye she noticed the glint from a pair of spectacles.

"OH!" she gasped, covering her breasts on seeing Ludwik standing in the drawing-room bay, looking directly at her and gripping the curtain beside him with a trembling fist. "OH DEAR!" she cried, throwing the curtains closed on one side, which frustrated their voyeur.

"What's wrong, dear?" Esther asked, stripping herself. "What is it?"

"Oh, er, nothing, dear." Minnie lowered herself ever so slowly into the steaming tub, not wanting to alarm her sister. "Just a spider, dear, you know what I'm like. Well what are you waiting for?" she asked. "It feels wonderful, dear, come on in."

Esther hung her robe and climbed in the opposite end of the tub, raising the water level to just below the rim. "Oooooh yes," she agreed. "I see exactly what you mean, this is heavenly."

After some awkward foot manoeuvring they relaxed to the sound of birdsong outside and the beautiful, although partially obscured view.

"Oooh, oooooh, yes," Minnie moaned with pleasure as the healing qualities of the mineral-rich local water worked its magic on her aching arthritic bones.

"Mmmmmmmm," Esther simply agreed, closing her eyes. "Heavenly."

Peshwari Nans

Topping the hot water occasionally, the contented sisters toyed with the bubbles, blowing them from their fingers towards one another and giggling like children.

Minnie eventually clambered, dripping, from the tub and wrapped a towel around her midriff. "Massage, dear?" she asked her sister, pressing a bell beside the bed. "With any luck it'll be administered by a hot middle-aged beef cake."

"You go ahead, dear," Esther said, reclining a little further. "I'll wait my turn, just go easy on the poor fellow will you, he'll need to save a little strength for me."

Minnie sat on the edge of the bed, swinging her legs in anticipation of the smouldering Adonis she was sure would arrive at any moment to run his slippery hot hands the length and breadth of her body. The door then opened and Monique marched in, rolling up her sleeves, her pinnie caked in baking powder. "You want massage?" she asked, a little peeved at the interruption.

"Oh!" Minnie said, sitting upright. "I thought…"

Esther sank lower into the bubbles with a broad smile on her face.

"No, er," Minnie said, holding up her hands. But Monique was having none of it, pushing Minnie down onto the bed and reaching for the liniment. "No, no, I don't!" Minnie cried, struggling, but Monique's manly hands were more than a match for her.

"You ring for massage," the Polish hotelier said, getting to grips with Minnie's lower back. "I give you massage. Be still!"

"Essy, heeelllp!" Minnie squealed, as Monique doused her with the pungent liniment and began kneading her spine, working her way vigorously towards her shoulder blades. "OW, OW, OOH NO!" she yelped.

"Oooh, you so tense," Monique said, applying a little more pressure to Minnie's neck.

Peshwari Nans

"Essy, please!" Minnie cried, reaching for her sister, who dipped below the rim of the tub out of sight, wincing at her sister's ill treatment as Monique began pounding on her back in a fierce chopping motion.

"OW, OW, OW, OH GOD NO!" Minnie pleaded.

Monique prodded, poked and pounded Minnie's neck, back and buttocks until they were flushed pink, before tossing her over like a side of beef onto her front. "Oh please, no!" Minnie begged, having her shoulders and breasts manipulated in such an invasive manner. "OOOOH OW!" she repeatedly screeched, feeling altogether violated and robbed of her dignity.

Monique applied more of the liniment to her hands, which reeked of cabbage and castor oil, her own repugnant recipe capable of lubricating the driest of places. "OH NO, NO, NO, NO, NO, NO!" Minnie cried when Monique's hands ventured lower, slapping her fiercely with the palm of her hand. "No, no, I forbid it!" Minnie yelped and although completely fatigued and bruised from her supposed 'therapeutic' body beating, pushed Monique aside and scrambled from the bed. "NO MORE, NO MORE!" she said, holding her hands up in surrender. "Please, no more!"

"Is good, yes?" Monique smiled, wiping her hands across her own voluptuous breasts.

"Oh marvellous," Minnie replied, not wanting a repeat of the sexually invasive pummelling as long as she lived. "Thank you, thank you so much. I believe I'm done."

Monique turned her attentions to the cowering Esther, who was almost completely concealed beneath the foaming lather. "You want massage?" she asked, brandishing the liniment.

Esther shook her head rigidly and jammed herself within the bathtub. "Thanks, but no thanks," she said, eyeing her breathless sister. "I'm fine as I am, thank you."

"Okay," Monique said, making for the door. "When you do, you tell me, yes? I come."

Before leaving she scooped a jug of water from a bucket beside the log burner and poured it over the iron top plate, sending a cloud of steam into the air. "Is good, yes?" she asked, tossing the jug down.

"Oh marvellous," Minnie said, struggling to stand. "It's just as I imagined." She also imagined Monique was not a woman to be trifled with, so thought it best to appease her with a white lie or two. "In fact the reviews hardly do it justice, dear."

Minnie hadn't read any of the reviews online. If she had then she may have rethought her choice of accommodation. In fact a scathing condemnation written by a group of backpacking Belgians was the reason for the chateau's reduction in visitors of late.

The Belgian party, mostly women, just like Minnie and Esther, had been pleasantly surprised by the quirky rest house, but the lack of promised facilities, the mysterious nocturnal noises and Monique's father's continuous lecherous advances caused them to cut their stay short and flee, utterly dissatisfied. Monique smiled and left the room to prepare dinner. "Has she gone?" Esther asked, emerging with a heap of bubbles on her head.

"I jolly well hope so!" Minnie moaned with a rosy glow all over. "Why didn't you help me, Essy?"

"Not likely!" Esther smirked, tugging the plug free and hoisting herself out of the tub. "God, I feel great," she said, stretching.

"If only I could say the same," Minnie said, grimacing. "I feel as though I've gone ten rounds with a mountain gorilla."

"Oh come on now, dear!" Esther laughed whilst throwing open the drapes. "OH GOOD GRIEF!" she then screamed on seeing Ludwik rooted to the spot in the opposite bay, staring back at her with a toothy grin. Snatching at the drapes, she quickly wrapped them around her naked body. "Minnie, that man!" she cried with her back to the wall.

"Oh yes." Minnie smiled, relishing the dose of karma. "I should have warned you, dear.

Esther peered cautiously around the window frame and received a polite wave from the randy onlooker. "The blighter's still there!" she exclaimed. "Minnie, dear, hand me my robe, quickly!"

"One moment, dear," Minnie replied, dressing. Considering the beating she had just taken she felt remarkably supple.

"Hurry, dear!" Esther said, daring to peep again "HEAVENS ABOVE!" she gasped, clutching her chest, having witnessed Ludwik, standing now in nothing but his underpants. "The filthy beast has no clothes on!"

"Really!" Minnie said, rushing to the window to see for herself. "Oh my word!" she too gasped, but unlike her sister Minnie, returned his gaze for a little longer.

"Minnie, what are you doing?" Esther snapped, inching along the wall. "Come away at once!"

"I tell you, dear." Minnie smiled, standing on tiptoe to see more of him. "He's in jolly good shape, jolly good. I mean even Cyril didn't have abs like that."

Although Ludwik was now a shadow of his former muscular self, there were still traces of a once formidable physique.

"Minnie!" her sister barked insistently. "I said come away, you'll give the twisted so-and-so the wrong idea!"

Esther snatched her robe and let the curtain fall back, obscuring Minnie's view. "Come dear," she said, grabbing her clothes and heading for the door. "That's quite enough of that."

Peshwari Nans

Minnie left with her sister with a devilish grin on her face, leaving Ludwik kicking at his wastepaper basket and in doing so stubbing his toe.

Sitting at their dressing tables the ladies preened themselves, firstly drying their hair with their towels. "He's obviously deranged," Esther remarked, still shaken at having seen Ludwik in the buff.

"Who, dear?" Minnie asked, slipping several bobby pins into her neatly brushed hair.

"You know exactly who!" Esther replied, looking across at her sister with a pin in her mouth. "That, that, peeping Thomas, that's who!"

"Oh him." Minnie smiled. "Oh I don't know, dear, the poor fellow can't help his carnal urges. After all, we are a couple of hotties now, aren't we?"

Esther failed to see the funny side. "Oh I'd help him," she sneered. "With a shot of bromide and a wooden ruler."

During their time at secondary school, if any lad was caught leering at the opposite sex his nether regions were briskly struck with a twelve-inch beech wood ruler to 'dampen his powder' as the head teacher would say.

The house bell rang to signal that dinner was about to be served and the sisters, now properly prepped, descended the stairs once again.

"Please, sit," Monique said at the head of her exquisitely laid out table. Minnie quickly sat at the opposite end, leaving only one chair free opposite Ludwik for her sister, who glared at her in return, knowing full well what she intended.

Lowering herself opposite the smiling gent, Esther did her utmost to avert her eyes. "This is lovely," she told Monique, remarking on the fine tableware. "It's not unlike our Royal Albert." She toyed with the gravy boat while Ludwik looked her up and down.

Peshwari Nans

"Quite lovely," Minnie agreed, tucking her serviette under her pearls.

"Soup," Monique said, ladling a quantity into her own bowl before passing the silver bowl clockwise to her father, who oddly enough never uttered a word again, an apparent side-effect of his life-changing fall in the garden.

"Mmmm it smells delicious," Minnie said when it was passed her way, with Ludwik stroking her hand in the process. "Thank you, dear," she said, smiling politely. "I don't believe I caught your name?"

"My father is mute," Monique said, speaking for him.

"Oh," Minnie said, open mouthed. "I see, I'm sorry I didn't know."

"Cream of mushroom is it?" Esther said, taking the bowl from her sister and changing the subject at the same time.

"Yes," Monique replied, producing one of the raw fungi from her pinnie pocket. "From our garden."

"Would you please pass the bread, dear?" Minnie said, eyeing a silver salver loaded with a thinly cut crusty cob.

During the first course Esther suddenly felt a shoeless foot brush against her inner calf and looked up from her bowl to see Ludwik grinning back at her whilst dunking his bread slowly and seductively. Esther snatched her leg back beneath her chair and stared wide eyed at her sister.

"How's your soup, dear?" Minnie asked, seeing her sister's face flushed. "Not too hot is it?"

"No, no the soup's fine," Esther said, her eyes flitting across to Ludwik.

"Jolly good, dear." Minnie smirked, savouring every moment of her sister's discomfort. "This is my sister Esther," she told Ludwik, much to her sister's horror. "She's a widow you know."

Peshwari Nans

"Minnie!" Esther said through gritted teeth whilst lashing out with her foot. "I doubt he wishes to know that."

But the news of Esther's apparent availability came as the most pleasant of surprises to the grinning gent, who straightened his tie and puffed out his chest yet again.

Esther was in the process of supping her soup when her sister asked Monique: "Does er, does your father work out by any chance?"

Esther spat the contents of her spoon back into her bowl with the unwanted vision of the near naked father in her head.

"He was Polish deadlift champion," Monique informed the ladies. "From 1970 to 1976, very strong man, very strong."

"Oooh I bet," Minnie said eyeing him again. "Did you hear that, dear?" she said to her mortified sister. "Deadlift champion. Isn't that something?"

Esther mopped her chin and cleared her throat. "What? Oh yes," she said, pushing her bowl away. "Yes that's em, really something alright."

"Show them, Father," Monique said, pointing to the grand piano in the corner of the room.

"Oh no, that won't be necessary, dear," Esther remarked, looking round at the half-ton instrument.

"Father, show them!" Monique insisted, prodding her father.

"Really, there is no need," Esther protested.

"Yes there is," Minnie added, relishing the spectacle.

Ludwik rose from the table, taking his cane from the back of his chair and shuffled, back bent, to one end of the piano.

"He'll hurt himself," Esther told a grinning Monique. "Please stop him."

Peshwari Nans

Minnie clapped her hands in anticipation as Ludwik set down his cane, and although his legs had been badly damaged, his lower back retained much of its former strength. Gripping the underside of the hulking piano, Ludwik crouched down.

"Oh this is silly." Esther laughed nervously. "Monique darling, there's no need for him to prove anything to us."

Taking several rapid deep breaths while eyeing the ladies Ludwik, with a grunt, a grimace and a groan, slowly raised one end of the piano off the floor.

"Good God!" Minnie gasped, dropping her spoon into her soup. "Essy, dear, the man's an ox!"

"Yes quite," Esther replied, marginally impressed herself.

Ludwik continued to raise the glossy black instrument until it was a full twenty centimetres from the carpet. He held it there until his arms began to shake and the veins on his forehead stood out.

"Thank you, Father," Monique told him, gesturing with her soup spoon for him to lower the piano, but Ludwik was eager to impress and maintained his grip, although he was turning a little blue in the face and grunting louder. "Enough, Father!" his daughter barked, tapping her spoon several times on the silver salver. Ludwik finally let the piano down with a thud and a chiming of keys, and, after straightening his back, retrieved his cane and crept back to the table.

"Well done!" Minnie cheered, pouring him a glass of water. "You must be positively pooped."

Monique lifted the lid of a large cooking pot that was in the centre of the table. "You like boar's head?" she asked.

Esther peered inside to see a complete boar's head surrounded by cabbage and potatoes. "Errrrrrm," she replied, instantly converting to vegetarianism. "Would you mind awfully if I just had the cabbage and potatoes?" she asked, not wanting to offend. "I'm veggie, you see."

"What?" Minnie said, pricking up her ears. "But we had corned beef yesterday, remember?"

"No, no, Minnie you're mistaken," Esther said, scowling. "I haven't eaten meat for quite some time."

"Well at least twelve hours, Essy dear," Minnie said, entirely unaware of her sister's intentions. "And not forgetting the baloney baguette we shared at the motorway services."

Monique and her father looked on as the sisters began a heated discussion with regards to Esther's culinary persuasion. "My dear!" Esther said, gritting her teeth. "As I said, you are mistaken. I truly believe it is morally and ethically wrong to eat the flesh of any of God's creatures."

"So, errr." Minnie smiled, the penny having finally dropped. "You won't be wanting any of the delicious parma ham we bought this morning then?"

"No," Esther said resolutely.

"Or the fois gras?" Minnie added, knowing full well that Vivien was packed with many of her sister's favourite edibles.

"Absolutely not!" Esther snapped, giving her teasing sister a loathing glare.

"Or the veal and ham pie?" Minnie chuckled.

"Oh shut up, Minnie!" Esther barked. "I'm a vegetarian and that's that!"

The revolting sight of the boiled boar's head did in fact give her cause to rethink her ethical stance.

"Well I'd love to try it," Minnie said, reaching for the pot. "Thank you, Monique."

Esther put her hand over her mouth while her sister fished around in the pot, hacking at the head with her knife and fork and loading her plate. Ludwik then reached inside and plucked an eye from its socket and popped it into his mouth.

"Oh God!" Esther cringed, having completely lost any appetite she may have had, and while Monique, Minnie and Ludwik tucked into their repulsive feast she toyed with a crust of bread, feeling altogether queasy and wishing for dinner to be over.

Minnie on the other hand was there to eat her fill and then some. "Mmmm you really should try this, Essy dear," she said, carving another slice.

Esther rose from the table. "Would you mind, Monique, if I took some air?" she asked.

"No, no, please go," her host told her, pointing the way to the rear door. "Go, see the garden for yourself."

"Thank you, do excuse me," Esther said politely. "Minnie dear, I'll see you when you've finished devouring that poor beast," she told her gorging sister.

"Okay, Essy darling." Minnie smiled, chewing an ear. "I'll be right out after dessert."

"Bon appétit," Esther said sarcastically in parting.

Leaving the dining room and passing through the kitchen, where the remainder of the disembowelled boar lay in quarters, Esther ventured outside, where the cool breeze ruffled the carrot and Brussel tops and toyed with the fallen leaves strewn in the kitchen garden. Esther walked along the rustic heavily worn red-brick pathways, running her hand lazily through scented lavender and coriander, tugging at a sage leaf and offering it to her nose. The chattering of a family of blue tits nesting in a dilapidated cedar greenhouse filled the air, as hungry open mouths were fed grubs, worms and damselflies. The three intertwining pathways each led towards a tall lilac hedge at the far end of the garden, the heady aroma of which was drawing Esther closer.

Peshwari Nans

On approach, the hedge seemed like an impenetrable barrier of contorted limbs and the lilac's distinctive heart-shaped leaves, but on closer inspection the living fortification was in fact a cleverly planted optical illusion, each plant overlapping the other to create a horticultural maze some forty feet thick. Like a moth to a flame Esther stepped inside, enticed by the hypnotic fragrant blooms. A pleasant form of narcosis gripped her and willed her on, first left then right with no end to be seen. The rustle of a rummaging vole in the leaf litter at her feet startled her at one point and the fluttering of a plump wood pigeon above sent a floating feather her way.

Turning three-hundred-and-sixty degrees, Esther could see no entrance nor exit, only the red brick path in its moss-covered state disappearing out of sight. Pressing on right, then twice left, through the thicket of lilac Esther suddenly gasped as an opening appeared, leading the would-be explorer to what could only be described as an enchanted oasis.

"Oh my!" she said, brushing a branch aside to stoop through. Right there was where the red-brick path ended and a velvety flower-strewn carpet of sweet grass began, soft as a downy pillow underfoot and the richest emerald green interspersed with sapphire and ruby perennial blooms.

Esther kicked off her shoes and plunged her feet into the cool and inviting grass, carefully navigating the daisies and plump bluebells and the foraging bees that bounced from bloom to bloom, their legs heavily laden with the plundered pollen.

Measuring exactly an acre, the hidden gem of a garden was bordered by sturdy oaks on three sides with rambling brambles and honeysuckle at their roots, forming a captivating corral, and just as the blue tits' chirping had accompanied the previous formal kitchen garden, so a turbulent babbling brook played the theme tune to this heavenly idyll. Entranced, Esther lowered herself onto a rock at the water's edge and dipped her toes into the gin-clear water, wincing at first at its immediate chilling effect, but soon her feet were submerged and swirling in lazy circles.

"Oh hello, gorgeous!" she then said, as a young muntjac deer stepped out through the brambles on the opposite side of the stream. The animal froze instantly on seeing her. As a regular visitor to the garden it was unaccustomed to sharing its watering hole.

"I won't hurt you," Esther said in a calming tone. The deer, who was a year or so old, sniffed the air, getting a faint whiff of Esther's lily-of-the-valley perfume, and took a cautionary step back.

"It's alright." Esther smiled. "It's fine, come on in."

The deer, although wary, eyed the thirst-quenching brook and stealthily crept forward.

"There you go," Esther said, watching its every move until it was within a few feet of her. It then lowered its head to drink whilst maintaining eye contact with the new garden invader.

"Oooh, you are thirsty, aren't you?" Esther said, leaning ever so slowly to scoop up a little water for herself. "Mmmm, so sweet," she added, wiping the drips from her chin with the back of her hand.

Soon having drunk its fill, the deer began to feel more at ease, sensing that Esther was no threat on the other side, and nestled down amongst the grass and chewed at the mosses therein.

Esther, with her skirt hitched up to her knees, sat captivated with her surroundings while brown and yellow butterflies danced and waltzed around her, and a cobalt-blue dragonfly balanced over the water on a bending reed. Closing her eyes, she took a deep breath as if to taste the natural beauty like a fine wine. But at the point when she thought she'd never ever want to leave, her sister's shrill voice rang out from beyond the lilacs:

"ESTHERRRRRRR! ESTHERRRRRRRRR!" her sister called, causing the muntjac deer to spring to its feet and flee to the relative safety of the bramble forest.

"ESTHER? WHERE ARE YOU?" Minnie called.

"IN HERE!" Esther called back, a little miffed to say the least.

"WHERE'S IN HERE?" Minnie yelled, stepping into the maze. "ESTHERRRR?"

"Alright, I'm coming!" Esther sighed, lifting her feet from the water. "Damn you," she mouthed, trudging back to the lilacs. "Follow my voice, dear!" she told her sister.

"Esther, Estherrrr!" Minnie cried, somewhat disorientated, turning this way and that. "Esther? I'm lost for Pete's sake! ESSYYY?"

"Calm down, Minnie dear!" Esther laughed. "I'm close by!"

"I know but I can't see you!" Minnie said, frantic at this point turning into a dead end. "OH ESSYYYYY!" she wailed, "What is this place?"

"It's magical, believe me!" Esther replied turning this way and thay and eventually appearing behind her sister. "This way Minnie dear."

"Oh there you are, Essy!" Minnie said, hugging her sister tightly. "What is this place, for heaven's sake?"

"Follow me," Esther said, taking her sister's hand and leading her to the heavenly secret garden.

"Oh my, Essy!" Minnie too gasped on setting eyes on the enchanted enclosure. "Essy, where are we?"

"I don't know, and quite frankly I don't care," her sister replied, making her way back to the stream. "Take off your shoes, dear," she told Minnie, taking her place on her rock and once again plunging her feet into the cooling water. "Come on in," she beckoned.

"Oooh, yes," Minnie said, joining her and kicking at the swirling current. "Oh Essy, this is simply wonderful."

"Shhhhhh," Esther whispered with a finger to her lips, seeing the fleeting figure of the deer amongst the brambles. "Watch."

Sure enough the yearling put its head out at and sniffed the air once more.

"Oh how beautiful, Essy," Minnie said under her breath.

"Yes I know," Esther agreed, coaxing the animal. "Come on darling, yes that's right, we won't hurt you, you know that, don't you?"

The muntjac deer approached with caution and again settled down, looking across at the sisters with its huge doey eyes whilst flicking its ears to disturb the irritating damselflies.

"Quite remarkable," Minnie exclaimed, slowly taking the tablet from her shoulder bag to capture the breathtaking image.

"Isn't it just?" Esther agreed. The sisters held hands and kicked their feet in the water until the light began to fade, and the deer took one last bite at the grass before clambering awkwardly to its feet and turning for the woods. "Good night," Esther called softly after it, and after a flick of its stunted tail the animal was gone once again and the sisters reluctantly left the tranquil stream.

"Can we come back tomorrow?" Minnie asked.

"I don't see why not, dear," her sister replied, keen to visit this little slice of heaven again.

"Did you find it?" Monique asked from the kitchen door.

"Indeed we did, dear." Esther smiled, leading her sister through the vegetable garden. "Indeed we did."

Peshwari Nans

Ludwik stood behind his daughter, daring not to venture outside but greeting Esther and Minnie with a lustful smile.

"Ludwik," Minnie said politely in passing, avoiding his wandering hand.

"Oooh you cheeky beast!" Esther snapped, swatting the same hand from her bottom.

"Father!" Monique said, tugging Ludwik back through the kitchen. "How many times? How many times must I tell you about this?"

Ludwik looked every bit the scolded child, but was leering over his shoulder all the same.

"You want nightcap?" Monique asked the sisters once she had safely stowed her father in his drawing-room chair.

"Oh no thank you," Esther said, raising her hand.

"Oooh yes please!" Minnie chirped. "Have you any sweet sherry?"

"Sherry?" Monique said, looking down her nose. "We do not have this, sherry. We drink vodka!"

"No, Minnie," Esther warned. "I forbid it."

"Oh Essy." Minnie smiled. "Come on dear, live a little."

"Minnie!" her sister snapped. "The last time we 'lived a little' as you call it, we spent the night hacking our way through a dense and dark forest at the mercy of the fiercest of God's creatures, so no we'll pass on the spirit thank you, Monique."

"Er, we'll take two please, Monique," Minnie said, ignoring her sister's sensible persuasion.

"Minnie, I said no!" Esther again protested.

"Oh silence, Essy!" Minnie barked. "Why on earth shouldn't we?"

"Yes, but—" Esther replied, struggling for any form of retort. "Minnie, we simply shouldn't, that's all."

"Two please," Minnie told their host, who disappeared downstairs to the basement.

Peshwari Nans

"Helloooooo!" Esther called several moments later when Monique failed to return. "Cooooeeeeee, you really needn't bother, Monique!"

"I have it," Monique said, appearing shortly afterwards with two dust-covered litre bottles of a clear spirit minus any labelling. "Vodka."

"Really?" Esther said, unconvinced.

"Oh it's just a nightcap, dear," Minnie told her sister to allay her fears.

But exactly one hour later the two of them were sitting at the kitchen table howling with laughter, and topping one another's shot glasses repeatedly up to the brim, toasting just about anything toastable, having exhausted the obvious.

"Here's to Garibaldi biscuits!" Minnie slurred. "And, and, and, and the Royal Albert," she added, toasting their tea set.

"Royal Albert!" Monique exclaimed. "Ahhh I have this." She left the table and opened the cupboard of a large French dresser to reveal her extensive china collection.

"Yes, that's it!" Esther said, raising her glass as did her sister. "Here's to the Royal Albert!" they both cried before draining their glasses.

Monique took three of her floral teacups and filled them with generous measures of her vodka: one for each of them. "Oooh now you're talking, dear," Minnie said, sipping with her pinky finger outstretched. "This really is rather refreshing," she added, licking her lips. "Is it locally produced?"

"Yes, I make," Monique told them.

"You!" Esther said examining the bottles "What, here?"

"Yes, come, I show you," Monique replied, leading the tipsy sisters to the basement stairs. "Careful it is steep," she warned them, gripping the handrail herself.

Peshwari Nans

"Hold me, dear," Minnie told her sister, a little unsteady on her feet.

A single flickering twenty-five watt bulb hung from the rafters above them, barely illuminating the dusty dank basement. "Mind your step, dear," Esther said, helping her sister down from the broken bottom tread. "Oh my!" she then gasped at seeing some five hundred or so bottles stacked in wooden apple crates from floor to ceiling.

"You made all this?" Minnie asked. "But, but, how?"

"I show," Monique said, leading the ladies through the cluttered basement that was littered with discarded furniture and rusting garden implements, to her huge copper still. "This is Clara," she told them, having lovingly named her illicit contraption.

"My word!" Minnie said, in awe of the network of copper and iron piping encircling the room. The still hissed and gurgled as the precious spirit that was produced dripped ever so slowly from one end and then stopped as she so often did.

"Damn you, Clara!" Monique cursed, picking up a heavy wrench and beating the loosely-fastened pipes, the sound of which reverberated through the entire house and appeared to be the obvious root cause of the previous tenants' sleepless nights and consequently their scathing reviews of the Secret Garden Chateau.

Esther took a moment to process Monique's clandestine operation. "Now hang on a minute," she said, backing away. "There are laws against this sort of thing, aren't there? I mean look at the likes of Al Capone during the prohibition era. He went to prison for his felonious activities. No, no, no, I want no part of this, it's nothing more than a hillbilly moonshine operation. Come, Minnie dear, before we're tarred with the same brush."

"No, no, you do not understand," Monique said in her defence. "I make for the orphanage in Niwiska."

241

"The orphanage!" Esther exclaimed. "You mean you give it to the children for heaven's sake? Dear God, woman, is there no end to your depravity? Minnie pack your things, we're leaving at once!"

"No, please!" Monique begged. "I sell to raise money for the children. Please, I explain."

"Hang on, Essy dear," Minnie said, breaking away from her sister's grasp. "What do you mean you sell it for the children, Monique? Why on earth would you need to do this?"

"Government," Monique told them. "They refuse to fund Saint Augustine's because many of the children are Roma, gypsies if you wish, abandoned as infants, sometimes at the roadside."

"Yes, but they're children," Minnie said, aghast. "Whether or not they are Roma or royalty, first and foremost they are children, innocent children."

"Why are they abandoned?" Esther asked, her tone changing somewhat. "Who would do such a thing?"

"Many are crippled," Monique explained. "Or possibly they have the Downs and are considered undesirable."

"Oh that's awful, how could they?" Minnie said, having seen at first-hand how loving and adorable someone with the Down's Syndrome can be. On occasion she had cared for her former neighbour's six-year-old Down's Syndrome son, Peter, who had the broadest of smiles and gave the warmest of hugs.

"Undesirable?" Esther said, her blood beginning to boil. "I'll give them undesirable! And you say your government do nothing to help them?"

"Nothing," Monique said, hanging her head. "So I make the vodka, an old family recipe. I know it is wrong but what am I to do? The children, they must eat."

Peshwari Nans

"I think it's very admirable of you," Minnie told their host. "And the vodka is jolly good," she added, both sisters still very much inebriated.

"Yes it is," Monique agreed. "The Russians come and give me good price and I buy food and clothing for the orphanage."

Minnie clutched her chest, touched by Monique's devotion and generosity. "Oh Monique, you are a saint, darling," she told her.

"Yes, yes, I quite agree," Esther added. "And I'm sorry for doubting you, it's just a crying shame that you must resort to such measures to ensure their survival."

"I have no choice," Monique said, beating at the piping once again. "CLARA NOT NOW!" she yelled, bringing the aging contraption back to life with a liberal beating.

"I tell you what." Minnie smiled, taking out her purse. "We'll take two cases, and we'll pay double the going rate for them too, I insist."

"Minnie!" Esther said, hesitant and well aware of the fraudulent implications. "If we're caught with it we'll be clamped in irons and thrown into a rat infested cell for the remainder of our days."

"Oh nonsense, dear." Minnie laughed. "Please excuse my sister Monique, she has what you might call an extremely vivid imagination. Like I said, we'll take two cases."

"But, but," Esther slurred, objecting adamantly.

"Quiet Essy!" Minnie insisted. "After all, it is for the children, am I right?"

"Well, well, yes I suppose so." Esther was forced to agree.

"And it isn't exactly unpleasant, is it dear?" Minnie continued fighting Monique's corner.

"No, no, you're right about that, dear," Esther again agreed, her argument now in tatters. "I was simply concerned about the possible ramifications of our purchase, that's all."

"My dear," Minnie said, looking her sister in the eye. "The only ramifications that should concern us are whether those darling children receive three square meals a day, a warm bed and a roof above their heads, don't you agree?"

Esther paused for a moment, steadying herself. "Yes you're quite right," she eventually said. "Two cases it is please Monique, and like my charming sister said, we'll pay double the price and not a farthing less."

"Thank you." Monique smiled. "Thank you so much, and bless you for your kindness, I will tell the children of you."

"Yes, you do that," Esther told her. "And be sure to give them our love too."

Esther and Minnie left Monique pounding at Clara's pipes, cursing in Polish as she did so. Helping one another up the rickety stairs, the swaying sisters made their way back to their room, passing Ludwik in the corridor, who in his knee-length paisley nightgown attempted to lure them into his bedchamber with a beckoning finger and a devilish grin. The intoxicated ladies merely burst out laughing, with their shoes in their hands like a pair of parting teens returning home from a night on the town. Saying nothing as usual, Ludwik stormed back into his room and slammed the door—spurned yet again.

"Those poor children," Minnie said, wrestling with her nightie. "Oh Essy dear, I'm stuck!" she then cried, with her head trapped inside the garment. "Help me, dear, please!"

"Stand still, dear!" Esther said, following her bumbling sister around the room as she careered into her dressing table in a blind panic. Esther grappled with her sister's nightdress, which she had inadvertently transformed into an escapologist's straightjacket.

"I said, stand still dear!" she said, getting to grips and firstly freeing an arm.

"Oh thank heavens." Minnie sighed, once she was released. "I do believe I've put on weight, dear."

"I'm not surprised," Esther scoffed. "What with the shrimp paste, Garibaldis and now the Polish boar's head."

"Oooh yes," Minnie said, licking her lips. "And not to mention dessert, dear, you left so I had yours too. It was a cranberry tartlet with hot cinnamon custard, oh Essy it was simply divine, it really was."

"I had to leave, dear," Esther replied, slipping into her side of the four-poster bed. "I couldn't bear the sight of that poor creature's head looking up at me from the pot. That and being violated by Ludwik's foraging feet, that awful man—he's like a perishing horny toad."

"Well I think, dear," Minnie said, slipping in beside her and pulling the blankets up around her chin, "as the Americans say, he just needs to 'get laid'."

"Oh, how revolting, dear!" Esther said, turning up her nose at such a thought.

"Well I think he's rather sweet, dear," Minnie confessed. "And after all, he is considerably younger than us."

"I don't care," Esther said, turning out the bedside lamp. "You're not to go near him, do you hear me? I expressly forbid it."

"Yes, dear," Minnie replied, punching her pillow into shape and settling down. "Of course, dear."

The sisters slept soundly in their stately bed, in fact more soundly than they'd slept in quite a while, numb from the neck down from Monique's home-brewed spirit.

"Morning, dear," Minnie said at around eight-thirty next morning, busying herself around the room when her sister opened an eye. "I don't know about you, Essy, but I feel absolutely marvellous this morning." She began to whistle as she folded her nightclothes.

Peshwari Nans

Esther paused for a moment, waiting for the throbbing in her head to begin but oddly enough it did not. "I er, I don't understand it, Minnie," she said, sitting up in bed and feeling no ill-effects whatsoever from their previous night's overindulgence. "I feel fine too. It's quite uncanny."

"Isn't it just, dear?" Minnie agreed, positively floating around the room. It seemed that the pure brewed spirit which contained no factory-added preservatives left the consumer without the slightest trace of a hangover. In fact the miracle spirit did quite the opposite. "I feel I could run a mile at the moment, darling," Minnie said, jogging on the spot.

Once dressed the sisters made their way downstairs for tea and hot buttered wholemeal toast. "Can we visit the garden again before we leave?" Minnie asked, longing to feel the cool clear water tumbling around her feet once more.

"Yes of course, dear," Esther replied, taking two carrots from the vegetable basket. "We can feed that delightful deer while we're there."

"Morning!" Monique then said, appearing from the basement with their two cases of spirit. "I will put in your car," she told the sisters.

"Good lord, have you been down there all night?" Minnie asked. "I mean we didn't hear a thing. We slept like newborn babies, didn't we dear?"

"We certainly did, dear," Esther agreed. "Whatever's in those bottles of yours is an instant cure for insomnia, that's for sure."

"Yes, quite," Minnie chirped. "And I leapt out of bed like a thoroughbred without an ache or a crick in my neck! It's the elixir of life, dear, that's what it is, the elixir of life."

"Yes, what's the secret?" Esther asked, feeling tickety boo herself.

Peshwari Nans

"It is the water," Monique explained. "From the stream. My father says it makes him feel half his age, with the stamina of a rutting buck."

"That explains it then," Esther joked, having been the focus of Ludvik's roving eye ever since she'd arrived. "The man's incorrigible."

"Oh look, dear!" Minnie then exclaimed, spying an artist's easel leaning in the corner of the kitchen. "You used to paint, didn't you?"

"Yes, that's right," Esther replied, recalling her early years when she'd sit and paint the daffodils and tulips in Victoria Park in the East End of London.

"I still have one of yours," Minnie confessed. "Monique, do you have water colours? My sister is really rather good you know."

"No Minnie I'm not, and Monique please don't bother yourself," Esther said, raising a hand. "At best I'm a rank amateur."

"Nonsense, dear!" Minnie protested. "I recall you sold several of your pieces at the church bazaar and even featured in the *Tower Hamlets Gazette* on one occasion."

"Well that hardly makes me a Constable or a Turner, does it dearest?" Esther replied abruptly. "No Minnie, my painting days are well and truly over I'm afraid."

"The water colours, Monique?" Minnie said, looking over her spectacles at their host.

"Yes, I have this," Monique replied, taking a paint-spattered box from her cupboard and opening it on the kitchen table to reveal several brushes, a palette and an array of paints.

"See Essy?" Minnie smiled. "You can paint the secret garden. That way we can take it with us wherever we go. Oh please say you will, dear, *pleeeeease*?"

Esther had seen that persistent look on her sister's face many times before and knew that any attempt at opting out would indeed be futile. "Do we have to do this, Minnie dear?" she asked with one last-ditch attempt to get out of it.

"Yes dear, we do," Minnie said, gathering up the easel and box. "Come along, Essy, I know once you get started you'll feel right at home again."

"Ohhhh, Minnie," Esther moaned, following her sister out into the kitchen garden.

"Look dear, the light is perfect," Minnie added, struggling with the cumbersome easel.

"Here, let me take that," her sister said, intervening.

"That's the spirit!" Minnie smiled, tossing the canvas box strap over her shoulder and making for the lilac hedge. "You lead the way, dear," she told Esther. "It's like a damned rabbit warren in there."

Esther confidently remembered the series of lefts and rights to bring them swiftly to the concealed garden.

Meanwhile, Ludwik had watched from his bedroom window, stamping his feet when they disappeared out of sight into the hedge, but he had a plan. Retrieving a pair of antiquated binoculars from his dressing-table drawer, the lustful Ludwik slid the heavy piece of walnut furniture across the polished floor to the window bay, grunting and groaning in the process. Then, with the aid of a crimson velour footstool, he clambered up on top, unsteady to say the least. Removing the leather lens caps from the binoculars Ludwik scanned the flowering hedge until he discovered the smallest of gaps, which partially closed from time to time as the subtle breeze toyed with the heavily laden branches. With his tongue hanging from the side of his mouth, Ludwik could just make out the sisters' figures on the other side, as he shuffled from left to right, tugging his curtains aside.

"God, it's simply divine, dear, isn't it?" Minnie remarked, kicking her shoes into the air.

Peshwari Nans

"Divine is definitely the word," Esther replied, standing the easel up and approaching the stream, where she stood breaking the carrots into bite-sized pieces and tossing them to the opposite bank. "Minnie, what on earth are you doing?" she asked, turning to see her sister stripping and discarding her clothes. "It's a little chilly to go skinny dipping, don't you think?"

"I want you to paint me nude," Minnie said, wrestling with her heavily elasticated underwear.

"What?" Esther exclaimed. "Don't be ridiculous, Minnie, put your clothes on for heaven's sake!"

Minnie tossed her bra over her shoulder. "Cyril and I once modelled at night school," she informed her bewildered sister. "They gave us tea, biscuits and five pounds each. Oh please, Essy, we're quite alone here, aren't we, dear?"

"Out of the question," Esther said adamantly, tossing the remainder of the carrots across the stream and kicking off her own shoes. "I don't know what's got into you lately Minnie, I really don't," she added.

Minnie, who was now completely naked, approached her sister, paintbox in hand. "Here," she said, thrusting it into her sister's hands. "I know you can do it. There's your easel thingy, here are your paints. I'll fetch you some water." She took a bean tin from the box and, crouching down, filled it from the swirling stream.

"Minnie, no!" Esther said, offering the box back. "I won't do it, it's not right, look at you for God's sake!"

"Why, what's wrong with me?" Minnie asked, looking down at her tired and sagging body. "I'll admit I'm no Grace Kelly, but I assure you, Essy I'm all woman, and I want to be painted as such before I shuffle off this mortal coil. Please, Essy, it would mean so much to me."

While Minnie stood without a stitch on, Ludwik could only make out her sister's frame beside the stream.

"But I've only ever done landscapes," Esther explained. "Minnie dear, I simply wouldn't know where to begin."

"With my muffins if you like," Minnie joked, lifting her breasts, which brought a smile to her sister's face.

"Muffins!" She laughed. "They're more like a pair of pitta breads, dear, I can remember when your chest could turn heads from Whitechapel to Westminster. God I was envious of you back then."

Minnie's face dropped as she let her aged breasts fall. "You're right, dear, what was I thinking?" she said, turning to gather her clothes. "I'm a damn fool that's what I am. Forgive me, dear."

Esther's heart immediately sank, recalling her own former taught physique. "Minnie, you are still a fine looking woman," she told her sister. "Look at you? You still have all your faculties, and your bottom, dear, it's as pert as a peach, I swear it."

"Thank you," Minnie said, reaching for her bra. "But I'll cover up all the same. I've embarrassed myself enough for one day."

"Alright, I'll do it!" Esther agreed. "But I must warn you it could be more Picasso than Rembrandt."

"You will?" Minnie squealed, ditching her clothes once again.

Ludwik craned his eager neck but could only catch a fleeting glimpse of an ankle, unaware of the positive 'flesh fest' that accompanied it.

"Where would you like me, dear?" Minnie asked, standing there in the buff.

"Beside the stream, dear," Esther directed her. "Sit down with your hair to one side. That's it, make yourself comfortable, this could take some time. Oh and I don't mind the muffins, dear, but I must insist you cover your crumpet."

Peshwari Nans

"Alright, dear." Minnie smirked, plucking a handful of bluebells and strategically placing them between her legs. "How's that?"

"Like the goddess Aphrodite herself," Esther said, putting her subject at ease. "Now please try to remain still, dear."

Settling at the easel, Esther arranged her paints on the palette and dipped her brush into the bean tin. "Okay, here goes," she said, a little apprehensive to say the least. "Oh look!" she then said, whilst setting out Minnie's basic outline.

Minnie glanced over her shoulder to see the friendly deer emerge from the wood, following the trail of carrot morsels before sitting on its hindquarters. "He's posing too, dear." Minnie smiled.

Mixing shades of pastel greens, blues and pinks, Esther soon picked up where she'd left off so many years previously, capturing the bluebells to a tee. "Go away!" she then snapped, as a buzzing bee circled her head.

"How's it looking, dear?" Minnie asked, her aching back seizing in position ever so slightly.

"I'm not happy with the composition, dear," Esther said, frustrated at her efforts, which by amateur standards were really rather good—she had captured her sister's wistful smile perfectly. "Will you please go away?" she again told the irritating bee.

Frustrated beyond belief, Ludwik eventually climbed down from his dresser and pushed it breathlessly back into place, tossing his binoculars onto the bed with a disgruntled sigh.

Adding the finishing touches to her watercolour, Esther rattled the brushed in the bean tin of water. "OW!" she then squealed as the bee settled on her neck, became entangled in her hair and in a panic stung her. "OW, OW!"

"Essy, are you alright?" Minnie asked, sitting upright and straightening her aching back as the deer bolted for cover.

"That blasted bee!" Esther stormed, rocking back and clutching her neck.

Minnie clambered to her feet, discarding the now wilted bluebells. "Essy, dear!" she said, approaching her rocking sister. "Essy, are you alright?"

Esther dropped onto one knee, feeling a little light-headed. "I, I, can't breathe!" she cried, with a hand clawing at her throat. "Min I can't breathe!"

"Oh Essy!" her sister shrieked. "Whatever's happened?"

Esther, having never before been a victim of a bee sting, was unaware that she was one of an unfortunate few to have a disastrous reaction known in the medical profession as 'Anaphylaxis'.

"Minnie, help me!" she croaked, grabbing at her throat, which was swelling rapidly.

"Oh Essy, I don't know what to do, dear!" Minnie cried, dropping to her side.

Esther's entire face had also begun to swell. "Get help Min, get help!" she said, clinging to her sister's hand. "Hurry, dear!"

"Yes, yes, of course" Minnie replied in a state of sheer panic. "But, but I don't want to leave you, Essy—"

"—Go Min, go please!" Esther said, rolling on her side onto the grass.

"Oh yes, dear, I will," Minnie said rubbing her sister's hand. "Oh dear gods, please hang on, Essy darling," she called back, making for the lilac hedge. "I'll be right back Essy, right back, I promise!"

Once inside the garden, Minnie, still very much naked as the day she was born, dashed this way and that, making several wrong turns and growing increasingly exasperated. "Oh hell, HELL!" she cursed, before stumbling across the exit. "MONIQUE, MONIQUE HELLLLLP!" she screamed. "MONIQUE!"

Ludwik hurried back to his window, having given up the ghost, grabbing his binoculars in passing. Then seeing Minnie with, as Esther described them, her 'pitta breads' swaying from side to side, he was immediately shocked to his very core, with the belief that all of his Christmases had suddenly come at once.

"MONIQUE!" Minnie again cried, rushing between the rhubarb and radishes until the chateau owner opened the kitchen door.

"What? Why are you like this?" Monique asked, stunned at Minnie's brazen appearance.

"Never mind!" Minnie said breathlessly. "My sister, my sister Essy, she's in trouble, please come quick!"

"What's wrong with her?" Monique asked.

"Please hurry!" Minnie replied, starting back through the vegetable garden, giving the stunned Ludwik a bird's eye view of her quivering bottom.

"WAIT, WHAT IS WRONG?" Monique asked, starting after her, bemused at her nudity. "And where are your clothes?" she asked, entering the lilac hedge.

"PLEASE HURRY!" Minnie cried, having now memorized the route through. "ESSY, ESSY, I BROUGHT MONIQUE!" she called to her sister, who lay wheezing on the grass, her airways gradually reducing due to the swelling.

"What happened?" Monique asked, dropping beside Esther and lifting her head. "What is wrong?"

"A bee," Esther cried, gesturing to her red and swollen neck.

"Bee?" Monique said, examining the affected area. "Be still!" she told Esther abruptly.

With her thumbnail and finger she quickly flicked the throbbing sting from her neck, but much of the damage

253

had already been done. "We should get her to the house," she told Minnie, scooping Esther up in her strong arms and racing back as best she could.

Minnie hurriedly gathered her things and ran after them, semi-dressed. "Will she be alright?" she asked Monique, brushing past the supported runner beans. "Monique, will she be alright?"

"I don't know why she is like this," Monique confessed, turning Esther through the kitchen door. "It was only a bee after all." Laying Esther on the chaise longe, Monique loosened her clothing and ran to the kitchen sink to fetch some water.

"Oh Essy, dear," Minnie said, fretting at her sister's side. "I never knew you had an allergy, dearest, I'm sorry but I don't know what to do."

Esther shook her head, now unable to speak as Monique hurried back, pushing Minnie aside. Firstly she held Esther's head and poured a quantity of water into her mouth to lubricate her sensitive throat.

"I must go for the doctor," she told Minnie. "Stay with her. Give her water."

"Yes, yes, yes of course," Minnie replied, sitting beside her stricken sister. "I never knew, I never knew, Essy," she kept saying.

"Here," Monique said, pouring a liberal amount of vinegar onto a tea towel. "Put this on her neck, it will help with the pain."

An old home remedy for bee and wasp stings, the acid in the vinegar counteracts the powerful alkaline in the insect's sting.

Esther face was now almost unrecognizable, her eyes red and puffed up to near bursting, and her normally wrinkled skin taught.

Peshwari Nans

"God, Essy dear, hang on! Monique's gone for the doctor," Minnie told her, rubbing her sister's hand vigorously. "She'll be back before you know it, I'm sure."

Minnie really hadn't a clue how long Monique would be or even how far the doctor was from the chateau, which was remotely situated a mile or more from the nearest village. "It'll be alright," she said repeatedly. "Here, have some more water, please Essy try to drink, Essy it's for your own good, dear."

Suddenly Ludwik appeared at her side, peering over her shoulder. "Oh, go away!" Minnie said, suspecting his philandering intentions. "Can't you see this really isn't the time?"

Ludwik pointed a shaking finger at Esther and, although he hadn't spoken in several years, cleared his throat and muttered, "Adrenalin!"

"What?" Minnie asked, looking round. "I told you this isn't the time! Now please will you go away?"

"Adrenalin!" Ludwik again said insistently. "Adrenalin, for her!"

"What are you talking about?" Minnie said, in no mood for interruptions. "What do you mean, Adrenalin?"

Having said this, Ludwik turned and disappeared.

"Wait!" Minnie called after him. "What did you mean?"

But Ludwik hurried upstairs to his room and rummaged in his chest of drawers for his EpiPen auto-injectors. He himself was allergic to the smallest of bites.

"Adrenalin!" he said, appearing behind Minnie. "For her, Esther, adrenalin!"

"Are you sure?" Minnie asked, eyeing the injector. But with her sister's face turning from crimson to white she had no choice but to trust Ludwik. "What do I do?" she said, taking the EpiPen from him.

"There, there!" Ludwik said, pointing to her thigh with a stabbing motion.

"Really?" Minnie asked, unsure and looking around for Monique, who had only just arrived at the doctor's house, a kilometre away.

"There!" Ludwik insisted with a genuine sense of urgency.

"Alright!" Minnie said, hesitating at first, not wanting to hurt her beloved sister. But Ludwik grasped Minnie's hand and plunged it into Esther's right thigh.

"Oh, oh, I'm sorry Essy!" Minnie cried, seeing her sister writhing on the couch. "Sorry, sorry dear. Ludwik, what have you done?" she asked abruptly.

"Wait!" Ludwik told her. "We wait."

Sure enough, Esther's breathing steadied somewhat and her heaving chest slowed. But she was far from well.

"Essy? How are you feeling, dear?" Minnie asked, but got no response. Esther could barely see through her eyes' narrow slits, but felt for her sister's hand. "I'm here, dear," Minnie told her. "I'm here."

Monique arrived shortly afterwards with the local doctor in tow, carrying his black medical bag. "Oh thank heavens," Minnie said, moving aside.

"Doctor Slavi," Monique said, introducing him.

"Hello, Doctor," Minnie said as he took out his stethoscope and listened at Esther's rasping chest.

"A bee?" he asked Minnie.

"Yes that's right, on the neck I believe," Minnie informed him wringing her hands. "I had no idea she was allergic, you see Doctor."

Doctor Slavi picked up the spent injector. "You give her this?" he asked.

"Yes we did, Ludwik and I," Minnie confessed. "Should we not have?"

"Yes, yes, you should, this is good," the doctor smiled. "Adrenalin is very good for her." The doctor had prescribed Ludwik the remedy himself, having treated the family for many years.

"Yes, yes, Slavi," Ludwik added, much to his daughter's surprise.

"Father!" she said, with a hand to her mouth. "Father! You speak!"

"Yes he does," Minnie piped up. "And I'm jolly glad of it I can tell you. Thank you Ludwik, thank you. What now, doctor?" she asked. "How long till my sister fully recovers?"

"She must rest," Doctor Slavi insisted, handing Monique a brown bottle of pills. "Monique give her these three times a day, without fail, do you hear?"

"Yes of course, Doctor," she replied, fearing yet another scathing review from her latest guests. "I am so sorry," she told Minnie, taking her hand.

"Oh don't be silly, dear," Minnie said, mustering a smile. "By no means is this your fault. It was an accident, and I fear the culprit has already paid the ultimate price."

The bee surely perished after leaving its sting in Esther's neck, having only one in its arsenal, unlike its savage counterpart the wasp, who was armed to the teeth, able to inflict pain and suffering at a whim with reckless abandon.

"Thank you, Doctor," Minnie said, wringing her hands. "For coming so quickly, I mean."

"It was Ludwik who saved your friend," the doctor replied, packing his bag. "Not me."

"She's my sister," Minnie informed him. "But you're right she's my friend too, my best friend for that matter, so I'm eternally grateful to the both of you, eternally grateful indeed."

She turned to Monique's father, who was leaving the room. "Ludwik," she said, approaching and embracing the quick-thinking gent, "You, sir, are a star, an absolute star, do you hear?"

Ludwik smiled, his hand slipping to Minnie's lower back tantalizingly close to her bottom. But before he could venture further, she broke away to be with her sister. "We should put her to bed at once, Monique dear," she then said, wanting the very best for her sister, who lay there, delirious and moaning,

"Yes, yes, of course," Monique said, lifting Esther once again. "Excuse me, Father," she added, passing the doddery Ludwik in the hall. "We will speak later, yes?" she told him, still somewhat stunned at him finding his voice after so long.

"Yes my dear." Ludwik smiled, eyeing Minnie's rear as she followed Monique up the stairs to their room.

"Thank you, dear," Minnie told the chateau owner as she drew the blankets up to her sister's chin. "Thank you so much, I don't know what I'd have done without you and your father, I really don't."

"I will fetch soup later," Monique said, leaving the sisters. "You have water, yes?"

"Oh yes, dear," Minnie replied, pouring Esther a glass from her bedside jug.

That evening while her sister slept, Minnie dined with Ludwik and his daughter, although her appetite wasn't what it usually was, not by a long chalk.

"You should eat," Monique said, witnessing Minnie stirring her soup in a daze. "You need to be strong for your sister when she wakes. Come on, eat."

"Yes you're quite right, Monique," Minnie said, raising her spoon and rewarding Ludwik with a flirtatious smile, for which he was extremely grateful.

CHAPTER SIX

With the morning sunlight creeping slowly across her face Esther stirred, pushed back the bed sheets a tad and opened her eyes, squinting in doing so.

"Essy!" Minnie gasped, dashing to close the slit in the drapes to shield her sister's eyes. "Oh Essy you're awake I've been so terribly worried." Minnie had hardly slept a wink that night, lying at her sister's side watching her breathe and call for Jack in a state of delirium.

"Yes, morning, Minnie," Esther said with a dry mouth. "Would you be a dear and pour me a glass of water, please?"

"Of course, of course," Minnie said, hurrying to her bedside cabinet. "Oh Essy, I'm so glad you're alright. How do you feel?"

"I feel fine, Min," her sister said, sitting up, although she did feel slightly groggy. "What, what time is it?" she asked, assuming she'd slept for an hour or so.

"Ten-fifteen, dear," Minnie said carefully, placing the glass in her sister's hand. "There," she added, handing Esther a tablet. "You're to take one of these too, dear, Dr Slavi's orders I'm afraid."

"Dr who?" Esther asked, popping the pill into her mouth as requested.

"Slavi, dear," Minnie informed her. "You don't remember do you? Monique went to fetch him after the accident."

"Oh, right," Esther said, none the wiser.

There was a knock at the bedroom door and Monique entered, carrying a tray of toast and poached eggs. "Ahhh good morning." She smiled, setting the breakfast down. "Tell me, how are you feeling?"

"Yes, fine thank you," Esther said, reaching for a slice of toast. "Minnie here tells me you brought the doctor to me. It seems I owe you a debt of gratitude, my dear."

Ludwik then entered the room, carrying a posy of wild flowers.

"Good heavens, it's that awful man," Esther told her sister. "Get rid of him, will you please?"

"No dear, you don't understand," Minnie said, greeting Ludwik. "Ludwik here saved your life, Essy," she told the frowning Esther. "If he hadn't acted when he did with the adrenalin, Dr Slavi said you could quite easily have died."

"Saved my life?" Esther exclaimed. "You mean—"

"—Yes dear," Minnie said as Ludwik handed her sister the flowers that he had picked, having also ventured outside for the first time since his own unfortunate incident. It seemed that Esther's brush with death had been the catalyst to his own 'rebirth', so to speak.

"Be careful of the bees," he told her with a smile. "You and I are the same."

Esther was overcome with emotion and guilt at having been so horrid to Ludwik. "Thank you," she simply said, cradling the flowers. "Thank you, Ludwik."

"Are you well enough to travel, dear?" Minnie asked, having packed their cases.

"Yes of course," Esther said, placing the breakfast tray across her legs. "I told you, I feel fine."

"Good," Minnie said, looking out of the window. "Because we've lost a little time since you've been unwell."

"A little time?" Esther said in between bites. "How long have I been asleep for heaven's sake?"

"Three days," Minnie informed her. "You had us all extremely worried, my dear."

"Three days!" Esther gasped, dropping her toast into her tea. "I can't have! Three days? Well why didn't you wake me, Minnie dear?"

Peshwari Nans

"Esther you were sick!" Minnie said abruptly. "You needed rest and lots of it, and I for one wasn't going to wake you, not for Ravi, not for anyone, do you hear me?"

Esther sat stunned into silence, the weight of her medical condition slowly sinking in. "Oh," she eventually said. "I see, I'm terribly sorry, Minnie, I had no idea."

"How could you have?" Minnie asked. "You were delirious half the time, calling for Jack and saying a whole load of nonsense in your sleep about mint imperials, Queen Victoria and Muffin the Mule."

"Was I really?" Esther asked, unaware of the extent of her mental state.

"Yes you were," Minnie continued. "At one point you grabbed my arm and yelled at me to run to the Anderson shelter because there was a doodlebug coming. Look, I still have the bruising." Minnie rolled up her sleeve to reveal a black-and-yellow handprint on her forearm, sustained during her sister's night terrors.

"Oh Minnie, I am sorry," Esther said, clutching her heart. "You know I'd never mean to hurt you."

"It's alright, dear,." Minnie said, dropping her sleeve. "The main thing is you're well again, that's all that matters to me."

Esther threw back her blankets. "Help me, dear, will you?" she asked Minnie, who offered her arm to steady her.

"Are you sure, dear?" Minnie asked in return. "One more day won't matter you know."

"It will to me, dear," Esther said defiantly. "Now where are my clothes?"

After taking another cup of fortifying tea at the kitchen table with Monique and Ludwik, the sisters prepared to leave.

"One moment, dear," Minnie said, stopping her sister and whispering in her ear.

"Yes if you want to, dear," Esther agreed.

"Ludwik my darling," Minnie said approaching Monique's father. "My sister and I would like you to have this, to remember us by, well me mainly."

She then presented Ludwik with the watercolour nude that Esther had painted of her, which delighted him beyond belief, and once again he was lost for words. A sinful grin then appeared on his face as he compared the likeness to the real thing.

"I thought you'd like it." Minnie smiled, noticing his obvious arousal.

"You earned it," Esther said at the door. "I'm just glad it's of my sister and not of me—she always had the more flattering figure."

"Oh I don't know, dear" Minnie protested. "You put me to shame in a pair of nylons time after time didn't you? You should have seen her, Ludwik, she absolutely oozed sex appeal, didn't you, dear?"

"Right, that's quite enough of that," Esther said, putting an end to Minnie's reminiscences. "Thank you Monique for your gracious hospitality and Ludwik, well, I don't have to tell you how grateful I am."

Ludwik immediately moved in and hugged Esther, still holding the painting in one hand.

"Ok, okay, yes, thank you Ludwik dear!" Esther said, breaking free from his roaming hands.

"Come back whenever you like," Monique told the sisters as they prepared to set off, with Vivien's engine quietly ticking over.

"Yes I'd like to thank you," Esther said, offering her hand.

"Goodbyyyyyye!" Minnie smiled, waving from her seat "Loved the garden!"

Ludwik waved and hurried back inside and up the stairs to appoint the risqué painting pride of place above his dresser at the foot of his bed, whilst Monique bid the sisters a fond farewell. "Be safe!" she called after them. She had grown mildly attached to the sisters, and had learnt the reason for their visit and subsequent onward journey, whilst sharing a glass or two of her potent spirit with Minnie during Esther's brief but traumatic illness.

Minnie patted her sister's knee as they left via the rusting chateau gates. "I'm glad you're alright, dear," she said with a loving squeeze. "Truly I am."

"Ahhh thank you, dear." Esther smiled, turning into the leafy lane, Vivien's tyres crunching the fallen twigs and acorns. "That was good of you to give away your painting though," she added. "I know how much you wanted it."

"Oh it's alright, dear," Minnie smiled, producing the tablet. "I took several photographs."

"What?" Esther said, wide-eyed, praying she hadn't shared the near pornographic image with one or two of their followers. "Minnie, tell me you didn't, you know…" she said, almost daring not to say it.

"Didn't what, dear?" Minnie asked, viewing the image in her online gallery.

"Please tell me you didn't," Esther again said, struggling to focus on the road ahead. "My God you haven't, have you?"

"You mean posted it?" Minnie replied, zooming in on her bunch of bluebells. "Of course I did, dear, why shouldn't I? It's a masterpiece, you should be proud of yourself, you have a real flair for it and don't you ever let anybody convince you otherwise."

"Minnie, have you no shame?" Esther snapped in sheer disbelief. "You have your whatsits hanging just above your knees and a few paltry blooms covering your lady bits. Oh hell I never should have painted you that way Minnie, the shame, the shame of it, you must remove it at once, at once do you hear?"

Peshwari Nans

"It's too late Essy, dear," Minnie informed her red-faced sister. "It's gone."

"Gone?" Esther asked. "What do you mean gone? Gone where?"

"Everywhere," Minnie confessed. "Cairo, Copenhagen, Corfu and even Kazakhstan, judging by the comments."

"Comments!" Esther cried. "Oh Minnie, how could you? Our reputations will be in tatters, just you wait and see!"

"No, on the contrary, dear," Minnie said, checking their Twitter feed once again. "Critics say that your use of light and shading shows a maturity only ever found in experienced artists, in other words, Essy, they love it. See? I told you you were good, didn't I? You just need to believe in yourself, that's all."

Esther's watercolour of her naked sister lounging provocatively beside a crystal-clear stream had indeed attracted attention from many well respected members of the art world, and with the ladies' ever increasing popularity adding provenance to the picture, the bids from private collectors and public galleries soon began to circulate. But Ludwik had no desire for monetary wealth, the painting to him was a sensual reminder of their brief encounter, a visual eroticism for his pleasure and his alone, to be viewed whenever his 'dander was up', so to speak.

"My God, what about Elizabeth?" Esther said, beside herself at this point as they were joining the motorway.

Esther was right to be concerned because news of the sensual sitting and images of the painting itself had reached their beloved homeland.

"WHAT THE?" Elizabeth shrieked, having taken a leave of absence from work to monitor her mother and aunt's progress twenty-four-seven, with an occasional tin of cold beans and a half bottle of scotch to sustain her.

Peshwari Nans

"Richard, don't look!" she told her son, covering her computer screen with a towel. "They'll be the death of me those two, I swear it," she added. "The bloody death of me!"

"It's okay, Mum, I've seen it," Richard confessed. "We discussed it at Uni today."

"You did what?" his mother gasped. "You mean you and your friends were laughing behind your hands like, like idiotic children!"

"No, Mum," Richard informed her. "We discussed it in class with Mr Brandon. Don't worry Mum, everyone thinks it's cool and gutsy, and I didn't know gran was such a great painter, she never said."

"Richard!" his mother barked, reaching for her medication. "I wouldn't call your Aunt Minnie's brazen behaviour cool or in any way gutsy. She's eighty-four, retired and wrinkled!"

"Lighten up, Mum," Richard told her. "And you really need to lay off the booze. Yeah, please Mum, it's eating you up, can't you see?"

Elizabeth looked long and hard at the glass of whisky in her hand. Perhaps her son was right, perhaps she had succumbed to a debilitating dependency, an all-consuming addiction that had sent countless consumers before her to an early pitiful grave.

"You don't need it, Mum," Richard added, appealing to her better judgment.

Elizabeth slowly lowered the glass to the side table but then, catching sight of Minnie in her birthday suit as the towel slipped from her screen, had her popping two tramadol tablets into her mouth and washing them down rapidly with the whisky. "Ohhhhh, Muuuum," Richard moaned, walking away and leaving his mother with her tremors.

Peshwari Nans

For the next hour or so Esther refused to talk to her sister, no matter how hard she tried to strike up a conversation. "Ooooh aren't those lambs simply adorable," she said at one point. "I could just eat them up, well I don't mean that literally of course," Minnie waffled as though nothing had happened between them. "You know I've never been a huge fan of it, in fact I'm considering giving up meat entirely when we return home, what do you think, Essy? Essy? I said I'm considering going veggie, or even vegan for that matter, Essy? Essy?"

"I have nothing to say to you," Esther said, defiantly gripping the wheel and staring into space.

"Perhaps I'll start with veggie," Minnie continued undeterred. "At least I'll be doing my bit, won't I dear? I said at least I'll be doing my bit, dear!"

"I heard you!" Esther snapped, unable to look her sister in the eye for fear of lashing out.

"Mind you I couldn't go without my shrimp paste," Minnie continued, thick-skinned to say the least. "I just won't eat the pretty ones, that's all."

Minnie's new selective diet, based on animals' outward appearance and factoring in their cuteness and huggability as she would later describe it, brought the slightest of smirks to Esther's adamantly aggrieved face.

"Huggability!" Esther eventually laughed. "I'd hardly call a scrawny chicken huggable, dear."

"Oh Essy you are mistaken, my dear," Minnie said, overjoyed at her sister's abating wrath. "I think they're gorgeous, and highly intelligent too by all accounts. There's a fellow on YouTube," she said, tapping at the tablet, "that has trained a flock of Rhode Island Reds to dance the hokey cokey and help pull a sledge with his team of huskies. It really is quite remarkable."

"No!" Esther gasped. "You're pulling my leg, surely?"

Peshwari Nans

"No, no, I'm not, dear," Minnie said, playing the three minute viral clip of the chickens dancing in formation, putting their 'left wings in' and their 'left wings out'. This of course had Esther howling with laughter and forgetting any grievance she may have had with her sister. "Whatever next." She chuckled. "Cows doing the Can-Can?"

"I don't know." Minnie laughed, searching the hugely popular site. "Let's see, shall we?"

Esther found it increasingly difficult to concentrate on the road ahead as her sister played clip after clip of household pets and farmyard animals alike doing the strangest of things. She was even forced to pull over at one point to watch a Shetland pony by the name of Bingo play a specially adapted piano a second and third time.

"And that's YouTube, is it?" she asked after a fit of the giggles.

"Yes, dear," Minnie said, shutting the tablet down to conserve the battery. "Isn't it really something?"

"Indeed it is," her sister replied as they approached Poland's border with Ukraine, where they noticed a heavy military presence.

The ladies were stopped and asked a series of probing questions while their passports were scrutinized.

There had been fierce fighting in the south of the country with pro-Russian militants and tensions were high. Armed guards who stood smoking around a personnel carrier ridiculed Vivien, while the sisters were detained for some time.

"Stick to the north," the Chief of Police said, thrusting their passports back into Esther's hand and ordering the barrier to be raised.

"Thank you, goodbye," she replied, but only received a cold hard look of distain in return. "How rude!" she said under her breath whilst proceeding.

Peshwari Nans

While the tiny vintage car entered Ukraine tens of thousands of online gamers were beginning similar journeys with their chosen classic vehicles, as the immensely popular *Gran Thrift Auto* game swept the globe. It was now time for Karl Bodine to make some serious money, by introducing a wider selection of vehicles, including Morgans, Triumphs and even the early Minis, which were to prove hugely popular indeed. His stable of silver-haired pensioners also increased, as did the tat on offer at his thrift shops, all in all causing the biggest ripple ever to be felt in the gaming industry for a very long time, with increasing numbers of the elderly taking up the console.

Financial analysts predicted record profits for Karl's fledgling company, from what they were now calling 'the grey pound', an otherwise untapped market that was positively bursting at the seams.

"So this is Ukraine, is it?" Minnie said, noting the distinct change in housing construction from their Polish neighbours. "I can't say I know too much about this lot."

The architecture wasn't the only difference between the countries as they soon found out when the weather began to deteriorate. "Oh blast!" Esther cursed when the icy rain turned to sleet. "Turn up the heat, will you dear?" she added, closing her window tightly and increasing the speed of Vivien's wipers.

A brisk south-easterly wind rocked the timber-framed vehicle, causing Esther to grip the wheel ever tighter.

Minnie reached into the back and retrieved two patchwork scarves. "Here, dear," she said, wrapping her sister's neck before her own.

"CRIKEY!" Esther shrieked as a high sided vehicle overtook them at speed, spraying her windshield with frozen slush and completely obscuring her view momentarily.

Peshwari Nans

"DAMN YOU!" Minnie yelled, opening her window and getting a face full of hail for her trouble. "OW, OW!" she cried, incensed even further.

"Close it quickly, dear!" Esther insisted, turning on Vivien's lights, even though it had just turned midday, "God, this is awful," she added, driving at a cautionary fifteen miles per hour. As a result she was repeatedly overtaken and showered with snow by speeding foreign lorry drivers. "Where are we, dear?" Esther asked, unable to distinguish any of the sleet-covered signs.

"We're thirty kilometres to the nearest town, dear," Minnie informed her, checking the tablet's GPS. "According to Mr Google and his exquisitely drawn maps."

"Thirty kilometres!" Esther exclaimed. "Isn't there anywhere closer for Pete's sake? This stuff's falling faster than my wipers can clear it."

"Absolutely nothing I'm afraid, dear," Minnie replied, noting the sparsely populated landscape. "We'll just have to hope it subsides." But her hopes and prayers for that matter were dashed, as the heavy snowfall increased, obliterating the road, leaving just two faint sets of tyre tracks from the vehicles ahead.

The surrounding countryside was engulfed in a thick blanket of crisp white snow, up to three feet thick in places and rising. "I've never seen anything like it, dear," Minnie remarked.

"And I, I never want to see it again," Esther said, leaning forward to focus. "It's no use, Minnie, we'll have to stop," she told her sister, as Vivien's wheels began to lose traction and they slowed considerably.

"Stop?" Minnie asked, looking around them. "Stop where?"

"Anywhere!" Esther cried, losing control sporadically. "If we don't we'll be killed by one of those lunatics for sure."

Yet another articulated lorry thundered by, the weight of its load providing all the traction it needed to maintain its breakneck speed.

"It's no use," Esther said, turning out of the tyre tracks and forcing Vivien into a snowdrift at the side of the road, where she immediately ground to a halt.

"CHRIST!" Minnie cried as she was thrown against her seat belt. "Essy dear, now what?"

"I don't know, dear," her sister replied, switching off Vivien's engine and removing her whitened knuckles from the wheel. "I just know we'd have come a cropper if we'd have carried on, that's all."

The sisters sat gazing out of their windows at the falling snow and up at the slate grey sky, wondering how much more those troublesome clouds could possibly hold.

With Vivien's engine off the temperature inside the draughty car soon plummeted, forcing the ladies to wrestle with their luggage and wrench on a further two layers of clothing. "It's getting deeper, dear," Minnie remarked, looking down at a foot of snow piled against her door. "What are we going to do?"

"Wait it out I guess," Esther replied with a furrowed brow. "I'm afraid we couldn't move now even if we wanted to."

The two chilled sisters sat blowing into their reddened hands and briskly rubbing their thighs.

"I have an idea," Minnie suddenly said, reaching behind her for the primus stove. "I'll make us some tea."

"Marvellous Minnie dear, well done." Esther smiled, rummaging for the teabags. Minnie set the stove between her legs on the floor and pumped the brass primer. "Be careful, dear," her sister said, setting a kettle of water on the blue flame, which pretty soon began to heat Vivien's interior.

Peshwari Nans

"Every cloud has a silver lining," Minnie said later, handing her sister a warming brew. But as well as a silver lining, every cloud around them also had a great deal more snow, which they deposited with increasing severity, helped by the harsh prevailing wind piling a drift against the passenger side until Minnie's view was obscured by a wall of snow. "I don't like this," she said, cradling her tea. "I don't like this one bit, Essy, not one bit."

"Me neither," Esther said, looking over her shoulder to maybe flag down another motorist. But unbeknown to her, the stretch of road they had been travelling on had been deemed unsafe and closed several miles behind them.

"It'll be alright though, dear," Esther said in a bid to calm her anxious sister. "We have enough fuel for the primus and we have food. If we sit tight and don't panic the snow will ease and someone will stop for us, you'll see."

She wound down her window and waved an orange head scarf above the car in the hope of attracting attention, but the sub-zero air temperature outside forced her to quit and tug her frozen hand back inside.

A further two hours elapsed without a break in the weather and Vivien was all but buried in the mounting drift.

"Richard!" Minnie suddenly said, reaching for the tablet. "Maybe he'll know what to do? I'll use the skype thingy to contact him."

"Yes dear, yes try it, he's a clever boy," Esther added with a sense of urgency. "Or that nice Mr Google? Maybe he could help us?"

"Richard, Richard dear!" Minnie cried, shaking the tablet. "Richard? It's Minnie, dear!"

"Oh hi Aunt Min," Richard replied sitting with his mother on the sofa. "Do you want Mum?"

"No, no, we need help, dear," Minnie told him. "Your grandmother and I are stuck under the snow."

"Under the snow!" Richard exclaimed.

271

"Richard, what is it?" his mother asked, leaning across to see. "Is that Minnie and my mother?"

"Yes Mum, yes it is," Richard replied turning the screen for her to see. "Apparently they're stuck under the snow."

"Under the snow!" Elizabeth shrieked. "What do you mean under the snow, MOTHER!"

"It's alright, dear," Esther called from her seat. "We're fine at the moment but we can't get out."

"Look, dear," Minnie told them, turning the tablet to all windows to reveal the extent of their situation.

"Oh my God!" Elizabeth cried. "Mother, how on earth?"

"It just started snowing, Lizzy dear," Minnie informed her. "And it hasn't stopped."

"Where are you, Aunt Min?" Richard asked, keeping a level head while his mother again went to pieces.

"Ukraine, dear," Minnie replied. "In the back of beyond by the looks of things. We haven't seen a solitary soul in well over an hour and we can't see a damn thing now."

"THAT'S IT!" Elizabeth stormed, leaping from the sofa "My mother's going to freeze to death in an icy tomb with her sister! I knew this would happen, I just knew it!"

She poured herself a double scotch and paced the room. "God it's my fault for letting them go," she added swigging from her glass. "I'll never forgive myself for this, never!"

"Mother please, be quiet," Richard said, mulling over the situation. "Aunt Min?" he said, checking over his own tablet. "Is your GPS switched on?"

"Yes dear, I believe it is," Minnie replied, flitting from one screen to another.

"Good," Richard said, watching his mother pour another drink. "So you have your coordinates. Could you let me have them? I'll tweet a distress call and I want you to do the same. Hopefully somebody in that region will be a follower of yours and get the message."

Peshwari Nans

"Do you really think that'll work, Richard?" Minnie asked, less convinced.

"Well I don't want to worry you two, but," Richard paused to hide his mother's pills behind the sofa cushion. "This really is your only hope. Okay hang up and get tweeting. I'll check back in an hour."

"WAIT, WAIT!" Elizabeth yelled, making a dash for Richard's tablet, but Minnie had gone. "Oh God no!" she cried, draining her glass. "Richard get them back! Get them back right now!"

"No, Mother, they have no time," Richard told his mother abruptly. "Now please, give me some space will you? I need to get on to this right away."

He began tweeting a message to all of the sisters' followers, requesting urgent assistance, and including the coordinates Minnie had supplied him with, while she did the same, only with a tad less dexterity.

"Mayday, mayday," she mouthed while typing her plea.

"Now what?" Esther asked when her sister had finished.

"We wait, dear," Minnie told her, setting the tablet down on the dashboard.

Vivien now had several inches of snow covering her roof, encasing the huddled sisters in the icy tomb that Elizabeth had feared.

"I know!" Esther suggested, reaching behind her seat. "We have the jigsaw of Prague castle to help pass the time, what do you say?"

"Wonderful idea, dear," Minnie agreed, rubbing her hands together and warming them on the primus flame.

"Okay, let's see what we have here, shall we?" Esther said, using the upturned box lid as a makeshift table. The sisters sat, plucking pieces at random.

"I have a corner, dear!" Minnie chirped. "Oooh and another!"

Peshwari Nans

With the four corners in place the ladies devised a plan as they so often did with their second-hand puzzles. "You do the river, dear," Esther told Minnie, handing her one or two corresponding pieces. "And I'll do the sky."

With this start they set about reconstructing the fifteen-hundred piece puzzle of the tenth-century castle, and if puzzling were a paid profession, these two ladies would be considered masters or their trade. "Oh well done, dear!" Esther commented as Minnie joined a large chunk to hers. The pair had completely forgotten their present perilous predicament.

Pretty soon the jigsaw was all but finished. "You do the honours, dear," Esther said, allowing her sister to place the final piece.

"Oh but there's two, dear," Minnie replied, peering into the box.

"Two?" Esther remarked with only one space left within the puzzle. "There can't be!"

The age-old problem of the missing piece in the 'thrift shop jigsaw' had just been turned on its head with the equally vexing discovery of 'one piece too many'.

"It looks like a foot, dear," Minnie told her sister. Having completed the jigsaw, she was examining the remaining segment.

"A foot!" Esther said, scanning the puzzle. "But there are no legs, dear."

"Well I never," Minnie said, flabbergasted. "I'll keep it anyway, dear," she said, popping the piece into her pocket. "We have a dozen at home minus a piece, so you never know, do you?"

The chances of the sisters having inadvertently stumbled upon the fabled 'missing piece', the holy grail that every persistent puzzler sought, was surely a billion or so to one, but as she so rightly said, you just never know.

Peshwari Nans

"My dear!" Esther suddenly said. "How on earth will they see us?"

She had a point. With Vivien now completely covered with snow, even with the correct coordinates any rescue attempt would be at a severe disadvantage.

"Quickly, dear, pass me the umbrella," she told her sister.

Minnie retrieved their lime-green brolly and handed it to her sister, who wound her window down halfway, allowing a little snow to fall inside. With all her might she pushed the point of the umbrella up through the icy covering until it popped clear. Feeling this lack of snow pressure, she pressed the button at the base, springing the lurid green brolly into shape.

"Oh you are clever, dear," Minnie said, warming a towel on the primus stove and handing it to her sister, who wound up her window, leaving their visual beacon on show. But with the perpetual snowfall in the region it wouldn't be too long before that too was engulfed.

After dismantling Prague castle brick by brick, the sisters sat in silence for a while with Minnie occasionally checking their Twitter feed.

"We've received over a thousand messages from concerned followers," she eventually informed her sister. "But none of them are in the area I'm afraid," Minnie said, reading several of the messages aloud to brighten the mood. "Oooh here's one from that charming weather girl on the BBC, dear, you know, the one you say looks as though she's been cosmetically enhanced."

"Oh the one with the big boobs," Esther replied, looking over her sister's shoulder. "What does she say?"

"Well," Minnie said, pushing her spectacles up the bridge of her nose. "Light to moderate winds in the south, heavy rain in the east with Yarmouth and Scarborough worst affected."

Peshwari Nans

"No dear!" Esther snapped. "About us!"

"Oh, oh yes, dear," Minnie said, reading further. "Sending all my love and best wishes to the Peshwari Nans and prayers for their speedy rescue, as more snow is expected throughout the night."

"Oh no," Esther muttered, sinking in her seat.

"Oooh here's another dear, from Prince Harry nonetheless! 'My family and I,' he says, 'are rooting for the speedy recovery of the Peshwari Nans, warm regards H', with two kisses dear, one for each of us. From a prince, dear, how exciting!"

"Such a charming young man," Esther remarked. "I do hope he meets the right girl, like his brother has."

Minnie read on. There were tweets from no less than a dozen countries, thirteen hundred in total and rising, each of them praying for their immediate rescue. "Ahhhh," Minnie sighed. "Barbra sends her love."

"Barbra Streisand?" Esther gasped. "Really?" The two of them were huge fans of her music. "My word!"

The primus stove at Minnie's feet may have been keeping the frostbite at bay, but it was also rapidly depleting the oxygen levels inside Vivien, and the sisters soon began to show signs of fatigue. Esther's head was dropping occasionally as she struggled to stay awake. "I think I may have a wee nap," she told her sister, who had already dozed off beside her, and in doing so stretched out a leg, leaving her heavy woollen skirt dangerously close to the flickering blue flame.

Very soon both sisters were sound asleep and the snow was piling up around the umbrella, with only half of it now visible. But as they slept soundly with very little oxygen left, an articulated lorry fitted with a powerful snowblade was heading in their direction. It was driven by an Irish father and son, Seamus and Kieran from West Belfast, who were hauling a consignment of oil exploration equipment from

276

Peshwari Nans

Dungannon to Shostka, in the north of Ukraine. Kieran had picked up Minnie's distress tweet on his laptop computer and was directing his father their way.

"This way, Daaa," he said, insisting his father turned left towards Turnapil.

"Where, son? Oy can't see nuttin," his father said, scanning the snow-covered horizon.

Kieran pressed his face to the window as his father's enormous Mercedes truck, specially adapted for the Ukraine weather, having made countless trips to the region, made good headway. "We're close Daaa," he said, checking the coordinates. "Real close."

By now the lime-green umbrella was completely submerged, leaving only the stainless-steel spike glinting in the sunlight, which broke through the heavy cloud on occasion.

"Wait Daaa, wait!" Kieran shrieked, flagging his father to a stop. "Oy saw suttin Daaaa!"

His father leaned across him and the two of them strained their eyes to look around them. "What was it, son?" Seamus asked. "Oy can't see a damn ting."

The brief spell of sunlight had passed, leaving the umbrella point a positive needle in the haystack. "It has to be around here, Daaa," Kieran insisted.

"We'll keep lookin', son," his father said, slipping his truck into gear and proceeding. But whether it was divine intervention or just sheer damned luck, a hole appeared in the snowy blanket of ashen cloud and a single ray of golden light shone down, hitting the umbrella point with astonishing accuracy.

"THERE DAAAAA, THERE!" Kieran cried, pounding at the window and throwing open the door while they were still moving.

"Jesus, son!" Seamus yelled, slamming on the brakes "What the feck are yeez doin?"

Peshwari Nans

"There daaa, over there!" Kieran exclaimed, leaping down from the cab into the heavy snow.

"WAIT!" his father cried, tossing his coat down after him. "You'll catch ya death of cold out there, sure ya will." Switching off the engine, Seamus donned his high visibility jacket and woollen hat and joined his son outside.

"There! Quick daaa," Kieran said as the sunlight faded.

"Here Kieran!" his father yelled, taking two shovels from the side of his truck and tossing one to his son.

Kieran fought his way through the snow and located the point. "Look Daaa, it's a brolly!" he cried, scratching around it with his bare hands.

"BeJesus, so it is!" his father gasped, readying his shovel. "We gotta dig 'em out, Kieran boy," he told his son. "And we gotta do it real fast d'ya hear me, boy?"

"I hear ya, Daaa!" Kieran said, setting to work, flinging shovelfuls of snow over his shoulder.

Unaware of the father and son above them, the sisters lay slumped in their seats, the primus stove flame diminishing until it was no more.

"Oy found suttin, Daaa!" Kieran yelled when his shovel hit Vivien's roof. "It's them Daaa, oy know it is, it's the Peshwari Nans, Daaa sure it is!"

"Keep digging, boy!" his father cried, plunging his own shovel in deep. Their hands now red raw, the father and son dug frantically as a howling gale whipped up the snow around them.

"Jesus Daa d'ya tink they're dead?" Kieran asked.

"Just feckin dig, boy!" his father snapped, with the whole of Vivien's roof now uncovered. "Find the winda boy!" he told Kieran. "Find the winda!"

"Oy got one Daaa!" Kieran shrieked, using his frozen hands to scoop the snow from Minnie's passenger window. "Jesus Daaa, Oy can see dem, oh no Daaa dere not movin, d'ya tink we're too late?"

"Shut up and dig boy!" his father barked, uncovering Esther's window and hammering on the glass.

"Ladies!" he yelled, wiping the snow from his eyes. "Ladies? Can ya hear me?"

"HEY!" Kieran screamed, banging on Minnie's door. "HEY LADY!"

"Hmmm, what?" Esther slurred, stirring. "Who? What? Oh, oh my—"

"WUNNA DEM'S ALOYVE DAAA!" Kieran said jubilantly.

"Keep diggin, Kieran!" his father told him, with much of Vivien still buried beneath the snow. "Keep diggin!"

Esther, although groggy, wound down her window a tad, letting in the chill but fresh air. "Oh thank heavens," she said, seeing Seamus's smiling face.

"Hello there, misses!" he said in his broad Belfast brogue. "We'll be gettin you out now, so don't you be worrying about a ting. What about your sister, is she…?"

"Minnie, Minnie dear!" Esther cried, tugging at her sister's overcoat, "Min dear, look we're saved!"

Minnie herself then stirred, wiping the drool from her mouth and opening her eyes to see Kieran staring back at her with the broadest of smiles. "Good God!" she remarked. "Essy dear, there's somebody at the window!"

"I know dear, look," Esther informed her.

Minnie turned to see Seamus smiling also. "Pleased to meet'cha ladies," he said, offering a sodden hand. "We'll have you outta here in no time, sure we will, now close ya window lovey, you'll be after catching ya death ya will."

"Thank you," Esther said, winding up her window. "Thank you ever so much, both of you."

"Yes, thank you!" Minnie mouthed to Kieran.

Sitting upright the sisters watched as the father and son worked tirelessly to clear the packed snow from around

Vivien. "Quick dear, light the primus," Esther told her sister. "We'll make the poor devils some tea."

Boiling a kettle of water Minnie popped a herbal teabag into two china cups.

"Cooooeeee!" she called, gesturing for Seamus to open the door. "Take this, dear," she told him with a smile. "You must be half frozen out there."

"Tank you me darlin," Seamus said, taking the fragile Royal Albert china in his fat fingers. "Kieran boy!" he called. "Here, get this down ya!"

"I'm afraid it's lemon and ginger," Esther told Seamus. "It's all we have at the moment I'm afraid."

"That's fine, me dear," Seamus replied, warming his hands on the side of his cup.

"What the feck?" Kieran said, sipping the herbal brew.

"Shut up boy and drink it!" his father barked. "It's hot, dat's de main ting."

Kieran reluctantly drank his tea, screwing up his face as it got stronger towards the bottom of the cup.

"Tank you misses," Seamus said, returning the cups to Esther. "Now oy'm gonna put a chain on ya little car here and pull you out. Where ya headin?"

"A place called Turnapil," Minnie informed him. "Do you know it?"

"Sure I do," Seamus replied. "It's only a mile or two down the road, Kieran and I pass through dere all the time, oy can tow ya there no problem."

"Only if it isn't too much bother," Esther said, handing the china to her sister. "However did you find us?"

"Kieran here," Seamus replied proudly. "He's always on that there laptop ting of his, always, oy told him it's not good for ya boy, he's even taken to Internet datin, Internet datin for Christ sake, have you ever heard anyting so ridiculous in ya loyf?"

Peshwari Nans

"Daaaa!" Kieran moaned, objecting strongly to his father's ridiculing.

"Anyways," Seamus continued, "he said he was tweetin, tweetin oy mean what in God's name's tweetin? Oy've told him countless times oy've said, Kieran get out ya room and go play football or suttin, but oh no, oh no he'd rather just sit dere tweetin and googlin and such loyk."

"Oh you know Mr Google too, do you?" Minnie remarked, getting a blank look from Seamus in reply.

"Anyways," Seamus again continued while his son dragged a chain from their truck. "While Captain Kirk here was tweetin on his ting he seen this message from yeez and here we are, and just in the nick of time no doubt."

"Thank you, young man!" Minnie said, winding her window down a little and waving to Kieran. "And do give my love to Mr Google next time you speak to him!"

Kieran gave her a sideways glance and dropped to his knees to attach the chain.

"Be sure to fix it tight!" his father told him. "Ya hear me boy!"

"Oy will Daaa!" his son replied.

"Thanks awfully," Esther again told Seamus. "I must admit I thought we were done for."

"Royt. Now me dear," Seamus said, rubbing his windburnt hands. "Oy'm gonne be towin ya real slow ya hear? So just take off ya handbrake and steer this little beauty behind me, ya got dat?"

"Yes, yes, of course and thank you once again," Esther replied, releasing Vivien's handbrake as Seamus and his son returned to their truck.

Thousands upon thousands of their followers waited eagerly for a tweet from the sisters, growing more and more frantic as time elapsed, but then suddenly their Twitter feed was alight when Minnie simply typed: "We're saved".

Peshwari Nans

A tide of emotional tweets swept the digital world, even the Prime Minister at the G8 summit in Geneva was interrupted during his speech and given the news.

"Ladies and gentlemen, I'm sorry," he told the gathered dignitaries. "But I've just been handed something I know you'll all wish me to share with you. The, er, the Peshwari Nans have been found safe and well."

A cheer erupted throughout the auditorium as members of each nation stood and clapped their hands, turning and hugging their counterparts, such was the love these two unassuming ladies had generated, an unstoppable love train that rumbled around the world, uniting the young and old, the French, the Swiss, the Chinese and just about everybody in fact who had access to the Internet, television, newspapers or radio. But the retired sisters knew very little of the global impact they had made, smiling sweetly to one another as Seamus put his giant truck into gear and eased away until the steel chain rose from the snow-covered ground, gently tugging Vivien free from the remaining drift.

"Dat's it, Daaaa!" Kieran said, leaning from his window "We gottem!"

Meanwhile, Elizabeth sat at her kitchen table with her head in her hands on the brink of a nervous breakdown, while Richard and Slider punched the air and hugged one another. "GET IN THERE GRAN!" Richard cried with tears streaming down his face. "GET IN THERE!"

"Oooh!" Minnie said, rummaging in the glove compartment and plucking out the last of their British toffees. "Here dear," she said, tugging the stubborn wrapper free. "You have it."

"Oh thank you, dear," her sister said, opening her mouth and allowing her sister to pop it inside. "That's very kind of you."

"Oh, wait a minute!" Minnie squealed, finding another. "Well now, isn't that just the icing on the cake, dear?" She smiled, twisting the sticky wrapper. The sisters screwed up their faces in sheer delight, proving that the simplest of pleasures shared with the ones you love can mean the most.

Esther steered Vivien in the truck's tracks while Seamus kept a close eye on his mirrors, crawling at a sensible eight miles per hour. "You did good, boy," he told his son. "Oy know oy'm always on at ya about dat computer ting, but ya did real good and oy'm prouda ya."

"Thanks, Daaa." Kieran smiled, leaning out once again to film the ladies behind, causing a second wave of elation throughout social media when he posted the footage, which was immediately snapped up by eager news channels and broadcasted globally to televisions, computer monitors and giant screens that had been hastily erected in Time Square (New York), Tokyo, Sydney and London's Piccadilly.

"Well, dear," Minnie eventually said after much sucking and gurgling of her toffee. "I think that turned out rather well, don't you?"

"All thanks to you, dear," her sister told her. "And your tweeter thing of course."

Minnie put her hand in her pocket and took out the random jigsaw piece. "And not forgetting my lucky foot, dear," she said, kissing the piece with the mystery foot on it.

"Er, shouldn't that be a rabbit's foot there, dear?" her sister asked with a smile. The two ladies burst out laughing as the sky above them slowly cleared and the snow abated.

Creeping slowly into the Ukraine town of Turnapil, Seamus pulled into a car park of the local supermarket, which had been cleared of all snow and spread with salt grit. Kieran hopped down from the cab, donning his own jacket and hat and went round to the back. "Are yeez alright, ladies?" he asked, leaning into Esther's window.

"Yes. Yes, we're fine thank you," she replied, winding it down a touch. "You, my dear, are an absolute saint, young man."

"Oh tanks, me love," Kieran said, blushing and removing the truck's chain from Vivien.

"Wonderful!" Minnie said, clambering out to greet Seamus. "How can we ever repay you?"

"You're safe, dat's all the tanks we need," Seamus replied, stowing the chain with his son. "Will you be okay from here?"

"Oh yes, thank you," Minnie told him, looking around. "We can get fresh supplies right here."

"Royt well, we better be goin," Seamus said, shaking the sisters' hands. "It was a pleasure meetin ya'z."

"Oh the pleasure was all ours, I assure you," Esther replied humbly. "And you, young man," she said, hugging Kieran and planting a kiss on his cheek. "You are a credit to your father, do you hear?"

"Yes, a credit to him," Minnie agreed. "I only wish there was some way we could repay you, that's all."

"Oh, wait a minute!" Esther said, scurrying to Vivien's back doors. "Here!" she said, retrieving a bottle of Monique's home brewed spirit. "A little something to keep out the winter chill, it's rather good you know," she told Seamus.

"Yes, I can vouch for that," Minnie confessed, having had her fill while her sister convalesced. "It's not for you though, young man," she told Kieran taking out her purse and popping fifty pence into his hand. "There." She smiled. "Get yourself something nice."

Kieran smiled politely as children the world over often do when they're given a pensioner's pennies.

"Tanks me dears," Seamus said, hugging the bottle. "Oy'll have a nip or two tonight, don't you worry about dat."

Peshwari Nans

"Do you have to, Daaa?" Kieran asked. "Dat means oy won't get a winka sleep wid ya snorin."

"Get back in the truck, ya cheeky little fecker," Seamus joked. "Be seein ya ladies," he told the sisters, bowing politely and returning to his truck.

"Yes, byyyye!" Esther called after them.

"Bye byyyyye!" Minnie said, waving. "Bye byyyyyyyyye!"

"Weren't they just the nicest?" Esther told her sister as they watched Seamus's loaded truck turn out onto the road.

"Indeed they were, dear," Minnie agreed. "Indeed they were."

Minnie turned to the huge sprawling supermarket with its windows emblazoned with special offers and the all-too-familiar two-for-one deals. "Shall we, dear?" she asked, eager to sniff out a bargain.

"Yes, why not?" Esther agreed. "Let's do this."

Retrieving their trusty 'bags for life' from Vivien, the sisters yanked a trolley free from the others and approached the automatic doors. "Where to first, dear?" Esther asked once inside the bustling store. It was brightly lit and a real shock to the senses, with its vivid advertisements and deafening tannoy announcements in the local tongue.

"There, my dear," Minnie said, pushing their trolley towards the confectionery aisle. "We'll begin with the essentials."

"Of course, dear," Esther agreed, cottoning on.

Esther and Minnie's faces lit up like those of children on Christmas morning on seeing the colossal sugar-coated selection of sweets on offer: a forty-metre-long aisle jam packed on either side with jellies, chocolate bars, bon bons, liquorice laces, marshmallows, lollypops and toffees to name but a few.

"We simply must have these, dear," Minnie said, dropping two large bags of toffees into the trolley. "Oh and we couldn't do without these," she added, snatching the bonbons. "Lemon or strawberry flavour?" she asked.

"Both of course," Esther said, choosing the chocolate eggs and sherbet dips.

"Ooooh oooooh!" Minnie squealed, tugging at the liquorice laces. "I'm sorry, dear," she explained. "I just have to have them. Cyril and I used to tie one another to the bedposts with these."

"Minnie!" Esther snapped, looking over her shoulder to see if anybody was within earshot of them. "I don't wish to know what you and that, that *sexual deviant* got up to, and I for one won't be having any liquorice laces, I don't think I ever will again after that disgusting confession."

"Suit yourself, dear." Minnie smiled, popping an extra packet in the trolley. "More for me."

The majority of the sweets on offer were of Russian or Ukrainian origin, but were direct copies of their western favourites. "Do you think these are parma violets, dear?" Esther asked, unable to decipher the label on a packet similar to their own beloved treats. But before Minnie could ask her, an elderly Ukraine couple reached between them and took two packets for themselves.

"I'd say so." Minnie smiled.

Having well and truly stocked up on all things sweet, the sisters turned their attentions to the day-to-day items. "They have no elderflower, dear" Minnie said, scanning the cordials. "They have something that look like gooseberry."

"Oh no, dear," Esther said, turning up her nose. "I had a rather unpleasant incident with a gooseberry tartlet once."

"What happened, dear?" Minnie enquired.

"Well let's just say," Esther said, looking over her shoulder a second time, "I had to leave the restraint early minus my undergarments."

Peshwari Nans

"Oh, oh dear." Minnie frowned, putting the bottle back. "Well we haven't enough knickers as it is, dear, so we'd best give that a wide berth I think. What about grape?"

"Grape is fine, dear," Esther replied. "And don't forget the mineral water—non sparkling, you know how that fizzy stuff affects my gout."

"Right you are, dear," Minnie said, hoisting two gallon bottles into their trolley. "D'you know what?" she remarked. "I couldn't have done that before Monique beat the living daylights out of me on the massage table. I now feel twice the woman I was—Monique has a real talent."

"What as?" Esther smirked. "A heavyweight boxer? I doubt if even Joe Louis would've stepped inside the ring with her."

Joe Louis, AKA the Brown Bomber, may very well have thought twice before raising a glove against a mauler such as Monique.

"Well, dear, I think we have everything," Esther later told her sister, checking their trolley. "Bread, milk, butter, cheese, shrimp paste, herbal tea…"

"Yes, dear," Minnie replied, looking very pleased with herself, with one hand behind her back. "And look what I found. Garibaldis!"

"Oh how wonderful, dear!" Esther squealed, clapping her hands and getting the oddest of looks from their fellow shoppers. "I was beginning to think we'd eaten our last until we returned home. It's nice to know that there is some modicum of decency outside of dear old Blighty."

"Indeed, dear," Minnie agreed. "But I'm afraid to say it was the last packet."

"What?" Esther stormed. "Well we'll see about that. You there!" she barked at a young shelf stacker. "Hey, yes you! What's the meaning of this?"

The trainee boy approached the ladies. "Excuse me?" he asked in Ukrainian, unfamiliar with the English language.

"There are no more Garibaldis!" Esther said abruptly. "Can you tell me why?"

"Pardon?" the boy said again in his native tongue, looking around for help.

"Garibaldis, dear!" Esther said, snatching the packet from her sister and waving them under the boy's nose. "This paltry packet just isn't good enough."

"Pardon?" the lad again asked, bemused.

"Ohhhh, fetch the manager," Esther snapped. "Man-a-ger," she went on, saying each syllable separately. "Well go on! What are you waiting for?"

The boy understood the word 'manager' and scurried off like a scolded child.

"My dear," Minnie said. "Don't you think you were a little hard on the lad?"

"My dear Min," her sister replied. "This is the Garibaldis we're talking about. They could quite easily be our national biscuit! There are principles at stake here."

"I suppose you're right, dear," Minnie eventually agreed after due consideration, taking the biscuits back and holding them close to her chest, just in case they really were the last.

"Ahhhh, are you the manager of this establishment?" Esther asked a suited gentleman who was heading their way.

"English?" the manager said, hazarding a guess.

"Unquestionably, dear," Esther told him.

"Without a shadow of a doubt," Minnie added.

"Quiet, dear," Esther told her sister, snatching back the biscuits. "I'll deal with this. Now look here my good man," she told the store manager. "I have a complaint to make about the Garibaldis, or rather the lack of them."

"Garibaldis?" the manager said, looking at the packet in her hand.

Peshwari Nans

"Yes. There aren't any," Esther told him abruptly. "Well there are these of course, but that simply will not do, it will not do I tell you."

"No, no it won't do at all," Minnie piped up.

"Quiet, Minnie!" her sister again snapped. "I said I will deal with it." She turned back to the manager. "Now have you an explanation for this horrendous failing on your behalf?"

"I am sorry, what?" the manager asked, his English not strictly true to the full Concise Oxford English Dictionary.

Esther waved the biscuits inches from his face. "Why haven't you any more Garibaldis?" she stormed. "It's simply unacceptable!"

"Simply unacceptable," Minnie echoed her sister.

"Minnie, dear!" Esther said, glaring at her sister. "What did I say?"

"You said it was unacceptable, dear," Minnie replied, blowing her nose into her floral handkerchief. "And I wholeheartedly agree, it's despicable that's what it is, despicable."

"I said," Esther growled, "that I'll deal with it. Now will you kindly be quiet while I give the manager a dressing down!"

"Yes, dear," Minnie said sheepishly. "But don't forget to tell him how much we love them."

"Of course, dear, I was coming to that," Esther agreed, although incensed with her sister's constant interruptions.

While the ladies conversed, the manager was having a heated discussion of his own with the young shelf-stacker, who informed him that a delivery had just arrived but would not be on the shelves for at least another hour or so.

"My dear fellow," Esther said, resuming her rant. "Us Brits are creatures of habit I'll have you know, and we like things to be just so, and the same goes for our biscuits.

Peshwari Nans

They're an institution like bangers and mash, the full English breakfast and Paul O' Grady."

"Paul O'Grady?" the manager said, pricking up his ears. "You know Paul O'Grady?"

"Yes, yes, of course," Esther replied. "Minnie and I never ever miss his show."

They were referring to the chat-show host and former drag queen, who was known back in the day as the glamorous and vivacious Lily Savage, a quick-witted 'comedienne' of sorts, who always shot straight from the hip.

Paul O'Grady, now a firm family favourite and a household name, has an army of fans the length and breadth of the country and as it now seemed, as far afield as Ukraine.

"Paul O'Grady," the store manager said dreamily. "Look, look!" he then said, reversing the lapel of his jacket to reveal an enamel badge with an image of his idol Paul, clutching one of his beloved pooches.

"Oooh, look dear," Minnie exclaimed. "The gentleman appears to be a fan too."

"Well, who isn't?" Esther asked, assuming the British celebrity's fame was universal.

"I am so sorry for this," the manager said, taking the biscuits from her. "Forgive me. I will see to it personally." He then turned and gave the young trainee a severe dressing down in Ukrainian, causing several shoppers to stop and stare. The red-faced youth set down his labelling gun and scampered off towards the stockroom. "One moment please," the manager told the ladies. "So, Paul O'Grady?" he added. "I am a huge fan of his work, a huge huge fan."

"Yes, I can see," Esther replied. "Perhaps I was wrong about you lot."

Peshwari Nans

The manager took a biro from his top pocket and a piece of paper. "Please?" he asked, requesting a signature, guessing that the ladies might have a direct connection with the chat-show host.

"You want an autograph?" Esther asked. "Whatever for?"

"Well dear," Minnie told her sister, "we are the Peshwari nans, after all."

"Oh yes, yes of course," Esther agreed.

In fact Gregor, the store manager and Paul O'Grady fan, was one of only a handful of people that actually had never heard of the Nans, but of course it was only a matter of time.

"Of course you can, dear," Esther said, taking the pen and paper.

"Can you sign for O'Grady too?" the manager asked eagerly.

"You want me to sign his name?" Esther asked, bemused.

"Yes please, if you would." Gregor smiled. "I would be forever in your debt."

"Well this is most irregular, most irregular indeed," Esther told him in no uncertain terms. "But I'll do my best, I doubt it'll stand up to scrutiny though, so please keep it to yourself, do you hear?"

As the manager lovingly examined Esther's crude forgery, his trainee hurried back carrying an entire box of Garibaldi biscuits, some thirty packets in fact.

"Good, good," Gregor said, dismissing the lad. "Please take these with my compliments," he told the delighted sisters. "In fact take all of it!" He gestured to their fully-laden trolley. "I insist, please!" He then clicked his fingers, attracting the cashier's attention. "ANNYA!" he called out (in Ukrainian). "NO CHARGE FOR THIS, NO CHARGE!"

"Are you sure?" Esther asked. "We really don't mind paying."

"Absolutely." Gregor smiled. "Please, take it."

The sisters were waved through the tills and their goods packed into boxes for them.

"Don't forget," Gregor called after them as they left dumbfounded, "when you see Paul O'Grady, tell him I said hi and that he can come shop in my store for free anytime he wishes, and if he needs a bed for the night my wife does not mind sleeping with chickens."

"Okay!" Esther laughed. "We will!"

"What an odd man," Minnie remarked.

"Yes, yes, indeed," Esther agreed. "But you have to admit dear, he does have impeccable taste."

"Oh without a doubt, dear," Minnie said, pushing the trolley across the car park. "Impeccable taste indeed."

Esther and Minnie now had enough Garibaldi biscuits to see them through to the end of their arduous journey, and they rejoiced as they filled Vivien with their kindly donated haul.

"So this is Turnapil, is it?" Minnie said, looking around, a tad unimpressed. "Where do you suppose one gets a spot of lunch, dear?"

"You and your stomach," Esther joked. "Come on, get in. There must be a cafeteria close by."

"With babka cake I hope," Minnie said, climbing in beside her sister, having already eaten the takeaway slices from their floating Prague hotel.

"Quite possibly, dear," Esther said as they drove out of the car park.

"Or maybe a nice Battenburg," Minnie added, licking her lips in anticipation. "Or a Victoria sponge with lashings of strawberry jam filling perhaps, orrrrr a lemon drizzle cake, oooooooh yes a lemon drizzle cake, wouldn't that really be something, dear?" Minnie waffled in a heady daze.

Peshwari Nans

"Or, or, a sumptuous coffee-and-walnut gateau, and, and maybe some individual bakewells, we like those, don't we dear? Don't we Essy dear?" she insisted.

"Yes, yes, alright!" Esther said, stopping at a halt signal. "I'll make sure they have cake, now will you please let me concentrate on the driving instead of your dietary requirements?"

"Oh," Minnie said, her head dropping. "Alright."

Esther looked left and right along the street approaching the town centre. "Shoes, electricals, children's wear," she mumbled to herself.

Minnie raised her hand as though she was in a school class.

"I don't want to hear it," Esther told her.

Minnie then opened her mouth to speak.

"Ah ahhhh!" Esther snapped, raising a finger. "Don't!"

Exactly fifteen seconds then elapsed before Minnie could contain herself no longer and blurted out: "I hope they have a gypsy tart!"

Esther slammed on the brakes.

"I'm sorry, dear," Minnie said, cowering. "I couldn't help myself."

"What?" Esther asked, pointing to an adjacent café. "I hope they have a gypsy tart too." She smiled.

"Oh," Minnie said again, like a turtle coming out of her shell. "Right, yes, er, I was rather hoping you'd say that."

"Come on." Esther laughed, applying Vivien's handbrake. "Don't forget the tablet and the tin," she reminded her sister.

"Right you are, dear," Minnie replied with renewed gusto.

Locking Vivien at the side of the road, Esther and Minnie tucked their handbags under their arms and entered the cafeteria, which at first sight appeared to be the equivalent of their own so called 'greasy spoons' back home. Cheap faded linoleum was laid throughout, beneath red formica tables heavily marked with copious amounts of gum pasted to their underside. The seating consisted of a few plastic garden chairs and crudely constructed wooden benches, which had worn timely grooves into the grubby flooring.

"Shall we find another one, dear?" Minnie asked, eyeing a bunch of builder types who were jostling one another and spilling their tea as they did so.

Esther was about to agree when the proprietor approached them, pen in hand.

"Tak?" (yes?) he asked.

"Oh hell," Esther said, having been put on the spot. "Er, tea?" she added, looking at his illegible menu that was in Ukrainian.

"Essy, let's go," Minnie said, tugging at her sister's arm.

"Ahhhhhh, American!" the man in the batter-splattered apron said, turning the heads of the builders.

"Oh good heavens no, dear," Esther said, clinging to Minnie's hand as she attempted to leave the premises. "We're from Whitechapel, young man," she informed him proudly.

"White chapel?" he replied quizzically before turning to the builders. "Hey, White chapel?"

The gang conferred with one another before shaking their heads.

"California?" one of them asked.

"No, no, no!" Esther insisted. "We're British, dear, the land of hope and glory, and it's not White chapel it's Whitechapel."

"Jack the Ripper!" another of the builders called out, raising his enamel mug, having been fascinated with the gruesome and yet unsolved killings of the late 1800s, known the world over.

Peshwari Nans

"Yes, that's right," Minnie piped up. "Those poor girls murdered by an absolute madman."

"Yes okay, dear," Esther said, bringing an end to the meaningless conversation. "Yes. Two teas please," she told the owner, taking a seat several tables away from the builders.

"Who do you think did it?" Minnie asked, sitting opposite her sister.

"Did what, dear?" Esther asked, trying to make sense of the laminated menu on the table.

"Why the murders, of course," Minnie said, resting her elbows on the table.

"I don't know, and quite frankly I don't care," Esther told her, taking her spectacles from her bag.

"Oh you must have a theory, dear," Minnie persisted. "Everyone has a theory."

"Minnie, I really don't care!" Esther snapped, peering over the menu. "Now will you please be quiet?" She scrutinized the faded pictures. "Now that looks like scrambled egg," she pondered.

"Well I believe," Minnie began while her sister was engrossed elsewhere, "it was that surgeon fellow. Well it's obvious, isn't it? The girls were dissected with skill and dexterity in a manner only a medical man could be familiar with. What do you think?"

Esther turned over her menu, oblivious to her sister's ramblings.

"Essy? I said what do you think?" Minnie again asked, tapping at her sister's menu. "Essy dear?"

"What?" Esther barked, removing her spectacles and glaring across the table.

"The Whitechapel murders, dear," Minnie reminded her. "Do you agree that the surgeon fellow must have committed them?"

"No I don't!" Esther said, stiff lipped. "In fact I do have my own theory."

"Oh yes?" Minnie said, leaning closer in anticipation. "Who dear? Pray tell."

"It was Professor Plum," Esther joked sarcastically. "In the library with the blasted lead pipe!"

It took a second or two for Esther's 'Cleudo' (board game) references to sink in with Minnie.

"Oh Essy!" she said, sitting back in her seat and picking up a menu, miffed to say the least. "I thought you were serious."

The owner then returned with two strong teas in blue-and-white enamel mugs. "Can I have this, please?" Esther asked him, pointing to a dated picture on her menu. "It is egg, isn't it?"

"No." The owner laughed. "Is dessert."

"Oh," Esther said, rethinking her lunch. "Meatballs?" she then asked, guessing at another picture on the menu.

"No, fish," the owner said, growing impatient.

"I say?" Minnie asked, raising her hand. "Do you by any chance have any gypsy tart?"

"No," the cafeteria owner again said. "We do not have, what you say, tart."

"Gypsy tart," Minnie informed him defensively. "Not just any old tart I'll have you know."

"Well what do you have?" Esther asked, opting for the easier approach and tossing down her menu.

"Fish!" was his reply without batting an eyelid. "And dessert."

"Well what about all this other stuff?" Minnie asked, waving the menu under his nose. "You can't tell me that's not a beef wellington."

"Fish," the owner reiterated, raising his eyes to the ceiling. "You want fish?"

Peshwari Nans

"No, no, we don't," Esther told him in no uncertain terms. "Not at this hour of the day, it'll repeat on me something wicked."

"You want dessert?" the exasperated owner asked abruptly.

"Oh really!" Esther moaned. "This is preposterous!"

"I'll have the fish wellington please," Minnie decided. "With the green dessert to follow—that one there, dear."

"Fish wellington!" Esther sneered. "I think I'd rather starve, dear."

"One must embrace the local culture, dear," Minnie said, supping her tea. "Oh," she then said, sniffing at her mug. "Excuse me, this tea, dear?" she asked the owner. "Is it Earl Grey by any chance?"

"No," he replied in the same monotonous tone. "Is fish."

"Fish tea!" Minnie exclaimed, lowering her cup. "What the devil?"

"Oh good heavens!" Esther also protested, pushing her cup away. "If there's one thing that should never be trifled with it's tea. This really does beggar belief. Come Minnie, we're leaving." She rose from the table, gathering her belongings.

"But Essy dear," Minnie said, rising slowly. "What about my wellington?"

"It's not a wellington, dear!" Esther reminded her sister. "A wellington is beef for Pete's sake, you know that, I know that and the majority of the western hemisphere knows it too! But this, this, *fish peddler* obviously does not!"

The owner and the builders watched as Esther stormed from the cafeteria, enraged that an institution as noble as tea could be so heinously violated. "Savages!" she cursed, with her sister shuffling behind.

"But dear!" Minnie called after her.

Peshwari Nans

"But nothing, dear," Esther replied, once she was behind Vivien's wheel. "Let me tell you something, Minnie," she ranted, wagging a finger. "Those poor devils on the plantations do not spend every waking hour picking the finest tips just so that the likes of that, that *philistine* can, can, brutalize it with the scent of raw herring. There ought to be a law expressly forbidding such atrocious behaviour."

"I quite agree, dear." Minnie nodded. "But what do we do now? I'm famished."

Esther reached behind her seat. "Have a Garibaldi," she told her sister, starting Vivien's engine. "At least there are some bastions of civilization that remain untainted."

"Well I rather fancied the dessert, dear," Minnie moaned, tearing open the packet of biscuits.

Esther, still fuming, said nothing. But if Minnie had indeed sampled the pea-green gelatinous dessert she would have undoubtedly had her first taste of raw halibut eggs in a spinach jelly, a local delicacy apparently, and one that oddly enough hadn't been adopted by neighbouring towns, let alone the wider world.

The gang of burly builders swigged their teas enthusiastically and tucked into their sturgeon and monkfish omelettes, mopping the remains with a fried slice dripping with fish oil.

Driving through town Minnie pointed out several more eateries but Esther flatly refused to stop. "Whatever next?" she asked, still vexed at the ghastly menu. "A sardine soufflé, or a mackerel meringue for heaven's sake?"

Minnie now couldn't help but laugh. "Or a dolphin doughnut, dear," she added, causing the two of them to roar with laughter as they left town, listing all things fish-related.

"A barracuda bagel!" Esther said, clutching her stomach and struggling to breathe.

Peshwari Nans

There was at least a three-day drive ahead of them before they'd reach the Russian border, but with much of the country languishing beneath a heavy blanket of snow, a hot meal and a warm bed was most definitely the order of the day, but they were now motoring through open countryside with hardly a cowshed in sight, let alone a hotel.

"We appear to be making good time," Esther remarked, sticking to the wide tyre tracks of whatever it was that was ahead of them. "Any idea where we are, Min dear?"

At this point they passed an upturned motor car in an adjacent field several metres below them, a casualty of the recent snowstorm, the unfortunate occupant having been airlifted to hospital only just recently. But unbeknown to the sisters, the panic-stricken driver veering out of control had taken out the one and only road sign of any significance to them in the process, burying it deep in the snow. It was the sign indicating a left turn ahead: critical to the sisters' safe passage around the war-torn region of the country.

Russia and Ukraine had been at loggerheads politically for some time, the spat finally erupting in all-out war in April 2014, culminating in a military stand-off around the city of Donetsk, with tanks from either side poised to wreak havoc on the other.

"We'll find somewhere, dear," Esther told her sister. "Trust me."

Driving straight past the important left-hand turn they needed to take, the sisters continued, blissfully unaware they were now on a collision course with the warring neighbours.

"Toffee, dear?" Minnie asked, delving into their fresh supplies.

"Ooh, why not?" Esther smiled.

Peshwari Nans

Minnie unwrapped her sister's sweet. "You first, dear," she said, pressing it to Esther's lips.

"Mmmmm, thank you," Esther replied, sucking loudly.

"You're welcome." Minnie smiled, unwrapping another of the Ukrainian sweets. "Mmmmmm, ooooh yes," she agreed. "Delicious."

After several minutes of chomping and chewing the sisters looked at one another, both of them struggling to consume the glue-like treacle treat. "Mmm, um, mmmmm," Minnie spluttered, unable to speak, pointing to her mouth.

"Mmmmm!" Esther agreed, equally frustrated. It appeared that the Russian refinery which processed the sugar used by the 'Vladimir confectionary company' used recycled uranium rods, purchased after the end of the cold war, and the phenomenal heat generated and subsequent radioactive properties, produced a granular product like no other.

Esther let out a whimper as her dentures ground to a halt, solidified as though fossilized in prehistoric amber. Minnie also screeched and gestured to her sister to stop the car at once.

Pulling over, Esther attempted to work her jaw loose with both hands while her sister examined her toffee-coated false teeth in the rear-view mirror. As a last resort, with her breathing soon affected, Esther wrenched the dentures from her mouth. "What in God's name?" she puffed, examining the teeth in her hand.

Minnie followed suit, the pair of them now completely toothless. "What do we do?" Minnie asked with a prominent lisp.

"I have no idea," Esther replied, trying to prise her teeth apart as if they were a spring-loaded bear trap.

Since they were very rarely seen without their teeth, the sisters were hesitant to continue their journey.

Peshwari Nans

"YouTube!" Minnie slurred, taking out the tablet, switching it on and troubleshooting their predicament via the video sharing site. As luck would have it, a twenty-one-year-old Chinese student by the name of Chao had visited the region during his gap year and posted a five-minute remedial clip after his own grandmother had suffered a similar fate when chewing on the exact same toffees he had brought her.

Esther and Minnie watched intently as the lad from the Sichuan province filled a large pan with water and brought it to the boil. He then soaked his grandmother's teeth for approximately three minutes, adding a spoonful of malt vinegar.

"Malt vinegar!" Minnie mumbled, the two of them springing from Vivian as fast as their aged bones would allow, and after donning their overcoats, hats and scarves, went round back of the car and opened the rear doors.

Minnie stood their primus stove down on the snow, stamping her feet to maintain her circulation while Esther filled their cooking pot with bottled water. The sisters stomped on the spot in temperatures just below freezing, willing the water to boil. Seeing the first bubble rise from the bottom of the aluminium pot, Esther tugged at her sister's arm to fetch the teeth, while she rummaged for the condiments.

The sight that followed would certainly have had dozens more vehicles skidding from the road, had there been any at all for miles around. The two elderly ladies from the East End of London were crouched beside a cooking pot in the middle of the snow-covered Ukraine wilderness, boiling their teeth!

Checking her wristwatch, Esther stirred the toothy brew while her sister warmed her hands, and after exactly five minutes had elapsed, and not a moment longer, Esther fished out the steaming teeth and dropped them onto the snow to cool. Wasting no time, Minnie snatched one set and popped them into her mouth, as did her sister. The pair huddled together, slurping and sucking their dentures into position, but after looking at one another quizzically and gumming the teeth a little further, the ladies hastily spat them into their hands and exchanged them with one another.

"Ahhhh, that's better." Esther smiled, working her jaw up and down.

"Undoubtedly, dear," Minnie agreed, fetching a cup from the car and scooping the vinegar water sweetened with treacle from the pan.

"What on earth are you doing?" Esther asked, watching her sister blowing on the brew.

"Surviving, dear," Minnie replied. "I'm sure Sir Edmund Hillary would have been glad of this during his ascent of Mount Everest."

"Minnie!" Esther said, the thought of the steaming cuppa having contained their teeth turning her stomach. "Firstly we are not and never will be attempting an ascent of Everest, and secondly!" she exclaimed, pointing to their open box of groceries, "we have Darjeeling for Pete's sake!"

"Oh," Minnie said, looking down into her cup. "Yes, right."

Esther snatched the cup from her and threw the contents down into the snow and did the same with the pan.

Very soon they were back on the open road with Minnie tucking the offending toffees into Vivien's glove compartment.

"You need to have a cast-iron jaw to get to grips with those darn things," Esther moaned.

"Well I suppose they keep the children quiet, Essy dear." Minnie chuckled at the thought of exasperated

Ukrainian mothers silencing their chattering children with the solidifying sweet treats.

"Well in that case," Esther added, "I'll take a handful back for that blasted Bijon dog the neighbours have just bought, yapping at all hours of the day and night, it really is completely unacceptable. I voiced my opinion on the doorstep but all I got was a volley of abuse and a door in my face, there really is no reasoning with some people, is there?"

"Oh but there is, dear," Minnie informed her. "I saw the young lady in question before we left."

"And?" Esther said expectantly. "What did you say?"

"I merely told her you were a gangster's moll, dear," Minnie said casually. "And that if she didn't keep the noise down you'd send the heavies round to fit her with a concrete overcoat."

"You did not!" Esther said, looking across at her sister, wide-eyed.

"Yes I jolly well did," Minnie told her. "I said you were once in cahoots with the Kray twins and a dear friend of Mad Frankie Frazer."

"What did she say?" Esther asked, intrigued now.

"Well she didn't say anything," Minnie replied. "She turned a whiter shade of pale and disappeared back inside, sliding three bolts across her door. I wouldn't be surprised if she's moved house by the time we return."

"Fantastic, dear," Esther squealed. "Did I ever tell you that Jack and I met the Kray brothers once? He took me for a babycham at the Blind Beggar pub one evening. I got the impression Jack knew the boys because he introduced me to them. Charming chaps I must say, very polite to the ladies and oh so dapper."

"Yes, so I heard," Minnie added. "I must admit I always found Reggie a very dashing individual, very dashing indeed."

Peshwari Nans

"Yes, I know what you mean," Esther remarked. "We were having a very pleasant evening chatting about their mother and the weather as you do, when suddenly Jack manhandled me outside and whisked me off home, leaving two bob in change on the bar and telling me it wasn't safe for some reason, but he wouldn't say why."

"How strange, dear," Minnie said, engrossed. "A spot of skulduggery on the twins' behalf no doubt, but at least the streets were safe to walk at night back then, dear. Which is more than I can say for this day and age."

"Oh good heavens yes, dear," Esther agreed. "Jack would hardly ever lock the shop after closing either, he always said that he had friends that looked after him. I guess he meant the market stallholders he drank with on a Thursday night in the Bow Bells—Jimmy Leadbetter and the others, they were all very close indeed."

In fact Jack had absolutely no fear of assault, or burglary for that matter, because the friends that watched over him were Ronnie and Reggie themselves, who had taken Jack into the fold after he repeatedly delivered fresh fruit and vegetables to their mother's house free of charge, thus proving himself a reliable stand-up fellow with, on occasion, a strong right hand.

Unbeknown to his wife, daughter and many friends, Jack was a silent enforcer, skilled in covert operations and only ever seen in the twins' company on rare occasions. Known to the twins and a select few as 'Jack the Veg', Jack would often slip out in the dead of night while his wife was sound asleep after Ronnie had thrown a small stone at his rear window to rouse him, returning before daybreak with a few pounds in his pocket and a bloodied knuckle or two. And the evening in question in which Jack had hastily escorted his love out of the Blind Beggar, was that fateful night when Ronnie Kray shot and consequently killed

George Cornell, a local hard man and continuous thorn in the Krays' side.

Jack, the unassuming greengrocer, led a model life and was well respected by his peers: the ideal cover for a man who secretly associated with the likes of Ronnie Biggs and Bruce Reynolds at around the time of the Great Train Robbery. But he was never implicated, although he may have been the shadowy figure at the back of the room when the daring caper was being plotted.

There was an honest living to be made selling Cox's orange pippins, conference pears and Victoria plums, and the odd white fiver to be made after dark, and whenever there was a raid on a jewellery store, for instance, Jack would be approached to hide the booty for a day or two, which he duly did in his cold store beneath several boxes of iceberg and cos lettuces.

Jack took those secrets to his grave so to speak, smiling briefly in those dying moments, safe in the knowledge that he hadn't once felt a bobby's hand on his shoulder, or served a single day behind bars, or more importantly hurt the one he loved, a rare quality amongst the underworld fraternity, of whom many had perished long before him.

"Any ideas where we are, dear?" Esther asked as they made their way south.

"Not a clue, dear," Minnie replied, searching for a road sign or a distinctive landmark.

Some sixty kilometres ahead of them Russian and Ukrainian forces were engaged in street-to-street skirmishes in the town of Donetsk, while their leaders voiced their own war of words via the world's media, with growing condemnation of their actions from NATO countries.

President Putin and his Ukrainian counterpart each refused to back down, despite the threat of sanctions from the Americans and many other concerned nations.

Peshwari Nans

"We're on the right road, dear," Minnie said confidently. "You know me—I have a keen sense of direction."

Esther glared at her sister. "If you mention a single word about your orienteering prowess I swear Minnie I'll, I'll…"

"Okay Essy, caaaaalm down," Minnie said, raising her hands, but then peering up into the sky, hoping for an early glimpse of the north star she'd relied on so often. But as the space station wasn't due to put in an appearance for another two-and-a-half hours, besides the occasional high-flying passenger jet, the skies were relatively clear.

"Don't even think about it, Min," Esther warned her sister. "The last thing I want right now is a repeat of our ghastly German episode. I doubt I'll ever fully recover from that night, so whatever it is you're looking for up there, I suggest you keep it to yourself. Do I make myself clear?"

"Crystal clear, dear," Minnie replied sheepishly. "Crystal."

Passing through remote villages with unpronounceable names, the sisters soldiered on, the snow eventually petering out. At one point their travels brought them parallel with the interstate train track, where a thirty-two car locomotive shadowed them for several miles.

"I just love a man in uniform, don't you dear?" Minnie said, eyeing the Russian troops leaning from the windows sharing cigarettes whilst clearly heavily armed.

"I wonder where they're headed," Esther said, looking across at her sister. "Anyone would think there was a war on."

"Don't be daft, dear," Minnie said, waving to them. "Anyone can see they're doing their national service, dear, you know, boot camp and all that, boys and their toys rolling around in the mud with wooden rifles and rubber grenades. It's quite pathetic really."

Peshwari Nans

"You could be right, dear," Esther agreed, although the wooden rifles did look awfully realistic from where she was sitting.

The troop train gathered speed and eventually left the sisters in it's wake, but the occasional armoured jeep or personnel carrier overtook them on the road, the occupants of which looking quizzically at the ladies in their Trafalgar-blue Morris Traveller.

"Perhaps they're having a jamboree, dear?" Minnie suggested, assuming the Russian and Ukrainian forces were engaged in some boy scout get-together, playing tag and singing along to a campfire chorus.

"What on earth?" Esther gasped, approaching a T-junction where an endless procession of Russian T-90 tanks were passing ahead of them. Esther stopped at the dotted line as the heavy war machines trundled by, their iron tracks chewing at the tarmac. Again the occupants gawped at the sisters from the turrets with their helmets and goggles on. Suddenly a tank ground to a halt as the dumbstruck driver radioed his commander to let him know there were civilians in the area.

"Oooh he's letting you out, dear," Minnie said with a courteous wave of her hand: again another wrong assumption on her behalf. Turning left, the sisters in their vintage car soon found themselves hemmed in between a line of some sixty tanks, sent to the region by President Putin as the world's media looked on.

The BBC back home along with CNN, Sky and Fox news and countless other media groups around the world broadcasted satellite images of the conflict to their viewers, including those who were in Elizabeth's house in England.

"Looks like the shit's really hitting the fan over there, Mum," Richard told his mother as he sat at the dinner table.

Peshwari Nans

"Language, Richard!" his mother snapped, tending to the oven.

"Oh my God!" Richard then gasped, seeing exactly what the whole world was seeing: a convoy of T-90 Russian tanks armed to the teeth with the latest military hardware, rolling into battle with a 1965 Trafalgar-blue Morris Traveller 1000, driven by his grandmother with her sister at her side wedged in the middle of the menacing convoy and keeping pace with it.

"What is it, dear?" his mother asked with her back to the table, and to the television for that matter.

"Er, er, nothing!" Richard said, dropping his spoon and springing from the table to block his mother's view.

"Richard? What are you doing?" Elizabeth asked. "Sit down, your dinner's ready."

"Oh er, I'm fine for a moment, Mum," Richard replied, glancing over his shoulder at the TV. "I'll have it in a minute if that's okay."

"Richard, sit down!" his mother insisted. "I haven't stood slaving over this hot stove, cooking your favourite just so you can let it go cold, now sit down, or this is the last pasta bake I ever make for you, come on!"

"But Mum," Richard protested as the news reporter struggled to explain what they were all seeing.

"Oooh ooooooh!" Minnie called from the window to the gobsmacked news crews at the side of the road, each with their cameras rolling and trained on the advancing convoy. "Bird watchers no doubt, dear," she told her sister.

"Twitchers," Esther said, correcting her.

"What dear?" Minnie asked.

"Twitchers, dear!" Esther reiterated. "The bird watchers, they call themselves twitchers."

"Oh yes, right," Minnie said, winding down her window. "Helloooooo!" she called out to them in passing. "If you're looking for the Willow Warbler we ran over the poor thing a couple of miles back, sorryyyyyy!"

The bemused news crews stood open-mouthed.

"I do hope they didn't come far to see it, dear," Minnie told her sister whilst winding up her window.

In England Elizabeth was losing her temper. "Richard!" she growled. "I sad sit!"

Richard reluctantly slipped away from the television and retook his seat.

"Thank you," his mother said, still wearing her oven gloves. "WHAT THE?" she then shrieked, catching sight of the television and of course her mother and Minnie en route to Donetsk, accompanied by an entire Russian tank regiment.

Richard put his head in his hands and waited for the inevitable fallout, and it came in spades. Firstly Elizabeth let the Pyrex dish of steaming pasta slip from her hands and crash to the tiled kitchen floor. She then lost all control of her legs and stumbled into the table, upsetting the drinks and condiments.

"Mum!" Richard said, leaping to her aid. "Are you okay?"

"I, I, I, I don't believe it," Elizabeth stammered uncontrollably. "Richard it's, it's your grandmother. She's, she's going, she's going into war with the damn Russians. Why Richard? Why?"

"I don't know, Mum," Richard confessed. "I really don't know."

The pair stood in stunned silence as the BBC's foreign correspondent faced his camera.

"I'm standing here," he reported, "just three miles outside of Donetsk, where a large contingent of Russian tanks under the command of General Russkoff are making their way to join the conflict, presumably as a show of strength to force the opposition to lay down their weapons and stand down. I er, I don't know whether you can see behind me that the war that rages between these two sides seems to have taken a rather bizarre twist, with the addition of what can only be described as a classic British car being driven by two elderly ladies. I strongly suspect that these travelling Brits have been kidnapped and are being used as a human shield to prevent the opposition from shelling the approaching convoy, like those used during the Gulf War by Saddam Hussein."

Elizabeth's eyes were wide and wild at this point. "My Mother!" she said, unable to comprehend what had been reported. "A human shield!" She clung to the table for support. "My mother!" she said again. "Is a *human bloody shield!*"

Elizabeth's eyes glazed over and she suddenly dropped like a stone to the kitchen floor, narrowly missing the shattered glass dish.

"MUM!" Richard yelled, ducking at her side. "MUM, MUUUUM!"

Seeing her stir, he rushed to the sink and filled a glass with water and returned, offering it to her lips. "Mum, are you okay?" he again asked.

Elizabeth sipped the water before pushing the glass away. "Water!" she said, coming to. "I don't need water, Richard, fetch me my whisky!"

"Mum you don't need it," Richard said, helping his mother to her feet and picking up the broken glass and scattered pasta.

"Richard perhaps you didn't hear the reporter," Elizabeth told her son, gripping his sleeve tightly. "He said my mother and Aunt Min have been kidnapped by the Russians for heaven's sake, and are going to be used in a war zone of all places, as human bloody shields! Human shields, Richard, my mother!"

Richard himself dropped into his seat, staring at the television, aghast, as were tens of thousands of the sisters' followers.

The forums and social networks lit up with the apparent news of the Peshwari Nnans capture and a wave of damning condemnations followed.

The tank commander was ordered by the general to escort the wandering strays to the nearest military base, where they would be detained for their own protection.

"He wants us to follow them," Esther said, heeding the commander's signal. "Perhaps he knows a shortcut."

"Perhaps, dear," Minnie agreed. "How kind."

Meanwhile Karl Bodine over in Ohio could hardly believe his luck. The ladies' growing notoriety increased his bank balance with every misguided mishap and he was tirelessly worked on the third edition of his ground-breaking game that featured a heavy military presence.

David Cameron, the British Prime Minister, was at home at number ten when his advisers switched on the television.

"Sir, you'll want to see this," one of them said. "The Russians really have gone too far this time."

"What? Get me Putin on the line!" the Prime Minister barked.

His aide arranged the call and moments later handed him the phone.

"Now you just listen here, Putin!" Mr Cameron barked, leaping quickly to assumptions. "You have our Nans and we want them back!"

"But, but we…" Mr. Putin said, struggling to be heard.

"I don't want to hear your buts!" the PM snapped aggressively. "I'm giving you an ultimatum right here and now! If they aren't set free within the hour you'll leave me no choice but to send in ground troops and mount an all-out assault against you. Do I make myself clear?"

Peshwari Nans

The Prime Minister's threatening tone angered the Russian premier, who pounded his desk with the palm of his hand.

"You dare to speak to me this way, Cameron?" he yelled. "You threaten me with war? Well I say no! No you cannot have these trespassers, they are now prisoners of Mother Russia and will be dealt with accordingly, so to hell with you I say!" President Putin slammed down the receiver and summoned his Commander-in-Chief.

"I want those British intruders placed under armed guard, do you understand?" he told him in no uncertain terms. "If the British want them then they will have to fight for them!"

"But sir," his Commander replied with a level head. "We really don't want to get into an argument with the British do we? They have the Americans and NATO on their side after all."

Putin leapt to his feet and stood toe-to-toe with his stunned commander. "Do as I say!" he bellowed. "Or I'll have you thrown into the guardhouse with the British! Do it now!"

His commander turned tail immediately and ran, donning his peaked cap.

Esther looked up out of Vivien's windscreen to see the thirty-foot gun barrel from the tank behind her looming over them as the convoy rumbled on for another kilometre before turning off the road, where the sisters were instructed to follow.

"You were right about the shortcut, dear," Minnie told her sister as they left the tarmac road and drove through a wooden enclave to a heavily fortified garrison.

"I'm not so sure I was, dear," Esther replied, seeing the armed guards waiting ahead with strict orders to place the sisters under arrest.

Peshwari Nans

"Oh!" Minnie cringed when the barrel of a semi-automatic weapon was thrust through her window. "Oh dear, what's happening Essy?" she asked.

"I don't know, dear," Esther replied as they were directed toward the makeshift barracks comprising of over a hundred camouflaged tents.

From this position the Russians could launch an offensive against the opposition and retreat just out of range of their mortars.

"OUT!" a Russian soldier barked when they were forced to stop. "OUT! OUT!"

"Er, there must be some mistake," Esther said, remaining seated. "We're on the road to Raipur you see."

"OUT!" the gun-toting foot soldier yelled again.

"I don't know what we've done to upset them, Essy dear," Minnie said, opening her door. "But I think we'd best do as they say, for now anyway."

Esther opened her door and was immediately dragged from her seat. "I say!" she cried, stumbling. "Do you mind?"

Minnie too was manhandled from Vivien and the pair marched at gunpoint towards an empty tent. "What's the meaning of this?" Esther asked, shrugging the soldiers hand from her arm. "Leave us be, do you hear? We've done nothing wrong! I said we've done nothing wrong! Do you speak English?" she asked, pulling Minnie behind her to keep her from harm.

"No English!" the soldier barked, forcing Esther and her sister inside the tent.

"Now you look here," Minnie protested. "We're British citizens I'll have you know, and you have absolutely no right to detain us. As my sister says we have done nothing wrong, I repeat we have done nothing wrong, so I demand that you set us free this instant."

Peshwari Nans

Minnie was shoved inside the tent and the flaps pulled closed. "Well I never," she said, stamping a foot.

"I don't like this, Minnie dear," Esther confessed. "I don't like this one bit."

The sisters peered from a slit in their tent at the forces amassing outside. "Oooh! Oooooh!" Minnie called to a senior officer. "Cooeeeee, I say!" She opened the flap a little and beckoned him over. "I was wondering if you could tell me why we are being detained? It's most irregular indeed."

"Putin's orders," the officer simply replied, leaving immediately.

"Whose orders?" Minnie called after him.

"President Putin," her sister told her. "The Russian leader. Now why on earth would he wish to detain us of all people?"

Back home, while Elizabeth went quietly insane the PM was in crisis talks with his generals and advisors.

"Sir we're under mounting public pressure to intervene and help the ladies," his intelligence officer told him. "They have unwittingly become political pawns in Putin's game and we simply cannot allow it. We should consider sanctions immediately."

One of the Prime Minister's political analysts stepped forward with his hand raised. "Now hang on a minute, let's not be too hasty here," he told the gathering. "The last thing we need right now is another conflict. We're still reeling after Baghdad for heaven's sake."

The PM paced the room. "Well what do you suggest we do?" he asked. "We can't just leave them to rot. By the sound of things I'll be lynched in the street if I even consider it."

"All I'm saying, sir," the analyst said, laptop in hand, "is that we need to proceed with extreme caution or we risk an all-out war with the Russians."

Peshwari Nans

"Look!" the PM said with both hands on his desk. "Those 'political pawns' as you call them are loyal tax-paying British subjects who deserve our help. Now I'm not going to order military intervention just yet but I won't be pushed around by Putin either. So get on your phones to your Russian counterparts and apply as much pressure as necessary, and somebody call the damned Russian embassy and tell them that if our citizens aren't released within twenty-four hours then they are to pack their bags and leave. Yes I'm deadly serious." He paced the room once again. "I'm prepared to expel all embassy staff if my demands aren't met. Now get on with it. We have an election looming and I don't need to tell you all that a situation like this could spell disaster for the party."

Esther and Minnie sat on the tent's groundsheet wondering what the hell they had got themselves into as a vast online campaign got underway to help free them. President Putin's personal email was hacked and leaked by bloggers, who urged their myriad of followers to bombard his mailbox with ranting requests, again crashing many of the overheating servers.

While the British and Russian governments were embroiled in political posturing their respective populations were furious that such a heinous crime against two sweet pensioners had been committed. Within the hour placard-bearing protestors had gathered in Red Square and Trafalgar Square screaming into bullhorns for immediate action and threatening all-out anarchy if their demands were not met.

"I suppose it could be worse, dear," Minnie said wistfully.

Esther gave her sister that look as if to say 'Minnie you cannot be serious'. "How, pray tell?" she simply asked.

"Well," Minnie replied, but then sat in silence for a moment.

Peshwari Nans

"Exactly!" Esther said, hugging her knees.

Later that evening the tent flaps were thrown open and a Russian infantryman ordered the ladies out.

"Oh dear," Esther said, clinging to her sister. "Do you think this is it?" she asked Minnie, who was literally quaking in her penny loafers.

"You mean, *it* dear?" Minnie said, having thought the same, namely that they were being led to the gallows or maybe a stone wall to face a dozen armed men and to be granted a last request.

"Well I'll be damned if I'm going out without a fight," Esther said, shielding her mouth with her hand.

"What do you have in mind, dear?" Minnie whispered as they walked behind the strapping soldier.

"Just follow my lead," Esther said with a steely resolve, whilst rolling up her knitted sleeves.

"Right you are, dear," Minnie said, clenching her wrinkled fists, although a little apprehensive to say the least. "We have nothing to lose, do we?"

Then without warning Esther flung her feeble arms around the burly Russian, toppling him off balance so that he fell flat on his face. "NOW MINNIE! NOW!" she cried, thumping his back as best she could.

Minnie gritted her teeth and kicked at his ribs before leaping on top of him with her sister,

"What are you doing?" the stunned corporal cried, his shocked expression soon turning to one of mild amusement.

"Take that, you horrid man!" Minnie yelled, twisting his right ear as her sister slapped him about the head with the palm of her hand.

"We have him, dear!" Esther grimaced, tiring somewhat.

But suddenly their escort flipped them both from his back with the greatest of ease and sprang to his feet unharmed and looked down on the two of them with his hands on his hips.

"Ah," Esther said, flat on her back.

"Let me get my breath back, dear," Minnie wheezed. "And then we'll really let him have it."

"Forget it, dear," Esther puffed, massaging the base of her spine. "It's no good. We're done for."

But Minnie was having none of it. Rolling onto her knees she pushed herself to her feet. "Right you!" she said, raising her fists and spoiling for a fight. "You've really got me riled now, I'll have you know!"

But the Russian bent and hoisted Esther to her feet, laughing in doing so, then he took hold of Minnie's arm. "Eat!" he snapped, pushing the pair of them into the huge swiftly erected mess tent.

"Oh," Minnie said with a look of abject realization on her face.

"Eat?" Esther asked. "Oh, I see."

It seemed the fate the Russians had in store wasn't as sinister as they'd imagined. In fact it was a full buffet lunch of boiled beef, cabbage and potatoes with a clear celery soup to start.

Minnie's eyes lit up and she rushed to the end of the queue. "Hurry, dear!" she called out to her bewildered sister. "They appear to be running out of roasties!"

Esther looked red-faced at the smiling soldier beside her. "I—er—I think we owe you an apology," she said, shrugging her shoulders. "I hope my sister and I didn't hurt you in any way."

"No." He laughed. "No I assure you, you did not."

With plates and trays in hand the sisters shuffled behind the Russian troops along the mess line. "Can I have another scoop of cabbage please, young man?" Minnie asked, pausing at the vegetables. "I have a vitamin deficiency you see, and Dr Kumali insists I don't skimp on my greens."

Peshwari Nans

Having collected their lunch, the ladies looked around for a place to sit. Several servicemen nearby slid their bottoms along their wooden bench to make room for the pensioners. "Thank you, dears." Esther smiled, setting her tray down beside them.

Minnie tucked straight in without hesitation, slurping her celery soup loudly.

"I'm sorry, you'll have to excuse my sister," Esther told the intrigued onlookers. "She has the manners of a ravenous hog at times, don't you, dear?"

"That's simply not true, Essy," Minnie protested with a leaf of limp cabbage draped from the side of her mouth.

"I'm sure the gentlemen beg to differ, dearest." Esther smirked, spooning her soup with an air of sophistication.

"Well I must say," Minnie eventually said, scraping her porcelain plate over and over, "that was absolutely divine."

"Yes quite," Esther agreed. She then watched as a middle-aged, broad-shouldered soldier on an adjacent table cursed and berated himself whilst attempting to thread a needle with the torn pocket of his tunic laid out in front of him.

"Ooh oooooh!" she called across to him. "Cooeeeee, allow me, dear," she said, beckoning to him.

Overjoyed, the Russian gathered up his sage-green tunic and hurried to her side. "Thank you," he said, laying it in Esther's arms. He then watched as she skilfully twisted the end of the black thread and gave it a lick.

"Ahhhhh." The soldier smiled when she passed it through the eye of the needle with ease.

"What have you been doing with this?" Esther asked, examining the three-centimetre hole in the breast pocket.

"Is war in Crimea," the Russian replied. "I lie in trench for two days."

"Boys will be boys, Essy," Minnie said, pinching a leftover potato from her sister's plate.

318

Peshwari Nans

"Leave it to me, dear," Esther told him, setting to work on the hole and leaving a seamless repair in just a few minutes.

"Essy dear," Minnie said, bringing to her sister's attention the line of soldiers forming behind her, each of them clutching a garment of one form or another, all of which were in need of her particular brand of attention.

"Oh," she said, looking over her spectacles. "That's quite alright, just leave them there, my darlings."

Soon a pile some four feet high sat on the bench beside her, comprised of socks, tunics and trousers, all them war torn and tattered.

"There, dear," she said, handing the first soldier his exquisitely stitched tunic.

The Russian bowed respectfully and gently squeezed her hand. "Thank you, thank you," he said with the faintest of tears forming.

Many of the soldiers had not seen their own elderly relatives in quite some time and warmed to the ladies instantly. Gifts of chocolate and tinned goods from their ration packs began appearing on the table in front of the sisters.

"There really is no need, you know," Esther told them while Minnie hastily unwrapped a bar of chocolate,

"I say, what's for dessert?" Minnie then asked, looking over her shoulder towards the field kitchen.

"Dessert?" a young recruit who clearly had a sweet tooth said longingly. "We have no dessert."

"What?" Minnie gasped. "No dessert? How preposterous!" She clambered from the bench and tugged her sleeves up to her knobbly elbows. "Our mother used to say that as long as you have a few basic ingredients," she added with an air of determination, "you can rustle up a veritable feast."

319

Peshwari Nans

Minnie and Esther's mother had lived through two world wars and was a time served aficionado of the 'make do and mend' culture, taking their meagre rations and preparing an extensive range of sumptuous, and more importantly nutritious, meals out of love and necessity, a gift that she had passed down to her beloved daughters, instilling in them a 'waste not want not' mentality.

"May I?" Minnie asked the military cooks, eyeing a spare workstation.

"Please, please, yes!" a sweating cook replied, handing her a black knee-length apron.

"Riiiight," she said, running a finger along the aluminium ingredients containers, plucking out one or two. "Oh yes!" She smiled, selecting the bicarbonate of soda. "Essy dear?" she called across to her sister, who sat busily stitching. "I'll rustle up a patriotic pudding!"

"Splendid idea, Minnie darling!" Esther replied. "One of Mother's favourites!"

The wartime recipe was a firm family favourite with just about everyone, proving that even in times of severe hardship and peril, children and adults alike could still enjoy a little sweet treat. Consisting of flour, fine oatmeal, fat, jam or treacle, bicarbonate of soda of course, syrup and a pinch of lemon or orange and a little water. Minnie floured her hands and mixed together the dry ingredients before rubbing in the fat. Dozens of the dining troops gathered at the makeshift counter, watching intently.

Next, Minnie stirred in the strawberry jam to the mix, turning it over and over in the porcelain bowl, and, unlike her mother's frugal rationed recipe, Minnie's mix was titanic in proportion, using three pounds of oatmeal as opposed to the recommended four tablespoons. Minnie greased a dozen bowls and filled them three quarters with her mountainous mixture, each of them were then covered with a dishcloth and left to steam for an hour.

Peshwari Nans

"Patience, my dears," she told the eager recruits, who were craning their necks at the counter.

Esther had all but finished the pile of garments at her side and set about dressing the wounds of some of the more minor injuries inflicted on the returning soldiers, whilst the camp surgeon dealt with the more severely maimed.

"Oh you poor dear," she said, removing the bloodied bandage of a grazing bullet wound. "You really should keep this clean, dear boy, tut tut," she added. "It seems this world hasn't learnt a single lesson from our generation, and look at you," she said, caressing the recruit's cheek. "You're just a boy. I have a grandson around your age, Richard his name is."

Minnie lifted the edge of one or two of the dishcloths. "COME AND GET IT!" she called, donning a pair of oven gloves to upturn the bowls onto a large tray.

The one hundred or so soldiers within the mess tent leapt from their seats and surged towards the counter, offering their empty plates. Minnie was handed a serrated kitchen knife by the cook. "Thank you, dear," she said, cutting each pudding into twelve equal portions and serving it across the counter to the jostling troops. "One at a time, my lovelies," she told them. "There's plenty to go round."

The camp commander then entered the mess tent to check on his prisoners.

"WHAT IS THE MEANING OF THIS?" he stormed, causing his troops to leap to attention.

"Sir, sir," his corporal said, approaching to calm his superior. "Look what they do, sir, look!"

The troops, whose morale had been at an all-time low of late after suffering heavy casualties, now seemed in high spirits, many of them with neatly sewn patches on their uniforms and having fresh field dressings, and not to mention a plate full of patriotic cake.

Peshwari Nans

"You?" the commander said to the sisters in turn. "You do this? For us?"

"But of course, dear," Esther replied. "A little human kindness goes a long way you know, especially in times of war, of which my sister and are are most familiar with."

"Quite right, dear," Minnie agreed, wiping a smudge of flour from her nose.

"Sir," a lieutenant said, offering his 'patriotic cake' to the irate commander. "Try it, it's good." He smiled.

The mess tent fell silent as the commander raised a morsel to his lips. "It is good!" he eventually said, having savoured the delicious doughy dessert. "My apologies to you," he told the sisters, examining a subordinate's pristine dressing. "This is war you see, we are not use to such things."

Esther reached for his lapel, which had a brass button missing. "Do you have the button?" she asked.

"Yes, yes, I do," the commander replied, producing the wayward button from his tunic pocket.

"Take off your coat and have a seat," Esther insisted.

"Oh no, it's fine," the commander replied, backing away a tad. "Do not trouble yourself."

"Ah, ahhh!" Esther said, holding out a hand. "I assure you it won't take a moment. Now hand it over, sit down and enjoy your pudding."

The commander did as he was told, sitting beside her. "I am sorry for detaining you both," he said while she reattached his button. "I have my orders you see, from Putin himself."

"I understand, dear," Esther said without looking up. "I wouldn't worry, it'll all turn out in the wash no doubt."

"I wish I shared your optimism," the commander said with a broad smile.

Meanwhile Minnie was busily dishing out second helpings until all of her patriotic pudding had gone. A loud cheer then erupted throughout the tent and she was embraced heartily when she emerged from behind the counter.

"Oh my!" She smiled. "That's quite alright, my darlings, maybe later I'll throw together a batch of rock cakes and a Saturday pie."

Another of her mother's regular bakes, the 'Saturday pie' consisted mainly of leftover table scraps, cold meats, potatoes, onions and herbs. "If chef will allow it of course," she added, turning to the overworked cook.

"Please, anytime," he said gladly.

The infantrymen slowly dispersed and went about their duties and the cook closed down his kitchen.

"I am so sorry," the Russian commander told the sisters. "But I must escort you back to your tent, again under Putin's express instructions."

"Oh don't worry about it, dear," Minnie said, helping her sister to her feet. "Essy and I are used to roughing it under canvas, aren't we dear? We camped at the Nürburgring en route you see."

Esther glared at her sister. "For all of five minutes!" she snapped. "And then Calamity Jane here decides to lead us up the garden path, literally!"

"Oh Essy, you aren't still mad about that, are you?" Minnie asked. "It was a simple miscalculation that's all."

"Yes!" Esther agreed with a frown. "*Simple* being the operative word."

The commander watched as the sisters began a heated debate. "Ladies, ladies!" he said, intervening. "Please!"

"Well she started it!" Minnie cursed. "I said I was sorry. If I hadn't lost sight if the north star we'd have been just fine."

"North star my foot!" Esther raged. "If you'd have listened to me and turned left when I said instead of following that idiotic instinct of yours we wouldn't have spent a hellish night in our nightgowns at a blasted bus shelter, would we? Well?"

"Well," Minnie said, her defence dwindling. "I suppose, but…"

"Ah ah ahhh!" Esther warned her. "Your confession of guilt is duly noted and appreciated, now shall we go?" She left Minnie pondering her case and followed the commander back to their tent. "Oh, I say!" she gasped on lifting the flap. Their previous empty canvas accommodation had been transformed by the grateful Russian troops, many of them donating blankets, pillows, night lights and further sweet treats from their rations and parcels sent from worried loved ones.

"Good heavens!" Minnie added, joining her sister.

"For you," a grinning soldier said.

"Oh you shouldn't have," Esther said, sitting on her bunk.

"Well I don't know about that, dear," Minnie said, reaching for a bar of nougat.

The camp commander called to his lieutenant: "Get me Putin on the telephone," he insisted. "Ladies," he said, peering into the tent. "Believe me when I say I will do all I can to see you freed."

"No rush, dear," Minnie called after him, pocketing a packet of peanut brittle. "I know what you're going to say, Essy dear," she told her frowning sister. "'A moment on the lips a lifetime on the hips', or so they say. To hell with it, dear," she said, holding out her haggard hands. "Look at us Essy. Look at us. I can remember back when you and I were bells of the ball, night after night in our satin knickers and nylons." Minnie's acceptance of her degenerative appearance brought a lump to her throat. "I miss those days, dear," she said, sitting on her bunk and hitching her skirt up to her knees in a most unladylike manner.

Peshwari Nans

"Now that's quite enough of that, Minnie dear," Esther told her, wagging a finger. "Yes we're old, there's nothing we can do about that I'm afraid and you know it, but I'm damned if I'm going to just roll over and let the almighty take me without a bloody good fight. And another thing, I'll be damned if I let him take you either, do you hear me Min? When I look at you I still see my sweet little sister, the sister who saved up her milk money to buy me those red shoes I so dearly wanted for my birthday. The same sister who took the blame when my yo-yo broke the window in Father's study, and also the sister who selflessly stood aside so that I could date Tommy Robbins when she had the most enormous crush on him herself.

"Minnie dear, beauty comes from within and you have it in spades my darling, you always have had, and the way you sat up with me night after night when that two-timing tike Tommy broke my heart was simply angelic."

Esther joined Minnie on her bunk and put a hand tenderly on her knee. "So come on, darling, what do you say we kick up our heels and show that grim reaper fellow that he'll get a whole lot more than he bargained for if he comes calling any time soon? Come on, dear, I hate seeing you like this, it's so unlike you. We may not have our looks but you see these wrinkles, dear? They're a map, a map to places our dreams have taken us, and boy have we been places, seen things and done unimaginable things, and through it all we have each other, Minnie, and I'll always love you no matter what, warts and all, as they say."

"Warts and all?" Minnie asked. "No matter what?"

"No matter what," Esther reiterated. "We've been so close for so long, dear, and I've never managed to stay mad at you for long, have I?"

"I was rather hoping you'd say that, Essy," Minnie said, finding it difficult to look her sister in the eye.

Peshwari Nans

"What do you mean?" Esther asked, knowing her sister oh-so-well.

"Well it's just that..." Minnie said, rolling the hem of her skirt between her fingers nervously. "Oh not to worry, dear," she added. "It really doesn't matter."

"What really doesn't matter?" Esther asked, pressuring her sister for an answer. "Come on Minnie, out with it."

"Oh it's nothing, Essy dear, I assure you," Minnie replied, backed into a corner somewhat. "Wasn't it nice of those chaps to fix up our tent?"

"Miniiiiie," Esther said, probing. "Don't you change the subject now. What's the matter? You know you can tell me, dear, I won't be mad I promise."

"You truly promise?" Minnie said, daring to look at her sister.

"Of course." Esther smiled, shaking her sister's knee. "We're sisters through and through after all, nothing you could possibly say would ever make me love you one iota less."

"Are you sure?" Minnie continued to ask, getting Esther's back up a tad by now.

"Minnie!" her sister snapped. "I won't ask you again, I've explained my position, now you know I won't be able to sleep tonight unless you tell me what's bothering you."

"Okay, okay!" Minnie said, edging away ever so slightly. "If—em—if you must know Essy it's, it's about Tommy Robbins."

"Tommy Robbins? That snake in the grass!" Esther said, stiffening her spine. "What has he got to do with anything?"

Minnie looked away towards the corner of the tent.

"Miniiiiie!" Esther said, pressing the subject. "What about Tommy blasted Robbins?"

"Oh let's just forget it, dear!" Minnie replied, getting up and pacing across the military tent. "Why rake up the past? That's what I say."

But her sister's curiosity was well and truly aroused at this point and she wasn't about to let those sleeping dog lie, not for one moment. "What about Tommy Robbins?" she insisted.

"Alright. It was me, Essy!" Minnie said, throwing her hands up in the air. "It was me he was fooling around with behind your back. And I'm so so sorry, but you knew how I felt about him from the start. There I've said it, and quite frankly, dear, I'm glad it's out. I've lived with the guilt my whole life."

"You?" Esther said, stunned to the core momentarily. "You? You and Tommy? Behind my back?"

"Essy, I never meant to hurt you, honestly I didn't," Minnie pleaded. "I tried to hide my feelings but I was young, we both were and a crush is a crush, you know that."

"Yes but he was with me!" Esther said, her blood now simmering. "*Me*, Minnie!"

"Yes I know dear. And you don't know how guilty it made me feel, you really don't," Minnie said, sitting on the opposite bunk, out of reach. "I was seventeen, dear, my head was all over the place and when he smiled at me at the corner shop my knees just turned to jelly."

"How long?" Esther asked, straight faced.

"I'm sorry dear, what?" Minnie asked.

"How long?" Esther asked, gripping her own skirt. "How long were you and that, that *lowlife* sneaking round behind my back?"

"Does it really matter now, dear?" Minnie asked, appealing for clemency. "We're sisters remember, through and through, like you said."

"Forget all that nonsense!" Esther stormed. "I want to know. How long?"

Minnie looked down at the canvas floor. "A month or two, three possibly," she mumbled.

"Three months!" Esther growled. "You were cavorting behind my back with my boyfriend for *three whole months* when you knew how I felt about him at the time. Minnie how could you?"

Minnie clasped her hands together. "Essy can we just forget all about it, please? It was a lifetime ago and a stupid stupid mistake on my behalf, a silly stupid mistake."

"A mistake?" Esther asked. "You call betraying my trust a simple mistake? I loved him, Minnie, and you knew that. I, I just can't believe you would do such a thing to your own sister."

Minnie hung her head, her mouth dry. "Essy I am so, so sorry," she said, shaking her head. "I really don't know what to say."

But Esther hadn't finished by a long chalk. "And you were…" she said, referring tactfully to their sexual infidelity. "With him?"

"Well yes, dear, but—" Minnie confessed.

"But what?" Esther snapped. "What? You were sleeping with my man behind my back. What more is there to say?"

"Well that's just it, dear," Minnie told her riled sister. "We slept for most of the time. Whenever we did, you know, do *it*, it was all over in a flash and the pathetic boy would roll over and light up a capstan as though he'd just conquered the blooming world."

The corners of Esther's mouth turned up ever so slightly at this. "I, I know what you mean," she admitted. "Although he was very charming and drop-dead gorgeous, the poor boy was absolutely useless at, well you know what, I mean."

Peshwari Nans

"Sex," Minnie said with a little less tact. "I'd say that's an understatement, dear. On one occasion the idiot bruised my breast, laddered my nylons and did his business in his trousers before he'd even taken the darn things off!"

Although Esther was mad as hell at her sister she couldn't help but laugh. "Oh he did that with you too, did he?" she said, rocking back. "I once had to lend him a pair of Father's trousers to go home in after his, well shall we say *dysfunction*. I mean to say he was premature wouldn't have quite done him justice."

"I know, dear." Minnie chuckled. "It was under a minute at Jenny Pendleton's party. If I'd have blinked I'd have missed it entirely."

The sisters sat comparing experiences with the sexually inadequate boy, eventually calming Esther completely and allowing her to forgive Minnie's apparent betrayal.

Passing Russian troops stopped and listened to the howling laughter coming from within the sisters' tent as the pair settled down in their beds for a night of confinement under canvas.

As the sisters slept the movement to free them gathered pace, with many high profile figures adding their weight to the case, but Putin remained resolute.

In the past the West had heaped pressure on him to comply and change his ways, causing him great embarrassment amongst his peers but now enough was enough. "NYET, NYET, NYET!" he roared, shaking his head when his Secretary of State approached him with news of the global outcry.

"I would rather see them hang than bow to those dogs, now get out of my sight or I'll have your head!" The President flung open his desk drawer and produced a large bone-handled hunting knife, forcing his secretary to flee the office immediately. The Russian premier was well known for his outdoorsmanship skills, riding bareback in the

Caucasus mountains to hunt down wild boars and brown bears.

Meanwhile crisis talks were being held at the British Embassy in Moscow and the Ministry of Defence back home in England.

"I've never seen anything like it, sir," said the Foreign Secretary to the PM. "These ladies, they seem to have created a wave of empathy that has literally encircled the globe. I'm getting letters, faxes, and emails from ex pats the world over demanding we act swiftly before the unthinkable happens."

"God forbid that," The Prime Minister replied. "I'll be out of office in a heartbeat if that ever happened."

"Indeed, sir," his minister agreed. "The crowds in Liverpool, Manchester, Edinburgh and Trafalgar Square are growing increasingly restless and I'd hate to see a return to rioting, especially those of Margaret's era."

He was referring to the infamous Poll Tax riots of 1989 and 1990, in which much of the capital was ransacked, looted and under the brief control of a chanting riotous mob. Countless arrests were made and millions upon millions of pounds were spent during the clean-up operation.

"Where are we on sanctions?" the Prime Minister asked his aide.

"Well, sir," his suited colleague said, slipping on his glasses to examine his notes. "If we wish to cease all trade with the Russians it will take several days to implement and the political fallout would be enormous. So therefore I would strongly advise against it."

"Quite frankly, Peter," the PM said, growing increasingly concerned for his future at Number Ten, "if it'll get the Peshwari Nans freed and on their way then I am willing to consider just about anything at this point, and that includes military action."

"But, but, sir!" his minister gasped. "You're willing to go to war with the Russians for these sisters? Sir, please take a moment to think what you're saying! The Russians for heaven's sake!"

"Yes I know!" the PM barked, flinging his fountain pen across the office. "But Putin leaves me no choice! The fool is forcing my hand!"

"But, but war, sir," the Foreign Secretary stammered. "Surely nothing or nobody is worth that."

The Prime Minister pulled back the curtains covering the windows. "Tell that to those out there, will you?" he insisted.

The minister joined him at the window to observe a gathering of some five hundred angry protesters at the Downing Street gates, baying for his blood unless he intervened and secured Esther and Minnie's release.

The following morning the sisters woke to the sound of marching boots outside their tent. "Mmmmm morning, dear," Esther said, stretching beneath her green blanket.

"Morning, Essy darling," Minnie replied, sitting up. "I don't know about you, dear," she told her sister. "But I had the most heavenly sleep, and as for my back, it hasn't bothered me the entire night."

"Me too, dear," Esther agreed. "These cots really are second to none."

Washing their hands and faces using the jug and bowl supplied by the troops, the ladies dressed, preened their hair and peered outside.

"I say, what are you doing?" Esther asked a group of soldiers surrounding Vivien. "Come away from her at once!"

But when they parted she and her sister could see that they had in fact buffed her paintwork and removed all of the dirt and grime accumulated on the previous leg of their journey.

"Oh," Esther said, feeling every bit the fool. "I am sorry, how awfully kind of you."

One young officer approached the ladies. "Service?" he said.

"What?" Esther asked, unsure of his intentions.

"Service?" the officer reiterated. "Your car, you want service? We have very good tank mechanic, he change oil, brakes and fluid, maybe clean carburettor."

"Oh I couldn't ask you to do that." Esther smiled. "No, no, no, thank you you've already done too much."

There was then the loudest commotion as a lieutenant came rushing through the camp, brandishing an open letter from home and a newspaper clipping, yelling hysterically in Russian, the only two words legible to Esther and Minnie being 'PESHWARI NANS!'

"I believe the penny has dropped, dear," Minnie told her sister.

Before long a tide of bodies surged forward surrounding Vivien and the sisters. "Peshwari Nans?" the officer asked the ladies. "Is this true?"

"Errrrr yes, it appears that way," Esther informed him. "It's a label that's been given to us several days ago and one that has stuck fast by the looks of things."

The officer turned and beckoned to two of his top mechanics. "Service!" he cried. "Good service you hear? You do everything, everything!"

"Are you sure, dear?" Esther asked. "We really don't want to be a burden."

"No problem." the officer smiled, swatting several of his men away from Vivien. "BACK, BACK!" he yelled, demanding for Vivien to be taken to the mechanics compound for a complete and thorough overhaul. "Come, you eat," he told the sisters, escorting them back towards the mess tent. "And please," he said, turning to Minnie. "You make for me this, rock cake?"

"Oh but of course, dear," Minnie said, again rolling up her sleeves. "ANYONE ELSE FOR ROCK CAKES?" she called behind them. The surging troops almost swept the sisters off their feet at the mention of home-made cake "Oh my!" Minnie cried as she was virtually carried to the camp kitchen.

"Right then," she said, composing herself and taking a pinnie from a peg. "Let's see what we can do, shall we?"

Esther was given pride of place at the head of a long table and surrounded by soldiers, each wanting to be close to the Nans, offering her chocolate and even cigarettes. "Oh no, dear, I don't," she told them, looking down her nose at the military issue smokes. "But I'm sure my sister would be more than grateful for the chocolate."

"Why you come to Ukraine in crazy car?" one lad asked her, unaware of the full extent of the sisters' travels. "My grandmother she sit in her chair that rocks," he told her, "and smoke her, what you call this, pipe?"

"Yes, a pipe," Esther replied. "I remember my father was rather taken with his, and I was quite fond of the smell of his rough shag too, I remember it so vividly. I would sit on his knee and watch in awe as he tapped the ash into the coal scuttle and refilled it with his thumb. I'm sorry dear, you say your grandmother?" she asked, cottoning on suddenly.

"Yes, yes, I have picture," the soldier said, rifling through his tunic pockets. "Many picture."

"Oh, oh yes, I er, I see what you mean," Esther said, exercising restraint at the first hilarious photograph of the lad's ninety-seven-year-old grandmother sitting in her wicker rocking chair in the corner of a smoke-filled room.

"She no travel," the recruit told her. "She just sit, every day she sit."

"Well you tell her from me, dear," Esther said, handing back the photograph and thumbing the others. "She might call that her living room but in fact it's quite the opposite. Life, real life, is out here, so sweet you can taste it. Take it from me I think I've lived more in the past days than I've done in a long long time."

"But she is old," the recruit added.

"Old!" Esther scoffed. "Age, dear boy, is a state of mind. It can either defeat you or set you free. Us old people, as you say, have no ties, no responsibilities, our children have long since flown the coop and more importantly, we just don't give a damn anymore."

The recruit barely got the gist of what Esther was saying but listened intently with the others all the same as she continued: "As my own darling grandmother used to say," she said, determined to get her point across, "'You're a long time dead Essy girl'. And she herself was seventy-two when she accompanied a party of climbers to the summit of Mount Kilimanjaro! God, that woman had a zest for life, was as strong as an ox and 'broad across the beam' as my grandfather used to joke. I'm sorry, dear boy," she told him. "I'm waffling, aren't I?"

But the gathering had moved in closer, enthralled at her take on life, a brief glimpse of escapism in their turbulent time of war.

"Africa!" one of them gasped.

"Yes that's right," Esther explained. "On the border of Tanzania and Kenya to be precise. She and the fifteen-man team set out from Nairobi and walked for three days to the foot of the mountain, encountering lions, elephants and rhino along the way. She told me she was trapped in her tent with a ravenous lioness tearing at the canvas, so in desperation and without a weapon, she slipped a big-band seventy-eight on her wind-up gramophone and let the beast have it at full volume!"

"What happened?" another soldier asked over his friend's shoulder. "What happened to your grandmother?"

"Oh she was fine, dear." Esther smiled. "The horrified lioness turned tail and fled across the open plain with its tail tucked firmly between her legs."

Whether this was just a wild fantasy that a grandmother would tell her granddaughter at bedtime or not, the troops listened in amazement nethertheless.

"Why she take gramophone?" the lieutenant asked from amongst his men. "To Africa. Why?"

"She never went anywhere without it, dear," Esther told him. "She was hugely patriotic, my grandmother. Do you know she had high tea at the summit of Kilimanjaro and played 'Land of Hope and Glory' while doing so. The natives found it all highly amusing of course, but she embodied everything that it was to be British, you see, and she would never for a moment let her impeccable standards slip a jot whenever she was away from her beloved home."

Meanwhile Minnie, with an audience of her own, had got to grips with an enormous bowl of crude rock cake mix, seconding two willing soldiers to help with the heavy mixing. "That's it, my lovelies," she told them, peering into the bowl and adding a little more water. "Splendid, splendid!"

Spooning the sticky mixture onto flat greased trays, Minnie offered the bowl to her onlookers, who all jostled to dip in a finger. "Esther was always first to the bowl whenever our mother made cakes," she told her keen kitchen helpers. "Until I slipped a packet of salt in the mix and taught her a lesson that is. Mind you, our mother was furious and made me eat two of the cakes every day until they were gone. I had to drink lashings of lemonade just to get rid of the taste."

Having enthralled and fed the Russian troops, Esther and Minnie were treated to a hearty military breakfast that was more than capable of sustaining a body through the rigours of battle. "Oh my, I'm stuffed," Esther said, leaning back and pushing her plate away. "Minnie dear, would you like the remainder of my beans?"

Minnie uncharacteristically shook her head whilst struggling to finish her own beast of a breakfast.

"Are you unwell, dear?" Esther asked, having predicted her sister's gannet-like response.

"No, no, er," Minnie said, rubbing her bloated stomach. "I had a rock cake or two with the chaps you see."

"Oh I might have known." Esther smiled. "I'm surprised the poor fellows got a look in." She looked across at the grinning troops tucking into Minnie's mouth-watering cakes.

"No I just had the two, dear," Minnie confessed, omitting the fact that while she was in the kitchen she'd eaten half a loaf of Russian black bread, which contained molasses, onion powder and instant coffee, a firm favourite with marching men and their fellow countrymen alike. She'd also willingly sampled the cook's cabbage rolls, stroganoff, salted cucumbers and tasted his powerful horseradish soup from the nine-gallon field pot that was permanently simmering on the stove.

"Just the two?" Esther asked, grinning.

"Oh yes, dear," Minnie replied, with a gurgling stomach. "I'd hate to make a pig of myself in front of strangers."

"Oh no of course not, dear." Esther laughed, knowing her sister oh so well. "Perish the thought."

Back home, while his mother switched from one satellite news channel to another, with a remote control gripped in one hand and a whisky glass in the other, Richard sat composing lengthy emails to the Prime Minister, begging for his help and replying to the countless well-wishing posts on their hugely popular social network platforms.

"Mum there's a tweet here from King Hussain of Jordon," he said over her shoulder.

Peshwari Nans

"Mmmmm?" Elizabeth said without batting an eye, sleep deprivation having got the better of her.

"Oh and Gran'll be pleased," he added. "There's one here from Paul O'Grady."

"Riiiiiight," his mother mumbled, her eyes glued to the television.

"You should get some sleep, Mum," Richard told her, spinning round on his computer chair. "Go on. I'll let you know if there's any developments."

Elizabeth stabbed at the remote buttons frantically as the batteries ran dry. "Shit!" she cursed, leaning closer to the screen. "Richard, be a dear and take the batteries out of the smoke alarm, will you?" she asked without a thought for the safety implications.

"No way, Mum," Richard protested. "I'm not taking the batteries out of the alarm for God's sake."

"Just get the damn BATTERIES!" Elizabeth yelled psychotically. "Now Richard!"

"Okay, okay!" Richard said, positioning a chair beneath the alarm. "But then I'm going straight to the corner shop for new ones."

Elizabeth snatched the triple-A batteries from her son and wrenched the back off the remote control.

"Mother, you really should get some rest," Richard said, standing at her side and stroking her hair. "Gran and Aunt Min'll be fine, they're not going to hurt a pair of sweet old ladies are they? Not with the entire world watching, anyway."

Elizabeth tossed the spent batteries aside and wrestled with the replacements. "Oh God, look there he is, the bastard!" she snarled, seeing President Putin standing before a Russian press conference.

"Sir, sir!" a representative of the Russian state owned news agency TASS called, raising his hand. "Sir, what do you make of the British and their increased military presence in the Baltic Sea? At present their HMS Richmond and Sutherland are within missile range of our beloved capital."

"I am aware of this," the Premier said, unflinching. "It is nothing, they would not dare fire on us, we have enough warheads standing by to sink the entire British fleet, so let them come. I will never concede to the West, never!"

The situation caused by two wayward ladies in a Morris Traveller had truly escalated to epic proportions. Never before had tensions between East and West been so high—even the Reagan/Gorbachev years paled into insignificance.

The US were on high alert with all military personnel refused leave and confined to base, ready for deployment at a moment's notice, and all this time Esther and Minnie were coping with their brief spell of confinement with true British resolve.

"Oh alright if you insist, dear," Minnie said, accepting yet another handful of chocolate from a Russian serviceman. "I'll pack it for our onward journey, although heaven only knows when that'll be."

"Putin must back down!" the lieutenant insisted, gathering his troops around him. "Do you agree?"

The fifty or so soldiers around him nodded. "Yes, yes, he must!" they yelled. "Putin must set them free!"

Minnie raised her hand. "No need to trouble yourselves, my dears," she told them. But a wave of rebellion had already formed within the forward Russian regiment, one that would soon turn the tide of loyalty the troops had for their president against him.

Slowly the resentment grew and grew within the superpower. A handful of Mother Russia's finest fighter pilots refused to take to the air and two nuclear submarine captains surfaced from deep beneath the polar ice cap, thus giving away their clandestine position. The President threatened court marshals and hard labour for such defiance, but the rapidly escalating numbers of conscientious objectors meant that his prisons would be full to capacity within a matter of days.

"DAMN THEM!" Putin roared, cursing the day the sisters had ever strayed into Ukrainian territory. "DAMN THEM TO HELL!"

"Sir," his general said, entering his office unannounced. "I'm afraid we have a situation."

"Boris, tell me something I did not know!" the President snapped, standing with his back to a roaring fire with a portrait of the Communist revolutionary Vladimir Lenin hanging over it.

"No, no, sir, a very serious situation," the general insisted. "Look, sir." Boris unveiled a global map on the President's desk. "The British now have destroyers, aircraft carriers and frigates here, here and here." He gestured to waters well within Russian territory. "Their hurricanes and tornadoes are fuelling as we speak, and, sir, we have detected long-range nuclear missile activity from their silos."

The President slammed the palm of his hand down hard onto the map. "I told you, let them come!" he barked, slathering at the mouth.

"But sir, we have no defence," Boris informed him. "No defence against this threat."

"What do you mean?" the President asked abruptly. "Of course we have a defence! Ready my fleet to intercept them and have my warheads armed immediately."

"But, but how, sir?" Boris asked, flinching somewhat at the President's violent gesture. "No one will fly. We have a mutiny on our hands, sir, our war in Ukraine has collapsed, with both sides laying down their weapons."

"WHAT?" the President bellowed. "I want a war, Boris! War with those British dogs and I want it now! Make it happen, do you hear me Boris? MAKE IT HAPPEN NOW!"

Boris backed away a foot or so. "But I am trying to tell you, Mr President, that we cannot go to war. Our armies are united in defiance, as is our air force and our fleet. Mr President we are sitting ducks, sir. If the British launch an attack we would undoubtedly face greater casualties, military and civilian, than both of our previous wars combined. In a word, sir, we cannot win."

"Then launch the nukes!" the President said, wild-eyed. "Launch them now and finish this before they strike. Launch them, Boris, I am giving you a direct order. What are you waiting for? I want the British wiped off the face of this planet.

"LAUNCH THEM NOW BORIS!"

"Impossible, sir," Boris said, taking another step back. "All of our warheads have been decommissioned and rendered useless by our own personnel. Our ground troops have disarmed and our fleet has returned to base. Mr President we are defenceless, completely."

The British prime minister had been informed of the Russian rebellion and placed another call to the Kremlin.

"It seems I have you at a disadvantage, dear boy," Mr Cameron told the Russian premier. "I am well aware of your rather embarrassing, shall we say *situation*. I am there in your backyard, so to speak, and there isn't a damn thing you can do about it. The security council are beside me on this as I'm sure you are well aware. Now, shall we talk terms?"

"Grrrrrr I will bury you all, Cameron!" the President snarled down the telephone. "Even if I have to arm every warhead myself, I will bury you!"

"Sir? Mr President?" Boris said at his side, producing projected Russian casualty figures by means of a pie chart.

Peshwari Nans

"We cannot win this. Look, sir, Mother Russia will be destroyed."

The President snatched the papers, screwed them up and tossed them into his fire, but deep down he knew his hands were well and truly tied, and his vast arsenal of weapons lacked powder.

"I don't think so, Putin," the Prime Minister said smugly. "At present you are a laughing stock. The world is watching you flounder helplessly while we bear down on you with everything we have, so I suggest if you wish to save the slightest bit of face in all this you listen to what I have to say, and you listen good, old boy, do I make myself clear?"

"GRRRR DAMN YOU!" President Putin raged, the most stubborn of men at the best of times. "Damn you and your pompous Britishness, with your tea and cricket and a 'jolly good show'! Damn you!"

"Nethertheless, Putin," the PM said, maintaining his composure while the President went into complete meltdown, "we will attack if my terms aren't met, and we will defeat you. Now do you really want to be remembered as the president that led his country to a crushing defeat? How would that read on your epitaph? It hardly ranks with your great predecessors, now does it?"

The Russian President lowered the phone and thought for a moment, looking up at Lenin's portrait, a legendary figure, a proud noble and adored by millions. "You will leave my waters?" he eventually said, resuming the conversation.

"You have my word," his British counterpart replied. "But you know what I want in return: the release and safe passage of the Peshwari Nans, and I repeat safe passage. Those ladies aren't to be harmed in any way, do you hear? It's not only your head on the line, I'll have you know."

"Your countrymen too?" the President asked.

Peshwari Nans

"Of course," the PM replied. "We are at a standstill here. I have all-out strikes throughout the British isles, within the transport infrastructure, electricity, gas, refuse, local government, you see I have no choice. If we do not broker a deal I must go to war or risk the collapse of democracy within the United Kingdom, and my place in history will be equally marred. So tell me, what's it to be?"

Biting his lip, the Russian leader was eventually forced to concede. "Okay, okay!" he said, snapping the pen in his hand in two. "You can have your Nans, I will see to their release immediately, just leave my waters and stand down your nuclear weapons. I too have strikes and rebellion here, I am besieged in the Kremlin by a crowd of thousands beating at my door. Tell me please, who are these Peshwari Nans to bring two great nations to their knees?"

"If I only knew," the PM replied, peering from his own window at the rocking Downing Street gates. The crowd had swelled and had begun hurling placards and street furniture over the railings at the cowering police officers ordered to guard him. "So we have a deal then?" he asked with fingers crossed.

"Yes, yes, we do," the Russian President told him, equally relieved. "You have my word. Boris?" he then called to his pensive general. "Give the order for the release of the British ladies."

A huge smile brightened Boris's face as he hurried from his president's office to break the good news.

"Thank you," the PM told Mr Putin. "Thank you for both our sakes. I will order the return of British forces immediately, goodbye Mr President."

He then summoned his aide. "Pete, call a press conference right away," he insisted. "Do it now, man, hurry!" the gates outside his home were beginning to weaken with the constant barrage of surging bodies.

Peshwari Nans

Exactly one hour later the British press were gathered with pens and Dictaphones poised. "Good morning ladies and gentlemen," the Prime Minister said, entering the room swiftly from the right. "Thank you all for coming at such short notice."

"What about the Nans?" an impatient hack yelled from the back of the room.

"Yes, yes, please give me a moment" the PM said, hands raised to calm the gathering. "I have some news on that matter that I think you'll all wish to hear. After lengthy negotiations with the Kremlin and of course Mr Putin, I am pleased to announce that the so called 'Peshwari Nans' are to be freed."

"YES!" was the instant reaction from many of the grinning reporters as they furiously scribbled onto their pads.

This meteoric news filtered through to the Internet within minutes and once again servers the world over struggled to cope with the intense overload. The giant electronic billboards that had once reported their imprisonment suddenly flashed continuously in a dozen different languages: THE PESHWARI NANS ARE FREE.

The PM was then whisked away to explain himself before the queen at Buckingham Palace as the British public rejoiced.

Premier league football matches were halted during play as their scores were erased from their screens and replaced with those five long awaited words, sending jubilant Mexican waves cascading around many of the stadiums.

Union officials called off their industrial action to the delight of their members and all those affected by the stoppages. While the sisters were waiting patiently for the news to filter through to their military encampment, huge parties were getting underway in all major British cities—an enormous boost to the economy as sales of alcohol, barbecues and carnival regalia reached an all-time high.

"Thank God," the prime minister said in the back of his limo as it swept through the palace gates, as his aide reported his rating rising out of the red.

Meanwhile at Elizabeth's house Richard raced in from the garden to find his mother in a drunken stupor, sound asleep slumped on the sofa, the TV remote in hand.

"MUM! MUM!" he cried, rounding the coffee table to shake her. "Mum, wake up! Mum they're fine!"

Elizabeth hardly stirred with the empty whisky bottle at her feet.

"Muuuuum!" Richard said again. "Gran and Aunt Min, they're free!"

"Mmmmm, what?" Elizabeth slurred, wiping her mouth. "Leave me alone, Richard!" she snapped, pushing her son away and grappling for the empty bottle.

"Mum!" Richard insisted, shaking her yet again. "The Russians are letting them go—Gran and Aunt Min! Look!" he gestured to the television, where the news crews were reporting the celebrations in Trafalgar Square. "Look Mum, that's all for Gran and Aunt Min," he told her. "Can you believe it?"

"Oh my God!" Elizabeth gasped, rolling from the sofa and clutching her throbbing head. "Richard, Mother's free!"

"That's what I've been trying to tell you, Mum," Richard said, exasperated to say the least. "You can stop worrying now, can't you?"

"Don't be ridiculous, Richard," his mother said, peering into the empty whisky bottle. "I won't rest until my mother is back from her ridiculous folly."

"Ohhh great." Richard sighed, having assumed the good news would finally put an end to her habitual drinking and neurosis.

Peshwari Nans

"Be a dear, Richard," Elizabeth asked, reaching for her purse. "Pop down to Romero's on the corner and get me a litre of Glenfiddich. Oh and while you're there see if his wife at the pharmacy counter has any Prozac. Tell her it's for me, she'll understand."

"You can't take pills with whisky, Mum," Richard told her as she thrust a fifty pound note into his hand. "You need help," he added, stroking her shoulder. "Why don't I make you an appointment with the doctor while I'm out, eh? Maybe he would prescribe you something a little more suitable, antidepressants maybe."

"Antidepressants!" Elizabeth stormed. "Is that what you think, Richard? That I'm depressed? Well thank you!"

"No Mum, look, you don't understand," Richard said, following his mother around the room. "Just let him check you over. You're not right, Mum, you know that."

"Richard!" his mother yelled, refusing to listen to reason. "Just get me the damn pills and whisky, that's all I need, not bloody therapy. Now go, Richard, and hurry back."

Richard reluctantly left his mother, forgetting that the media was encamped outside the front door.

"SON, SON, OVER HERE!" several reporters yelled.

"Excuse me," a female CNN journalist said, tugging Richard to one side. "Can you tell us what your relationship is to the Peshwari Nans?"

"Who? Oh yes, right," Richard replied, wincing at the countless flashes aimed his way. "Well one of them, Esther, is my grandmother and the other is her sister, my Aunt Minnie."

There was a murmur of "Esther and Minnie" throughout the eager crowd.

"And your name is?" the journalist asked, thrusting her microphone closer to Richard's face.

"Richard. But look," Richard said, trying to break away. "I really have to go. I have to run an errand for my mother."

"Your mother?" she said, looking over his shoulder. "Is she at home?"

"Yes, but," Richard replied, knowing his mother was in no fit state to be plagued. "She's, she's, not well and can't be disturbed, so if you'll excuse me—"

"—One more question please!" another jostling reporter said, waving yet another microphone. "If Esther and Minnie are your grandmother and great aunt, who is Vivien?"

"The car of course," Richard informed them. "Not just any old car though, she's a classic with bundles of character and olde-worlde charm. My friends and I fixed her up before they left for India."

"India?" another hack gasped. "Why on earth are two pensioners going to India, for Christ's sake? Just how old did you say they were?"

"I didn't" Richard replied abruptly. "But if you must know my Gran is eighty-seven and Aunt Min is eighty-four, and I'm very proud of both of them."

"No doubt you are," the CNN reporter agreed. "And your mother, how did she feel when her own mother at the ripe old age of eighty-seven you said, decided to hop in a classic car and drive halfway around the world through treacherous war-torn territories?"

"Well," Richard said struck speechless momentarily. "She, err, she's behind them all the way of course, we all are."

This was a huge untruth of course but entirely necessary, considering his mother's present mental condition. "I really do have to go now," he added, shoving his way through to the gate past the gathered media representatives. "Seeya!" Richard marched quickly off in the direction of the corner shops, still hugely relieved and overjoyed that the family elders would soon be free.

Almost fifteen hundred miles away as the crow flies, in their temporary military encampment where the sisters had been held, a guard at the main gate was the first to receive the news from Moscow from an arriving troop carrier. "Really!" he said, flinging his hat into the air. "This is true?"

"Yes, yes, from Putin himself," the smiling driver replied as the barrier was raised.

"Thank you, thank you!" the guard yelled, starting off across the compound, leaving his mud-splattered hat "HEYYY, HEYYYYYYY!" he cried, waving his hands in the air and heading for the mess tent. "PUTIN, PUTIN HAS GIVEN THE ORDER!"

Hearing this and assuming that the president had ordered their execution, the troops within rushed to the entrance to form a human shield to protect the sisters, with side arms drawn.

"NO!" their commander barked. "Not while I draw breath!"

"Me too, me too," his men said, standing adamantly at his side. "He will have to kill us all first." Four heavily armed officers surrounded the sisters' table, each of them prepared to take a bullet to save them.

"This doesn't look good, dear," Esther said, taking her trembling sister's hand.

"Ohhhh Essyyyy!" Minnie said, cowering. "I love you, dear."

"I love you too, dear," Esther said with her head down and an arm around Minnie, pulling her close.

"STAND DOWN!" the commander yelled at the approaching guard, aiming his pistol at the hysterical Russian's head. "I SAID STAND DOWN OR I WILL SHOOT!"

Peshwari Nans

"No, wait, you do not understand!" the guard replied, skidding to a halt as his commander fired a warning shot, inches from his head. "Putin has given the order!"

"And I said NO!" the camp commander bellowed. "Not today, not tomorrow, never you hear! You tell Putin he will never take the lives of these ladies, NEVER!"

"No, no." The guard laughed. "Putin has set them free, he has given the order, our ladies are free to go!"

"Free?" the commander said, lowering his weapon slowly. "Is this true?"

"Yes, yes, of course," the guard said, punching the air. "Our ladies, they are free." His use of the term 'our ladies' was shared with each and every individual within the camp, all of them touched in some way by the sisters' timid sweetness and their ever-present zest for life.

The commander turned and pushed his way back inside the mess tent, yelling to the sisters' four personal guards in his native tongue that their leader had buckled under mounting global pressure and rubber-stamped their release.

"What did he say, dear?" Minnie asked, still clinging, white knuckled, to her sister's sleeve.

"You are free!" one of the four guards said, turning to help the two of them to their feet. "You are free."

"It is true," the commander reiterated. "Our president has given his word. You will not be harmed and we are to help you on your way as soon as possible."

"Really?" Esther cried. "Oh God, I thought—"

"—Me too, dear," Minnie added, still visibly shaken.

"No, no, I assure you it is correct." The commander smiled, taking their hands. "I too thought the worst for you but believe me you would not have been taken from us without a fight, and a bloody fight at that!"

"Why thank you, dear," Esther said, squeezing his hand. "My sister and I have grown rather fond of you all, thank you, thank you for being so kind and hospitable."

Peshwari Nans

"Yes, we've thoroughly enjoyed our stay," Minnie told the surrounding troops. "And we're going to miss each and every one of you."

"Ahhhhhhh," some of the soldiers sighed, rubbing the sisters' backs. "You have been so good to us," one of them said, speaking for everyone present. "And Minnie, we are really going to miss your cakes." A huge cheer of agreement rang out throughout the mess tent.

"And who will darn my undergarments?" another called out, waving his threadbare pants.

"You're on your own there, Gustav," one of his friends joked, backing away out of range.

Esther and Minnie were followed back to their tent by the entire camp contingent, who all waited outside in high spirits while they gathered their belongings. Vivien was driven out of the mechanics' compound, having been completely overhauled once again. Parts had been delivered by army helicopter from the city of Volgograd, where the Russian arm of the Morris Minor Owners Club were based, and whatever was no longer available had been hand crafted by the ingenious military mechanics.

The sisters emerged from their tent to a sea of smiling faces. "Oh look, dear!" Minnie told her sister. "Doesn't Vivien look absolutely stunning again."

"Oh my, yes dear, doesn't she just," Esther agreed, looking at her reflection in the gleaming bonnet.

The surrounding troops hastily removed their hats and caps and fussed over the sisters, carrying their bags and opening Vivien's doors.

"Thank you." Esther smiled. "Thank you all, you're so kind, it's, it's really quite touching."

The camp cook approached Minnie and handed her the pinnie she had worn, with its Russian insignia and a parcel of food, enough to last them a day or two. "Ahhhhh, thank you, Vassily," she said, hugging him. "Now," she said, brushing crumbs from his lapel. "You do remember the recipe for the patriotic pudding don't you?"

Vassily produced a piece of paper from his pocket "Yes, yes I have it," he said chirpily. "And those cakes of rock of yours, I will make them every day."

"Rock cakes, dear." Minnie laughed. "I'm so glad you liked them. My father always went to work with one tucked in his pocket, he used to say there were three things he could never live without: a pipe, a pint and one of Mother's rock cakes. Mother wasn't best pleased of course, not getting a mention and all."

Esther approached a munitions box. "Could you help me, dear?" she asked an adjacent soldier, who carefully lifted her aloft.

"Ahem!" she said, clearing her throat. "I er, I know many of you will not understand so I'll expect your friends to translate for you. My sister and I, although delayed from our journey, have learned so much from your culture. You are a warm and loving people with loving families no doubt."

Many lowered their heads at the mention of their loved ones.

"This is not at all how you have been portrayed by the rest of the world, I assure you," she continued as they shuffled closer. "This, this war of yours," she said, taking a handkerchief from her sleeve and wiping her nose, "it's so unnecessary don't you think? The fighting and bloodshed that goes on day after day causes so much pain and suffering to those left behind. Minnie and I, being as old as we are, have witnessed more than our fair share of heartache associated with battle during our lives, so I suppose what I'm trying to say is surely enough is enough? Sometimes there has to be an end to the killing for the sake of humanity itself, for the sake of your mothers, fathers, brothers, sisters and for the sake of your children. What message do we send to the children? I say we send them one of hope, hope for a brighter future. What do you say?"

Esther's speech for peace in the region had more than a few of the surrounding troops wiping a tear from their eyes, thinking of home and for the first time of those they were sent to kill. Esther was helped down from the box to rapturous applause as she rejoined her sister,

"Beautifully put, Essy dear," Minnie told her, pecking her cheek. "Beautifully."

"Ladies," the camp commander said, offering his hand once again. "It has been a pleasure and indeed an honour to have been in your company, and it's Stanislav," he told them. "You wanted to know my name, it's Stanislav. On behalf of me and my men I wish you a safe journey and want you to know you will always be held with the greatest esteem amongst us. I have instructed an armoured unit of my finest men to escort you back to the Russian border where you will be safe, and you are right about this war, it is senseless, my men are tired and wish to go home."

"Then take them home," Minnie insisted. "To hell with your orders. We are free because of you, now free yourselves! Go home, all of you!"

A murmur of rebellion reverberated throughout the camp as many threw down their weapons in defiance of their tyrannical leadership.

"Beautifully put yourself, dear," Esther said, patting her sister's back.

"I learned from the best, dear." Minnie smiled, climbing aboard Vivien.

The sisters waved to the troops, who parted, applauding them wholeheartedly. "Goodbyyyyye, goodbyyyyye!" they said from their open windows as they followed the personnel carrier out of the gate. Looking in the rear-view mirror, Esther followed them out onto the road with their hands in the air.

Peshwari Nans

"What a delightful bunch they were," she told her sister, who had already started on Vassily's kitchen gifts.

"Mmmmmm, yes indeed," Minnie replied with her mouth full. "Delightful, dear."

The war in Eastern Ukraine turned a new and dramatic corner that day with the capital Kiev and rebel leaders signing a fresh peace agreement, a truce in which each side would begin to withdraw heavy artillery and weapons from the front line immediately. Thousands of lives had already been lost in the bloody conflict, but for Stanislav and his men the news came as a great source of comfort, knowing they could all be home in a matter of days.

"Black bread, dear?" Minnie said, offering her sister a slice whilst showering her lap with crumbs.

"No thank you, Minnie dear," Esther replied, smiling as she turned toward the Russian border. "I haven't been able to pass anything since you gave me those blasted rock cakes. You did follow the recipe to the letter, didn't you?"

"Well," Minnie replied, scooping the crumbs from her dress. "In times of war, dear, one has to make do and use whatever is at hand. I'm sure Mother would agree, don't you think?"

The camp commander himself was soon hovering over an open pit clutching his stomach, cursing Vassily, who hovered beside him red-faced, with his trousers at his ankles.

"What do you mean, make do?" Esther snarled, as the gurgling in her lower intestine grew louder. "Minnie!" Esther's eyes widened as her sister listed the replacement ingredients she had used, the end result being a far cry from their dear beloved mother's original recipe.

CHAPTER SEVEN

Having bid a fond farewell to their Russian escort the sisters finally crossed into the motherland at Milerovo, where the border guards checked their papers and swiftly waved them on, following strict orders from above.

"How odd," Esther said, seeing the streets ahead lined with ecstatic locals held back by a police cordon. She then checked her rear-view mirror to see if maybe a limousine containing a visiting VIP had followed them across but the road behind was clear.

"Essy I think this is for us, dear," Minnie said on seeing a small child holding up a crudely drawn image of two elderly ladies, both bent over with overly long noses, crooked backs and bent canes.

"Are you sure, dear?" Esther asked, seeing absolutely no resemblance to them whatsoever. But a young boy sitting in a wooden box cart by the name of Vivien swayed her. "What on earth?" she gasped, passing slowly by as rice and scented blooms were tossed toward them.

They were then stopped by two motorcycle police officers.

"You are the Nans?" one of them asked in a deep officious tone.

"Errrr yes, yes, I suppose we are," Esther said, very much in awe of their welcoming committee, while her sister leaned from her window and accepted the juvenile's amateur caricature.

"Oh thank you, my darling," Minnie told the five-year-old Russian girl. "You seem to have captured my sister to a tee."

The child blushed and ran back to her mother's arms, having slipped through the jostling cordon.

"We are to escort you to Moscow," the rider added. "The President's orders, please follow."

"Moscow!" Esther said. "But we were hoping to avoid the capital. We have some ground to make up, you see."

"You follow!" the second rider barked, donning his helmet and kick-starting his motorcycle.

"Ohhhhh phooey!" Esther said, starting after them. "Now what?"

Minnie waved regally to the bystanders, lapping up the adoration. "Who do you think you are, dear?" Esther scoffed. "Camilla Parker Bowles?"

"How did you guess, dear?" Minnie smiled, acknowledging their cheers. "You know, if she hadn't snapped up our Charles when she did I think I might have made a play for him myself."

"You!" Esther laughed, following closely behind the police riders. "Whatever gives you the impression he'd look twice at a commoner like you?"

"Essy, dear," Minnie said, puffing her chest somewhat. "I may be several years his senior and not cut from exactly the same cloth, but I think I have the wherewithal to float his boat, so to speak. I've always found him oddly alluring, do you know I bet he's an absolute dynamo beneath the sheets."

"Minnie, dear!" Esther snapped. "I'll remind you that's our future king you are talking about, not some lecherous beast from the bowls club!"

"Oh don't be such a fuddy duddy, dear," Minnie scoffed, plucking a flower from Vivien's wing mirror and putting it to her nose. "They're just the same as you and I behind closed doors. No I'd imagine he finds a mother figure quite arousing, as many men do. My Cyril often dressed in short trousers and insisted on six of the best with a bamboo cane."

"Minnie!" Esther remarked, horrified at her sister's candour. "Would you kindly keep your shameful shenanigans to yourself! I'd rather not know if it's all the same to you."

"Oh Essy, you have led a sheltered life, haven't you?" Minnie chuckled, placing the flower on the dashboard in front of her, having been a tad more adventurous in the boudoir than her sister could ever imagine. "There's more to life than meat and two veg and the missionary position I'll have you know. Cyril used to do this thing with a stick of rhubarb and melted wax that drove me absolutely—"

"—Minnie, that's enough!" Esther snapped, feeling altogether queasy. "Jack and I would never dream of such, such, *debauchery.*"

"And you ran a greengrocer's, dear." Minnie smiled, imagining the endless possibilities therein. "What a waste."

Esther blushed and hurriedly changed the subject. "Get on to our Mr Google will you please, dear?" she told her sister. "Find out just how far this blasted detour is taking us out of our way. President or no president we have a pressing engagement in the opposite direction."

"Right you are, dear," Minnie said, tapping at the tablet whilst delving one handed into the Russian tuck box again. "Eight hundred and seventy kilometres to be exact, dear," she informed her sister, brushing the breadcrumbs from the screen. "A trip of around twelve hours in a modern automobile."

"Eight hundred and seventy!" Esther gasped. "Eight hundred and seventy kilometres!"

"Yes, around five hundred and forty miles, my darling," Minnie added.

"Oh no, dear, that's quite preposterous," Esther said, shaking her head. Then, without any warning whatsoever, she pulled off the main road and into a side street while the motorcyclists continued, distracted momentarily by a shapely leg in a short skirt.

"What are you doing, dear?" Minnie asked, looking over her shoulder whilst nibbling her black bread.

"What we came to do," Esther replied, checking her mirrors, turning left then right to evade their escort.

"HEY!" one of the Russian police officers called to his colleague, looking behind them. The pair stopped, dismounted and looked all around. "Where are the Nans?" he asked.

"They were there!" his colleague said, flabbergasted. "Why were you not watching them?"

"Me?" his friend barked. "I thought you were watching them!" The pair began a heated argument in the middle of the road.

"Putin will have our heads for this!" one of them cried, leaping back onto his purring motorcycle. "FIND THEM! FIND THEM AT ONCE!".

Taking separate streets, the two Russian cops sped from left to right, craning their necks to find the distinctive car and its runaway occupants, who had somehow escaped them.

Esther could hear the hum of the powerful police machines somewhere behind them and turned into narrow alleyways, upsetting several brimming refuse bins. "Ooooh, how exciting!" Minnie squealed, holding on to her hat.

"Hang on, dear!" Esther cried, mounting a hump in the road which dislodged them from their seats and rattled the Royal Albert china behind them.

"Careful, dear!" Minnie cried, clinging to the tablet and the tea tin.

"Don't worry, Minnie darling," Esther said confidently, whilst speeding through a bustling marketplace, honking her horn to alert the innocent bystanders, who snatched their bags and children out of harm's way.

Peshwari Nans

"SORRYYYYYY!" she called out of the window in passing.

"Ooooooh look, dear!" Minnie shrieked, observing the surrounding stalls. "They have the tie-backs and matching velvet drapes we've been looking for."

"Not now, dear," Esther insisted. "We haven't time I'm afraid."

Ordinarily the sisters would never pass up the opportunity to browse a market stall of two, haggling with the stallholders over a few coins, which increased the thrill tenfold.

"Shame." Minnie sighed with the bountiful bargains beyond her reach. "They had the scatter cushion covers too."

"What?" Esther exclaimed, slamming on the brakes. "In blue velvet?"

"Yes dear, with the exact same gold braid," Minnie explained, looking over her shoulder.

"Well, well, what are you waiting for?" Esther said, leaning across her sister to fling her door open. "Go and get them at once!"

"But, dear, those men!" Minnie protested.

"Minnie!" her sister said forcefully. "An opportunity like this does not present itself every day I'll have you know, so go and get those curtains, covers and tie-backs at once, and don't forget to barter, dear, like your life depended on it, alright?"

"Alright, dear," Minnie agreed, taking the money from her sister's hand. "Shall I pick up something for our tea too, dear?" she asked.

"No of course not!" Esther barked. "Just the chintz, dear, just the chintz, now do hurry!"

With the frantic motorcyclists speeding up and down the adjacent streets, desperately searching for the Morris Traveller, Esther sat checking her appearance in the mirror, adjusting her hat and applying a little extra foundation. Minnie on the other hand, queued behind a group of locals perusing the furnishings.

"Excuse me!" she said over their shoulders, attracting the stallholder's attention. "I'd like the blue cushions and tie-backs please if you don't mind, the blue with gold braid!"

The stallholder ignored her and continued to plump his cushions "I sayyyy!" Minnie called a little louder. "I am in rather a hurry if you don't mind, COOOOEEEEEE!"

An angry customer in front spun round and glared at her. "You wait!" she said with her arms folded across her ample chest.

"No, no, you don't understand," Minnie explained. "We haven't time you see, my sister and I are being pursued by the police."

"Police!" the market stallholder said, pricking up his ears. "You bring police? Go, go!" He pushed Minnie away, only too aware that he'd just received a consignment from a highly questionable source. "GO PLEASE!"

"I'm not leaving without those cushions," Minnie said defiantly, with her eyes firmly fixed on the prize. "So I guess we'll both just have to sit and wait till they arrive."

"No, no, please you go!" the stallholder begged. "You want cushion, I give you good price!"

"Okay, now we're getting somewhere." Minnie smiled, rolling up her sleeves in anticipation. "Shall we say five hundred rubles?" (this equated to a little under six English pounds) "For the set and another two hundred for the tie-backs?"

"WHAT?" the stallholder said wide-eyed. "I pay more than you offer for this. You give me two thousand rubles for all."

"Ohhhh no no no no no." Minnie laughed. "Five hundred and not a ruble more."

Peshwari Nans

"Five hundred!" The man again gasped. "Please I am a poor man, my children are hungry, my wife is sick."

"Yes yes yes, I know exactly how this works, young man," Minnie warned him. "You bleat and whine about your hardships and I'm supposed to up the ante, but I'm afraid you've met your match here, matey boy. I've haggled with the best of them and emerged victorious every time. Five hundred is my final offer, take it or I'll make myself comfortable right here and wait for our mounted friends to arrive. What's it to be?"

"Fifteen hundred, please!" the stallholder replied, breaking into a sweat. "And I make no profit for this. Please madam, please!"

"Five hundred," Minnie said, stiff lipped. "I'm sure you'll fleece the less educated and make up the shortfall." Minnie held firm at five hundred rubles as the sound of motorcycles could be heard nearby.

The desperate stallholder eyed his illegitimate stock, which if it was seized would earn him a heavy sentence of hard labour and solitary confinement for a very long time indeed.

"Please!" he begged, hands clasped. "One thousand, for my family, my dead dog and for my mother. She is like you, old and crazy in the head."

"I beg your pardon?" Minnie scoffed, pocketing half of her rubles. "Crazy in the head am I? Well my good man if I am crazy I will offer two-fifty for the cushions, tie-backs and two of your lace tablecloths."

"TWO-FIFTY!" the man cried, clasping his hands to his head. "You really are crazy. I would be cutting my throat to do this. Okay, this is what I do. I will take seven hundred, but not for the lace."

"Two-fifty," Minnie said, straight faced. "And I want that lace." She then turned in the direction of the approaching motorcycles, who were still a street away. "OVER HERE!" she called out. "I'M OVER HERE!"

"Wait, please wait!" the stallholder begged. "Okay, okay, I give you for two-fifty."

"And the lace?" Minnie asked.

"Oh damn you, yes!" the holder begrudgingly replied. "The lace too."

"Sir, you have yourself a deal," Minnie said, handing over the pittance with a smile.

The furious stallholder hastily bagged Minnie's booty and thrust it into her hands. "You go!" he snapped. "Go, go!"

"With pleasure, dear." Minnie smiled, turning for the car. "Good day to you."

The stallholder returned to his previous customers, who each stood clutching a few measly rubles, expecting the exact same deal as he'd given Minnie: a sale to end all sales that would surely bankrupt the peddler and his bootleg business.

"Any luck, dear?" Esther asked as her sister loaded her wares into Vivien's rear.

"Of course, dear," Minnie replied confidently. "Like taking candy from a baby." Their proven technique had netted the sisters a houseful of haberdashery over the years.

"Well done, darling," Esther told her sister as she climbed back in beside her, leaving the stallholder pulling his hair out as his stock dwindled before his eyes. "Right, shall we go?" she added.

"I think so, dear, don't you?" Minnie replied without a shred of urgency.

The pair set off once again, turning left as the motorcycle cops rounded the corner into the marketplace and stopped at the near ransacked soft furnishings stall with the owner close to tears. "You want the old ladies?" he cried, baying for Minnie's blood.

Peshwari Nans

"Where?" the policemen both called back, revving their engines, desperate to find the sisters.

"That way, that way!" the stallholder yelled. "Get them, get them quick, look what they do to me!"

The riders sped off once again, turning in Vivien's direction. "Putin will have our heads for sure," one called to the other.

The President had requested the sisters' presence in the Kremlin purely for propaganda purposes, using their notoriety to pressure certain western countries to lift their sanctions against him. Many of them had been angered by his treatment of the people of Crimea and his numerous NATO violations. A photocall with the famed Peshwari Nans would go a long way towards restoring his global credibility, especially with his online ratings at an all-time low. To be accepted by a fraction of Esther and Minnie's vast following would certainly be a political dream come true, and one he wasn't about to pass up on, therefore failure on the motorcyclists' part just wasn't an option.

Esther was especially determined to evade the riders and resume their road trip, refusing to play any part in those costly diversions, again turning left and right at every opportunity, she remained out of sight of the pursuing officers.

"Look, dear," Minnie said with the lace on her knee. "It has the same embroidery as our standard lamp, how wonderful."

"Yes, dear, quite," Esther replied, swerving to avoid a stray dog. "Now get the map, dear, and get us out of here. If I'm not mistaken we seem to be going around in circles at present."

"Oh yes, right you are, dear," Minnie said, placing the lace behind her. After wrestling with the giant global paper map turning it this way and that, sometimes in front of her sister's face, Minnie eventually gave up and screwed it into a ball, frustrated with the folds and creases.

"Use the gadget thing, dear!" Esther insisted, snatching the paper ball and tossing it over her shoulder whilst cutting through an industrial area, wrenching Vivien's wheel from side to side to skirt the countless potholes in the road.

It certainly wasn't Vivien's pace and manoeuvrability that helped them evade capture, it was simply blind luck and several astute decisions on Esther's part, such as stopping abruptly behind a line of steel shipping containers while the motorcyclists sped by, and crawling through a crowd of some four hundred governmental protestors.

"Ahhhh here we are, dear." Minnie smiled, seeing themselves as a flashing blue dot on the tablet's GPS. "According to this, dear, we need to head back to Volgograd and then on towards the Kazakhstan border, a distance of approximately three hundred kilometres."

"Okay, which way?" Esther said at an intersection whilst checking her rear-view mirror repeatedly.

Minnie held the tablet in front of her in both hands, like a games controller, turning it from side to side directing her sister and the blue dot out of town. "Left dear," she'd say, "another left then two rights and a left. There should be a bridge ahead and a cemetery to our right."

"Yes, yes I have it, dear," Esther replied, looking across at the regimental rows of eerie tombstones.

"Ooooh yellow car!" Minnie then called out, pinching her sister's arm, resuming the game they had started several days earlier.

"OW!" Esther shrieked. "Damn you, Minnie, this really isn't the time for such tomfoolery." But then moments later the gift of another yellow car proved too much of a temptation for her. "Oh to hell with it, yellow car!" she too said, nipping at her sister's thigh with her thumb and forefinger, startling her as she scrutinized the screen.

Peshwari Nans

"OW, that hurt!" Minnie cried, inching away.

Soon the two frantic motorcyclists were forced to give up the search and radio in to their commander.

"WHAT?" their superior yelled, leaping from his seat. "What do you mean, you lost them? Putin is expecting them today!"

"Sorry, sir," one of the red-faced officers said, switching off his engine. "We have been outfoxed."

"OUTFOXED!" the commander bellowed. "BY TWO OLD LADIES? I'LL HAVE YOUR HEADS FOR THIS, BEFORE PUTIN HAS MINE!" the commander gripped the receiver ever so tightly, as though it were his officers' throats. "FIND THEM!" he insisted. "I'm sending every man we have to assist you, now go, and do not call me unless you have them. Arrest them if you have to, chain them, drug them and lock them in a box, JUST GET THEM TO PUTIN!" With this he slammed down the phone and then, with one single furious swipe, cleared everything from his desk onto the floor in a fit of rage. But moments later, to his horror the telephone rang again and his eyes widened as he scrambled on the floor to find the phone and took the call. "Mr President," he said, hastily getting up and standing to attention and straightening his tunic. "The ladies, yes, yes, we have them, my men are escorting them to you as we speak. Yes sir, Mr President as we speak, you have my word."

The Russian Premier had invited the world's press once again to the Kremlin with the promise of a personal interview with the travelling Nans, an interview the media craved so desperately to appease their news-hungry readers and viewers. "Hurry!" he stormed. "If I am made to look a fool I assure you, Sergei, I will have your head in a basket, I promise you!" This time it was the President who slammed down the phone, leaving his Commander-in-Chief trembling and flushed blood red.

Peshwari Nans

Summoning his lieutenant, the petrified commander ordered his entire complement of officers off their day-to-day duties and insisted they join the search for the sisters, to continue through the night if they had to.

"We appear to have given them the slip, Essy dear," Minnie said, looking over her shoulder. "Do you think we could stop for a cup of tea?"

"Absolutely not," her sister said resolutely. "I'd like to put at least fifty kilometres between us and that town before we even think of stopping. Now which way? Right or left?"

"Well dear," Minnie said, pushing her luck somewhat. "According to Mr Google there's a charming little cafeteria to the left that serves cinnamon buns and iced tea, and they have a roof terrace with excellent views of the river."

"Which way, Minnie?" Esther asked, having none of it. "It's right, isn't it?"

"Yes dear, but…" Minnie said, looking to her left as her sister turned right.

"We haven't time for 'buts', dear," Esther told her, accelerating to thirty-five miles per hour. "Have some cordial and be done with it."

Whilst Minnie rummaged for refreshments behind her, some seventy men, women and canines had been mobilized to find them in over forty vehicles, including a spotter plane. "Would you like a pickle, dear?" Minnie asked, delving into a huge jar of gherkins and fishing around for the largest specimen.

"Oooh I don't mind if I do, dear," her sister said, plunging her free hand in. "Come here, you little perisher!" she cursed, chasing the lengthy pickle around the jar. "Ooooops!" she cried, clipping the kerb and plucking out the gherkin. "Gotcha!" she added with a smile. Fishing for more pickles, each of the sisters gorged themselves, unaware of the sheer scale of the operation to locate them.

Peshwari Nans

However, each time the tiny Russian plane passed overhead by pure chance it turned out that Vivien had entered a motorway tunnel or an avenue of sycamore trees, obscuring its view. Either way the gods, whoever they may be, appeared to be with them. At one point a patrol car passed them on the opposite carriageway, the officers inside gesturing wildly to the driver, pointing at Vivien, but it was at least a further six kilometres before they could make a U-turn, affording Esther valuable time to turn off the busy road and disappear into the narrow and twisting country lanes.

"Well this is nice, dear," Minnie remarked as she looked at the flowering verges and hedgerows. But the net was closing in on them after the motorway cops had radioed their position, and the spotter plane turned in their direction.

"Blast!" Esther said, catching a fleeting glimpse of the twin-engined plane in her wing mirror. "Why won't they just leave us alone?".

The anxious Russian President had no intention whatsoever of leaving them be with the world watching and waiting for his photo opportunity. And to make matters worse, the Obamas had flown in from the States to help ease the tensions between the two superpowers, and of course so they could meet the now fabled Peshwari Nans themselves, leaving President Putin extremely red-faced indeed.

"SERGEI!" he yelled into his telephone, having been kept waiting a further two hours for news of their arrival. "Tell me, where are my Nans?"

"Close, Mr President, very close," his Commander replied, looking out from his window and loosening his collar. "I just need more time, sir, and you will have them, I promise."

"MORE TIME?" Putin roared. "I DON'T HAVE MORE TIME! The damned Americans are here breathing down my neck, so bring me those ladies NOW SERGEI, NOW!"

"Well, er, Mr President," Sergei said, petrified of his leader to say the least. "If I could possibly have another hour or two I assure you I will find them."

"Find them?" the President asked fuming. "Sergei what do you mean *find them*?, You do have the Nans don't you?"

"Well, well, sir, I did," Sergei replied apprehensively.

"WHAAAAAT?" the President roared into his telephone. "SERGEI TELL ME YOU HAVE THE NANS, SERGEIIIII?"

"Mr President," Sergei said, wrestling with his conscience. "We had them, I assure you but…"

"What do you mean HAD!" the President growled. "Sergei, what are you saying? WHERE ARE THE DAMNED NANS?"

"I, er, I don't know, Mr President," Sergei confessed, holding the receiver a short distance from his ear and awaiting the President's violent backlash, which came in spades.

"YOU DON'T KNOW?" Putin yelled, furious beyond words. "YOU DON'T KNOW? SERGEI YOU IMBECILE WHAT HAVE YOU DONE?"

"I'm so sorry, sir, they got away from us," Sergei pleaded, trembling as he stood at the window. "I have every man at my disposal out looking for them. Mr President, I am confident we will find them."

At that point the President's aide entered his office. "Excuse me, Mr President," he said, raising a finger. "The Americans, sir, they're growing restless and are calling for you."

"GET OUT!" the President barked. "GET OUT I SAY!" his aide scurried from the office, clipboard in hand, to issue a further false statement on his President's behalf. "Find them, Sergei!" Putin ordered his commander. "Find them and bring them to me now, do you hear? FIND THEM, or God help me, I'll strip the flesh from your back!"

The President produced a hunting knife from his boot and drove it deep into his mahogany desk. "FIIIIIND THEEEEM!" he roared, wild-eyed and drooling.

"Yes sir, yes, yes sir," Sergei stammered, having been on the receiving end of Putin's wrath once before and carried the scars to that very day. "I promise, sir, I will have them to you, you have my word, I will see to it personally."

"DO IT!" the President said abruptly. "I want them within the hour!" He slammed down the receiver dramatically once again and kicked out at his surrounding furniture. His aide then knocked sheepishly at his door, waiting this time to be invited in. Receiving no answer, he dared to knock again a little louder.

"WHAT?" the President yelled, his blood now boiling in his veins. His aide knocked once more, positively shaking in his shoes. "YES, WHAT?" the President snapped, hurling a silver plated inkwell at the door.

The anxious aide opened the door and peered inside. "Mr President," he said, keeping his distance. "The press, sir, if we don't give them something soon our public relations exercise could be a complete disaster, and, er, as for the Americans, sir—"

"—TO HELL WITH THE AMERICANS!" the President yelled, kicking his chair across the room. "When I have the Nans I will meet with them and not a moment sooner!"

"But, sir, I thought you had the ladies," his aide said, with his back to the door. "I have informed the media of this. When will you have them, Mr President? When will you have the Peshwari Nans? And the Americans, sir, what shall I tell them?"

The fuming president wrenched his hunting knife from his desk and hurled it toward his stuttering aide, with every intention of killing him, instead embedding it an inch into the door, a hair's breadth away from his head. "If you don't get out of here right now," he raged, "I will hang those blasted Nans and go to war with the American dogs! Now get out, GET OUT, GET OUUUUT!"

"Yes, Mr President," his aide said, eyeing the knife beside him. "I'll tell them the Nans will be here very soon, sir." With this he rounded the door and hurried back to the waiting press conference, to tell a few more untruths and soothe the baying media, who were growing ever more restless.

"Where are the Nans?" they continued to call. "What is Putin hiding?"

Bitterly incensed, the Russian President flew into a blind furious rage, wrenching a fire iron from its stand and beginning to beat at his panelled office walls.

"I'LL KILL THEM, I'LL KILL THOSE BITCHES!" he stormed, hurling a stack of books across his office. Such was his venom that the President snatched his copy of the communist manifesto from above the fire and tore it to shreds: the act of a complete madman, as this was a priceless first edition, signed by none other than Karl Marx himself, co-author of the historic document, setting out all that was wrong with the capitalist ideal and written in 1884.

The manifesto was traditionally handed down from president to president but now lay in tatters at his feet. With his eyes now white and his fists firmly clenched, the President tore the lock from his personal gun cupboard and took out his high powered Kalashnikov rifle, his preferred weapon when hunting in the Caucasus mountain region. He then stuffed several boxes of ammunition into a black holdall and swung it and the rifle over his shoulder, tugged the knife from the door and left his office ransacked, cursing under his breath.

"Mr President, where are you going?" his chief of staff asked in the corridor. "Mr President, the Americans?"

The President said nothing, barging past the chief and making for the elevator. "Mr President, the press are waiting!" the astonished chief called after him. "Mr President!"

But the crazed Russian Premier had only one thing on his mind: hunting down the Nans, who had been a bloody thorn in his side for days, and bringing them back to the Kremlin. Dead or alive. Storming from the Kremlin, he pulled a guard away from his armoured jeep and leapt in, tossing the holdall onto the seat beside him, unaware that the world's press and the Americans for that matter, were watching from an upper window.

"Look!" a Russian reporter yelled. "It's Putin. What is he doing?"

Within seconds, the entire gathering was at the window, recording the departing President with his hunting rifle cocked.

"My God!" his aide said, forgetting momentarily where he was. "He's going for the Nans!"

"The Nans!" a CNN cameraman replied, capturing the footage live for their global viewers. "But I thought the Peshwari Nans were here?"

At that point the American President stepped in. "Excuse me, but why does your president feel the need to carry a gun?" he asked.

"Oh, er," the aide replied, thinking fast on his feet. "Merely for his own protection. We have many bears in our country, just like your grizzly bears."

"He's going to kill the Nans!" a French reporter yelled, starting a panic in the room, and there was a furious flashing of cameras as the President sped from the Kremlin with the scent of blood in his nostrils.

"No, no, no, please!" his aide squealed, attempting to calm the maddening crowd. "Putin would not do such a thing!" But the cat was well and truly out of the bag and yet another media storm surrounding the sisters had begun.

Blissfully unaware of the Russian Premier's manic intentions, Esther and Minnie continued their cross-country game of cat-and-mouse with Sergei's determined men, who were now hot on their heels. "There dear, there!" Minnie yelled, eyeing an open barn as the spotter plane approached from the west, temporarily blinded by the setting sun.

"Are you sure, dear?" Esther asked, turning off the road. "We'll be sitting ducks."

"Trust me, dear," Minnie replied, glancing over her shoulder. "I've seen all the movies."

"Ohhh great." Esther sighed, navigating the bumpy approach. "May I kindly remind you, dear," she told her sister, wincing as their car careered over the rough terrain. "We are not the flaming Dukes of Hazard and my Vivien is in no way the General Lee. She's a lady of the highest order and you'll do well to remember that."

"Esther!" Minnie snapped. "Just get in the damn barn will you!"

Hopping from Vivien, Minnie closed the dishevelled double doors behind them as her sister drove into the straw that was strewn around, just as three patrol cars crammed with police officers sped by and the plane passed low overhead. "Genius if I may say so myself." Minnie smiled, brushing the dust from her hands as Esther stepped from Vivien into a cow pat.

"Oh blast!" Esther cursed, dragging her dung-covered shoe through the straw. "Genius, my foot!"

Peshwari Nans

Minnie opened Vivien's rear doors and set up the camping stove. "Tea dear?" she asked her frustrated sister.

"Yes, yes, whatever," Esther moaned, eyeing her shabby surroundings. "Don't be too long though, Minnie," she told her sister. "I want to make a break for the border before nightfall."

"But we could spend the night in here, dear," Minnie suggested. "It's warm, dry and cozy, after all."

"Absolutely not!" Esther said resolutely, on seeing evidence of bat activity up in the rafters. "I'd rather die than spend one night in this filthy place."

"Oh Essy, don't be so melodramatic for heaven's sake." Minnie smiled, putting a kettle of water on the stove.

The pair settled on a straw bale in relative comfort, while the gun-toting Russian President sped to their last reported position, running every red light in doing so and brandishing his loaded weapon at all who dared to confront him. The frantic news crews fell over one another, racing from the Kremlin to their satellite vehicles to set off after him to record all of the sensational mayhem in glorious high definition, a ground-breaking scoop which would bring the viewing world to a standstill. And, just like the lunar landings and the Kennedy assassination, for generations to come the world would remember where they were when the Russian leader went berserk on a rage-fuelled manhunt, or 'Nanhunt' to be exact, through his capital and out into the Russian countryside.

"OUT OF MY WAY!" he yelled at an astonished school-bus driver, who swerved to avoid him, toppling many of the children from their seats.

"Putin, it's Putin!" one lad shrieked, picking up his school cap and peering over the rear seat, his bruised and bewildered classmates rushed to join him, having learnt of his tyrannical presidency in school that very day.

371

Peshwari Nans

"MOVE, MOVE DAMN YOU!" the President snarled, shooting out the bus's rear tyre, single handedly sending the children tumbling once again.

The racing news crew had caught up and was tailing the President. "Tell me you're getting this," the CNN reporter asked his cameraman. "The man's a complete maniac!"

Esther and Minnie sipped their tea in silence, contemplating the events of the past few days. "Last tablet, dear," Esther said, finishing the course of antibiotics that doctor Slavi had prescribed her.

"How are you feeling now, dear?" Minnie asked, examining her sister's neck. "I must say you gave me quite a fright."

"Fine, dear," her sister replied, putting Minnie's mind at rest. "Thanks to Ludwik."

"Yes, what a remarkable man," Minnie agreed. "Quite remarkable."

"Indeed he is, dear," Esther added, setting her cup down in its china saucer, the sound of which was disturbing something in the stall behind them.

"What was that?" Minnie asked, looking over her shoulder and clutching her chest as the sound of rustling straw grew louder.

"I have no idea," Esther said, standing and backing away. "And I have absolutely no intention of finding out either. Come along Minnie, let's go."

"Wait, dear," Minnie said, ever the inquisitive one.

"Come away, dear!" Esther snapped, but Minnie simply had to see for herself.

"Oh quiet, dear!" she whispered. The stall door was open as Minnie approached with caution and her heart was in her mouth and, with her sister now locked inside Vivien, she peered over the top of the stall. "Oh it's a cow, dear!" She smiled looking down on a heavily pregnant dairy cow, stretched out on the aging straw bedding. The cow was predominantly white with random black patches and an identification tag stapled to her ear. "Essy!" Minnie called to her sister, who sat in the car with all the doors and windows firmly locked shut. "Essy, come and look!"

"What is it, dear?" Esther asked, winding her window down a half inch or so.

"It's a cow, dear, not a crocodile!" Minnie informed her. "Now get out of the car and come and see for yourself. She won't bite you—I think she's in labour."

The expectant mother let out a pitiful groan and kicked out at the straw, unable to stand.

"Did you say a cow, dear?" Esther asked, venturing out of Vivien.

"Yes, and I think she's about to have a baby," Minnie replied. "And really soon by the looks of things."

"Oh how wonderful," Esther said, joining her sister. "Hello darling," she added, addressing the writhing cow.

The mother-to-be had escaped from a dairy farm several kilometres away and had wandered the countryside in search of a safe place to give birth to her baby. Ordinarily cows bred for their milk would be impregnated over and over again, in order for them to maintain their milk production, but the resulting calves when born would be cruelly snatched from their mother's teat and the parent and offspring would never ever see one another again. Mothers would grieve for days on end, only for the cycle to be repeated yet again. For this particular cow though, enough was finally enough and she had broken free during the night, kicking at the steel gate over and over again until it broke away, but there were obvious complications and her calf was now long overdue.

"Something's wrong, dear," Esther remarked, seeing the cow's stomach moving violently.

"Oh no!" Minnie said, daring to step inside the stall.

"Careful, dear!" her sister warned her.

Peshwari Nans

"Shhhhhhh, shhhhhhh," Minnie said, attempting to calm the distressed animal. "I think the baby's breeched, dear," she told her sister.

"How on earth can you tell?" Esther asked, joining her with extreme caution. "You're not a vet."

"No dear, but the flying doctor is," Minnie said, rubbing the cow's nose. "I never miss an episode, and the week before last he had an expectant rhino to deal with."

"But this is a cow, dear," Esther reminded her.

"Oh dear, Essy," Minnie said sympathetically. "You have led a sheltered life, haven't you? There really is no difference whatsoever, dear. We are all mammals, don't you know?"

"Well," Esther remarked, getting her back up. "Why is it I've never seen this flying doctor or whatever the heck he is, eh?"

"Because it's on on a Wednesday, dear," Minnie informed her. "You're at the bingo remember? With that snooty cow from next door—no offence," she then said hastily to the groaning heifer beside her.

"What is it about Muriel?" Esther asked. "You never have liked her, have you?"

"No, no, I haven't," Minnie said, scowling. "Always thinks she's better than everybody else, with her Fortnum and Mason delivery and her diamond white dentures. I don't know what you see in her, Essy, I really don't."

Esther was about to reply, extolling the virtues of her one and only bingo buddy, when the pregnant cow cried out and kicked at the stall walls. "Oh dear, the poor thing," Minnie said, lifting her tail. "We'll have to help her, Essy dear. Now if I remember," she said, rolling up her sleeve.

"Wait. What are you doing?" Esther asked, aghast.

"Delivering the baby," Minnie simply replied. "Now be a dear, will you, and go fetch the Vaseline from the overnight bag."

"But, Minnie dear," her sister protested. "You've never…"

"Just do it, dear!" Minnie insisted, "or this beautiful creature could die, along with the baby! Now please hurry!"

"Oh alright, but," Esther moaned, returning to Vivien. "How?" she said, moments later. "I mean if you think for one moment I'm putting my hand in there you are much mistaken, my dear."

"Just give it here," Minnie said, taking charge and lubricating her right arm up to above the elbow. "Right!" she said, taking a deep breath. "Hold the tail please, Essy," she told her horrified sister. "Essy, the tail please!"

Esther did so, holding it between her thumb and forefinger while her sister slowly inserted her hand into the cow's orifice. "There, there, my darling," she told the moaning animal. "Shhhhh now, I'm just trying to help."

"Oh God, Minnie, how could you?" Esther asked, turning away as her sister's arm disappeared.

"Necessity, dear," Minnie puffed. "Necessity."

Feeling the calf inside, Minnie grappled for its feet. "Oh dear, it's worse than I thought," she remarked. "The poor thing's stuck fast."

No matter how hard she tugged, the wriggling calf would not budge. "Essy, fetch me the tow rope," she told her sister. "Do it now Essy, please!"

Shell-shocked at her sister's abruptness, Esther scurried back to the car to retrieve Vivien's tow rope. "What are you going to do, dear?" she asked.

"We, dear," Minnie replied, removing her arm to tie a noose in one end of the blue nylon tow rope. "You mean what are *we* going to do. I'm going to tie this to the baby's feet and you and I are going to pull the little fellow out."

"So, er," Esther said, wanting further confirmation. "I don't have to put my hand in there?"

"No dear, you don't," Minnie replied, gently pushing the noose into the cow's swollen womb. "Just grab hold of the end of the rope, dear," she told Esther. "And pull when I say."

With her tongue out, Minnie foraged inside the cow for a minute or two. "Almost there," she said, with beads of sweat forming on her brow. "Come on my darling, just move a little for me. Got it!" She smiled, tightening the rope around the struggling calf's front feet. "Okay Essy, dear," she said, removing her arm again and gripping the rope. "Now pull like your life depends on it!"

The sisters tugged and tugged while the moaning mother mooed loudly. "I know, I know," Minnie told her, digging her heels into the dirt floor. "Pull Essy! Pull!" she puffed.

"I am pulling, dear!" Esther snapped behind her. "It's no use, Min," she then added, clutching her back. "We just haven't got it in us."

"You're right, my dear," Minnie agreed. "But Vivien has."

"What?" Esther said. "Vivien?"

"Yes! Back her up a little, dear," Minnie told her sister. "Hurry please, Essy! It's her only hope!"

"Yes, right dear," Esther replied unconvinced. "Are you sure this'll work, dear?"

"Never mind, just do it!" her sister barked, doing her level best to calm the cow. "Don't worry yourself, my darling," she told the mother-to-be. "If anyone can get your baby out Vivien can."

Esther reversed Vivien slowly back to the stall and sat looking over her shoulder.

"Now when I say dear!" Minnie called to her as she attached the end of the rope to Vivien's rear bumper, "drive gently forward. Just a few feet, mind!"

Peshwari Nans

Esther gave her sister the thumbs up and sat riding the clutch.

"Okay, dear!" Minnie called. "Off you go!"

"Okay, dear!" Esther said, filled with trepidation "I don't want to hurt her though!"

"If you don't she will die!" Minnie yelled. "NOW GO ESSY! GO!"

Slowly raising Vivien's clutch, Esther crept forward at a snail's pace. "That's it dear!" Minnie said, watching the rope rise from the floor and tighten. "Slowly now, slowly!"

The cow let out a deafening cry as the baby within her began to turn.

"Don't stop, dear!" Minnie called, waving to her sister. "Gently does it now, gently!"

Inch by inch the rope emerged until Minnie's crude knot was in sight. "Splendid dear!" she remarked, then two cloven feet appeared. "Oh my!" she gasped, controlling the rope.

"Is it out?" Esther called back, whilst skilfully manoeuvring.

"No, keep going!" Minnie told her as a dripping nose appeared. "There you are, my darling." She smiled. "Come on, out you come!"

The exhausted mother attempted to push but had absolutely nothing left to give at this point, she merely lay groaning, wide-eyed. "Almost there, dear!" Minnie cried, tugging a little herself to free the shoulders. "Almost!"

Then suddenly without warning, with its upper half now free, the calf slipped out like a bar of wet soap.

"STOP!" Minnie cried when the sodden calf slid across her, pinning her to the ground, followed by a tide of its mother's fluid, which engulfed her.

"Is it out?" Esther said, reversing ever so slightly and hurrying from the car. "Oh my word Minnie!" she gasped with a hand to her mouth, seeing her sister flat on her back with the hefty calf draped across her. "Are you alright?"

"Yes, yes, but it's not breathing," Minnie replied, clearing the mucus from the infant's nose and mouth from her prone position beneath it.

"Oh dear, is it…" Esther asked, not daring to say.

"Not if I can help it," Minnie cursed, beating at the calf's chest over and over until it stirred.

"There dear!" her sister cried. "You did it, you did it!"

Sure enough, the calf kicked and bucked, taking its first full deep breath of free air.

"Oh my beauty!" Minnie said as the mother turned to lick her baby, and Minnie too for that matter. "Help me, dear," Minnie asked gently, pushing the calf off her and dragging herself to her feet.

"Look at you, dear," Esther said, keeping her distance from her placenta-splattered sister. "You're a mess."

"Oh I'm fine, dear." Minnie smiled, watching mother and baby bond. "There is nothing in this world more amazing and beautiful than new life," she told her sister. "Don't you think?"

"Yes, yes, you're right," Esther was forced to agree. "But, er, we'd best get you out if those clothes Minnie dear, I'll fetch a towel." She turned but paused at the stall door. "Min," she said calmly. "Well done. Well done you."

"Why thank you, dear." Minnie smiled, flicking the fluid from her hands. "I couldn't have done it without the flying doctor."

Esther returned to her car. "Remarkable," she said to herself. "Quite remarkable."

Using three towels, her discarded clothes and a fistful of straw to clean herself, Minnie dressed at Vivien's back doors and returned to the stall, where mother and baby were doing just fine, the calf suckling its mother's precious milk as it should. "It's a girl, dear," she told her sister, who

378

busily bagged the sodden clothes. "I think I'll call her Betty after Betty Davis. I mean just look at those eyes, aren't they adorable?"

"I tell you what," Esther said, bringing up the prickly subject of her sister's dearly departed daughter. "Why don't you call her Sophia?"

"No dear!" Minnie said, straightening her back. "No, I'm, I'm sorry I couldn't."

Esther took Minnie's hand. "Sit down, dear," she told her, perching on the edge of a bale of hay herself. "And listen." Esther had begged her sibling for years to open up and talk about her deceased daughter, to release the knot of sorrow and on occasion rage, that had remained churning deep within her.

Minnie immediately tensed rigid, as she had done on countless occasions when her sister had broached the subject.

"Now Min, dear," Esther began. "We are a million miles from God knows where right now, and we aren't going anywhere just yet, wouldn't you agree?"

"Yes Essy, but," Minnie said, shuffling from side to side. "I'd really rather not if it's all the same to you." She attempted to leave the bale but Esther tugged her back down.

"I said sit down," Esther insisted. "Now, Min you're going to hear me out this time whether you like it or not, do you hear?"

Minnie kicked at the loose hay on the dirt floor whilst looking for an exit.

"Ah, ahhhhh," Esther said, turning her sister's chin to face her. "Minnie look at me," she told her. "Now let's talk about Sophia."

Minnie again attempted to stand. "We really should be going, dear," she said, looking towards the door, but was restrained once again and pushed back down onto the bale of hay. "Please Essy I can't," she added, with a quivering lip. "Please don't."

"Minnie, look at me," Esther said abruptly. "Look at me! You're my sister and I love you with all my heart and, believe me, I'd never ever do anything to hurt you, you know that, don't you? But, Minnie dear, I've watched you go through hell and high water carrying this, this burden. Yes you loved Sophia, yes she was your world and, as a mother, I fully understand that, any mother would. But Minnie, she's gone my darling, although it breaks my heart to say it, believe me it does, but it's time you let go, dear. I don't mean forget her, because neither of us ever will, but free yourself from the guilt that I know you carry to this day. Minnie, please, it's not your fault."

"No, dear, no I can't!" Minnie replied, shaking her head continuously. "I can't, Essy, I just can't. It is my fault, all my fault, and I've had to live with it. If only I'd insisted on more tests Essy, if only, if only. I trusted those, those people with my daughter's life and they failed me. They failed Sophia, God Essy, it kills me to say her name it honestly does."

Sophia's misdiagnosis when she contracted meningitis at such a young age, haunted Minnie terribly as it did so many parents in similar circumstances.

"Please, Essy, I've got to get out of here, I really need some air I can't breathe, dear, I can't breathe!" Again she tried to stand with tears welling in the corners of her eyes. "God, Essy, please don't make me do this," she begged. "Please don't, not now."

"It's for your own good, dear," Esther said with a firm hand bearing down on her sister's shoulder. "Trust me. You had absolutely no counselling after her death, did you?"

"Oh, what good would that have done?" Minnie protested. "Would it have brought Sophia back?" Her attitude had turned to one of bitter rage in an instant. "No, no it wouldn't have, so don't you stand there, Essy, and lecture me about counselling. I dealt with it the best way I could!"

"By getting drunk!" her sister replied with equal venom. Her plan was to get her sister to talk no matter how aggressively she had to behave. And it was working.

"Yes!" Minnie barked, slamming her fist down onto her knees. "Yes I got drunk, and I won't make a single excuse for it, I was a raging alcoholic for that matter. I'D LOST MY CHILD, ESSY, MY SOPHIA!" The tears now dripped from her chin into her lap.

"Yes, dear, I know," Esther said, calming slightly and sitting close to her trembling sister. "I know, but you needed to talk too, and you didn't. I tried and I tried but you just wouldn't, and I watched it destroy you. And I know, Minnie darling, I know it still eats away at you. I see it in your eyes when you are quiet sometimes. You have to let it out, dear, please, let it out."

Minnie's insides tightened, causing her to bend double. "I can't, Essy, I can't! It hurts too much!"

"I know, dear," her sister said, holding her tightly. "Of course it hurts, but I'm right here for you, I've always been right here for you."

Minnie began to crumble. It started with her legs shaking uncontrollably, but soon it consumed her until she rocked back and forth, clutching her stomach. "I can't, Essy!" she sobbed. "I loved her so, so much!"

"Love her, Minnie, you love her," Esther reminded her. "You don't stop loving someone because they simply aren't here. I still love Jack with all my heart and I always will until the day I die—I know it."

"OH GOD!" Minnie cried out, looking up to the rafters.

"Minnie, you can get through this," Esther told her, wiping her sister's cheek. "You are so strong, one of the strongest women I know in fact. I just watched you deliver a calf without hesitation, for Pete's sake! Minnie you are an amazing courageous woman. I've watched you do things this last week that I'd never dream of doing."

Minnie's face was now bitterly contorted as the well within her bubbled to the surface. She let out an unearthly cry similar to that of the mother cow in labour who'd been desperate to see its infant.

Esther rose to her feet and held out her arms. "Come, dear," she said, beckoning for an embrace.

But the weight of sorrow and the sheer pain pinned Minnie down. "Help me, Essy!" she sobbed, holding out her quivering hands. "Please, help me!"

Esther's own heart was breaking as she stooped and gathered her sister up into her arms and raised her to her feet, taking her entire weight. "I've got you, dear," she said softly. "I've got you."

"Oh Essy, Essy!" Minnie said, bursting into full-blown tears. "Essy! My baby, my baby!"

"I know, dear," Esther replied, rubbing her sister's back. "Go on, dear, let it out, let it all out, I'm here for you."

"My baby, my Sophiaaaaa," Minnie cried repeatedly within her sister's tightening embrace.

Esther rocked Minnie whilst gently caressing her hair. "Thaaat's it," she said, kissing her forehead. "Thaaat's it, my darling."

"SOPHIAAAAAAAAAA!" Minnie screamed toward the heavens at one point, but Esther held on tight. She had her sister and she wasn't going to let her go, not until her demons had been vanquished, even if the Russian President himself burst through those barn doors and put a gun to her head.

Sure enough after a further five minutes of struggling rage, Minnie tired and slumped exhausted into her sister's arms. "Sophia," she merely said, closing her eyes.

Peshwari Nans

"There, there, shhhhhhh," Esther whispered, kissing her sister tenderly. "I've got you, dear, I've got you."

The pair stood and swayed a while before parting, looking into one another's eyes momentarily. "Thank you," Minnie said, drying her eyes. "Thank you, Essy." She felt somewhat light on her feet with an overwhelming sense of relief and release. The burdensome load that she had carried for much of her life had been lifted from her, leaving only the sweetest memories of a bubbly beautiful child that had brought her so much joy and love.

"Would you like some tea, dear?" Esther asked, patting her sister's hand. "And possibly a Garibaldi?"

"Oh good heavens, yes." Minnie smiled. "That would be absolutely splendid right now."

Shortly afterwards the two sisters stood side by side, sipping and nibbling watching the cow and her newborn calf become acquainted. "You did that," Esther told her sister proudly, with a gentle prod. "You."

Meanwhile, frantic media crews pursued the Russian Premier, who by now was way beyond all reasoning, smashing the wooden wheel off a hay cart in passing and toppling the petrified driver into the dirt.

"MOVE, MOVE!" he screamed, tossing his mobile phone into a drainage ditch when his Secretary of State called to calm him and beg him to return to the Kremlin.

The spotter plane moved away from the area where the sisters sheltered to widen its search, and all this played out on prime-time television, giving Karl Bodine, the young computer gaming entrepreneur, plenty of food for thought. His next addition to his award-winning game would undoubtedly feature maniacal world leaders hunting his elderly characters with their respective arsenals at their disposal: yet another sure-fire hit in the making.

"Shall we go, dear?" Esther asked her sister, who stood staring dreamily into the calf's eyes.

Peshwari Nans

"You're right, dear," Minnie agreed. "Sophia it is."

"Are you sure?" Esther asked, delighted at her sister's eventual acceptance.

"Yes, yes, of course," Minnie told her. "I mean, look at her Essy? She's gorgeous."

"Yes, she is indeed." Esther smiled.

The pair left the mother and baby to an uncertain future, but for the time being at least Sophia would feel the warmth of her mother's side and suckle her rich sweet milk.

"All clear, dear," Minnie said, peering outside and listening for the plane, which was flying low over a small village several kilometres away.

"Right you are, dear," Esther replied, steering Vivien slowly from the barn while Sophia and her well-rested mother clambered to their feet and peered from the stall.

"Goodbye my darlings," Minnie called back to them, leaving one door ajar so that they could drink from a nearby stream whenever they so desired. "D'you think they'll be alright, dear?" Minnie said, climbing in beside Esther and glancing over her shoulder. "The cows."

"Oh I'm sure of it, dear," Esther replied, patting Minnie's knee. "We all will."

Returning to the dual carriageway, neither sister had the slightest idea that along with the Chief of Police and every man at his disposal, a far deadlier threat was fast approaching from their rear.

"MOVE DAMN YOU!" the President again screamed, ramming the rear end of a packed taxi cab. "MOVE!" And like many others, the taxi driver wound down his window to barrack his would-be assailant but then veered violently off the road in abject horror, when seeing his leader with his Kalashnikov rifle trained on his taxi.

"Lovely day, dear" Minnie remarked, feeling altogether positive about her life as a whole.

"Isn't it just?" Esther smiled. "Just lovely."

Peshwari Nans

Looking over his shoulder, the Russian President opened his glove compartment and rummaged for the pistol inside, then, yelling at the top of his voice, fired a volley of shots toward the news-hungry crews behind him.

"This is pure gold!" the Fox News anchor man laughed, ducking down in his van. "I hope you're getting this, Jerry!"

"Every crazy second!" Jerry said, sitting beside him in bulletproof clothing, with his camera on his shoulder, but fearing for his life nethertheless. "We should back off a little though, don't you think?" he told his colleague.

"Are you kidding me?" the anchor exclaimed. "This story's mine, do you hear me? Mine!"

Esther checked her mirrors with a sigh of relief. "I think we've lost them all, dear," she said, seeing a sign up ahead for the Kazakhstan border, which was just an hour away.

"Did you know, dear?" Minnie asked, swiping through the web pages on her tablet, "Kazakhstan has a population of sixteen million and is between two and three hundred metres above sea level?"

"Riveting, dear," Esther said sarcastically. "Is that it then?" she asked. "An entire country described in two brief sentences?"

"Oh no, dear," Minnie replied, her eyes widening as she scoured the Internet. "For instance did you also know that Kazakhstan is the largest landlocked country in the world? Isn't that just amazing? And Kazakhstan is situated both in Europe and Asia, with the Ural river being the boundary and it's four times the size of Texas."

"How interesting," Esther said with her mind elsewhere.

"Isn't it just, dear?" Minnie said enthusiastically. "I for one can't wait to try the fried doughnuts and salted cheese balls, they look delicious."

"Well I for one won't be," her sister said adamantly. "I'm afraid I don't have your constitution."

"No you haven't, have you?" Minnie replied, switching off the tablet. "You refused to try Father's tripe and onions, didn't you?"

"Yes I jolly well did!" Esther said, turning up her nose. "Just the thought of it was enough to put me off my supper."

"And the faggots, dear," Minnie added. "You'd push those around your plate until Mother said you could be excused, didn't you?"

"Ooooh, faggots," Esther said, screwing up her face. "Father did love his offal, didn't he?"

"Yes," Minnie said wistfully. "I still miss them both terribly you know," she confessed. "Not all the time, I mean occasionally I might see somebody of Father's stature, or hear that characteristic laugh, just like Mother's."

"Oh yes, dear," Esther agreed. "It was quite infectious, wasn't it? Whenever I was in a foul mood I'd only have to hear Mother laugh out loud beside the wireless listening to the *Goon Show*, and I'd eventually be in fits myself."

As the sisters reminisced, the President rounded a corner and got his first glimpse of Vivien, several hundred yards ahead.

"Yes!" he growled, drooling at the prospect of causing them harm. With his foot firmly to the floor, Putin raised his rifle, resting the barrel on the dashboard, shooting out his windscreen first.

"My God, look it's the Peshwari Nans!" the CNN anchor told his driver. "And the President is shooting at them! He really is going to kill the Nans!"

Veering from left to right across the carriageway and taking aim, the President fired a volley of shots towards the Morris Traveller.

"What was that, dear?" Minnie asked as a 39mm cartridge struck the ash frame of Vivien's rear doors.

Peshwari Nans

"I don't know, dear," Esther said, checking her mirrors. "What on earth?" she gasped, seeing the President's jeep closing in on them from a distance.

Rival news crews stepped up the pace, jostling for position, their mirrors colliding as they barracked one another.

"HE'S MAD!" the Fox anchor yelled to his CNN counterpart, through their vehicles' open windows. "STARK RAVING MAD! HE MEANS TO KILL THE NANS, AND WE HAVE TO STOP HIM!"

"BUT HE HAS A GUN!" was the reply from the CNN truck. "A VERY BIG GUN!"

The Fox anchor's driver tapped him on the shoulder. "Perhaps we should back off a little," he suggested, easing back on the accelerator.

"NO WAY, MAN!" the anchor yelled. "Those old ladies are a media sensation and my ticket to a corner office and journo of the year! But I don't want it to be for recording the deaths of the biggest cash cows to come along in decades. Now we gotta stop him, step on it!" he told his driver. "Run him off the road if you have to!"

"But, sir!" the driver replied sheepishly, "that's the Russian President!"

"No, it's a madman!" the anchor yelled. "And if we don't do something right now he's gonna kill those sweet old ladies. Now do you want that on your conscience? Coz I sure as hell don't! Now step on it, goddamn you!"

"What is it, dear?" Minnie asked, turning in her seat. "Who is that?"

"I have no idea," Esther replied, accelerating. "But I don't like the look of him, not one bit."

"Is that, is that, a gun?" Minnie asked, sinking lower in her seat. "Essy, dear, he has a gun!"

"Good God!" Esther shrieked. "Why on earth would he have a gun?"

Peshwari Nans

Another of the President's whizzing bullets struck Vivien's rear chrome bumper, then another hit her vintage number plate. "Crickey, dear, he's shooting at us!" Esther cried, ducking and accelerating further.

"Why, dear? Why?" Minnie asked, cowering in her seat. "Oh Essy, what's happening?" she too cried, as the President's jeep drew ever closer.

Esther dared to glance behind. "It's obviously a case of mistaken identity, dear," she told her terrified sister, catching a glimpse of the crazed President in her wing mirror.

"In a Morris Traveller, dear?" Minnie asked, peering cautiously over the back of her seat. "Surely not."

Esther took Vivien to previously unchartered territory by accelerating to a whopping sixty-eight miles per hour, but the President was still gaining on them.

The convoy of news truck and vans with their respective cameramen leaning from their windows, raced behind them. "Come on, goddamn it!" the Fox anchor gestured to his driver. "Ram the President's damn car!"

Esther and Minnie had hardly ever seen a gun, let alone been fired upon by one, as they realised that yet another whistling shell had struck Vivien's bodywork.

"Essy, I'm scared!" Minnie squealed. "Why is he doing this? Why is he doing this to us?"

"I told you, I don't know," Esther snapped, attempting to drive evasively, with the notion that a dodging target would be more difficult to hit. She was right.

The Russian President cursed, wild-eyed and unable to lock his sights on them, as the world watched in horror at his insane actions.

"COME ON, COME ON, GO, GO!" countless supporters yelled at their television sets, willing the sisters on. "NO, NOOOOO!" they also cried, seeing the jeep gaining on Vivien.

Peshwari Nans

"We gotta do something right now!" the Fox anchor yelled, several metres behind the manic President, "or we'll have two dead ladies on our hands!"

This time it was Minnie's door mirror that was shot out, sending her into a blind panic. "ESSY, ESSY!" she screamed, clinging to her sister. "HELP! HE'S GOING TO KILL US! HE'S GOING TO KILL US!"

"Shut up, dear!" Esther snapped, pushing her sister away whilst swerving to keep the President from pulling alongside them. "Come on Vivien darling," she added, coaxing her car. "Don't fail me now, dear, don't fail me now please!"

The world held its breath as round after round was fired toward Vivien, several of the shots piercing her fragile rear doors' panelling and shattering one or two jars of Minnie's precious shrimp paste.

"The blighter!" Minnie cursed, getting a whiff of that oh-so-familiar paste. "He's shot my potted paste!" She held the tablet above her head and took several snaps of the advancing President in his jeep.

"What are you doing?" Esther asked, tugging at her sister's arm.

"Evidence, dear," Minnie replied. "If we get out of this alive I'll see that menace in court if it's the last thing I do!"

"Get down!" Esther barked.

Once again the drooling president set down his rifle and swung around with his pistol in hand and took a pot shot or two at the pursuing news crews.

"SHIT!" the Fox driver screamed as their windscreen was penetrated, the shell lodging in the bulkhead behind him.

"Don't worry, I'm getting all this," the cameraman cried, cowering, with his lens resting on the dash.

"Okay, hang on!" the driver yelled, enraged at his damaged vehicle. "You goddamn bastard!" he said with the

389

President in front of him. Accelerating rapidly, he jolted the jeep's rear bumper, dislodging the President in his seat.

"What's happening back there?" Esther asked, seeing the fleet of vans. "Who are they?"

"God only knows," Minnie replied, peering behind them. "But I dearly hope they're here to help us."

"American dogs!" the President yelled, flinging his pistol behind him and clumsily reloading his rifle before turning to shoot out the lead van's headlight. "I have you!" he snarled, firing on Vivien and closing in.

"Arrrrgh!" Minnie screamed when the Russian jeep rammed them from behind. "ESYYYYYYY!"

"ALRIGHT, ALRIGHT!" Esther yelled. "I'M TRYING!"

The President began to laugh, eager for the kill, which as he thought was now imminent. "DIE! DIIIIIIIIIIE!" he roared, ramming Vivien a second time and shooting out the indicator glass.

"NOW! NOW!" the Fox anchor stormed, slamming his hand down on the dashboard. "DO IT NOW!"

Taking a deep breath, the Fox driver pulled alongside the speeding jeep and wrenched his wheel violently to the side to slam his vehicle into the President's jeep.

"Grrrrrrr, American pigs!" the Russian leader raged, veering back to repay the favour.

"AGAIN! AGAIN!" the anchor cried, looking down on the President and the petrified sisters ahead. "GET HIM!"

Esther gripped Vivien's wheel as tightly as she could, applying more pressure to the accelerator pedal and watching the speedometer increase to seventy-five. "Come on, old girl!" she told the car. "Help us, please!"

With his jeep buffeted by the news van, the persistent President took aim at the rear of Esther's straw hat. "Bitch!" he snarled, his finger tightening on the trigger.

Peshwari Nans

"NOW!" the anchor screamed, seeing the President's fiendish grin. His driver swung away before crashing it into the side of the jeep with great force, sending it careering across the road and sending the President into a panicked rage.

Attempting to correct his steering, the Premier overcompensated considerably and swerved violently into the path of an oncoming fuel truck.

"SHIIIT!" he cried, tugging at his wheel to avoid a catastrophic collision. But in doing so he clipped the opposite kerb and mounted the pavement, sending his rifle toppling to the floor and jamming his accelerator. "ARRRRRRRRGH! NOOOOOO!" he screamed, approaching a tight hairpin bend in the road which Esther had just taken, hanging onto her hat.

"WOAAAAAAW!" Minnie squealed, sliding across her seat toward her sister.

But the President fumbled for his brake far too late and took a much wider line into the bend, the bumpy grass verge causing him to lose control and veer towards the adjacent marshland.

"NO, NO!" he cursed, striking a fallen birch trunk and taking to the air. Strapped in and unable to bale out, the President in his jeep, vaulted the remainder of the verge and, after clearing several metres of boggy marsh, splashed down bonnet first, sending a surge of water and weed out across the marsh and splattering the President at the same time.

"Where did he go, dear?" Esther asked, checking her mirror yet again at the far side of the bend, upon seeing that the road behind was suddenly clear.

"I, I, don't know, dear," Minnie said, rising in her seat apprehensively. "Just keep going, please."

The fifteen or so news vehicles slowed and pulled up alongside the marsh, leaping out to record the dramatic

391

scene as the Russian President lay groaning, slumped across the dashboard and out over the bonnet, stuck fast in six feet of boggy wetland, and surrounded by inquisitive geese, which quickly returned in search of food after the initial splashdown.

"Are you alright, dear?" Minnie asked her shell-shocked sister.

"Yes, yes, I think so," Esther replied, checking herself over before looking across at the broken wing mirror. "But my dear Vivien has suffered terribly. I haven't a clue who that maniac was back there," she added breathlessly, "and I don't intend to stick around to find out either." Checking her rear-view mirror, Esther maintained her hair-raising speed.

"Ahem," Minnie said, tapping the central speedometer. "A tad too hasty, wouldn't you say, my dear?"

"Oh good Lord!" Esther remarked, stunned at the needle's position, which was way beyond anything she had ever experienced. "My apologies, Vivien dear," she said, raising her foot a little to relieve the strain on her automobile's aging engine.

"She saved us, Essy," Minnie said, stroking Vivien's dashboard.

"Didn't she just?" Esther added, tapping the wheel lovingly but still checking behind them at regular intervals.

With more than a dozen cameras rolling in his direction, the Russian President came to and began pounding the partially submerged bonnet of his jeep, knowing full well that the Nans had eluded him.

"Sir, Mr President!" Sergei, his Chief of Police called as he and his men arrived at the scene.

"AFTER THEM!" the President barked furiously. "AFTER THEM I SAY!" But his reputation as a world leader was now in tatters and the majority of his men refused point-blank to obey him.

Peshwari Nans

"We should get you out, Mr President!" Sergei said, kicking off his shoes and socks and wading in the water up to his knees.

Meanwhile, the world rejoiced, elated at the President finally getting his comeuppance, hundreds of thousands of them sharing the photographs Minnie had busily uploaded. The resulting political fallout would lead to the complete collapse of the President's government and yet another record-breaking YouTube viral video.

"How far to Kazakhstan, dear?" Esther asked her sister, eager to leave the former Soviet Union. "God, I so need a drink."

"Six kilometres, dear," Minnie replied, checking their global position on the tablet. "I think a sip or two of Monique's wonder brew is in order this evening, what do you say?"

"Maybe three of four," Esther said, holding out a trembling hand.

"For medicinal purposes?" Minnie asked.

"Hell no!" Esther exclaimed. "I intend to get completely smashed, my dear, it's the only thing that'll steady my nerves."

Approaching the Kazakhstan border and putting as much distance between themselves and the rampaging Russian President as they could, the sisters finally began to relax, having been traumatized beyond their worst nightmares.

"Here we are" Minnie remarked on crossing the border. "Shall we stop, dear?"

"No, no, no, no," Esther replied, shaking her head. "I'll drive till dusk, dear, then we'll rest Vivien for the night."

"Right you are, dear." Minnie smiled, foraging for Monique's illicit liquor. "I'll just have a nip to be going along with." She unscrewed the cap and took a swig from the neck of the bottle.

"Minnie!" Esther gasped at her audacity.

"To hell with it, dear," Minnie replied, wiping her mouth with the back of her hand. "We've just been shot at by a raving lunatic, so I think the least you can do is excuse my manners. It won't happen again I assure you."

"Very well, dear," Esther agreed, turning a blind eye to her sister's guttural gluttony.

"Did I tell you, dear?" Minnie said, supping some more of the drink, "that Kazakhstan has a population of just sixteen million?"

"Yes, dear," Esther said, looking across disapprovingly. "You did."

"Oh," Minnie replied, cradling the bottle. "And that it is the largest landlocked country in the entire world?"

"Yes dear, and that too," her sister replied. "Right that's enough for now," she then said, wrenching the spirit from her sister's grasp. "You'll be three sheets to the wind before we even stop."

"I'm fiiine, dear." Minnie smiled, although Monique's miracle home brew had already got to work, relaxing her limbs and soothing her frayed nerves. "Perhaps you were right, dear," she said, at ease with herself. "About it being a case of mistaken identity. I mean, these eastern Europeans types fall in love with a lot of our vintage cars. I hear the Triumph Herald was extremely popular with the Poles."

Again the sisters suspected nothing sinister, and soon resumed their journey in the manner in which they had begun, although Vivien's scars told a completely different story.

Back at Elizabeth's house meanwhile, Richard followed the doctors, who had his mother strapped to a wheelchair that was being taken to the front door.

"You'll be fine, Mum," he called over their shoulders. "You just need some rest, that's all."

Peshwari Nans

Richard had been forced to make the call when his mother suddenly 'lost it completely', so to speak. Seeing her mother and aunt on television yet again, this time being pursued by a gun-toting madman, Elizabeth could neither be calmed nor reasoned with, and constantly screamed the house down, popping pills like lemon drops and drinking her drinks cabinet dry.

"RICHAAAAAAARD! RICHAAAAAAARD!" she cried, reaching behind her in the chair. "DON'T LET THEM TAKE ME, RICHAAAAAAARD!"

"It's for your own good, Mum, really it is," Richard said, handing one of the doctors her overnight bag.

"Don't worry, son," the medical man said, raising the wheelchair wheels over the threshold. "We'll take good care of her."

"Thank you," Richard said, seeing them to the garden gate. "It's her mother you see, my grandmother. She's, she's away at the moment."

"Could be worse," another doctor joked. "She could be related to one of those Peshwari Nans on the telly!"

Hearing this, Elizabeth began foaming at the mouth and wrestling with her restraints. "We're gonna have to sedate her," the doctor told his colleague, reaching for his bag.

Elizabeth was later sectioned under the mental health act, for her own protection, and housed with other like-minded individuals. "That's, that's my mother that is!" she said sitting in the hospital's day-room in a white medical gown, staring at the television set, having grappled the remote control from another inmate's hands to change the channel.

"Yes, dear," the nurse said, humouring her. "Of course it is." She then snatched back the remote control to appease the majority of the patients, by switching to the cartoon channel which played constant reruns of *Tom and Jerry*.

"No, no, it really is!" Elizabeth insisted. "It's my mother I tell you!" She then leapt from her seat and set about the nurse, knocking her to the floor. "Give me that!" she cursed, reaching for the remote. "Give it to me, or by Christ I'll kill you, I swear it!"

The alarm was then raised by security officials watching on CCTV, and a rapid response team was sent in to restrain the ranting woman.

"NO! NO!" she cried as they dragged her kicking and screaming from the day-room. "NO THAT'S MY MOTHER I TELL YOU! MY MOTHER!"

Elizabeth's medication dosage was increased until she sat passively, rocking to and fro in her room, wearing woollen mittens to prevent her from harming herself, her arms now heavily bandaged from her constant scratching.

Skirting the Caspian Sea which stretched out to their right, the sisters trundled on through country number eight, having covered some two thousand-nine-hundred miles of their arduous journey, a journey with rather more hiccups than they'd initially anticipated. That's if you can call getting lost in a German forest, bed-ridden by a bee sting and shot at by a Russian President 'hiccups', that is. All in all the sedate road trip that they had hoped for had been more of a disaster than a voyage of discovery and wonderment.

"Do you know that Genghis Khan once roamed these parts, dear?" Minnie informed her sister, having again trawled the Internet for the relevant facts and figures. "He was the founder and great Khan of the Mongol empire, you know." She began to reel off the Mongolian warlords' Wikipedia page word for word.

"That's it!" Esther barked, eventually having heard enough of the finer details. "Switch it off, switch it off right now, Minnie, or so help me I'll throw the damn thing out the window!"

Peshwari Nans

"But, Essy dear," Minnie said, defending her font of knowledge. "It's important we learn the history of these places so we can better understand the people, wouldn't you agree?"

"I don't want to understand them," Esther insisted. "I just want to get by with a nod and a smile and go about my business. And you, my dear, are not helping one iota with your constant dictations. I don't wish to know who defeated who several hundred years ago or what Genghis blasted Khan had for his breakfast. I just want to know where to turn left or right and how far it is to the next petrol station, which I might add is a matter of some urgency."

"Oh, oh yes, let me see," Minnie said, hastily consulting the oracle on her lap. "Three kilometres, dear," she added, checking the fuel gauge. "Have we enough?"

"I hope so," Esther replied, tapping the glass, as if doing so would somehow magically replenish their dwindling supply. But Vivien made it with a drop or two to spare as the sisters pulled off the highway into a service station.

"Petrol?" the elderly pump attendant asked.

"I'm sorry," Esther replied, stepping from the car and straightening her back. "Oh, oh yes, petrol please," she said with a smile. "You'd better fill her up," she added, looking along the dusty road. "Heaven only knows when we'll find another station."

The attendant opened the petrol flap and inserted the pump nozzle spitting on the floor in doing so. "Oh good grief!" Esther remarked, turning up her nose and muttering under her breath. "Filthy beast."

The attendant spat again whilst filling Vivien's tank.

"Please don't do that," Esther asked, sidestepping his spit to visit the kiosk. "Minnie dear!" she called back from within the building. "Would you like a cinnamon whirl?"

Peshwari Nans

"Ooooh, yes please!" Minnie replied, retrieving the bottle of Monique's vodka substitute out of sight of her sister, and sipping twice while her back was turned, much to the amusement of the pump attendant.

"How much, dear?" Esther asked the female cashier, who was dressed in a gaily coloured smock. Unable to decipher the pensioner's language, the cashier merely gestured to the cash register the sum of three Kazakhstan tenge, giving her a customary smile.

"Tenge? Tenge?" Esther said, rummaging in her bag "Don't worry my dear, I have them here somewhere. It's my daughter, you see," she explained. "She's one of life's organizers, and believe me I'm very grateful for it indeed, because believe you me I wouldn't know a tenge from a thai bart."

She then paused, looking at the woman's blank expression. "You haven't understood a word I've said, have you?" she told her. "Well, dear," she added, gathering her pastries, "I won't waste any more of your time, nor mine for that matter." She handed over her Kazakhstan currency. "There's four of your tenge whatsits," she told the cashier. "Keep the change my dear and I'll bid you good day." Esther left the bemused cashier and returned to the car. "Here, dear," she said, handing Minnie the cakes. "I did ask if they were fresh but the dear girl directed me to the lavatory instead."

Minnie was sitting there with a huge grin on her face, having quickly tucked the bottle behind her. "Are you alright, dear?" Esther asked her. "Your face, it's glowing."

"I'm fine," Minnie said, with the faintest of slurs. "Couldn't be better in fact."

"Riiiiight!" Esther said, unconvinced. "You haven't been at the vodka again, have you?" she asked, checking around her sister's person.

"No, no!" Minnie said, shaking her head theatrically. "Not a drop, not one teensy weensy drop, cross my heart and hope to die."

"Hmmmm," Esther mumbled beginning to tear off pieces of the cinnamon bun on her lap. "What on earth?" she soon remarked, examining the cake closely. "Is that meat, for God's sake?"

"I hadn't noticed, dear," Minnie said, licking her fingers clean. "I thought you said it was a cinnamon whirl."

"Well I asked the damn girl!" Esther moaned, spitting a morsel out of the window in a most unladylike manner and tossed the remainder after it towards a stray dog at the side of the road. The treat she had purchased did actually resemble a British bakery favourite, but instead of the customary cinnamon and vanilla extract filling, it contained a mixture of boiled goat's liver and fennel, a local delicacy confined to the region.

"Savages," Esther remarked, looking every bit as though she'd just licked a battery.

During the following two-and-a-half hours, Minnie sang along to one of their 'wartime greats' compilations on Vivien's stereo. "There'll be bluuuuuebirds over, the whiiiiite cliffs of Dover!" she warbled out of tune somewhat, and: "Hang out ya washing on the Sieeegfried line!"

"Do you have to?" Esther asked, wincing.

"Of course, dear." Minnie smiled. "Oh come on, Essy," she said, goading her grumpy sister. "You used to love a good old singalong in the old days, with Jack and his harmonica."

"Yes, yes, I did," Esther said, raising a smile herself. "I remember the winter evenings in the parlour with a glass of cherry b—"

The next classic tune started up. "Oh I remember swaying arm in arm with my Jack to this," Esther told

Minnie, breaking into song: "Weeeeeee"ll meeeeet agaaaaain, don't know where don't know wheeeeen…" Minnie then joined her: "But I know we'll meet again some sunny daaaaaaaay!"

The sisters laughed as they sang a further accompaniment to such bygone classics as 'When I'm cleaning windows' by the inimitable George Formby, 'Wish me luck as you wave me goodbye' by Gracie Fields, and 'The Chattanooga choo choo' by Glenn Miller, one of their mother's firm favourites. Then there was a song that always brought a smile to their faces and a burgeoning sense of patriotic pride. "Turn it up, dear," Esther said as the two of them puffed out their chests and launched into song:

"THERE'LL ALWAYS BE AN ENGLAND, AND ENGLAND SHALL BE FREEEEEE, IF ENGLAND MEANS AS MUCH TO YOUUUUUU, AS ENGLAND MEAAAAANS TO MEEEEEEEEEEE!"

"Marvellous!" Esther said, wiping away a tear.

"Yes it gets you right there, doesn't it?" Minnie agreed, patting her breast.

With Vivien's windows wound down, the sisters turned more than a few Kazakhstani heads as they passed through a small village, warbling: "Run rabbit run rabbit run run run, don't let the farmer have his fun fun fun!"

Children playing in the gutter stopped, stood and stared as they drove merrily by. "He'll get byyyy without his rabbit piiiiiiie…" they continued whilst waving at the gawping locals. "So run rabbit run rabbit run run run!"

Ahead of them lay the vast meandering Ural River, which began its watery life far away in the Ural Mountains and eventually drained into the shimmering Caspian Sea.

"Can we camp by the river, dear?" Minnie asked. "We've travelled far enough today, don't you think?"

"Yes, very well dear," her sister replied, turning down the music. "I need to straighten my back anyway, otherwise you'll have to chisel me out of this seat, I swear it." She then wagged a stern finger at her sister. "But I'm warning you Minnie, tonight we stay put in our tent, do you hear me?"

"Yes, of course dear." Minnie smiled, relishing a night under canvas and a drop or two more of Monique's elixir.

Reaching the Ural River, Esther drove alongside it, looking out at a flotilla of tiny fishing boats eking out a living catching sturgeon and beluga in their drift nets. "Oooh what about here, dear?" Minnie piped up, seeing an area of open grassland leading down to the water's edge. "Can we? Can we?" she said, bobbing in her seat.

"I don't see why not, dear," Esther said, pulling in off the road and onto the coarse meadow grass.

Much of Kazakhstan was arid and rocky but the banks of the Ural in places were lush and inviting. The air was cool and sweet with the subtle scent of water lily and wild tulips to further enrich the idyllic location.

"Wow is the only word that springs to mind, dear," Minnie said, stepping from Vivien and clinging to the door as she straightened up, with a crack of bones. "Ooooooh that's better," she added, rotating her swollen ankles.

Esther rounded the car to inspect the damage inflicted by the Russian President's Kalashnikov. "Oh my poor darling," she sighed, running a trembling hand over the bullet holes. "Look at you."

"Never mind that, dear," Minnie said, opening the rear doors. "Look I've lost five jars of shrimp paste because of that blighter. Ooooh if I could get my hands on him I'd, I'd—"

"—Calm down, Minnie dear," Esther said, taking her sister by the arm. "It's not as if you're short of the stuff, is it? Now help me clean up this mess and erect the tent."

The goods and chattels they had carried with them had undoubtedly saved their lives that day, preventing four of the President's bullets from reaching them in the front of the car. "I'll keep it as a souvenir," Minnie said, plucking a buckled shell from their picnic basket. "Would you like one, dear?"

"No I would not!" Esther stormed. "I'd just like to put the whole sorry affair behind me thank you! Hopefully Richard and his friends can work their magic on my Vivien when we return."

While Esther struggled with their tent, Minnie wandered down to the riverbank, gazing out and listening to the relentless lapping of the waves at her feet. "Errrr Minnie, dear!" Esther called, wrestling with the many ropes and poles. "A little help here would be greatly appreciated, helloooooo!"

But Minnie was miles away, dreaming of the time she and Cyril went boating on Lake Windermere in a sixteen-foot day cruiser, anchoring up in a sheltered bay to canoodle in the cabin.

"Minniiiiiiiie!" Esther yelled, getting into a flap with the pegs. "Ooooh I'll give you what for if you don't give me a hand with this BLASTED TENT!"

Minnie returned a short while later, just as the final peg was hammered home by her exasperated sister. "Oh well done, dear," she said with a smile. "I'd have helped with that, dear, you know I would, you only had to ask."

Esther glared at her sister, her hand tightening on the hammer's shaft. "I was calling you!" She grimaced. "Didn't you hear me?"

"I heard a squawking, dear," Minnie informed her, "but I thought it was a mating goose. Anyway now that the tent is up we can relax. I don't know about you, Essy, but I'm positively pooped." Minnie retrieved her deckchair from Vivien and set it up beside the tent and sat down, locking her fingers behind her head. "Ahhh, well this is nice, isn't it?" she said, kicking off her shoes.

Peshwari Nans

Esther flopped down on the grass on her backside, aghast at her sister's flagrant disregard.

"Be a love, Essy dear," Minnie said, pushing her luck to the very limit. "Fetch the vodka and biscuits, will you? I'm settled now."

"Minnie!" Esther growled, pulling herself onto the side of her sister's chair. "I am not here to wait on you hand and foot! Now I'm going to unpack the bedding, so I suggest if you want anything from the car that you get up off your backside and get it yourself!" She stormed over to Vivien and pulled their blankets from the boot.

"Oh," Minnie said, unaware she had overstepped any mark at all. "Right I'll er, I'll get it myself, shall I?"

"Yes, you do that!" Esther snapped over her shoulder.

Minnie, as thick-skinned as she was, hauled herself from her chair and approached her brooding sister, failing miserably to give her the space she so desired. "Are you alright, Essy?" she asked. "You seem a little tense. Have you been taking your supplements?"

"Yes, Minnie, I've taken my damn supplements," Esther said, seething. "I'm tired and I'm hungry and I just want to be left alone."

"Oooh what's for tea?" Minnie asked, her own hunger pangs returning. They had ample provisions from their recent shopping spree, and while Esther arranged the blankets inside the tent, Minnie ferretted around in the cardboard apple boxes. "Omelette dear?" she called.

"Nooooo," Esther replied drearily. "Not today."

"Hmmm, me neither," Minnie replied, replacing the half dozen eggs. "Sausages?" she asked, brandishing a six-pack.

"Nooooo," Esther droned. "I was saving those for breakfast."

"Oh," Minnie said, delving a little deeper. "Alright, how about a suet pudding?"

"Too heavy," Esther said, in no mood for conversation.

"Riiiiight." Minnie sighed, reviewing their remaining options. It was then that the two of them were startled by a voice from behind them.

"Missy!" a young boy no older than ten or twelve called out to them from the water's edge "Missyyy!"

"Oh heavens!" Esther exclaimed, turning to see the sparsely dressed lad standing up to his knees in the water holding two small sturgeon. "Fish Missy—you buy?" he called, nodding his head. "Fish. You buy?"

The sisters looked at one another and then at the plump fish. "Are you thinking what I'm thinking?" Minnie asked.

"Of course, dear," Esther said changing her tone towards her sister instantly. "Fetch the tartare sauce, will you?"

Esther approached the river and the young Khazi boy. "Good evening, young man," she said with a smile. "How much for the two?"

The boy at first looked puzzled "Fish. You buy!" he insisted.

"Yes, yes, dear, I'm trying to," Esther told him. "How much?

"I'll handle this, dear," Minnie said, joining them at the water's edge. "Give me some of their funny money, will you, dear?" she asked.

Esther dished out a handful of coins to her sister, who rattled them under the boy's nose. "How much for the fishes?" she asked, speaking slowly and holding up one coin at a time. "One, two, three perhaps?"

The boy's eyes lit up as he leapt from the water, snatched the coins from her hand and dumped the slippery fish into her arms. "Oh!" Minnie at first cried, jostling the lifeless fish. "Er, thank you, what's your name?" she asked, stooping to his level, but the boy turned and dived, plunging back into the murky Ural River and swimming back towards the fisherman's nets, which he regularly plundered to help feed his poverty-stricken family.

The fishermen in question left their nets strung across the deepest stretch of the Ural to catch the migrating fish, and had caught the boy red-handed on several occasions, and each time they had beaten him with the soles of their sandals and warned him never to return. But needs must as they say, and with his own father having drowned during a fishing expedition to the Caspian Sea, he was now left to fend for his mother and three younger siblings.

"My God, the boy swims like a fish," Minnie marvelled, watching him dive some fifteen feet below the surface to check the nets.

"Where is the boy's mother, that's what I want to know?" Esther asked, adopting a more maternal stance. "He should be at home, not swimming in this filthy river peddling fish, for God's sake."

"Speaking of fish, dear," Minnie asked as they returned to the campsite, "how do you like it?"

Esther stood looking out over the water and waiting for the boy to surface and breathing a sigh of relief when he eventually did, although empty handed. "In a pan with a little butter and lemon," she told her sister, turning away too.

The sisters set up their camping stove and cookware and huddled around, moving the sizzling fish around the pan. "It smells delicious, dear," Minnie remarked as her sister dished up her serving, along with a ladle full of boiled potatoes.

"Doesn't it just?" Esther agreed, sitting beside her. "Do you think he's gone home?" she then asked.

"Who, dear?" Minnie replied, tucking into her fish supper.

"The boy," Esther said, looking out across the water. "I haven't seen him in the last hour. I do hope he's alright."

405

"Oh I don't know, dear," Minnie remarked without averting her eyes from her plate. "Yes maybe, would you pass the salt please, dear?"

"The what?" Esther said, turning back to her sister.

"The salt, dear!" Minnie reiterated. "It's there by your foot."

The young Kazakhstani boy had indeed returned to his mother's humble home to hand over the few coins he had earned that day and to consume his daily ration of rice and black beans. But unlike most children of his age he would not be lounging in front of the television that evening or playing video games. Come nightfall he would venture back out onto the river to raid the drift nets once again, with nothing but a simple waterproof torch to assist him.

Extinguishing the stove and washing their pots and pans, the sisters settled down to watch the sun descend below the horizon. "Now about that drink, dear," Esther said, feeling more at ease with a full stomach and, as she hoped, the worst of their journey behind them.

"Oh yes, of course dear," Minnie chirped, scurrying to the car. "A nip or two before bed would be just what the doctor ordered." She returned moments later with the full bottle, minus her earlier indulgence of course, and two china cups. "Chin chin!" she then said after pouring two ample measures and settling back in her chair.

"Ahhhhh." Esther sighed, cradling her cup in both hands and reclining, at peace for the first time in days. "Isn't this just heavenly?" There was no reply from her sister, who was busily refilling her cup. "Steady on, old girl," she warned her.

"Oh quiet, dear!" Minnie said, reaching over to top up her sister's cup. "It'll be plain sailing from here," she said, reassuring her rattled sister. "I can feel it, so just relax, dear."

Peshwari Nans

Esther thought for a moment and then raised a smile. "You're quite right, dear," she said, taking another hearty sip and toasting her sister. "Here's to plain sailing."

Although Esther agreed to lighten up and relax, a little of her remained pessimistic about their onward journey, considering their track record of late. She looked across at her sister, who hadn't a care in the world, and was gazing up into the evening sky.

"Have you ever wondered, dear," Minnie suddenly asked, startling her sister somewhat, "how infinite space really is? I mean really sat and wondered? It's something that's plagued me for years."

"I can't say that I've ever given it any thought, dear," Esther replied, looking skyward herself. "It's just, there."

"I know it's there, dear," Minnie remarked, beginning a philosophical rant. "Of course it's there, but how far does it go, that's what I want to know. I mean it can't just stop somewhere, can it? And the whole question of alien life. Do you know, I truly believe there is, somewhere out there."

Esther rolled her eyes and took another sip from her Royal Albert cup.

"I read an article in the *Evening Standard*," Minnie continued with Monique's cure-all working its magic on her tired limbs, "suggesting there could be a parallel universe just like this one, where Esther and Minnie also exist."

"Really?" Esther exclaimed. "Well I hope the other Esther is having better luck with her Minnie than I am, that's all."

Minnie pondered her sister's remark for a few seconds. "What do you mean, dear?" she then asked. "Haven't I always been an absolute rock at your side? Haven't I?"

"Well." Esther smirked. "I wouldn't say always, perhaps most of the time, dear."

This flagrant attack on Minnie's loyalty got her back up in an instant. "Well I've never been so insulted!" she said, with her nose in the air. "When have I ever let you down, eh? When? Just tell me one time I wasn't there for you, eh? One time, Essy!"

"Well." Esther thought for a few moments. "There was the time I asked you to pick up my wedding dress from the dry cleaners, and with just half an hour to go before the service you show up with a bag containing six pillow cases and a duvet cover. And yes, I know they were wrapped in brown paper, but you really should have checked."

"Okay, okay maybe there was just that one time," Minnie admitted. "But I've never failed you since, have I? Not once."

"What about my Elizabeth's christening?" Esther blurted out, recalling a particularly harrowing event. "You said you'd sort the buffet, I said ohhhh no, but you insisted on helping out. Well what did our guests have to choose from? I'll tell you, shall I in case you don't remember? You brought one hundred-and-fifty shrimp-paste sandwiches and a packet of cheese straws."

"Oh I thought the cheese straws were wonderful, dear," Minnie replied, topping up her cup again. "They were Waitrose you know. I spared no expense for our little Lizzy."

"Oh no, dear!" Esther said angrily. "Nobody but you touched the shrimp paste, so there were angry scuffles over the cheese straws. By three o'clock we had an angry mob on our hands, threatening to trash the place!"

"But I thought everybody liked shrimp paste, dear," Minnie said in her defence. "I made enough to go round."

"Yes you did, didn't you?" Esther snapped. "That was the problem" It was thirty-five degrees in that church hall, the bread was beginning to curl and the stench of that damn paste was making everyone feel nauseous. Even the vicar's dog turned his nose up at the blasted things."

Peshwari Nans

"Okay, okay!" Minnie again said, holding up her hands. "But apart from the pillow cases and the shrimp paste, when have I ever let you down?"

"Do you really want me to go on, dear?" Esther asked with a knowing smile. "I have all night you know."

"Perhaps not," Minnie said rapidly, changing the subject. "More vodka, dear?" she asked, offering the bottle.

"Not for me, dear," Esther replied, with a hand covering her cup. "I think I'll turn in."

"Right you are, dear," Minnie replied, tucking the bottle between her legs. "If it's all the same to you, dear, I'm going to sit for a while and watch for shooting stars."

"You do that, dear," Esther remarked, dragging herself up out of her deckchair. "With a little luck you'll be beamed up by one of your alien friends," she added under her breath.

"What was that, dear?" Minnie asked with a hand to her ear.

"I said I'll bid you good night," Esther said, heading for the tent. "Good grief!" she then said, staggering somewhat. "What on earth's in that stuff?"

"Marvellous, isn't it dear?" Minnie smiled, caressing the bottle.

"Well I shall sleep like a log, that's for sure," Esther said, stooping to crawl on all fours into their tent. "Good night, dear!" she called back.

"Night night!" Minnie replied, reclining and gazing up into the star-filled night sky once again.

Minnie's mind soon wandered as it so often did, transporting her to a far-off galaxy where shrimp paste was the accepted norm and bingo was played by the gods in giant arenas.

Esther's nasal snoring was the only sound that pierced the silence, but Minnie hadn't noticed. Her thoughts were a billion light years away, and a warm fuzzy vodka-fuelled feeling engulfed her.

Some time later Minnie's eyes grew heavy and the china cup she was holding slowly slipped from her hand, landing unbroken at her feet. She was neither awake nor asleep, she was in the space between, her head nodding as she fought the tiredness, a fight she would sooner or later undoubtedly lose. But no sooner had she succumbed to the phantom fatigue than something then quickly brought her round. "What? What?" she said, wriggling in her chair and shaking her head in a bid to rouse herself. "Who's there?" she asked, looking behind her chair.

A splashing sound could be heard out on the river as Minnie struggled to focus. "What the?" she said, leaning forward and donning her spectacles. An intermittent light could be seen swaying from side to side before disappearing momentarily. Minnie groaned as she heaved herself wearily to her feet and shakily approached the water's edge until her toes felt the cool ebbing Ural. "My God, it's the boy!" she gasped, with a hand above her eyes. "Esther it's the boy!"

It was now ten-thirty at night and the young Kazakhstani boy was still out on the river in search of trapped fish. But something was wrong, he was waving frantically, before disappearing beneath the swell for what seemed like an age, but was in fact several seconds.

During his last dive, to work the length of another of the fisherman's drift nets in which he had held his breath for a staggering twenty-five seconds, his left foot had become entwined in the fine nylon. After attempting to free himself with his tiny lungs near bursting, he was forced to swim to the surface, dragging a large section of the heavy net with him. Breaking the surface, he gasped the precious air and waved his torch above his head, too exhausted to cry out before the weight of the net dragged him back under and he knew he'd have to fight to reach the surface once again, all the time tugging at the noose around his foot.

"God, he's in trouble!" Minnie cried, turning for the tent. "ESTHERRR!" she yelled, stumbling and staggering as best she could. "ESTHER! THE BOY! ESTHERRRR!" But her sister remained dead to the world. "Esther!" Minnie barked, opening the tent flaps, the urgency sobering her a tad. "Oh blast!" she cursed, turning back to the river. "HANG ON!" she called out to the stricken boy. "HANG ON, I'LL GET HELP!"

Unable to see more than a few feet ahead of her, Minnie held out her arms and hurried along the riverbank as best she could. "HELLLLLLLP! ANYBODYYYYY! HELLLLLLLP!" she screamed, but the boy's village was half a kilometre away, with its lights barely visible.

"Ohhhhhhh!" she moaned, looking back out at the splashing boy, who was beginning to tire whilst choking on the water he had swallowed.

It was then that Minnie noticed the bow of a small boat wedged into a reed bed, with a wooden plank for a makeshift seat. "Oh hell," she cursed, not having been in a rowing boat for some considerable time. "HANG ON!" she again called, taking a deep breath and venturing into the freezing water up to her knees, the muddy riverbed clogging her toes and the silkweed clinging like nylons to her legs.

Tugging at the tiny craft while keeping a watchful eye out for crocodiles, she had convinced herself inhabited these waters, Minnie stooped to look inside, and as luck would have it, the fisherman's craft contained a pair of hand-crafted oars. With the boy's light disappearing for an ever-increasing amount of time, Minnie had no choice but to cock one leg over the side of the boat and drag herself aboard, clinging on tightly as it rocked violently from side to side.

"Right, you can do this, Minnie," she told herself, sliding the oars through the two brass gunnels. Pushing herself away from the bank with her head still a little fuzzy, Minnie attempted to row, but her timing and rhythm left a lot to be desired and she began to turn full circle. "Damn, damn!" she cursed, struggling to keep the boy in her line of sight. "Come on, Minnie, you can do this!" she said, berating herself. "Pull yourself together woman!"

Eventually she managed to keep the small boat on an even keel and in a relatively straight line, heading out towards the nets. "I'M COMING!" she yelled over her shoulder. Arriving at the boy's last sighted position Minnie searched all around her boat but there was no sign of the boy. "Oh no!" she cried, peering over the side. "Where are you? Where are you?" she called. Then, rolling up her sleeve, she plunged her arm into the blackened water, reaching this way and that. "Dear God, where is he?" she said trying the opposite side.

The boy, now exhausted, had been dragged to the bottom yet again, panic stricken and unable to hold his breath a moment longer. Inhaling a mouthful of water, the boy had convulsed and gave one last-ditch attempt to reach the surface, pushing hard off the soft silt bottom of the Ural. Cupping his hands, he thrust the water behind him and screamed with gritted teeth, swimming for his very life, but in fact making very little headway.

Minnie, now frantic, suddenly saw the faint glimmer of the boy's flashlight, which he'd tucked in his shorts.

"HERE! I'M HERE!" she screamed, pounding the surface of the water with both her hands. "SWIM, BOY, SWIM!" She then reached down even further into the water, leaning precariously over the edge of the boat.

Peshwari Nans

Suddenly she felt the tips of the boy's thrashing fingers, which came as a complete shock to the Kazakhstani lad. "Gotcha!" she cried, grasping the boy's hand and leaning back into the boat, heaving him breathlessly to the surface, where he emerged, coughing and spluttering.

"Help. Help me, please!" he said in his garbled dialect, before coughing a stream of water from his lungs. The boy clung to the side of the boat, limp and exhausted but still very much entangled in the net.

"I've got you, don't worry, I've got you," Minnie reassured him, gripping his shoulders and dragging his torso up from the water. "Oh my!" she gasped, seeing the heavy net trailing behind him, pulling and straining her fragile back.

The boy managed to flop into the boat, where he lay panting in an inch or so of water, with his leg draped over the side, the thin tensile nylon cutting deep into his tender skin. "Thank you, Missy," he said, taking deep lungfuls of air. "Thank you."

"Oh heavens," Minnie said, taking the torch from him and examining the fisherman's netting.

At the same time, Esther stirred and rolled over in the tent. "What? What?" she said drowsily. "Just the one crumpet for me, Minnie dear," she said, emerging from a blissful dream. "Minnie?" she then added, rubbing her eyes and seeing the empty blanket beside her. "Minnie, where are you?"

Stoll woozy and feeling the effects of the alcohol, Esther rolled from her blanket and pushed herself shakily up onto all fours, poking her head out of the tent flaps. "Minnie? Come to bed, dear," she said, looking at the empty deckchair and the discarded vodka bottle. "Minnie?" she called. "Where the devil are you?"

Crawling out, Esther clawed at the tent pole to pull herself to her feet. "Heavens!" she moaned, clutching her

413

head. "Minnie dear!" she called out, still in her night dress. With no immediate reply, Esther grew increasingly concerned. "MINNIIIIE? MINNIIIIE? WHERE ARE YOUUUU?" Fearing her sister may have been abducted by foreign nationals or even the very aliens she spoken of, Esther flew into an animated panic, striding around Vivien with her hands to her mouth. "MINNIIIIE!" she again called at the top of her voice. "MINNIE DARLING!"

It was then that she heard a faint reply,

"Essyyyyy I'm herrrrrre!" Minnie replied from out on the river.

"Minnie, Minnie, where are you, for heaven's sake?" Esther yelled, hardly thinking to look towards the river.

"HERE!" Minnie again replied, waving the boy's torch above her head. "ESSY, I'M OVER HERE!"

"WHAT?" Esther cried, spinning in her bare feet. "MINNIE!" She clasped her hands to her head. "Minnie no!" she shrieked, heading hastily to the water's edge. "MINNIE, WHAT? WHY?"

"I'M ALRIGHT ESSY!" Minnie called back in a bid to calm her frantic sister.

"GET BACK HERE THIS INSTANT!" Esther beckoned to the figure way out on the Ural. "WHAT DO YOU THINK YOU'RE DOING?"

Esther couldn't see the young Kazakhstani boy, who was lying panting in the bottom of the boat. "WHAT ON EARTH ARE YOU DOING IN THAT DAMN BOAT FOR CHRIST'S SAKE?" she asked, struggling to come to terms with the precarious situation. "I CAN'T LEAVE YOU FOR A MOMENT, CAN I?" she added "NOT FOR ONE BLASTED MOMENT!"

"ESSY, I CAN EXPLAIN!" Minnie shouted in reply, whilst tugging at the nylon net.

"THAT'S IT, THAT IS IT!" Esther raged, stamping her foot. "I'M PUTTING YOU ON A PLANE FIRST

THING IN THE MORNING, YOU'RE A BLOOMING LIABILITY YOU ARE, A LIABILITY I SAY!"

"BUT ESSY, WAIT!" Minnie replied with no time to explain.

"I DON'T WANT TO HEAR IT!" Esther said angrily. "I'VE MADE UP MY MIND! YOU'RE GOING HOME AND THAT'S THAT!"

Minnie tugged at the nylon, with it cutting into her fingers too, until eventually she miraculously managed to free the boy's foot, discarding the nest of twine over the side, letting it sink back to the bottom of the unforgiving river. "Right, let's get you back," she then told the shivering boy.

"I'M WAITING!" Esther yelled, with her hands now firmly gripping her hips.

"ALRIIIIGHT!" Minnie snapped back. "I'VE BEEN A LITTLE BUSY OUT HERE YOU KNOW!"

"BUSY?" Esther barked "I'LL GIVE YOU BUSY, SCARING ME HALF TO DEATH IN THE MIDDLE OF THE NIGHT AND BOBBING AROUND IN A BLOOMIN BOAT. WHATEVER'S GOT INTO YOU?"

Minnie grappled with the oars once again, firstly rowing in the wrong direction. "Oh hell!" she cursed, missing the water completely with several strokes.

Esther grew increasingly irate, grinding her teeth and threatening all sorts of things under her breath. "Where are you going?" she asked as her sister neared the bank but then veered to the right.

"I'm trying, dear!" Minnie puffed.

"I'll say!" Esther replied sarcastically. "And then some!" She kicked at the water lapping over her feet. "I mean it, Minnie," she growled. "First thing in the morning you are on a plane home, this really is the final straw, you have overstepped the mark by a mile my dear, by a mile!"

"I told you I can explain, dear!" Minnie barked in reply, growing tired now of her sister's constant barracking.

"Save it!" Esther said defiantly. "I'll even help you pack." Minnie's boat drew closer and Esther reached out for the bow. "I can't tell you how disappointed in you I am, Minnie," she told her sister. "You could've got yourself killed out there, and for what? Tell me, dear, what were you doing?"

She tugged the boat into the shallows, wedging it firmly in the muddy bank, but her jaw then suddenly dropped on seeing the young boy flat out in the bottom at Minnie's feet. "What?" she simply said, aghast. "What, what's he doing in the boat for Pete's sake, Minnie? What's going on?"

"I told you I could explain, dear," Minnie said, stepping gingerly into the water and out onto the bank to her sister's side. "The boy was trapped, in the fishing nets. I heard him and tried to wake you."

"Trapped?" Esther gasped, suddenly feeling extremely foolish. "Oh, I see."

She and Minnie helped the boy from the boat. "Minnie, I…" Esther said, unable to find the words. "I, I'm afraid I misjudged you—"

"—Save it, dear," Minnie replied, looking the boy up and down. "Are you alright, dear?" she asked him, stooping down. "What were you doing out there?"

"Fish," the boy merely said, pointing out across the river and then at his mouth. "Fish."

Esther hastily retrieved a towel from Vivien and wrapped it around the boy's shoulders. "Young man, you shouldn't be out at this time of night," she told him, rubbing him dry. "Fish or no fish."

"Perhaps he does it to feed his family, dear" Minnie proposed, hitting the nail directly on the head, as the boy stood shivering, in a state of shock.

Peshwari Nans

"My God, do you think so?" Esther asked. "Minnie, fetch a bag quickly," she said, shoving her sister aside. "And you, young man, come and sit inside Vivien here for a moment."

The boy clambered behind the wheel and sat staring into space for a while until coming to. A smile then slowly crept across his face as he ran his hands across the polished dashboard and sat pretending to steer from left to right, while Esther and Minnie filled two bags with the majority of their groceries. "Here you are, young man," Esther told the boy at the car's door. "Take these home with you. Tell your mother it's not much, but you're more than welcome to it. Oh and please stay out of the river, it's really not safe."

The boy was reluctant at first to leave the car. He had seen pictures of automobiles in discarded magazines, but never before had he been behind the wheel of one.

"We have chocolate, too," Minnie informed him, producing a bar from her pocket. The boy's eyes lit up as he leapt from the driver's seat and snatched the milk chocolate treat, tore open the wrapper, and stood chomping greedily,

"Will you see that your mother gets this?" Esther added, placing a quantity of notes into the boy's hand, a sum equivalent to a month's wages for the average Kazakhstani.

The young lad looked down at the money and then up at each of the sisters before throwing his arms around them in turn. "It's alright." Minnie laughed. "Now go on, get yourself off home it's late."

"Tank you tank you tank you," the boy said, attempting a little English, taking the bags from Esther and turning towards the distant lights.

"Please forgive me, dear," Esther said, slipping an arm around her heroic sister's shoulder as the pair watched the boy skip along the riverbank, eager to present his beleaguered mother with his haul. "I've been such a fool," Esther confessed to Minnie. "I should learn to trust your judgment."

"Yes, yes, you should, Essy dear," Minnie replied, crawling into their tent and flopping exhausted on top of her sleeping bag.

Esther stood outside for a few moments until the boy disappeared out of sight, shaking her head in disbelief at the sheer enormity of her sister's selfless actions. She then smiled as Minnie soon began to snore even louder than she had done before. Crawling inside the tent and zipping the flaps shut, Esther, without a thought for herself, opened up her own sleeping bag, lay beside her sister on the groundsheet and pulled it over the pair of them, snuggling in close and chuckling at Minnie's open-mouthed gurgling.

For the remainder of the night, Esther tossed and turned to avoid an obvious lump beneath the tent, while her sister slept soundly. But eventually her own exhaustion got the better of her, and she drifted off to sleep with an hour to spare before daybreak.

Esther opened an eye around nine-fifteen, stiff as a board, shivering and aching all over. She reached behind her, assuming her sleeping bag had slipped from her shoulders, only to find that her sister had dragged it from her during the night and cocooned herself completely, leaving her with absolutely no cover at all. "Thank you very much!" she said, wincing as she stretched, the lump beneath her digging into her bottom yet again.

Minnie, on the other hand, lay with a contented smile on her face as though she'd slept the sleep of kings, but she too eventually woke up, only she was fresh and invigorated, unlike her tetchy sister. "Morning!" she said in remarkably high spirits. "Essy where on earth is your sleeping bag, dear?" she asked over her shoulder, still heavily wrapped up herself.

"You have it!" Esther snapped, on edge whenever she was deprived of sleep. "You have all of it in fact!"

"Oh, I am sorry, dear." Minnie smiled. "You should have woken me, dear," she told her irate sister. "I'd have shared it with you."

"It's mine!" Esther growled. "And I shared it with you, remember? But you robbed me of it as I slept, you, you despicable wretch you!"

"Put the kettle on, will you dear?" Minnie said, resting her head down once again. "You really aren't yourself until you've had a cup of tea."

"Oh really!" Esther grimaced, crawling out of their tent and immediately shielding her eyes from the hazy sunshine, remaining on all fours for a moment, too stiff to stand. "Oh God!" she said, her knees clicking as she dragged her aching frame up their tent pole. "I feel a hundred-and-fifty years old and not a day less."

Minnie threw back both sleeping bags and stretched out her arms. "Ahhhhh," she sighed contentedly. "What a beautiful morning." She could hear the larks and reed warblers at the water's edge gathering flies and mosquitoes for their hungry chicks. "Any chance of some breakfast, Essy dear?" she called out to Esther, who was struggling to light the primus, the dampness having affected their matches.

"Any chance of you shutting the hell up?" was Esther's rattled reply under her breath, as she leaned from side to side to the chorus of creaking bones.

"What was that, dear?" Minnie asked, cocking an ear. "Was that a yes to breakfast?"

"Alright, alright!" Esther stormed, walking bow legged up to Vivien. "I'll get us some eggs on the go. How would you like them? Poached or scrambled?"

"Not for me, dear," Minnie informed her, poking her head from the tent. "I'm off eggs now for good, I should have told you."

"What?" Esther said, turning in astonishment. "Off them? But you love your eggs in the morning."

"Not any more I don't, dear," Minnie replied, crawling out and springing to her feet. "I had this dream last night."

"Well lucky you," Esther scoffed. "I'd have dreamt too if I'd have slept long enough."

"You should have had a nip or two more of Monique's elixir, dear," Minnie said, stretching again and bending to touch her toes, something she hadn't done in some twenty years. "It really is quite the tonic you know."

"What I need is my own damn tent!" Esther said, in no mood for her sister's jubilance. "Now, what was that about the eggs? Do you want them or not?"

"Not, thank you," Minnie said, striding purposefully towards the car. "Like I said I had this dream about the suffering of these poor animals and I do believe it's affected me profoundly dear, I really do."

"No dear," Esther said drearily. "I think you'll find it was Monique's alcohol that profoundly affected you."

"I'm deadly serious, dear," Minnie insisted. "I did tell you I was considering going veggie. Well to hell with it. I'm going to go the whole hog, so from this day forth, Essy, I am a vegan."

"Vegan!" Esther scoffed. "You? Well that'll be the day."

"No dear, today's the day," Minnie said adamantly. "From now on I will not be eating meat, fish or any other dairy derived product."

"What, no meat?" Esther asked.

"No meat," Minnie reiterated.

"No fish?" Esther asked, aghast.

"Absolutely not, dear," Minnie informed her. "None whatsoever."

Peshwari Nans

"None, dear?" Esther continued to ask, unable to come to terms with her sister's sudden drastic change of heart. "But, but, what will you eat, for heaven's sake?"

"Well I'll have good old beans on toast this morning," Minnie told her flabbergasted sister, plucking a tin from the remainder of their provisions. "No butter on the toast of course, and, er, possibly couscous for lunch."

"Couscous?" Esther sneered. "Couscous?"

"Yes dear, couscous." Minnie smiled. "So good they named it twice, you know."

Esther then delved into Minnie's hoard. "Ahhhhhh." She smiled confidently. "Well what about your shrimp paste then, eh dear? Are you really willing to give that up too?"

Minnie thought long and hard for a moment or two. Had she indeed been too hasty in ascending the moral high ground?

"Yes, yes I am," she eventually said after much deliberation. "I'll have no more of it and that's that."

"What?" Esther said, wholeheartedly stunned at her sister's apparent resolve. "Are you sure, dear? I mean this is your shrimp paste we're talking about here, the same shrimp paste you've been eating for the last forty years."

"Not any more, dear," Minnie said, turning her face away. "If I'm to do this I'll need to make a clean break, cold turkey so to speak. Only without the turkey of course."

"Cold turkey!" Esther laughed. "Minnie dear, you're not a heroin addict."

"Essy," Minnie said, straight faced. "Never underestimate the power of the paste. As you say, I had my first sandwich forty years ago but by Christ I was hooked in an instant..." Minnie went on to compare the innocent potted paste to the most dangerous of class A amphetamines. "I was craving the stuff day and night, Essy dear," she added, trying desperately not to look at the alluring jar in her sister's hand. "Throw it out, dear, please, before I weaken!" she begged.

"I'll do nothing of the sort," Esther replied, bagging the jars. "I'll give it to the needy. It's a crime to throw away perfectly good food when the homeless are starving in our streets. An absolute crime."

"Very well, dear," Minnie agreed. "Just keep it away from me if you will. I usually have it on a cracker for my elevenses, so I'll be climbing the walls a little later no doubt."

"Oh don't be ridiculous, dear!" Esther scoffed. "It's just shrimp paste for God's sake."

"I wouldn't be too sure if I were you," Minnie warned her.

Esther examined the seemingly harmless jars. "The power of the paste." She smirked, never having partaken herself. "I'll try it myself while you warm the beans."

"Are you sure, dear?" Minnie asked, concerned to say the least. "May I just remind you that you are dealing with forces here that you couldn't possibly begin to comprehend."

"Oh fiddlesticks!" Esther laughed, taking a slice of bread and the toasting fork. "I told you, it's just paste, nothing more."

While Minnie warmed her baked beans on the primus, Esther sat browning her bread on the excess flame until it was crisp and slightly charred. "Here," she said, handing the fork to Minnie. "Now let's see what all the fuss is about, shall we?" she added.

Minnie looked on knowingly as her sister prised open a jar of the ominous shrimp paste and spread a liberal layer onto her toast. "And so it begins," Minnie said to herself, watching Esther take the first bite, wincing as the barrage of flavours assaulted her taste buds.

Peshwari Nans

"Mmmmmm," Esther mumbled, taking another bite instantly. "It em, mmm, it is rather good, isn't it?" she said with her mouth full. "Minnie dear, would you do me another slice please, my dear?"

"Oh dear." Minnie frowned, handing her sister the slice she had browned for herself. "I warned you, Essy."

Esther consumed a further three slices of shrimp paste toast before replacing the jar with a loving caress.

"What about the needy, dear?" Minnie asked, scooping a spoonful of beans into her mouth.

"Oh to hell with the needy, dear," Esther said, guarding her stash of paste. "Charity begins at home, isn't that what they say?" Esther's uncharacteristic actions resembled those of a user taking their very first hit, like the first snort or tote on a crack pipe. She had a feeling of instant euphoria and she liked it. Could this truly be the power of the paste, she wondered? Could dark forces really be at work beneath that humble lid? Only time would tell. For Esther, her forthcoming addiction had only just begun, but for her sister the traumatic task of kicking her forty-year habit was about to prove a truly mammoth undertaking and would require a will of iron and nerves of steel.

After breakfast, Esther single handedly (as usual) took down their tent, with Minnie standing beside her doing very little indeed, a skill she had perfected to a tee. "What are you doing, dear?" Esther asked, stowing the tent into Vivien.

"I'm, I'm, sorting the spoons, Essy," Minnie replied, shuffling the cutlery. "You know how frustrating it can be searching for a dessert spoon amongst the soup spoons."

"No, no, I don't actually," Esther confessed, snatching the spoons from her sister's hand and tossing them back into the box with the others. "A spoon is a spoon. Now make yourself useful and pack away the primus, will you?"

"Yes but…" Minnie said, stalling. "But I haven't sorted the forks yet, dear."

"Minnie!" Esther barked, pointing to the stove.

"Oh alright." Minnie sulked. "As if I haven't done enough already."

With Vivien neatly packed, the sisters were about to set off when they heard the sound of a child calling.

"Oh look, dear!" Minnie said, nudging her sister. "It's the boy from the river."

Indeed it was the Kazakhstani lad hurrying along the riverbank with his mother following close behind him. "MISSY! MISSY!" he yelled, waving.

"Hello," Minnie said, greeting the child. "And how's our little friend today?"

The boy waffled in the language of his forefathers, introducing his mother in doing so.

"Pleased to meet you, dear," Minnie said, getting the gist of the garbled conversation. "You must be his mother. I'm Minnie and this here is my sister Esther."

The boy's mother stood with her hands clasped together, bowing repeatedly, having been told by her son of the white lady's heroics. She then took the money the sisters had given her son and offered it back to them, pleading for them to accept it.

"Oh no, dear, that's for you," Esther insisted. "For you, my dear."

"No dear," Minnie added when the mother persisted. "We would like you to have it." She pushed the woman's hand away. With this the grateful boy's mother reached into her crudely constructed backpack and took out a loaf of stoneground bread and offered it to her son's saviour.

"Okay dear, that's awfully kind of you," Minnie said, accepting the token.

Peshwari Nans

"Yes, very kind indeed," Esther agreed. "I shall have a slice or two with paste for my elevenses," she informed the bewildered Kazakhstanis.

"See? I told you," Minnie said, grabbing at her sister's arm. "Beware the potted paste!"

"Oh shut up, dear," Esther scoffed. "I can take it or leave it."

But Minnie knew otherwise, harking back to the days when she herself was a slave to her own delusional dependency. "You were warned, dear," she simply said before turning back to the boy. "And you, young man, remember what I said. No more river, do you hear?"

The lad nodded in agreement although much of what Minnie said was a complete mystery to him.

"Make your mother proud," Minnie added, ruffling the lad's hair. "Go to school."

The boy's mother again bowed respectfully and led her son away, the pair of them waving back at the sisters.

"Take care!" Minnie called after them.

"Yes byyyyye!" Esther said, pondering for a moment how many others like the lad risked their lives on a daily basis just to put a hot meal on their mother's table. "It's criminal," she said to herself.

"What is, dear?" Minnie asked, still waving beside her.

"We live in a world of perpetual waste," Esther explained. "And yet here a crust of bread could mean the difference between life and death. It's an injustice Minnie, a rotten injustice and it sickens me to my stomach, it really does."

"It's not just here though, dear, is it?" Minnie reminded her sister. "We have it back home too. Do you know I'd never even heard of a food bank until I was asked to donate at the supermarket. But when the nice young lady explained that there were those among us in our own community that simply couldn't afford the bare necessities

I just had to do my bit. I left them three tins of spaghetti hoops, a jar of marmite and a lime jelly."

"Well that's awfully decent of you, dear," Esther said, climbing behind the wheel, ready for the off.

"Well not really, dear," Minnie confessed. "The spaghetti hoops were dented and marked down, the marmite was out of date and I'd nibbled half the lime jelly on the way round. But I suppose it's the thought that counts isn't it, dear?"

"I, er, I suppose it is, dear," Esther replied after a moment's contemplation. "You really are a regular Mother Teresa, my dear."

"Well I wouldn't go so far, dear," Minnie said as they left their riverside campsite. "But I'll confess I do sleep a little more soundly now, knowing I've helped the poverty stricken in some small way."

"Emphasis on the word 'small', Minnie dearest," Esther joked, turning the car out onto the dusty highway, her comment going way over Minnie's head, as her level of sarcasm often did.

The sisters kept their windows wound fully up as they trundled behind a convoy of dust-covered trucks loaded with rocks. "Can you not pass them, dear?" Minnie asked as Vivien was repeatedly showered with windswept grit.

The terrain was mountainous and the makeshift road meandered from left to right. "I daren't pass them, dear," Esther said, unable to see beyond the last of the trucks. "Perhaps we should stop for a while? Until they're gone I mean."

Minnie glanced over her shoulder at several more laden trucks approaching behind them. "I'm afraid that's out of the question, dear," she said as they were hemmed in. "You'll have to pass them, dear, it's no use," she added desperately. "Before dear Vivien here is pebble-dashed to pieces."

Peshwari Nans

"Yes I know what you mean," Esther said, wincing as a sizable stone struck the windscreen "Dear lord!" she gasped, veering to the right and briefly glancing along the line of some six or seven heavy trucks ahead.

Soon the road ahead widened, offering ample room for the sisters to safely pass the convoy, and a sturdy steel barrier was situated at the cliff's edge to prevent any potential fatalities. This was a recent addition to the accident black spot, after approximately thirty bikes, cars and trucks had strayed over the edge and plummeted down the treacherous ravine in as many weeks, culminating in almost certain death for the unfortunate riders and drivers.

"What are you thinking, dear?" Minnie asked her sister.

"Well we can't stay here, that's for sure," Esther agreed. "And these lorries are moving particularly slowly, so I'm thinking maybe this old girl could get by them after all."

"That's the spirit!" Minnie smiled, unfazed by the obvious complexities of such a manoeuvre.

Esther kept pace with the rear truck, winding down her window to lean out to increase her view ahead.

"What are you waiting for, dear?" Minnie asked impatiently. "Just go around them, will you?"

"Hush will you!" Esther cursed over her shoulder, her hair instantly clogged with the dry reddish dust flicked up by the worn truck tyres.

"Now dear, now!" Minnie cried, goading her apprehensive sister. "Go on!"

"Minnie!" Esther again snapped, turning with a dust-spattered face. "You, my dear, are not helping!"

"Sorry dear," Minnie replied, zipping her mouth.

Esther again held her breath and leaned from her window and watched out for a long straight section of road. "Here goes!" she said, tugging Vivien's wheel to the right and pushing the accelerator to the floor, passing one, two and then three trucks with relative ease.

Peshwari Nans

Minnie waved politely to the Kazakhstani drivers in passing, each of them heavily tanned on one side only, as many within the haulage industry so often were.

But suddenly when they were rounding a bend the road ahead began to narrow gradually. "Oh dear!" Esther remarked, thumping the pedal harder to the floor and gripping Vivien's wheel tightly.

"Hurry, dear!" Minnie said, a little on edge now with the trucks beside her maybe a foot or so from her door and towering above her.

"I'm trying!" Esther replied, passing another until only two remained ahead of her.

"Okay Essy dear, you really to need to hurry now!" Minnie squealed, shifting closer to her sister and watching the trucks' hefty wheel nuts rotating at speed desperately close to her door."

"Yes dear!" Esther barked, gaining on the lead truck but then gasped open mouthed as she saw that the steel barrier beside them ended abruptly.

"WHAT?" she cried. Unable to pull in between the thundering trucks full of rocks, she had fully committed Vivien and themselves and now had absolutely nowhere to go but ahead. Esther leaned on Vivien's horn to alert the Kazak truck driver beside them to their perilous predicament, but he sat there oblivious, staring straight ahead with his radio belting out hits from the Kazakhstani cow bell choir, to which he swayed rhythmically, completely ignoring what was in his truck's mirrors.

"HEY!" Esther yelled from her window, but only succeeded in inhaling a large quantity of fine choking desert dust.

"Essyyyyyy!" Minnie said, inching closer to her sister. "Do something!"

"HEYYYYYYYY!" Esther screamed, honking the horn over and over. "HEYYYYYYYYY!"

Peshwari Nans

By now the driver's colleagues behind could see the obvious danger and also tugged on their air horns, but the lead driver merely waved nonchalantly and increased his speed.

"No, no, no, no, no!" Esther shrieked, with Vivien's offside tyres now inches from the cliff edge.

Minnie reached and wound down her own window and waved her handkerchief in an attempt to attract the day-dreaming driver's attention. "YOU THERE!" she called. "LET US PASS YOU FOOL!"

The sound of horns was now deafening, drowning out the cow-bell choir and antagonizing the lead truck driver somewhat, so much in fact that he leaned from his window, momentarily shaking his fist at his friends. It was then that he got his first glimpse of Vivien below him, but it was too late. Two of her wheels were now off the road and rumbling along the rocky slope, shaking the wheel in Esther's hands violently. "Oh God, oh God, oh God!" she cried, looking down at the river at the bottom of the steep ravine.

The startled truck driver quickly applied his brakes and pulled sharply to the left as best he could, considering the weight he was carrying, scraping his wing mirror on the limestone rock face beside him in doing so.

"ESSYYYYYY, WHAT'S HAPPENIIIING?" Minnie shrieked, clinging to her seat and clenching her eyes tightly shut.

Ignoring her petrified sister, Esther fought tooth and nail to maintain control, but a huge bolder up ahead sent a shiver along the length of her spine. "God damn it!" she yelled with her options severely dwindling and Vivien's aged suspension battering their backsides.

Minnie opened one eye and peered between her fingers, but she too gasped on seeing the gargantuan rock looming ahead and clasped her hands in prayer, begging the almighty for a miracle. The entire convoy of rock-laden trucks slammed on their brakes, locking their rear wheels and gouging the dirt road, sending plumes of choking dust into the humid air.

With precious seconds to spare Esther tugged as hard as she possibly could on the wheel. "Help me, dear!" she cried, with Vivien's tyres stuck in a rocky rut. "Minnie help me! Help me please!" She thumped her sister's arm until she opened her eyes and grabbed at the wheel. "Pull Minnie! Pull for Pete's sake!" Esther said through gritted teeth. "Come on Vivien my darling, come on girl!"

"I'm trying, dear!" Minnie said, leaning and clawing at the wheel.

Suddenly Vivien struck a smaller rock which forced her back onto the road and narrowly missed the fallen bolder by a whisker.

"Oh thank heavens." Minnie sighed, looking over her shoulder and slumping in her seat, mopping her brow with her handkerchief. "May I remind you, dear?" she told her panting sister. "That you should not overtake until it is safe and legal to do so. Page one hundred-and-sixty-three of the Highway Code I'll have you know."

"It was you, you damned fool!" Esther yelled, removing her straw hat to thrash her sister's thigh. "'What are you waiting for?' you said, 'Just go round them' you said! Well next time don't say a damned thing, do you hear me? Not a damned thing!"

Minnie sat staring at the cliff face. Having been scolded she was refusing to even look at her sister. "I fail to see how it was my fault," she eventually said to her own reflection. "After all, I am merely the passenger, you on the other hand, Essy, should know better. You could've got us both killed with your irrational behaviour."

Peshwari Nans

"My irrational behaviour!" Esther exclaimed. "It was you, it's always you, ever since we were babies, Minnie, it's always been you. You are a liability—a blasted liability!"

"Well," Minnie huffed. "There's gratitude for you."

Esther spun to glare at her sister. "Tell me, what on earth am I supposed to be grateful for?" she asked, changing gear with real venom. "Eh? Tell me Minnie, because I am more than intrigued to know, believe me!"

"Well." Minnie thought long and extremely hard. "We did get out of that dust bowl back there, didn't we?"

"Oh yes we sure did, didn't we?" Esther laughed. "Out of the frying pan and into the blooming fire! Well done you!"

"Why thank you, dear." Minnie smiled, taking her sister's sarcasm literally. "As I said before, dear," she reminded Esther, "it's sure to be plain sailing from—"

"—Don't say it!" Esther interjected swiftly. "Just don't say it, because nothing about this trip has been remotely plain, nothing whatsoever."

A short while later Minnie tapped her sister's shoulder and then her wristwatch. "Elevenses, dear?" she asked.

The sisters were devout creatures of habit and very rarely broke their daily routine, and no matter how aggrieved Esther was with her sister, the routine remained. "Of course," she said, sternly at first.

"Paste?" Minnie then asked, tempting a smile from her sister.

"Well." Esther's mood switched in a heartbeat. "Ooooh now you're talking, dear!" she said, as though no harsh words had passed between them. "Liberally spread, of course."

"Of course, dear," Minnie agreed, flipping over the tablet in readiness for the food. "I'll of course abstain from anything animal-derived," she added proudly. "Er did I mention, dear, that I am now a fully-fledged couscous-touting vegan?" she then asked. "And I must say I believe I feel better for it already."

"Yes, dear, you did," Esther said, rolling her eyes. "And may I remind you that you have only been a vegan for two-and-a-half hours. So how could you possibly feel any better?"

"Spiritually, dear." Minnie smiled, patting her chest. "Spiritually, it's like I've been reborn, cleansed even." She puffed out her chest a little further. "Do you know, dear, that the former US President Bill Clinton is now a paid-up member of the veggie club? Quite admirable I'd say, and I think in light of this we can now forgive him for the whole Monica Lewinsky affair."

"Forgive him!" Esther sneered. "How can you possibly forgive the President of the United States of America for having a torrid affair with a White House intern and then lying about it under oath, for heaven's sake? What was it he said? 'No I did not have sexual relations with Miss Lewinsky'. Well, tell that to her dry cleaner."

"Yes, dear, I know that but," Minnie said, retrieving the bread and cutlery, "I believe that anyone who converts to veganism should be absolved of all sin, I truly do. Their slates should be wiped clean so to speak."

Esther could hardly believe her ears. "So let me get this straight. If what you say is true, then if our very own Jack the Ripper had been apprehended and confessed to all of the grizzly Whitechapel murders, but on the day of his hanging also informed the executioner that he'd suddenly adopted a plant-based diet, then his life should have been spared?"

"Well," Minnie said, mulling it over. "Possibly not. But armed with this crucial information I believe the defence would have certainly given the prosecution a run for their money."

Peshwari Nans

"Poppycock!" Esther scoffed. "I've never heard so much nonsense in my entire life. You're a vegan, dear, that's all, you haven't been canonized by the blasted Pope."

Minnie ignored her sister's ridiculing while she reluctantly spread the fishy paste on Esther's slice of Kazakh stoneground bread. "How could you?" she asked, turning her nose up as she handed it to her sister between her thumb and forefinger, so as not to make contact with it. "Those poor shrimps, hunted down and forced into that tiny jar against their will." She revelled in the piety of her new-found vocation.

"Quite easily, dear," Esther said, driving one-handedly while she devoured her sandwich. "Mmmmm, mmm, mmmmm!" she moaned with pleasure. "Deeelicious, what'll you be having, dear?" she asked.

Minnie rummaged through the remaining provisions, examining each and every label in turn. "Eggs, milk, cheese," she mumbled, listing her banned ingredients. "Oh hell," she then cursed, opting for a dry slice of bread. "It's fine," she said, putting on a brave face whilst chewing the firm seedy crust. "Mmm, not bad," she added, lying blatantly. "I'll admit it'll take some adjusting to, but I'll persevere for the sake of the animals, dear."

"Well that's extremely noble of you, dear," her sister said, licking the fish paste from her fingers. "I'm very happy for you." She then snatched the shrimp paste jar from her sister's lap and scooped a large dollop out. "I'm happy for me, too," she added, sucking the paste greedily.

"That's enough, dear," Minnie said, removing the jar from her sister's manic grasp, but not without a fight. "I said that's enough!" she added through gritted dentures, replacing the lid and stowing the hypnotic paste away. "I knew this would happen," she told her frustrated sister. "It's got hold of you, Essy. I warned you of the power of the paste, didn't I?"

Peshwari Nans

"Yes and I told you I can control it!" Esther snapped. "But if I could just have one more slice, Minnie dear," she pleaded, "I'd be enormously grateful, indeed I would."

Minnie crossed her arms and completely ignored her sister's constant pleas for another 'fix' of the powerful paste to maintain her heady high.

During their passage through Kazakhstan the sisters marvelled at the breathtaking terrain, a glorious cinematic backdrop. "Have I told you, dear," Minnie said, with the tablet illuminated on her lap, "that Genghis Khan ruled the vast majority of this mystical land during the thirteenth century."

"No dear," Esther said, disinterested to say the least. "You did not."

"And that—" Minnie continued reading from the Internet's Wikipedia page word for word, "The word Kazakh is derived from the ancient Turkic word meaning independent, a free spirit. Isn't that fascinating, dear? I said isn't that fascinating Essy? Essy?"

"Wonderful, dear," Esther eventually said, paying very little attention.

"Kazakhstan itself," Minnie rambled on. "It says here, has been inhabited since the Neolithic age. Well I never," she exclaimed. "Fancy that, dear? I said fancy that, Essy? The Neolithic age!"

"I heard you," Esther said, staring blankly ahead, concentrating on avoiding the countless potholes in the ancient road surface. "Blast!" she cursed, hitting a particularly deep rut, jostling the pair of them in their seats.

"Apparently, dear," Minnie said, unfazed, "Kazakhstan was the last of the Soviet republics to declare independence following the dissolution of the Soviet Union in 1991. Are you listening, dear?" she asked. "Essy?"

"Switch that damned thing off, will you?" Esther stormed, having heard enough mindless trivia for one day.

Peshwari Nans

"Haven't I told you it's for emergencies only. Not for you to give a relentless running blasted commentary."

"Oh," Minnie said abruptly. "Okay dear." She switched off the tablet and turned it face-down once again before strumming her fingers rhythmically. "Are you alright, dear?" she eventually asked her sister. "You've been awfully cranky all morning and it really isn't like you at all."

"No, no, I'm not actually," Esther confessed. "You don't remember, do you?" she added. "Well today would have been Jack's birthday."

"Oh God, Essy, I'm so sorry, my darling," Minnie said, with a hand to her mouth. "How could I have forgotten? Please forgive me."

Jack's birthday had long since been a memorable occasion. Almost all of his extended family, including grandchildren and great-grandchildren would take time out to visit him for the ceremonial cutting of his favourite fruit cake, and the all-important singalong, which became a yearly tradition in the Reynolds' household, and one that would indeed be sorely missed now that he was dead.

Minnie placed a hand on her sister's knee. "You must think me such an insensitive fool," she told her. "Waffling on about Genghis Khan on such an important day. You should have stopped me, dear."

"Minnie." Esther smiled. "It would take a bullet to the head to stop you when you're 'in the zone', as the young types like to say."

"Yes, you're probably right, dear," Minnie agreed. "Happy birthday, Jack," she then said, looking skyward.

"Yes, happy birthday, darling," Esther reiterated with a lump in her throat.

"Don't worry, dear," Minnie said softly. "He's there."

"Yes," Esther replied. "Yes, I know he is."

The sisters sat in reflective silence for a few moments until Minnie slowly and calmly began to chant Jack's favourite party song, the one he'd always sing, when sitting in his sagging armchair clutching a tin of stout, with his entire family around him. "I don't care, I don't care," she began, "I don't care if he comes round here."

Esther looked across, not knowing whether to laugh or cry as her sister warbled on: "I've got my beer in the sideboard here let Mother sort it out if he comes round herrrre."

Esther herself soon began to mouth the words, gradually raising her voice. "I don't care, I don't care, I don't care if he comes round herrrre."

Soon the pair of them were swaying and belting out the tribute to her late husband: "LET MOTHER SORT IT OUT IF HE COMES ROUUUUUUND HERRRRRRRRE!"

Esther had the broadest of smiles on her tear-stained face. "Thank you, Min," she said, squeezing her sister's hand. "Thank you. I needed that."

"You're welcome, dear," Minnie replied, reaching to turn Vivien's wheel, so as to avoid a crumbling crater in the road ahead.

"Oh dear Lord!" Esther shrieked, coming to her senses. "Well done, dear". Many of the road signs along the way were either illegible or faded into obscurity. "Okay, you win," Esther conceded after a while. "Will you please ask Mr Google where the devil we are?"

"Certainly, dear." Minnie smiled, flipping back the tablet and consulting their dear friend, as she thought Mr Google was. "Well, dear," she told her sister. "I think we may have caught him at an inopportune moment, because he's taking his time replying."

"Oh dear." Esther frowned. "Please send him our sincere apologies and tell him we'll fetch him a little something back for his troubles."

Peshwari Nans

"Will do, dear," Minnie replied, tapping at the screen with her tongue protruding from the corner of her mouth. "Oh hang on, dear!" she then squealed, utterly delighted. "Here's the map I requested now. Never mind bringing him a little something, I think we should bring him a *big* something back, wouldn't you agree, Essy dear?"

"Well yes, he has been an absolute darling, hasn't he?" Esther said, nodding in agreement.

"I'll say." Minnie smiled. "Do you know, Essy, I think he could be older," she added, referring to the imaginary Mr Google. "Maybe closer to my age."

"Whatever gives you that idea?" Esther asked.

"Well he's so wise, dear," Minnie explained. "So surely it would take a lifetime to become the font of all knowledge, don't you think? Do you know, I asked him earlier if he had a vegan replacement for my beloved bacon double cheeseburger, and do you know the genius came straight back with a mung bean and chick pea patty with a lime and coriander garnish! I simply can't wait to try it."

"Really?" Esther said, tempted by Minnie's meatless dish. "What did he say about your corned beef hash? You know how you crave it at times, dear."

"Oh yes, dear," Minnie said, full of herself at this point. "That'll be the chick pea and mung bean mash. Sounds mouth-watering, doesn't it?"

"Hmmmm," Esther said, suddenly having reservations. "And your chicken curry, dear?" she asked. "What could he possibly do with that? Answer me that?"

"Simple, dear." Minnie smiled, tapping the tablet. "Mr Google recommended the mung bean madras with a chickpea chapatti."

"Really, dear?" Esther smirked. "It is rather limited this diet of yours, wouldn't you say? I suppose for breakfast you'll be having the chickpea cheerios with semi-skimmed mung bean milk?"

"Precisely, dear!" Minnie chirped. "Aren't they just so versatile."

"Aren't they just?" Esther said, entirely unconvinced. "But let me tell you something, dear," she warned her sister. "If you think I'm travelling halfway around the world in this tiny car with you and your belly full of beans you are much mistaken."

"A small price to pay, dear," Minnie merely said in reply. "For the greater good and all that."

"Greater for who, dear?" Esther asked. "Certainly not for me that's for sure. No, no I really must insist you broaden your dietary consumption. Surely there's more to this veganism than just peas and blasted beans for heavens' sake."

"Oh yes of course there is, dear," Minnie replied confidently. "I can have—" She paused, whilst considering her options.

"Go on!" Esther said with a wry smile. "You can have what exactly?"

"Yes, yes, give me a moment, dear," Minnie said, pondering. "Cauliflower cheese! Yes, yes I can have cauliflower cheese," she said, bobbing in her seat. "Oh no, wait." She then sulked. "That contains cheese, doesn't it?"

"Errr, as the name suggests," Esther said sarcastically. "As do cheese puffs, cheese balls, cheesy chips and would you believe it? Cheese on toast."

"Oh yes, alright!" Minnie snapped, backed into a corner somewhat. "I'll have a word with Mr Google later and get back to you. I don't want to bother him right now—the poor fellow must be exhausted answering to my every beck and call."

Minnie sat, quietly contemplating her forthcoming dietary intake while her sister steered them through sprawling built-up towns and sparsely inhabited dirt-track villages. "There dear, look!" Minnie eventually said, seeing the first legible sign for well over a hundred kilometres. "Uzbekistan to the right."

"Yes dear, I can see that," Esther said, indicating and cutting across the path of a speeding motorcycle who was attempting to overtake her, causing the startled rider to lose control, mount the adjacent grass verge and plunge fifteen feet down into a drainage ditch, where he lay cursing the elderly road hog. "What was that?" she asked, checking all mirrors but seeing nothing.

"What was what, dear?" Minnie asked, oblivious. The sisters passed a further road sign indicating that in fact Uzbekistan was still at least a further four hours away.

"Uzbekistan," Minnie said, bored and restless. "Uuuuuuzbekistaaan."

"Stop it, dear!" her sister snapped, irritated to say the least. "Why don't you read your book or something?"

"What a splendid idea, dear," Minnie replied, reaching round the back for her paperback and thumbing her way to the final four pages.

"How was it, dear?" Esther asked, peering over her sister's shoulder.

"How was what, dear?" Minnie asked, looking over her reading spectacles.

"The pavlova!" Esther said again, with more than a hint of sarcasm. "The book of course, silly! I'll read it after you if you don't mind."

"Well I'd hardly call it a romance," Minnie informed her whilst brandishing her soft porn spin-off of the *Fifty Shades of Grey* saga entitled *A Rough Trade*, the story of jobbing builder, Billy Strange, a multi tradesman who with his inimitable cockney charm worms his way into the undergarments and bed sheets of countless lonely housewives, who answer his advertisement in the local rag.

Within minutes of first unloading his trademark white van on site, Billy goes to work on the wanton wives, many of them starved of affection, showering them with the compliments they so eagerly crave whilst stripping to his waist to flaunt his sagging six-pack and, of course, the ever-present 'builder's crack'. No sooner were they under his cheeky spell than Billy would unleash upon them an array of specially adapted power tools to pleasure them, while their husbands worked to pay the endless stream of overinflated invoices foisted upon them when the jobs in hand overran as they so often did.

On one occasion Billy was called in to lay a simple garden path for a rather heavily chested brunette, but managed to stretch out the project for a whopping three-and-a-half months, after bedding her for the first time in a record-breaking twenty-five minutes of his arrival on site. Consequently her clueless husband was fed every line of bull from the builders' handbook, from 'late deliveries', 'unavailable materials' and the great British weather either being 'too hot', 'too cold', 'too wet' or 'too windy' to work, under the guise of his own distorted version of the Health and Safety at Work Act. And what little progress he did achieve was always accompanied by Billy's customary catchphrase: "Ya pay peanuts, ya get monkeys mate." In fact, had the client actually employed a team of trained chimpanzees, the task in question would have undoubtedly been completed on time and, more importantly, to budget.

Billy's final invoice for said garden path including 'Incidentals' as he called them, had the customer clutching his chest and writing a cheque for a staggering fifteen thousand pounds. "Cushty geez," Billy said, pocketing the small fortune and covertly slapping his customer's wife's bottom. "You know it makes sense."

"The lead character's a colourful chap," Minnie explained to her sister. "But for a builder he doesn't actually do a great deal of, well, building. Mind you I'm not surprised, what with the harem of housewives falling over themselves to bed him. The man's a stallion in steel toe-capped boots, dear, a hard-hatted horny toad."

"A stallion, you say?" Esther said, peering across at the paperback in Minnie's hands.

"Yes dear," Minnie confirmed. "In a tea-stained high visibility jacket. I tell you, Essy, when he goes to work on those women with his cordless hammer drill and G clamps, they're like putty in his hands. I mean can you imagine it, dear?"

"I'm trying not to, dear," Esther said, getting a little hot under her faux-fur collar at the mention of Billy and his DIY debauchery.

"Well I wasn't expecting that!" Minnie exclaimed, reaching the end of her steamy novel.

"Don't tell me!" Esther cried. "I don't want to know dear, just give me the damn book!"

"Okay dear, but..." Minnie said, popping the paperback onto the dashboard.

"No buts!" Esther snapped. "I told you, I don't want to know what happens, it'll spoil the surprise."

"Oh it's a surprise alright." Minnie smiled knowingly, whilst positively bursting at the seams to tell all.

"Don't!" Esther said as her sister opened her mouth. "I mean it."

Esther struggled to concentrate on the road ahead with the x-rated read in front of her. "Shall we stop at the next village, dear, and get a room for the night?" she asked Minnie, eager to delve between the book's pornographic pages to see for herself if Billy really was the extra marital master craftsmen that her sister had made him out to be.

"No dear, let's press on for the border," Minnie insisted. "I'm itching to try out my Uzbek."

"Ohhhhh, very well, dear," Esther conceded. "But we're stopping the moment we cross over, and not a kilometre further, do you understand?"

"Yes, yes of course dear," Minnie agreed. "Now are you sure you wouldn't like to know what happens to Billy the Brazen at the end of the book? It involves a cement mixer, a roll of duct tape and a cricket bat."

"NO!" Esther insisted. "Don't you dare, Minnie! Or so help me I'll, I'll—"

"—Okay, okay !" Minnie said, holding up her hands. "My lips are sealed."

Minnie sat beside her sister, itching to reveal the twist in the final chapter, but knew also that her sister would be furious and possibly put her on the same flight home that she had earlier warned she might do.

"It's the sheer audacity of it that gets me, dear," Minnie piped up some ten minutes later, unable to contain herself.

"Of what, dear?" Esther asked, navigating a crude roundabout with a sleeping mule at its centre.

"Billy, dear," Minnie added. "And the wife of the future king." She couldn't help but hint at the fact that the builder with the roving eye had somehow charmed the royal undergarments off the newlywed wife of a prominent prince, after landing a contact to repair the guttering at Buckingham Palace.

"Minnie!" Esther stormed. "I swear I'll put you out on the side of the road and leave you there if I hear one more word about that book. Do you hear me? Do you?"

"Yes, yes," Minnie said, flinching as her sister raised a fist. "Sorry dear, it just slipped out."

"I'll give you slipped out in a minute," Esther warned her. "Will you just forget you ever set eyes on the damn book?"

"Okay I'll try, dear," Minnie promised. "But I must warn you, dear, the content is rather racy."

"And I'm warning you, Minnie!" Esther said, glaring across at her sister. "One more word, just *one more word* and so help me I'll…"

"Uzbekistan!" Minnie then squealed, startling her sister. "Look, dear!"

The timely distraction had surely saved Minnie from a further ferocious verbal assault, as she was just about to blurt out the tacky novel's cliffhanger of an ending: would Billy be discovered by the future king and spend the remainder of his days locked in the Bloody Tower and the whole sorry affair kept under wraps? Or would the shameless adulteress run away to his caravan in Canvey, causing possibly the greatest scandal the country had ever known, and one that would rock the monarchy to the point of complete collapse? Either way the sequel was set to be an instant bestseller within hours of its hotly anticipated release.

"So it is, dear," Esther said, crossing the unassuming outpost. "Now let us find that bed for the night."

"Right you are, dear," Minnie agreed, looking out at a row of sun-bleached cottages by the side of the road, many of them without windows, or doors either for that matter.

"What's it to be, dear?" she joked. "The Ritz or the Dorchester?"

"Preferably somewhere without a hole in the roof," Esther replied, aghast at the state of dilapidation of the buildings. "Perhaps I may have been a little hasty and we should try a little further down the road, dear."

"I quite agree, dear," Minnie said, waving to a group of native children playing on a broken cart. "Look at them, dear," she then remarked. "They haven't a care in the world, have they?"

The children leapt down excitedly and chased Vivien for a dozen or so yards, before giving up and returning to the baby they had left precariously balanced on the abandoned cart.

"This looks promising, dear," Minnie told her sister, a mile-and-a-half later down the road, when they entered an altogether more prosperous-looking village.

"Excuse me, sir!" Esther said, winding down her window and stopping at the first sign of life: a robust gentleman in a simple shawl, carrying a bundle of firewood. "I say, could you please point us in the direction of a hotel?"

Of course the gentleman spoke no English and totally ignored her.

"Ahem, excuse me!" she again called.

"Essy, leave it to me, dear," Minnie insisted, opening her door and stepping out, stretching her back yet again in the process. "I say, cooeeeeee!" she too called, waving and approaching the Uzbek man and racking her brains for the correct Uzbeki phrase that would informing him that they required a bed for the night and could he please recommend a boarding house. But her Uzbeki was as bad, if not worse, than his Queen's English, and what she in fact said was: "We would like to ride a brown bear and sleep with your brother."

The gentleman quickened his step immediately and disappeared between the heavily-laden fruit stalls of an open market.

"How rude!" Minnie remarked.

"There, look dear!" her sister called out. "If that isn't a guest house then my name isn't Esther Reynolds."

Minnie crossed the street and Esther drove the short distance to a stone coloured building with a crudely drawn symbol of a sleeping guest swinging from a rusting nail outside. Handing the tea tin out of the window to her sister, Esther snatched the paperback from the dashboard and clambered from her seat.

Peshwari Nans

"Call the bellboy, will you dear?" Minnie told her sister while she opened Vivien's rear doors and gathered their bags.

"Right you are, dear," Esther replied, stepping up onto the timber porch.

"Oh!" she then said on opening the door and stepping inside. "Leave the bags, dear!" she then called back. "We won't be stopping!"

The interior of the roadside shack-cum-hotel was dilapidated beyond belief and near derelict, with flaking plastered walls, the colour of which had long since faded, a partial dirt floor with several loose boards covering an open sewage pit and a dozing elderly gentleman perched on a wooden box in one corner. "Pardon, dear?" Minnie asked from the car.

"I said we're not stopping!" Esther yelled a little louder, waking the sleeping proprietor.

"AHHHHHH!" he said, rubbing his eyes and throwing his hands in the air, springing to his feet with a toothless grin. "American. Yes?"

"No, we are not!" Esther growled. "Why on earth do people on this godforsaken side of the planet assume that my sister and I are American, for Pete's sake?"

"Ahhh you stay, you stay!" the gent cried, tugging at her arm. "Come, you stay!"

"Errr, actually we'd rather not," Esther informed him, attempting to free her arm.

Minnie then arrived with the cases. "Tell them not to worry, dear, I brought them myself," she said entering the room. "No need to bother the bellboy. Oh!" she too then said.

"Yes, 'oh' indeed," Esther sneered, wrenching her arm free from the eager proprietor. "Take back the bags, my dear," she said, swatting a fly from her face. "I said we're not stopping."

Peshwari Nans

"Oh, but Essy dear," Minnie moaned, "granted the foyer leaves a hell of a lot to be desired, but I'll wager the rooms are a vast improvement. And I don't know about you, but I could kill for a hot bath right now."

"Absolutely not, dear," Esther said defiantly. "We'll find another place to stay nearby, you just wait and see."

"No place, no place!" the grinning gent said with his hands in the air. "You stay *this place*!"

"You've got to be kidding me," Esther said at the door. "There has to be another hotel."

"No place!" the owner again cried, leading the ladies to his box which doubled as his reception desk. "Two bed, yes?" he asked.

"Yes please," Minnie blurted, overriding her sister. "For one night only, please."

"Minnie, what are you doing?" Esther grimaced. "If you think I'm spending the night in this, this…"

"Oh hush, dear." Minnie smiled. "How much, dear?" she asked the hotelier.

"Yes, yes!" he replied holding out his hand.

"No, how much?" Minnie again insisted.

"Yes, yes, yes," he said, waving his grubby hand.

"Essy dear," Minnie asked while signing the broken slate register with a stub of chalk. "Let me have some of our Uzbek cash, will you darling?"

"Are you out of your mind, Minnie?" Esther asked, reluctantly handing her sister a quantity of Uzbeki Som.

"How much, deary?" Minnie again asked the grinning gent, waving the notes under his nose. "How much of your funny money for one night?"

"Yes, yes," he said, swiftly snatching three notes and handing the slate to Esther. "Yes!"

"How primitive," Esther remarked, scrawling her name and snapping the remaining chalk in doing so. "Now my good man," she said sternly. "Kindly direct us to our room if you would, but I must warn you that my sister and I are extremely particular, if you get my drift."

"Yes, yes!" he replied, pocketing the cash and taking the bags from Minnie.

"Right you are, dear, lead on," Minnie said, optimistic about the whole experience, while her sister on the other hand remained severely sceptical. She had every right to be it seemed, as they were led to an equally shabby back room and then out into the backyard.

"What the devil?" Esther said, tapping the gent firmly on the shoulder. "Our room!" she barked. "Where is it?"

"Yes!" he replied, nodding and pointing proudly to a timber outhouse with an ill-fitting door and a grass-thatched roof.

"There?" Esther gasped. "Are you out of your mind?"

"Oh I think it's quaint, dear," Minnie said, taking back their bags. "Come on. Nothing ventured and all that."

"Dear Lord!" Esther sighed, following her sister. "Have mercy on us."

Shoving open the door with her shoulder, Minnie smiled, pleasantly surprised on first impressions. "Oh look dear," she called behind to her trudging sister. "All the comforts of home."

The owner had indeed gone out of his way to spruce up the dated cabin. There was a faded Persian-style rug fitting wall to wall, dowdy beige drapes hanging at the shutters and a boxwood table and three chairs.

"A little basic," Minnie added. "But homely, wouldn't you say?"

"Basic!" Esther scoffed, peering inside. "Minnie that's an understatement my dear! This place makes Mother's outside loo seem positively palatial!"

"Oh come now, dear," Minnie said, setting the bags down inside the room. "It'll be cozy enough with just the two of us. Turn on the light, will you please?"

Peshwari Nans

Esther tugged at a tangled cord several times but to no avail. "Oh really this is ridiculous!" she stormed, turning for the door. "I SAY!" she yelled to the owner, who was scattering corn to a flock of fattened chickens. "ELECTRICITY?"

"Yes, yes!" he again replied, setting down the feed and hand-cranking a huge diesel generator, which roared into life before settling to a monotonous drone. "Yes?" he added, raising a thumb as the cabin's light illuminated.

"I'll give him yes!" Esther raged, slamming the cabin door closed.

"Well it appears we have a choice of beds, dear," Minnie informed her sister, sitting on the first of a row of seven.

"Yes, how odd," Esther remarked, prodding a firm mattress disapprovingly. She continued poking the beds along the line, and examining the wafer-thin and suspiciously stained bedding, before settling to the one furthest from her sister.

The crooked door did very little to drown out the hulking generator, which grated on Esther's nerves, but Minnie remained oddly unfazed as she opened her case and removed a quantity of confectionery. "What more could we possibly want, Essy dear?" she said, reclining contentedly.

"Hmmmm," Esther growled. "A four poster and a foot spa for starters," she said, positively dreading their stay. "I'll take the first bath if you don't mind," she told her sister, feeling somewhat tainted from the very moment they had arrived.

"You go right ahead, my dear," Minnie told her whilst getting to grips with a stick of liquorice.

Esther opened a door at the rear and immediately staggered back at the sight of a putrid, faeces-covered toilet pan and a bucket of stagnant water that appeared to double as a washbasin. "Oh good heavens!" she said, wrenching her handkerchief from her sleeve and clutching it to her mouth.

"How is it, dear?" Minnie asked, tying a strawberry lace sweet into a bow and popping it into her mouth.

"Indescribable!" Esther mumbled, closing the door quickly before the swarm of bluebottles escaped. "Indescribable!"

"Oh don't be such a prude, dear," Minnie said, wrapping a lace around her finger and rising to see for herself. "OH GOOD GRIEF!" she cried, peering inside and getting a heady waft of excrement.

"Shut the door, quick!" Esther yelled as the feeding bluebottles took to the air from the filthy toilet's rim.

"Did I say quaint, dear?" Minnie said, clutching her beating chest, mortified to say the least. "I er, I'd say I may have been a little hasty in that respect."

Minnie beat a hasty retreat to her bed. "Well I can hold it if you can, dear," she told her sister, determined to avoid the facilities at all costs.

"I'd rather wet the bed," Esther confessed.

"What?" Minnie smirked, caressing the crumpled and odious bedding. "And spoil the fine linen, dear?"

"Hmmmm," Esther huffed, laying her overcoat out on her bed so as not to make contact with the sheets, and turning over the pillow before gingerly reclining and reaching for the paperback and raising it in front of her face.

Minnie was about to speak when Esther raised a hand. "Not a word," she simply warned her sister. "Not a single word, do you hear?"

Minnie lay silently, staring at the bare rafters above her before delving into her pocket and retrieving the mysterious extra jigsaw piece. "Who's do you suppose it is, dear?" she asked, examining it closely. "Essy?"

"What?" Esther barked, having barely turned a page. "What are you talking about?"

"The foot, dear," Minnie said, raising the solitary jigsaw piece. "I can't help but wonder whose it is."

"Does it really matter?" Esther said, glaring across the room before returning to the first page.

"Well, yes dear," Minnie piped up. "Somewhere out there there's a jigsaw minus a foot. I know if it were mine I'd be mortified." She scrutinized the piece further. "Hmmm, no shoes or socks," she added. "Could be a Greek god, What do you think, dear? I said what do you think, dear? About it being a Greek god I mean. Or perhaps it could even be a cross-Channel swimmer. Essy? What do you think?"

"FOR GOD'S SAKE, MINNIE!" Esther raged, slamming the book down on the bed beside her and removing her reading glasses. "I'm reading, can't you see? And what blasted difference does it make whose damn foot it is? It could be Laurence of bloomin' Arabia's for all I care! Now will you please be quiet?" She raised the book once again and wriggled into a semi-comfortable position.

"Oh no, dear," Minnie said, shaking her head. "It couldn't possibly be Laurence of Arabia, he wore a riding boot, don't you remember? Father took us to the Odeon to see it. No, no, my money's definitely on a Greek god, possibly Zeus, or maybe Apollo. Which would you say, dear, if you were to hazard a guess I mean? Essy?"

Her sister gave her a look of pure hatred, that had Minnie quickly tucking the piece away and wriggling down her bed.

But it wasn't too long before Esther herself gasped on reading the grizzly and graphic sexploits of 'Billy the ballsy builder'. "My word!" she exclaimed with her cheeks now flushed. "I wouldn't have thought that possible!"

Peshwari Nans

"He is rather good, isn't he dear?" Minnie remarked. "I take it you mean in the JCB digger with the twins?"

"Yes dear, and the plasterer's whisk," Esther replied, picturing the steamy scene in the big yellow excavator. "The man's insatiable."

Minnie smiled, knowing full well what fornication was to come. "He most certainly is," she merely said, tugging another lace from the packet of liquorice.

It wasn't too long before Esther slapped a hand to her mouth.

"Good grief!" she cried, in awe of the builder's stamina. "How does he do it?" This was closely followed by "I don't believe it!" and "Good heavens!"

Eventually she slammed the paperback closed in disgust and tossed it down beside her. "I'll not read another word of that, that filth!" she cursed. "I said I'll not read another word, Minnie. Minnie?" She looked across to see her sister sound asleep with her arms folded across her chest and a strawberry lace dangling from the corner of her mouth. "Great," she said, folding her own arms and settling down herself. But moments later she opened an eye to check on her sister once again, and rummaged for the book beside her, thumbing feverishly to where she had left off. It was all that she could do to prevent herself from shrieking and crying out whenever Billy bent yet another willing wife over his cement-splattered concrete mixer and later invoicing her for the pleasure.

Esther eventually succumbed to fatigue halfway through chapter four, at the end of a particularly erotic scene involving a builder's level and a pallet of plasterboard. She ditched the 'mummy porn' as the industry calls it, and turned onto her side to sleep with thoughts of Billy's 'builder's bottom' weighing heavily on her mind.

Both sisters were sound asleep and snoring contentedly by around nine-thirty, when the sound of approaching footsteps caused them to stir. Esther opened one eye and froze. "Min," she whispered. "Psssst! Minnie!"

"Mmmm, what dear?" Minnie asked, rolling over to face her sister. "Go to sleep, dear."

"Somebody's coming!" Esther said, staring at the cabin door.

"What? Who?" Minnie said, coming to.

Suddenly the door opened and a group of middle aged Uzbeck men entered in jovial mood. The mortified ladies clenched their eyes tightly shut, playing dead as it were, and praying the men would turn and leave immediately. But instead the five of them, all passing through and wanting a bed for the night, glanced over at the supposedly slumbering sisters and went about their business, as though it were an everyday occurrence. They stripped down to their ghastly underpants and prepared for bed.

Three of the would-be guests visited the lavatory in turn, the vomitous belching sounds which accompanied their prolonged toiletry eruptions turning Minnie and Esther's stomachs. However, neither of them dared say a word let alone flinch. Without a care in the world, or indeed a second glance at the sisters, the Uzbek men, all of them travelling around to seek employment, settled down in the bunks between the English elders. And after the odd and quite frankly odious 'bottom belches' they performed, each of them pulled the shabby sheets up around their necks and drifted off to sleep, leaving Esther and Minnie wide awake and fearing for their lives.

At opposite ends of the row of beds, Esther and Minnie both considered fleeing into the night but thought better of it, and opted instead to remain vigilant and ride out the night without a wink of sleep. But sleep they eventually did, when fatigue overcame them and defeated the weary travellers. It was only the crowing of a nearby scrawny cockerel that roused the two of them at around six-thirty

Peshwari Nans

the following morning. Esther yawned and stretched then froze once again, looking slowly to her right, having completely forgotten about their impromptu 'visitation'.

"They're gone!" she said, looking around the room. "Minnie! They're gone!"

"Who dear?" Minnie replied, rubbing her eyes.

"Those men. Who do you think?" Esther snapped, annoyed at herself for letting her guard down.

"Men?" Minnie said, still half asleep. "What men?"

"Ooooh I'll come over there and give you what for in a minute!" Esther ranted. "The blasted men that barged in here and spent the night! I was frightened half to death!"

"Ohhhhh, those men," Minnie replied, unfazed. "Yes I'll admit I was a little perturbed at first, Essy, but I also found it mildly titillating too."

"Titillating!" Esther said, throwing her hands in the air. "A gang of stinking savages bursts in here in the middle of the night with God knows what on their minds, and you find that titillating? Are you out of your mind?"

Minnie said little more in her defence, not daring to mention the dream she had as she lay beside a particularly brutish Uzbek with hairy hands and the broadest back she had ever come across on a man. It had been a dream tinged with fantasy, almost leading to consensual consummation, but thwarted in the nick of time by the noise of the strutting cock outside.

"Oh God, no!" Esther then gasped, looking up to see the swarm or bluebottle flies circling overhead, and the lavatory door ajar.

"I've got it, dear!" Minnie said, climbing from her bed and arching her back. "Leave it to me."

Firstly, she flung open the door and waved the buzzing flies out using a discarded Uzbek newspaper, then instinctively glanced inside the lavatory. "Good lord, those animals!" She cringed, covering her nose with her sleeve

453

when seeing the pan further encrusted and the woodworm-riddled floor saturated with urine. She bent double, retching over and over with her eyes streaming. "My word!" she said, wheezing breathlessly. "I, I've never seen anything like it in all my days, Essy. And I mean it when I say I'd rather spend an eternity in the bowels of hell than one minute in there."

"Me too, dear," Esther agreed, rising from her bed and snatching her bag, having slept fully dressed. "Come dear, we're leaving at once," she added, striding purposefully out of the open door with Minnie scurrying behind her, gathering up her things in passing.

"Ahhhh, yes," the hotel owner said when they met him in the cockroach-infested foyer, greeting them with open arms.

"I'll give you 'yes'!" Esther snarled, shaking her bag in his face. "I don't know what sort of establishment you're running here, you filthy little man, but it's certainly not how we British do things. Not by a long chalk."

"Not by a long chalk," Minnie echoed her sister in time honoured tradition, as the elderly so often did.

The perplexed proprietor again hadn't understood a word and wrongly presumed that they had been more than satisfied with the standard of their lodgings. "Yes!" he said, handing Esther another broken slate and gesturing for her to write a glowing review. "Oh so you'd like a comment, would you?" she said, snatching the chalk. "Well I've got one or two for you."

She then proceeded to scratch the underlined words: DESPICABLE, DILAPIDATED, DEPLORABLE and DISGUSTING, with a fearsome full stop, before thrusting the slate back into his chest. "There!" she said. "Stick that in ya pipe and smoke it!"

"Yes in ya pipe!" Minnie reiterated.

Peshwari Nans

"Yes, yes, you like!" the grinning Uzbek said, offering a tray of stale mints to his parting guests.

"Oooh!" Minnie said, hoping to freshen her breath, but her hand was snatched away by her sister, who escorted her quickly from the premises, as the owner looked proudly at Esther's scrawled slate before hanging it above his crumbling fireplace, tipping it from left to right until it was perfectly aligned with the crooked mantelpiece.

"Yes," he said to himself, displaying the harsh criticism with an overwhelming sense of pride.

Without looking back, the sisters climbed aboard Vivien and left, kicking up a cloud of dust in their haste. "I'm half starved, dear," Minnie told her sister, plucking the last of her sweets from her pocket. "Could we please find an eatery, do you think?"

"Yes, one with washroom facilities preferably," Esther added, feeling altogether grubby from head to toe.

Just eleven kilometres down the rugged highway the sisters came across the sprawling town of Chirchik.

"Ahhhh, civilization at last!" Minnie said, clapping her hands. "I tell you dear, I could eat a horse."

"Horseradish I hope?" Esther remarked. "What with you being vegan and all."

"Oh, oh yes, yes of course" Minnie said, remembering her solemn vow. "That's me, vegan through and through." With her stomach now rumbling, she struggled with her conscience and thoughts of bacon butties. "Nobody said it would be easy, dear," she added in a bid to convince herself. "It takes grit, determination and a high moral standing, of which I'm proud to say I have all three by the bucketload, don't you agree, Essy dear?"

"Of course you do, dear." Esther smirked, having been a lifelong carnivore with absolutely no intention of converting. "I want you to know I'm behind you every step of the way."

Peshwari Nans

"Why thank you, dear." Minnie smiled with her faith renewed. "I knew I could count on you. Now are you sure you wouldn't like to try the mung bean mash? It really is rather delicious."

"Sorry, I couldn't possibly, dear," Esther said, refusing to be lured to the green side. "It's the beans you see. I just can't keep the perishing things down."

Even in deepest darkest Uzbekistan there were large pockets of the sisters' Twitter and Facebook followers, many of them residing right there in Chirchik.

"How odd," Esther said, looking across the street at a bystander who had recognized the car immediately and had dropped his morning coffee onto his open toed sandals. However, that wasn't the reason he was hopping up and down like a lottery winner.

"PESHWARI NAN! PESHWARI NAN!" he shrieked, doing a sort of Irish-cum-Uzbek jig. "PESHWARI NAN!" he continued, waving his shirt above his head. "PESHWARI NAN!"

"How on earth do they know?" Esther asked, waving discreetly back and seeing no trace of a satellite antenna. The Uzbek began slapping his chest and gyrating his hips while eyeing Minnie, as though he was performing some primitive mating ritual. "I think he likes you, dear" Esther told her sister. "Would you like me to stop?"

"Don't you dare!" Minnie snapped, ducking in her seat. "The man's an imbecile, a complete imbecile."

Esther was forced to accelerate as the clearly besotted man pursued them along the street, flexing his muscles and rubbing his groin.

Back in the UK, Elizabeth had been admitted to the Glory Peak Sanitarium for a stress-related breakdown. The staff there were compelled to keep her heavily sedated for much of the time, after a series of altercations with staff colleagues and her fellow residents. She had become increasingly delusional, and violent for that matter, when overhearing the most innocent of conversations, flying into an uncontrollable rage when she assumed that the Peshwari Nans had been mentioned, trashing the day-room and screaming from the barred windows.

Poor Elizabeth lay strapped to her bed by night, hearing a dozen or so imaginary voices whispering: "Peshwari Nans, Peshwari Nans" over and over. The walls of her secure room had been daubed with these two words too, the letters written with lipstick and strawberry custard scooped from her lunch bowl.

Richard had visited daily, bringing his mother fresh fruit and flowers. "Richard darling, you've got to get me out of here!" she repeatedly begged. "They're all mad, all of them! I hear them Richard, I hear them whispering behind my back. I know what they're doing Richard, they don't think I do but I know." She leapt to her feet and began beating on her door. "I KNOW WHAT YOU'RE DOING, I KNOW, I KNOW!"

"Mum, calm down, please," Richard said with an arm around her. "They just want to help you."

"Help me!" his mother replied, breaking away and rocking on the edge of her bed, scratching at her arm. "Richard there is nothing wrong with me, you know that, don't you? Richard, tell them, tell them to let me out, tell them I'm fine. You will do that, won't you Richard? You will tell them."

Elizabeth was far from fine, in fact she was Glory Peak's most disturbed patient, housed separately from all the others for her own safety and theirs.

"I'll speak to them, Mother," Richard said in a bid to calm her. "But seriously a few more days' rest in here would do you the world of good. Oh and Gran sends her love too, I spoke to her this morning. She and Min are in Uzbekistan, can you believe that?"

Peshwari Nans

"Uzbekistan!" Elizabeth yelled, leaping from her bed and pacing the room, scratching feverishly. "Richard, what are they doing in Uzbekistan? Tell me, Richard! Kazakhstan, Uzbekistan, what next AFGHANI BLOODY STAAAN!"

"Mother, please?" Richard begged, following her around her room.

Elizabeth wrenched at her locked door. "Richard help me, will you?" she said, kicking and punching at the door frame. "I have to stop them. I have to stop the Peshwari Nans. RICHARD PLEAAAASE!"

"Mother please, Gran's fine," Richard said, prising his mother away from the door. "Come and sit down. I'll pour you some juice."

"JUICE!" Elizabeth stormed. "My mother and Minnie are halfway to hell and you want to give me juice!" She pushed her son aside and rushed back to the door. "It's a bloody conspiracy that's what it is," she growled over her shoulder. "A conspiracy to drive me insane, and you, Richard, you're in cahoots with them, aren't you? Yes, yes, you are, my own son is out to get me! What's in the juice, Richard? Drugs? Yes I know—you want to drug me, just like them out there!"

"No Mum, please," Richard said with his head in his hands. "We all want what's best for you, honest! I just want you well and back home where you belong!"

"Well help me escape then, Richard," Elizabeth replied, rushing to the window and tugging at the steel bars. "Help me, Richard! I can't stay here. They all talk behind my back, they think I can't hear but I can. If I had a gun I'd kill them all! Yes that's it, a gun! Richard, you have to get me a gun! Richard get me a gun and I'll shoot my way out if I have to!"

Peshwari Nans

"Mum, I am not getting you a gun," Richard told her, becoming increasingly concerned for his mother's sanity. "Like I said, you just need rest and plenty of it."

Richard looked around at the plastered graffiti in his mother's room in despair. "You'll be home soon, Mum," he said reassuringly. "I promise. I've kept the place tidy, just the way you like it," he told her. "I've put the rubbish out and even scrubbed the pots and pans."

"What did you say?" Elizabeth snapped, glaring at her son. "Richard? What did you just say?"

"I, I, said I've scrubbed the pots and pans, Mum, why?" Richard asked quizzically.

"No you didn't!" his mother said. grabbing at her son's arm. "You said Peshwari Nans, didn't you? DIDN'T YOU?" She shook her son violently. "YOU'RE IN IT WITH THE OTHERS, AREN'T YOU?" she screamed. "OUT TO GET ME! YOU'RE ALL OUT TO BLOODY GET ME!"

"No, Mum, no!" Richard pleaded. "Please, Mum, you're hurting me!"

Elizabeth began to hear the whispering voices again, teasing and taunting her. "SHUT UP!" she screamed at the empty chair. "SHUT UP, ALL OF YOU!"

She snatched her juice jug from her bedside table and hurled it across her room. "I'LL KILL YOU, I'LL KILL YOU ALL I SWEAR IT! I'LL KILL YOU ALL!"

The key then turned in the door and a burly member of staff entered. "Now now, Elizabeth," the man said, approaching her with caution and with his hands raised. "Let's not have a repeat of yesterday. It's almost time for your medication, so you need to calm down."

Elizabeth made a dash for the open door, but was restrained by a second member of staff. "I'm sorry, but I'm going to have to ask you to leave," he told Richard. "Don't worry about your mother, she'll be fine."

Peshwari Nans

"Bye Mum, love you," Richard said as he passed, greatly disturbed by her mental state. "I'll be back tomorrow, I promise."

"Get me a gun, Richard!" Elizabeth yelled, wrestling with the porters. "RICHARD GET ME A BLOODY GUUUUUUN!"

She was again medicated and strapped to her bed for the remainder of the afternoon while her episode subsided, and at a briefing each and every member of staff were warned never to mention the Peshwari Nans in her company or anything remotely connected with them for that matter.

Back in Uzbekistan, Esther parked outside a popular Uzbekistani fast food outlet that was selling kebabs, falafels and flatbreads. "Here, dear," she said to Minnie. "This looks just the place."

Locking the car, the sisters made their way inside, with Minnie tucking the tablet and the tea tin into her bag. "Oooh this is nice, dear," she said, looking in awe at the smart sleek interior. "And falafels are vegan, Essy. I know that for a fact."

"Well I'm having the chicken kebab," Esther said defiantly. "Excuse me!" she called to the girl behind the counter. "Do you mind if my sister and I use the washroom to freshen up?"

"Please, please," the girl said, pointing the way. "Of course."

"Thank you, my dear," Minnie said, following her sister.

The ladies washed as best they could and availed themselves of the toiletry facilities, chatting to one another through the cubicle walls.

"Do you know?" Minnie said while swinging her legs, seated on the lavatory. "That Uzbekistan is one of the only double landlocked countries in the world? The other is Liechtenstein. That means, Essy dear, that they are completely surrounded by countries which are themselves landlocked. Isn't that fascinating?"

Esther said nothing whilst reading the scribblings on the rear of her cubicle door.

"And did you also know?" Minnie continued, "that the elephant has no knees, so therefore it cannot jump. Did you know that Essy? Essy?"

"WHAT?" her sister snapped. "What is it?"

"Elephants, dear!" Minnie replied, talking to the wall beside her. "They cannot jump!"

"Neither can I!" Esther huffed. "Big deal."

"And mayflies, dear!" Minnie added. "Do you know that they only live for one day? Can you imagine that, Essy? Trying to fit an entire lifetime into a single day?"

"Yes dear, I can," Esther said sarcastically. "Every day with you feels like a lifetime to me."

"What was that, dear?" Minnie asked, cupping her ear.

"Nothing, dear," Esther called back. "Oh drat!" she then cursed, reaching for the empty tissue holder. "Min dear, would you please pass some tissue?" she asked.

"Of course, dear," Minnie replied, rolling a wad around her fingers and slipping her hand under the dividing wall. "Did you know, dear," she said in doing so, "that the ancient Romans used wool soaked in rose water before toilet paper was invented?"

Esther snatched the tissue from her sister. "No dear!" she snapped. "And I don't wish to know either. As far as I'm concerned it's a taboo subject that should remain that way, so I'll thank you kindly to keep any such trivia to yourself in future."

"Please yourself," Minnie said, unfazed as usual.

Having made themselves as presentable as humanly possible considering their circumstances, the sisters returned to the counter. "I'll have the chicken kebab with salad please," Esther told the assistant, who turned to Minnie.

"And the same for you?" the girl asked, with her finger poised at the cash register.

"Oh good heavens no!" Minnie exclaimed with a hand to her chest. "I'm a vegan, my dear, not a barbarian. No, I'll have the falafel flatbread with salad and a vinaigrette dressing."

"Oh yes," Esther piped up. "And I'll have the barbaric salad cream with mine also please, and a glass of full cream milk."

Minnie glared at her sister disapprovingly. "Don't go there Minnie," Esther remarked. "A day or two ago you'd have eaten three kebabs and bitten the hind leg off a donkey. Now you think you're the next veggie Messiah!"

Minnie took her order from the counter, snubbing her sister and headed for a window booth.

"Oh don't look at me like that," Esther said, following close behind with her tray. "I'm just teasing you. Actually I think it's rather admirable of you to make a stand for what you believe to be right." So saying, she picked up her fat-drenched kebab and took a bite. "Mmm, mmmm, delicious," she said with her mouth full. "Ohhhh Min, ohhh wow this is—"

"—Do you mind?" Minnie said, nibbling her falafels. "I'm making a stand, remember."

"Oh yes of course, sorry dear," Esther replied, wiping the fat from her chin. "I forgot. But you really don't know what you're missing, Min, you really don't. This is delicious."

"Yes, and so are my falafels!" Minnie said defensively. "Very tasty indeed actually."

"Yes, they look very appetizing," Esther said, mocking her sister's plate, but then after taking another bite of her

Peshwari Nans

kebab she winced and cried out: "OUUUCH, OW OWWW!"

"What is it, dear?" Minnie asked, setting down her flatbread. "What's wrong?"

Esther rocked back and forth, reaching into her mouth and plucking out a small sharp obstruction from her dentures. "Oh Christ!" she said on inspection.

"What is it, dear?" Minnie asked, leaning across the table.

"It's a—it's a beak!" Esther said, aghast.

"A beak?" Minnie cried, covering her mouth with her hand. "You mean a chicken's beak?"

Esther flung the offending body part down onto her plate. "Well it wouldn't be a damned duck's now, would it?" she cursed "Considering it was a chicken kebab I ordered!"

Minnie sat back looking extremely pleased with her menu selection. "Falafel, dear?" she asked, sliding her plate towards her sister.

Esther tossed the remainder of her kebab down and sat picking at her salad with a face like thunder. "Don't say it!" she told her smug sister, who sat opposite, tucking into her chickpea derived falafels.

"Mmmmmm, marvellous," Minnie said, wiping her mouth and setting her knife and fork down neatly on the side of her plate. "Well I must say those were amazing, dear, do you know I think my transition may be easier than I first imagined. Such a shame about your chicken, Essy, a crying shame." Minnie's teasing remarks made her sister's blood boil as she sat with clenched fists.

"That's it!" Esther cried, pushing herself up from her seat. "I have every right to complain and demand my money back!"

"Good for you, dear." Minnie smiled. "Let them have it, dear, and don't you take no for an answer."

Peshwari Nans

"Don't you worry Min, I won't!" Esther said, spoiling for a fight. "I know my rights," she added, heading for the counter. "I SAY!" she called to the young lady. "I SAY, excuse me, I have a complaint!"

The assistant was busily handing another of their ghastly chicken kebabs to an unwitting customer.

"I wouldn't eat that if I were you," Esther told the middle-aged gent beside her, who understood nothing of what she said. "I found a beak in mine. God only knows what's in yours—the parson's nose, no doubt."

The customer had absolutely no idea that Esther was referring to the chicken's bottom and took a bite right there and then.

"Oh well, on your head be it," Esther told him. "Don't say I didn't warn you."

The gentleman left, devouring almost half his meal by the time he reached the door, and didn't at all seem fazed when he tugged a feather from his pitta bread, as though it were the norm in this establishment.

"I said I have a complaint!" Esther again informed the assistant. "It's about my kebab!"

"Kebab?" the girl replied. "You like another?"

"No I would not!" Esther barked, slamming her hand on the counter. "I want a refund, and I want it now!" she ranted. "There was a blasted beak inside it. A beak, do you hear me?"

"Beak?" the girl said, scratching her head. "What is beak?"

"Ohhhh, go and get me the manager!" Esther told the girl, growing increasingly irate. "Go on! I demand to see the manager, get him out here right now!"

"You want Boss?" the girl asked.

"Yes, I want Boss!" Esther stormed. "Now hurry, before I really lose my rag!"

Peshwari Nans

"I fetch Boss," the assistant replied, heading for the rear door.

"God give me strength." Esther sighed, shaking her head. "You tell him I'm not happy!" she called after the girl. "Not happy at all!"

"Stand your ground, Essy dear!" Minnie called from their booth. "Show them some of our bulldog spirit, that'll put the fear of God into them!"

"Oh I will, don't you worry!" Esther replied over her shoulder, whilst rolling up her floral sleeves. "I can be most determined when I wish to be."

"That's my girl!" Minnie said, giving her sister the thumbs-up. "Eye of the tiger, dear, eye of the tiger!"

Minnie had watched the first of Sylvester Stallone's 'Rocky' movies when she visited a video rental store to take out Elizabeth Taylor's *Cleopatra*, but when returning home found that the cassettes had been switched. Needless to say she thoroughly enjoyed the boxer's epic battle with Apollo Creed. "YO ADRIAAAAN!" she then yelled, shadow-boxing in the booth, goading her sister.

Esther leaned on the counter, ready to give the restaurant owner a piece of her mind when suddenly there was a loud thud from the backroom and the door was flung open. What emerged shook Esther to the very core. There was a mountain of a man in a blood-spattered white string vest. In one hand he held a dripping cleaver and in the other a twitching chicken, minus its head.

"Complaint?" he asked, slamming the blooded bird down onto the counter and wiping the cleaver across his chest.

"Me?" Esther said, rooted to the spot. "Good heavens no, oh no, no no, I just wanted to say how much I thoroughly enjoyed your kebab. Very tasty, very tasty indeed."

Peshwari Nans

"Ahhh you like!" The manager smiled, picking up his headless bird, which had pumped a quantity of its blood onto the marble counter. "Good, good!" he said, turning for his kitchen. "I make for you another, special for you."

"Oh no, don't bother yourself!" Esther called after him. "There really is no need."

"I MAKE!" the owner insisted, raising his cleaver. "YOU EAT!"

"OH yes alright," Esther relented, fearing for her life. "That's awfully kind of you, I'll have it later. For my tea perhaps."

"You eat now!" the manager told her, licking the remainder of the blood from his blade. "Here, now!"

"Oh right, yes of course." Esther nodded, forcing a smile. "Of course. I was only saying to my sister a moment ago how I could eat another, wasn't I dear?" she turned to her sister who merely raised her thumb again, unaware of her sister's plight.

"Good, good." The chicken-killer then smiled a toothy grin. "You wait, I make."

Esther stood exactly where instructed, petrified of enraging the hulking restaurateur. Within minutes and after further chopping and slashing, the owner returned with another of his grisly creations, handing it proudly to Esther.

"Why thank you," she said in as convincing tone as she could muster. "Oh look, and it's extra large, how thoughtful of you."

"You eat!" the owner told her, wiping his hands on his already filthy vest. "You tell everybody come to my place for kebab, yes?"

"Oh but of course, dear," Esther replied. "I'll make a point of it, I assure you."

"Gooood." The owner smiled, returning to his kitchen, leaving Esther trudging back to their booth, kebab in hand,

Peshwari Nans

"What happened, dear?" Minnie asked when her sister sat opposite her with yet another chicken kebab, this one almost twice the size of her first. "I thought you were demanding a refund?"

"I was," Esther said, peering cautiously inside the pitta bread. "But after extensive negotiations I stood my ground and demanded a free meal instead."

"Are you out of your mind?" Minnie asked. "After the incident with the beak, for Pete's sake?"

"Oh I'm sure that was a one-off, dear," Esther said in a bid to convince herself as well as her sister, "Besides, I am still a tad peckish."

"Well on your head be it, dear," Minnie said, reclining in her seat. "Personally I couldn't eat another thing. Anyway, bon appetit."

Esther herself had absolutely no appetite, but on seeing the owner waving his bloody dishcloth from the kitchen door, she raised the kebab to her lips, much to Minnie's disgust. Closing her eyes, Esther nibbled tentatively at one corner while her sister took out the tablet as a welcome distraction.

"Oh good Lord!" Esther then moaned, covering her mouth to prevent herself from vomiting when she felt the gristle between her teeth.

"Smile, dear," Minnie said, snapping her sister with a gaunt expression on her face and a giant kebab cradled in both hands. "Oh heavens, look dear!" Minnie then said, turning the screen towards her sister. "We have a message from the Prime Minister!"

Esther hardly flinched, focused only on finishing her mammoth 'Gran versus food' challenge, and getting the hell out of there.

"Essy, I said we have a message from the PM, dear!" Minnie reiterated. "The Prime Minister himself has taken time to message us in person, isn't that marvellous? I'll read it, shall I? Okay here goes:

"'My dear Esther and Minnie I am writing to express my heartfelt joy and relief at your release from your Russian captors. The level of love and support you both have back home and abroad for that matter is quite staggering, and a credit to you both. Considering your achievements thus far, my wife and I look forward to taking tea with the two of you on your return, but for now God be with you and a safe journey from all at Number Ten, regards David.'

"Well, isn't that something, dear?" Minnie said, flabbergasted. "How nice of him to take the time to write to us."

Esther remained stony faced, having forced down half of her kebab, but had also deposited three feathers, a claw, a number of bones and yet another beak on the side of her plate.

"Are you alright, dear?" Minnie asked, noting her sister's pale complexion. "Eaten something that didn't agree with you perhaps?"

Esther glared across the table at her gloating sister and then turned to see that the chef had vanished. "Quick let's get out of here," she said, wrapping the remainder of her revolting meal in a napkin and dropping it into her bag.

Minnie picked at the crumbs of falafel on her plate. "Are you sure you wouldn't like the dessert menu, dear?" she asked, relishing the moment. "God only knows what you'll find in the strawberry fool."

"Hush Minnie, please," Esther said, clutching her stomach and pushing the gruesome remains away.

"No bones in a chickpea, dear." Minnie smiled contentedly.

"OK, OK!" Esther blurted out, dragging herself from the booth. "The only thing worse than that hideous kebab is your self-righteous gloating. You were right, there I said it! Now, can we please leave before that butcher returns?"

"Right you are, dear," Minnie smiled, hurrying after Esther out of the fast-food establishment and into Vivien without a moment to lose. "Parma violet?" she then said, offering her sister a packet of sweets.

"Oh God, yes," Esther said, snatching several and popping them all into her mouth while depositing the remainder of the kebab into an adjacent bin.

"So," she said whilst crunching the candies to rid her of the taste of her previous meal as they drove off. "This vegan thing of yours. Tell me more."

Minnie began to explain the health and ethical benefits of life choice, but then suddenly froze in her seat. "Essy, my bag!" she shrieked, looking down at her feet. "I don't have it!"

"What?" Esther slammed on the brakes, having reached the end of the street. "What do you mean you don't have it?"

"I left it in the loo, Essy," Minnie confessed. "I took out the tablet and popped the bag on the floor. Oh God, Essy, it has Jasvinder's tin inside it."

"You fool!" Esther yelled. "Minnie you damned fool! How could you be so stupid?" Hastily attempting to manoeuvre in the road, Esther was hampered by a row of parked bicycles. "Blast!" she cursed, panic stricken at this point. "Minnie how could you? How could you? Ravi will need that money and you trash his wife's memory by leaving it in the lavatory of all places!"

Reversing at speed, Esther clipped one of the bicycles, sending the entire line tumbling to one side. "Damn it!" she cried, refusing to stop for the irate owners, who came dashing from the barber shop.

"I'm sorry, Essy," Minnie said, hanging her head. "You're right, I am a fool. And after all we've been through."

Esther thrust her foot to the floor causing a passing truck to veer violently to the opposite side of the road, trashing a vegetable cart in the process.

"Careful, dear!" Minnie said, looking over her shoulder at the trail of destruction in their wake.

"To hell with careful!" her sister raged, with the restaurant in sight. "Just you pray it's still there, Minnie my girl, just you pray!"

Minnie was doing exactly that and cursing herself at the same time. With a screech of Vivien's brakes, the sisters swung their legs out of the open doors and hauled themselves from their seats. "Quickly, dear!" Esther yelled, flinging open the restaurant door and stepping aside to let a young man leave with his kebab tucked beneath his arm. "Hurry, Minnie!" she called to her sister, who was in some considerable pain, having jarred her back exiting the car so hastily. "Hurry, will you!"

"I'm trying, dear," Minnie replied, hurrying as best she could.

"Ahhhhhh!" the owner smiled on Esther's return. "You want kebab, yes?"

"No I do not!" Esther snapped ferociously. "I wouldn't feed that garbage to a dog!"

"Dog?" the Uzbek chef replied. "Yes we have dog, chicken, goat and donkey. You like donkey? I make for you special donkeybab, is good yes?"

"NO!" Esther raged while Minnie ducked back into the lavatory. "Is not good, not good at all!"

The restaurant's 'donkeybabs' were a local delicacy that oddly enough hadn't been embraced by the wider world.

"IT'S HERE!" Minnie called from the lavatory. "IT'S OKAY ESSY, I HAVE IT!" She rejoined her sister with a smile on her face, looking tremendously relieved. "Thank goodness for small mercies, eh Essy?" she said, brandishing her shoulder bag.

"Hmmmm," Esther snorted, snatching the bag from her sister and rummaging inside. "Minnie, where's the tin?" she asked, frantically tossing Minnie's personal effects aside. "Where is it?"

"What?" Minnie gasped, looking for herself. "Essy it was right there, I swear."

"Well it isn't now, is it?" Esther stormed. "Minnie where is the damn tin? Where is it?"

"That young man!" Minnie said, pointing to the door. "He must have it!"

The two of them looked across at the gents toilet, which was displaying an 'out of order' sign in the Uzbeck language, and the penny suddenly dropped. He had been wearing a loose-fitting robe, which could have quite easily concealed the Lipton's tea tin.

"After him, Minnie!" Esther yelled, pushing her sister towards the door.

"YOU WANT DONKEYBAB?" the owner called after them.

"Shove it!" Esther yelled back. "Shove it all!"

Once outside, the sisters looked both ways before catching sight of the culprit crossing the street. "HEYYYYY!" Esther called, raising a hand and starting after him. "HEYYY YOU THERE!"

Glancing over his shoulder and seeing the approaching pensioners, the lad quickened his step, discarding his kebab and clutching the tin tightly against his chest.

"HEY YOU!" Minnie yelled. "STOP, STOP THIEF, SOMEBODY HELP, HELLLP!"

Assured he could easily outrun the old ladies the lad slowed and even turned to taunt them, brandishing the tin with a devilish grin.

Peshwari Nans

"Hurry, dear!" Esther again cried, but they were no match for his youthful legs.

"It's no use, dear," Minnie said wheezing and clutching her aching back. "I'm sorry I can't, I just can't."

"Minnie, we must catch him," Esther said, stopping to take her sister's hand. "We must, HELLLLLP SOMEBODY HELLLP!"

The thief stopped and stood laughing with the tin in his hand, beckoning to the sisters to pursue him, but his jubilant expression suddenly changed to one of horror when he felt a firm hand on his shoulder. It was the bare-chested man whom Minnie had wrongly assumed was a complete imbecile. Quick as a flash the have-a-go hero plucked the tin from the youth's grasp, hoisted him off the ground single handedly, and dumped him backside first into a nearby refuse bin, pushing him down hard until he was firmly wedged.

"Oh my dear God, thank you!" Esther said, arriving moments later and clinging to a lamp post for support. "I don't know how we can ever repay you."

The man said nothing but merely handed over the precious tin. "Oh thank heavens, Essy," Minnie said, arriving shortly afterwards, clutching her chest. "Thank heavens. And thank you sir, thank you ever so much."

"Peshwari Nans!" the Uzbeki man said, ecstatic at meeting the ladies face to face. "Peshwari Nans!" He took a pen from his pocket and insisted the sisters scrawled their names across his bare chest.

"My pleasure, dear." Minnie smiled, encircling his right nipple with a heart and adding two kisses for good measure. "You don't know how much this means to us," she added, planting a kiss on his cheek. The man flung his arms around the two of them, hugging them both tightly.

Peshwari Nans

"Okay, okay!" Esther gasped. "Thank you, that's quite enough," she said, pulling away and casually patting his shoulder and avoiding any further advances.

"And you!" she growled at the lad crammed in the bin beside them. "You should be ashamed of yourself."

"Yes, truly ashamed!" Minnie echoed, wagging a finger at the flinching boy.

Bidding a fond farewell to their saviour, the grateful sisters returned to Vivien with Minnie clinging ever so tightly to the precious tin. "I am sorry, dear," she said, tucking the tin between her legs. "You do believe me, don't you?"

"Hmmmm," Esther merely said, setting off for the second time with an overwhelming sense of relief. Their stay in the sleepy Uzbek village had not been a pleasant one and Esther did her level best to put some distance between them and the place, deciding also to skirt the remaining major towns and cities and push on across the open rocky plains, following the ancient silk route. "Gooood girl," she said, patting Vivien's dashboard after reaching the top of a particularly arduous incline. "Goood girl."

With nothing but rocks, mountains and tumbleweed on the horizon, the sisters soon found themselves truly alone and at the mercy of the elements. "Are you alright, dear?" Minnie asked, seeing her sister squirming in her seat.

"No, dear," Esther confessed. "I am not. I think I have a touch of Deli belly, if you catch my drift."

"Oh, oh, I see," Minnie said, turning her nose up. "It seems the chickens are coming home to roost."

"Oh God, please don't mention the chicken!" Esther replied, clenching her knees together. "How far to the next village, dear? Minnie please, how far?"

"Darling," Minnie said, shrugging her shoulders, "there are rocks as far as the eye can see, so I think it's safe to say we won't be seeing civilization for some time to come."

"Oh hell!" Esther squealed. "I'm in dire need right this minute, dear, and I mean *right this minute!*" Beads of sweat began forming on her forehead and she wriggled from side to side.

"You'll just have to do what the bears do, dear," Minnie said, trying not to laugh. "Only there are no woods."

"What do you mean?" Esther asked, horrified at the thought. "Out there?"

"Well dear." Minnie smirked. "It's either out there or in here, and I'm afraid the latter simply isn't an option. So I suggest you grab yourself some three-ply and go find yourself a discreet rock."

"I'll do nothing of the sort!" Esther said defiantly. "I'm a lady and ladies don't, well, you know—"

"—Poop." Minnie smiled. "It's quite alright, dear, there isn't a living soul around for miles."

"I said no, Minnie!" Esther snapped. "Never! I'd rather soil myself."

"Well I'd much rather you didn't," Minnie replied, opening her window. "You'll just have to hold it then, that's all."

"Yes, yes, that's what I'll do," Esther said, clenching her knees a little tighter. "I'll hold it, dear. There, that's not so bad."

But Esther then suddenly slammed on the brakes and threw open her door. "Where did you say the three-ply is, dear?" she asked, with a genuine sense of urgency.

"In the basket, dear!" Minnie called after her. "Beneath my surgical supports!"

Esther rummaged hastily amongst Minnie's elasticated bandages, plucking out a roll of toilet tissue before waddling off in the direction of a cluster of boulders. "Ohhhhhh Lord!" she moaned, accompanied by the sound of an ominous drainage-like gurgling.

Peshwari Nans

Minnie watched, laughing at her sister's baby steps as she shuffled out of sight. It was during Esther's 'call of nature', so to speak, that Minnie turned on the radio and tuned into an Uzbeki country station. She sat there, tapping her feet and slapping her thigh to the rhythm of the nation's favourite flutist, whilst humming along to his nonsensical wailing.

Esther crouched behind a large moon-like boulder whilst her sister turned up the volume a little louder, joining in with a little wailing of her own.

"Daft mare" she said to herself, unaware of the impending threat nearby: a Caspian cobra. One of the most venomous species of cobra in the world slithered from its rocky retreat and approached her from the side, flicking its probing tongue in and out. It reared up, extending its hood whilst poised to strike.

Esther stood and adjusted her skirt, thoroughly disgusted with herself for stooping so low, but as Minnie had warned her, there was no acceptable alternative. Turning to head back with the swaying serpent recoiling in readiness, Esther suddenly leapt several inches in the air, clutching her chest when the sound of a single gunshot shattered the deathly silence.

"ARRRRRRRGH! WHAT THE?" she screamed, ducking quickly with her heart thumping in her chest. She then heard the sound of horses' hooves approaching, and peered cautiously over her shoulder to first see the deadly Caspian cobra, splayed out as dead as dead could be.

"JESUS!" she cried, inching away as an old man on a rickety cart approached her with a rifle cocked in his right hand. "What?" Esther gasped, instantly dismissing the deceased and altogether headless snake. "WHAT ARE YOU DOING?" she called to the aged Uzbeki. "Were you, were you spying on me? You were, weren't you, you beastly pervert! Get away with you, get away I say!"

She groped on the ground at her feet, plucking several small pebbles to toss in his direction. "I SAID GET AWAY WITH YOU, YOU HEAR? GET AWAY, MINNIE HELLLLLLLP!" she yelled towards the car. "MINNIIIIIIIIIE!"

But her hapless sister had picked up on the repetitive and quite frankly relentless Uzbek country chorus, and sang along to that year's Eurovision hopeful.

The Uzbeki man pulled back on his reins, stopping his horse in its tracks and sat staring at Esther, completely bewildered as to why a white woman close to his own age would be crouching behind a rock on his ancestors' land, with Minnie and Vivien out of sight at this point.

"GO AWAY!" Esther screeched, hurling a larger rock but missing by a yard-and-a-half. "YOU, YOU PEEPING THOMAS YOU! GO AWAY OR I'LL CALL THE POLICE! YES THAT'S IT, I'LL CALL THE POLICE, MINNIIIIE, DAMN YOU!"

The elderly Uzbek calmly patted the seat beside him, offering Esther a ride to his village.

"Absolutely not!" she barked from behind her rock. "I wouldn't go with you if you were the last man on earth I can assure you of that. Now turn your silly cart around and sling your hook, go on, sling your hook I say!"

Minnie eventually grew tired of the monotonous flutist and switched off the radio, looking around for her sister. "Oooooh," she moaned, massaging her calves before opening the door to stretch her legs.

"Are you alright, dear?" she called towards the larger rocks, but got no answer. "Ohhhhhh no," she then cursed, walking around Vivien to increase her circulation and discovering a flat rear tyre. "Essy, dear, we have a flat!" she yelled with a hand to her mouth. "ESSYYYYYY!"

Peshwari Nans

Hearing Esther's companion, the Uzbeki man breathed a sigh of relief and flicked the reins on the horse's rear to turn his cart.

"Yes go on, off you go you despicable little man!" Esther cursed, emerging from behind her rock.

"ESSYYYYYY, WHERE ARE YOU?" Minnie continued to call. "ESSYYYYYY!"

"Yes, yes I'm coming!" Esther barked, looking over her shoulder at the retreating horse and cart. "Come on dear, we're leaving," she said, hastily returning to her sister and Vivien. "Get in, dear," she insisted. "There are some pretty unsavoury characters lurking around these parts. Minnie what are you waiting for? I said we're leaving."

"No we're not, dear," Minnie informed her. "I was trying to tell you. We have a flat."

"A flat?" Esther asked climbing back out of the car. "A flat what?"

"Tyre of course," Minnie pointed out. "But it's worse than that, dear. I've checked the spare and that's flat too."

"What?" Esther gasped, with a hand to her head. "Good God, no."

"I'm afraid so, dear." Minnie sighed. "What are we to do? And where have you been, anyway?"

"Where have I been?" Esther remarked. "Where have I been? I'll tell you where I've been. I've been fending off the lecherous advances of a blasted Peeping Tom, that's where I've been."

"A Peeping Tom?" Minnie replied, wide-eyed. "Was it a man?"

"Yes of course it was a man!" Esther said abruptly. "But I sent him packing with a flea in his ear, the filthy beast."

"Well, what was he doing?" Minnie asked, rushing to view the disappearing cart.

"The damn fool shot a snake and almost blew my head off in the process," Esther said, kicking at the deflated tyre.

477

"A snake!" Minnie gasped, returning to the car. "Essy dear, has it not occurred to you that the poor chap may have just saved your life? And you repaid his heroics by tearing him off a strip. Oh Essy, how could you?"

"Well I, I..." Esther stammered, "I assumed..."

"Yes you assumed, didn't you?" Minnie said disapprovingly. "Like the time you assumed Jack and I were having an affair, do you remember? When all the time he and I were merely planning your surprise birthday party! You were left with egg on your face though, weren't you, when you burst into the British Legion with a bread knife in one hand and your wedding ring in the other, screaming for a divorce only to find your entire family, the vicar and a handful of your closest school friends waiting in the dark with balloons and streamers!"

"Yes, yes, okay," Esther conceded. "I said I was sorry, didn't I? I thought—"

"—Yes, you thought," Minnie said, wagging a finger. "You always think, or assume the worst Essy, that's your problem. If it wasn't for that Good Samaritan on his cart you may have been bitten on the backside by a black adder or whatever the hell it was. And furthermore, sister dearest, you have frightened off the one person who may have helped with our present predicament." She gestured to their stricken vehicle.

"Oh gosh, yes!" Esther exclaimed. "Quickly, Minnie, we have to call him back. Hurry!" Esther waved her arms in the air. "COOEEEEEEE!" she called towards the tiny figure in the distance. "I SAYYYYYYY, HELLOOOOOOOOO!"

"Oh Essy, that'll never do," her sister said, leaning inside Vivien. "Cover your ears, dear," she added before leaning on the horn for a full thirty seconds. She then joined her sister, the pair of them shielding their eyes and watching, as the cart, now a good quarter mile away, stopped and the gent glanced over his shoulder.

"HEYYYYYYYY!" the sisters both yelled, waving frantically. "HEYYYYYYY COME BAAAAACK, HEYYYYYYYY!"

With another flick of his reins, the Uzbek native turned yet again and started back toward the stranded sisters.

"He's coming, he's coming!" Esther shrieked. "Minnie he's coming back!"

"Yes I can see that, dear," Minnie said breaking away from her sister, who had shaken her violently. "Now just you remember to mind your manners. And above all, apologize for your deplorable behaviour."

"Yes, yes, of course," Esther said, relieved to say the least, and waving at the approaching cart some more. "Oh thank you kindly, sir!" she called several moments later, having changed her tune, and with her sister looking on over her spectacles.

"Now don't forget, be nice, dear," Minnie insisted.

"Yes, dear I know!" Esther snapped under her breath. "Ahhhh good day to you," she said, greeting the elderly Uzbek. "It er, it seems I owe you an apology."

The Uzbek man had a face that was as wrinkled as a tatty leather couch. He sat staring, with his arms resting on his knees, unable to decipher their foreign tongue.

"What my sister's trying to say," Minnie interjected, "is that she's deeply sorry for any offence she may have caused you, and begs you to accept her heartfelt apology."

The two sisters stood and waited for a verbal response, but instead were treated to a broad toothless grin.

"Apology accepted I believe, dear," Esther said, ushering her sister aside to reveal the flat tyre. "We, er, we have a situation here, as you can see, and we were wondering if you'd be so kind as to lend a hand. I have arthritis you see, and Minnie here has trouble with her

Peshwari Nans

pipes. Any heavy lifting and she pees uncontrollably, isn't that right, dear?"

"Quite right, dear," Minnie agreed unashamedly. "I recall a rather embarrassing incident at the library when I requested six volumes of the Encyclopaedia Britannica. Well, after getting the blasted things stamped, I staggered, puffing and panting out of the door, but not before leaving a deposit on the foyer floor."

"Yes, yes alright, dear!" Esther intervened before her sister could offer a more detailed description of her library leakage. "We get the picture. Now my good man," she said, appealing to the elderly Uzbek whilst stroking the nose of his horse. "Would you mind helping a damsel in distress?"

"Damsels, dear," Minnie added, straightening her hat and striking a pose beside the car. "We would be ever so grateful, I assure you."

The elderly Uzbek looked over their shoulders and began rambling.

"I'm sorry, what?" Esther asked, approaching his side. "We're from the United Kingdom, dear, do you speak English by any chance?"

He continued to chatter, laughing occasionally, exposing a scattering of yellow teeth that looked like listing tombstones.

"I say!" Minnie attempted to intervene. "I say, yoohooo!"

Without warning, the crooked-backed gent then sprang from his cart, put his back to Vivien, grasped the wheel arch and lifted one side clear of the ground.

"Good God!" Esther remarked, clutching her chest as he gestured to the sisters to roll a rock beneath the car.

"What's he saying, dear?" Minnie asked, observing his fabulous physique, especially considering his advancing years.

Peshwari Nans

"The rock, Minnie! Help me with the rock, will you!" Esther said, hitching up the hem of her dress and stooping.

"Oh, yes, yes, of course dear," Minnie said, rolling up her sleeves and scrambling at her sister's feet.

The Uzbek gent raised Vivien several inches higher. "Ha, ha, ha!" he said, which unbeknown to the sisters meant 'yes' in Uzbeki.

"What the devil's he laughing at?" Esther puffed as they flipped the rock over once. "Minnie dear, are you helping?" she asked.

"Yes of course, dear," Minnie replied, in fact being of very little assistance. "I'm doing my level best!"

The pair huffed and puffed while the gent held Vivien aloft.

"Ha, ha, ha!" he said until the rock finally toppled beneath the car, and he gently lowered the chassis.

"Well done, dear," Esther said, straightening her back and helping Minnie to her feet. "And you, sir, that was quite remarkable," she told their gallant new friend. "But you really needn't have bothered. Vivien has her own jack you see."

Of course, the Uzbeki man understood nothing.

"I say!" Minnie called, producing a tyre iron from Vivien's rear. "You may find this of some use."

"Ha, ha!" The Uzbek smiled and set about removing Vivien's wheel.

"Remarkable, quite remarkable," Esther commented at the speed and agility at which the man worked. "I doubt if this man's ever seen a doctor in his entire life."

"No dear," Minnie agreed, finding herself strangely attracted to the terrain-hardened tribesman. "He's um, he's quite a specimen, isn't he? I, I mean he's a picture of health, Essy dear." Her cheeks flushed red for a moment or two as he removed his tattered cotton shirt, that had once red but was now bleached a faded pink by the desert sun.

Peshwari Nans

"Would you like some tea, dear?" Esther asked him. "Minnie, be a dear and put the kettle on, it's the least we can do, don't you think?"

"Splendid idea, Essy dear," Minnie replied, rummaging in the back for their camping stove.

"I hope you like chamomile, my dear," Esther said as the Uzbek skilfully removed the tyre. "Oh good heavens!" she then gasped as he poked a withered finger through a gaping hole in the tyre's side wall. "Oh Minnie darling, it's worse than we thought."

"Hechqisi yo'q, Hechqisi yo'q." he said, smiling, meaning: "No problem, no problem!"

He took a knife from his belt and proceeded to cut a patch of leather from the side of his boot.

"What on earth?" Esther asked, confused to say the least.

"Essy dear, what's he doing?" Minnie asked as she poured three cups of herbal tea.

"I haven't the foggiest, dear," her sister said, looking on, but what was to follow would astound and horrify the sisters and stay with them until their dying days.

The Uzbki man set about creating a makeshift patch by first tearing a handful of tinder-dry grass from the stony ground and placing it between his rotten teeth. But it was what he did with the swatch of brown leather that sent a shudder down the sisters' spines, causing them to turn away with a hand clasped to their mouths.

Lifting the horse's tail, the gentleman inserted the patch into the animals rear end whilst stroking it's rump to calm it somewhat, and buried his hand inside up to his wrist.

"Oh good Lord have mercy!" Minnie cried, peeking through her fingers. "Essy, he's—"

"—I don't want to know!" Esther said, raising a hand, with her back to the horse. "Minnie I do not want to know."

Peshwari Nans

Removing the swatch that was now coated in steaming dung, the Uzbeki gent added the straw to the foul-smelling mix and manipulated the mess between his grubby fingers.

Esther got a whiff of the concoction on the breeze and began to gag. "Minnie dear," she said, retching. "Whatever it is he's doing, please ask him to stop and leave us at once. At once Minnie, do you hear?"

"I say!" Minnie said, backing away a tad. "We were rather hoping you could mend our puncture without fornicating with your dear horse, but if you must insist on doing so then I'm afraid we'll have to ask you to leave."

"Kut, Kut!" the Uzbek replied, insisting that they wait and be patient. Then he plastered the patch of leather, dung and straw, over the hole and rested the tyre in the sun to dry, and again asked them to wait, by saying, "Kut!"

"Ohhhh I see." Minnie smiled, cottoning on. "Essy dear, perhaps we may have been a little hasty in our scathing. I do believe the gentleman's concocted some form of repair."

"What?" Esther replied, almost not daring to look. "From a horse's—" She paused to compose herself. "—From a horse's bottom?"

"It does appear so, yes," Minnie said, scurrying to the rear doors of the car. "I'll fetch the dear fellow some tea."

Offering the Uzbeki man a china cup of chamomile, Minnie took care not to make contact with his dung-smothered hands. "I do hope you like it," she told him, snatching her hand away.

"Rakhmat, rakhmat!" he said, thanking her and bowing his head respectfully.

"Do be careful, it's hot!" Esther warned him as he drained the cup of its piping contents in a single gulp before offering the china back. "You keep it, dear," she then said, turning up her nose. "Please, consider it a gift."

"Keep it, dear" Minnie insisted, eyeing the dung-smothered cup. "It's for you."

"Rakhmat!" The gentleman smiled, placing the Royal Albert piece on his cart and checking the tyre. His unorthodox repair had baked hard in the sun and adhered to the rubber wall as successfully as any modern-day tyre repair material would have been.

"Quickly, dear!" Esther told her sister, while their saviour reassembled the wheel at her feet. "The pump, fetch the pump."

"Oh yes, yes, of course dear," Minnie said, settling down her tea. "I have it, I have it Essy!" she could be heard saying in the back of the car, before emerging with a tarnished brass vintage foot pump. "Shall I do the honours, dear?" she asked, eager to help.

"No, no dear, give it here," Esther insisted, stooping to attach the nozzle to the tyre's valve. "Phew," she said moments later, after a mere half dozen pumps of her right foot. "Maybe, maybe I was a little hasty."

Before Minnie could step in to replace her sister the generous Uzbeki ushered Esther aside and, after a brief examination of the strange apparatus, began pumping with incredible vigour.

"My, my, look at him go." Minnie smiled, watching the tyre rapidly inflate and Vivien's body rise. "Splendid, splendid!" she shrieked, clasping her hands together.

"Okay thank you, that'll do nicely," Esther told him, kicking at the side wall of the tyre. "Thank you!"

But the Uzbeki man continued to pump, nodding his head rhythmically and relishing the experience. "Stop for heaven's sake, stop!" Esther said, waving her arms, fearing the tyre would rupture once again. The Uzbeki man desisted, and Esther quickly removed the pump. "Thank you, dear, that's quite sufficient."

Peshwari Nans

Minnie admired his handiwork. "Will you look at that dear, she's as good as new!" she told her sister, who stood downwind of the obvious stench.

"Yes, quite," Esther remarked, unconvinced. "Now my good man, you must allow us to pay you," she added, taking out her purse. "Please, name your price."

"Yok, yok yok!" the Uzbek said, backing away and shaking his head, refusing to accept a penny from the sisters.

"Oh please, you must," Esther insisted.

"Yok!" he again replied adamantly, before hopping up onto his cart and taking up the reins.

"Wait, wait!" Minnie said, ducking inside the car. "Here, take this!" she said moments later, handing the gentleman a jar of shrimp paste and a box of chamomile tea. "It's the least we can do, you've been so kind."

Smiling, the Uzbeki man placed the goods on the back of his cart and held out his hand, which Minnie duly shook.

"Minnie!" Esther shrieked. "His hands, his hands!"

"Oh good God!" Minnie cried, snatching her hand away. "Heavens, Essy, what have I done?" she cursed, sniffing gingerly at her fingers and eyeing the horse's rear.

The Uzbeki gent roared with laughter whilst turning his cart and heading back towards the horizon, waving his hand above his head.

"Thank youooooo!" Esther called after him, while her sister stood mortified, with her hand hanging limply at arm's length.

"Essy dear, help me, will you please?" Minnie begged, approaching her sister, who ducked the other side of Vivien.

"You stay away from me, Minnie," Esther warned her, clambering aboard and slamming her door closed. "Stay away!"

Peshwari Nans

Minnie scrubbed and scrubbed, using an entire packet of wet wipes, until all traces of the dung were erased. Then and only then was she permitted to retake her seat beside her sister.

Esther sniffed in her sister's direction, satisfied that she was now hygienically acceptable. "Right then," she said, turning the key. "Let's be off, shall we?"

The sisters watched as the Uzbek cart snaked across the arid plain, kicking up a wisp of dust from each of its wooden wheels as they, too, set off on their journey.

Minnie turned to her sister when they'd travelled a mile or so along the dirt track. "Course it's all your fault you know," she said, with her arms crossed defiantly.

"What?" Esther said, taken unawares. "What do you mean? What's all my fault?"

"Well," Minnie added with her nose in the air. "None of this would have happened if you hadn't eaten that ghastly chicken kebab. That's called karma that is, dear, 'Thou shalt not kill'—that's what the good Lord said." She was on her high horse at this point. "'No sin shall go unpunished', 'He who casts the first stone' and all that—"

"—Oh shut up, Minnie!" Esther snapped, taking her eye off the road momentarily. "I didn't kill the damn bird, did I? OH HELL!" she then cursed, as Vivien was violently shaken after mounting the rocky verge. "Damn you, Minnie!" she cried, wrestling with the wheel to maintain control.

"Karma, dear," Minnie said with a self-righteous smile, whilst clinging to her safety belt. "That's what that is."

"Minnie!" Esther growled, as Vivien's contents rattled behind them. "I'll have you know my conscience is clear! The blasted chicken was already deceased when I ate it! Now will you kindly keep your opinions to yourself? I'm having a hard enough time as it is, can't you see that?"

Peshwari Nans

But Minnie was determined more than ever to get her point across and dogged her shaken sister a little further. "You can wash away the blood, dear," she told her, "but you can't wash away the guilt."

"I am not guilty!" Esther stormed. "For God's sake it wasn't a living breathing chicken when I purchased it, it was a damned kebab! A kebab, Minnie, and a week ago you'd have bitten my hand off for a bite! Now if you don't wish to walk the rest of the way to Raipur I suggest you leave me the hell alone. And don't you think I wouldn't do it, Minnie, don't think I wouldn't leave you out here at the mercy of the snakes and the elements, because I would, I'd do it in a heartbeat if it meant I'd be spared your pious preaching. Yes you are right, I shouldn't have eaten the kebab! Now let's just leave it there, shall we? For both our sakes."

Minnie turned her face away and shunned her sister for a further five minutes. "Well it wasn't me that ate the poor defenceless chicken," she eventually mumbled. "So why should I have to walk to Raipur? Why Essy? Why?"

Esther turned up the radio to drown out her sister's constant protestations "What is this garbage?" she said, wincing at the wailing flutist.

"Oh leave it, Essy," Minnie said, making a grab for the radio. "That's Papa Yamo. Apparently he's huge in Uzbekistan. This is his latest track—it's entitled 'Bringing in the goats', and he's accompanied by his wife and seven daughters on the spoons. He reminds me of a young Frank Sinatra."

"God, it's awful," Esther remarked, listening to the hypnotic ditty recounting the tale of a young goat herder who fell in love with a girl from a neighbouring village and a whirlwind romance ensued, a romance that was destined to last for all eternity, until one fateful day while she was out picking wild flowers she was killed by a freak rock slide, burying her beneath thousands of tons of Uzbek mountain scree. Her lover, Muzaffar, went quite insane and disappeared into the wilderness with his entire flock, leaving the village devoid of all livestock. Each night the inhabitants would gather together and call out to him to 'bring in the goats, bring in the goats'.

"It's hideous," Esther reiterated, switching off the radio.

"Ohhhh Essyyyyy," Minnie moaned. "Granted he's not everybody's cup of tea, but if you bear with it you'll be swinging your petticoat in next to no time, I promise you."

"And I promise you I won't," Esther said, steering around another rut in the road.

Minnie sat quietly humming to herself but eventually broke into song, emulating the charismatic Papa Yamo:

"Bring in the goaaaaaats
bring in the goaaaaaats,
there is nothing colder
than a dead girl under a bolder,
but please bring back our goaaaaats
we've no milk for our oaaaaaaats,
bring in the goaaaaats
Bring in the goaaaaaaaaaaaaats!"

Esther found her sister's rendition hilarious and couldn't help but laugh. "A dead girl under a bolder." She chuckled. "I've never heard anything so ridiculous in all my life."

"Catchy though, isn't it dear?" Minnie smiled. "It's easy to see why the man's as big as Elvis out here."

Esther could barely contain herself at Papa Yamo's comparison to the legendary king of rock and roll. "Are you serious?" she asked, aghast. "Bring in the goats? I mean it's hardly 'Jailhouse Rock', is it? A story about a manically depressed goat herder and a dead girl under a rock."

"Well I like it," Minnie confessed.

Peshwari Nans

"Well I don't!" Esther replied defiantly. "And I certainly wouldn't buy it."

Minnie sat humming until she caught sight of her sister glaring across at her and abruptly stopped and cleared her throat. "Sorry dear," she said lowering her head.

But in less than a minute the humming started up again, only this time it wasn't Minnie, it was Esther who sat bobbing her head from side to side. "There is nothing colder," she quietly sang, "Than a dead girl under a boulder, OH HELL!" she then cursed. "Now look what you've done Minnie? I can't get the damn tune out of my head."

"I told you, dear." Minnie nodded in agreement. "It's a catchy ditty, isn't it?"

"Ohhhh alright I suppose I'll have to agree with you there," Esther confessed. "Pathetic, but catchy nethertheless."

The pair of them began to sway side by side in their seats. "Bring in the goaaaaaats!" Minnie warbled.

"We've no milk for our oaaaaaaats!" Esther added. The pair then joined hands momentarily and raised the roof: "BRING IN THE GOAAAAATS, BRING IN THE GOAAAAAAAATS!"

Papa Yamo, a middle-aged crooner, was held in the highest esteem by the entire Uzbek nation and was one of only a handful of millionaire musicians to hit the big time, although one million Uzbek Som was the equivalent in total to around four hundred US dollars. But in the eyes of his people Yamo was a superstar, even if the mainstream global music industry had refused to give him the time of day, assuming his demos were an elaborate hoax, or indeed the work of a complete madman.

That afternoon, having been rocked and rattled around relentlessly for a number of hours crossing the deserted Uzbek plains, the sisters grew weary and somewhat saddle sore. "Look dear!" Minnie piped up, having sat silently fidgeting for quite some time.

A faint wisp of smoke could be seen emanating from the horizon ahead, a welcome hint of civilization.

"Thank goodness." Esther sighed, shifting uncomfortably in her seat. "I don't care what it is, dear," she told her sister whilst accelerating a tad. "We're stopping. My back and backside must be black and blue, I swear it."

"I know what you mean, dear," Minnie agreed, rotating her ankles to maintain the flow of blood and prevent a reoccurrence of her former thrombosis attack. "I haven't been in this much pain since I was caned for smoking behind the bicycle sheds with Suzie Watson."

"And well deserved it was too," Esther scoffed. "Filthy disgusting habit. I remember Father was mortified when he found out."

"Not half as mortified as I was, dear," Minnie said, smirking, "when he sat me down in his study and made me smoke an entire Cuban cigar until I was sick to my stomach."

"It certainly did the trick though dear, didn't it?" Esther smiled, recalling her sister's harrowing ordeal and the violent vomiting that had followed.

"Did it hell!" Minnie laughed. "I got the taste for them after pinching the butts from Father's ashtray and sharing them with Suzie in the garden shed. We'd come out coughing and spluttering with our eyes streaming, ahhh those were the days."

"Weren't they just?" Esther said, less convinced.

The sisters in their Morris Traveller drove into a sleepy windswept village similar to those featured in gun-toting wild west movies, only carrier bags and other associated litter replaced the customary tumbleweed. Uzbeks of all ages sat at the side of the road outside crude huts, with their arms crossed on their knees as they did each and every day of the year, with unemployment running at ninety-nine per cent and the prospects of getting employment being a flat zero.

"Are you sure you want to stop, dear?" Minnie asked when the residents rose to their feet to observe the strange spectacle approaching, one that they were highly unlikely to ever see again in their lifetimes. It was rather like seeing Halley's Comet: two eighty-somethings in a vintage British automobile.

"I don't think I've ever seen a more menacing bunch of cutthroats," Minnie added, locking her door and sliding Jasvinder's tin further beneath her seat.

"It's alright, dear," Esther assured her sister, winding down her window. "Leave this to me. Excuse me!" she called, slowing to a stop. "Oooh oooooh, excuse me my dears, would you happen to know where we might get a cup of tea?"

The Uzbeks stared blankly back at her. "Tea!" she called again. "Is there a cafeteria nearby perhaps?"

"I doubt that very much, dear," Minnie told her sister, without making eye contact with the locals. "We're more likely to get mugged than get a muffin and a mug of tea."

"Oh don't be daft, Minnie dear." Esther smiled. "That's always been your problem, you will judge a book by its cover, won't you? You know you really should learn to look for the good in people and have a little faith."

As she said so, a young Uzbek drew a long knife from his sash and approached the car. "OH GOOD GRIEF!" she squealed, hastily winding up her window. "Minnie, Minnie, help!"

But the heavily tanned teen moved behind the car and stooped and cut a stream of tangled garbage from Vivien's axle and held it proudly aloft.

"Oh," Esther said, opening her eyes to see him grinning at them.

"You know you really should have more faith, dear." Minnie smirked with her own heart racing. "That's always been your problem."

"Oh shut up, Minnie!" Esther said, swatting her sister's hand from hers and winding down her window. "Thank you," she said, red-faced. "Thank you kindly, young man."

"Yes, thank you for not slitting our throats," Minnie called across her sister.

"Minnie!" Esther barked. "As I said in the beginning, leave this to me. I say?" she asked the boy. "As I was saying, could you recommend a cafeteria or a tea room perhaps? You do have tea, don't you?"

"Teaaaaaa!" The youth smiled.

"Yes, that's right." Esther smiled too, turning to her sister. "See dear?" she said smugly. "Now I've established a line of communication we'll be fine, you mark my words."

"Teaaaaa!" the lad said again.

"Yes that's right, dear," Esther said, nodding politely. "Tea. Now if you would be so kind as to point us in the right direction I'd be much obliged."

"Teaaaaaaaa!" the Uzbek youth called back to his family and friends, who each joined him in what they perceived was their impromptu visitors' customary greeting call: "TEAAAAAAAAA!"

"You were saying, dear?" Minnie asked, gloating a little.

"TEAAAAAAAA!" they again called, waving frantically.

"Yes, yes, tea!" Esther said persistently, determined to break down the near impenetrable language barrier. "Tea, teaaaa!"

Minnie reached behind her and plucked a Royal Albert china teacup from the box and gestured to her lips. "Tea my good man!" she called to him.

Peshwari Nans

"Ahhhhhh choy!" He eventually smiled, slapping his forehead. "CHOY!" he called back to the others. "CHOY!"

"Well if choy means tea, then yes," Esther told him. "Now as I say if you could just point us in the direction, we'll be on our way."

"Come, come!" the lad insisted, opening Esther's door. "Come!"

"Oh no, that's quite alright, dear" Esther said hesitantly. "Perhaps we'll try a little further in town."

"Come!" the youth said, taking her arm and gently tugging her from her seat.

"Oh no, I assure you we'll be fine," Esther protested.

"Essy, we'd best do as he says, dear," Minnie said, doing a quick head-count of the toothless locals, "or things could turn uglier than they already are, I might add if that's at all possible."

Minnie unclipped her seat belt and stepped out from Vivien. "Helloooo," she said with her back firmly pressed against the car. "No sudden movements, dear," she said through clenched teeth to Essy, observing the arsenal of weapons openly on show. "Whatever you do, don't spook them."

"Spook them!" Esther exclaimed. "What about me for Christ's sake!"

"Come, come!" the Uzbek lad said, leading the sisters toward his mother's hut.

"Teaaaaa!" each of the natives said as the sisters passed by.

"Yes teaaaa," Minnie said, appeasing them and scurrying after her sister into the Uzbeks' family home, where the two of them were instructed to sit on upturned apple boxes at a three-legged table.

"Oh hello, hello," Esther said, looking around the dimly lit hut at the dozen or so relatives dotted around the place, seven of them being children. The lad's grandparents and great grandparents were also there, as well as his mother, who stood drying her hands on her shawl, bowing respectfully to the sisters.

"Hello, my dear," Esther said, reaching out a hand. "What a lovely home you have."

The mother sheepishly offered her own hand whilst covering a tear in her smock.

"Very homely," Esther added, momentarily lost for words.

"Yes, very minimalist." Minnie smiled, observing the decaying roof timbers and dry dirt floor. "I swear if this place were in Mayfair or Chelsea you'd be sitting on a fortune, my dear, an absolute fortune. Sorry, but I didn't catch your name. I'm Minnie and this is my sister Esther."

The mother merely understood the introductory gesture. "Lusa," she said, bowing again.

"No need to bow, dear." Esther smirked. "We're not the Windsors you know."

"Choy choy!" the son said in a flap as his seven young siblings dashed outside to gather round Vivien, making faces and laughing at their distorted reflections in her chrome bumpers. His mother disappeared behind a tattered beaded curtain which served as a crude partition.

"We, er, we're just passing through," Esther said nervously as the lad stood in the doorway.

"Yes, we can't stop long I'm afraid," Minnie added, shuffling closer to her sister, unsure of the Uzbeks' intentions.

The grandparents sat staring at the travelling Brits. Since the family had no television these visitors were a welcome distraction from the four peeling and cracked mud walls. The great grandmother held a copy of their religious text tightly on her lap, raising it to her face occasionally to focus on the minute print.

Peshwari Nans

"Excuse me," Esther said, reaching into her bag. "Perhaps you'd like to try these, my dear." She produced a spare pair of spectacles and offered them to the ninety-something lady. "Go on, it's alright," she added, leaning forward on her box seat. "They're not prescription glasses, dear, I get them at poundland," she informed the wrinkled relative as the lady shakily donned them. "But they do just fine for my sudoko."

"Ahhhhhh!" The great grandmother smiled, looking down at the text with abject astonishment at it loomed up at her as clear as day. She then popped the spectacles onto her husband's face and waved the text in front of him. He too marvelled, as though he was having his sight restored after decades in the dark.

"Here, dear," Minnie said, rummaging for her spares. "Try mine, my dear."

The great grandparents sat grinning for ear to ear, eyeing one another up and down and also looking at their surroundings, before removing the glasses and offering them back.

"No, no, keep them please," Esther said, raising a hand. "We have more where those came from, because my sister here will insist on losing them, won't you dear?"

"I do not!" Minnie protested. "That's a lie, Essy, and you know it."

Esther turned and looked her sister in the eye. "Alright!" she said, grimacing. "So where are my mother-of-pearl glasses? You know, the ones with the butterfly case?"

"Oh, those," Minnie replied, shuffling awkwardly. "Well I told you I had them when I got on the bus, dear," she added in her defence. "But I dozed off, missed my stop and ended up at Saint Pancras. By the time I got home I was minus the glasses, my umbrella, my woollen mittens and half a chocolate orange."

"Exactly!" Esther said knowingly. "And my Burberry check pair? I suppose you left those on the bus too, did you?"

The Uzbeks looked on in wonderment as Esther tore a strip off her sister.

"Ahhh no, no I didn't actually," Minnie said, raising a finger. "I left those in the library."

"I rest my case," Esther said, crossing her arms. "She'd lose anything, this one," she told the onlookers. "Do you know she once mislaid twenty-five rolls of three-ply toilet tissue? I mean who in their right mind could possibly lose twenty-five rolls of toilet tissue, for Pete's sake?"

The Uzbeks sat wide-eyed, not understanding a single word but enthralled netherthless.

"It wasn't my fault, dear," Minnie replied with a hand on her sister's knee. "I put them down while browsing in the Heart Foundation thrift shop and must have left without them. But Essy, I did manage to purchase that delightful tea cosy, didn't I? Oh and the crystal fruit bowl of course. I know it's chipped but what do you want for two pounds?"

"I was waiting on the lavatory!" Esther said through gritted teeth. "I sent you out for tissue and you were gone for over an hour for heaven's sake! My knees were killing me, my back was aching and don't get me started on my bottom. And what do you come back with? A tea cosy and a blasted fruit bowl!"

"Oh but it was genuine crystal, dear," Minnie reminded her sister. "You must admit it does look gorgeous on the sideboard with a pound of Cox's in and a bunch of grapes."

"But I was waiting for the damned tissue!" Esther stormed, with their audience open-mouthed, looking from one sister to the other during their exchange.

"Yes I know, dear," Minnie said, shuffling away ever so slightly. "I did tear you a page or two from the *Radio Times* though, didn't I?"

Minnie's quick thinking substitute at the time had only enraged her sister further.

"I told you then and I'm telling you now, Minnie," Esther said, wagging another finger. "There was absolutely no way I was going to wipe my bottom on that dear sweet Paul O'Grady's face! I, I wouldn't be able to live with myself."

Before the lavatorial conversation turned ugly, the Uzbek mother returned with two odd cups, bowing again as she handed them to the warring sisters. "Oh thank you, my dear." Esther smiled whilst snubbing her sister. "How kind."

"Yes, very kind indeed," Minnie said, eyeing her blue plastic cup complete with unhygienic staining. "What is it, dear?" she asked her sister under her breath.

"Tea, I hope," Esther said, still very much miffed at her sibling.

"Teaaaaaaa!" the Uzbek family called out, raising their hands in the air.

"Tea it is then," Minnie said, taking a sip. "Oh good grief!" she shrieked, sniffing at the odourless brew again. "No it isn't, it's coffee, Essy, and strong enough to stun a bull elephant."

The Uzbeks gathered on the couch opposite the sisters and watched intently as they cradled their cups, hesitant to say the least. "Oh hell," Minnie cursed. "We'd best drink it dear, I'd hate to offend them."

"Me neither," Esther agreed, noticing the son's handgun tucked in his trousers and the antiquated rifle that stood in the corner of the room. Sipping at the mud-like brew, the sisters gagged at the caffeine overload. "I doubt I'll sleep for a month," Esther said under her breath whilst smiling politely at their hosts.

"I know it's making my dentures rattle," Minnie added. "Very nice, dear!" she told the mother. "Is it Columbian by chance?"

"Teaaaaaa!" the mother replied, rocking and clapping her hands.

"Really?" Minnie said, taking another tentative sip. "You could have fooled me, my dear."

Feeling positively queasy, the sisters begrudgingly drained their plastic cups and sat trembling and twitching.

"That was lovely, thanks," Esther said, rising to her feet. "Come along Minnie, it's high time we were on our way," she said, dragging her sister to her feet. "Hurry will you!"

"Yes, yes, thanks for the coffee, tea or whatever," Minnie told the mother, who rose to bow yet again.

The son leapt from the sofa and barred their way once again. "Choy, choy!" he told his mother, who scurried back into their kitchen.

"Oh hell," Esther said taking her sister's hand. "Stay calm, Min, whatever you do stay calm. Now you look here!" she told the youth, puffing out her chest. "You can't keep us here against our will. It really isn't the done thing, you know."

"No it's not the done thing," Minnie echoed, ducking behind her sister. "Tell him Essy, tell him," she added, cowering.

The son called out anxiously to his mother, who ducked from behind the curtain, bowing as she handed Esther a cloth bag containing a quantity of their home-ground coffee. "Teaaaaaa!" She smiled, clasping her hands together.

"Oh, I see," Esther said, red-faced. "Yes, er, thank you, my dear."

"Oh," Minnie also said, emerging from behind her sister. "How, er, how kind."

Peshwari Nans

The Uzbek great grandparents dragged themselves from the sofa and hugged each of the sisters, thanking them wholeheartedly for the gift of sight.

"That's quite alright, dear," Esther said, shuffling out of the door. "Don't mention it."

"Don't lose them now, will you?" Minnie said, following closely behind.

"That's rich coming from you," Esther said, turning to frown at her sister. "I swear you'd lose your head if it were possible, you really would."

"Oh Essy, I'm not that bad, dear," Minnie moaned.

"Not that bad, not that bad!" Esther scoffed as the Uzbek children fussed at their feet. "Why do you think I haven't given you another door key, eh?"

"Oh Essy, everybody loses their door keys." Minnie smiled, ruffling the children's hair. "It's a fact."

Esther climbed behind the wheel of their car. "Minnie!" she snapped. "You've had five keys and you've mislaid them all! Thank youooo!" she then said, waving to their gracious hosts. "Hurry Minnie, and get in," she added, eager to leave.

Minnie waved from the window as the village children chased them down the dirt street. "Here you are my lovelies," she said, retrieving a packet of sweets from the glove compartment and tossing them into the air, then she watched in the rear-view mirror as the ecstatic children stopped and shared them equally amongst themselves. Minnie sat looking ever so pleased with herself as the sisters drove from the quiet village.

"OH GOD!" she then suddenly shrieked.

"What, what is it?" Esther asked. "Minnie, what's the matter?"

"I gave them the toffees," Minnie said with her hands clasped to her face.

Peshwari Nans

"And?" Esther asked, but then it suddenly dawned on her too, that the village children were now in possession of the same uranium-enriched treacle treats that had gummed their dentures so solidly together in the Ukrainian wilderness. "Heavens Minnie, what have you done?" she asked. "We should go back!"

"Oh please God, no," Minnie said, clutching the tin of caustic coffee. "I doubt my nerves could stand it, dear."

"I know what you mean," Esther replied, still buzzing from head to toe. "But what about the children?"

The usually boisterous village infants sat at the side of the road, picking at their teeth without a peep from any of them.

"Oh dear," Esther said, seeing the funny side eventually. "There's a lot to be said for dentures, isn't there dear?" she said, jostling hers around in her mouth. The children on the other hand, did not have the luxury of removable molars and were forced to resort to some bizarre do-it-yourself dentistry with a hammer and a crude chisel.

The sisters drove unhindered for a further four hours with Minnie wide awake and wired after their coffee break, chatting non-stop while Esther strummed her fingers repeatedly on the wheel. "Only another fifteen kilometres to China, dear," Minnie rattled on. "I can't wait, I really can't wait. Do you know they have a population of one-and-a-half billion? One-and-a-half billion, Essy! And the Great Wall of China, dear, do you know it can be seen from outer space? Outer space, dear!" Her heart was pounding in her chest as the caffeine rush reached fever pitch. "And did you know, dear, that the Chinese use some forty-five billion chopsticks per year? Forty-five billion, dear, can you imagine it?"

"Remarkable, dear, quite remarkable," Esther replied, unable to stop her knees from trembling. "From space you say?"

Peshwari Nans

Soon the horrendous 'caffeine hit' wore off, and the sisters approached the Chinese border.

"There it is, dear, there it is!" Minnie squealed, pointing up to the mist-covered mountains, with the awe-inspiring Great Wall snaking along the rocky slopes and peaks. "There it is, all thirteen thousand miles of it. Isn't it spectacular!"

"Magnificent," Esther agreed, marvelling at the wonder of the ancient world, that dated back as early as the seventh century, constructed to keep out invading Eurasian nomads, who were desperate to seize Chinese lands and wealth.

After several rubber-stamped formalities the barrier was raised and the sisters entered the ninth country of their arduous and all-consuming quest, a country unlike any other. It was vastly overpopulated, a country where on one hand a new skyscraper is constructed every five days and on the other an estimated thirty-five million people still reportedly live in primitive caves.

The sisters soon found rural western China to be a lush temperate oasis with rice and soybean terraces stretching as far as the eye could see. Minnie waved at every soul they passed, from hordes of identically dressed schoolchildren to crooked elders hauling huge bundles of firewood or sacks of rice, wheat and barley on their backs. Many of them were travelling several kilometres to market, giving the sisters much food for thought, their own three-minute stroll to the supermarket proving that they led a guilt-ridden pampered existence.

The roads were soon transformed from narrow baked clay tracks, where a single motorcycle might pass them every thirty minutes or so, to rolled crushed rock and eventually concrete and tarmac, where a myriad of buzzing mopeds like swarming flies, weaved in and out in formation, skilfully avoiding any collisions, although they were within a hair's breadth of one another—and of Vivien for that matter.

"Oh, ohhh!" Esther gasped, seeing entire families pass by on a single machine. "Hellooooo!" she then called to a two-year-old child, who was perched precariously on her father's shoulders.

Recent traumatic events had rattled the sisters somewhat and Esther had decided that the two of them quite rightly deserved at least one night of luxury in the very best hotel their purses would allow.

"Ohhhh, can you imagine it, dear?" Minnie said dreamily. "A hot bath and a real bed. a real bed, Essy."

"I've thought of nothing else all day," Esther confessed, the spasms in her lower back growing in intensity. "Although I'd settle for a spinal board right now."

"Oh dear," Minnie said sympathetically. "Perhaps a shot of Monique's elixir might help?" She reached behind for another bottle. "It's worked wonders on my sciatica, and you know how I suffered terribly with it, don't you dear?"

"Don't I just?" Esther replied, rolling her eyes. "I swear if I had to listen to you grunting and groaning one more night I'd have, I'd have…"

"Ooooh, look dear!" Minnie said, stopping her sister's rant in mid-sentence to point out a procession of revellers following a dozen dancing men in a snake-like dragon costume, many throwing firecrackers into the air to herald the new moon and to give thanks for a bountiful rice harvest, after three consecutive years of drought.

"Oh how lovely," Esther agreed in awe, as her sister downed another cheeky nip of Monique's moonshine and hastily replaced the bottle. "Cracker, dear?" she said, offering her sister a dry morsel from their wicker basket.

Esther looked down her nose and raised a hand. "I'd hate to ruin my appetite, dear," she said sarcastically.

"Besides, I've decided to treat us both to a slap-up meal tonight. I'd say we've earned it, wouldn't you?"

"Ohh! Can we have Chinese, dear? Can we? Can we?" Minnie squealed, positively bobbing in her seat. "Oh please, Essy."

"Of course, dear." Esther laughed realising there was anyway absolutely no alternative in sight. "When in Rome—"

"—Rome, dear?" Minnie asked, looking out at the traditional gaily coloured lanterns strung from one noodle vendor to another, while perspiring rickshaw runners navigated the narrow cobbled streets, skilfully skirting the overabundant stray dogs and bamboo-laden bicycles, "But Essy this is—"

"—China, yes dear, I know," Esther said, honking Vivien's horn to disperse a pack of emaciated mongrels from the gutter. "It was a figure of speech."

"Oh, oh, right, I see," Minnie replied, lurching forward as her sister hurriedly applied the brakes when one brazen hound refused to leave the flattened feast of foo young that had been trampled underfoot into the pedestrian crossing.

"Out of the way for heaven's sake!" Esther moaned, peering over the bonnet and leaning on the horn once again. The dog, of no particular breed, stood hunched over its find, baring it's teeth at any of its kind that dared to approach, who might be hoping for a share of the pickings.

"Oh Essy, you'll frighten it," Minnie said, objecting to her sister's apparent lack of empathy. Taking a handful of crackers, she then tossed them onto the pavement amid the hungry pack, thus clearing the obstruction when the stubborn stray left the crossing, twitching its inquisitive nose and jostling with the other dogs for Minnie's strewn offerings.

"There," she said, brushing the crumbs from her lap. "Sometimes, Essy dear, you just need to think outside the crate."

"Box," Esther said, proceeding. "It's box, dear."

"What is?" Minnie asked

"Outside the box," Esther explained. "You said crate."

"Are you sure?" Minnie asked, mulling over the two alternatives in her head. "I mean crate does seem a little more plausible, don't you think?"

"Minnie," Esther remarked sternly. "Trust me. I've only ever missed three episodes of Catchphrase since it was first aired in the eighties, so believe me I should know."

"Yes but," Minnie piped up, "I think—"

"—It's box!" Esther snapped. "I distinctly remember Jack and I screaming at the television and the half-witted contestant who, like you, repeatedly said, 'Outside the damned crate'!"

"Oh," Minnie replied. "I see." She toyed with a loose button on her cardigan for a moment, watching the squabbling dogs in the door mirror. "I hope they have pineapple fritters," she then suddenly said out of the blue.

"What?" Esther asked, hastily winding up her window when a wok full of water was tossed into the road beside them. "Who?"

"The Chinese, of course," Minnie said, raising her eyebrows. "Do pay attention, dear. Cyril and I simply adored our fritters. We used to visit the Mandarin Palace on the Hackney Road. It was two-for-one for the over-seventies you see. Anyway Mr Lee would always put fresh carnations in our vase and give us a calendar at Christmas."

"Yes, yes dear, alright," Esther remarked, familiar with the inner workings of an oriental restaurant. "Everybody gets a calendar at Christmas."

"Mind you," Minnie rambled on, unhindered, "Cyril preferred the calendar he got from the garage that serviced his beloved VW Beetle. The ones with those scantily clad grease-covered girls jacking up a Jaguar or buffing the bonnet of a Bentley. He papered the inside of his potting shed with them, and spent hour after hour in there pricking out his seedlings."

"I bet he did." Esther smirked. "I would never allow Jack to keep them," she confessed. "Anyway he had me, so why on earth would he ever want to look at another woman?"

In fact Jack would very often sit in the rear courtyard of their shop on a hot summer's evening in his striped deckchair, barefooted with his trousers rolled to his knees and a bottle of stout at his side, waving to his beloved at the kitchen window with a copy of the *Greengrocers' Guide* in his hands. But like the majority of red-blooded men, he would covertly secrete a copy of a well-known top-shelf 'totty' mag between the centre pages, unbeknown to his spouse of course.

"Anything interesting this week, darling?" Esther would call, whilst preparing supper.

"A couple of things caught my eye," Jack once said, turning the centrefold on its side. "That reminds me, I must order more peaches."

"No, no, Jack wasn't the sort to gawp at pictures of naked women," Esther told her sister adamantly, whilst flanked by a wall of mopeds, many of them carrying two, three and up to five family members, not to mention the livestock.

"My word!" Minnie gasped when a yellow Yamaha passed by with a dozen or so squawking ducks huddled in a basket behind the rider. But very soon, just when the two presumed they had seen it all, a young husband and wife overtook them, cradling a small child and the majority of their worldly possessions, clearly forgoing the expense of a costly removal company. Instead they balanced a divan bed, table, two folding chairs, a portable television and a standard lamp on the remainder of the seat and handlebars.

"Great Scott!" Esther marvelled. "Whatever next?"

And yet there were more precarious acrobatics from an entire hockey team perched on a humming Honda, to a fish farmer with a hundred plastic bags containing koi carp, hanging like teardrops around his speeding Suzuki.

"Ohhhh Essy, look," Minnie chirped as the four-star 'Komodo Dragon Hotel and Spa' came into view. It had a classic swooping pagoda-style pantiled roof, crimson fluttering flags, hand-painted with mystical Chinese symbols depicting wealth, prosperity and happiness. These lined the approach to a shimmering smoked-glass foyer, where two huge fire-breathing bronzes sat greeting the guests.

"Shall we, dear?" Minnie squealed. "Shall we?"

"We shall indeed." Esther smiled, pulling in off the road as dusk descended.

"Thank you, young man," she said, handing Vivien's keys to a smartly dressed valet, who bowed and opened her door. "Now you you will treat her with the upmost respect, won't you?" she warned him. "She's a lady not a Lamborghini, I'll have you know."

The valet, who spoke no English, bowed a further three times and stood aside as a bellboy hurriedly descended the stone steps and gathered up the sisters' bags. "Welcome, welcome to the Komodo Dragon," he said, bowing also. "Please, follow me."

"Right you are, dear," Esther said, clutching her purse while her sister tucked the tablet and tea tin under each arm. The pair followed the eager employee into the hotel foyer, where they were both instantly struck by the majesty and splendour of the opulent interior.

"Good grief, Essy," Minnie said, tugging at her sister's sleeve. "Do you think we can afford it, dear?"

Peshwari Nans

"I have my savings, Minnie dearest," her sister replied, patting her purse. "Jack always said we should save save save, but now I think to hell with it. Let's enjoy it while we still can, and hang the expense."

"Well if you're sure, dear," Minnie said, tottering after her sister to the desk.

"Good evening, ladies," the clerk said. He was dressed in a neatly pressed silk tuxedo with his jet-black hair swept to one side and lathered in place with a proprietary cream. "It is my pleasure to welcome you both to the Komodo Dragon. Would this be your first stay with us?" His English was without a doubt impeccable, indeed he had been schooled in West Sussex at a private boarding academy.

"Yes, yes, it is," Esther replied, resting her hand on the scaly back of a gleaming marble dragon beside her. "And may I say it's simply breathtaking," she told him.

"Breathtaking," Minnie echoed, as she so often did. "Simply breathtaking my dear, is it Ming?" she then asked, tapping a jade-and-enamel vase on the desk.

"Ming?" the clerk scoffed. "Madam, you can buy Ming from a common street peddler. Much of what you see here at the Komodo Dragon predates the Ming dynasty by several centuries at least."

"Hmmmm, just as I thought," Minnie muttered. having very little knowledge of the world of antiquities. "I tell you I saw one just like it at a bring-and-buy sale at Saint Benedicts, but there was no way I was parting with the asking price of four whole pounds. Oh no, I stood my ground and beat them down to two-fifty and insisted it was gift-wrapped too." She lifted the vase from its gilt base and checked the underside, as any astute dealer would.

"Please madam!" the desk clerk said, snatching the valuable piece from her. "I assure you this vase is priceless. Now I take it you'll be requiring a twin room?"

"Oh yes, of course," Esther replied, signing the elaborate register. "And could we please order room service for, say, six-thirty?"

"Ask him dear, ask him," Minnie insisted. "Ask him if they have pineapple fritters."

"Yes, yes, alright dear!" Esther snapped, shrugging off her sister's nudging hand. "Alright."

"I'm sorry madam," the clerk said, pre-empting her. "We only serve food in our Michelin-star restaurant. May I remind you," he added proudly, "that this is the Komodo Dragon, not the Ritz or the Radisson. We have a reputation unparalleled by any other. We are without a doubt the jewel of the orient, putting all others to shame—a star fallen from the very heavens," he continued to gush about his illustrious place of employment.

"Yes, yes," Minnie said, unimpressed to say the least, and prodding at his desktop. "But I'm telling you that if you don't serve pineapple fritters just the way Mr Lee at the Mandarin Palace does I'll be voicing my opinions to the chef in no uncertain terms."

"Quite right, dear," her sister agreed. "And we'll be leaving a forwarding address too, so we'll be expecting a calendar later in the year."

The clerk stood speechless, mortified in fact at the preposterous comparison. "Madam I, I, mean we..." he stammered, lost for words.

"Now about that room," Esther reminded him. "Do please hurry. I need to use the facilities, if you catch my drift."

"I beg your pardon?" the clerk asked, still very much taken aback.

"She needs a wee!" Minnie informed him with far less tact than her sister.

Peshwari Nans

"Yes! Do please hurry," Esther added, fidgeting from left to right. "I must warn you I have very little control these days."

"You're telling me," Minnie scoffed. "She filled a builders' bucket while shopping for curtain rings at the DIY store."

"Yes, yes, of course." The clerk flapped around, getting the gist of it and handing over a swipe card. "Third floor, room two-seventeen. Dinner is served from six-thirty, elevators are situated at either end of the corridors, oh and one last thing. I must stress that the top floor is strictly off limits to all guests, strictly ladies. Do I make myself clear?"

"Off limits?" Minnie said as Esther bobbed beside her. "And why, pray tell, would that be? I was hoping to take a few photographs, you see." She produced the tablet.

"No!" the clerk said, shaking his head adamantly. "Out of the question. Any guests found in the prohibited area will be escorted from the hotel, immediately."

"But, but, why?" Minnie added, ever the inquisitive one.

Esther took her sister's arm and coaxed her from the counter. "You heard the man, Min," she said as they headed for the elevator. "It's prohibited."

"Yes, but…" Minnie said, looking back over her shoulder, "I'd just like to know why, that's all."

"What's got into you?" her sister asked with a firm grip on her sister's coat sleeve. "You've always had a problem with authority, haven't you?"

"Ohhh, you know me, Essy," Minnie said, entering the sleek glass elevator reluctantly. "Tell me not to do something and I want to do it even more. It all began when Father told us never to touch his crystal brandy decanter."

"Oh yes, I remember." Esther smirked, pressing the lift button for the third floor. "You were ill for three days, Father was furious and grounded you for the entire summer holidays. I would have thought you'd learnt your lesson and discarded your rebellious streak."

Minnie wasn't listening. Her eyes were fixed on the number eight, the top floor the clerk had so vehemently warned them away from.

"But I was wrong, wasn't I?" Esther added. "You've been nothing but trouble ever since, getting caught in the boys' dormitory at summer camp, sitting in first class with an economy ticket, scaling a barbed-wire fence to see the Rolling Stones for heaven's sake! I mean whatever were you thinking, dear?"

"Oh Essy, it was worth every scratch," Minnie confessed as the elevator stopped and they alighted. "Nobody moves quite like Jagger," she added. "He has the kind of hips that make you go all weak at the knees."

"Yes, quite." Esther sighed, heading along the tapestry-lined corridor to where the bellboy was waiting with their luggage outside room two-seventeen. "Thank you, dear," she told him as he held open the door. "Minnie, do come along dear," she called to her trailing sister.

Minnie's defiant streak had got her into hot water on numerous occasions over the years and had even seen her hospitalized at one point, when she fell from the neighbour's heavily laden cherry tree and struck her head on a terracotta gnome, leading to an overnight stay in hospital and half a dozen stitches.

"There you are, young man," Esther said, slipping a few yen into the bellboy's open hand. The boy left pocketing the pittance with a disgruntled glare.

"Well isn't this just charming?" Esther told her sister, admiring the beautifully embroidered drapes, bedding and scatter cushions en route to the bathroom, while Minnie slipped her coat from her shoulders and flung it on the adjacent bed.

Peshwari Nans

Esther returned to find her sister hunched over, plucking a bottle of champagne from the mini bar. "Shall we, dear?" Minnie asked, seeking her elder sibling's approval for such an extravagance.

"Well I don't see why not, dear." Esther smiled, retrieving two flutes as her sister wrestled with the cork until a loud pop startled them both. "OHH!" Esther laughed, rushing to catch the escaping froth in her glass.

"Cheers, my dear," Minnie said, chinking glasses with her and sipping the fizzing bubbly.

"Yes, cheers," Esther replied, letting out the tiniest of ladylike burps. "Ohhhh excuse me," she said with a hand to her mouth. "I can't tell you the last time I drank champagne. Jack was never a fan. Fizzy piss he used to call it, if you'll pardon my French." She strolled casually around the spacious room, closely admiring the painted paper screens with scenes of bonsai gardens and carp-filled lily ponds and of course a dragon or two.

"Oh my, Essy look," Minnie gasped, tugging back the full length drapes to reveal their balcony, that looked out over the blue glazed tile roofs below, lit now by street lights and lanterns.

"Ohhhh, Minnie!" Esther too marvelled at the truly oriental spectacle. "Isn't it just…" She let slip another burp and the two laughed heartily.

The transfixed sisters stood draped over the sandstone balcony wall watching the townsfolk below winding down after a hectic day's street trading.

"Minnie dear," Esther said, setting down her glass. "How many yellow cars have you now seen to my sixty-three?"

"Oooh errrrm," Minnie pondered, the pair having kept up their tedious travel game throughout their previous eight countries. "I think I tail you by twenty-two. Why do you ask?"

"Well," Esther replied with a confident smile, "that means I get first dibs in the bath, am I right?"

Leaving Minnie open-mouthed, she ducked back inside to rummage for her washbag.

"Yes, but!" Minnie called after her, but then realized she hadn't a leg to stand on: a wager was a wager.

"But what, dear?" Esther asked, popping her head back outside, towel in hand.

"Nothing, dear," Minnie replied, turning away. "You go right ahead, don't mind me."

"Right you are, dear," was her sister's reply as she entered the ornate ensuite bathroom once again, to run a tub of steaming water.

"Ohhhhhhhh," she soon groaned upon lowering her aching frame into the scented lather and reclining opposite the fearsome hot and cold dragon-headed taps. Esther lay soaking away the stiffness associated with prolonged driving and one or two other age-related symptoms.

"Ahem!" Minnie later called, tapping on the bathroom door, clutching her own washbag and robe. "I say, Essy!"

Esther had drifted off into a deep heavenly sleep with her head tipped to one side, open mouthed.

"Essy!" Minnie called a little louder whilst wrenching at the door handle. But her sister, not wishing to be disturbed, had slipped the lock on the inside.

"Esther darling, are you alright?" Minnie asked, but her feeble knocking had very little effect on the robust rosewood door. Lowering herself steadily onto one knee, Minnie peered through the tiny keyhole. "Oh my word, Essy!" she cried, catching sight of her slumped sister and instantly fearing the worst, as relatives of the elderly so often did. "God no, Essy dearest!" she gasped, hoisting herself to her feet and turning this way and that in a blind panic. "Oh please God no, not my Essy. Not now!"

Peshwari Nans

Shoving at the door with her shoulder in a bid to break it down, Minnie's efforts proved futile to say the least. "Ohhhhhhh!" she moaned, dashing out into the corridor. "HELLLLLLLP!" she called, turning back and forth. "HELLLLLP, ANYBODY!"

But there wasn't a soul in sight. "Ohhhh blast!" she cursed, hurrying back inside and snatching at the telephone receiver above the mini bar. "Hello, hello, hello!" she called, stabbing randomly at the buttons until eventually the desk clerk answered. "Hello, hello, come quickly!" she begged on hearing his voice. "Hello!"

"Room two-seventeen?" the clerk asked. "What seems to be the problem, madam?"

"The problem?" Minnie asked, forgetting herself momentarily. "Oh, oh yes, yes, it's my sister! You must hurry, please I think she's d…" The word stuck in her throat like a knot of barbed wire. "She's d…"

"She's what, madam?" the clerk asked as he sat at his busy reception desk. "What is your sister doing?"

"Doing?" Minnie asked, positively trembling at this point.

"What do you mean, what is she doing? She isn't doing anything! She's dead for Christ's sake! Do you hear me, you pathetic little man? I said she's dead! My Essy, my beautiful Essy!"

"Dead!" the clerk said, wide-eyed. "What do you mean, she's dead?"

"Deceased, you fool!" Minnie raged, welling up and wiping a tear from her cheek. "Oh God, please do something! She's locked in the bathroom, it's so undignified!" Minnie's head and heart were all over the place at this moment in time.

"I see madam, do please try to remain calm," the clerk said, attracting the attention of his assistant and covering the receiver with one hand. "Call the police," he told his number two. "The fire department, an ambulance and the coroner. Hurry, yes the coroner, damn you!" he snapped when his motive was questioned.

The emergency services were alerted and en route within minutes. In the meantime the clerk paced the entrance in readiness to greet them, and Minnie sat rocking on the plump sofa, unable to come to terms with the apparent horrendous tragedy. "Oh God, Essy," she sobbed, clutching her stomach. "My dear, sweet Essy."

Three police officers were the first to arrive at the Komodo Dragon, followed closely by two paramedics, four firemen, a district coroner and a priest.

"This way, gentlemen," the clerk said, ushering the ensemble to the elevator under the watchful eyes of several inquisitive guests. "There's nothing to worry about ladies and gentlemen, I assure you," he told them before leading the emergency services, the coroner and priest to the third floor and room two-seventeen, where he knocked courteously. "Madam?" he softly called.

"Oh thank heavens," Minnie sobbed, opening the door and ushering them all inside. "Oh please, you have to get her out! I, I can't leave her there like that, not my Essy, we were only talking on the balcony a short while ago," she began to ramble nonsensically. "She'd seen more yellow cars you see."

"Yellow cars?" the clerk asked.

The fire crew and police officers turned their attentions to the bathroom door, shoving it bodily and picking at the lock, causing Esther to stir from her slumber inside the bathroom.

"Damn you, Minnie," she said, aggrieved at being woken and clambering shakily from the bath.

"Break it down," a police officer told the fire crew, who readied with their shoulders as Esther reached for the door.

"Minnie will you wait, for Pete's sake!" she snapped, tugging the door open with just a loose-fitting towel tied around her waist.

"ARRRRRRGGGHH!" she immediately shrieked when confronted by the team of uniformed men, who were lurching towards her. "MINNIE WHAT THE?" she added, grabbing her robe and ducking behind the door. "MINNIE, MINNIE? WHAT IN GOD'S NAME IS GOING ON?"

"ESSY!" Minnie gasped, pushing aside the priest who had been comforting her. "Essy you're, you're alive!"

The gathered officers and paramedics turned on Minnie. "Where is the deceased?" one of the policemen asked, with his hands firmly clasped on his hips.

"Deceased?" Esther said, emerging tentatively. "Minnie? What's he talking about? What's going on? Come on, out with it!"

"Essy I, I—" Minnie stammered, red-faced. "I'm sorry Essy, I thought—"

"—You thought what?" Esther growled, tugging her robe tightly around her body "What are these gentlemen doing here? Minnie what have you done?"

The officers then confronted the hotel clerk, who took a step or two back.

"Gentleman, gentleman, I assure you I was informed we had a fatality," he grovelled, knowing full well the penalty for wasting the officials' time. The clerk was torn off a strip during a heated dressing down, before the officers stormed from the room, leaving Esther still terribly confused.

"It appears there has been some sort of misunderstanding," she told the clerk whilst glaring at her sister. "Hasn't there, Minnie? And will somebody please tell me why we have a priest in our room?"

"To ease the suffering in your time of loss," the priest said solemnly.

"Loss!" Esther exclaimed, still very much in the dark. "What loss? Minnie, what's he talking about? Who on earth has died?"

"You have!" the disgruntled clerk raged. "Well at least you're supposed to have!"

"Me?" Esther gasped. "Me? Minnie will you kindly tell me what's going on?"

Minnie hung her head.

"Minnie!" Esther said insistently. "Minnie tell me, what have you done?"

"Well I saw you through the keyhole, dear," Minnie confessed. "You weren't moving and I'm sorry, but I feared the worst. Oh but Essy I'm so glad you're alive, honestly I am." She rose from the sofa and approached her sister, arms outstretched. "Thank God."

"Get away from me, you fool," Esther said, stepping back and escorting the furious clerk to the door. "I'm ever so sorry, it's my sister she's—" She paused, unable to justify her sister's actions. "She's a damned fool!" she eventually blurted out, grimacing at Minnie over her shoulder.

"May I remind you, madam," the clerk said, standing at the door, "that this is the Komodo Dragon. We have entertained emperors, kings, queens and celebrities here, even your own Paul O'Grady has graced us with his presence. Our standards are second to none, therefore we will not tolerate unruly behaviour of this nature, is that clear?"

"Yes, yes, it is quite clear," Esther said, positively seething beneath her humble exterior. "I can't apologize enough and I assure you, sir, that we will not trouble you again, you have our word. Doesn't he Minnie? Minnie?"

"Oh, oh yes, cross my heart," Minnie said sheepishly at her sister's side. "Well unless my sister does in fact breathe her last and shuffle off to the pearly gates during our stay. Then I suppose we could simply put tonight's fiasco down to a dry run, what do you think dear?" she asked her speechless sister.

"Minnie!" Esther then growled, shoving her sister towards the bathroom. "Get in there before we really do have a fatality in the family."

"Wait, wait, which room?" she called over her sister's shoulder. "Which room?"

"What?" the clerk replied, helping the aging priest to his feet.

"Which room?" Minnie again asked whilst being manhandled by her sister. "Paul O'Grady! Which room did he stay in? Please tell me it was ours."

The clerk merely looked down his nose at the wrestling sisters and disappeared with the confused clergyman.

"I bet it was this room, dear," Minnie said, relenting and kicking off her shoes. "I know him, he'd simply die for these curtains."

"I wish you'd simply die!" Esther raged, pushing her sister inside and dragging the door closed. Whilst Minnie undressed and ran a fresh bath, Esther took several deep breaths out on the balcony to lower her racing heartbeat, looking over her shoulder towards the bathroom once or twice and shaking her head in despair.

No matter how mad Esther may have been with her sister at that particular moment, one thing troubled her during the following thirty minutes or so—it was those parting words fired in anger: "I wish you'd simply die".

Stepping back inside she approached the bathroom door and tapped gently with an index finger. "Min?" she said softly, "Min are you alright?"

Getting no answer, her heart suddenly raced once again. What if those really were the last words between the two of them? How would she ever forgive herself?

"MIN!" she yelled, beating on the door. "MINNIIIIIE!"

Peshwari Nans

Suddenly the door was flung open and her sister appeared in the altogether, her hair a dripping matted mess.

"What is it Essy, what's happened?" she asked, having leapt from the bathtub as best she could, fearing a fire or something worse. "What's wrong?"

Esther clutched her chest and breathed a huge sigh of relief. "No, no, nothing's wrong," she said, mustering a smile. "I, I just wanted to say sorry that's all, for being mad at you I mean. You were upset and clearly did what you thought was right. I should never have called you a fool, will you please forgive me, dear?"

"Oh that's quite alright, dear," Minnie said, standing in a puddle of her own making at this point. "It's water off a duck's back that's all it is." She shook a leg and looked down at her feet. "And mine for that matter," she joked.

"I'm glad," Esther agreed, leaning in to kiss her sister's cheek. "My apologies for disturbing you, dear."

"Oh that's quite alright, Essy," Minnie said, examining her hands. "I was beginning to wrinkle anyway."

Esther couldn't help but laugh. "My dear Minnie, how on earth could you tell?" she asked, eyeing her sister's furrowed skin.

"Ooooh, you cheeky mare!" Minnie smirked before checking her neckline in the mirror. "Hmm come to think of it, dear, do you think it's too late for Botox?"

Minnie was in fact deadly serious but her sister could hardly contain herself. "Oh stop it, dear," Esther said, clutching her side. "You're killing me."

"I hope not, Essy dear," Minnie said, straight faced. "I think the clerk would have kittens if I telephoned him a second time." She too then burst out laughing and the pair embraced, the very best of friends once again.

The sisters dressed in readiness for their evening meal, putting their earlier differences behind them. "Oh that's a charming dress, my dear," Esther said, caressing Minnie's floral pleats. "I can't say I've seen you in it before. Is it new by any chance?"

"Yes, yes, it is and I simply adore it," Minnie replied with an elegant twirl. "Sydney at the bowls club bought it for me."

"Sydney!" Esther remarked, taken aback. "But, but he's, he's ninety-two, isn't he?"

"Yes I know." Minnie smirked. "I call him my sugar daddy. He's absolutely loaded by all accounts."

"Well maybe he is," Esther said with a disapproving glare. "But there's no need to take advantage of the poor fellow now, is there?"

"Oh no Essy I'm not, I promise," Minnie said, stepping into her patent shoes, another gift from her wealthy benefactor. "We just enjoy one another's company that's all—a game of cribbage, afternoon tea and suchlike. He really is rather sweet you know. He's asked me to accompany him to Vienna with the operatic society, all expenses paid of course."

"Yes dear," Esther said quizzically, suspicious of the aged Sydney's intentions. "But what does he expect in return? That's what I'd like to know."

"Oh really, dear," Minnie scoffed. "The poor thing's crippled with arthritis, partially sighted, hard of hearing and borderline incontinent. On top of all that he gets out of breath opening a packet of custard creams, so I'd say his only intentions are to avoid the grim reaper, wouldn't you say?"

"Yes, well," Esther said, unconvinced. "You don't want to toy with his affections now, do you? Or with anything else for that matter."

Unbeknown to Minnie, Sydney had bedded several widows and spinsters at the 'Green Bowls Club', first showering them with expensive trinkets, designer dresses and lavish Continental escapes until they were obliged to repay his kindness between the sheets so to speak. The deed was done with the aid of reinforced undergarments, a lumbar support, breathing apparatus and a handful of tiny blue pills.

"Well I hope you know what you're doing, that's all," Esther warned her sister as they left the hotel room.

Descending to the lobby the sisters waved in the clerk's direction but were treated to his cold shoulder in return. "How rude!" Minnie said, lowering her hand and forming a tight fist. "Somebody needs to teach that arrogant buffoon some manners."

"Leave it, dear," Esther said, taking her sister's hand and guiding her in the direction of the restaurant. "Let's just eat, I'm famished. Table for two please, my dear," she then told the stunning young waitress. She was dressed in a shimmering black gown with two ebony chopsticks keeping a tight jet-black bun in place on her head, her face powdered white and accentuated with ruby-red lips.

"Of course, please, this way," the girl said, bowing before leading the sisters to their table.

"Could we have a pot of tea, my dear?" Esther asked over her menu once she was seated. "PG if you have it."

"I do not know this tea," the girl confessed. "But we have many traditional Chinese tea here at the Komodo Dragon."

"Such as?" Esther asked while Minnie perused her menu for the vegan options.

"Okay, we have," the waitress said, pausing to take a breath before reeling off the hotel's extensive locally cultivated list of available teas: "Chun Mee, Keemun, Jin Fo, Oolong, Wong Lo Kat, Lapsang souchong, Jin Jun Mei, Lei Cha, Longjing, Bai Mudan and Golden Monkey."

"My word," Esther exclaimed, her head spinning. "Perhaps we'll try the Golden Monkey. What do you think Minnie? Minnie dear?"

Peshwari Nans

"Sorry dear, I wasn't listening," her sister replied, looking over her spectacles and lowering her menu."

"I said we'd try the Golden Monkey, dear," Esther reiterated. "If that's okay with you."

"Golden Monkey!" Minnie gasped. "Esther dear, if you think for one moment I am going to retract from my beliefs and consume the flesh of another sentient being then you are much mistaken."

"No, no, you don't understand," Esther said, attempting to intervene.

"Oh, I understand alright!" Minnie said, rising from the table and flinging her napkin to the floor. "You expect me to sit here with these, these *savages,* and scoop the brains from a living monkey's skull with a dessert spoon! Well Essy, I am now seeing you in an entirely different light."

"No Minnie you've got it all wrong," Esther said, pleading to be heard, "it's—"

"—I know precisely what it is!" Minnie said, raising her voice so that all the people around could hear. "It's the kidnap, torture and consumption of our closest living relatives. Essy, do you realize that's tantamount to cannibalism? CANNIBALISM!"

"Minnie, it's tea!" Esther said insistently. "Tea for heaven's sake!"

"And another thing," Minnie barked. "What?" she then asked her sister. "What do you mean, tea?"

"Golden Monkey tea," Esther said, tapping at the beverage menu.

"Tea?" Minnie replied, shrinking somewhat. "As in, tea?"

"Yes, tea," Esther said, red-faced, glancing over her shoulder at a dozen curious faces looking their way. "Now if you've quite finished insulting our hosts I suggest you sit down and keep quiet or you'll have us both deported, or worse for that matter!"

Peshwari Nans

"Tea?" Minnie mumbled to herself with her head down. "Well how was I supposed to know? I'm sorry, my dear," she told the waitress. "I've taken the pledge, you see."

"No problem," the girl said with a smile. "I tell chef make for you special dish, no meat and no monkey brain." She and Esther laughed at Minnie's expense.

"Alright, alright," Minnie said, raising a smile herself. "I suppose I asked for it."

The Golden Monkey tea arrived and Minnie again blushed as it was poured into two shallow willow pattern cups. She then looked down her nose as her sister's starter of crispy aromatic duck and butterfly prawns arrived.

"Not a word, Minnie," Esther warned her, catching sight of her sister's shaking head. "Not a damned word."

Minnie's platter then arrived and immediately turned Esther's head. It was a steaming sizzling assault on the senses, vibrant in colour, with an aroma like nothing either of the ladies had experienced before.

"Crickey," Esther said, comparing her seemingly mediocre morsels with the dish. "What is it?"

"Yes, what is it?" Minnie asked the waitress, pulling the platter closer to her, wide-eyed and wanton.

"Salt and chili tofu," the waitress explained. "On a bed of Singapore rice noodles with fresh water chestnuts, bamboo shoots in a satay sauce and glazed beansprouts. You like?"

"Like?" Minnie said positively salivating as she wrestled with her chopsticks, eventually discarding them and opting for the western alternative. "I love it!"

"Tofu, you say?" Esther asked.

"Oh Essy, it's amaaaaazing," Minnie said with a look of pure orgasmic bliss on her face. "It, it just melts! I'm telling you—"

"—Melts you say?" Esther said, eyeing the sumptuous spread. "I must say, dear, it does look rather tantalizing."

Peshwari Nans

"Try it, dear," Minnie said, offering a forkful of tofu.

"Oh no," Esther said, turning up her nose. "I couldn't possibly, no no, I'll be fine with my duck and prawns."

"Esther, you always have duck and prawns," Minnie said, rolling her noodles around her fork. "You really should take the plunge and live a little. Before it's too late I mean."

"No, no," Esther replied resolutely. "I'll be just fine, you know me, I'm a creature of habit, meat and two veg on a Sunday, fish on a Friday and liver and onions on a Thursday. And on the rare occasion Jack and I had a takeaway it was always duck and prawns, without exception."

"That's precisely my point," Minnie mumbled, whilst spooning water chestnuts into her mouth. "You need to broaden your horizons dear. I mean take sex for instance."

"Minnie!" Esther snapped, ducking and glancing across at the adjacent tables. "Will you please keep your voice down! And what the devil has that got to do with anything?"

"You mean sex, dear?" Minnie smiled. "It's alright, everybody does it, and believe it or not, everybody's talking about it, it's all over the inter web thingy—who's doing what to who and how many times. I find it all rather titillating."

"Minnie stop, please!" Esther whispered, cringing in her seat. "I'm sure there is a time and place for such vulgarity but this certainly isn't it."

"A time and place?" Minnie scoffed. "My dear Essy, sex should be spontaneous and exhilarating. Take Cyril for instance. He used to grab me from behind whenever I was blanching my sprouts or waxing the gramophone. I'd put up a fight of sorts, but that only got his dander up even further."

523

Peshwari Nans

"My God, Minnie, have you no shame?" Esther said, sinking further into her seat. "Jack would never dream of manhandling me in such a malicious manner! He was a gentleman through and through. Of course we, well you know, did it, but there was no spontaneity involved, none whatsoever." She peered over the back of her seat before continuing. "Everything was planned meticulously. Jack would shut up shop half an hour early on the third Friday of every month and fetch a fish supper from the Happy Halibut on the corner."

Minnie rolled her eyes at her sister's sorry tale.

"Anyway," Esther added with yet another furtive glance around, "after supper we'd each have a cherry bakewell and watch *Countdown* before retiring early for, well you know what."

Minnie sat open-mouthed at her sister's blatant confession. "Cherry bakewells and *Countdown*! Are you serious?"

"Yes, dear," Esther said in a hushed tone. "Once a month, religiously. But there was no funny business I assure you, oh no, it was all over by the time I'd turned the page on my Mills and Boon."

"Good God!" Minnie gasped, mortified.

The waitress then approached the table. "Is everything satisfactory?" she asked.

"Oh yes, yes thank you," Esther said blushing and rising slowly in her seat. "Yes it's lovely."

"Would you care for dessert?" the young lady asked, producing a second menu.

"Ooh yes," Minnie said in an altogether mischievous mood. "Do you by any chance have a cherry bakewell? My sister tells me they're quite the aphrodisiac."

"Minnie!" Esther cursed, pushing an elbow into her sister's side. "Please! I told you that in the strictest of confidence."

Peshwari Nans

"Cherry, bake well?" the waitress replied. "What is cherry bake well?"

"Never mind, dear," Esther said hastily. "Just another tea for me, dear."

"And for you, madam?" the waitress asked Minnie. "Dessert?"

"But of course, my dear." Minnie smiled, pushing away her empty dish and thumbing the menu, drooling in contemplation.

Esther sat sipping her Golden Monkey tea, looking every inch the lady, while her sister on the other hand slurped and slobbered her way through two bowls of lychees, a caramelized apple, a dozen brandy-infused strawberries and not one but two pineapple fritters, with ice cream of course.

"Have you quite finished?" Esther asked as the scraping of Minnie's plate grated on her.

"Oh heavens yes," Minnie said, reclining with her hands on her stomach. "You know me, dear, I'm not one to make a pig of myself."

"Really?" Esther smirked, giving the waitress several tables away the customary hand gesture to request the bill.

Full and content, the sisters retired to their room and after dispensing with their costume jewellery, slipped into their night attire.

"My I'm positively pooped," Esther confessed, yawning and stretching out her arms with her feet up on the sofa, whilst Minnie switched from channel to channel on the television.

"Ooh look dear!" Minnie said, seeing a familiar face and a rerun of the aforementioned *Countdown* programme dubbed in Chinese. But on glancing over her shoulder she saw that her sister had reclined a little further and was fighting a losing battle with fatigue.

Peshwari Nans

Minnie sat close to the television set, struggling to keep up with the subtitles. "Oh hell!" she guessed, running out of time to guess the *Countdown* conundrum. "I said that, I said that!" she squealed when the solution was revealed. "Essy didn't I say that?" she asked her sister, who merely groaned and rolled onto her side. "Essy?"

Following Mrs Vorderman and her *Countdown* cohorts, Minnie stabbed at the remote control, incensed that all fifteen channels had chosen to simultaneously cover the opening of the Chinese Parliament in Beijing, a riveting ten-day affair with topics such as planning targets and budgeting decisions to whet the appetite of the Chinese population.

"Damn and blast," Minnie cursed, having harboured a deep mistrust of all things political ever since the early eighties, when the 'Iron Lady' as the PM, Mrs Thatcher, was known, imposed the infamous poll tax, causing a good friend and neighbour of hers to take her own life when plagued with final demands from courts and collectors.

Switching off the television and tossing the remote away, Minnie retrieved the tablet and began snapping their apartment, including the novelty heated musical lavatory seat and 'his' and 'hers' Haribo dispensers either side of the bed. Venturing out onto the balcony, she captured the star-filled night sky with its vivid crescent moon. Standing on tiptoe, she again cursed when attempting to photograph the silhouetted ancient ruins of a ninth century temple on the edge of town. It was partially obscured by an adjacent apartment building. With her tablet poised, Minnie looked around for an alternative vantage point, the obvious solution being higher ground—possibly the rooftop.

Dismissing the warning concerning the upper floor, given to them on arrival by the insistent clerk, Minnie stepped back inside.

Peshwari Nans

"Essy I..." she said, peering over the back of the sofa and finding her sister sleeping contentedly. She buttoned her lip and chose not to bother her, convinced she could take her pictures and be back in no time with Esther none the wiser and unable to protest.

Tiptoeing gingerly to the door, Minnie tweaked the handle without making a sound and slipped out into the seemingly deserted corridor, still dressed in her flowing nightgown, and made her way towards the elevators. "Oh hell!" she said, ducking into the emergency stairwell when the elevator suddenly arrived and the sound of voices could be heard within.

Holding her breath as best she could, Minnie stood with her back to the wall out of sight and waited, but the three guests that alighted lingered in the corridor chatting amongst themselves, in no hurry to return to their rooms.

"Oh go awayyyy," Minnie said under her breath. Several moments later Minnie had no choice but to take to the stairs, puffing and panting in doing so. A thought then crossed her mind: if she bypassed the top floor and took the fire escape instead to access the roof, then officially she would not be breaking any house rules. But all the same in passing, she couldn't help but wonder what lay beyond the top floor door. Her hand hovered inches from the handle with her curiosity silently goading her. "No, no," she told herself with a rare display of common sense. "Leave it Minnie, leave it."

Minnie clung to the stair rail and pulled herself up the final flight, wheezing and a little light-headed, with her calves throbbing and her chest tightening. She suddenly pricked up her ears at the faint sound of a baby crying, a distressing screech that was rhythmic and high pitched. But unable to ascertain the direction of the tearful tot, Minnie ventured on, shoving open the fire escape door that led to the roof terrace.

Peshwari Nans

"Bingo!" she said, stepping out into the prevailing wind, which whipped up the hem of her nightdress. "Oh my!" she exclaimed, holding her hair in place and proceeding across the hotel's private helipad. The rooftop itself was dotted with a dozen or so hexagonal skylights, illuminated from the floor below, one in particular stopping Minnie immediately in her tracks as she passed.

"What the devil?" she asked, peering down upon what appeared to be row after row of infant cribs, more than thirty at a quick count, each of them occupied by a near newborn baby.

"This is a hotel not a hospital," she thought to herself. "And why are the infants tethered by their right hands?"

Her suspicions were further aroused when a group of men entered the room. They wore expensive Italian designer suits and highly polished brogues, and, after examining the wriggling children, all of whom oddly enough appeared to be female, one of them instructed a subordinate to place a tearful child into what could only be described as a canine 'carry cage' and remove it from the room.

Minnie took a step back and held out the tablet in order to capture the clearly clandestine proceedings before approaching another beacon of light. There she witnessed a surgical team in masks and gowns, scrubbing their hands and forearms vigorously while three infants lay heavily sedated on trolleys with each of their internal organs marked on their skin as a series of dotted lines with an array of razor-sharp sterile instruments at their sides.

It was at that precise moment that the grizzly truth struck Minnie rigid, and sent a shiver through her aged bones. "The girls!" she said with a hand to her mouth. "Oh my God the girls!"

Just days before the sisters had embarked on their global journey, whilst travelling London's Underground, the

528

Peshwari Nans

Northern line to be precise, Minnie had picked up a discarded copy of the *Daily Telegraph* and thumbed the pages to pass the time. One article in particular caught her eye amid the tedious stock exchange predictions and business analysis. An undercover journalist had delved deep into the ugly side of China's much documented 'one child policy'. The brainchild of former leader Deng Xiaoping in 1979, the strict decree forbidding multiple births had been in place for more than thirty years.

Designed to limit the rapidly increasing population, the one child policy applies to some ninety per cent of Chinese citizens, with the threat of employment termination and withdrawal of state benefits hanging over the heads of any who dared to violate the decree. In extreme cases women had reportedly been forcefully sterilized and persecuted for flouting the law.

Poorer families, who were dependent on a male child to continue the family line and earn a greater wage to support them, more often than not aborted a female foetus prior to birth, but for thousands upon thousands of those who were too late to abort, an equally harrowing fate awaited them with cases of neglect, abandonment and even infanticide: infant murder, rife throughout the country. A virtual selective genocide was taking place, hidden from the wider world.

Subsequently criminal organizations had learnt to exploit this unwanted resource, offering mothers a few paltry coins for their infant daughters and the assurance that they would be placed with loving western families. Although a very small percentage of the infants were sold on the black market to foreign clients eager to adopt, it was discovered that the vast majority met a more gruesome end in makeshift operating theatres like the one Minnie had just stumbled upon.

Peshwari Nans

The market for infant organs, bone marrow, tissue and even DNA was huge, with vast pharmaceutical companies preferring to test their products on human material, because they were under growing worldwide condemnation of their treatment of laboratory animals.

Whether it be a skin sample, an eye or an entire frozen corpse, unscrupulous companies were willing to trade in this readily-available commodity, with staggering profits to be made. Profits which allowed this particular criminal cartel to rent the entire top floor of the Komodo Dragon Hotel, using its helipad to transport the children to and from the hotel.

"Oh no, those poor babies!" Minnie said, unable to contain her emotions. Again she fumbled with the tablet, taking a series of incriminating photographs. "Oh hell!" she cursed. With a wealth of evidence in her possession, should she burst in and confront the perpetrators? Or approach the hotel clerk and insist he alert the authorities?

Either course of action would undoubtedly land her in hot water, and the gang members would obviously be prepared to stop at nothing to protect their business interests and the hotel clerk would be unappreciative of her snooping and only too glad to serve the sisters with an eviction notice, he himself being on the payroll of the criminal gang.

"Damn, damn, damn!" Minnie cried, in a complete flap, and the innocent children below only moments away from dissection. It was then that she realized what a powerful weapon she had right there in her hands: the tablet, a window to the world and a means of communication. The finger, it seemed, was now more powerful than the sword, with vast multinational conglomerates being brought to their knees by a single tweet, blog or email.

Frantically, Minnie began uploading the images to all the forums at her disposal, with the words SEND HELP

NOW emblazoned above them, before activating the tablet's GPS. Repetition and constant tinkering meant that she had become quite adept and computer literate in recent days.

As a result of her desperate plea her images were flagged up on no less than seven-and-a-half million devices worldwide, including those of NATO and the International Security Council, whose analysts hastily deciphered the data and gave the green light for 'Operation Rickshaw'. A cross-Continental rapid response team was briefed and given diplomatic dispensation to enter Chinese airspace and deploy ground troops or 'gangbusters' as they were known; these were elite bands of special forces personnel from Great Britain, France, Germany, and the US to name but a few.

The very best of the best were mobilized and scrambled within minutes from a number of locations, armed and prepared, having trained relentlessly and carried out countless covert humanitarian and military operations in the most hostile of environments, from El Salvador and Somalia to Uganda and the Gaza strip.

"Help me, Mr Google!" Minnie said, shaking the tablet.

A single tweet from a NATO source came bouncing back, four words in fact, saying: "SIT TIGHT WE'RE COMING."

"When, how long?" Minnie keyed in, fearing for the children below.

Back in their hotel room Esther stirred, the crick in her neck waking her. "Ooooh," she said, pushing herself upright and turning her head from left to right to ease the pain. Figuring that her sister had retired for the night, Esther dragged herself to her feet, turned out the light and made for her bed in a sleepy daze. Had she woken fully she might have found her sister's bed to be empty, but instead

Peshwari Nans

Esther flopped onto her own, pulling the sheets up around her neck and resumed her slumber in a matter of seconds.

Minnie in the meantime, tapped maniacally at the tablet's screen. "Hurry, hurry!" she cursed, returning several anguished tweets whilst watching the proceedings beneath her. Ice-filled Medicare boxes sat in readiness to preserve the precious organs during transit, but, unlike the genuine donor scheme where consent was given in advance in order to save another human life, this was literally 'murder for profit', plain and simple. The poorly trained doctors who doubled as surgeons had each previously been struck off their respective registers for a series of botched medical procedures and subsequently the deaths of innocent patients who would have otherwise undoubtedly survived.

"Oh no, no, no no no noooo!" Minnie squealed, on seeing one of them don his mask, tug on his latex gloves and select a scalpel before prodding the sleeping child about the abdomen. "No please God no!" she gasped, looking desperately for any sign of help arriving.

But she was alone and a child's life hung precariously in the balance below her. As the gleaming blade approached the blue dotted line that ran from the girl's neck to her navel, Minnie had absolutely no choice but to take matters into her own hands, no matter how foolhardy it might be. "HEYYYYY, NOOO!" she yelled, stooping to pound on the glass skylight. "HEYYYYYYY!"

The startled would-be surgeons and nurses froze and looked up at their elderly voyeur and began yelling between them in a blend of European tongues, flinging open the door to raise the alarm and summon the men in suits.

"Oh hell," Minnie said, backing across the roof terrace and peering over the side in search of an alternative escape route, but there were none. And with the sound of approaching footsteps and indecipherable rantings growing louder, her only means of evasion was to duck behind a large ventilation duct, clutching her beating chest.

The voices grew louder, as did the footsteps so Minnie, thinking fast on her feet, switched off the tablet and slid it along the floor out of sight, moments before a pistol was pushed into her face.

"YOU!" a henchman barked in a broad Albanian dialect that was incomprehensible to Minnie, astonished to find a pensioner in her nightdress on the roof of the hotel at that hour. "What are you doing here?" he asked, lowering his gun and still speaking in his native tongue.

"I, I'm sorry I don't understand," Minnie replied, shaking in her carpet slippers. "I don't know what you're saying."

Her only hope was to play for time. "I'm English you see, you understand English?"

The three aggressors turned to one another, shrugging their shoulders.

"I'm looking for my cat," Minnie informed them, offering what she deemed to be a plausible explanation. "You haven't seen her, have you? She's a tortoiseshell with a white nose and three white socks? Answers to the name of Babs after Barbara Windsor, because she's a bubbly little thing you see." She began looking around, making a coaxing sound and calling for her fictitious feline. "Baaaaaabs, Babs darling? She will wander off, you see," she told them.

"English!" the Albanian man snapped. "What you do here?"

"I told you," Minnie replied, eyeing his heavily armed associates. "I'm looking for my cat."

"Cat?" the Albanian asked.

"Yes I told you, my Babs," Minnie said. "White nose, three white socks. Have you seen her?" Before the gunman could reply, Minnie continued to ramble and stall them.

"She was a stray, you see," she informed them, perpetuating the lie. "The blasted thing used to poop in my garden until I gave it a saucer of milk. Well after that she moved straight in without so much as an invitation and now she does her business on the newlyweds' lawn next door. Mind you, they aren't what you'd call gardeners."

While the gunmen stood, looking completely perplexed, Minnie longed for the cavalry to arrive. "Mind you," she added, trembling in her nightie, "I doubt they get much time."

"Who?" the Albanian asked, his head now spinning as he struggled to process the extraordinary situation.

"The newlyweds!" Minnie exclaimed. "Oh do pay attention. Anyway they're at it half the night, well you know how newlyweds are, funny how they won't do it in their own garden though isn't it? The cat I mean, not the newlyweds."

"STOP!" the Albanian barked, having heard quite enough. "Stop talking you crazy old woman, go, go!" He shoved Minnie back towards the fire escape door. "Go back to your room and do not return!"

"But what about my Babs?" Minnie asked, wincing as he gripped her arm and pushed her inside. She glanced over his shoulder for the help that NATO had so faithfully promised. "Where are they?" she said a little louder than she'd intended.

"They?" the Albanian asked, his suspicions again aroused. "What you mean, they?"

"Oh, er," Minnie stammered. "Didn't I tell you? Babs has a brother Wilbur, you see. Wilbur was the name of the chemistry teacher I had a crush on at high school, I used to go all weak at the knees at the mention of magnesium and copper sulphate. There's something quite provocative about a man in tweed don't you think?"

Peshwari Nans

"GO I SAID!" the Albanian bellowed in Minnie's face, causing her to jump. "To hell with you and your cats, just go!"

"Okay okay!" Minnie replied, turning for the stairs. "Please, just don't hurt the children."

"What?" the Albanian said, making a grab for her and hoisting her back. "What did you say?"

"Oh, er," Minnie said, stuck for words for once. "I, I…"

"Take her!" the gunman told his associates, who wrestled Minnie from the stairwell and into the top floor corridor.

"Wait, what are you doing? Let me go!" Minnie cursed. "Let me go I say, let me go!"

But she was no match for the muscular men who dragged her to a sparsely furnished room and thrust her down onto a firm wooden chair. "What, what are you doing? Hey I said what the devil are you doing?" she asked as her hands and feet were bound. "Let me go!"

The men then huddled in the corner of the room, talking out of earshot of their captive.

"I sayyy!" Minnie called to them whilst tugging at her restraints. "My er, my husband will be wondering where I am you know. He's a huge brute of a man and not one to be trifled with, I assure you, so I suggest you untie me and send me on my way if you know what's good for you, helloooo, you there!"

The Albanian approached Minnie and thrust his handgun into her face once again. "Your husband," he said menacingly. "Does he have one of these?"

"Er, no, not exactly," Minnie said, cringing and inching away. "He's more of a Jiu jitsu man you see, or is it kong fu? I could never tell the difference. Anyway that Brucey Lee stuff, so you really do need to untie me before he arrives and wipes the floor with the lot of you."

Peshwari Nans

The gun was pressed into her cheek with greater venom. "So, you saw the children," the Albanian said, gritting his teeth. "That is very unfortunate."

"Yes, yes, I did," Minnie said defiantly. "And I know your game Sonny, ohhhh yes I know just what you're up to alright, you murderous barbarians. They're babies for heaven's sake, how could you?"

The Albanian pocketed his pistol and made for the door. "Kill her," he told his men in passing.

"What?" Minnie cried. "Wait, no, no wait!" She again wrestled with the sturdy nylon ties that bound her. "Wait, you need to leave right away!" she warned them all. "My friends are coming you see, lots of them. Yes that's right, so you'd better get going before they arrive or you'll be sorry!"

The Albanian stopped at the door and turned around with a wry smile. "More of your kung fu fools I suppose?" He laughed. "Let them come. We have weapons, many weapons." He then quietly instructed his men how best to dispose of Minnie's body.

"Well don't say I didn't warn you," Minnie continued, although she was absolutely terrified at this point. "They're coming alright, and when they do you'll be sorry, you mark my words, ohhhh yes you'll all be sorry."

"You know what I think," The Albanian growled, taking a step towards her and retrieving his weapon once again. "I think nobody is coming, no friends, no crazy kung foo man, no Babs, no—"

"—Wilbur," Minnie reminded him. "His name is Wilbur, do pay attention. He's a ginger Tom with half his right ear missing, he got into a scrap with the Persian twins at number forty-two over an empty tuna tin—"

"—STOP, STOP, STOOOOP!" the Albanian roared. "STOP OR I WILL KILL YOU MYSELF, RIGHT NOW!" He cocked his weapon and held it close to Minnie's right eye. "There are no cats, do you hear me?" he added, spraying saliva into her face. "Just a crazy old woman who has seen too much, and for that you will pay with your life, what little of it you have left."

"Oooh, you horrid man," Minnie said, scowling at the crook. "Untie me and I'll show you how much life I have! I'll, I'll box your ears you, you brute."

Suddenly the sound of approaching helicopter rotors could be heard above them. "You see? You see?" Minnie said, overcome with relief. "I told you my friends were coming, didn't I? Now I suggest you each lay down your weapons and surrender. Oh and get me out of this blasted chair!"

"Go!" the Albanian barked, ordering his men up to the terrace while he remained with Minnie. "Your friends, you say," he said, putting a foot up onto the arm of her chair. "Well, well. What are we to do?"

"Untie me and I'll have them spare you," Minnie replied, wriggling. "Well? What are you waiting for?" she listened for a moment for the sound of gunfire which ordinarily accompanied the storming of an enemy encampment, but there was none.

"I am waiting for my boss," the hoodlum said, opening the door for the criminal overlord who had just arrived by helicopter. Accompanying him was a fresh consignment of infant girls, some thirty or so, heavily sedated in cramped wooden crates.

"Mr Hoff," the Albanian said, standing rigidly to attention. "It's good to see you, sir."

"What is this?" the Dutch billionaire and mastermind of the lucrative enterprise immediately asked, marching into the room and gesturing to the bound pensioner.

"Sir she, she…" the Albanian stammered, clearly afraid of his superior.

537

Peshwari Nans

"I SAID WHAT IS THIS?" the Dutchman yelled as his minions carried in the children. "And why have the operations ceased? WHY NIKOLAS, TELL ME WHY?"

Rinze Hoff, an Amsterdam-born petty criminal, had literally fought his way to the very top of Interpol's 'most wanted' list with a string of no less than thirty murders to his name, the majority of those by blade or leather garrotte. "Tell me, Nikolas, or you will be replaced!" he added, slipping his hand into the pocket of his knee-length cashmere overcoat.

Nikolas knew only too well what his employer meant by 'replaced'. His predecessor and several before him had each perished at Rinze's hand.

"She, she was up on the roof, sir!" Nikolas blurted out while Minnie froze in her seat. "She said, sir, she said she was looking for her cat."

"Cats," Minnie piped up. "Babs and Wilbur."

"SILENCE!" Nikolas yelled, having heard enough of Minnie's imaginary pets. "I TOLD YOU THERE ARE NO CATS!"

"Nikolas!" Rinze snapped, confused to say the least by this farcical situation. "Nikolas look at me, look at me!" He removed his blade and pointed it in Minnie's direction. "Tell me Nikolas, why is this woman still breathing? Why Nikolas? Why?"

"Breathing, sir?" Nikolas replied, losing track momentarily on seeing the switchblade glinting in his boss's hand.

"Yes, *breathing* you fool!" Rinze said, losing his cool and spinning the blade in his hand. "If I have to ask you once more I will kill her myself and then, Nikolas, I swear I will gut you while my blade still runs with her blood."

"No, no sir!" Nikolas begged. "I was about to kill her when you arrived. Please, sir, I will do this!"

"He's lying," Minnie piped up, adding her own brand of fuel to the fire. "He said I could go free with his blessing."

"WHAT?" Rinze Hoff exclaimed. "NIKOLAS, IS THIS TRUE?"

"WHAT?" Nikolas also asked, spinning to confront his captive. "What are you saying?"

"You said you hadn't the stomach to kill me," Minnie said, relishing his squirming. "You even promised to help look for my pussies."

"WHAT? NO I DID NOT!" Nikolas shrieked with his boss breathing down his neck. "Mr Hoff, Mr Hoff, she is lying, sir," he pleaded. "I did not say these things, you must believe me, sir."

"But I do not believe you, Nikolas," Rinze said, prodding his back with the rapier-sharp blade. "I do not believe you. Do you know why?"

"No Mr Hoff, why?" Nikolas asked, with beads of perspiration appearing on his forehead. "Why do you not believe me, sir? I have never let you down, never sir never, why do you not believe me?"

"BECAUSE SHE IS STILL BREATHING!" Rinze roared, applying greater pressure to his blade.

"OW SIR, PLEASE!" Nikolas grovelled.

"So, er," Minnie said amid the fracas. "Can I go now?"

"NO, NO YOU CANNOT!" Nikolas screeched in the midst of a really bad day.

"But you said," Minnie added with the merest hint of a smile. "Don't you remember, shortly after you made me a cup of tea."

"You made her tea?" the billionaire barked. "Nikolas I am beginning to think you are surplus to requirements."

"Sir, please!" Nikolas said, thinking fast on his feet. "Look, sir, look I will do it now, I will kill her sir, for you!"

He cocked his weapon and thrust it against Minnie's temple, pushing her head to one side. Minnie winced and closed her eyes as his finger tightened on the trigger. There was a loud clicking sound, but miraculously the pistol misfired, much to Nikolas's horror.

"What?" he cried, looking over his shoulder.

"You disappoint me, Nikolas," Rinze snarled, growing ever impatient.

"Wait, sir, I can do this!" Nikolas said, removing and replacing the bullet clip from his gun. "I can do this, Mr Hoff!"

Rinze gripped his knife ever tighter. "Nikolas," he simply said, "you know there are no second chances in my organization."

"But sir, wait!" Nikolas pleaded, whilst fumbling with his weapon. "Wait! I beg of you!"

But the crime lord did not suffer fools, nor was he merciful, having brutally murdered his own son earlier that year for a foolhardy business decision made in his absence. Without warning or hesitation, Rinze plunged the blade deep into Nikolas's back, piercing his heart with pinpoint accuracy.

"Arrrrrgh, sir, no!" Nikolas screamed, reaching behind and buckling to his knees. "Mr Hoff, please! No!"

Minnie gasped and again closed her eyes, turning her head away as the Dutch villain wrenched his blade free and, in an instant, slit the Albanian's throat and watched as his blood-soaked body collapsed at his feet and bled out before him.

"Oh good grief!" Minnie cried, glancing down at the twitching body convulsing, as the life literally drained from it. "Oh God no, no, no, no!"

"You must understand, old woman," Rinze said, taking a step towards her. "This is business, nothing personal I assure you." Again he drew back his blade as a pool of blood formed at his feet.

Peshwari Nans

"OHHH ESSYYYYYY!" Minnie cried, reeling back in her seat.

Rinze had no qualms about killing a woman, elderly or otherwise. To him they were merely obstacles standing in his way and therefore deserved to die, for life was cheap. Besides, he enjoyed it, the word psychopath somehow fell short in describing his depravity, malice and cold-blooded cruelty. Grabbing at Minnie's arm, Rinze relished his next kill.

But suddenly the night sky above them was lit up by the powerful searchlights of four approaching apache helicopters.

"What the...?" Rinze gasped, pausing, blade in hand. "What is this?"

"I did try to warn your friend," Minnie informed him with the knife inches from her pounding chest. "I told him they were coming."

"Grrrr, damn you!" Rinze snarled, screwing Minnie's sleeve in his left hand and drawing back his blade. "Damn you to hell!"

The door was then flung open and two of his men rushed in with their guns raised. "Sir, sir, we have to go!" one of them yelled, panic stricken. "We have to go right now!"

Rinze released Minnie and looked up through the skylight as a dozen ropes were dropped from the hovering helicopters, on which the multinational special forces team descended to the roof terrace, dressed from head to toe in black Kevlar and carrying semi-automatic weapons. The bogus doctors and nurses fled down the hotel stairs, leaving the fifty or so infant girls behind, three of them still prepped for surgery and anaesthetized.

In all, two dozen special forces personnel stormed the roof terrace of the Komodo Dragon Hotel that evening, their laser-guided scopes searching for a target.

Peshwari Nans

"GO GO GO!" an SAS commander yelled, ordering an all-out assault on the fire escape door.

"SIR, NOW!" one of Rinze's men barked, looking down at his dead colleague and briefly forgetting his place amid the chaotic scene

Enraged by his subordinate's insolence, Rinze gathered up Nikolas's pistol, cleared the chamber and fired a single shot into his henchman's temple, dropping him like a stone to the horror of his colleague, who backed slowly out of the door into the corridor and inadvertently into the path of a Navy Seal's rifle scope. Two rapid shots traced the laser dot on the base of his skull and felled him on the spot.

"FUCK, FUCK, FUUUUCK!" Rinze Hoff screamed, now trapped in the room with the tethered Minnie, who sobbed uncontrollably with two slain gunmen in close proximity.

Two thirds of the special forces team split to sweep the entire top floor, bursting into room after room with their weapons at the ready. But instead of the anticipated armed resistance they found only crying babies traumatized by the commotion. "CLEAR, CLEAR, CLEAR!" they yelled in turn after finding no combatants present, several of them hanging their weapons over their shoulders and hoisting a child from its crib into their arms.

"SIR, IN HERE!" an SAS operative called when entering the makeshift operating theatre.

"Good God, man!" his commander gasped, discovering the three tots with the ink lines marking their skin for immediate surgery. "MEDIIIIC!" he yelled out of the door. "MEDIIIIC!" A field doctor, dressed in similar military fatigues, rushed in with a large backpack of medical supplies and immediately set to work reviving the girls.

Rinze Hoff peered out of the door and fired several shots towards the approaching troops, sending them ducking into an adjacent room. "HELLLLLP,

HELLLLLLP!" Minnie called, desperate for the ordeal to be over. Rinze turned in a bid to silence her with a single bullet, but a Seal's shell struck his trailing arm, shattering his radius bone and sending him reeling to one knee. Fearlessly, Rinze clambered to his feet, screaming in anger as well as agony, and fired a further three shots along the corridor while Minnie cowered behind him.

Ground troops had sealed off the hotel entrance and lower floors, escorting any curious or petrified guests from the building. Esther however, hadn't stirred throughout her sister's ordeal. Countless hours behind the wheel had taken its toll, every rattle, bump and roll reverberating and aggravating her rheumatoid arthritis. The sumptuous hotel divan bed was so warm and inviting that it enveloped her, transporting the weary traveller to a place beyond sleep, a dream-filled nirvana, making her feel weightless and heavenly.

In the meantime, Rinze was now cornered, but, as the advancing forces were about to discover, that was when he was at his most dangerous. Dripping with blood and seething, he stepped over Nikolas's corpse, cut Minnie free, and hoisted her to her feet.

"Please, please don't hurt me!" Minnie cried, stumbling over the lifeless bodies at her feet.

"Silence, bitch!" Rinze grimaced, thrusting her towards the door.

"HOLD YOUR FIRE! HOLD YOUR FIRE!" a Seal yelled, raising his hand on catching sight of the elderly Brit as she was shoved out into the corridor, where a dozen flitting laser beams illuminated her floral nightgown.

"Stop, please!" Minnie told Rinze, who ducked behind her for cover. "You're hurting me!"

"BACK OFF!" Rinze ordered the troops with his gun rammed against Minnie's skull. "BACK OFF OR I'LL KILL HER, I SWEAR IT!"

Minnie struggled to break free, but only succeeded in enraging the crime boss further. "STOP!" he snarled, smacking the pistol hard against the side of her head, drawing blood immediately. But Minnie was equally angered and kicked back at his shin bone with equal venom.

"BIIITCH!" Rinze screamed, striking her again and again before throwing her to the ground in a blind rage, and in doing so forgetting the armed servicemen ahead of him. Taking aim at Minnie's head he suddenly became aware of the dozen or so laser dots grouped around his heart "DAMN YOUUUUU!" he roared, but before he could squeeze the trigger and put an end to Minnie's meddling once and for all, he was literally blown off his feet by a sporadic burst of high velocity bullets, the majority of which passed straight through him and pierced the panelled wall behind him, against which he stumbled and slid to the floor, dead from the very first bullet.

Two special forces' personnel rushed to the Dutchman, rifles poised, and kicked the pistol from his lifeless hand, while another stooped to help a shell-shocked and battered Minnie to her feet.

"It's okay, ma'am," the Navy Seal said, supporting her in his arms. "You're safe now."

"Thank you." Minnie sobbed, clutching her bloodied head.

"MEDIIIIC!" the Seal called.

"No, no!" Minnie said, raising a hand. "Please, see to the children, see to the babies."

"They're fine, ma'am," the Seal replied as his colleagues filed by with an infant in each arm, wrapped in surgical blankets. "All of them are fine."

"All of them?" Minnie asked.

"Yes, miss," a British officer replied, cradling a six-month-old girl who was smeared with surgical fluid and drowsy from the anaesthetic. "All of them."

"Thank heavens." Minnie sighed before her legs buckled beneath her.

"I gotcha ma'am, I gotcha," the Seal said, supporting her frail frame with ease. His superior then arrived, clutching Minnie's tablet.

"We tracked your signal, ma'am," he told her, referring to the device's Global Positioning System. "I just wanna tell you, you did a mighty fine job, ma'am, mighty fine."

Minnie sat on the stairs and had her head wound tended to by the field medic. "Does it hurt anywhere else, miss?" he asked, swabbing the blood from her silver hair.

"No, no, I'm fine," Minnie replied, recoiling at the application of an antiseptic gel. "Ow, ow, owwww!" she squealed when his fingers probed for signs of fracture.

"We need to get you to a hospital for a thorough examination," the medic told her whilst shining a flashlight into each eye. "I'd say you've experienced severe concussion at the least."

"No, no I told you I'm fine, really," Minnie insisted. "I don't want to cause a fuss, I'll simply take an aspirin or two and sleep it off."

"But miss," the medic urged, "I really think—"

"—And I really think!" Minnie said, dashing his concerns in an instant, "that a stiff drink and a good night's sleep will do me the power of good! Now if you don't mind I really should be going." She clawed at his fatigues, hoisting herself to her feet. "If my sister Essy wakes and I'm not there." She paused to steady herself. "Well to say she'll be worried sick is an understatement."

"Essy?" the medic asked. "Do you mean Esther?"

"Yes," Minnie replied quizzically. "But how…?"

"So you must be Minnie." The medic smiled.

Peshwari Nans

"Yes, yes, I am," Minnie replied. "I don't understand. Do I know you?"

"No, but I know you," the medic said. "You're one of the Peshwari Nans, aren't you? I'm right, you are, aren't you?"

"Yes, that I am," Minnie replied proudly, having accepted the title.

The army medic rallied his colleagues. "Hey, hey, guys, do you know who this is?"

The top brass had been privy to Minnie's identity but word hadn't yet filtered down to the lower ranks.

"She's a Peshwari Nan!" the medic said excitedly. "Look, it's Minnie!" The penny slowly dropped with each of the surrounding special forces operatives as they jostled to shake her hand.

"Well I'll be damned!" a Navy Seal gasped, removing his black beret. "It's an honour to meet you ma'am, an honour."

"Oh the pleasure's all mine, believe me," Minnie said, posing amongst the men as they each hastily captured the moment for posterity. After all, their profession might have been daring, dangerous and high octane for much of the time, but meeting one of the now legendary 'Peshwari Nans' in the flesh, would prove to be the very pinnacle of their careers, with their hard earned military decorations paling into insignificance.

"You should have this, maam," a Seal said, removing the medal of honour he carried in his pocket, awarded for bravery above and beyond the call of duty in Afghanistan's Helmand Province. The young soldier had selflessly run a hundred-and-fifty yards under heavy enemy fire to embrace a dying marine and offer precious words of comfort. "You earned it," he told Minnie, offering it to her.

"Oh no, don't be ridiculous," Minnie said, raising a hand. "I couldn't, I mean I, I, didn't really do anything."

546

"Are you kidding me?" the Seal said, pinning the prestigious mark of accolade to her chest. "What you did took guts, lady, real guts."

An echo of agreement rang out around them as Minnie's protests fell on deaf ears.

"Well, thank you," Minnie said humbly. "I shall cherish it I promise, and thank you all for risking everything to save us. I for one will never forget you."

Kissing them on the cheek one by one, Minnie said her goodbyes. "Now be sure to buckle up in those whirly birds, won't you?" she advised them in parting. "Take care now, take care!"

The medic was ordered to escort Minnie to her room while his colleagues assembled on the roof terrace, bagging and tagging the bloodied and lifeless profiteers of this sickening infant 'chop shop' as they often jokingly referred to it.

"Are you sure you'll be alright?" the medic asked at Minnie's hotel room door. "You know I'd be much happier if you were examined more thoroughly."

"Young man," Minnie replied, still very much shaken by the night's harrowing events but resolute netherthelesss. "I truly appreciate your concerns, honestly I do, but I come from a bygone generation of Brits that were repeatedly bombed out of our homes, forced to endure great hardship through poverty, rationing and consequently hunger during the darkest of dark times. But I'm still here when so many perished, so so many." Her head bowed at the thought of the fallen, many of them children in the eyes of their grieving mothers, and remembered only briefly with the respectful purchase of a paper poppy.

"I'm sorry I didn't mean…" The medic stammered, "I was just—"

"—Oh it's alright, I know you mean well." Minnie smiled, caressing his cheek. "But I'll be fine, you get on home, and thank you once again."

Minnie's steadfast resolve and sheer backbone touched the young serviceman deeply. "No, thank *you*." He smiled, leaning forward to hug her, finding comfort in that briefest of moments and vowing to visit his estranged grandparents on his return and put an end to the petty family feud that had driven a wedge between them. "Goodbye Minnie," he said in parting. "You take care, and give my love to your sister, you hear?"

"I will. Goodbye," Minnie said, waving as she pushed open her door. "Byyyyyyyye!"

Closing the door behind her, Minnie clutched her pounding head and felt her way towards the bedroom without turning on the light. "Essy?" she whispered, looking across at the outline of her sister's back. "Essy dear?"

Esther had slept through the evening's traumatic events, purring contentedly as she strolled hand-in-hand with her beloved Jack along the scenic Brighton promenade, a recurring dream of late and one she hated to wake from.

"Psssst, Essy dear," Minnie said a little louder. "You will simply die when I tell you what happened to me this evening, Essyyyy." She reached to nudge her motionless sister. "Esther darling, please it's important!"

"Mmmmm?" Esther mumbled, burying her head further beneath the duvet.

"Essy!" Minnie insisted. "I've been—" Before she could describe her grievous injuries, her sister partially came to.

"Minnie, go to sleep!" she said, seething as Jack's image began to fade. "Whatever it is it can wait!"

"But, but Essy, you don't understand," Minnie pleaded with a hand pressed to her bandaged head in an attempt to relieve the throbbing.

Peshwari Nans

"Go... To... Sleep!" Esther growled, repeating her late husband's name over and over in her head as though to call him back for one more ride on the waltzers and to enjoy a lap full of vinegar-drenched chips on their favourite bench, whilst fending off the tenacious Herring gulls.

"Oh," Minnie said, turning away and rolling back her own sheets. "Alright Essy, I'm sorry I woke you."

Minnie's words fell on deaf ears, with Esther having sprinted back to the spot where she had left her Jack. "Jaaaack, Jaaaack!" she called, turning this way and that, but her love was nowhere to be seen. In fact the promenade was now deserted and more importantly derelict, the waltzers which once whirled them together in a heady daze with their monotonous jaunty jingle standing idle behind a shabby advertisement hoarding. "Jaaaaaaaack!" she called, now frantic and restless in her bed.

Her dream, her beautiful dream, was barely recognizable as she ran to where the chip shop once stood, the path ankle-deep in litter and heavily overgrown with bramble and briar which tore at her nylons and the hem of her pleated skirt. Minnie's intervention had destroyed the fantasy she had so lovingly conjured and crafted to perfection, and her day trip was now a hellish nightmare trapped in a post-apocalyptic resort, and, worst of all, her Jack was gone. Again.

Minnie knew nothing of her sister's heartache and anguish under the cover of darkness, for her screams were inaudible to those on the outside of this windswept wasteland where it seemed she would wander lost and alone, calling his name a thousand times until morning, when she woke up exhausted and wet through, having turned three dozen times during the course of the night.

"Thank God," she said croakily whilst wrestling her legs free of the tangled sheets and vowing rashly to never close her eyes again for fear of returning to that place of torment and eternal damnation. Shaken somewhat by her restless encounter, Esther stretched out her arms, yawned and breathed a sigh of relief, then looked around for a familiar face to reassure her that all was just as it should be.

"GOOD LORD, MINNIE!" she screeched, horrified immediately by her sleeping sister's battered appearance.

"MINNIE DARLING, WHAT HAPPENED?"

During the night her sister's condition had deteriorated dramatically, and the trauma she had suffered at the hands of the now deceased Rinze Hoff, had manifested into a severe swelling to the visible side of her face, which was yellow and blue in colour and also completely encompassing her right eye. The bandaging applied by the diligent army medic was seeped in congealed blood, as were her pillow and pressed cotton sheets.

"MINNIE!" Esther cried, clambering hastily from her bed, mortified and clueless as to the root cause. After all, Esther reasoned, she'd been fine when they last spoke, but then again, this was Minnie. "Christ, Minnie darling, Minnie, Minnie!" She nudged her sister but failed to wake her. "Min my love, what on earth have you been doing? Miniiiiiiie!"

Her sister let out a pitiful whimper, reassuring Esther she was still with her, for the time being at least.

Opening her undamaged eye, Minnie reached for her sister. "Essy, Essyyy," she groaned, wincing as the slightest movement sent an electrifying spasm through her head.

"Minnie, please, tell me what happened?" Esther begged. "Who did this to you? Tell me, darling?"

Minnie reached for the tablet beside her bed. "Baaaaad men," she slurred, tapping at the screen.

"What is it?" Esther asked, turning the device this way and that. "What am I looking at? You know I'm no good with this sort of thing."

Peshwari Nans

Minnie raised her pounding head from her pillow to focus with her one bleary eye. "Baaaad men," she said again whilst clumsily opening the tablet's gallery of pictures.

"What's this?" Esther asked. "Minnie is that the roof, for heaven's sake? Please tell me you haven't been on the roof. You have, haven't you? And you fell, didn't you? Yes that's it. Minnie, you fell from the roof! My God, Min, whatever possessed you?"

Minnie shook her head from side to side and in doing so burst several more blood vessels close to the base of her brain. "MMMMMMMM?" she whimpered, clawing at the bedcovers and grabbing her sister's hand.

"Oh darling, darling, what can I do?" Esther asked, now frantic. "You need a doctor, yes, yes, that's it I'll fetch a doctor. Wait there darling, I'll be right back!"

Minnie shook her head again but was unable to utter a single legible word as her fretting sister dragged her heavy coat over her nightclothes, paying very little attention to her haphazard buttoning. "Really Minnie!" she cursed. "Will you ever learn? I thought your reckless stunt at the municipal baths was foolish and juvenile, but this, Minnie, this time you really have gone too far. I mean look at you? You could have got yourself killed, for Pete's sake!"

Minnie shook her head and gestured to the discarded tablet to set matters straight, but her sister would not hear of it.

"Falling from the roof!" she exclaimed, shaking her head in disbelief. "Minnie dear, have you lost your mind?" she then asked, tugging her carpet slippers onto the wrong feet in her exasperated state. "I'll ask reception to send for a doctor right away," she told Minnie, who had suddenly lapsed into unconsciousness. "That's it, you get some rest," Esther said, heading for the door. "Damn it!" she cursed en route, before kicking off the ill-fitting slippers and scurrying along the corridor towards the elevator, with the vision of her blundering sister toppling from the rooftop and miraculously surviving the fall of an estimated ninety feet or more.

With a resounding 'DING' the elevator ground to a halt at the lobby level and the doors slid open.

"What the...?" Esther remarked when confronted by a bank of restless reporters occupying the majority of the foyer.

"MINNIE, MINNIE, MINNIE, OVER HERE!" the camera-wielding paparazzi called, dazzling Esther with a barrage of flashes. "NO, WAIT!" a Swedish reporter yelled over the others. "That's not Minnie, that's Esther, ESTHER, ESTHER! WHERE IS YOUR SISTER, WHERE'S MINNIE?"

"YES, WHERE'S MINNIE?" another journo called, jostling the competition.

"What?" Esther asked, dazed and confused. "What? What do you want?"

"We want Minnie. Where's Minnie?" came the resounding reply. "Is she coming down?"

"No, no, she isn't!" Esther snapped, pushing her way towards the front desk. "She needs a doctor right away!"

"Yes we heard," the Chinese Chief of Police replied. "Esther let me tell you, your sister, she very brave lady."

"Brave?" Esther remarked, pushing a lens from her face. "I'd hardly use the word brave where Minnie's concerned. Irresponsible, now there's a more fitting summarization, or moronic even! Now if you'll kindly step aside please, my halfwit of a sister is in need of medical attention, out of my way I said!"

"I'd hardly call her a halfwit," a British news anchor replied. "Your sister saved those babies, Esther! She saved them all!"

Peshwari Nans

"Babies?" Esther said, spinning round to confront him. "What are you talking about? There were no babies. My sister fell from the roof, didn't she?"

The world's press had once again got wind of a scoop concerning the Peshwari Nans, or Minnie to be more precise. Her impassioned plea for help had been streamed throughout the world, sending their notoriety rocketing into the stratosphere. A-list celebs, rock gods and world leaders alike saw their popularity dwindle as millions upon millions turned away to follow these two remarkable retirees.

"PLEASE COULD SOMEBODY CALL A DOCTOR?" Esther yelled above the murmuring media circus.

"Madam," an Asian gentleman said, pushing his way towards her. "I am a doctor. How may I be of service?"

"Oh thank heavens." Esther sighed. "It's my sister Minnie, she's fallen from the roof, well, at least I think she has, now I'm not so sure. Can you please take a look at her?"

"Yes, yes, of course, I'll fetch my bag at once," the doctor said, scurrying to the front desk where he had just proceeded to check in. The news hounds surrounded Esther, hungry for the lowdown on her sister's condition.

"ESTHER, ESTHER, OVER HERE!" they again pleaded. "Esther, how serious are your sister's injuries?"

"I'm sorry!" Esther told them, tugging the doctor's arm towards the elevator. "I can't do this right now, all I can say is that Minnie is hurt, she's hurt really badly and I for one am worried sick about her, so if you'll excuse me."

She left the network crews grappling frenziedly for their phones to relay the disastrous news to their editors and director generals, who in turn ordered the front pages of every tabloid and broadsheet held and the story of Minnie's heroism and subsequent suffering sensationally relayed to their deeply concerned readership. Radio and TV shows were interrupted simultaneously, just as they were when the deaths of JFK and Princess Diana brought the planet to a complete standstill, and in time-honoured tradition, the story became contorted and grossly exaggerated, with every 'Chinese whisper' as it were, with sensational headlines such as: 'Minnie Maimed by Mob Maniac' and 'National Treasure at Death's Door'.

An attack of this heinous nature on any senior citizen would undoubtedly incur the wrath and condemnation of every decent law abiding citizen, but somehow this time it was different: it was Minnie, a household name who had, just like her sister Esther, become everybody's Nan, symbols of all that was good and sweet in the world, when all around there was war, famine, poverty, disease, and the perpetual threat of unemployment. The Nans had given their followers renewed hope in uncertain times, a reason to believe once again in the impossible.

"This way," Esther said, hurrying from the elevator with the doctor in tow. "Here." She fumbled for her key, her hands trembling somewhat.

"Please, allow me," the doctor said, taking the fob from her and letting them both in.

"Minnie, Minnie dear, I've brought a doctor," Esther called, heading through the lounge toward the bedroom, but to her shock and bemusement Minnie's bed was empty, with the bloodied sheets turned back. "Minnie!" she called, flitting around the room. "Minnie dear!"

"There!" the doctor said, following a faint impassioned moaning.

"Oh dear God!" Esther cried, brushing past him and dashing to the bathroom. "Minnie? Minnie it's me!" The door was ajar but jammed for some reason. "Minnie darling, are you alright?" she asked. Esther suddenly caught sight of the bathroom mirror, seeing her sister lying slumped beside the bathtub. "MINNIE!" she shrieked, pushing at the door. "Doctor, please help me!"

In Esther's absence, Minnie had foolishly ventured from her bed to the bathroom in order to see for herself the extent of her facial bruising. But being unsteady on her feet and with her head spinning, she took a tumble and found herself too weak to stand. "Essy," she groaned on hearing her sister's voice, her speech still very much impaired.

"Minnie I can't get in, what's wrong?" Esther asked, anguished and fearful.

The doctor dropped to his knees, reached around the door and slid Minnie's feet to one side, allowing Esther to slip inside. "Oh, Minnie darling," she said, lowering herself beside her sister, using the washbasin for support. "Doctor, hurry!" she called, beckoning him in. "You have to help her, please!"

Crouching at her side in the now cramped bathroom, the oriental doctor first offered Minnie a few words of comfort: "Hello Madam my name is Kim and I am here to help you. I am a doctor and I would like to examine you if I may."

Minnie nodded while Esther clung to her, caressing her hand lovingly. "It's alright dear," she assured her, "Essy's here, shhhh, shhhhhh," she added when Minnie tried to speak. "You should have stayed in bed you silly, silly girl."

"May I ask how old she is?" the doctor asked Esther, in order to ascertain his patient's physical capabilities.

"She's eighty-four," Esther replied, smiling at her sister, "going on eighteen, aren't you dear?"

"Minnie?" the doctor said, leaning over her. "Minnie, do you mind if I remove the bandages?"

Minnie agreed and raised her head an inch or so from the tiled floor with the help of Esther. "Oh you poor thing," her sister said, looking on as the dressing was unwound and the horror beneath revealed.

"Okay madam," the doctor said, opening his bag and removing a roll of fresh wadding. "I need to clean some of this blood from your head to see more clearly. I'll be as gentle as I can, I promise." Running the basin taps for a moment he soaked the wadding in warm water and dabbed at Minnie's head wound. "She has severe swelling," he told Esther, "I am concerned that there may be some internal bleeding, madam, we must get your sister to a hospital right away."

"Oh please, no!" Esther gasped, clasping her free hand to her mouth.

"Right away, Madam!" the doctor reiterated with a sense of urgency. "Quickly! You must call for an ambulance, there is no time to waste."

"Yes, yes, of course!" Esther said, gripping the basin once again. "Minnie my love, I'll be right back, I promise," she said, first kissing her frail sister's hand before stepping over her and rushing into the lounge, while the doctor applied a cool press to Minnie's near unrecognizable face.

The injury Minnie had so bravely dismissed the previous night was fast becoming a far more serious affair, exacerbated of course by her advancing years.

"Hello? Hello?" Esther called, jabbing at the telephone buttons with the receiver pressed to her ear. "Hello? Hello? Yes it's Mrs Reynolds in room two-seventeen," she told the receptionist. "Yes, that's right, Esther," she added when questioned by the girl, who was also a huge fan of the Peshwari Nans. "Never mind the Peshwari nonsense!" Esther snapped. "We need an ambulance right now, and hurry girl, hurry!"

"An ambulance!" the receptionist gasped. "For Minnie?"

"Yes, yes, for Minnie!" Esther barked, gripping the receiver. "Now hurry, please!"

Several reporters close by had overheard the young Chinese receptionist utter the words 'ambulance' and

'Minnie', and pretty soon the entire hotel lobby was in complete pandemonium. The startled receptionist was besieged and questioned vigorously by a dozen hungry news hounds, thrusting microphones and mobiles in her face. "IS SHE ALRIGHT?" they asked. "HOW'S MINNIE?"

"Please, please!" the girl replied, shielding her eyes from the flashing cameras. "I must phone for ambulance, she need hospital. Minnie! Minnie need hospital!"

Again the rumours rapidly circulated among the ever increasing media representatives, one or two conveying back home the information that one of the Peshwari Nans was now in fact deceased.

"No, no, she not dead!" the receptionist called, waving a hand with her telephone poised. "Minnie alive for now, but need hospital!"

She called the nearest hospital and requested an ambulance and paramedic, ASAP. "Yes, Yes the Komodo Dragon Hotel, come now please!" she told them, whilst swatting a microphone from under her nose.

Esther left the receiver dangling and hurried back to the bathroom. "How is she, doctor? How's my sister?" she asked, shuffling in beside them and handing the doctor a cushion she had wrenched in passing from the sofa.

"I have given her something for the pain," the doctor informed her, slipping the cushion beneath Minnie's head. "The bruising will subside, but your sister must undergo a thorough medical examination at the hospital to assess whether or not she needs surgery."

"Surgery?" Esther gasped as the enormity of her sister's condition came to light. "Why doctor, why would Minnie need surgery? What's wrong with her? Tell me, doctor?"

"Please try to remain calm," the doctor said, concerned now for Esther. "Did you call for an ambulance?"

"Yes, yes, of course I did," Esther snapped. "But you haven't answered my question. What's wrong with Minnie, doctor?"

"Well," the doctor said, hesitating. "I am hoping it is just mild concussion, which would explain the dizziness and possibly the fall."

"And if it isn't?" Esther insisted. "What else could it be?"

"Madam, I don't wish to alarm you," the doctor said, lowering his voice. "Your sister is not a young woman as you well know."

"Neither am I," Esther said, angered at his presumption, "but I'll have you know, young man, that we are far from infirm, and my sister here is as fit as a flea." She looked own at her groaning sibling. "I said you're as fit as a flea dear, aren't you?"

Minnie raised a thumb and half a smile.

"So come on, out with it, doctor," Esther said, pressing the medic to answer. "If it isn't just concussion, what else could it be, eh?"

"Bleeding in or around the brain," the doctor told her. "In cases of severe trauma, a haemorrhage can occur when blood vessels or arteries burst, causing localized bleeding."

"Haemorrhage!" Esther said, shaken by his terminology.

"Yes, sometimes leading to a stroke," the doctor continued. "But we must not jump to conclusions. The hospital will undoubtedly provide a more accurate assessment."

"Oh, Minnie dear." Esther sighed, sitting with her sister once again. "What's this I hear about babies? I thought you'd fallen from the roof."

Minnie raised her eyebrows at the absurdity of her sister's assumption. "No Essy, the babies," she said, slurring her words and reaching out to her.

"I'm here, dear," Esther said reassuringly. "Don't worry, we'll get you to hospital and straightened out in no time."

In the foyer below there was a frenzied surge as the ambulance arrived to the sound of sirens, as cameramen and reporters alike jostled for position in readiness for Minnie's emergence.

Paramedics hastily lowered the wheels on a bed trolley and fought their way towards the elevator. "Room two-seventeen," the receptionist told them, rounding the counter to lead the way, illuminated by a thousand watts of halogen light beamed by bustling broadcasting teams.

"Hellooooo," the receptionist called, entering the sisters' room. "The ambulance has arrived."

"In here!" Esther called as the doctor rose to greet them and briefly explained his basic understanding of the situation.

"Okay, thank you," the paramedic replied, placing a hand on Esther's back. "I'm sorry madam, I am going to have to ask you to step outside."

"Oh, oh, right, yes of course," Esther said, leaning firstly to kiss Minnie's forehead. "I'll be right outside, dear," she said softy. "I'm sorry, but could you help me?" she asked the paramedic, her back having seized somewhat. The paramedic helped Esther to her feet and out of the bathroom, before donning his latex gloves in order to examine Minnie prior to moving her.

"Hello madam," he said gently, raising Minnie's chin from the cushion to see the extent of her bruising, which now covered two-thirds of her face. "With your permission I am going to shine a light into your eyes."

Minnie nodded, although she offered only one open eye, the opposite one being puffed up and clamped shut.

"Okay, okay," the paramedic continued, taking a closer look at her cleaned but seeping wound. "My colleague and I are going to get you out of here and take you to the hospital, is that okay?"

Again Minnie nodded, desperate to be off the bathroom floor and growing tired of the prodding and poking.

Once she was loosely strapped and covered with a warm crimson blanket, Minnie was wheeled from their room and into the elevator, with her sister and a hastily packed bag close at her side. "Oh I almost forgot to tell you, dear," Esther told her sister as they descended. "There are one or two people here to see you."

The elevator doors opened to a riotous scene, with crews pushing and shoving one another in order to catch a glimpse of the battered heroine, each of them under enormous pressure from their employers to pip the opposition to the post in a ratings war that could literally make or break an entire organization.

"Minnie, Minnie, do you have a word or two for your fans?" one pushy reporter asked, getting a little too close for Esther's liking.

"Get away from her!" she snapped, lashing out with her bag. "All of you, step aside, step aside, for heaven's sake!"

Chinese police officers forced the crowd in two with batons and lined a path to the waiting ambulance, with every second of the chaotic proceedings captured and again aired live across all networks.

Meanwhile on the opposite side of the globe, from whence the sisters came, Elizabeth had just been overpowered by four porters in the day room of the secure facility she'd been housed in. She had caught sight of her heavily bandaged aunty on the wall-mounted television and once again completely flipped, flinging chairs about the place and screaming at the top of her voice.

"WHEN WILL IT END?" she yelled. "WHEN WILL IT END?"

The struggling porters wrestled Elizabeth into a straightjacket for her own protection, and that of her fellow patients.

"WHY ARE THEY DOING THIS TO MEEEEEEEEEEEEEE!" she screeched, salivating and kicking out at anything within range. "WHYYYYYYYYYYYY!"

A doctor rushed to assist, brandishing a hypodermic loaded with a powerful tranquillizer.

"STAY AWAY FROM ME!" Elizabeth stormed, catching sight of the syringe. "NO, NO, NO LET ME GO, LET ME GO!"

Suddenly she broke free and ran around the day room, shackled within the jacket with the porters and doctor in pursuit, ramming the barred windows in an attempt to break free.

"Elizabeth, Elizabeth please calm down," an approaching porter said in a soothing tone. "It's alright, nobody wants to hurt you."

Elizabeth ducked behind a crowd of emotionally traumatized inmates, barging one or two of them towards the approaching porters. "STAY AWAY FROM ME!" she screamed. "I MEAN IT! YOU STAY THE HELL AWAY FROM ME, YOU BASTARDS!"

Rushing the disturbed Elizabeth, the porters soon regained control and bundled her from the room shortly after she had been administered with a double dose of sedative. Escorted back to her padded room, Elizabeth was fastened down to her bed by her wrists and ankles and the door was then bolted on the outside.

"WHEN WILL IT EEEEEEEEND!" she cried, tugging at the sturdy buckles and shaking her head violently from side to side.

Due to Elizabeth's ever increasing psychotic episodes, all visitations had been suspended whilst various pharmaceutical remedies were given to her in an attempt to calm and eventually eradicate the demons within her. Her anxious son Richard had kept the news of his mother's mental breakdown from Esther and Minnie, assuming that the duo had far more pressing matters to contend with. And of course he was right.

Minnie was driven at high speed a kilometre away to Kashi Hospital, where further news crews were already encamped in anticipation of her arrival, and after a barrage of questions, Minnie delighted them with a raised hand and an extended thumb. This image from beneath the crimson blanket prompted a deafening cheer the world over, when many thought that all was lost. It was as iconic a moment as Neil Armstrong's lunar footprint or the collapsing of the Berlin wall. It would literally write a new chapter in the history of such publications as *Time* and *Okay* magazines. This time the gathered members of the media parted respectfully, giving Minnie a resounding round of applause that lasted long after she was wheeled inside, where a nursing team was waiting to admit her.

"Can I go with her, please?" Esther asked, as her sister was whisked along a maze of corridors.

"Of course," a nurse replied. "We at the Kashi Hospital are honoured to have you and I for one will see to it that your sister receives the very best of care during your stay with us."

"Why thank you, dear." Esther smiled. "But we aren't looking for handouts or special privileges. I'm sure there are many patients here just as deserving as my Minnie, but thank you all the same."

Minnie was taken to the hospital's Intensive Care Unit, where she was examined more closely, before it was decided that a cranial CT scan was necessary to detect any potential inner bleeding which, if left untreated, could undoubtedly prove fatal. When the scanning process was explained to Minnie, she immediately became agitated and attempted to climb from her bed. "Minnie, please," Esther said, taking her arm. "It's for your own good, darling."

"No, Essy, no!" Minnie said, shaking her head and wrestling with her sister. "I'm fine!"

"Minnie dear, you are far from fine," Esther insisted. "You know it and I know it and so do these good doctors. So please do as they say, Minnie, please!"

In June of 2007, Minnie has been admitted to the Royal London Hospital at Whitechapel after repeated nosebleeds, and consequently a CAT scan was advised and she willingly agreed to it, after enduring weeks of the frustrating condition, with outbreaks causing anguish and embarrassment, like those aboard the bus or during a particularly intimate interlude with her former suitor, Cyril. But the procedure, which generally takes between ten and twenty minutes, turned into quite an ordeal after the computerised tomography machine suffered a series of mechanical and electrical malfunctions. At one point the radiation that Minnie was being exposed to increased to five times the clinically acceptable level, causing extreme nausea and vomiting.

The cause of the bleeds had eventually been diagnosed as hypertension, or high blood pressure, and Minnie was advised to make several alterations to her diet to counteract it, such as having a reduction in the amount of salt she'd habitually shake over her fish-and-chips, increased physical activity, and a cutting down of her sweet sherry intake. This had been a regime she had rigidly adhered to for several months, after cultivating a deep mistrust of medical radioactive technology.

"You must, Minnie," Esther added, looking to the nurses for support.

"She's right, Miss Minnie," one of them said, fetching a paper gown. "If you wish I can give you a mild sedative to help you relax."

Minnie was backed against her bed with nowhere to go. "I promise you will not feel a thing," the nurse added, handing Minnie the gown. "I can also arrange for some music to be played if you like. Many of our patients say it helps them to remain calm."

"Oooh, have you any Sinatra?" Esther asked, knowing the crooner was a firm favourite of her sister's. "My sister simply adores him, don't you dear? I said don't you dear?"

"Ahhhh sorry, no," the nurse replied whilst tugging at Minnie's clothing. "We have very very good musician for you, Yang Liu, Gigi Leung, Shen Sinyan and my favourite Chan Wing-wah. He very good, very very good."

"Chan Wing-wah?" Esther said, utterly bemused. "Does he do anything from the rat pack? You know, Sammy Davis? Dean Martin?"

"No no no." The nurse laughed. "Sorry. Only Chinese." Her associate then leaned and whispered into the nurse's ear and retrieved a CD from her bag. "Ahhhh yes of course, of course!" the nurse said with a smile. "What was I thinking? We have Po Po!"

"Po Po?" Esther said quizzically. "Who on earth is Po Po?"

"Not *who*," the grinning nurse replied, clutching the CD to her breast. "*What.*"

"Okay?" Esther again asked with a huff. "Well, what is Po Po?"

Each of the nurses fell about laughing, astonished that there was a living soul who had not heard of their beloved idol.

"Never mind," the nurse said, slipping the CD into a player. "You will like, I promise you."

Peshwari Nans

"Well, whatever," Esther said dismissively. "Right Minnie, let's get you out of those clothes."

Minnie, although filled with trepidation, relented and changed into the disposable surgical gown and approached the CT room door. But she paused with her spine tense and her heels glued to the floor so to speak.

"Minnie please, it's for your own good," her sister reminded her. "Besides, it'll be over before you know it."

Minnie shook her head with a look of dread in her one good eye.

"I tell you what." Esther smiled. "I'll come in with you and hold your hand. How does that sound?"

Minnie smiled and nodded but the nurse intervened. "I'm sorry, but that is not possible," she informed them.

"Why ever not?" Esther asked defensively.

"Only the patient," the nurse replied. "Because of the radiation, you see."

"To hell with the radiation!" Esther exclaimed, taking her sister's hand. "Whatever it is you're going to do to my sister you can do to me too, with my blessing, I might add."

"But Mrs Esther," the nurse explained. "I cannot subject you to radiation unnecessarily. We have rules here at the Kashi, as I'm sure you have in your country. I'm sorry."

Esther was about to retaliate once again when Minnie this time intervened: "Essy," she said, grasping the door handle. "I'll do it, please don't come inside."

"But, but Minnie, I…" Esther said before Minnie raised a finger to her sister's lips to silence her.

"Wait for me," Minnie simply said before entering with a nurse.

"Well of course I'll wait!" Esther called after her. "I'm not going anywhere without you, I promise."

The door was closed in Esther's face and she was directed to a viewing window, where she stood wringing her hands and watching her apprehensive sister being talked through the process before the nurse herself left her alone in the room. Esther tapped on the glass and waved to let Minnie know she was close at hand. Minnie attempted a smile in return, but deep down she was petrified.

Lying on the padded table, Minnie closed her eyes and waited as the circular tomography machine began to hum and move towards her, shining a red crosshair laser down onto her face. Heeding the nurse's strict instructions, Minnie remained motionless, breathing steadily.

However, moments later she completely broke the scanning protocol and fell about laughing, although it pained her to do so, when a speaker in the ceiling above her linked to the CD player outside began playing as promised the nurse's suggested soothing song, a firm favourite with the entire nation, having remained at the top of the Chinese charts for an unprecedented thirteen months.

The smash hit, a jaunty tale about a mythical magic panda named Po Po that lived high up in the mountains in a giant red shoe, had propelled the class of under-fives who had recorded it into the record books, and overnight 'Po Po mania' was born. The panda's image was plastered the length and breadth of the country, from cereal packets to billboards, earning the young female teacher that penned the delightful but dotty ditty, millions in sales of merchandising alone. Every child in the land had to have a 'Po Po' backpack, tee shirt, lunch box and bicycle. Television and movie deals were signed within a matter of days of the CD's release.

"Please, you must remain still," a voice called to Minnie over a separate loudspeaker.

"How can I?" Minnie laughed, rolling from side to side, clutching her sides. "What on earth is that?"

Several nurses swayed outside, singing along to the ridiculous but strangely hypnotic lyrics, accompanied by a piercing penny whistle, sounding like that of the fabled Pied Piper of Hamelin.

Esther listened too, her smirk turning to a chuckle and then full blown laughter until she too, mouthed the words:

"*High up on a mountain*
there lives a magic bear
beside a crystal fountain
you will find him there,
he's fearless and he's humble
and wise beyond compare
if you hear the mountains rumble
you'll know that Po Po's therrrrrrre"

"Stop, stop!" Minnie called, with a tear on her cheek and a knot in her stomach. "Oh please stop!"

Esther stood transfixed at Po Po's popularity, every nurse, doctor and surgeon within earshot immediately stopped what they were doing and swayed in time with their hands in the air. She too, tapped a toe in time to the ensuing ludicrous verses.

"You're all mad!" She laughed, swaying with them. "Only in China," she added. "Only in China."

The nurses were eventually forced to cut short the tale of Po Po the Panda in order to calm a now hysterical Minnie, and they proceeded with the CT scan as scheduled, but that was to prove more difficult than they had imagined, with their patient humming to the mesmerising melody that had been firmly implanted in her head: "*He's fearless and he's humble,*" she began to slur, "*And wise beyond compaaaaare*"

"Mrs Minnie, please!" the nurse called to her over the loudspeaker. "You must remain perfectly still, Mrs Minnie!"

"I'm trying," Minnie replied, trying to blot out all thoughts of Po Po and his mountain home.

Peshwari Nans

After several aborted attempts, Minnie settled and a successful scan was taken. "You are finished Mrs Minnie," a smiling nurse told her, entering the room and helping her from the table.

"There dear," Esther said, wrapping an arm around her emerging sister. "That wasn't so bad, was it?"

Minnie was escorted to a private ward and helped into bed while the results of her scan were analysed.

"You'll be fine, dear," Esther said reassuringly whilst plumping Minnie's pillow and fussing over her.

It was then that it began, the seemingly endless procession of flower-laden delivery men and women, entering the ward with baskets, balloons and bouquets of all shapes, colours and sizes.

"What the...?" Esther gasped as the room filled with scented blooms sent from well-wishers the world over, each carrying messages of love and support to their beloved Minnie, their adopted Nan, whom they had taken to their hearts and idolised.

"Are they for me?" Minnie asked, reaching to pluck a card from a floral heart sent from 'Sheila and the Crawley Hells Angels', the band of motorcyclists whom the sisters had encountered at the Nürburgring during the German leg of their journey. The card simply read: *We love you Nanna, stay strong.*

"Ahhhhhh, that's nice." Minnie smiled.

"Oh look, dear!" Esther said, opening a card from Minnie's previous admirer Ludvik, the father of the moonshine-brewing Monique. "It's from Ludvik."

"Ooooh, what does it say?" Minnie said as the nurses stood open-mouthed and jostled by further floral arrivals.

"Well, he sends his best wishes and..." Esther began.

"And?" Minnie asked. "And what, Essy?"

Peshwari Nans

Esther's cheeks flushed as she read on to herself. "The filthy beast!" she exclaimed, slamming the card closed against her chest.

"Oooh let me see," Minnie said, reaching out.

"No dear, I'm sorry," Esther warned her. "It could have a devastating effect on your blood pressure, and we both know where that could lead." She was making a reference to Minnie's former nosebleeds and the whole CT scan debacle. "Maybe another time," she added, handing her sister a pink fluffy bear sent by the Russian troops they had encountered en route in the Ukraine, with an accompanying card containing some three hundred signatures.

"Oh how lovely," Minnie said, quite overcome with emotion. "But how did they know?"

"I think that lot may have had something to do with it," Esther said, pointing out the hordes of camera-wielding journalists camped right outside the window.

"Oh hellooooo!" Minnie said, giving them a wave and then wincing once again.

"Be still, will you?" Esther barked, tucking Minnie's sheets tightly under her mattress to restrict her movements. "You're in no fit state for acrobatics, my dear."

Along with the flowers, parcels of fresh fruit and provisions arrived, as well as warm clothes, including a staggering forty-five scarves, seventy pairs of mittens and enough additional knitwear gifted from fellow pensioners to last a lifetime.

Soon a doctor squeezed his way into the room, showering himself in pollen and petals in doing so. "Ahh Mrs Minnie, there you are," he said, peering over the mountain of gifts. "I have the results of your CT scan."

"What is it, Doctor?" Esther asked hastily. "Is she alright? Is Minnie alright?"

"Well," the doctor replied, plucking an image of Minnie's brain from his folder.

"What do you mean, well?" Esther blurted out. "Well what? What's wrong? What aren't you telling us?"

"Essy, let the man speak," Minnie insisted. "Do excuse my sister, Doctor," she added. "She means well."

"I understand." The doctor smiled.

"He's hiding something, Minnie!" Esther again said, theorising and cutting the doctor short. "Well, out with it! You can't pull the wool over our eyes, she's my sister and I demand to know what it is you're trying to hide!"

"Madam, I assure you," the doctor said in his defence.

"You haven't assured me of anything!" Esther stormed, taking a step too far to protect her sister. "Will somebody please tell me what the hell's going on around here?"

"Essy, he's trying!" Minnie snapped. "Now button it and let the man speak! You're giving me heartburn with your constant jabbering. I'm sorry, Doctor, you were saying?"

"Well," Esther huffed. "Excuse me!"

"Yes, as I was saying," the doctor said. "We have the results."

"Well get on with it, man!" Esther again intervened.

"And," the doctor added, a little rattled by Esther's aggressiveness, "there is very little cause for concern. A little fluid and swelling around the brain, but nothing we cannot treat with ice and anti inflammatories."

"You mean," Esther said, open mouthed, "you mean she's going to be alright?"

"Yes, yes, of course," the doctor said with a smile. "I predict a full recovery within forty-eight hours, but, er," he added looking around the ward, "we may have to move Mrs Minnie to a larger room to accommodate her gifts."

"Ohhhh, Minnie!" Esther said, dropping onto the bed beside her and scooping her sister into her arms.

"Ow, ow, owww!" Minnie squealed when Esther pulled her to her chest. "I'm alright Essy, you heard the doctor." she told her. "A handful of happy pills and a packet of frozen sprouts and I'll be as right as rain." She then beckoned to a nurse. "Right. Now young lady, if I'm to stay here we need to discuss my dietary requirements. I trust you have a vegan option? If not, I'll be taking it up with the board of governors."

Esther looked the bewildered nurse in the eye. "You have my deepest sympathy," she told her, knowing full well that her sister's stay at the Kashi Hospital would indeed be a memorable one.

Over the course of the next two days Esther travelled to and from the hospital, keeping tabs on her sister, each time running the gauntlet of the paparazzi and media hordes while Minnie on the other hand, savoured the attention and adoration that poured her way from hospital staff and patients alike.

During the day, restless Minnie would wander from her private room, visiting the adjacent wards and distributing the overspill of flowers from her generous well-wishers and sitting with the terminally ill, sharing her recent experiences with them to bring a little light into their darkest hour.

"So I said to my sister," she explained to a young leukaemia sufferer as she shared the tale of their harrowing night spent wandering the German forest. "Trust me, I know what I'm doing."

Minnie and the patient, a terminally-ill teenage lad by the name of Kim, fell about laughing. "Well how was I supposed to know it was a statelite?" she added. The boy coughed and spluttered and only caught his breath when Minnie offered a glass of juice to his lips. "There, I think that's quite enough excitement for one day, young Master Kim," she told him, mopping his chin. "Now you get some rest and I'll pop along and see you later, my love."

The boy's penniless parents had been forced to abandon him at the hospital steps when his medical bills far outweighed their meagre government handouts, and although every effort had been made by the authorities to locate them, the fruitless search was eventually called off and the boy rubber-stamped as an orphan. When Minnie learned of this and the lad's short life expectancy, she endeavoured to help in the only way she could.

"PSSSSSSSST!" she called later that day from her window, summoning a reporter from a leading Chinese newspaper, offering a tell-all interview in exchange for their help in locating Kim's mother and father.

A nationwide hunt was soon set in motion, with every city, town and village canvassed until a distant relative of Kim was finally located, who knew the whereabouts of Mr and Mrs Chung.

"Goood morning, my sweet," Minnie chirped as she attended Kim's bedside the very next day. "I've brought your breakfast, and before you ask, no it isn't those beastly beans. I had a word with matron and got you the chocolate ice cream you wanted. Well, you did say it was your favourite."

The boy, who was now withered and pale, smiled and insisted that Minnie should sit with him and tell him once again how she came to be trapped in the gents lavatory surrounded by a coachload of French footie fans. The tale particularly tickled the terminal teen, and Minnie for that matter, as she lovingly brushed his thinning fringe from his face.

Suddenly Kim reached out to something that was beyond Minnie, behind her.

"What is it? What is it, Kim my love?" she asked, turning round to see his guilt-ridden parents standing at the door. "Oh hello!" she said, rising to greet them, her own wounds having healed considerably by now. "Are you Mr and Mrs Chung?"

The pair nodded solemnly.

"Do come in, please," she told them, beckoning. "Kim has told me so much about you."

The mother ran to his bed with her arms outstretched, while his father remained deeply moved and remorseful. "It's alright," Minnie told him, taking his hand. "Really, it's alright Mr Chung."

Heaping apologies onto their only child, Kim's parents wept continuously, begging for their boy's forgiveness. Minnie brushed the ailing lad's hand. "Kim my sweet, I'll leave you now," she said softly. "I'll pop along and see you later, dear, and if you're up to it, let's have another round of dominoes."

Kim nodded with a smile, while his parents looked on in dismay at the tangle of ventilation tubes and saline drips attached to their son.

"Thank you," Kim's father said, rising to hug Minnie. He looked over his shoulder at his waning child and dropped his head. "You think we are bad parents," he added shamefully. "Maybe you are right."

"No, no, not at all," Minnie insisted. "You did what you thought was best for Kim, so who am I to judge? The fact is that you're here now and Kim is delighted. Look at him."

Kim clung to his mother as he had done as an infant, scrutinising every line on her ashen face, deep furrows formed through years of longing and regret. "My baby, my baby," she said over and over, rocking rhythmically with his head pressed to her chest. Mr Chung bowed and held Minnie's hands to his forehead, shedding several tears onto her fingertips.

"Father!" Kim called, reaching for him. "Father, please!"

"Yes, yes, my son," Mr Chung said, wiping away his tears out of sight and forcing a smile, before the three embraced tighter than ever.

Peshwari Nans

"Minnie!" Kim called, stopping her at the door. "Do you think matron has any more of that delicious chocolate ice cream?"

"Well if she doesn't, my sweet," Minnie promised, "I'll send to the ends of the earth for it—the ends of the earth, I promise you."

Minnie left the reunited family to continue her rounds, having built up quite a list of dependants. "Afternoon Mrs Yoong!" she called cheerfully, entering another ward. "How's your haemorrhoids today?"

Mrs Yoong, a middle aged mother superior, replied with a pained expression.

"Oooh, that bad eh?" Minnie said, rummaging in her pinny for a bottle of baby oil. "Well I'm afraid this won't cure the blighters but it'll certainly help with the chaffing. Oh and Mr Whan!" she then called across the ward. "I managed to get those mucky mags you requested, but don't worry, I wrapped them in brown paper just like you asked—greaseproof of course."

The aged Mr Whan, hospitalised with a kidney disorder, snatched the parcel of top-shelf titillation publications from her and thrust it hastily beneath his bedcovers.

"Oh and I hope you don't mind," Minnie added, without a shred of discretion. "I took the liberty of thumbing through the classifieds in the back pages and telephoning a rather fetching 'bbw' on your behalf." She turned to Mrs Yoong. "That means a 'big beautiful woman', in case you were wondering Mrs Yoong," she called out. "Or is it a 'big buxom woman'? I can't remember. Anyway Mr Whan, I know you like your ladies a little broad across the beam so to speak, so consider it a parting gift, as I'll be leaving in the morning."

Mr Whan's eyes lit up and his temperature soared. "Miss Minnie I, I, can't…" he stammered.

Peshwari Nans

"Yes you can, Mr Whan." Minnie smiled, slipping three Viagra tablets into his hand. "Ahhh here she is now, good afternoon mistress."

A hefty oriental 'hooker' entered the ward. She was wearing black patent knee-length boots, a purple PVC mac that was positively bursting at the seams and had two mother-of-pearl chopsticks speared through a bun on her head. Her face was as round as a watermelon, with a beaming smile which puffed her powdered cheeks. Glimpses of cellulite were clearly visible between her taut buttons, leaving little or nothing to the imagination.

"Mr Whaaaaan, you ready for your bed bath?" she shrieked, tottering on her heels toward his bed, where he sat clutching his sheet tight to his chest, stunned and speechless.

"But, Miss Minnie!" he eventually blurted out.

"You're more than welcome, Mr Whan," Minnie said, drawing the curtains around him and his hired help.

"No, no, no, no, no, no!" he could be heard squealing as Minnie left the ward. And then: "Ahhhhhhh. Yes."

Young Kim lost his fight with leukaemia that evening, and passed away peacefully with Minnie and his mother and father at his bedside, in his final moments managing a smile for his new found friend and for a distant orbiting satellite visible from his window.

Minnie's tears eventually ran dry around 3 a.m. as she lay in her bed unable to sleep, experiencing a bag of mixed emotions from anger to sorrow, to love for the lost child. Sheer exhaustion finally got the better of her and an hour later, she sank into her tear-strewn pillow.

Esther packed that morning at the Komodo Dragon Hotel, having stayed considerably longer than they'd intended. She ascended in the elevator and approached the desk, where a few lingering reporters sat sipping coffee, the majority of them having relocated to the Kashi Hospital.

"I'd like to settle my bill please," she told the girl at the counter, while cameras flashed around her. "Room two-seventeen," she added, sliding the keys across the counter.

"Bill?" the girl replied, checking her records. "There is no bill for room two-seventeen."

"I beg your pardon?" Esther said, peering over the counter at the register. "Of course there's a bill. I've been here since Friday for Pete's sake, room two-seventeen, in the name of Reynolds."

"Yes I know, Mrs Reynolds," the girl said, closing the register. "But I assure you there is nothing to pay for that room."

"But, but, what about the restaurant, and the mini bar?" Esther asked, bemused. "Here, take my card will you?" she offered her credit card.

"Mrs Reynolds," the girl reiterated, "you do not understand. There is no charge to pay. Because of you and your sister the Komodo Dragon Hotel is fully booked for the next fifteen months. Hundreds of people are requesting to stay in room two-seventeen, your room, Mrs Reynolds."

"Oh," Esther replied, taken aback. "I see. Well, thank you I suppose."

"No, thank you," the grinning receptionist replied. "And please come and visit us again any time you choose, anytime Mrs Reynolds. And please give our love to your sister, she's quite a lady."

"Yes," Esther said, pondering. "Yes, I suppose she is."

Esther said her goodbyes after a brief interview in the foyer and followed the bellboy, who eagerly carried her bags.

"Mrs Reynolds?" the lad said as he was loading Vivien. "Mrs Reynolds, may I ask something of you?" he said, straightening his tunic and standing to attention, hastily buffing his cap in the process.

Peshwari Nans

"Of course." Esther smiled. "Ask away dear, I won't bite you know."

"Bite?" the boy said, confused at first. "Oh, oh yes, Mrs Reynolds. I wish to ask a favour if I may?"

"Yes, yes, what is it Chen?" Esther asked as she stood at Vivien's door and checked her wristwatch.

"Mrs Reynolds, my dream," the bellboy explained, rocking on the balls of his feet, "my dream, Mrs Reynolds, ever since I was a small boy, was to fetch and carry the bags of the rich and famous at your London Savoy Hotel. The likes of Richard Branson, Mr Sugar and, dare I say it, Paul O'Grady."

Esther smiled, warming to the lad. "So you're a fan too, are you?" she asked.

"A fan, Mrs Reynolds?" the boy exclaimed. "I was raised by my grandmother, who worships the ground Mr O'Grady walks upon. If I could meet him, Mrs Reynolds." The lad's eyes sparkled. "If I could meet him for coffee or maybe just a selfie, my grandmother would be so so proud of me."

"Well." Esther pondered. "It just so happens that the hotel's owner is rather smitten with my younger, and considerably more promiscuous, sister, so I'd say we may have a little leverage where your case is concerned. Leave it to me, Chen my dear, I'll see what I can do."

"Ohhhhhhh, Mrs Reynolds!" Chen rejoiced, flinging his arms around her. "You are truly everything they say you are and much much more. Be sure to give him my name, won't you? It's Chen, Chen O'Grady—that was my grandmother's idea."

"Well, the woman has taste, Chen, I'll give you that." Esther smirked, lowering herself into the driver's seat. "I dare say I'll see you in London, young man," she added. "Bye bye."

Peshwari Nans

Chen closed Esther's door and punched the air triumphantly. "Oh thank you, Mrs Reynolds, thank you, thank you!"

Watching her leave and waving ecstatically, Chen then raced back inside to hastily pen his letter of resignation and sprint the mile or so to his grandmother's house.

Still relatively uneasy at accepting the Komodo Dragon Hotel's 'gratis' hospitality, Esther pulled into a service station en route to the hospital. "What do you mean, no charge?" she said when visiting the kiosk to pay. "But I've filled my tank. Of course there's a charge."

"No, no charge," the pump attendant replied, employing a friend to take a candid snap of the two of them as proof of her visit to his humble franchise. "No charge," he said, smiling and gesturing to a wall plastered with photographs of himself and visiting A-list celebs, including Mr Schwarzenegger himself, George W. Bush, Oprah, Madonna and now, the pièce de résistance, a Peshwari Nan.

The owner quickly took Arnold's polaroid down from the top spot and replaced it with the picture of him and Esther, and stood in awe of his family of friends, as he so often boasted. "Here!" he said, filling Esther's arms with groceries. "Take these with my blessing, and please, do come again."

Esther wandered back to Vivien dazed, confused and laden with provisions. "How odd," she said, having always paid her way and quite rightly assuming that charity was meant for the needy—in short, those far less fortunate than she was.

"Wait, wait!" the owner called, rushing to Vivien to squeegee the splattered bugs from her windshield and dangle a scented cardboard tree from her rear-view mirror. "Please drive carefully, madam," he added, standing proudly beside his petrol pump and waving to his neighbours. "MY FRIEND!" he called, gesturing to Esther. "A PESHWARI NAN!"

"Yes, well, goodbye," Esther said as the whispering onlookers gathered and headed her way.

Minnie was dressed, packed and waiting in the foyer of the hospital when Esther arrived.

"Hello dear, how are you feeling?" Esther asked, rubbing her sister's back sympathetically. "I am ever so sorry to her about your friend."

"How am I feeling, dear?" Minnie repeated, blowing her nose and tucking her handkerchief into her sleeve before putting on a brave face. "Oh I'm fine. The doctor said he's delighted with my recovery, and look Essy? The bruising is barely noticeable."

"You know what I mean, dear," Esther said, questioning her emotional state.

Minnie sidestepped this prickly subject and approached the Kasha staff, who had assembled to bid her farewell.

"Ladies," she said, addressing a huddled group of diligent nurses. "I must say it's been an absolute pleasure. And Doctor, your bedside manner has been impeccable. You should all be extremely proud of yourselves, extremely proud."

The nurses curtsied respectfully, just as they had done for the visiting Chinese leader several weeks previously.

Esther gathered her sister's belongings and escorted her outside, where she turned and waved up at the numerous fellow patients she had got to know so well in a relatively short space of time, each of them leaning from a window bidding her farewell. There was Mrs Yoong with her bottom-soothing baby oil, Mr Whan, red-faced but eternally grateful, and many many more. But her heart sank a tad when she looked up at the empty window of Kim's room.

Peshwari Nans

Esther looked on, speechless at the outpouring of affection for her sister, that and her own recent freebies bringing home the reality of their unlikely celebrity status.

"Goodbyyyyyye! Goodbyyyyye!" Minnie called from the passenger seat as they drove out of the hospital gates to continue their journey.

"Here, dear," Esther said, handing her sister a packet of cinnamon buns. "You aren't the only one with connections I'll have you know."

Uncharacteristically, Minnie raised a hand and refused, having left the Kashi Hospital with mixed feelings.

"Okay, dear," Esther added, replacing the buns. "I quite understand."

Their onward journey would take them south through rural China, with the mountains of Tibet on the distant horizon. Beyond that formidable formation lay Nepal and its capital Kathmandu, then India, and finally Raipur.

CHAPTER EIGHT

With Esther's daughter Elizabeth now having to be medicated twenty-four-seven following increasingly psychotic episodes, the maximum security hospital where she was now housed had decided she would be an ideal candidate for a revolutionary and altogether groundbreaking new procedure. This was the brainchild of an eminent Swiss Psychologist, Doctor Schultz, and although the procedure had been well received internationally, it had never been trialled in the UK.

The 'Shultz Theorem', as it had become known, consisted of a series of micro-fine electrodes placed strategically about the patient's body, the fingertips and toes etc., and while these were pulsating with seventy-five volts of electricity, images of the patient's childhood were flashed simultaneously before their eyes in an attempt to, as doctor Shultz described it, 'retune and realign their psyche to happier times and hopefully banish all destructive tendencies'.

Early experiments at the Swiss maximum security facility where Dr Shultz worked on multiple murderers, had yielded promising results, with only one in five patients having an adverse reaction and suffering permanent neurological damage. Consequent to this, these unfortunates had to remain incarcerated, and were devoid of all sanity, and also posed an even greater threat to themselves and society as a whole than they did before the treatment.

The risks were high. But in Elizabeth's case the procedure was deemed worth a shot. Richard was asked to gather any such images and possessions from his mother's house that had at one time or another evoked happiness in her life, and more importantly been associated with a state

581

of calm, such as the patchwork throw her mother had knitted her, the holiday snaps from the Greek islands and the lock of Richard's baby hair she lovingly kept in her jewellery box. Together these and other cherished keepsakes, plus the awe-inspiring soundtrack of Humpback whale calves calling to their mothers, were specifically tailored to reconnect Elizabeth with her birth mother.

Administered in three, four-hour stints, the Shultz Theorem had very little effect on Elizabeth in the early stages. But with a little tweaking and fine tuning: namely the replacement of Humpbacks with howling Orangutans, and an additional fifteen volts of electricity, her progress greatly improved. But to ensure complete realignment the procedure would need to be rigorously repeated over a matter of weeks, to guard against the danger of remission.

In the meantime, Minnie and Esther had been making excellent progress at a cruising speed of forty-eight miles per hour with a gusting tail wind, at times pushing them to the mid-fifties. They were heading towards Ngari, situated on the China national highway, the famed G219, which was sometimes known as the Tibet Highway.

It was noticeable that Minnie hadn't been herself since leaving the Kashi Hospital, where she had witnessed the life drain away from young Kim, and another mother grieving for her child caused echoes of her own tragic loss to come to the fore.

"How about a nice cup of tea, dear?" Esther asked in an attempt to lift her sister's spirits. "I know I'm parched. How about you?"

Minnie stared blankly ahead, lost in her thoughts and oblivious to the breathtaking passing scenery.

"Minnie?" Esther asked again. "I said would you like some tea? I have some loose rosehip and elderflower, enough for a generous pot I'd imagine."

Peshwari Nans

Esther pulled over to the side of the road, switched off the engine, and turned to her solemn sister. "Min darling," she said, placing a hand on hers. "What you did for Kim and his parents was simply wonderful. I can't even begin to imagine how awful his death would have been without his family at his bedside. Promise me you'll be there for me when I, well, you know."

"When you what?" Minnie blurted out. "Essy please don't say such things. I don't know what I'd do if you ever left me." She squeezed her sister's hand. "I really don't. I'm as dotty as a dodo, dear and you know it. I'd never cope on my own, Essy, they'd put me in a home, I know they would. Aunt Ethel went into a home and within a week we were cremating her."

"Minnie dear," Ester reminded her sister, "Aunt Ethel had glaucoma if you remember, and she couldn't see further than the end of her nose. The poor dear got out the wrong side of the bed, put a foot in her bedpan and slipped, hitting her head on the nightstand. That's why we cremated her, dear, it was an accident, nothing more."

"Well, nevertheless," Minnie added, "I'd rather go first if it's all the same to you. Or perhaps we could go together, to save any arguments? What do you think?"

The sisters then began a heated discussion as to which sibling should outlive the other.

"I'm the eldest!" Esther said insistently. "Therefore the odds are heavily stacked in my favour. Hold on, what am I saying?" she then asked. "Minnie neither of us are going anywhere soon, do you hear? Aside from the usual aches, pains and bladder complaints, Dr Kumali said he sees absolutely no reason why the two of us shouldn't maintain our independence for several years to come."

"Yes, but—" Minnie said but was cut short.

Peshwari Nans

"—No buts, dear," Esther informed her. "We're stuck with one another for the foreseeable future and that's all there is to it. Now, about that tea…"

"Rosehip and elderflower you say?" Minnie said, feeling somewhat relieved but in no way jovial. "Okay dear, I'll light the primus."

Setting out the Royal Albert, with silver teaspoons and a lace cloth on their folding table, the sisters sat facing the picturesque terraced rice paddies that were several kilometres away, with Vivien shielding them from the occasional passing vehicles, which were indeed few and far between, leaving the two of them in complete silence at times.

"Any word from Elizabeth?" Esther eventually asked.

Minnie reached for the tablet to check their recent messages. "No dear, nothing from Lizzy at all," Minnie replied. "Perhaps she's mellowed and finally come to terms with your absence. What do you think?"

"Hmmmmm," Esther said unconvinced. "I'd like to believe that, Minnie dearest, but you know what she's like."

Little did the ladies know, but at that precise moment Elizabeth was hardwired to the national grid, twitching with every burst of electricity, and screaming for her mother. It was hoped that the patient, Elizabeth, would come to associate pain with anxiety, and subconsciously learn to control her feelings of rage and angst and eventually eradicate them completely. But with Elizabeth only time would tell, and was likely to put the Shultz Theorem to the ultimate test.

"Richard sends his love though," Minnie added. "As do …" She paused to double check the number at the head of the screen. "Seventeen million four hundred and eighty-five thousand two hundred and eighty-three others."

"How many?" Esther gasped, pausing with her cup to her lips.

Peshwari Nans

The staggering total increased minute by minute as their fan base ballooned, coming from all walks of life, including nursery-school children, death row inmates, Kuwaiti Sheikhs and Polynesian pearl divers alike. The love for these ladies was truly infectious, sweeping through towns and villages like a wave, leaving empathy and awe in its wake, and unwittingly Esther and Minnie had become ambassadors for the elderly, restoring people's faith in life after retirement.

A revolution amongst senior citizens the world over had begun, with tens of thousands rising from their easy chairs to take back a life that was once theirs. Gymnasiums had been overwhelmed with enquiries from those once considered infirm and irrelevant by modern day society's standards, while economic growth had taken a new turn, with businesses and entrepreneurs alike eager for a slice, following in the footsteps of Karl Bodine and his gaming consortium, who now boasted that one-in-three games controllers purchased was now in the hands of a senior citizen, whether arthritic or otherwise.

"Thank you, dear," Minnie said, setting her cup down and reclining, thankful once again for her sister's tea and sympathy.

During their roadside recess Esther and Minnie had failed to notice a connection between the half dozen or so vehicles that had passed them by. Each of them in one way or another was transporting caged canines, either a single dog or as many as forty, mostly mongrels rounded up from the gutters of neighbouring towns, villages and even cities.

These desperately distressed animals cowered submissively, cramped and fearful in appalling conditions, but oblivious to the sinister fate that awaited them at their destination, Guangxi Province and the infamous Yulin dog meat festival, an annual tradition that saw upwards of ten thousand dogs slaughtered for their meat.

Peshwari Nans

International condemnation thus far had failed to stop this barbarism, where victims were mostly burned alive in open markets, or barbequed for the baying crowd's pleasure. Reports had surfaced of household pets being stolen and transported along with the strays, fuelling increased anger and attracting greater scrutiny of the horrific practice. Celebrities the world over had added their weight and signatures to a growing list of well over four million who were in direct opposition to the ten-day traditional gathering.

"Ready dear?" Esther later asked, having given her sister ample time to collect her thoughts.

"Yes dear." Minnie smiled. "Yes I do believe I am."

Approaching the sprawling Tibetan prefecture of Ngari, with its population of just ninety-five thousand, Esther and Minnie had thus far travelled a little over six thousand miles, five times Vivien's recorded mileage over the previous two decades. But on she trundled, her aspirated petrol engine purring with the occasional startling misfire.

The pair shared the last of their liquorice allsorts as they entered the built up Burang township, situated four-and-a-half thousand metres above sea level, making it the highest region on planet earth, with Mount Everest as its towering pinnacle rising majestically from the Tibetan plateau.

"Oh God, look dear!" Minnie suddenly gasped, choking on her coconut ring as a moped sped by them with what appeared to be a small dog tied in a hessian sack hanging from one side, the rider an aged and weathered gent with a hand-rolled cigarette wedged between his teeth.

"What the devil?" Esther too exclaimed, appalled by the obvious ill treatment of the creature. The overhead traffic signals changed from green to red and the motorcyclist slowed to a stop.

"HEY, YOU THERE!" Minnie called, leaning from her window.

Peshwari Nans

"Minnie, what are you doing?" Esther asked apprehensively.

"HEY, EXCUSE ME!" Minnie yelled, oblivious to her sister. "YOU THERE, YES YOU, THAT'S NO WAY TO TREAT THAT POOR ANIMAL, YOU OUGHT TO BE ASHAMED OF YOURSELF!"

"Oh no," Esther said as the lights changed and a truckload of captive canines overtook them at speed. "I know what this is, dear."

"What, Essy?" Minnie asked. "What's going on? Where are they taking those dogs?"

"It's Yulin," Esther said with a rigid look of dread on her face.

"Yulin?" Minnie said, none the wiser. "What's Yulin, dear? Essy, tell me darling, what is it?"

"Believe me," Esther warned her sister. "You don't want to know, Minnie dear, it's awful."

"Tell me!" Minnie insisted. "Essy, what's Yulin?"

"Leave it, dear," Esther said adamantly. "Wind up your window, please."

"Essy!" Minnie protested. "Essy what's Yulin? Essyyy!"

"Alright alright!" Esther snapped. "If you must know, Minnie, Yulin is a festival."

"A festival?" Minnie replied. "Well, what's wrong with that?"

"A dog meat festival, Minnie," Esther added. "These dogs are going to be eaten."

"Eaten!" Minnie said aghast. "Eaten as in, eaten?"

"Yes dear. It happens every year apparently," her sister informed her, sickened at the idea herself.

"But why?" Minnie asked. "Why, Essy?"

"Tradition," Esther replied. "I read an article in the *Standard* when I was wrapping the Royal Albert. Animal rights activists have been campaigning for its abolition for some time, but you have to understand dear, this is China."

587

Peshwari Nans

Driving behind the moped, Minnie looked into the terrified mongrels' eyes with the bag's cord tied way too tightly around its neck. "Oh Essy, we should do something," she said with a heavy heart. "Essy we must!" She wound her window down a little further. "HEYYYYY!" she yelled once again. "HEYYYYYYY!"

"Minnie please, what are you doing?" Esther asked, slowing somewhat.

"Never mind, dear!" Minnie snapped. "We have to stop him, hurry dear, hurry!"

"And do what, dear?" Esther asked, thinking rather more rationally than her sibling. "Minnie? Do what?"

"I don't know!" Minnie raged. "But that poor creature needs our help and it needs it now, so will you please get a move on, NOW ESSY!"

As luck would have it, the rider slowed again with the signals against him.

"Gotcha!" Minnie snarled, clambering from Vivien. "YOU THERE!" she called, approaching his machine with the bit firmly between her teeth at this point and prodding the gent's shoulder. "I'm talking to you!"

"Minnie, will you please come back?" Esther called from the safety of her seat. "Minnie!"

But Minnie rounded the moped and stood astride the front wheel, gripping the handlebars in her whitened knuckles. "You're going to this Yulin thingy, aren't you?" she said, confronting the startled rider. "You understand? Yulin?"

"Ahhhhh, Yulin." The gentleman smiled, removing his cigarette with a smile and pointing down at the trussed up pooch. "Yulin!"

"No you can't," Minnie said, seething by now. "Please don't do this, please! Just turn around and go home."

"Yulin!" the Chinese national said, pointing ahead. "Yulin!"

"No, no Yulin!" Minnie insisted. "Not today, not with that little dog you're not, I won't let you!"

The traffic signals changed once again and the gentleman put his bike into gear. "Wait!" Minnie said, refusing to step aside. "Please sir, please don't do this!"

Esther stepped from Vivien. "Minnie there's nothing you can do, darling!" she called, sympathetic to her cause but realistic nevertheless.

"Yes there is!" Minnie growled, gripping the handlebars ever tighter. "Give it to me," she told the Chinaman. "You don't need to eat it."

"Yulin!" the rider again gestured, attempting to move off.

"PLEASE!" Minnie begged. "Let me have it!"

"Minnie we can't!" Esther said, approaching cautiously. "We can't have a dog, for Pete's sake."

"So what becomes of it, Essy?" Minnie said angrily. "Tell me, are you comfortable with the fact that this adorable creature will be somebody's main course? Because I'm telling you, Essy, I for one am not!"

"Yulin," the agitated rider again said, revving his engine.

"NO, NO YULIN!" Minnie yelled, shaking his motorcycle. "No, goddamn it!"

"I'm awfully sorry," Esther told the rider. "It's my sister you see, she's—"

"—I'll buy it!" Minnie blurted over her sister's apology. "Yes, yes, that's it! I'll buy the dog. How much?"

"What?" Esther asked. "Minnie dear, what are you saying? You're not thinking straight."

"Yes Essy, I am!" her sister replied, wild-eyed. "I am Essy. Now give me the money."

"But…" Esther said in an attempt to dissuade her adamant sister.

"Just give me the damn money, Essy!" Minnie barked. "I'm sorry, but I have to do this."

Peshwari Nans

Esther could tell that Minnie's opinion would not be swayed, no matter how hard she tried. "Very well, dear," she said, reaching into her cardigan pocket for her purse. "I just hope you know what you're doing, that's all."

Minnie snatched a quantity of notes and waved them under the traveller's nose. "This for the dog!" she said forcefully. "Do you hear me? I want to buy the dog."

The Chinaman's eyes lit up on seeing at least a month's wages before him. "No Yulin?" he asked.

"No," Minnie agreed. "No Yulin." She thrust the notes into his hand. "The dog goes with me, okay?" she added.

There was a moment or two of tense contemplation before the gentleman nodded his head and hastily pocketed the cash before slipping the knot and handing Minnie the grubby sack.

"Thank you," Minnie sighed. "Help me, will you Essy?" she added, enlisting her sister's help in releasing the clearly malnourished mongrel. "It's alright," she said, cradling it in her arms. "It's alright you're coming with us." The pooch stretched out and licked Minnie's cheek repeatedly, and suddenly the bond between them was set.

"Well I hope you know what you're doing, Minnie," Esther said, stomping back to Vivien to the sound of disgruntled drivers behind them. "Yes, yes alright!" she added, swinging her leg inside. "Come on Minnie, and put that wretched creature in the back."

"I'll do nothing of the sort!" Minnie protested. She checked beneath the dog's tail before continuing. "She stays with me, Essy. Look at her? She's traumatised, the poor little mite." She climbed in beside her sister with a defiant glare.

"And what about me?" Esther snapped. "I'll be traumatised with that, that, *sewer rat* sat beside me! I doubt if it's had a decent bath in its entire life." She wound her window all the way to the bottom and looked down her nose at the bundle of tousled grubby brown fur on her sister's lap.

"She's not a sewer rat, Essy," Minnie said, objecting fiercely to her sister's jibes and looking her new pet up and down. "She's a, well actually I don't know what she is, but she's no rat I can tell you. She's not a Shitzu though, that's for sure. She has the look of a King Charles about her. What do you think, Essy?"

"Nonsense." Esther smirked, moving steadily in traffic. "It's a mongrel, plain and simple."

"Don't be ridiculous!" Minnie laughed. "You can tell just by looking at her she has breeding. You know I wouldn't be surprised if she has a pedigree."

"Pedigree my foot!" Esther smirked. "Anyway we can't keep it of course, so you'll just have to find a home for it, and sooner rather than later if you don't mind."

"What?" Minnie exclaimed. "What do you mean we can't keep her? Why not, Essy? Please tell me why not?"

"We just can't, that's all," Esther huffed. "We'll get it to a safe place and then be rid of it. I can't say fairer than that now, can I?"

"*Her*, Essy, you mean be rid of *her*," Minnie informed her sister. "And there's no safer place than right here with us. Look, she's taken to us already."

The new arrival continued to lick at Minnie's hand.

"*You*, Minnie!" Esther said, honking at a daydreaming pedestrian. "It's taken to you, not me. No we can't keep it. I mean her. Oh you know what I mean. Anyway Minnie, I'm not a doggy person, I never have been. They take up far too much of your time and, quite frankly sister dear, that's the one thing we have very little of, wouldn't you agree?"

"Yes dear, but look at her," Minnie said, appealing to her sister's sensitive side. "Isn't she adorable?"

Peshwari Nans

"Minnie!" Esther said, losing her cool somewhat. "I for one am not going to spend the remainder of my days going for walkies and picking up doggy doo doo! Do I make myself clear?"

"Oh but Essyyyyy," Minnie whined, "I'll walk her I promise, and I'll pick up her doo doo too, but I doubt there'd be more than a handful anyway, judging by the size of her. Rather like a walnut whip wouldn't you say?"

"Oh really, dear!" Esther said with a look of disgust contorting her face. "You know how partial I am to a walnut whip. No, no, she's going and that's that."

With this, the tiny dog crawled from Minnie's lap across to Esther's.

"Minnie!" Esther shrieked, navigating through bustling rush-hour traffic. "Minnie what's it doing? Get it off me! Get it off at once!"

"She's alright, dear." Minnie smiled. "She's just saying hello, that's all."

"Well I don't want to say hello," Esther said, looking down momentarily. "I'd rather say goodbye quite frankly. Now please Minnie, if you don't mind."

Minnie turned her face away, smirking while the dog nuzzled beneath her sister's cardigan.

"Minnie, I'm warning you!" Esther raged while the animal nestled down, at ease with its new mistresses. "Oooh, just you wait," she growled.

Stopping from time to time amid the hustle and bustle of the town centre, Minnie watched out of the corner of her eye as Esther's hand dropped occasionally to instinctively pet the now sleeping dog on her lap. "I told you." She smiled. "Didn't I, Essy? I told you just how adorable she is."

"What?" Esther said, snatching her hand away. "I wasn't, I mean I—"

Peshwari Nans

"—Oh yes you were." Minnie smirked. "Admit it, dear, she's gorgeous, simply gorgeous."

"No, no, she isn't!" Esther insisted, prodding the stray awake and pushing her over to Minnie's side of the car. "And my opinion remains unchanged, Minnie. She has to go."

Minnie picked up the pooch and placed it back onto her sister's lap. "Very well, dear," she said, crossing her arms over her chest. "You do it then."

"What do you mean, do it?" Esther asked. "Do what exactly?"

"I don't know," Minnie said defiantly. "Throw her from the car if you're desperate to be rid of her."

"Me!" her sister said, looking down as the pooch looked up into her eyes. "Why me, Minnie? It's your damned dog!"

"No Essy, she's ours," Minnie replied, gesturing to the window. "Well? What are you waiting for?"

"What? No!" Esther protested, clutching the animal tightly. "Minnie I couldn't, I couldn't harm a hair on her head."

"Her?" Minnie asked, tongue-in-cheek. "A moment ago, dear, she was an 'it'."

"Yes, yes, I know, but…" Esther stammered.

"But?" Minnie said hastily. "But Essy? But what?"

Esther found herself lost for words with the rescued hound burying it's snout deeper. "Ohhhhhhh!" she then growled, frustrated and on the verge of conceding.

"Well?" Minnie asked with an air of confidence. "Can we keep her Essy? Can we?"

Esther said nothing for a moment of two, her eyes flitting from the road ahead and the wriggling bundle stretched across her knees, "Ohh damn you, Minnie," she eventually blurted out.

"Is that a yes?" Minnie chirped. "Is it Essy? Is it? Is it?"

"Alright, alright!" Esther stormed. "But I'm warning you Minnie, if she—"

"—Yes, yes, yes!" Minnie squealed, cutting her sister's terms and conditions short. "Did you hear that, darling?" she added, snatching the contented canine back and holding her aloft. "You can stay with us, yes you can, oh yes you can, ohhhh yes yes yes!"

Esther looked on disapprovingly at her sister's juvenile gesticulations, with the pooch hanging like a rag doll between her hands, its tiny tail thrashing from side to side.

"Ohhhhhh, yes you can you gorgeous girl," Minnie continued. "Yes yes yes, yes yes yes!"

"Minnie!" Esther finally snapped, having seen and heard quite enough. "Put her down for heaven's sake, you'll shake her half to death!"

"Oh, oh yes, of course dear," Minnie replied, clutching the dog to her chest. "I promise you, Essy, she'll be no trouble, no trouble at all."

"Hmmmmm," Esther mumbled reluctantly. "And I promise you, Minnie dear," she said, adding a condition of her own, "the moment she is I'll be cutting the both of you adrift and proceeding alone, do I make myself clear?"

Minnie sat toying with her new pet's tail, oblivious to her sister's threats of eviction. "Who's a poochy woochy woo?" she chuckled, rubbing its belly. "You are, yes you are, ohhhh yes, yes, yes you are."

"MINNIE!" Esther again barked, quite literally at the end of her tether. "Give the damn dog a name and use it for heaven's sake! I don't care what it is, just as long as it isn't poochy-blasted-woochy!"

"A name?" Minnie smiled. "Oh yes, yes of course dear, she must have a name, errrrrrm." She sat, mulling over countless possibilities. "Daisy, Duchess, Isabella, Lulu…" none of which suited the bedraggled street stray. "Any ideas Essy?" she asked. "Essy?"

Peshwari Nans

Esther refused to be drawn into this ludicrous affair as she saw it. "None whatsoever," she replied adamantly. "I've made my position quite clear, Minnie, she's your responsibility, not mine. Jack and I never wanted so much as a canary let alone a dog, so please just keep her out of my way."

Minnie covered the animal's ears. "Don't listen to her, darling," she said in that annoying childlike tone. "She's just a little cranky that's all, she'll come around you'll see."

"Huh," Esther mumbled. "I wouldn't hold my breath if I were you."

While Esther drove, unwilling to fully accept the new addition to the family, Minnie posted several pictures of their recent rescue online and appealed to the masses for a suitable name and enlist their help in pressing the Chinese government to once and for all outlaw such barbaric practices as the Yulin dog meat festival, which consequently went hand-in-hand with the hideous trade in canine leather, which was stitched into everyday consumer goods and sold globally to the unsuspecting public.

Minnie's revelation struck an immediate chord with animal lovers and resonated the world over. Shock and repugnance soon turned to outrage and civil unrest by the more militant of activists. Minnie had literally 'blown the lid' off the little-known practice and caused a stir that would bring shame and condemnation heaped at the Chinese door.

On the flipside, pet names came flooding in within minutes, by the tens of thousands in fact, from Britney to Beyoncé, Miley to Madonna, Kylie, Carmen, Candice, Courtney and Clarisse. But when they were relayed one by one to the docile dog over the course of several miles, and much to Esther's despair, not a single suggestion caused a stir.

Peshwari Nans

Eventually Esther could stand no more. "THAT'S IT!" she stormed, applying the brakes and pulling to the side of the road. "Choose a blasted name, Minnie, or so help me I'll, I'll…"

"Okay, okay!" her sister replied, cringing. "It's not that simple, Essy."

"Yes it really is that simple!" Esther remarked. She then cupped the dog's snout and turned it to face her. "Beady eyes, facial hair and a runny nose. Just like Aunt Sissy. There. Sissy it is!"

"Oh I loved Aunt Sissy," Minnie said, remembering their now deceased relative with affection. "She made the best eccles cakes I think I've ever tasted, and she always let me sleep over on a Saturday night with cocoa and cookies. Oh I do miss her so, and anyway, Essy, she didn't have beady eyes, you were just jealous because I was her favourite."

"Jealous!" Esther scoffed. "Don't be ridiculous!"

"It's true!" Minnie replied defensively. "Ever since she bought me a bicycle and you a skipping rope."

"Well I should have had the damn bicycle!" Esther snapped after her sister opened an old wound. "I'm the eldest, but oh no, little Miss goody two shoes gets a shiny pink bicycle, with a bell I might add, and all I got was a stupid skipping rope!"

The incident, that happened some seventy-five years ago, still grated on Esther. "A skipping rope!" she moaned. "I mean it hardly compares to a new bicycle, does it? I mean, does it?"

"No dear," Minnie said, rolling her eyes, having endured that very same conversation more times than she'd care to remember. "Yes dear, no dear, no dear, of course not, dear," she replied to her sister's continued ranting.

"Well I adored Aunt Sissy," she eventually blurted when Esther paused to draw a breath. "So yes, I think it's a wonderful choice." She cradled the pooch once again. "What do you think, Sissy?" she asked. The dog wagged its stubby tail and licked at Minnie's face. "Oh look, dear, she likes it!" Minnie gushed. "Sissy it is then."

"Whatever," Esther said dismissively whilst pulling away.

"I'll take Sissy to the cemetery when we return home," Minnie said, bouncing the dog on her lap. "And take Aunt Sissy some gladioli. Aunt Sissy did love her gladioli. Perhaps you'd like to join us, dear?"

Esther refused to comment as she sat, quietly seething over the gross injustice served upon her, as she saw it, at the hands of her late aunt.

"Essy?" Minnie said, pressing for an answer. "I said perhaps—"

"—Yes I heard you!" Esther snapped. "I'm sorry Minnie, but if the tables had been turned I'm sure you'd have felt the same."

"Well actually no, no I wouldn't," Minnie confessed. "If the truth be told it was I who was jealous of you, dear. I'd have much rather had a skipping rope than that rotten bicycle that tore my nylons every time the blasted chain came off. Essy if only you'd have asked, instead of screaming the house down, I'd have been only too happy to trade."

"Trade?" Esther asked, momentarily dumbstruck. "You mean…"

"Of course," Minnie replied with a smile. "In a heartbeat, dear."

Esther's cheeks flushed a little. "Well I'll admit, dear, I may have overreacted a tad," she confessed.

"A tad!" Minnie laughed. "If you've mentioned that bloomin' bicycle once, Essy Reynolds, you've mentioned it a thousand times, so I'd hardly call that a tad. An obsession maybe, a fixation, a bitter resentment, a—"

"—Alright, alright!" Esther said, holding up a hand. "I'm sorry, I'm sorry Minnie, for being such a damn fool all these years. There, I've said it."

Minnie looked on aghast, as though a great storm that had troubled them had now finally passed. "Oh," she said, stunned and shaken. "Right, well, that's the end of that then."

"Yes, yes it is," Esther said with the weight now lifted. "That's the end of that."

Moments later Minnie raised a finger. "Although," she said hesitantly, "you were rather miffed, dear, when I got the ballet shoes and you got a banana."

Esther flew into a rage once again. "You had to mention those damned ballet shoes, didn't you?" she cursed. "And what did I get? What did I get? You're right, Minnie, I got a blasted BANANA!"

Minnie sank into her seat, having roused the envious monster within her sister and listened sheepishly to her heavily punctuated profanity until the bitter resentment was well and truly off her chest.

After a much lengthier spell of blissful silence, Minnie again composed herself. "She always said I ought to have married, you know," she said out of the blue.

"Who?" Esther asked, snapping out of her daydream.

"Aunt Sissy, of course." Minnie sighed whilst feeding Sissy the remainder of their custard creams. "Just moments before she passed away, God rest her soul, she beckoned me to her bedside and told me to find a good man and marry the blighter. Well under such circumstances I promised faithfully that I would, but alas it just wasn't meant to be."

Esther struggled desperately to see any significance in her sister's ramblings.

"I mean Cyril popped the question several times," Minnie continued unabated, "but I guess I just wasn't ready to settle down. Mind you I'll say one thing for him, he kept a spotless home."

Esther looked away, disinterested to say the least.

"His linen was always crisp," Minnie informed her. "And his curtains, Essy, they were always immaculately pleated, and do you know, dear Cyril even ironed his—"

"—Minnie!" Esther snapped. "I swear if I hear one more word about Aunt Sissy or your blasted Cyril I'll, I'll throw myself from the Great flipping Wall I will!"

Minnie sat, momentarily positively stunned. "Oh," she eventually said, her mouth downturned. "I see."

"No Minnie, you don't!" Esther continued. "That's just the point. It's 'Cyril this' and 'Cyril that', well if the truth be known, my dear, I can't say I was very fond of the fellow at all, and believe it was a blessing when your grubby relationship finally ran its course. There I've said it. So now you know."

"What? Do you mean you didn't like him?" Minnie asked, aghast at her sister's revelation. "Essy, what do you mean?"

Esther remained tight-lipped but Minnie persisted: "Essy!"

"If you must know," Esther finally confessed, "I didn't think he was right for you from the start. I know he was merely a casual acquaintance, but I truly believe you could have done so much better for yourself."

"Ohhhhh, I see," Minnie replied, nodding. "This is about Harold, isn't it?"

"No, no, of course it isn't," Esther said defensively whilst braking sharply to avoid a chicken that had wandered onto the road. "It's purely my personal opinion, that's all."

"Balderdash!" Minnie said, glaring at her sister while Sissy licked at the biscuit wrapper. "You wanted me to marry Harold, didn't you? Admit it!"

Peshwari Nans

Harold was Jack's twin brother, older by just forty-five minutes. When Esther began dating Jack almost sixty years previously, she'd got it into her head that the two sisters should marry the two brothers and live the model fairy-tale life of wedded bliss, maybe even as neighbours. But although Harold was charming and more than willing, Minnie simply didn't share her sister's utopian view, and shunned his constant advances and her sister's relentless matchmaking.

"Well, well, yes of course I did," Esther blurted out. "He was perfect for you."

"No dear," Minnie said, raising a finger. "He was perfect for you and your 'grand plan' as you called it. Well I'm sorry but I wasn't ready to settle down. Not with Harold, not with anybody. I was having far too much fun."

"But Harold was fun," Esther said in his defence. "Don't you remember?"

"Ohhh yes, I remember alright." Minnie smirked, raising her pencilled eyebrows. "He collected stamps and rang church bells at the weekend."

While Harold found the pastimes of bird watching, train spotting and brass rubbing riveting, Minnie was a young lady in the prime of life with a string of admirers, each of them willing to spend a shilling or two on a cinema ticket or a sparkling glass of babycham to win her affections.

"I suppose Jack blamed me for what happened, did he?" Minnie asked, referring to Harold's death at sea aboard a Royal Navy mine sweeper.

Spurned once too often, Harold upped sticks and enlisted in Her Majesty's Navy to forget the apple of his eye. Eventually, after rigorous basic training, he was stationed in the Far East with the rank of petty officer pinned to his chest. It was while he and the rest of the crew were assisting in the removal and decommissioning of Second-World-War ordinance, that a collision occurred and blew a gaping hole in the forward hull. The ship went down in a matter of minutes, claiming the lives of every living soul on board, leaving nothing but an oil slick and a few personal effects.

Jack was visited in his humble greengrocer's shop by two naval officers carrying a handwritten letter from the Admiral himself.

"Did he?" Minnie again asked. "Did Jack blame me for Harold's death?"

"Well, if he did," Esther replied, honking Vivien's horn to clear a path ahead, "he never said, but I knew it affected him deeply."

"Yes, yes, of course dear," Minnie said sympathetically. "No doubt he was devastated, we all were. Harold was a sweet sweet man, but Essy, he and I were worlds apart. I mean we wanted different things. Harold wanted a doting wife to take rambling, narrow boating and beachcombing, while all I wanted to do was paint my nails and party with my friends. But I'll never ever forget his kindness, Essy. I'd only have to call and he'd pick me up at all hours of the day and night in his father's Ford, and drive me home. But Cyril was different, dear. He was fun and exciting, spontaneous if you wish. He'd leave notes about the house and hearts drawn in the steamy bathroom mirror, and of course that's not to mention his experimental side."

"Yes okay Minnie, that's enough," Esther said, recoiling somewhat. "I've told you before, I'd rather not know what you and that man did or didn't do between the bed sheets."

"Between the bed sheets!" Minnie chuckled. "My dear, that's where we slept for heaven's sake. Oh no no no, the majority of our, shall we say 'lustful encounters', were conducted a little more publicly."

"Publicly!" Esther exclaimed, mortified at the suggestion. "What do you mean, publicly? On second thoughts, I really don't think I want to know."

"Yes, publicly," Minnie proceeded. "It's called 'adding spice', dear, maybe you and Jack should have tried it once in a while."

"We had our moments," Esther said proudly. "I remember one Friday after our fish supper, Jack and I were, well you know, when I suddenly realised I'd left the curtains open."

"Oooh that's more like it, you minx!" Minnie said, rubbing her hands together. "And were the neighbours watching?"

"Good heavens no!" Esther abruptly replied. "Perish the thought. A pigeon perhaps might have seen us, but I shushed it away, closed the curtains, and turned out the lights."

"Good God." Minnie sighed. "And that's it, is it? That's the extent of your wild abandon?" She again raised her eyebrows. "Well let me tell you, dear," she added, "Cyril and I once took the train to Liverpool to cross the Mersey. Well while we were aboard, Cyril came over all amorous, dragged me to the engine room and gave me the most amazing—"

"—Minnie!" Esther cried, slamming on the brakes once again. "What have I told you about keeping such depravity to yourself? Harold would never have dreamt of such a thing."

"Exactly!" Minnie smiled. "That's precisely my point, dear."

Now midway between Ngari and the mountains of Nepal, the tiny ash-framed classic car trundled across the rugged Tibetan plains on a route that at times tested the most robust of 4x4 vehicles. Esther and Minnie's passage to India in a fifty-year-old Morris would undoubtedly be a world first if, and only if, Vivien was up to the task.

But neither sister could have possibly prepared for what was to come, and they drove on in blissful ignorance through traditional villages, many of them unchanged and untainted by western influence, unlike China's sprawling cities, which had succumbed to the heavy hand of globalization, which on one hand brought increased trade and prosperity but on the other unleashed a plague of western fast-food outlets onto an unsuspecting population who, until then, had maintained a simple diet, predominantly rice, fish, vegetables and a little meat. The result was an almost immediate spike in the rates of obesity, coronary heart disease and associated conditions, which was alien to the vast majority of Chinese people before then.

"What are you doing, dear?" Esther asked, glancing across at her sister, whose constant tapping at the tablet screen had begun to grate on her.

"I'm bidding, dear," Minnie replied without averting her eyes.

"Bidding?" Esther asked. "What do mean, bidding?"

"Bidding, dear," Minnie reiterated. "I was browsing the web, I think that's the correct terminology, when I stumbled across a selection of online auction houses. Essy dear, I haven't had this much fun since Cyril and I—"

"—Yes yes alright!" Esther interjected. "Bidding on what?"

"Hang on, dear," Minnie said, tapping again. "I'm just upping the ante." She continued to raise the stakes and was arousing her sister's curiosity further.

"Well?" Esther asked, leaning across to glance at the screen.

"Oh, sorry dear," Minnie said, momentarily breaking her concentration. "I'm bidding on a cake stand, dear, not just any old cake stand though I'll have you know. It's a rather fine piece of Wedgewood. I've offered a pound thus far, and the auction ends in fifteen minutes, so fingers crossed."

Peshwari Nans

"A cake stand, you say?" Esther said, pricking up her ears and leaning a little closer and slowing somewhat.

"Yes dear, look," Minnie said, turning the screen so her sister could see. "It has a small chip on the top tier but I can cover that with a slice of Battenberg. Oh damn and blast!" she then cursed, having taken her eye off the ball so to speak.

"What is it, dear?" Esther asked, intrigued to say the least. "What's happened?"

"I've been gazumped," Minnie explained, tight-lipped. "A rival bidder has offered one-twenty, the perisher."

"Well offer more dear, offer more!" Esther said excitedly. "We simply must have it! I mean, can you imagine the look on the face of Marjorie, from number thirty-two? She'll be green with envy. She still hasn't forgiven me for purchasing the walnut-and-wicker sewing basket from the Bow church bring-and-buy bazaar. She swore blind she'd seen it first, but I was in there like a shot with my elbows fending her off, and stole it right from under her nose, it was an absolute bargain at seventy-five pence, and well worth falling out with Marjorie for. She refused to speak to me for weeks after I smugly informed her that the basket contained a dozen or so rolls of the finest quality thread, a pair of commemorative Charles and Diana thimbles, and a dressmaker's pattern for knee-length knickers."

"Oh yes, I remember, dear," Minnie chirped. "You made me a pair in powder-blue crimplene for Christmas, I still have them and I must say, Essy, the stitching is of the finest quality, dear, and ever so robust too. If I ever had my hands full at the market I could always tuck a pound or two of maris pipers and a head of broccoli down each leg and waddle home like Jemima puddleduck. I call them my 'practical pantyhoses'."

Peshwari Nans

"Well I'm glad you like them, dear," Esther said, having personally hand-stitched somewhere in the region of a hundred-and-fifty pairs of the passion killing panties for Oxfam, who had appealed for garments to clothe the recently displaced refugees in southern Sudan.

"Offer another twenty pence, dear!" Esther said, goading her sister on.

"I'll do nothing of the sort," Minnie scoffed, raising her bid by a measly five pence. "There, that ought to seal the deal," she said confidently. "What?" she then growled when she was informed once again that she'd been outbid.

Minnie's auctioneering opponent was an equally persistent pensioner from Barnsley by the name of Miriam.

"Well, we'll see about that," she stormed, offering a further five pence more. The two tenacious ladies began a furious bidding war in miniscule increments, each determined to procure the much coveted willow pattern Wedgewood.

"What's happening?" Esther asked, mounting the grass verge on occasion.

"Don't worry, dear, I know what I'm doing," Minnie replied, grabbing at the wheel with her free hand. "Just concentrate on the road, will you? Anyway I'm just about to fire a warning shot across their bows and offer a further fifteen pence."

"Good idea, dear." Esther smiled. "Let them know we mean business."

"Precisely," Minnie said, puffing out her chest. "After all, it's a matter of principle now, dear, a battle of wills, a test of our metal so to speak."

The bidding then ceased, with Minnie's offer standing firm. "It appears the opposition has left the arena, dear, with their tail between their legs no doubt."

"How long, dear, how long?" Esther asked, positively bobbing in her seat as the auction timer turned red. "I'll get a Victoria sponge when we return. Marjorie could never resist a Victoria sponge, and of course I'll serve it on our new Wedgewood stand. Oh I can't wait to see the look on her face, Minnie dear, it'll be priceless, absolutely priceless!"

"Sixty seconds, Essy dear," Minnie replied with a confident grin.

But Minnie was a novice when it came to online auctioneering, unlike her opponent in this tug of love for this damaged but nethertheless desirable collectable. Miriam was a time-served aficionado, skilled in the art of the long game, and with twenty seconds remaining, in her eyes the auction was far from over.

Miriam sat in her lounge poised in her housecoat and fluffy carpet slippers, with one hand teasing her tabby tomcat with a woollen mouse on a string, and the other hovering over her keyboard. Then while Minnie reclined with both hands behind her head, grinning like the proverbial Cheshire feline, Miriam dealt the decisive blow, hammering home a last-ditch bid of one pound seventy-three pence with just four seconds remaining.

"WHAT?" Minnie cried, wrenching her hands apart. "What the...?"

"What? What is it?" Esther asked as her sister jabbed and poked at the screen. But her bid of one pound eighty was rejected by the electronic auctioneer, and Miriam was hailed the victor once again.

"We have it, Arthur," Miriam told her playful tabby, whom she'd named after the plucky Arthur Scargill, a politician and staunch trade unionist who defied Margaret Thatcher and her Conservative government in the mid 1980s and led his members out on the famed miners' strike. But after violent clashes, the picket lines were eventually dispersed and the pits that had produced the nation's fuel since the 1800s were forced to close.

Peshwari Nans

"We have the Wedgewood!" Dropping the makeshift mouse, Miriam clasped her hands together in sheer delight and marvelled once again at her private collection of cake and confectionery stands which filled every nook and cranny of her two-up two-down end-of-terrace house.

"Minnie, what is it?" Esther insisted while her sister sat open mouthed. "Have we secured the cake stand?"

"I don't believe it." Minnie gasped, still jabbing at the tablet in the hopes of a last minute reprieve. "I, I thought we had it. I honestly did."

"Thought!" Esther said, grimacing. "What do you mean you thought? Are we or are we not, the proud owners of a Wedgewood cake stand?"

"Not, dear," Minnie replied in a state of shock. "We appear to have been pipped at the post. I, I don't know what to say."

"WE?" Esther raged. "You mean you were pipped at the blasted post? Oh Minnie, how could you be so stupid."

"I'm, I'm sorry, dear," Minnie stammered, staring at the stand that had simply slipped through her fingers.

"I knew it, I knew it," Esther said, pounding the wheel. "If it were me I'd have bid a whole two pounds—possibly two-fifty, but oh no, not you," she raged, such was her anguish at losing out. "As usual, Minnie knows best," she continued to vent her frustration. "Well it's because of you and your penny-pinching, Minnie, that I now have nothing to display my muffins on when Marjorie comes calling. Nothing, Minnie!"

Little did Esther know at the time but when it came to cherished Chinaware, her neighbour and bitter rival had recently stumbled across the holiest of holy grails at a charity jumble sale: a stunning Clarice Cliff pot pouri bowl, with an estimated value of well over four hundred pounds. She however had parted with the meagre sum of just three pounds for this once-in-a-lifetime find.

Peshwari Nans

Beside herself with excitement, Marjorie scurried home with the bowl clutched tightly to her chest. "Oh yes yes yes!" she squealed, positively peeing herself as she polished the hand-made fine china limited edition piece. "You know what you can do with your Royal Albert, Esther Reynolds," she sneered, setting the table in readiness for Esther's return. Marjorie sat staring out of the window, willing Esther to turn the corner. Occasionally she tweaked her table arrangement for maximum jaw-dropping effect.

"How could you, Minnie?" Esther asked as her sister sat with her head hung and Sissy asleep at her feet. "You simply must find another, you must!"

"Okay, okay!" Minnie said, inching away. "I'll try, Essy."

But try as she did, after scrolling and scrutinizing page after countless page, her search proved fruitless.

"Well?" Esther asked, strumming the wheel.

"Wait a minute, dear, I'm bidding," Minnie told her sister.

"On a cake stand?" Esther asked enthusiastically.

"No dear, on a foot spa," Minnie said, having been well and truly bitten by the bidding bug.

"A foot spa!" Esther sneered. "Minnie, for heaven's sake what do we want with a foot spa?"

"Ah ahhhh, don't knock it until you've tried it, dear." Minnie smiled. "My Cyril swore by his. He said he could sit and bathe his bunions whilst blanching his broad beans at the same time."

Esther thought for a moment. "You mean…?" She said, picturing Minnie's ex with his canker-covered feet immersed in a bath of bubbling beans.

"Oh yes, dear," Minnie added, singing the gadget's praises. "You have to supply your own water of course, but its versatility is limitless. Apparently a lady in Carmarthen has taken to breeding shubunkins in hers."

Peshwari Nans

"Breeding what?" Esther asked, swerving to avoid yet another pothole.

"Goldfish, Essy," Minnie informed her sister. "And a couple in Felixstowe have reportedly…"

Esther wrenched at the wheel, narrowly avoiding an oncoming truck which had emerged suddenly from a blind bend, while Minnie, unfazed, explained in elaborate detail how the bygone gadget had seen something of a resurgence of late, after a certain aged British Bake Off presenter confessed on national television to bleaching her bloomers twice weekly in the diverse device.

"You mean?" Esther gasped, referring to the household family favourite whose mouth-watering desserts, cakes and canapés had wowed the nation for decades.

"Yes dear, I do." Minnie smirked, having read a tell-all in the Sunday tabloids.

"Noooooo," Esther again exclaimed as her sister divulged further extraordinary exerts from the culinary Queen's serialized autobiography, telling of her romps on the flour-covered kitchen table with a handsome young sous chef. "With a whisk and a wooden spoon?"

"Ohhhhh yes." Minnie nodded. "And I daren't tell you what she wrote in piped icing on his bare bottom."

Esther could hardly believe her ears as her sister elaborated. "She did not!" she said, stunned at the promiscuous and somewhat perverse picture her sister had painted.

Ascending a Nepalese rocky mountain pass Vivien slowed to a stately fifteen miles per hour. "Good grief!" Esther said with her heart in her mouth.

"Yes, quite," Minnie agreed as she clung to Sissy, not daring to look to her right at the near vertical drop of almost half a kilometre, with only a haphazard row of irregular white-painted stones planted to define the edge.

Peshwari Nans

Every so often a break in those stones would signify a fatal miscalculation on behalf of a former road user. Freshly laid flowers and incense burners marked the more recent tragedies, as did the valley floor below, that was littered with the twisted and tangled remains of iron ore trucks, motorcycles and not one, but two school buses that had fallen foul of the perilous pass within a matter of weeks of one another, leaving forty grieving families and an eerily silent schoolhouse. "Dear God, please be careful," Minnie said as conditions worsened.

"Yes, yes, please be quiet," Esther said, dropping another gear as Vivien laboured on another steep incline. "Damn it!" she then cursed, steering close to the edge to avoid a rotting goat carcass in the road, the unfortunate creature having stumbled on the loose scree high above them—a further reminder that lady luck and the fickle hand of fate toyed with the lives of all who dared to undertake a crossing of this nature through the famously formidable Himalayas.

Carrion crows picked at the goat's rancid corpse as Esther inched by, dislodging several of the painted markers in doing so.

"Essyyyyy," Minnie said, sliding further towards her sister and holding Sissy ever tighter and tugging at her sister's knitted sleeve. "Essy let's go back, please!"

"Are you out of your mind?" Esther said, attempting unsuccessfully to shrug off her petrified sibling. "We couldn't turn around even if we wanted to! Now will you please let go, Minnie. Minnie let go, or you'll have us over the edge, LET GO!"

Minnie by now had convinced herself without a shadow of a doubt that that fateful day would be their last and grappled with her sister. "Essy, please stop!" she pleaded, making a desperate grab for the wheel. "Stop!"

Peshwari Nans

"MINNIE!" Esther barked. "WHAT ARE YOU DOING? NO, NO YOU'LL...!"

But it was too late. Minnie's foolhardy intervention, albeit with the best of intentions, was to have immediate catastrophic consequences.

"NO, NO, NO!" Esther cried three times in rapid succession as Vivien veered to the left, colliding with the jagged rock beside them, which tore at the aging classic's wing, leaving a streak of Trafalgar-blue behind them.

"MINNIE YOU FOOL!" she screamed, steering away but overcompensating at the same time. "OH NO, OH NO!" she cried, skidding on the dirt track while her sister closed her eyes. Vivien's brakes barely slowed them as Esther thumped at the pedal repeatedly but to no avail. Her front wheel toppled the marker stones over the edge and rolled over behind them.

"OH NO MINNIIIIIE!" Esther screamed, clinging helplessly to the wheel with her antiquated roadster's rear wheels locked and dragging dirt. The panic-stricken pensioners were both thrown violently forward in their safety belts when Vivien's dust-covered bumper struck a withered and wind-tortured birch tree, one of only a few to eke out a precarious existence on the harsh Himalayan slopes. The sudden impact and abrupt stop had the sisters mortified but also perplexed.

"Oh dear Lord!" Esther gasped, opening her eyes and stiffening immediately at the enormity of their predicament. All four wheels had left the mountain track and they were now wedged at an angle of forty-five degrees, facing the valley floor far below them. "Minnie dearest, whatever you do," she said, the colour draining from her wrinkled face. "Don't move."

Minnie opened her eyes whilst slumped against the canvas belt. "What is it, dear?" she asked, peering over the dashboard, hardly daring to look. "OH GOOD

HEAVENS!" she shrieked, grabbing at her sister's hand, the two of them now literally staring death in the face. "Essy, Essy, what do we do? What do we do, Essy?"

Suddenly the car lurched forward several inches when the birch buckled somewhat under the strain, its shallow roots barely clinging to the dry mountain grit.

"ARRRRRGHHHH!" the ladies cried in unison, grabbing at one another.

"Essy, Essy, we're…" Minnie mouthed with very little sound, "we're!"

"Yes, yes, I know," Esther exclaimed. "I know Minnie, please just don't move, don't move a muscle."

Sissy, who had tumbled into the footwell, began barking at Minnie's feet. "Oh you poor thing," she said, stooping to comfort her but shifting her weight in the process.

"I SAID DON'T MOVE!" Esther yelled, pushing ever harder on the brake pedal, with Vivien shifting forward, increasing the force on the bending birch tree tenfold.

"I'm sorry, I'm sorry, I'm sorry," Minnie whimpered, dragging Sissy slowly back onto her lap. "It's Sissy, dear, she's scared."

"She's scared!" Esther said, retracting further into her seat. The sisters sat speechless for a moment or two before Minnie reached slowly for the door. "NO!" Esther snapped, making a grab for her sister. "Minnie don't!"

"But Essy," Minnie replied, unable to curtail her survival instinct. "We must!"

Vivien's undercarriage creaked as did her faltering brakes. "We must remain calm," Esther told her insistently. But the word calm was immediately followed by an anguished appeal to the almighty when Vivien slid a further six inches, removing the dappled white bark from the bending birch. "Okay, you're right!" Esther hastily agreed. "We'll go on three."

Peshwari Nans

The pair gripped their respective door handles with Minnie wrenching Sissy to her bosom by the scruff of her neck.

"One!" Esther cried, feeling sick to her stomach at the thought of losing her beloved car. "TWO!" Several of the isolated tree's roots were now visible as the hillside heaved under mounting pressure.

"WAIT!" Minnie said, relaxing her poised posture. "I can't do it, dear," she confessed. "I thought I could but I just can't Essy, I'm sorry."

Fear had got a grip and locked her joints and tendons solid. "This is all my fault, darling, I am honestly so so sorry."

"Shh, shh, shhhhhh, it's alright," Esther said, silencing her anguished sister. "It's alright Minnie dear, really it is." Since the demise of her lifelong love, Esther no longer feared death. In fact during her darkest hours she longed for an end to the hurting and a chance to join Jack wherever his soul might now reside. "Honestly dear, it's okay."

"I love you, Essy," Minnie said, releasing Sissy and the door handle and offering a hand.

Esther tugged Minnie's trembling fingers to her. "Ditto," she simply said, planting a tender kiss.

The Himalayan birch which had first prevented their catastrophic descent, bowed to the ever increasing forces of gravity and the combined weight of Vivien, her occupants and their shackles, which included their precious Royal Albert chinaware, a must have for any self-respecting senior citizen, but a weighty extravagance nethertheless.

Minnie reached into her pocket and retrieving the random jigsaw piece she had so eagerly prized as a talisman, that had brought them good fortune until now. "Maybe I was wrong, dear," she said, reaching to toss the segment featuring a human foot from the window.

Peshwari Nans

"Minnie wait!" Esther urged, plucking the piece from her hand and kissing it for luck. "If you believed, dear," she added with a half-hearted smile. "Then so do I."

"But Essy we're…" Minnie replied, stopping short of the inevitable.

"Yes I know, darling," Esther said, slipping the piece between their clenched hands. "I know, I'm only sorry we let Jazzy down, that's all."

"Oh I don't think we did, Essy dear," Minnie insisted. "From the moment you decided on this, this pilgrimage for want of a better word, you expressed more love for that girl than she ever could have imagined, and wherever she is, God rest her soul, I'm certain she knows. You did Jasvinder proud, Essy, and I won't hear a word on the contrary, do you hear me?"

"We, dear," Esther corrected her sister. "*We* did her proud, I could never have got this far without you, never, I mean that Minnie. And if it has to end right here like this then, then, so be it." She raised her sister's hand triumphantly.

"You're right," Minnie agreed, feeling oddly at ease considering the circumstances. "No regrets, Essy?"

"No regrets, dear," her sister said calmly.

Sissy began barking and leaping from Minnie's lap towards the window, scratching at the glass. "Let her go, dear," Esther said calmly, then watched as Minnie reluctantly released the frantic animal, which scrambled free of Vivien and raced back up to the dirt track, still yapping repeatedly.

Esther and her sister reclined and barely flinched as Vivien's chassis tore the birch roots one by one from the ground and rolled towards the inevitable. The pair took a deep breath, closed their eyes and braced themselves. "SISTERS!" Esther yelled, squeezing her sibling's hand hard enough to bruise.

Peshwari Nans

"YES DEAR, SISTERS!" Minnie echoed her rallying cry, when suddenly, without warning, Vivien came to an abrupt halt with a resounding jolt.

"What the…?" Esther cried with her heart near bursting, and again the two of them sat hanging in their restraints.

"Essy, what is it?" Minnie shrieked, refusing to open her eyes.

"Dear Lord!" Esther blurted out, catching a flash of flesh in the rear-view mirror.

"What is it? What is it Essy?" Minnie asked, tugging at her sister.

"I, I, don't know," Esther confessed, wide-eyed and open mouthed, checking the mirror again to see several near naked men scrambling in the scree behind them.

Sissy's frantic departure was in no way the actions of a coward deserting a sinking ship. She had gotten wind of a party of shaolin monks heading in their direction along the pass and had raced to attract their attention, averting them from their daily ritual of walking barefoot for fifteen miles swinging scented burners to cleanse their path.

Without uttering a word or having a moment's hesitation for that matter, the twenty or so devout Buddhists whipped off their bright oranges robes, strung them together and fashioned a crude rope. Several of the more youthful and agile Tibetans had scrambled down to the stricken car and hastily tethered Vivien by her rear axle while their brethren dug their callused heels into the dirt and took the strain.

"Heaven?" Minnie asked, squinting and following her sister's gaze. "Oh good heavens!" she cried when confronted by a smiling monk. "Essy what?"

"I, I, don't know," Esther too gasped, flabbergasted beyond belief. The monk waved courteously and turned to rejoin the others, flashing the majority of his pert bottom, that was loosely wrapped in a loincloth.

"Dear Lord, Essy. He's wearing no trousers," Minnie said, momentarily averting her eyes.

"None of them are," Esther replied, tweaking the mirror.

"You mean there's more of them?" Minnie asked, winding down her window a little further and looking behind to the road above. "Essy, Essy, they're here to save us!" she cried, wrenching her hand from her sister's. "Essy!"

"Yes, yes, it's a miracle!" Esther cried with her hands clasped in prayer. "A miracle, Minnie darling!"

"No dear," Minnie said, holding the jigsaw piece proudly aloft. "It's my lucky foot. I knew it. I knew it you little beauty," she chirped, kissing the segment and tucking it safely back into her pocket.

There was a further jolt as the company of monks, whose combined age topped twenty-two hundred, began to heave on the makeshift rope slowly, hand over fist, clearing Vivien of the splintered birch without breaking a sweat. The sisters were gradually being plucked from the jaws of death without a doubt in the nick of time. But while Minnie bobbed in her seat, Esther wisely curtailed her enthusiasm whilst staring down at the rocky valley floor and the upturned battered and burnt family saloon, with its erstwhile inhabitants' sun-bleached possessions strewn over some distance.

Vivien's rear wheels soon rolled back onto the mountain track with the coil of robes piling at their rescuers' feet.

"Thank youuuuu!" Minnie called from the window and raising a thumb to the would be heroes. "Oh my God, thank you so much!"

Finally, with the dirt scuffed by numerous feet, Vivien was hauled to safety with her relieved and reprieved occupants. Esther was the first to let out an extended sigh of relief and relax her grip on the wheel. "Thank you," she said, looking up at the roof lining.

The Shaolin monks hastily dismantled the lifeline and donned their robes.

"Hellooooo," Minnie said, opening the door to greet them. "I don't know what to say. My sister and I honestly thought we were, well you know, gonners so to speak."

The monks each bowed, then turned to leave.

"Wait, wait!" Esther called, flinging open her door to thank them personally whilst Sissy ran around in circles, tugging playfully at their hems. "How can we ever repay you?" she asked, distancing herself from the treacherous edge.

The simple order of monks from the opposite side of the valley turned and smiled without breaking stride as an elder occasionally rang a cow bell to signify purity of mind, body and spirit, but a few of the trailing members paused to glance through Vivien's rear windows, tugging at one another's robes and pointing out the Royal Albert.

"Sissy, get down!" Esther snapped, shushing the little dog from the master's robes. "I am sorry, she's a little unruly you see," she explained before glaring at her sister. "Rather like her owner."

"Oh Essy, that's not fair," Minnie protested, oblivious to the monks' enthusiasm for their china. The strict order forbade any items of luxury or the trappings of the opulent western world, but with their own crude dinner set carved from boxwood blocks that were now cracked and riddled with woodworm, mealtimes were fast becoming a penance too far.

"Fair!" Esther said raising her voice "Have you forgotten it was you that almost got the pair of us killed with your reckless tomfoolery?"

"But Essy I said I was sorry," Minnie pleaded. "It was a mistake, that's all it was."

"A mistake?" Esther scoffed, crossing her arms as the master looked on bemused. "The mistake, Minnie, was fetching you along in the first place. You've been nothing but trouble from the start. And will you please control that damn dog of yours."

Sissy's teeth had clamped down on the aged master's robe, tearing a yard or so of material as she ran rings around him.

"NO, SISSY!" Minnie yelled, rushing to separate them. "Forgive me," she said, scooping the snarling pooch and tugging the shredded hand-woven wrap from her mouth while her sister did her level best to hide her embarrassment.

"Oh you like the Royal Albert, do you?" she asked the mesmerised monks, who had their noses pressed to Vivien's windows. "I said you like the Royal Albert?" she reiterated.

"Oh I see, I am sorry," she said when the monk closest to her raised a finger to his lips, thus informing her of their vow of silence, but then nodded in agreement.

"It was my mother's," Esther told them, opening the door and removing a cup and saucer from the collection. Passing the delicate pieces between them and attracting the attention of the others, the monks marvelled at the exquisitely preserved collectables before offering them back.

"If you like it, it's yours," Esther told them, refusing to accept the return of her precious inheritance. "In fact," she added, leaning inside and removing the entire box. "Have it all with our blessing. Please, it's the least we can do."

The monks backed away but eventually relented when Minnie arrived, carrying Sissy beneath her arm. "Yes you must have it, my dears," she said, standing shoulder to shoulder with her sister. "I'm certain Mother would have approved, wouldn't she Essy?"

Esther, although miffed once again with her sister, was inclined to agree. "Without a doubt, Minnie, without a doubt."

The younger monks looked to their master for his approval, as in the past it had been known for members of the centuries-old order to be stoned, so as to banish any wanton cravings for such earthly possessions from them.

"Please," Esther said, appealing to the master's better nature, one that he had kept under wraps for the past fifty years. But he too had grown tired of sipping his cherished juniper tea from a leaking bowl, and after a tense stone-faced stand-off with his followers, turned up the corners of his mouth and nodded.

"Excellent!" Esther chirped, clasping her hands together. "Please, help yourselves."

A jubilant yet deathly silent scene followed, with the ecstatic fist-pumping monks delving into the sisters' delicate treasure trove, holding each piece of the hand-painted, gold-rimmed service aloft, as though offering it to Buddha himself, or maybe seeking his blessing. Nethertheless, to say they were overjoyed would be a gross understatement.

"You're welcome, dear," Minnie told a beaming Buddhist, who was brandishing her late mother's butter dish, his fellow worshipper grinning with the gravy boat clutched lovingly to his chest. The ringing of their master's cowbell suddenly brought the crockery carnival to its senses and one by one the shaven headed devotees filed after him.

"Goodbyyyye!" Minnie called with a wave. "And thank you once again, all of you!"

Without looking back, the monks raised the shared Royal Albert in salute to their benevolent benefactors.

"Ahhhhh," Minnie sighed. "What a charming bunch."

"Yes, quite," Esther agreed, closing Vivien's rear doors and scowling at her sister once again.

"What?" Minnie asked, climbing aboard. "It was an accident dear, plain and simple."

"My dear, plain you are not," Esther fumed, examining the damage to Vivien's panelling, running her hand along the deep gouges now exposing the buckled bare metal below. "But simple," she added, climbing in beside her sister, who sat with Sissy lapping at her face. "Oh boy, where do I begin?"

"Oh Essy, lighten up dear." Minnie smirked. "All's well that ends well, eh? And Essy darling," she continued, "we did get to see a bunch of half-naked ninjas or whatever they were."

"Monks," Esther said, tight-lipped. "They were monks, not ninjas."

"Monks, ninjas," Minnie said without a care. "It matters not, dear. I for one definitely would."

Esther turned the key, relieved when Vivien's engine whirred into life. "Would what?" she then asked, letting curiosity get the better of her.

The mischievous Minnie could hardly contain herself. "Tug on their bell ropes." She chuckled, holding a hand to her mouth.

Pulling away, Esther struggled to maintain her composure and remain displeased with her jovial junior. "Bell ropes!" she suddenly blurted out. "Minnie you saucy minx you!"

"Yes I know." Minnie laughed with a glint in her eyes. "But don't say it didn't cross your mind too, my dear."

"Not for a moment," Esther replied defensively whilst keeping a watchful eye on the marker stones beside them, and lying of course in the process. Unlike Minnie's shameless leering, Esther had allowed herself a fleeting glimpse of the bare-breasted monks and maybe another at their scantily clad nether regions. "Well," she then confessed with her cheeks flushed, "okay, maybe I did find them mildly alluring."

"Alluring!" Minnie laughed. "Essy my dear, they were hot to trot, I'm telling you they could have buttered my crumpet any day of the week. Even master Yoda or whatever his name was, the man had buns of steel, dear."

"And quite a lunchbox by all accounts," Esther added, tongue-in-cheek, whilst navigating a series of punishing bends. The two sisters shrieked with laughter, sharing a confession or two, having got quite hot under their collars during their daring but altogether silent rescue.

For several miles the brutal terrain hampered their progress with dangerous inclines and steep, stomach-churning descents.

But unlike her modern counterparts, that were constructed of wafer-thin alloys with speed and fuel efficiency in mind, the Morris Traveller was built with pride to last, right up until the very last of her kind rolled off the production line in 1971.

"Hold onto your hat, dear," Esther said, slowing to roll cautiously over a deep crack in the road, then doing the same for another and another still.

"What is it, Essy?" Minnie asked, observing the aftermath of a giant rockslide across the valley. "What's happened?"

"God only knows," Esther said, praying for conditions to improve. But what the sisters were witnessing first hand was evidence of a powerful earthquake and reported aftershocks that had devastated vast swathes of Nepal and its capital Kathmandu in recent months.

A magnitude 7.8 earthquake first struck to the east of Kathmandu at approximately 11.56 on April 25th 2015, killing over 9,000 people and instantly levelling many poorly constructed outlying villages. A state of emergency was immediately imposed, but rescue efforts were hampered by further tremors and the threat of more to follow. The roads were barely passable, with much of the debris having been cleared by hand, while the death toll rose steadily as more victims of this tragic natural disaster were exhumed from the rubble.

Aid agencies such as the British Red Cross struggled to cope with the limited resources at their disposal, and donations were slow to filter through, with the world still reeling from the catastrophic Japanese tsunamis, one of which in 2011 initiated the Fukushima nuclear disaster.

The monks who had so bravely and selflessly rescued the sisters earlier, now practised their Buddhist beliefs beneath a makeshift canvas awning, after their cherished 15th-century hilltop monastery was completely destroyed during the quake, along with precious and irreplaceable scrolls. The Royal Albert china gifted to them would come to symbolise more than just a token of gratitude to the silent order. Taking pride of place on their temporary altar it would come to signify a new beginning, rebirth as it were, and unlike their hallowed scrolls, the quintessentially British chinaware's true value lay in its beauty and effortless simplicity—a mantra that the remote brotherhood of monks had lived by for centuries.

Reaching a remote settlement miles from the capital, the sisters were startled when a small boy no older than five or six, wearing nothing but a tattered pair of yellow shorts and threadbare sandals, ran from the rubble that was once his family home and approached Vivien with his hands outstretched. The remainder of his family, three generations in fact, were huddled beneath a blue tarpaulin amid the broken clay and splintered timber.

"Oh Essy, stop dear!" Minnie said, tapping her sister's arm insistently. "Please Essy!"

Peshwari Nans

Esther slowed and Minnie immediately stepped from the car. "Hello my darling," she said to the boy, who spoke no English but repeatedly gestured to his mouth. "Heavens, dear, he's hungry," she told her sister. "Hurry Essy, we have more than enough."

"Oh yes, yes, of course," Esther replied, clambering from her seat and opening the rear doors as the child beckoned to his family and craned his neck to see the sisters' plentiful provisions, his village having been largely overlooked by the underfunded and overstretched emergency services.

"It's alright," Minnie said to his apprehensive relatives. "Come, we have food and water and you're more than welcome, please."

The otherwise proud Nepalese family emerged, helping one another from the ruins, clearly traumatised and fearful of further quakes. Esther and Minnie filled the child's arms with tinned beans, cereals and chutneys until he could carry no more, before greeting his sheepish relatives.

"Hello, my dear," Minnie said to his mother, whilst plying her with fresh water and toiletries. "What happened here?" she then asked, assuming the country to be at war and recalling a similar scene in the East End of London when the German Luftwaffe levelled her own home during the Blitz, which began on the eve of her mother's birthday, the 7th of September 1940 and lasted for a staggering seventy-six consecutive nights, the family sitting huddled along with four hundred other Londoners on the platform of Mile End Tube Station, while the streets above them were pounded relentlessly by the aerial bombardment.

"The earth," the shell-shocked mother said. "She shakes."

"Of course," Esther said with a hand to her mouth. "The earthquake. Forgive me, dear, I feel such a fool. Look at you, you've lost everything, you dear sweet thing."

"We are the fortunate ones," the mother went on to explain. "Many have lost their lives, my own sister and her family cannot be found. We pray, we pray they have been taken to the shelters."

"And you?" Minnie asked. "Why are you not at the shelters? Why do you stay?"

"We wait," the lady's husband replied, "for the trucks, but they not come."

Esther looked the ladies up and down. "Here," she said, wrenching the majority of her clothing from her suitcase. "Perhaps you could make use of these. I'm sure my sister has one or two things also, don't you Minnie?"

"Oh yes, yes, of course," Minnie replied, hurriedly reaching for her own luggage. "It's mostly second hand," she told them, emptying several pockets of mothballs, "but you're more than welcome to it my dears, more than welcome."

The husband delved into his trouser pocket and produced several coins.

"Oh no dear," Esther insisted, raising a hand. "We couldn't possibly accept payment. Like my sister says, it's mostly second hand, no, no you take it with our blessing."

The boy scurried to their temporary tarpaulin to deposit their donations before returning to look the curious little car up and down.

"Shall we, dear?" Minnie asked her sister, holding her father's primus stove aloft.

"But of course, dear," Esther replied without hesitation as she was bagging their entire inventory of dry goods. "How else are they to heat their cuppa soups and chamomile?"

"Thank you," the mother said, bowing with her arms piled with the sisters' belongings, leaving them with just the one change of clothes and their now trademark straw hats which, under the circumstances, would be of very little use to the stricken Nepalese family.

"Oh please," Esther said, humbled by her courtesy. "I only wish we could do more."

"Here, my dear," Minnie said, slipping the coat from her back and wrapping it around the trembling grandmother's shoulders. "Now, now, I insist," she added when the elder backed away. "Come now, you'll catch your death otherwise." Minnie buttoned the coat to her neck, turned up the collar and slipped her knitted mittens over her crippled fingers. The grandmother, overcome with emotion, stooped to kiss Minnie's hands.

"Oh my dear, there really is no need," Minnie said, straightening her immediately, with a lump forming in her throat. "Like my sister says, we only wish we could do more."

The sisters then turned to see the boy smiling at Vivien's window, where Sissy was leaning out and lapping at his face. "Oh I see you've found my Sissy," Minnie said, reaching for the door. "Come on darling, out you come," she added, releasing Sissy, who leapt to the ground and ran rings around the chuckling child.

"Sissy?" the boy asked whilst tossing a stick.

"Yes, that's right." Minnie smiled, brushing the boy's fringe from his grubby face.

"It's the eyes." Esther smirked, harking back to her late aunt's likeness to the dog once again.

The group watched the young boy skip gaily around the site of his former home. "SISSY, SISSY!" he called, with the little dog nipping at his heels.

"And the facial hair," Esther told the Nepalese family, who looked on, none the wiser.

The mother tugged at her husband. "Aardesh, Aardesh, look!" she said, filled with a sense of renewed hope on seeing her child at play.

The boy, named Balmani, meaning 'young jewel', had suffered from what psychiatrists would term as post-traumatic stress syndrome, a state of deep distress, since being thrown from his bed in the dead of night and waking to witness his world's violent destruction, a horror that would undoubtedly haunt the most hardened person, let alone a five-year-old boy. "Look Aardesh!" she rejoiced.

"SISSY, SISSY, SISSY!" Balmani shrieked, pursued relentlessly by a yapping bundle of overexcited fur.

Minnie took her sister's hand. "I say, dear, are you thinking what I'm thinking?" she asked, observing the heart-warming scene.

"Do you know?" Esther smiled. "I do believe I am."

"Sissy," the child said, panting on his return.

"Balmani, is it?" Minnie asked his mother.

"Yes," she said proudly. "My child."

"Well, Balmani my darling," Minnie said, bending to look the boy in the eye with his mother echoing her words in translation, "I don't expect you to understand the meaning of the word fate, perhaps your mother and father will explain it to you one day. Anyway my sister and I gave Sissy here a second chance when she needed it most, and now I truly believe she can do the same for you, if you'll have her, that is?"

There was a moment or two as the boy listened intently to his mother's quivering interpretation. His eyes then widened as the earth-shattering revelation hit home. "SISSY!" he cried, dropping to his knees in the dirt and cradling his new companion in floods of tears. "Sissy, Sissy," he sobbed, unable to breathe at times.

"Bravo," Esther said quietly, choking back a tear herself and rubbing her sister's back. "Bravo."

Balmani leapt to his feet and wrapped his arms around Minnie's legs and then Esther's, his heart thumping.

"Thank you," his mother again said, nestling close to her husband. "You are a blessing, both of you."

"Oh we're nothing of the sort, dear," Minnie remarked. "And I'd like to think, my dear, that if the tables were turned you would do the same for my sister and I."

The family bowed while the ecstatic child once again rolled at their feet sobbing tears of joy, whilst fending off his slobbering playmate, who lunged repeatedly at his face.

Esther took the mother by the hand. "We wish you the very best of luck," she said, gently squeezing. "We really do, my darling."

"Yes," Minnie agreed. "The very best." She then picked the wriggling Sissy from Balmani's chest and offered her to Esther. "Do you have a kiss for Sissy, dear?" she asked, tongue-in-cheek.

Esther ducked and weaved away, avoiding any contact. "Minnie!" she snapped aggressively, "I didn't have a kiss for her namesake so I certainly haven't one for that, that, hairball."

"Ooooh, what is she saying, Sissy darling?" Minnie cooed, allowing Sissy to remove a layer of rouge with her flitting tongue. "Goodbye my precious," she added, handing her back, feeling conflicting emotions.

Climbing into their near empty car, the sisters sat there, reluctant to leave. "Are you sure you'll be alright?" Esther asked before raising her eyes. "What am I saying?" she added. "Of course you're not alright, look at you, you poor things."

"You should go," the mother told them. "It is not safe on these roads after dark."

The sisters still had an hour or so's driving to reach Kathmandu, and the light was fading fast. "Goodbye my darlings!" Minnie called as her sister turned the ignition key. "Take care!"

Peshwari Nans

"Damn, damn!" Esther growled, pulling away and glancing in her rear-view mirror to see the family waving, all with the broadest of smiles. "I do hate to leave them Minnie, I really do," she confessed, slapping Vivien's wheel in sheer frustration.

Balmani and Sissy ran alongside for several yards, inseparable it seemed. "Goodbye my sweet!" Minnie again called, blowing a kiss. "Goodbyyyye!"

The boy and his pet stopped and watched the sisters turn a bend in the road and disappear out of sight, before rejoining his family beneath their meagre shelter.

Esther and Minnie sat in quiet contemplation for a mile or two before the weathered track they had travelled ended and joined the highway on the approach to the capital Kathmandu, where the havoc wreaked by the series of earthquakes became more apparent, with open farmland bordering the highway on either side. Piles of rubble, broken tiles and scattered possessions were all that remained of once-thriving homesteads, their cattle, chickens and sheep wandering aimlessly, foraging untended.

Several trucks thundered by, rocking Vivien and her occupants in the swirling vortex created between them.

"Darling, look!" Minnie suddenly cried, breaking her silence when one particular truck caught her eye—it had the tell-tale red cross emblazoned on its rear. "We have to tell them, Essy!" she said, sitting bolt upright. "We have to tell them about Aardesh and his family Essy, we must!"

"Heavens, you're right!" Esther remarked, springing to life and bearing down on the accelerator.

Minnie wound down her window and began waving her straw hat, but the driver of the relief truck failed to spot them in his mirror and left them in his wake, rapidly increasing the distance between them.

Peshwari Nans

"HEYYYYYYY!" Minnie screamed against the wind, waving frantically as her sister leaned on Vivien's horn. "Hurry dear, hurry!" Minnie insisted, goading her sister on.

"I'm trying!" Esther snapped, thumping the horn, but Vivien's horn, factory fitted in the 1960s during a more sedate motoring era was of very little use, some would describe its sound as pathetic.

But since dusk was descending, Esther switched on the headlights and began repeatedly flashing towards the Red Cross vehicle, now a quarter of a mile ahead of them.

"HEYYYYYYYYY!" Minnie continued to yell, leaning from her window. "STOOOOOOOP, PLEASE WAAAAAAAAAIT!"

The truck eventually began to slow on reaching the urbanised outskirts of the capital, much of which was showing some evidence of quake damage, from hairline cracks in buildings to complete cave ins.

"Quickly dear!" Minnie urged as road conditions improved in their favour until they finally drew alongside the aid vehicle, racing at Vivien's top speed of sixty miles per hour.

"HEYYYYY!" Minnie called until she was hoarse and the ribbon was fluttering from her hat, until the unsuspecting driver glanced down at them. "Heyyyy stoop, pleaaaaase!" Minnie begged. "You have to go baaaack!"

Vivien's horn was now barely audible and her flashing lights were illuminating the highway.

"Cut him off, dear!" Minnie urged, prodding her sister frenziedly. "Cut him off!"

"Yes, yes, of course," Esther agreed, taking both their lives into her hands and wrenching the wheel to veer into the path of the speeding sixteen-and-a-half-ton truck. There was a sudden screech of brakes and plumes of smoke as the startled truck driver slowed dramatically, causing those behind to do the same, whilst furiously venting their frustrations.

Esther stopped on the highway and the pair wormed themselves from their seats. "GO BACK!" Esther yelled, approaching the truck. "YOU MUST GO BACK!"

Minnie pounded on the shell-shocked driver's door until he wound down his window.

"What the bloody—" he said, stopping short.

"Go baaack!" the sisters yelled in tandem.

"Blimey you're English!" the driver exclaimed, switching off his radio.

"As are you," Esther said, equally surprised.

"Peterborough born and bred," the driver said proudly. "I heard the Red Cross were looking for drivers so I quit my job, bought a plane ticket and here I am," he went on to explain. "The wife weren't best pleased but when I showed her the pictures of the babies sleeping on the streets she was right behind me. I tell ya she can be a hard-faced cow at times my misses, but underneath it all she's got a heart of gold."

"Yes, well, that's precisely why we're here," Minnie said, assuming they were singing from the same hymn sheet when it came to the homeless children. "That's why you have to go back for our friends."

"Friends? What friends?" the burley driver asked, then stooped to look the sisters up and down. "Hang on a minute!" he suddenly said. "It's you, it is isn't it? The Nans I mean?"

"Yes, yes, but never mind all that," Minnie said, prodding at his door once again. "You must help those friends of ours."

"Oh……my……God!" the driver gasped, dismissing Minnie's plea. "My Denise is gonna die when I tell her. She's been driving me up the wall she has, ringing me every day, saying have you seen the nans yet, have you seen the nans yet."

"Excuse me!" Esther insisted. "About our friends."

The driver began hyperventilating and bobbing in his seat. "She is gonna die I swear, wait, wait there!" he told the irate sisters. "Don't go anywhere! I'm gonna call my Denise, she's gonna die I just know it!"

"I sayyyyy!" Minnie called when he turned his back to rummage for his mobile phone. "It really is a matter of some urgency. I sayyyyy, oh blast!"

"Cupcake, cupcake it's me, muffin!" the ecstatic driver said when his beloved answered the telephone back home in her kitchen. "Cupcake, can you hear me? It's your chubby muffin."

The sisters looked at one another incensed, but a little perplexed at the same time. "Chubby muffin" Minnie mouthed.

"Yes darling, yes it's me," the relief driver continued. "Listen, listen cupcake, you'll never guess who I just bumped into, never in a million years. Go on have a guess babe, go on!"

"Oh really!" Esther groaned, kicking at one of his mammoth tyres as he rocked back and forth in his seat.

"No not the Dally Larma." He laughed. "Bigger babe, bigger than the Dally Larma!"

"Helloooo," Minnie again called. "Mr Muffin, Mr Muffiiin, MR MUFFIN FOR PETE'S SAKE!"

"One minute ladies," the driver said, raising a finger. "No Cupcake it's not Ghandi ya daft mare, I'll give you a clue shall I? There's two of 'em, grey hair, straw hats and wrinkles."

"Ooooh you cheeky beggar!" Esther remarked, hastily checking her reflection in his door mirror.

Peshwari Nans

The penny suddenly dropped back home in the UK, and Denise, aka Cupcake, shrieked with excitement, so loud in fact that the sisters winced.

"Yeah babe, it's really them," the muffin replied. "It is, it is I swear. You don't believe me, do ya? I'm telling you love it's the Peshwari Nans, right here outside my truck as God is my witness, babe! Okay, okay, I'll prove it, shall I?" he said abruptly.

"Mr Muffin, please!" Minnie raged. "We really haven't the time for such nonsense!"

"Please," the driver said, offering Esther the phone. "Just say 'ello to me misses will ya? She don't believe me she don't, go on just say 'ello, I'm telling ya she's gonna—"

"—Die, yes, yes, we know," Esther said, snatching the mobile. "Hello? Hello?" she said sharply. "Cupcake. I mean Denise. It's Esther here, yes, yes that's right a Peshwari Nan, for what it's worth."

Denise erupted in her kitchen, howling with a hand to her forehead. "Oh my God, oh my God!" she blurted out, rocking back against the dishwasher. "You're not winding me up, are ya?"

"No, no, Denise it's me I assure you," Esther replied, rolling her eyes. "I am here with my sister Minnie but I really must speak with your husband if it's all the same to you, dear."

"No, no, wait!" Denise cried, clinging to this once-in-a-lifetime opportunity. "Get a selfie with him, please Esther! Please, I wanna photo of you two with my Cupcake, so I can show the mums at the nursery. They are gonna die, I tell ya, can I speak to Minnie?"

"With pleasure," Esther sneered, thrusting the phone into her sister's hand, somewhat relieved. "Apparently," she told the husband, "we've got to get a selfie with you, but really Mr Muffin, we have a far more pressing agenda."

"Mike," the driver informed her. "It's Mike, my Denise calls me Muffin coz I call her Cupcake, you see."

"Yes, quite," Esther said, decidedly disinterested. "Now look here, Mr Mike, you must turn this vehicle of yours around, do you hear?"

"Yes, yes, yes," Mike said, rooting in his glove compartment and retrieving a permanent marker. "You gotta sign my wagon first," he insisted, gesturing to the driver's door. "Please! It'll really make my day."

"Oh this really is too much," Esther groaned, decidedly vexed at this point. "And then you'll go back for our friends, right?"

"Friends?" Mike asked. "What friends?"

"Aardesh!" Esther said, raising her tone, "and his family. Dear God, why on earth do think we hijacked you, for Pete's sake?"

"Excuse me," Minnie said, interrupting the pair. "Apparently Mr Muffin, Denise is decorating little Millie's nursery and would like to know if you've a preference between matt or vinyl silk emulsion."

"What?" Esther snarled. "Minnie what are you talking about?"

"The nursery, dear," Minnie replied with Denise waiting expectantly at the other end of the line. "I told her personally I'd go with the vinyl silk. Well it's far more practical where grubby little hands are concerned, wouldn't you agree, dear?"

"Minnie have you lost your mind completely?" her sister raged. "Have you forgotten why we are here? Have you forgotten young Balmani, and his family?" she added, jogging Minnie's memory.

"Oh! Oh yes, of course dear," Minnie said, turning to Mike. "Mr Muffin?" she asked.

"I'm with you, Minnie love," Mike agreed. "Vinyl silk all day long, our Millie's a messy little moo she is, wait a minute I've got a picture here somewhere." Mike turned his back to them once again.

"God give me strength!" Esther cursed as her sister resumed her long-distance conversation whilst irate motorists sped by.

"Yes, Denise darling, Muffin agrees with me," Minnie rambled on, oblivious to her sister's aggressive posturing. "The vinyl silk my love, oh and should little Millie moo decide to try her hand at graffiti, may I suggest a little lemon and baking soda applied with a lint cloth in a circular motion?" Minnie turned to receive Esther's frosty glare. "What?" she asked.

"MINNIE!" Esther bellowed, clenching a fist in readiness. "I swear I'll swing for you in a minute!"

"One moment, Denise dear," Minnie told Mike's beloved. "I won't be a moment, Essy dear," she said with a hand over the mouthpiece. "The dear girl's getting herself into a flap over the bedding and drapes." She then returned to Denise before Esther could interject. "If you want my advice, my love," she told the mother of one troublesome three-year-old, "I'd stick with the floral theme, it's chic and girly and a godsend when it comes to vomit stains. Anyway dear, I must dash. It's been lovely talking to you, yes and you, bye bye, bye bye, my sweet."

"Have you quite finished?" Esther ranted, her cheeks red. "Between you, Cupcake and Muffin here, I do believe I'm finally losing the will to live, I honestly do."

"Sorry dear," Minnie said solemnly. "You're right we must think about our friends back there. Right Mr Muffin!" she said assertively. "If you don't turn this vehicle of yours around this instant, Essy and I will be forced to take matters into our own hands, do you hear?"

Her thinly veiled threat yielded very little in the way of response as Mike turned his back a second time and returned moments later with a fist full of photographs.

"This is Millie on her first birthday," he explained, handing his cherished snaps out one by one. "I don't know how she managed to get chocolate cake in her ear, but that's our little moo, oh and that's her biting Father Christmas at the shopping centre."

"Ahhhhh," Minnie sighed. "Isn't she just adorable?"

Esther speedily flipped through the images. "Yes, yes, very nice," she said, offering them back. "Now Muffin, or Mike or whatever your name is, I really must insist you go back and collect our friends, without further delay."

"Okay," Mike finally agreed. "But let's get that selfie first, otherwise Denise'll kill me." Turning his back yet again, Mike stretched out his mobile in front of him with an exaggerated smile. "Say cheese!" he said, ensuring both sisters were in the frame.

"Oh really," Esther growled whilst Minnie adopted a more pleasing pose.

"Cheeeeeese!" Minnie chirped.

"One more, one more!" Mike called over his shoulder, turning his mobile ninety degrees to capture a landscape shot of the three of them.

"Have you quite finished?" Esther said angrily.

"Yes thanks," Mike said, stowing his phone and photographs away.

"Right. Now what can I do for you?" he asked.

"Fiiiinally," Esther said, quite exasperated at this point. "Like we've been trying to tell you all along, you have to turn around and go and fetch some friends of ours that seemed to have been overlooked. A Nepalese family living back a ways on the road to Ngari. But you must hurry, they truly are in dire straits."

"The Ngari road, you say," Mike confirmed. "Yeah I know it well, it's on our list but with what's been going on elsewhere that region has been declassified."

Peshwari Nans

"Declassified?" Esther stormed. "Declassified? Those poor things are living under a windswept tarpaulin, drinking rainwater and surviving on handouts from passers-by, which as I'm sure you are well aware, are few and far between. Have you any idea what that must be like? Have you?"

Mike hung his head. "Listen, I'm sorry Esther, I really am," he conceded. "But orders are orders, you know how it is."

"Orders!" Esther said, pointing an aggressive finger. "I'll give you—"

"—Essy dear, please, leave this to me," Minnie said, halting her sister's furious tirade.

"Yes, but…" Esther added, eager to press home her point.

"Essy please!" Minnie reiterated, ushering her sister aside bodily. "Now look Mike," she said, clambering up onto his door step and clinging to the truck's mirror. "They have a small boy, Balmani and several frail relatives. It would be a crime to allow them to spend another bitterly cold night out there, an absolute crime I tell you."

"A boy, you say?" Mike asked.

"Yes, a dear little thing," Minnie informed him. "How on earth they've managed until now under such horrendous conditions heaven only knows. Now I'm no driver, but I'd say if you turned around now you'd be there in approximately half an hour. What's half an hour, Mike, compared to the suffering of that family? Please, Mike."

"Minnie babe," Mike said, patting her hand, "you don't have to say another word love. If there's a kiddie back there I'm going, and I'll get 'em, don't you worry about that."

"Really?" Minnie said, her heart suddenly a flutter. "You're not, 'winding me up' as your Denise would say?"

"No, Minnie love." Mike laughed. "I'm not winding you up, I don't care how far it is or how long it takes, I'll get 'em, I promise."

"Thank you," Esther said with a resounding sigh, "Muffin."

Minnie was helped to the ground by her sister and the pair took a cautionary step back.

"Now remember," Esther told Mike. "Look for the blue tarpaulin, and be sure to give them our love, won't you?"

"No worries," Mike said, firing up his powerful truck and sending a plume of black smoke into the air. "You two take care, yeah?" he added, selecting first gear with a resounding crunch. "You're amazing, do you know that?" he told the sisters, who stood clinging to their hats with the wind whipping at their skirts.

"No Mike, you are amazing," Esther said, raising her voice. "You should be immensely proud of yourself."

"Ahh thanks darling," Mike replied with a renewed sense of purpose surging within him.

"Miiike!" Minnie called as he pulled away from them. "Give little Millie Moo a big hug from me when you return home, won't you?"

"Definitely!" Mike smiled and gave them a wave. "Be lucky, ladies!" he added, heading off towards the next junction to make an immediate U turn.

"Yes!" Esther said clenching a fist, safe in the knowledge that salvation and sanctuary was now imminent for Aardesh, Balmani and the others.

"Yes indeed," Minnie agreed, leading her sister back to Vivien as night fell in what seemed like an instant.

Restoration works had begun in haste in the capital, with much of the essential services having been restored, a true testament to the enduring will, courage and resilience of the people of Nepal, but a tragedy of such biblical magnitude in human terms would leave a vast open wound that would take decades to heal and eons to forget.

Kind-hearted volunteer workers such as Mike, aka Muffin, who freely gave up their time sought no praise for their humanitarian assistance, for the gratitude etched on the faces of those fortunate enough to survive the devastation was payment in itself.

Running low on funds at this point, the sisters spent the night in a simple three-storey hostel that was a stone's throw from the centre of Kathmandu. Ordinarily a Mecca for mountaineers and backpackers alike, the city was suffering both physically as well as financially in the wake of the quakes, with tourists the world over having been warned to steer clear of the region until further notice by their respective foreign offices.

The generous proprietor of the hostel from whom Esther and Minnie had rented a room, had opened his doors to a dozen homeless families, allowing them to occupy over half of his hostel free of charge, and also went so far as to personally deliver a quantity of groceries to their doors each morning. And this was no isolated occurrence. Tibetans and Nepalese people rallied in support of their fellow countrymen, offering shelter against the harsh Himalayan elements with the help of charitable aid organisations.

Although deeply fatigued, Minnie woke at around 5.30 the following morning after a restless night with thoughts of Balmani, his family and little Sissy, racing through her mind. Esther, on the other hand, slept soundly, having driven hard for so many days—further in fact than she'd driven in her entire lifetime combined, having clocked up a whopping six-and-a-half thousand road miles in total thus far.

Minnie crept from her side of their timber-framed double bed, with its sagging mattress and creaking headboard, while her sister purred contentedly with the sheets pulled up close under her nose. The washing facilities were primitive but adequate: a porcelain jug and bowl and half a broken mirror taped to the lime mortar wall.

Dressing as quietly as humanly possible, Minnie sat on the one and only chair at the window, brushing the lace curtain aside to observe a new dawn breaking over this ancient city, which had suffered so terribly. At street level trolley buses running on overhead power lines offered a skeleton service, with much of the system having been destroyed and awaiting repair. Shutters on small businesses were rising noisily, rousing the zombie-like street-sleepers from their doorways, each of whom clambered bleary eyed to their feet, gathering up their cardboard matting and pitiful possessions.

Intrigued, Minnie watched some sixty to seventy vagrants of all ages and gender trudge to one end of the block to a small communal garden where they sat, each of them looking in the same direction as though in anticipation. Minnie found herself inquisitively following their gaze until a middle-aged city gent in a neatly pressed deep-blue cotton suit rounded the corner, with his regulation briefcase in one hand, but oddly enough dragging a child's box cart in the other, with a canvas covering the contents. The homeless gathering bowed their heads, greeting the gent respectfully as if he was an old friend. In fact this man, Gopal, rose every morning a full three hours before he needed to, to perform his morning ritual in the kitchen of his humble residence, baking fresh bread rolls, roasting potatoes and filling several urns with hot sweet tea.

Gopal's decision to open the blind eye that he had turned for so many years against these forgotten people came in an epiphany after the tragic death of his wife and childhood sweetheart during the opening minutes of the very first quake, when an apartment block collapsed onto the bus in which she was travelling home. Two-thirds of the salary Gopal now earned as a bookkeeper went directly to improving the lives of those less fortunate than he was.

Spellbound, Minnie reached for the tablet computer and began recording the remarkable scene. It started the moment Gopal folded back the canvas sheet and broke the warm bread rolls and handed them, along with one or two potatoes, to each of the desperate down-and-outs, who neither pushed nor shoved as the tea was poured into paper cups and distributed. "Remarkable," Minnie softly said, while zooming in to capture more clearly what followed.

Whilst his briefcase was closely guarded by the rag tag ensemble, Gopal poured a quantity of water into a bowl and, after removing his suit jacket and rolling up his shirtsleeves, proceeded to cleanse and shave the faces of the more infirm amongst the homeless. "Why does he do it?" Minnie thought to herself. "Why would somebody of his obvious social standing drop to his knees to help these people?"

Checking his wristwatch, Gopal soon rolled down his sleeves and donned his jacket before chaining his cart to the garden fence to be collected on his return that evening. Then, giving a bow, he placed a single note into each of the now-nourished Nepalese hands. This money was enough for a hot meal during the course of the day. Then, with briefcase in hand, he was gone.

Minnie sat stunned and in awe at this selfless act of human kindness, a pure and simple concept almost entirely forgotten in today's supposedly 'advanced' society.

Esther soon opened a bleary eye, just the one at first. "Mmmmmmorning," she said, gathering the ruffled sheets around her. "What, what are you doing?" she then asked, opening the other.

"Morning dear," Minnie replied. "I've, I've…" she then stammered. "Essy, I've just witnessed something quite remarkable, quite remarkable indeed."

"Really dear?" Esther said, showing little interest. "Minnie dear, have you seen my slippers?" she asked, hanging from the side of the bed and lifting the sheets from the floor.

"Essy, there was a man," Minnie continued unabated, "not just any man, a truly remarkable man in my opinion."

"Yes, yes dear, but have you seen my slippers?" Esther again asked.

"They're here, dear!" Minnie said, retrieving them from the foot of the bed. "Right where you left them. Anyway he bathed their feet and even cut their hair, heaven only knows why. But Essy, Essy, it was beautiful to see, it touched my heart, it really did."

"Who?" Esther asked, climbing from the bed and donning her slippers and housecoat. "Who cut whose hair? What are you talking about Minnie? You're not making any sense, woman."

"The maaan!" Minnie exclaimed. "Across the street. Look, I'll show you."

She sat Esther back down on the edge of the bed and settled beside her with the tablet on her knees. "Look dear, here he comes," she said, pointing out Gopal and his cart. "Watch, dear. Watch what he does next. It's, it's, well—you decide for yourself."

"Yes, yes, be quiet!" Esther told her, now mildly intrigued.

There then followed a lengthy spell of complete and utter silence. Esther held her breath at times, thunderstruck by the phenomenal footage.

Minnie looked closely, to see a single tear creep from a crow's foot in the corner of her sister's eye.

"Wow," Esther simply said, when Gopal left the garden.

"I know," Minnie agreed. "Have you ever seen anything so, so, wonderful in your entire life, dear?"

"Well," Esther said, drying her eyes. "Aside from the birth of my child no, no, I can't say that I have." She crossed to the window to see for herself the enchanted scene that Gopal had left in his wake. "Look at them Minnie, look," she said, beckoning and tugging the curtain aside. The weight of despair and desperation had been temporarily lifted from the shoulders of the people huddled across the street, many of them laughing and complimenting one another's freshly groomed appearance. "Remarkable," Esther gushed. "Quite remarkable."

"Isn't it?" Minnie again agreed.

Esther then suddenly made a grab for her sister's arm, startling her. "Minnie that's it!" she said, turning to the discarded tablet. "We have to get them to see it!"

"What are you talking about, Essy dear?" Minnie asked, oblivious to her sister's idea at this point. "Get who to see it?"

"Everyone!" Esther shrieked, pacing the room purposefully, deep in thought with a finger pressed to her cragged lips.

"I don't understand, dear," Minnie said, following Esther to the left and then to the right.

"Wait!" Esther said, silencing her sister whilst formulating her plan, her 'eureka moment' so to speak. She then made a grab for the tablet and shook it in Minnie's face. "What do they say?" she asked, unnerving her sister somewhat. "It has to go virus, right?"

"Virus?" Minnie asked, taking a step back. "Ohhhh you mean viral, dear," she added knowingly—this was the Internet term meaning that a particular uploaded clip had been viewed and shared by the masses and consequently achieved global recognition. "Yes of course!" Minnie blurted out, cottoning on at last. "But Essy, I haven't the foggiest idea how to go about it."

"What? Oh blast!" Esther cursed, pacing once again. "Richard!" she suddenly cried, throwing her hands in the air. "Minnie get hold of Richard. He'll know what to do. He's a whiz with that sort of thing."

"That he is, dear," Minnie said, tapping at the screen. "I'll call him up on the Skype thingy at once."

"It's all gibberish to me," Esther confessed. "Just make it happen, dear, if you can."

Minnie sat at the window, tapping at the tablet. "I do hope he's available," she said, awaiting Richard's reply.

"Minnie dear," Esther said, tongue-in-cheek. "It's noon on Saturday. If I know my Richard, he's just got out of bed. Keep trying, dear."

"Aunt Min!" Richard then said, his flushed face suddenly appearing on her screen. "Errrrr, hi. Is everything okay? Is Gran alright?"

"Yes, yes dear, Essy's fine," Minnie replied as her sister leant over her shoulder.

"Morning, my darling," Esther called to him. "Or should I say good afternoon?"

"Oh, Hi Gran!" Richard said. "Is everything alright? Where are you? The last I heard you were in China of all places."

"Yes we're fine, dear," Esther said, brushing her hair. "We're in Kathmandu, darling. How's your mother? Is she there?"

Richard hadn't the heart to divulge the seriousness of Elizabeth's present condition, even though early tests showed she was responding well to the 'Doctor Shultz's Theorem' course of treatment. "Oh she's okay," Richard said as a voice could be heard off-screen.

"Lizzy!" Esther called to her daughter. "Richard dear, put your mother on, will you?"

"Errrrrrr, she's bust, Gran," Richard replied hastily, his face reddening further. "Look, errr, can I call you back later?"

"No!" Esther and Minnie both barked. "Richard, it's important," Minnie added.

The sisters then watched open mouthed as a semi-naked woman several years Richard's senior came into view. "Richie, come back to bed," she said, draping her arms around his neck and pecking at his ear.

"Richard!" Esther crowed. "Richard, what the devil's going on?"

Her grandson quickly shrugged his female companion aside, and they heard him say, "Not now please, it's my Gran!"

In fact the typically red-blooded teen had been seduced by a persistent and extremely provocative journalist who was working on behalf of a popular tabloid newspaper. The lad put up very little in the way of resistance, since girlfriends of late had been thin on the ground to say the least.

"Richard, who was that woman?" Esther stormed.

"Ohhh leave the boy alone, dear," Minnie told her sister. "He's at that age, and is obviously wrestling with his emotions."

"He looks like he's been wrestling with more than his emotions," Esther said, decidedly unimpressed.

In a moment of weakness when confronted with unimaginable temptation, Richard had given the journalist everything she wanted in exchange for a night he would dine out on for the rest of his life. The cat was well and truly out of the bag where Esther and Minnie were concerned, and the tabloid was now privy to their entire life story from humble beginnings to their present day heroic quest and, more importantly, their final destination. There was enough information and photographs from their family albums to serialise their story in the centre pages for several days, earning the media enterprise millions in daily sales.

"Your grandmother?" the journalist said, jostling with Richard. "Can I have a quick word?"

"No, no, you should go!" Richard replied, gathering up her discarded clothes and pushing her towards the door. "Please, I've given you what you wanted, now you really do have to go."

"Okay sweetie," the unscrupulous redhead said, planting a kiss on Richard's cheek, flinging her jacket over one shoulder and marching confidently down the garden path, armed with the story that would undoubtedly secure her a five-figure bonus and possibly that corner office she so craved.

"Richard! Richard!" Esther called until her grandson reappeared. "Richard, will you please tell me what's going on? And where on earth is your mother?"

"Essy!" Minnie snapped. "Never mind all that. We need his help, remember?"

"Oh," Esther said, agitated. "Oh yes, alright go ahead Minnie, but—"

"—Ah ahh," Minnie said, stopping her sister mid-sentence. "Now, Richard dear, we require some assistance," she said, returning to the tablet. "As you know your grandmother and I aren't exactly rocket scientists when it comes to computers."

"Oh I don't know, Aunt Min," Richard replied. "You've been doing a brilliant job uploading your holiday snaps. The two of you are famous, do you know that?"

"Oh I don't know about that, dear," Minnie said modestly. "Anyway, we're far too old for the limelight."

"Get on with it, dear!" Esther insisted, prodding her sister. "Tell him about the virus."

"Virus? What virus?" Richard asked. "Gran are you sure you're alright?"

Peshwari Nans

"Viral dear, viral!" Minnie reiterated. "Richard dear, we have a recording, a video recording I think it's called, of a Good Samaritan here in Nepal and we'd like your help to make it go viral, you know, around the world if possible, with a message attached, urging viewers to donate whatever they can afford to help these beautiful people in their darkest hour."

"Yeah I heard about the earthquakes, Aunt Min," Richard recalled. "A group of friends shaved their legs at Uni and raised six hundred and fifty-five pounds for the appeal."

"Well that's highly commendable," Minnie said, resting on her forearms, "but we need everybody to pitch in, Richard. If this humble gentleman can transform the lives of a handful of victims, just think what a million just like him could achieve? Or two million, five million even? I'm sure, Richard dear, that if they were to see this, this saintly man and the looks on the faces of those he has helped they'll undoubtedly feel the same as we do."

"Great idea, Aunt Min," Richard agreed. "Don't worry, I know exactly what to do. Send it over, will you? Just like you did with the Chinese babies, remember? But attach it to my email, yeah?"

"Attach it to your email?" Minnie said with a blank expression. "Attach it to your what, dear?"

"Don't panic, I'll talk you through it, Aunt Min." Richard laughed. "And leave the message to me, okay? Mum always says I've got a way with words."

"Err, speaking of your mother," Esther called from behind her sister, "I'm amazed she hasn't been in touch of late. What's got into her?"

"Ooooh it's sending!" Minnie squealed. "Richard dear, it's sending. Essy look, I've sent an email."

Peshwari Nans

"Riveting, dear," Esther said, raising her eyes, but not letting her grandson off the hook. "Richard, Richard!" she persisted, "about your mother?"

"Well done Aunt Min," Richard said, opening the mail's attachment. "Leave it to me, yeah? I'll get back to you later. Bye Gran!"

"Richard, Richard!" Esther said, reaching to tap at the screen, but her grandson had signed off and disappeared from view. "Richard? Ooooh that boy!"

"Ohh Essy, he's not a baby anymore," Minnie said, switching off the tablet. "He's a young man, doing exactly what young men do."

"Yes!" Esther snapped. "I can see that!"

Richard watched the footage for himself, over and over again, relieved to be by himself and able to shed many a tear. Charged thus with emotion, Richard set to work uploading the precious clip to every social media platform at his disposal, accompanied by a heartfelt footnote urging, *demanding* even, that the world as a whole should unite and donate as little as a penny, or a nickel, or a cent even, to the floundering fund that had seen donations dwindle because of the reduced media coverage.

Richard went on to name and shame big businesses putting greed before the greater good, and calling for an all-out boycott on them unless they openly agreed to help, and boy did it hit the spot. From the moment the footage went live, a tsunami-like surge bouldered through the Internet, knocking dancing dogs and cats in hats off the top spots of viewed videos, and as Esther had wished, causing a viral virus that corrupted every monitor as the story reached fever pitch.

The phrase 'Together we can do great things' echoed on lips the world over, loosening purse strings, cash registers and safety deposit boxes all at the same time.

"Shall we go, dear?" Esther asked her sister, once they'd packed.

"Yes, let's," Minnie agreed, unravelling a scribbled note. "According to my calculations, dear," she added, holding it closer to her aging eyes, "we have a little over a thousand miles to go before we reach Raipur, and should cross the Indian border later this afternoon. If we make good time, that is."

"Well I don't see why we shouldn't," Esther said, now recharged and invigorated.

Leaving Kathmandu, the sisters headed south and, despite numerous landslips and the consequent diversions, as expected they approached the Nepalese-Indian border a little after 4.30 p.m.

"Essy," Minnie said as their timber-framed veteran vehicle crept in traffic toward the checkpoint.

"I know," Esther replied, watching the to-ing and fro-ing of the gaily coloured Indian buses, mini cabs and pedal powered Tuctucs. "India," she added with an extended sigh of relief.

Thus far Esther and her sister Minnie had visited nine consecutive countries and were about to enter number ten, the home straight as it were.

Trailing some three hundred metres from the border crossing behind a cattle truck, the sisters wound down their windows when an almighty commotion could be heard up ahead. "What is it, dear?" Minnie asked, leaning as far as she dared.

"I have no idea, darling," Esther said, leaning out also. "I do hope we're not delayed."

"Perish the thought," Minnie agreed. But the commotion was no delay, in fact it was the exact opposite.

Border officials who had learnt of the Nans' imminent arrival, dashed from vehicle to vehicle, barking and gesturing for them to pull aside immediately, thus giving up their place in the slow-moving queue to allow the Peshwari Nans to proceed unhindered. "Please, please!" an official called, waving the sisters on.

"It's alright!" Esther replied, raising a hand. "We'll wait our turn."

But the Indian Prime Minister himself had given strict instructions to border staff to do everything within their power to assist in the Nans' swift and incident-free passage, for any hindrance or altercation at this point would undoubtedly heap shame on the current political regime.

"No, please!" the official insisted, halting all incoming traffic and waving the sisters on once again before saluting them as they passed. The sisters looked on, astonished at their unexpected reception.

"No need, madam," a sari-clad woman in passport control said when Esther stopped at her window and offered their documents.

"No need?" Esther said in reply. "Are you quite sure?"

"Of course,." The official smiled. "Please enjoy your stay in our country." She turned to her envious friends in her office, squealing with delight at having addressed the famed Nans.

"Well I never," Minnie said as they breezed on through whilst those behind had their papers closely scrutinized, and more often than not their vehicles searched.

Exiting the border compound, Esther suddenly slammed on Vivien's brakes, awestruck at the sight ahead of them.

"Essy, what?" Minnie gasped, rising in her seat and clutching her sister's arm.

"What indeed?" Esther concurred.

A welcoming committee of as many as seventy vehicles of all shapes, sizes, makes and models, lay in wait at the roadside, each and every one of them adorned with thousands upon thousands of fresh golden marigold blooms, a carnival of colour and an attack on the senses.

One by one horns began to sound and the exuberant drivers leapt from their seats, unfurling makeshift banners and placards expressing their adoration for the visiting sisters, and dashing to shower Vivien with perfumed petals.

"Oh!" Minnie said, alarmed at first when the car was surrounded by the merry mob.

"Hellooooo!" Esther called to the myriad of smiling faces jostling for an optimum viewpoint. "Oh thank you, how kind," she added when a floral garland was strung around her neck through the window, and then another, and another.

Eventually, Esther was forced to give Vivien's horn the tiniest of toots to part the crowd in order to proceed, albeit at a snail's pace.

"Well I never," Minnie said from beneath a mountain of marigolds.

"Excuuuse meeee!" Esther called when further supporters dashed into the road ahead, desperate for a glimpse of the now famous Peshwari Nans.

Many of the Indian nationals raced back to their vehicles and hastily tagged along behind the sisters, cheering and tooting until a three-hundred-metre long carnival procession snaked its way from the border checkpoint.

Esther cleared Vivien's screen with her wiper blades and removed several garlands in order to breathe, whilst her sister sat engulfed in blooms.

The joyous welcoming committee remained in tow even as the sisters left the border town of Raxaul and made their way through lush wetlands teaming with strutting egrets that were stabbing at the small fry at their feet.

Quickening the pace now to thirty miles per hour, Vivien left a flurry of petals in her wake as did the jubilant autocade behind. Further evidence of their global notoriety came when a near naked gent who was a day over ninety years of age, and wearing what could only be described as a sagging sumo-like wrap, leapt to his feet at the roadside in his home village of Chapwa. He hopped and bobbed with both hands clasped to his head, wild eyed. "YOUUUUUUU, YOUUUUUU!" he shrieked, pointing the sisters' way as they slowed to pass an ox in the road. "YOUUUUUUU, YOU ARE THE PESHWARRRI NANS!"

Esther waved sedately, mildly embarrassed at his outlandish exhibition. "Yes." She nodded "I suppose we are."

Minnie, having received twice the number of garlands that her sister had, tugged them from her face and eyed the gent from head to toe, admiring his enduring agility and of course the wrap that was tethered about his groin.

"Apparently, dear, that's what's known as eye candy," she told her sister, who quickly averted her eyes when the animated village elder, in a heightened state of hysteria, whipped off the said wrap and swung it in a circular motion above his head. "PESHWARRRI NANS, PESHWARRRI NANS!" he continued to call.

"Candy, you say?" Esther sneered. "Thank you dear, but I think I'll stick with my sugared almonds."

"Suit yourself, dear," Minnie said, turning a full one hundred-and-eighty degrees to watch him to the last.

"Minnie!" Esther barked, bringing her sister to her senses. "Have you no shame?"

"Shame, dear?" Minnie replied. "Oh I left that behind in gym class when I traded a kiss for a yo-yo behind the trampoline."

"A yo-yo?" Esther scoffed. "Sister dear, I must confess I always thought you a little cheap, but to sell your dignity for a mere trifle is low by any stretch of the imagination."

"In that case, dear," Minnie said, tongue-in-cheek, "I daren't tell you what I had to do for the slinky."

"Oh dear God, please don't!" Esther said in haste whilst attempting to blot out all thoughts of her sister's adolescent amorous bartering. Minnie on the other hand sat with a knowing smile, recalling in vivid detail the titillating terms and conditions of the trade.

At regular intervals along Highway 28, groups of buoyant Indians gathered to greet their country's honoured guests, tossing flowers and confetti ahead of them to provide a spectacular scented carpet. "Oh how lovely," Esther gushed, rounding a bend to see a mile or so of straight road hidden beneath a rich tapestry of orchids, lilies, jasmine, azalea and rhododendron blooms, a mesmerising mosaic lovingly laid as far as the eye could see.

Minnie busily snapped the spectacular sight and the smiling faces gathered nearby for the benefit and delight of their global audience. Spellbound by the route ahead, the sisters failed to notice the cortège growing rapidly in length, as more and more motorists rushed to join them.

Their arrival had been broadcast the length and breadth of the Indian subcontinent, interrupting every network channel, even their beloved test cricket, for which much of the country ordinarily ground to a halt.

But soon it wasn't just the Indian nationals following the two weary travellers in their Trafalgar-blue Morris. Three Americans in a camper van, six Dutch motorcyclists and a coachload of Australian tourists detoured from their planned vacations to join the growing movement, eager to be a part of something colossal and yet so captivatingly charming.

Esther at one point pulled to the side of the road, assuming that the pomp-fuelled procession behind wished to pass, but was dumbstruck when each and every reveller did exactly the same and sat with bated breath, waiting for them to proceed. It appeared that the GPS attachment to each of Minnie's uploaded images drew willing participants from across the continent like moths to a flickering flame.

Never before had such a gathering been witnessed, it was a carnival to dwarf the likes of Rio De Janeiro, London's Notting Hill and Trinidad and Tobago. Media teams were dispatched in private jets from as far afield as Nova Scotia, Canada to capture the event that gripped every man, woman and child who had taken the Nans to their hearts.

Three hours from the border, a staggering eight-hundred vehicles now trailed the Morris, whilst bombarding Facebook, Twitter and Instagram with more images than their combined steaming servers could cope with. And an hour later Russian cosmonauts aboard the international space station who were photographing China's Great Wall, turned their attentions, and lenses for that matter, towards central India, marvelling at the miniscule millipede-like movement that was now visible almost four hundred kilometres beneath them.

Offerings of steaming chai were handed through the windows to the sisters en route, while ribbons and streamers were attached to Vivien's mirrors and bumpers.

"Essy!" Minnie suddenly said, sitting bolt upright and rigid, startling her sister. "Look!"

Esther slammed on the brakes as did those behind, and the two elderly Londoners' jaws dropped on seeing the name Raipur for the very first time on an adjacent sign, with the figure 75 km beneath it. It was a stone's throw away in comparison with their past meteoric endeavours.

"Raipur," Minnie said, reaching down to retrieve Jasvinder's tin. "My God, Essy."

Esther switched off Vivien's engine and slumped back into her seat. "My God indeed, dear," she said, quite overcome and tearful.

Peshwari Nans

"Hey, hey, heyyyy," Minnie said, rubbing her sister's arm. "Shh, shh, shhh, don't cry, my darling, don't cry, believe me I know exactly how you feel, but we must remain strong to the last, for Jasvinder's sake."

"I'm sorry." Esther sobbed. "I don't know what came over me, Minnie."

"Pride, dear," Minnie informed her. "It was pride, at what the two of us have accomplished, thus far that is. As the sign says, we still have a ways to go."

"You're right," Esther said, popping open her door. "You don't mind if I savour the moment, do you dear?"

"Of course not," Minnie replied, following Esther out of the car.

The two eighty-somethings stood shoulder to shoulder at the roadside in awe of the simple crooked yellow sign, saying 'Raipur 75 km'. It was approximately forty-six miles to their journey's end.

"Quickly, dear!" Esther blurted, embracing technology for the first time. "Take a selfish, take a selfish!"

"You mean a selfie, dear." Minnie smirked as the pair turned their backs on the sign, with Minnie raising the tablet. It was then that the true extent of their following hit home. Slowly lowering the device Minnie, along with her sister, tilted their heads and took a step to the side to see the sheer scale of the travelling supporters behind them.

From their elevated vantage point Esther and Minnie could quite easily see some seven or eight miles to their rear, but still the motorcade extended further, each of them stirred and stimulated into taking part in by now what was fast becoming the longest single-file procession ever recorded.

"Why, Essy?" Minnie asked. "Why?"

"If only I knew, Minnie dear," her sister said, waving sheepishly to their army of joyous admirers, who hung on their every move. "O......kay, perhaps we should go," she then said, sliding back into Vivien and checking the line again in her rear-view mirror to confirm it was no dream.

"COOOOEEEEEEEEEE!" Minnie called back in a far more animated manner. "LOVELY DAYYYYY!"

"Minnie, get in!" Esther said, pushing open her sister's door, unnerved by the masses in tow. Minnie was given a rapturous reply which reverberated like a Mexican wave along the line of exhilarated followers.

"Buckle up, dear," Esther told her sister, turning Vivien's ignition key.

But instead of the reliable whir of Vivien's 48 brake horse power engine, there was nothing. Esther tried again. And again.

"What is it, dear?" Minnie asked, buckled up in readiness. "What's wrong?"

"I don't know, dear" Esther replied, tweaking Vivien's choke and pumping her accelerator.

"Try it again," Minnie said, offering very little in the way of constructive advice. "Wiggle the thingy!"

"I am, I am!" Esther snapped, beginning the starting procedure from scratch and step by step, but still there was nothing.

Several minutes passed and Esther grew increasingly concerned. "Oh hell!" she cursed. "Not now, Vivien dear, not now!"

A concerned driver behind stepped from his decorated taxi and approached the sisters, keeping a respectful distance from Esther's window.

"I'm sorry, but it won't start!" Esther called to him, twisting the key over and over and fearing a possible road-rage altercation. "I'm sorry if we appear to be blocking the road."

The taxi driver, who only spoke in Bengali, realized her predicament straight away and began yelling and beckoning to several of his fellow countrymen behind. He then gestured to Esther to release Vivien's bonnet as a crowd gathered beside him. "No wait!" Esther called out. "It's probably nothing, really!" but again he and the others gestured for her to open up the bonnet.

"You'd best do as they say, dear," Minnie said, peering over the dashboard. Vivien's bonnet was raised and supported and a dozen raven-haired heads peered beneath, each of them vying to be heard above his neighbour and offering their own high-pitched diagnosis.

Soon wrenches of all sizes were being thrust into Vivien's engine bay as the crowd jostled, dislodging several of their turbans in the process. "Oh Lord," Esther said, deeply concerned for Vivien's wellbeing. "What are they doing?"

With each of the would-be mechanics yelling above those beside him, the indecipherable din and consequent rocking of Vivien from side to side had the sisters quaking in their pixie boots, but what was to follow had Esther clutching her pounding heart, when suddenly Vivien's engine, in all its entirety, was plucked from its housing before her very eyes.

"Essy dear!" Minnie gasped. "Isn't that?"

"Yes!" Esther replied, wide-eyed. "Yes, yes it is. HEYYYYY!" she yelled from her window. "Hey, what in God's name do you think you're doing? You put that back, do you hear me? You put that back right now!"

Unwilling to leave their seats and confront the mechanical mob, the sisters watched in horror as the engine was lowered onto the grass verge and dismantled, piece by antiquated piece.

"Hellooooo!" Minnie called. "Is that really necessary?"

But her protestations fell short of the Indians' cacophonous chattering.

"I sayyyyy!" she added. "Yoohooooo!"

Peshwari Nans

Although the scene appeared chaotic and alarming to say the least, the Indians were in fact doing what they do best: making do with the limited recourses at their disposal. Three men raced to a rusting abandoned harvester in an adjacent field, wrenching the engine cover free and tugging at the belts and pulleys, while a fellow motorist was flagged down and persuaded to donate all of his spark plugs, thus rendering his own vehicle redundant.

This riotous cannibalism went on for a full half hour before a cheer erupted, and Vivien's reassembled engine was proudly raised above the mechanics' heads and paraded for a moment like the arc of the covenant itself, before being ceremoniously lowered back into place, as though they were setting a precious gemstone in its gilded mount.

"What on earth?" Esther asked, as once again Vivien was buffeted by the beavering Bengalis, Sikhs and Hindus alike, who meticulously reassembled her beloved car until eventually Vivien's dust-covered bonnet was lowered, revealing a swarm of perspiring but smiling faces.

"Kooshish kooshish!" an Indian in a grease-spattered robe shrieked at Esther's side, which in Hindi means "Try try!"

"Sorry, what?" Esther replied, shrugging her shoulders.

"Try the key, dear," Minnie exclaimed, hazarding a guess. "Go on, try it."

"Okay, okay," Esther said, springing upright. "Right, here goes."

Miraculously, on the very first twitch of the key Vivien leapt into life and responded beautifully to Esther's prodding of the accelerator.

"Woopeeeeeee!" Minnie squealed, clapping her hands. "Oh how marvellous, thank you, thank youuuuu!" she added, reaching out to shake one or two oily hands. "Thank you ever so much."

Peshwari Nans

Esther reached for her purse. "Now you must let me give you something for your troubles, dear," she told those passing by her window, but not a single soul stopped to take advantage of her generosity. "I sayyyyyy!" she called out, waving a note. "Please! It's only right!"

But in an instant they were gone.

"Onwards and upwards, dear," Minnie told her sister, fastening her belt.

"Precisely, dear," Esther agreed, pocketing her purse and gripping the wheel. "Riiiight," she sighed, selecting first gear and together with her sister, eyed the sign for Raipur in passing.

Were the sisters to maintain an average speed of thirty miles per hour, which in Vivien's newly refurbished condition would be a breeze, then the two could expect to reach their destination within the following ninety minutes.

This was a destination also now known to the wider world, thanks to Richard's loose tongue at the hands of a cunning seductress. Their current position and previous progress was now the subject of discussion on television and radio channels broadcasting across every continent.

NASA satellites had been reprogrammed to track the tiny car, and even the multi-billion dollar Hubble telescope, which scoured the universe in search of black holes and nebula such as the famed 'Pillars of creation', was rotated one hundred-and-eighty degrees and directed earthward, beaming breathtaking, high resolution imagery of the travelling circus. And again the masses assembled to witness the spectacle in greater numbers, in streets, parks and stadiums alike on huge concert screens, the largest gathering of like-minded souls since Live Aid in the 1985 festival. And all for two uber-sweet sisters and their tiny classic car. If the feelgood factor could have been bottled and labelled as 'Esther and Minnie's elixir of life', then the populous would queue to drink it, bathe in it even.

Peshwari Nans

Huge sporting fixtures such as the Superbowl, The Ashes, Wimbledon and the Ryder Cup were postponed due to lack of interest. All eyes were on that car and its precious occupants.

Raipur, the aforementioned rice-bowl of India, was soon a mere twenty kilometres away from the aged travellers, and Ravi's family farm a stone's throw from the centre. The hooting and cheering behind grew louder and louder it seemed with every yard gained, as it did across the globe.

And then, there it was: Raipur. Rising resplendent from the Indian state of Chhattisgarh, west of the mighty Mahanadi, or Great River, and dating back to the ninth century. Esther and Minnie rose in their seats, lengthening their crooked spines to take in the panorama.

The tension inside the British motoring icon grew and grew as it did in living rooms and stadiums thousands of miles away.

"This is it, dear," Minnie said as Vivien rolled as gracefully as her namesake from the dirt track dividing two rice paddy fields and onto the approach road, while kings, queens and presidents set aside all official engagements to share in this meteoric moment.

Esther reached and took Minnie's hand and the inseparable pair held their breath when crossing a line that separated dry dirt from concrete.

"Essy!" Minnie gasped, squeezing her sister's fingers.

"I know, I know," Esther squealed with a dry mouth and her heart thumping in her chest.

At that precise moment a simultaneous cheer erupted worldwide, from modest terraced houses to the palaces and stately homes of the ordinarily stiff-upper-lipped monarchy. With cheeks flushed, Minnie now crumbled and put her head in her hands, unable to curb her emotions a moment longer.

Peshwari Nans

"We did it, Minnie my love," Esther said, caressing the small of her back as she bent double. "We did it."

The road led directly to the centre of town, where the majority of the followers stopped, alighted and joined their fellow countrymen and visitors alike to revel in the achievement.

"Excuuuse meeee!" Esther called to a local stallholder, who was peddling fine silks and linens. "I wonder, could you help me, dear?" She produced the basmati rice bag that the dying Jasvinder had given her. "I'm looking for this address. Is it far, do you know?"

The salesman took the bag from Esther. "Ahhhhh," he said, flashing his yellowing teeth. "Ravi, Ravi."

"Yes, yes, that's right," Esther replied, gripping Minnie's arm. "Do you know him?"

The stallholder prodded the symbol on the rice bag and pointed to the left-hand fork in the road and jabbered in Hindi.

"I'm sorry, what?" Esther asked. "I don't understand dear, my sister and I are from out of town, you see."

The animated gentleman thrust the symbol of a wallowing water buffalo under Esther's nose and again gestured to the left fork.

"That way?" Esther asked. "Ravi? That way?"

"Haan haan," (meaning 'Yes yes') The Indian nodded, handing back the rice bag and ushering them on. "Ravi!" he added with yet another toothy smile.

"Okay, left it is." Esther smiled. "Thank you. And good day to you, sir."

"Where to, dear?" Minnie asked, assuming that Esther had confidently conversed with the natives.

"I haven't the foggiest," Esther confessed, shrugging her shoulders and tossing Minnie the rice bag.

While their followers prepared to celebrate with wine, fine food and firecrackers in the centre of town, Esther and

Peshwari Nans

Minnie proceeded alone for several hundred yards, taking a left as instructed to the rural side of Raipur, where they passed the gates of the capital's lesser known rice producers.

"What are we looking for, dear?" Minnie asked, looking in either direction. "Oh wait!" she then shrieked, prodding the rice package herself. "Look dear, look!"

Sure enough, the sacred beast depicted on the basmati bag matched that on an adjacent smallholding entrance.

"That's it!" Minnie added. "Essy stop, look! Look! It's Ravi's farm!"

Esther slowed, turned into the open broken five-bar gate and stopped beside the sign, unable to decipher the inscription. But the logo's similarity was undeniable.

"Minnie dear, I do believe you're right," she told her sister, proceeding along the track that was bordered on either side by a rush-filled drainage ditch, until they came up to Ravi's family home.

"Oh how charming," Minnie said and sighed, gazing out at the simple timber construction, hand painted in canary yellow, with fly screens at the windows and galvanised corrugated sheets forming the shallow pitched roof.

Staying put in their seats while the dust cloud whipped up by Vivien's wheels settled, Esther and Minnie quietly gathered their thoughts. The last time the two of them had seen Ravi, he and his beautiful Jasvinder had lovingly prepared pakoras, Dahl and chapattis to share with them the night before his journey home, to be at his father's bedside.

The ill-fitting screen door opened and Ravi's grandmother appeared, shielding her eyes with one hand whilst stabbing at the veranda with her cane, unsteady on her feet, wearing a plain white sari pulled up over her head.

"Oh hello, my dear!" Esther called, stepping from Vivien and beckoning to her sister, who hurried along behind, clutching the Lipton's tea tin. "I er, I hope you don't mind us turning up unannounced like this," Esther added, dragging her sister close to her side for moral support. "Out of the blue as it were."

The aged Indian matriarch looked beyond both sisters at their unorthodox mode of transport. "Vivien!" Esther called to her. "She's called Vivien, my name's Esther and this fine upstanding individual is my sister Minnie. We were friends of Jasvinder's, the best of friends I might add."

"Jasvinder!" the grandmother said, raising a hand to her ear.

"Yes, yes. Jazzy!" Minnie piped up. "She lived upstairs you see, back home in Whitechapel, that's in the UK in case you were wondering. Anyway she asked us to come, no, no actually she was quite insistent we came, to see Ravi that is."

"Is he home?" Esther asked, looking over the grandmother's shoulder. "I dare say he'll be surprised to see us."

"Surprised indeed" Minnie echoed.

Ravi's aged relative turned and took several tottering steps towards the family's five-acre rice paddy.

"Raviiiiii, Raviiiiii!" she called, waving her stick above her head to a group of labourers, who were bent over, ankle deep in caramel-coloured water.

Ravi rose from amid them with a hand to his aching back, having planted several thousand basmati shoots that morning alone. On seeing the warm familiar faces of his former neighbours, Ravi froze for a moment, letting the bundle of lush green basmati fall from his hand. Of course he had learnt of the sisters' courageous efforts to reach Raipur, but the reality of them actually succeeding was almost too much to bear. He put a hand to his quivering lips and wept openly, while his companions continued working with their heads bowed.

Peshwari Nans

"Ravi, my darling!" Esther called, raising a hand while Minnie removed her straw hat and waved it above her head.

Ravi, in turned-up trousers, sandals and a wrinkled paisley shirt, tugged his feet from the sodden mud and made his way toward them, extending both arms as he approached in floods of tears.

"Oh come, my dear," Esther said, offering her own arms until the two embraced, with the basmati farmer bawling on her shoulder. "There, there, my darling," Esther said, rubbing his back tenderly. "It's so wonderful to see you, it really is, Ravi dear."

"Yes, wonderful," Minnie agreed.

Ravi reached and pulled Minnie to them, hugging the sisters tightly. "Hello, Ravi dear," Minnie said, wiping a tear from her eye. "We found you, we found you at last!"

Ravi eventually pulled away and dried his eyes on his shirtsleeves. "Mrs Esther, Miss Minnie," he said, emotionally charged. "I, I don't know what to say. I heard you were coming but I had no idea why."

"For Jazzy," Esther informed him while his grandmother hobbled back to the house to prepare chai and edibles for their guests. "I was with her you see, when she…" Esther paused to clear her throat. "When she…"

"You were with my Jasvinder?" Ravi asked.

"Yes," Esther replied solemnly. "Yes I was. She spoke of you, Ravi, in fact she spoke of nothing else, God bless her."

Minnie took his hand. "She loved you deeply, you do know that, don't you?" she said, trembling at the knees "Without a shadow of a doubt."

"She is here," Ravi said, gesturing towards a clump of banyan trees, which cast a long cool shadow across the family's neatly cultivated lawn. Jasvinder's body had been flown back to India and buried beneath the banyan boughs a week before the sisters arrived.

"Jazzy's here?" Esther asked, following Ravi tentatively. "Oh Minnie, look dear," she then said, observing the tranquil setting and the freshly turned mound of soil with its simple headstone.

"Please, come." Ravi beckoned when the sisters paused within feet of their friend's shallow grave. "I told her you were coming," he continued. "I talk to Jasvinder every day."

He stooped to jostle the fresh flowers he had recently laid, and to brush the fallen debris from the banyan trees. "I told her," he added with a fondness in his voice. "I said Jasvinder my love, Esther and Minnie are coming, I do not know how, but apparently they are coming to Raipur."

"Well, Ravi darling," Esther explained, "it's been something of an ordeal I have to admit. But I know I speak for my sister too, when I say we'd do it all again in a heartbeat for our Jazzy."

"Oh yes in a heartbeat, dear." Minnie nodded. "A heartbeat."

Esther lowered herself onto one knee with Ravi's help and placed a hand onto the crumbling clay. "Oh Jazzy my darling," she said, her voice breaking along with her heart. "My friend," she added, driving her fingers into the dirt. "And your father, Ravi?" she asked, looking up. "Is he?"

"Taken by the fever," Ravi replied, pointing to a second grave several yards away. The yellow fever that Ravi's father had contracted had been an extremely virulent strain, taking his life in a matter of days. He had been laid to rest beside Ravi's mother, who had perished giving birth to the youngest of his brothers.

"Oh Ravi, I'm so terribly sorry," Esther said, clambering to her feet. "I can't imagine how you must be feeling, I truly can't."

"It's alright, Mrs Esther," Ravi said, flashing the bravest of smiles. "They are here, all together."

Peshwari Nans

Minnie took his hand. "And you're a credit to them, Ravi dear," she told him, nestling in close. "And might I add, so brave."

"Yes ever so brave indeed," Esther agreed.

"Me?" Ravi replied, shaking his head. "It is you who are brave, look at you. You are here, in Raipur!"

"Ohhhhhh it was nothing, dear," Minnie joked.

"Really!" Esther smirked.

Minnie produced the tea tin. "I believe this is yours, my dear," she said, handing it to Ravi, and in doing so completing their quest. "Jazzy wanted you to have it."

Ravi's hand shook as he took the savings he and his love had scraped together through hard work, sacrifice and sheer determination. Ravi cradled their money box close to his chest, the link to his sweetheart at his feet.

"Jasvinder always said we should save for the future," he told the sisters. "I wanted a holiday but she said it was a shameful extravagance, and she was right. Jasvinder was always right."

"Oh I don't know, my dear," Esther said, looking about the place. "I'd say you should allow yourself that extravagance, shameful or otherwise."

"No, no, Jasvinder would never forgive me," Ravi replied resolutely. "Besides, the harvest has been weak this year and we are behind with our payments."

"Payments?" Minnie asked.

"Yes," Ravi added. "My father was forced to remortgage the farm with a Bengali bank, but rising interest rates and falling basmati prices mean that one day we could lose everything. Many of our friends and neighbours await a similar fate."

"Oh heavens, no!" Esther said, taking Ravi's wrist. "Haven't you suffered—"

Peshwari Nans

Before she could finish the three of them looked skyward on hearing the whir of approaching helicopter blades, a rarity for Raipur to say the least.

"What the devil?" Esther asked, shielding her eyes from the dazzling afternoon sun.

"I can't see a damn thing," Minnie moaned, removing her spectacles and polishing the lenses on the hem of her skirt.

"There!" Ravi suddenly said, pointing out a blurred silhouette approaching from the west.

Ravi's three bothers and an uncle rose from the rice paddy and made tracks for the bank in the ankle deep water. There they ducked out of sight among the banyans.

"I do believe it's heading this way," Esther said, reaching for her sister. "Minnie, stay close," she warned her.

"American," Ravi remarked, making out the familiar outline of a Black Hawk. "American military."

"Military!" Minnie said, donning her spectacles. "Essy what would the American military want with us?"

Esther glared at her sister. "I was about to ask you the same question," she said with her hands on her hips. "What have you gone and done?"

"Nothing dear," Minnie said in her defence. "I swear."

"Miniiiiiie," Esther said disbelievingly.

"Honest, dear." Minnie squirmed. "Oh wait a minute," she then said, suddenly recalling an online altercation. "There was that one thing."

"One thing?" Esther growled as the helicopter sped their way, swooping low over the rice paddys and dispersing the water with its powerful rotors. "What one thing?"

"Well," Minnie said, inching away.

"Well what?" Esther insisted. "Come on, out with it!"

"It wasn't my fault," Minnie said, reluctant to divulge the details of the sensitive incident.

Peshwari Nans

"Minnie!" her sister barked, reaching for her sister as the Black Hawk touched down on the opposite side of the banyan grove, sending the uncle and brothers scurrying to the house for cover, while Ravi stood firm. "What have you done?"

Ravi plucked up the courage to investigate, leaving Esther at Minnie's throat.

"It was just my personal opinion, that's all!" Minnie squealed, with her sister's hand on her collar. "That's all, Essy, I swear!"

"Minnie, if you don't tell me right now I'll, I'll," Esther said, pausing to face Jasvinder's grave. "I'm sorry Jazzy dear," she told her departed friend, "but knowing my sister as well as you do, I'm sure you'll forgive my frustrations. Okay Minnie, out with it. What did you say to bring the American military down on us, hmmmm?"

"I merely suggested," Minnie said sheepishly, "that maybe instead of wasting billions of dollars waging war in foreign parts, their money would be better spent tackling their growing obesity epidemic perhaps, or homelessness, that's all."

"Oh," Esther said, stunned somewhat. "I see. Well I must say for once I wholeheartedly agree with you, dear, well said."

"And," Minnie added, taking yet another step back.

"And?" Esther said as the rotor blades slowed behind them. "And what exactly Minnie? What did you say?"

"That, 'em," Minnie stammered, "that JFK was clearly assassinated by the CIA, as well as Abe Lincoln, Malcolm X, Martin Luther, Marilyn, Mahatma Gandhi and possibly, Elvis."

"WHAT?" Esther shrieked, slapping a hand to her forehead, horrified at her sister's ludicrous and somewhat brazen accusations. "Minnie what have you done, you fool?"

Peshwari Nans

Fearing the self-same fate from the Black Hawks' occupants, Esther took her sister firmly by the arm and marched her bodily towards Vivien. "How could you be so stupid?" she raged.

"But, but dear, it was just my opinion," Minnie said, her feet barely touching the ground.

"Your opinion!" Esther snarled. "I'm surprised you haven't blamed the Americans for the demise of Julius Caesar and the BLASTED DINOSAURS. Now get in the car! Hurry damn you!"

"Ahhhhh ladies," a voice behind suddenly called out. "Boy am I glad to finally meet you."

"Damn!" Esther said, freezing rigid to the spot and turning moments later to see a smiling Karl Bodine, with Ravi at his side.

"Look I'm sorry," Esther confessed. "I'm sure she meant nothing by it, did you Minnie?"

"No, no, not at all," Minnie agreed, ducking behind her sister and peering over her shoulder. "It was just my opinion, that's all. I assure you it wasn't my intention to offend you, not my intention at all."

"Offend me?" Karl laughed. "Why in God's name would you have offended me? Quite the opposite in fact ma'am."

"I'm sorry, but I don't understand," Esther said, shielding her sister. "Who are you?"

"Bodine, ma'am," Karl said, approaching and offering his hand. "Karl Bodine, and I've been wanting to meet you ladies and shake you by the hand."

"Bodine, you say?" Minnie said, peering round her sister and recalling the gaming guru's rise to fame on the Internet. "The boy with the Midas touch, isn't that what they say?"

"Yeah, thanks to the both of you," Karl replied, removing his mirrored shades and tucking them into the breast pocket of his Italian designer jacket. "The Gran

Thrift franchise has outsold all of its major competitors combined and turned the industry on its head overnight."

"Gran thrift?" Esther mouthed. "I'm sorry, why are you here?" she then asked, eyeing the Black Hawk behind him. "And what's with the military whirly bird? I'll have you know you gave the two of us quite a start."

"Yes, quite a start," Minnie said, peering around her sister.

"She's a beaut, ain't she?" Karl said proudly. "The Pentagon was having a yard sale so I bought three of these babies."

"Three of them?" Minnie exclaimed, raising an eyebrow.

"Yes, yes!" Esther remarked, unimpressed. "That's all very nice Mr Bodie but—"

"Bodine," Karl interjected. "It's Bodine, ma'am."

"Yes of course it is, but why are you here?" Esther asked, vexed at the untimely intrusion.

Karl turned to his waiting Helicopter. "Hazel honey!" he called, summoning his PA, a stick-thin brunette, whose buoyant breasts came into view before the rest of her. "Come on out here, baby!"

Hazel had ruby red lips, and tiptoed from the Black Hawk in Parisian heels, wearing a figure-hugging lycra body suit in lime green.

"I figured I owe something to you two," Karl told the sisters as Hazel tottered to his side. "How does thirty-five million sound?"

"I'm sorry?" Esther bid, bewildered as to Karl's intentions. "Thirty five million what exactly?"

"Dollars, pounds." Karl smiled. "Hell you can have it any way you please, ma'am." He gestured to his lovely assistant, who tapped at a digital pad. "Little Miss Cutie pie here's ready to wire the payment directly into an account of your choosing, just say the word."

Peshwari Nans

"Wire the payment?" Minnie asked "Mr Bodie am I right in assuming—"

"Bodine!" Karl said, correcting the second sister. "It's Bodine, ma'am, and you must be Minnie."

"Yes, yes that's right," Minnie replied, rooted to the spot beside her sister. "So let me get this straight, young man," she added apprehensively. "You have flown here from the United States in your whirly bird to offer us a mountain of money, am I right?"

"Hell yeah." Karl smiled. "Believe me, you earned it, every cent." Karl went on to explain how the globetrotting sisters inspired not only himself but an entire generation of gaming retirees, yielding unprecedented revenue for his fledgling company.

"I'm sorry, but we cannot accept your money," Esther eventually said, having heard enough. "We did this for our dear friend Jasvinder, not for monetary gain."

"Essy, Essy!" Minnie whispered, tugging her sister's arm. "May I remind you that we currently have eleven pounds to our name and our pensions aren't due until a week Thursday. We're broke, dear. To put it bluntly we haven't got a pot to…"

"Yes, yes I get the picture!" Esther stormed. "But it wouldn't be right I tell you. No I'm sorry Mr Bodie, it's awfully kind of you to offer but—"

"—Esther Reynolds!" Minnie said with increased conviction, tugging her sister aside and conversing in private, occasionally gesturing towards the bemused Ravi.

"Oh," Esther eventually said. "Yes I see what you mean, perhaps I was a little hasty."

"Hasty?" Minnie scoffed before turning her attentions to the young entrepreneur. "We'll take it," she said abruptly. "All of it, every penny. Thank you."

"Yes indeed," Esther agreed. "But as my sister has quite rightly suggested, there are some far more deserving beneficiaries than ourselves. Minnie dear, would you do the honours?"

"Yes of course, dear," Minnie replied, approaching Karl's pretty PA. "Hazel my darling, might I have a word?" she said, taking the girl to one side and informing her of upwards of a dozen cash-strapped charities, the plight of the Nepalese quake victims, and of course Ravi and his fellow rice farmers, who were indebted to the Bengali bank, whose bully-boy tactics of foreclosures and repossessions had led to many of their kind taking their own lives rather than face the indignity of eviction.

"Consider it done," Hazel eventually said, having listed the worthwhile causes. "But our lawyers insist that you ladies receive a monthly dividend from the company and have settled on three per cent, do you have any objections?"

"Oh no, I don't think so, deary," Minnie agreed. "Three per cent, Essy darling!" she told her sister. "I think we can live with that, don't you?"

"Well," Esther pondered, "I suppose a few extra pennies would come in handy. There's that balding lavatory brush I've been meaning to replace, and as you are well aware, Minnie dearest, our clothes pegs have certainly seen better days."

"Precisely, dear," Minnie said, clasping her hands together. "And perhaps, dare I say it, we could replace the Royal Albert. I've seen a partial set on a bric-a-brac stall on Petticoat Lane. They're asking five pounds but there's a chip on the teapot spout, so I'd imagine if the gods were in our favour we could barter them down to three-fifty."

"Splendid idea, Minnie," Esther said, patting her sister's crooked back.

The extra pennies the sisters presumed would be coming their way would be more in the region of a five-figure salary, paid on the first of each month for the remainder of their days. Profits in 'Bodine Gaming' were expected to reach an all-time high in the run-up to Christmas, while merchandising also boosted its quarterly accounts. The pint-sized Esther and Minnie figurines were literally flying off the shelves, with scenes on occasion reminiscent of the Black Friday disturbances following reports of empty shelves and a delay in delivery by the Chinese importers.

Collectors clambered for miniature Morris Travellers, of which the Trafalgar-blue coloured model was undoubtedly the most popular. But more surprising was the unprecedented demand for the life sized 'woodys' (the colloquial name for the timber framed cars) themselves, so much in fact, that many of Morris's former aged employees were lured back from their allotments and pigeon coops to take their place once again on the historic production line, with an order book filled until the foreseeable future. The British automobile industry was about to regain a strong foothold in a global market that had formerly been dominated by the Germans, the Italians and the Japanese.

Karl shook the ladies by the hands. "Listen I gotta fly," he told them as Hazel crossed the Ts and dotted the Is, bequeathing the sisters' healthy lump sum to their chosen beneficiaries. "Why don't you let me give you a ride home?" Karl suggested, heading back to his Black Hawk with Hazel in tow. "It really is quite a rush, I tell ya."

"Oh good heavens no," Esther replied insistently. "I couldn't possibly, not with my thrombosis. But thanks all the same."

"Minnie?" Karl asked. "How about you?"

"Thank you kindly Mr Bodie," Minnie said, standing firm at her sister's side. "But it's all for one and one for all, as the Three Stooges would say!"

"Musketeers," Esther said, correcting her sister.

"I'm sorry, what was that, dear?" Minnie asked as the Hawk's rotors began to whir.

"IT WAS THE MUSKETEERS!" Esther yelled above the din.

"WHAT WAS, DEAR?" Minnie again asked, with a hand to her ear.

"ALL FOR ONE AND ONE FOR ALL!" Esther yelled, waving to Karl and co. as they rose into the air and turned across the rice paddys. "IT WAS THE MUSKETEERS, FOR PETE'S SAKE!"

"Are you sure, dear?" Minnie pondered with tranquillity soon restored. "I believe I beg to differ, but in the spirit of harmony and sisterly love we'll simply agree to disagree, don't you think?"

"No, no, I don't think!" Esther raged, with Ravi still very much in the dark and his in-laws returning to the paddy. "I know I'm right, hell everybody knows I'm right. IT WAS THE THREE MUSKETEERS!"

"Esther!" Minnie snapped at Jasvinder's graveside. "Please, show some respect won't you?"

"Oooh, one of these days," Esther growled under her breath.

Ravi's grandmother served refreshments on the porch a short while later. "How can I ever repay you?" Ravi told the sisters as they sipped sweet chai (tea) in the shade. "To know our home is now safe is truly a blessing, a blessing from Vishnu himself." Ravi looked out across the family paddy with the Lipton's tin held tightly in his hands. "You know," he added decisively, "I will take that holiday after all. I have a sister in Mumbai I have not seen in many many years, and when I return I will buy more land, and invest in the modern machinery my father always wanted for our farm. I will make them proud, all of them, you will see."

The wind rustled through the banyan trees as though the deceased were voicing their approval. Ravi's dream of forming a coalition with his fellow basmati farmers would soon become a reality, with the weakest amongst them having an equal share in the profits and access to technology thus far denied to them. This cooperative would also serve to stabilize the local economy and to bring prosperity to those that deserved it the most, those that broke their backs day in and day out cultivating a staggering seventy per cent of the world's basmati rice.

"And you will succeed, Ravi darling," Esther told him whilst reaching for the tandoori chicken. But then out of the corner of her eye, she caught sight of her sister's disapproving glare, and recalling her gastric fiasco with the Uzbeki kebab, and it's cringe-worthy contents of buttocks and beaks, she swiftly opted for the vegetable samosas instead.

The sisters, along with Ravi and his grandmother, were later startled when an aerial display of fireworks broke high above the banyans, the sight reflecting beautifully in the shallow waters of the rice paddys.

"Oh good heavens!" Esther shrieked, clutching her chest and her sister's arm simultaneously.

"Ooooh, look dear," Minnie said, delighted. "How wonderful!"

"Ravi, what is it?" Esther asked, flinching with every thunderous explosion and kicking the samosa she'd dropped to the scavenging yard dog.

"It is Holi!" Ravi informed them. "Our festival of colours. It is held every year in the centre of Raipur. We should go."

"Ooooh, can we Essy? Can we?" Minnie chirped, bobbing in her wicker chair. "Pleeeeeease, Essy dear?"

"Only if you promise to stop that pathetic whining," Esther replied, brushing the crumbs from her lap for the mongrel at her feet.

Peshwari Nans

"Yes, yes, yes!" Minnie squealed. "I read about Holi in the National Geographic at the library, Essy dear. It looks like tremendous fun."

"Oh Miss Minnie, it is," Ravi reiterated. "But I must warn you do not be wearing your best clothes to Holi."

This was because revellers attending the annual festival hurled brightly coloured powders and water at one another, and sang and danced in the open street. It was a period of thanksgiving where broken relationships are often restored and good is seen to prevail over evil.

"My dear Ravi," Esther said, wincing once again as a barrage of rockets detonated in rapid succession. "The last time Minnie and I wore our best clothes, the Germans had just surrendered to the western allies and Mother bought us both matching pinafores for the street party."

Ravi helped the sisters from their seats. "I assure you, you will have the most wonderful time," he said, before racing to the edge of the rice paddy to summon his relatives. "COME, COME, HOLI HAS BEGUN!" he yelled, beckoning wildly. "HURRY NOW!"

The eager farmers threw aside their basmati shoots and squelched from the water, jostling one another playfully and bursting with anticipation. Holi was a chance for them to forget their woes and join with their friends, neighbours and countrymen in the centre of town, to party and parade late into the evening, sharing food and drink with loved ones and strangers alike in a rare humanitarian display of love and harmony.

With Vivien now devoid of all clutter, Esther held open her rear doors. "Perhaps my sister and I could give you a ride," she told Ravi and the others, whilst Minnie buckled herself into her seat.

Marvelling at the vintage classic, the boisterous basmati farmers leapt aboard barefoot, and huddled together, ruffling one another's hair.

Peshwari Nans

"Vivien is a rare and beautiful jewel, Mrs Esther," Ravi remarked, caressing the hand-carved widow framing.

"Isn't she just, dear?" Esther said, closing the doors and sliding in beside her sister, who sat brimming with excitement. "Yes, yes, yes alight, dear," she told her whilst following the Highway Code to the letter and only releasing the handbrake after checking both mirrors and signalling, even though there was not another motor vehicle in sight, just a grazing goat, four chickens and a rusting plough.

"Riiiight," she said, pulling away and waving to Ravi's grandmother, who had opted to remain behind.

"Hurry dear, hurry," Minnie squealed once they were out of the farm gates. "We don't want to miss it."

"Do not be worrying, Miss Minnie," Ravi assured her. "Holi will go on and on long into the night, I promise you."

"Thank you, Ravi dear," Esther said smugly on the approach to town, whilst flashing her sister a look of contempt and cruising at a fraction of the legal speed limit.

As newbies to the festival of Holi, nothing could have prepared the sisters for the sight that greeted them when rounding the final corner.

"Dear Lord!" Esther gasped at the thousand or so strong gathering that was barely visible beneath a kaleidoscopic cloud of swirling powdered painted people, each and every one of them lost in a heady euphoric haze. Small children ran about the place amongst the revellers, brandishing plastic pistols loaded with lurid liquid paints, whilst the adults danced to the rhythmic beat of wooden spoons on copper pots and clanging cow bells.

The delirious Hindus immersed themselves completely in this cultural phenomenon, with a haze of vibrant colours hanging above their heads as fresh fistfuls of cerise, violet, magenta and saffron were hurled from all directions.

To those unfamiliar with Holi, these proceedings may appear a riotous battleground, a violent demonstration of civil unrest. But the looks of ecstasy and sheer unadulterated bliss would soon tell a different story.

Esther approached with caution, her right foot hovering over Vivien's brake pedal until a solitary reveller caught sight of the distinctive Morris and tugged at his neighbour's robe.

"Peshwari Nans!" he shrieked, yanking again and again. "PESHWARI NANS!".

His message reverberated throughout the festival like the ripples on a pond, until the volume decreased and all heads turned in their direction. The heavily spattered gathering parted to allow Vivien to enter the square whilst a rainbow of paint particles descended all around. Soon a deathly silence fell in central Raipur as Esther slowed further still and stopped beside a marble fountain that featured a host of chiselled Hindu gods. All eyes and beating chests now faced the tiny car, with Minnie being the first of its occupants to emerge, with a resounding click of Vivien's passenger door. Esther soon followed suit, releasing Ravi and the others in doing so.

There was a moment or two of wonderment on everybody's part, the sisters included, before Minnie reached into a reveller's muslin bag.

"Well?" she said, tossing a handful of crimson powder paint into the air. "What are you waiting for?"

The square immediately erupted, mimicking Minnie until an explosive cloud of colour obliterated the sun itself. "Oh my word!" Esther cried in awe.

"Isn't it just amazing?" Minnie squealed as she and her sister were hoisted up onto Ravi and his brother's shoulders and were paraded along, clinging to their hats and handbags around the square, the crowd bowing majestically as the sisters passed by.

Peshwari Nans

"Minnie dear!" Esther said above the din, "I have never in all my days witnessed anything quite like it, have you?" she then asked before a purple haze engulfed her.

"What was that, dear?" Minnie laughed, admiring her own 'coat of many colours'.

Vivien sat amid the frenzied festivities awash with paints and powders of every hue, her former regal Trafalgar blue now undetectable, whilst Esther and Minnie were carried three times around the fountain and set down upon a granite plinth overlooking the town square and the revelment therein.

"Oh my dear, look at you." Esther laughed, brushing her sister's polka dot cheeks. "You look as though you've been at Mother's cosmetics again."

As a child, Minnie had often resembled an oriental geisha in miniature, after repeatedly plundering their mother's make-up purse and lathering on her rouge, mascara and lip liner, before stomping about the place in oversized heels, a flowing velvet evening dress trailing behind her and a string of pearls hanging at her feet.

"Look at the both of us." Minnie also chuckled.

The sound of laughter and strumming sitars which kept a repetitive but altogether hypnotic beat, coaxed mothers and daughters into the street to dance in satin saris, twirling feverishly hand in hand, with golden charms on chains running from their ears to their nostrils, flaying at their sides, and although Holi had been adopted by a string of foreign countries, only in India was it performed with such vibrancy and passion.

Eventually the masses tired and the colourful cloud descended and settled at their feet as they breathlessly embraced one another. "Amazing, simply amazing," Esther said, slipping an arm around her sister's waist.

"Ditto," Minnie said, resting her head on Esther's shoulder. The sisters examined their paint-speckled attire and complexions with the same burning thought at the forefront of their minds: how on earth would it be removed without them stripping off right there in the street. But the solution soon presented itself, as those around them gathered at the fountain side and stepped beneath the arching sprays spewed from the exquisitely sculptured lips of Kali, Shiva, Krishna and Hanuman, the mischievous monkey god.

"Help me down, will you dear?" Minnie said, taking her sister's hand.

"You're not seriously suggesting we…" Esther said, finding the cleansing ritual a tad too much.

"Oh but of course, dear," Minnie insisted, clambering down from the plinth. "Come dear, I have you."

Again the gathering parted to allow the sisters safe passage to the water's edge. "In for a penny, dear," Minnie said as she was helped over the granite lip and into the knee-deep water, which now ran with the heavily diluted remains of the Holi festival.

Hand in hand, Esther and Minnie hobbled beneath the fountain to rapturous applause and mutual adulation. There they removed their straw hats, closed their eyes and let the cooling waters strip the powdered pigments from them while their supporters, in ever-increasing numbers, cupped their hands and ferried water to Vivien, restoring her with great affection to her former glory in a matter of minutes.

Saturated, the sisters kissed and hugged each other tightly before turning to their followers and each raising a fist, in defiance it seemed at the odds that had been so steeply stacked against them from the very beginning. Their age, which as a mere number now paled into insignificance, and as far as death was concerned, while it was inevitable at some stage, would now simply have to wait because an eternal flame now burned brightly within the humble elders, filling them with youthful exuberance and igniting their imaginations and, more importantly, their aspirations for a future that had previously appeared bleak.

Yet again the proceedings were captured and beamed around the globe, evoking a surge of emotion like never before. Motorways, airport terminals and city streets ground to a halt as a deathly post-apocalyptic silence fell, with heads bowed, the people watching the sisters on a multitude of electronic devices.

What was to follow that day would herald a new dawn for those who were presumed by society to be in their twilight years. Scenes of pure anarchy erupted in nursing homes after viewing the proceedings in Raipur. Tens of thousands rose from their rockers and easy chairs and cast aside their canes and walking frames, breaking free of their artificially heated environments to feel the sun on their cragged faces and the grass beneath their feet. Families that had once deposited their senior members in such places, cutting adrift an emotional burden, now welcomed them back into their family's bosom with open arms and a heavy heart.

An awakening of epic proportion swept through God's waiting rooms like a powerful enema, provoking a movement, but not of the bowel, of the soul. A zest for life so intense that it hoisted those from the deepest and darkest pits of despair back from the brink as it were, back to the tea dances and promenades that had once enthused their youth so richly.

And all this happened unbeknown to Esther and Minnie, the very epitome of sweetness and innocence, loved by one another, but adored by a million more.

Invigorated, the sisters clambered clear of the technicolour soup and stood dripping amid the panting crowd. A breath of wind tumbled over them from the east, drying their hair and drawing steam from their sodden clothes. Along with the scent of dampened laundry came the delirious aroma of Indian herbs and spices, as a sumptuous feast was laid before them on silken sheets at the roadside.

Esther and Minnie, as guests of honour, were invited to 'first pick' over the lavish spread of locally produced basmati, that was lovingly infused with cumin, fresh coriander and cardamom pods and sweet mango chutneys to delight the taste buds, whilst fluffed Bombay aloo, bajis and breaded naans, including the obligatory peshwari, bolstered and refuelled the weary revellers.

Soon the sisters were dry and heartily fed as all eyes turned to the sun setting in a turmeric sky to the west. Ravi could be heard making his way towards the sisters, holding their tablet aloft.

"Mrs Esther, Mrs Esther!" he called, having retrieved the flashing device from Vivien. "Mrs Esther you have a call!"

"For me?" Esther said on his approach. "Whoever could it be?"

"Oh look dear," Minnie said, glancing over her sister's shoulder. "It's Elizabeth."

Sure enough, Elizabeth's face loomed on the screen. "Hi Mother, Aunt Min," she said in a surprisingly buoyant tone. "How are you?"

"Errrrrrrr," Esther said, caught completely off guard by her daughter's apparent U-turn. "Okay, I guess."

Elizabeth had responded remarkably well to Dr Shultz's ground-breaking treatment and had eventually been allowed home for an initial trial period.

Richard could be seen crammed into the corner of the screen. "Hi Gran!" he called with a wave. "Congratulations!"

"Thank you, Richard darling," Esther said with Minnie at her side. "As you can see we made it, and Jasvinder is here too, in a simply idyllic setting."

"Ahhhh." Richard smiled. "I'm glad Gran, really I am."

"Yes, yes," Elizabeth said, inching her son out of the frame. "So er, now that you've reached Rajasthan or wherever it is you've ventured to—"

"—Raipur." Esther corrected her. "It's Raipur, Lizzy dear."

"Of course it is," Elizabeth said, fidgeting in her seat. "Anyway," she continued, "I assume now that this silliness is over you'll be coming straight back home."

Esther froze momentarily. "Home?" she then said, turning to Minnie.

"Yes, home," Elizabeth reiterated. "When exactly can we expect you? I trust you'll leave the car and fly back immediately."

Minnie gripped her sister's sleeve. "Essy I..." she said, catching her breath. "I don't know about you. but I—"

"—Me neither," Esther blurted out before her sister could finish. "Elizabeth darling," she then said, caressing the screen. "Minnie and I, well we won't be coming home. Not just yet anyway."

"What?" Elizabeth said, straightening her back. "What did you say, Mother? For a moment then I thought you said you won't be coming home."

"Yes, that's right dear," Esther informed her, clutching her sister's hand. "We're going to press on."

"Press on?" Elizabeth said in a heightened tone. "Press on? What do you mean, press on? Mother? Mother, what do you mean?"

Richard put an arm around his mother. "Mum, Mum, calm down please," he asked. "Remember what the doctor said."

Elizabeth shrugged her son aside. "Don't tell me to calm down!" she barked. "Mother, I insist you return home right away! Do you hear me? I said do you hear me?"

Peshwari Nans

Minnie nestled closer into her sister's side. "You know I rather fancy Kenya," she said with a smile. "With Kilimanjaro and the Congo."

"Oooh yes!" Esther said, wide eyed. "Or the Inca trail, Ecuador and the Amazon!"

"Mother!" Elizabeth snapped, gripping Richard's laptop computer. "Mother, your place is here, just around the corner, where I can keep an eye on you! Now stop this foolishness at once and come home!"

"Oooooh!" Minnie again squealed. "What about Madagascar, dear?"

"Madagascar!" Elizabeth raged. "Madagascar Minnie, oh no, ohhhhh no, you bring my mother home right now, do you hear me?"

"Or Dubai," Esther said, dismissing her daughter's insistence. "Brunai and Borneo, Vietnam and Cambodia!"

"No, Mother!" Elizabeth growled. "I forbid it, I forbid it, do you hear?"

"Shall we, dear?" Minnie said, leading her sister towards Vivien.

"Oh but of course, dear." Esther smiled, patting Vivien's gleaming bonnet. "Goodbye Ravi, my dear," she told their friend with a peck to his cheek. "I fancy we shall meet again some day."

"Nothing would make me happier, Mrs Esther," Ravi replied, returning the kiss. "Goodbye and good luck, and to you Miss Minnie."

"Thank you, Ravi love," Minnie said, opening the passenger door. "Thank you everybody!"

"Mother, Mother!" Elizabeth ranted from the screen held beneath her mother's arm. "Mother no, no, no, no, do you hear me?"

Again Richard pleaded with her. "Muuuuum you need to calm down, honestly."

But Elizabeth was having none of it.

"Get away from me!" she said, shoving him bodily. "MOTHER!" she then yelled, pounding the kitchen table.

The sisters climbed aboard and fastened their seat belts. "Elizabeth darling," Esther said, with her finger hovering over the power button. "I assure you that Minnie and I will be home, eventually."

With that and a resounding prod, she severed the lines of communication with her now frantic daughter, whose blood pressure soared immediately.

"EVENTUALLY?" Elizabeth asked, shaking the screen. "EVENTUALLY, MOTHER? DON'T YOU DARE MOTHER, MOTHER, MOTHERRRRRRRRRRRRRRRRR!".

It was all that Richard could do to prevent his mother from destroying the family home whilst he was telephoning the secure unit that had recently housed her. Meanwhile, his grandmother and her sister waved one last time to their army of supporters and set off out of town en route to rural India, the horizon, and the setting sun.

The End.

Peshwari Nans

Nepal appeal

Do something amazing today and help the people of Nepal rebuild their shattered lives.
Together, we can make a difference.

www.dec.org.uk/**appeal/nepal-earthquake-appeal**

www.savethechildren.org.uk/about-us/.../**nepal-earthquake**

www.redcross.org.uk/.../Donate-to-the-**Nepal-Earthquake-Appeal**

www.oxfam.org.uk/what-we-do/emergency.../**nepal-earthquake**

Thank you

Made in the USA
Middletown, DE
08 December 2017